THE CANTERBURY TALES:
NINE TALES AND THE
GENERAL PROLOGUE

AUTHORITATIVE TEXT
SOURCES AND BACKGROUNDS
CRITICISM

A NORTON CRITICAL EDITION

Geoffrey Chaucer

THE CANTERBURY TALES: NINE TALES AND THE GENERAL PROLOGUE

AUTHORITATIVE TEXT
SOURCES AND BACKGROUNDS
CRITICISM

Selected and Edited by

V. A. KOLVE

THE UNIVERSITY OF CALIFORNIA AT
LOS ANGELES

GLENDING OLSON

CLEVELAND STATE UNIVERSITY

W · W · NORTON & COMPANY · *New York* · *London*

Published simultaneously in Canada by Penguin Books Canada Ltd., 2801 John Street, Markham, Ontario L3R 1B4.
Printed in the United States of America.

First Edition

Library of Congress Cataloging-in-Publication Data

Chaucer, Geoffrey, d. 1400.
The Canterbury tales : authoritative text, sources and
backgrounds, criticism / selected and edited by V. A. Kolve, Glending
Olson.—1st ed.
p.   cm.—(A Norton critical edition)
Bibliography: p. 547
1. Chaucer, Geoffrey, d. 1400.   Canterbury tales.   I. Kolve,
V. A.   II. Olson, Glending,   III. Title.
PR1866.K64 1988
821'.1—dc19   87-32084
ISBN 0-393-95245-2

W. W. Norton & Company, Inc., 500 Fifth Avenue, New York, N.Y. 10110
www.wwnorton.com

W. W. Norton & Company Ltd., Castle House, 75/76 Wells Street,
London W1T 3QT

1 2 3 4 5 6 7 8 9 0

Contents

Criticism   439

for
Ingrid Kristine Olson
and
Ellen Winter

Preface

The first part of this edition of *The Canterbury Tales: Nine Tales and the General Prologue*—the glossed Chaucer text—is addressed specifically to students making their first acquaintance with Chaucer in his own language, and it takes nothing for granted. All difficult words and constructions are translated, in glosses at the margins of the page or in footnotes at the bottom when longer explanations are required. Because we hope the book will serve several sorts of introductory courses in literature, the glossing is complete for each of the tales. They may be assigned in any number and in any sequence. We have selected tales generally considered among Chaucer's finest, and whenever possible we have included from Chaucer's framing story passages that locate each tale in its immediate dramatic context.

The glossing is frankly pedagogic, intended to help the student understand Chaucer in the original language rather than to provide a steadily idiomatic modern translation. *Thou*-forms of the verb, for instance, are glossed as such, though a modern translation would express them as *you*. Verbs are glossed in their exact tense, though medieval texts often shift between past and present forms in ways modern English declares ungrammatical. The glosses sometimes provide both a cognate word (which can help fix the original in mind) and a synonym that better conveys its contextual meaning. Chaucer's language is not so far removed from modern English that translation need be the aim of anyone's study. The poet can be understood in his own voice from the beginning.

The text is likewise conservative and pedagogic. This has not seemed to us an appropriate occasion to attempt a radically new edition of Chaucer's text, even if there were general agreement concerning the shape such an edition should take. Although some eighty-two manuscripts of the *Canterbury Tales* survive, in full or in fragment, none is in Chaucer's own hand and none possesses his final authority. He died before the work was complete, and what has come down to us is, in even its earliest examples, scribal and implicitly editorial. Since we have neither autograph nor archetype, Chaucer's "original text" is in fact irrecoverable—and for editors attempting a definitive edition, as for critics specially concerned with Chaucerian metrics and stylistics, that is a great frustration. But the best manuscripts of the *Canterbury Tales* are, on the whole, very good, and the variations between them, word by word, reasonably few and only seldom of substantive importance. In the present case, we have used Skeat's landmark edition as our copy-text; but for many specific readings we have consulted facsimile editions of the Ellesmere and Hengwrt manuscripts, the editions of Manly & Rickert, Robinson, Baugh, Donaldson, Pratt, and Fisher, and the new *Riverside Chaucer*, 3d ed., under the general editorship of Larry D. Benson. Skeat lightly normalized the spelling in the manuscripts—a feature we have retained as a convenience for beginning students, along with his use of a hyphen before the *y*-prefix in past participles. We have, however, moved in the direction of Robinson's handling of the final *-e*, even though that risks making Chaucer's meter somewhat more regular than scholarship can confidently affirm. Our most systematic change has been to repunctuate the text, for the sake of clarity and in accordance with both medieval and contemporary usage. In matters of punctuation, less has seemed to us more.

The second part of this book offers a collection of documents of various kinds—sources, analogues, or other medieval writings—which represent ways in which Chaucer or his first audiences might have known these stories from elsewhere, or ways in which they might have thought about certain aspects of their meaning. Such documents can help students think in historically relevant ways about Chaucer's art and meaning. In such study, they will find the differences at least as revealing as the similarities, for the differences help identify choices made, emphases added, roads taken and not taken.

To that end we have worked with a more generous definition of the relevant than did Bryan and Dempster in their magisterial collection, *Sources and Analogues of Chaucer's Canterbury Tales*.[1] We have brought together writings that cast an interesting and suggestive light on the tales included here and have made those writings accessible (as Bryan and Dempster do not) to students untrained in the several languages of medieval Europe. Some of the translations that follow have been made specially for this volume; certain others, though previously published, have been difficult to come by and seem worth reprinting here. We have not glossed the Middle English writings in this section as extensively as we have the Chaucer texts, but even here we take for granted only a beginner's knowledge of Chaucer's language; a good deal of help is provided. Again, we have normalized certain features of these texts, substituting the appropriate modern letters for Middle English letters no longer current, regularizing *u/v* and *i/j*, eliminating certain scribal idiosyncracies, and modernizing punctuation and capitalization. We hope that both the new translations and the gathering together of what has been widely scattered or out of print will prove welcome, to teacher and student alike.

The third part of the book brings together a number of critical essays on Chaucer. Instead of trying to select a single most authoritative and illuminating essay on each tale—a task increasingly impossible as the secondary literature on Chaucer becomes a library in its own right—we have chosen historically influential essays that treat the broader critical questions, ques-

---

1. W. F. Bryan and Germaine Dempster (1941; New York: Humanities Press, 1958). We refer to this book throughout as *Sources and Analogues*.

tions that arise whether one is considering the stories individually or collectively. Hence Hoffman on the double focus, sacred and secular, of the pilgrimage and Mann on the complexities of the portraits in the General Prologue; hence Donaldson, Howard, and Leicester on the nature of the poem's voices; hence three markedly different approaches to the structure and meaning of the *Canterbury Tales*, ranging from Kittredge's seminal work focusing upon "the marriage group" as demonstrating Chaucer's interest in psychological realism and dramatic interplay between the pilgrims, to Robertson's insistence upon an allegorical intent, to Josipovici's examination of the fiction as play and game. Preceding all these is a biographical essay by the historian F. R. H. Du Boulay that not only sets out the essential facts of Chaucer's life but evokes something of the social and intellectual environment in which he wrote. It can usefully serve as an introduction to this volume as a whole. In the selective bibliography at the back of this book, we offer suggestions for further reading, tale by tale.

Though this edition includes only nine *Canterbury Tales* and the prologue that introduces them, they have been chosen as exemplifying Chaucer's highest achievement in the art of story. His is a Gothic art, full of variety and contradiction, tension and transcendence—an art that dared to look at human life under so many guises and from so many points of view that it lays convincing claim, even in the late twentieth century, to having seen life whole.

In the making of this book, the editors gratefully acknowledge the assistance of Betsy Bowden, Thomas Cannon, Jr., Raymond Cormier, Rosa DelVecchio, Julie Bates Dock, Mary Dugan, Rita Hammond, Betty Hanson-Smith, and Jeanne Vanecko. We thank Carol Stiles Bemis and Marian Johnson at W. W. Norton for their careful and cooperative editorial work.

Chaucer's Language

There are many differences between Chaucer's Middle English and modern English, but they are minor enough that a student can learn to adjust to them in a relatively short time. We have sketched below just a few of the principal differences. For fuller treatments see the section on language in the bibliography.

I. Pronunciation

The chief difference between Middle English (ME) and modern English (NE) is in pronunciation. The best way to learn ME is to hear it spoken—by a teacher, or on records or tapes. A number of good records are available, including those by J. B. Bessinger, Jr., on the Caedmon label. The discussion below will pinpoint the principal sound differences, but it takes practice—listening and reading aloud—to develop a good ME pronunciation.

A. VOWELS

ME distinguished between long and short vowels, whereas NE does not, even though it takes longer to say the vowel of "bad" than of "bat." In addition, ME long vowels underwent, over an extended period of time, a change known as the Great Vowel Shift, in which they systematically acquired new sound values. The beginning student can best cope with these differences by working backward from NE pronunciation and spelling, a procedure that will ensure reasonable though not perfect accuracy in ME pronunciation. Accordingly, in the following table of sounds, we have indicated not only Chaucer's spelling and pronunciation (both in International Phonetic Alphabet symbols and in NE equivalents) but also how the vowel sounds have evolved in NE.

Two further aspects of the pronunciation of vowels may be considered in connection with Chaucer's principles of versification. Although scholars are not in complete agreement about the nature of Chaucer's metrics, most assume that his lines are basically iambic pentameter, with a good deal of metrical variation. Vowels occurring in combination should all be pronounced, as the meter often makes clear:

And plesaunt was his absolucioun

More complex is the question of finale *e*. Originally there was no such thing as "silent *e*" in English: the final *e* in ME words often represents a reduction of more distinctive Old English inflections. By Chaucer's time it is likely that in normal speech the final *e* was silent, but in his poetry it is frequently pronounced, with the schwa sound [ə] that we use in unstressed syllables, such as those at the end of *sofa* and the beginning of *about*. Always pronounce final *e* at the end of lines, and within lines pronounce it or not depending on the requirements of the meter. In the following example the final *e*'s that should be pronounced are italicized:

Wel coude he sitte on hors, and faire ryde.
He coude songes make and wel endyte

As these instances indicate, final *e* is usually not pronounced when it appears before words beginning with vowels or weakly pronounced *h*'s.

B. CONSONANTS

ME consonants are pronounced as in NE, with some exceptions:

1. In general, pronounce all consonants in clusters: *g* and *k* before *n* (*gnawe, knife*), although *gn* in French borrowings (*digne, signe*) is [n]; *w* before *r* (*write, wroth*); *l* before *f, v, k, m* (*half* or *halve, folk, palmer*); *ng* is usually pronounced [ŋg], the consonant cluster in *finger* rather than *singer*.

2. *gh* is pronounced with the guttural sound in German *ich*. There is no comparable sound in NE, except for *loch* when pronounced with a heavy Scots accent.

CHAUCER'S SPELLING	EXAMPLES	ME PRONUNCIATION	EVOLUTION IN NE
VOWELS			
a	after, at	[a], as in NE top	usually becomes [æ], as in NE after, at
a, aa	take, caas	[a:], as in NE father	becomes [e], as in NE take, case
e	best, hem	[ɛ], as in NE best	no change
e, ee	heeth, ese, see	[ɛ:], as in NE bed	becomes [i], spelled ea, as in NE heath, ease, sea
e, ee	swete, be, see	[e:], as in NE take	becomes [i], spelled e or ee, as in NE sweet, be, see
i, y	hit, in	[I], as in NE hit, in	no change
i, y	I, ride	[i:], as in NE seed	becomes [ai], as in NE I, ride
o	of, oxe	[ɔ], as in NE long	usually becomes [ə] or [a], as in NE of, ox
o, oo	go, hope, so	[ɔ:], as in NE law	becomes [o], as in NE go, hope, so
o, oo	roote, to, good	[o:], as in NE note	becomes [u] or [ʊ], as in NE root, to, good
u, o[1]	up, but, come	[ʊ], as in NE put	usually becomes [ə], as in NE up, but, come
ou, ow	hous, town	[u:], as in NE to	becomes [aʊ], as in NE house, town
u, eu, ew	vertu, salewe	[y], as in Fr. tu[2]	no NE equivalent
DIPHTHONGS			
ai, ay, ei, ey	day, sayn, they	[æI], somewhere between NE hay and high	becomes [e], as in NE day, say, they
au, aw	cause, draw	[aʊ], as in NE out	becomes [ɔ], as in NE cause, draw
eu, ew[3]	newe, reule	[ɪu], close to NE few	becomes [ɪu] or [u], as in NE few, rule
oi, oy	joye, point	[ɔI], as in NE joy	no change
ou, ow	thought, bowe	[ɔʊ], a glide between the vowels of NE law and to	becomes [ɔ] or [o], as in NE thought, bow

1. A few words with the short [ʊ] sound in ME are spelled with o instead of u: *sone* (NE *son*), *sonne* (NE *sun*), *come, love, some*. These words were originally spelled with u in Old English; the o spelling is an orthographic change only.
2. This sound occurs only in a few words recently borrowed from French.
3. A few words—the most familiar are *fewe, lewe, shew, shrewe*—should be pronounced [ɛɪ] instead of [ɪu].

3. *ch* is always pronounced [č], as in NE *church*.

4. *r* should be trilled.

5. *h* is not pronounced at the beginning of words borrowed from French (*honour, hostelrye*); at the beginning of short ME words like *he, his, hit, him, hem*, it is also silent or only weakly pronounced.

6. Final *s* should not be voiced to [z] in stressed positions. At the end of lines Chaucer rhymes *was* with *glas* and *cas, is* with *this*.

II. Morphology

NOUNS: The usual ending for plural and genitive singular forms is *-es*, sometimes *-is*, generally pronounced as a separate syllable. The plural ending *-en* is more common than in NE: e.g., *eyen* instead of *eyes*.

PERSONAL PRONOUNS: Second-person pronouns have both singular forms—*thou, thy* or *thyn, the(e)*—and plural forms—*ye, youre, you* or *yow*. The latter set can be used with singular meaning in some cases.

The third-person singular neuter pronoun may be spelled *it* or *hit*; the possessive case of *it* is *his*, not *its*, which did not enter the language until the Renaissance.

Chaucer's third-person plural forms are notably different from those in NE. *They, their*, and *them* are Scandinavian borrowings, which were assimilated into the language at different times in different ME dialects. Chaucer uses the nominative *thei* but retains the native forms for possessive and accusative case: *hir(e)* or *her(e)* instead of *their*, *hem* instead of *them*.

RELATIVE PRONOUNS: Chaucer uses *which, that*, or *which that* instead of *who* and *whom* when referring to human beings, as in "But I, that am exiled" and "a wyf, / Whiche that he lovede."

VERBS: The old infinitive form in *-en* appears frequently in Chaucer, but not consistently. For example, in the opening sentence of the *General Prologue* the infinitive of *seek* appears both as *to seken* and *to seke*.

The past participle is usually prefixed by *y-*, as in *hadde y-ronne*.

Verbs are inflected in the present tense as follows:

Indicative—Singular: 1. *take* 2. *takest* 3. *taketh*
Plural (all persons): *take(n)*

Subjunctive—Singular: *take*
Plural: *take(n)*

As in NE, ME verbs form past tense either by adding *-ed* or by a sound change within the word (e.g., *speke, spak*); the only difference is that some ME verbs that use a sound change have since shifted to the *-ed* form: in Chaucer the past tense of *shape*, for example, is *shop* rather than *shaped*.

ADVERBS: In addition to using -*ly* and -*liche*, Chaucer also uses the suffix -*e* to form adverbs, as in "ful loude he song."

III. Syntax

Chaucer's ME is more flexible in word order than NE, and he uses syntactic patterns no longer common today. Among the most frequent are:

object—subject—verb	But Cristes lore, and his apostles twelve, / He taughte
object—verb—subject	A Yeman hadde he
complement—subject—verb	Curteys he was
complement—verb—subject	Short was his gowne
verb—subject—object	Thus hath this pitous day a blisful ende
subject—auxiliary—object—verb	I have thy feith and thy benignitee . . . assayed

Other features of Chaucer's syntax also differ from standard NE practice. Often he shifts tense within a sentence:

> And doun he *kneleth*, and with humble chere
> And herte soor, he *seyde* as ye shul here . . .

The relative pronoun may be omitted:

> With him ther was dwellinge a poure scoler,
> Hadde lerned art . . .

As in spoken English, grammatical construction may shift in mid-sentence, or the subject may be repeated:

> The reule of Seint Maure, or of Seint Beneit,
> By cause that it was old and somdel streit,
> This ilke monk leet olde thinges pace . . .

> Upon that oother syde Palamon,
> Whan that he wiste Arcite was agon,
> Swich sorwe he maketh . . .

Negation is handled on the principle that if one negative element in a sentence creates denial, further negative elements make the denial even more emphatic. Hence one can find double, triple, and even quadruple negatives in Chaucer:

> He *nevere* yet *no* vileinye *ne* sayde
> In al his lyf, unto *no* maner wight.

Finally, Chaucer uses some verbs in impersonal constructions that have since become personal. "*Me thinketh it*" means "I think" (cf. "It seems to me"). Sometimes the "it" in such constructions is omitted: "*hym liste* ryde so" = "it pleased him to ride in that way."

Selections from
THE CANTERBURY TALES

The Canterbury Tales

The General Prologue

Whan that Aprill with his shoures sote°   *sweet showers*
The droghte° of Marche hath perced to the rote,°   *dryness / root*
And bathed every veyne° in swich licour,°   *vein / such moisture*
Of which vertu° engendred is the flour;   *By power of which*
5 Whan Zephirus° eek with his swete breeth   *the west wind*
Inspired° hath in every holt° and heeth°   *Breathed into / wood / heath*
The tendre croppes,° and the yonge sonne   *sprouts*
Hath in the Ram his halfe cours y-ronne;[1]
And smale fowles° maken melodye,   *birds*
10 That slepen al the night with open ye°—   *eye(s)*
So priketh hem Nature in hir corages[2]—
Than longen° folk to goon° on pilgrimages,   *Then long / go*
And palmeres for to seken straunge strondes,[3]
To ferne halwes,° couthe° in sondry londes;   *far-off shires / known*
15 And specially, from every shires ende
Of Engelond to Caunterbury they wende,
The holy blisful martir[4] for to seke,°   *seek*
That hem hath holpen,° whan that they were seke.°   *helped / sick*
Bifel° that, in that seson on a day,   *It befell*
20 In Southwerk at the Tabard° as I lay°   *(an inn) / lodged*
Redy to wenden° on my pilgrimage   *depart*
To Caunterbury with ful devout corage,°   *heart*
At night was come into that hostelrye°   *inn*
Wel nyne and twenty in a companye
25 Of sondry folk, by aventure° y-falle°   *chance / fallen*
In felawshipe, and pilgrims were they alle,
That toward Caunterbury wolden° ryde.   *wished to*
The chambres° and the stables weren wyde,°   *bedrooms / spacious*
And wel we weren esed° atte beste.°   *made comfortable / in the best (ways)*
30 And shortly, whan the sonne was to° reste,   *at*

---

1. Has run his half-course in the Ram; i.e., has passed through half the zodiacal sign of Aries (the Ram), a course completed on April 11. A rhetorically decorative way of indicating the time of year.
2. Nature so spurs them in their hearts.

3. And pilgrims to seek foreign shores.
4. Thomas Becket, archbishop of Canterbury, murdered in 1170 and canonized shortly thereafter. The place of his martyrdom was the greatest shrine in England and much visited by pilgrims.

So hadde I spoken with hem everichon° *each and every one*
That I was of hir felawshipe anon,
And made forward° erly for to ryse, *agreement*
To take oure wey, ther as I yow devyse.° *(will) tell*
35 But natheles,° whyl I have tyme and space, *nevertheless*
Er that I ferther in this tale pace,° *pass on*
Me thinketh it acordaunt to resoun [5]
To telle yow al the condicioun [6]
Of ech of hem, so as it semed me,° *seemed to me*
40 And whiche° they weren, and of what degree,° *what / status*
And eek in what array° that they were inne; *clothing*
And at a knight than wol° I first biginne. *will*
 A KNIGHT ther was, and that a worthy man,
That fro° the tyme that he first bigan *from*
45 To ryden out,° he loved chivalrye, *ride (on expeditions)*
Trouthe and honour, fredom and curteisye. [7]
Ful worthy was he in his lordes werre,° *war(s)*
And therto° hadde he riden, no man ferre,° *in such / further*
As wel in Cristendom as in hethenesse,° *in pagan lands*
50 And evere honoured for his worthinesse.
 At Alisaundre° he was whan it was wonne; *Alexandria*
Ful ofte tyme he hadde the bord bigonne° *headed the table*
Aboven alle naciouns in Pruce.° *Prussia*
In Lettow hadde he reysed and in Ruce, [8]
55 No Cristen man so ofte of his degree.° *rank*
In Gernade°at the sege° eek hadde he be° *Granada / siege / been*
Of Algezir,° and riden in Belmarye.° *Algeciras / Benmarin (in Morocco)*
At Lyeys° was he and at Satalye,° *Ayas / Adalia (both in Asia Minor)*
Whan they were wonne; and in the Grete See° *Mediterranean*
60 At many a noble armee° hadde he be. *armed expedition*
At mortal batailles [9] hadde he been fiftene,
And foughten for oure feith at Tramissene° *Tlemcen (in Algeria)*
In listes° thryes,° and ay slayn his foo.° *tournaments / thrice / foe*
This ilke° worthy knight hadde been also *same*
65 Somtyme with the lord of Palatye,° *Palatia*
Ageyn° another hethen in Turkye; *Against*
And everemore he hadde a sovereyn prys.° *reputation*
And though that he were worthy, [1] he was wys,° *prudent*
And of his port° as meke as is a mayde. *deportment*
70 He nevere yet no vileinye° ne sayde *rudeness*
In al his lyf, unto no maner wight.° *any sort of person*
He was a verray,° parfit,° gentil° knight. *true / perfect / noble*

---

5. It seems to me reasonable (proper).
6. Character, estate, condition.
7. Fidelity, honor, generosity of spirit, and courtesy (the central chivalric virtues).
8. He had been on campaigns in Lithuania and in Russia.
9. Tournaments fought to the death.
1. I.e., valiant.

But for to tellen yow of his array,
His hors° were gode, but he was nat gay.°   horses / brightly dressed
75 Of fustian° he wered° a gipoun°   rough cloth / wore / tunic
Al bismotered with° his habergeoun,°   stained by / coat of mail
For he was late y-come° from his viage,°   recently come / expedition
And wente for to doon° his pilgrimage.   make
　　　With him ther was his sone, a young SQUYER
90 A lovyere, and a lusty bacheler,²
With lokkes crulle, as they were leyd in presse.³
Of twenty yeer of age he was, I gesse.
Of° his stature he was of evene lengthe,°   In / average height
And wonderly delivere,° and of greet strengthe.   agile
85 And he hadde been somtyme in chivachye°   on expeditions
In Flaundres,° in Artoys,° and Picardye,°   Flanders / Artois / Picardy
And born him wel, as of so litel space,⁴
In hope to stonden° in his lady° grace.   stand / lady's
Embrouded° was he, as it were a mede°   Embroidered / meadow
90 Al ful of fresshe floures, whyte and rede.
Singinge he was, or floytinge,° al the day;   fluting (whistling?)
He was as fresh as is the month of May.
Short was his gowne, with sleves longe and wyde.
Wel coude° he sitte on hors, and faire ryde.   knew how to
95 He coude songes make and wel endyte,°   compose verse
Juste° and eek daunce, and wel purtreye° and wryte.   Joust / draw
So hote° he lovede that by nightertale°   hotly / at night
He sleep° namore° than dooth a nightingale.   slept / no more
Curteys he was, lowly, and servisable,⁵
100 And carf° biforn his fader at the table.   carved (meat)
　　　A YEMAN hadde he, and servaunts namo⁶
At that tyme, for him liste° ryde so;   it pleased him to
And he was clad in cote and hood of grene.
A sheef of pecok-arwes° brighte and kene   arrows
105 Under his belt he bar° ful thriftily.°   bore / carefully
Wel coude he dresse° his takel° yemanly: keep in order / equipment
His arwes drouped noght with fetheres lowe,
And in his hand he bar a mighty bowe.
A not-heed° hadde he, with a broun visage.°   closely-cropped head / face
110 Of wodecraft wel coude° he al the usage.   knew
Upon his arm he bar a gay bracer,°   fine wrist-guard
And by his syde a swerd and a bokeler,°   shield
And on that other syde a gay daggere,

2. A lover, and a vigorous young man, one preparing to become a knight.
3. With locks as curly as if they'd been pressed (by a
curling iron).
4. And conducted himself well, considering his
inexperience.

5. He was courteous, humble, and willing to be of
service.
6. He [the Knight] had a Yeoman [a servant one
step above a groom in rank; this one seems to be a
forester] with him, and no other servants.

Harneised° wel, and sharp as point of spere;   *mounted*
115 A Cristofre° on his brest of silver shene.°   *St. Christopher medal / bright*
An horn he bar, the bawdrik° was of grene;   *shoulder-strap*
A forster° was he, soothly, as I gesse.   *forester*
   Ther was also a Nonne, a PRIORESSE,
That of hir smyling was ful simple and coy°—   *modest*
120 Hir gretteste ooth was but by Seynte Loy°—   *Eligius (Fr. Eloi)*
And she was cleped° madame Eglentyne.   *called*
Ful wel she song° the service divyne,   *sang*
Entuned° in hir nose ful semely;°   *Intoned / becomingly*
And Frensh she spak ful faire and fetisly,°   *elegantly*
125 After the scole of Stratford atte Bowe,[7]
For Frensh of Paris was to hire unknowe.
At mete[8] wel y-taught was she with alle:
She leet° no morsel from hir lippes falle,   *let*
Ne wette hir fingres in hir sauce depe.°   *(too) deeply*
130 Wel coude she carie a morsel, and wel kepe[9]
That no drope ne fille° upon hire brest.   *fell*
In curteisye° was set ful muchel° hir lest.°   *etiquette / much / delight*
Hir over°-lippe wyped she so clene,   *upper*
That in hir coppe was no ferthing° sene°   *small drop / seen*
135 Of grece,° whan she dronken hadde hir draughte.   *grease*
Ful semely after hir mete she raughte,°   *reached*
And sikerly° she was of greet disport,°   *certainly / cheerfulness*
And ful plesaunt, and amiable of port,°   *deportment*
And peyned hire° to countrefete chere°   *took pains / imitate behavior*
140 Of court, and to been estatlich° of manere,   *stately*
And to ben holden digne° of reverence.   *considered worthy*
But, for to speken of hire conscience,°   *sensibility*
She was so charitable and so pitous,°   *compassionate*
She wolde wepe, if that she sawe a mous°   *mouse*
145 Caught in a trappe, if it were deed or bledde.
Of[1] smale houndes hadde she, that she fedde
With rosted flesh, or milk and wastel-breed.°   *fine white bread*
But sore° wepte she if oon of hem were deed,   *sorely*
Or if men° smoot it with a yerde° smerte;°   *(some)one / stick / sharply*
150 And al was conscience and tendre herte.
Ful semely hir wimpel° pinched° was,   *headdress / pleated*
Hir nose tretys,° hir eyen° greye as glas,   *graceful / eyes*
Hir mouth ful smal, and therto softe and reed.
But sikerly° she hadde a fair forheed—   *certainly*
155 It was almost a spanne° brood, I trowe°—   *span / believe*

---

7. I.e., in the English fashion, as it was spoken at Stratford at the Bow—a suburb some two miles east of London and home of the Benedictine nunnery of St. Leonard's.

8. I.e., at table.
9. She knew well how to raise a portion (to her lips) and take care.
1. I.e., some.

For hardily° she was nat undergrowe.° · certainly / undersized
Ful fetis° was hir cloke, as I was war.° · elegant / aware
Of smal coral² aboute hire arm she bar
A peire of bedes, gauded al with grene;³
160 And theron heng a broche° of gold ful shene,° · ornament / bright
On which ther was first write° a crowned A,⁴ · written
And after, *Amor vincit omnia*.° · Love conquers all
     Another Nonne with hire hadde she,
That was hir chapeleyne,° and PREESTES three. · chaplain, assistant
165 A MONK ther was, a fair for the maistrye,° · a very fine one
An outrydere° that lovede venerye:° · estate supervisor / hunting
A manly man, to been an abbot able.
Ful many a deyntee° hors hadde he in stable, · valuable
And whan he rood, men mighte his brydel here° · hear
170 Ginglen° in a whistling wind als° clere · Jingling / as
And eek° as loude as dooth the chapel belle, · also
Ther as° this lord was kepere of the celle.⁵ · Where
The reule of Seint Maure° or of Seint Beneit,° · Maurus / Benedict
By cause that it was old and somdel streit,° · somewhat strict
175 This ilke° monk leet olde thinges pace,° · same / pass away
And held after the newe world the space.° · meanwhile
He yaf° nat of° that text a pulled° hen, · gave / for / plucked
That seith that hunters ben° nat holy men, · are
Ne that a monk, whan he is reccheless,° · negligent of his vows
180 Is lykned til° a fish that is waterlees° · likened to / out of water
('This is to seyn,° a monk out of his cloistre); · say
But thilke° text held he nat worth an oistre.° · that same / oyster
And I seyde his opinioun was good:
What° sholde he studie, and make himselven wood,° · Why / mad
185 Upon a book in cloistre alwey to poure,° · pore over
Or swinken° with his handes, and laboure, · work
As Austin° bit?° How shal the world be served? · Augustine / bids
Lat Austin have his swink° to him reserved! · work
Therfore he was a pricasour° aright:° · hard rider / truly
190 Grehoundes he hadde, as swifte as fowel° in flight; · bird
Of priking° and of hunting for the hare · riding
Was al his lust,° for no cost wolde he spare. · pleasure
I seigh° his sleves purfiled° at the hond · saw / trimmed
With grys,° and that the fyneste of a lond;° · gray fur / land
195 And, for to festne° his hood under his chin, · fasten
He hadde of gold y-wroght° a ful curious pin: · made
A love-knotte⁶ in the gretter° ende ther was. · larger

2. I.e., small coral beads.
3. A string of beads (a rosary), its groups marked off
by special stones, called "gauds," of green.
4. The letter A with a symbolic crown fashioned

above it.
5. A priory or dependent house.
6. An elaborate knot symbolizing true love.

His heed was balled,° that shoon as any glas, — *bald*
And eek his face, as° he had been anoint.° — *as if / annointed*
200 He was a lord ful fat and in good point:° — *condition*
His eyen° stepe,° and rollinge in his heed, — *eyes / prominent*
That stemed as a forneys of a leed;[7]
His bootes souple,° his hors in greet estat°— — *supple / condition*
Now certeinly he was a fair prelat.
205 He was nat pale as a forpyned goost;° — *tormented spirit*
A fat swan loved he best of any roost.
His palfrey° was as broun as is a berye.° — *horse / berry*
    A FRERE° ther was, a wantowne° and a merye, — *Friar / gay (one)*
A limitour,[8] a ful solempne° man. — *distinguished*
210 In alle the ordres foure[9] is noon that can° — *knows*
So muchel of daliaunce and fair langage.
He hadde maad° ful many a mariage — *arranged*
Of yonge wommen, at his owne cost.[1]
Unto his ordre he was a noble post.° — *pillar*
215 Ful wel biloved and famulier was he
With frankeleyns over al in his contree,[2]
And eek with worthy wommen of the toun;
For he hadde power of confessioun,
As seyde himself, more than a curat,° — *parish priest*
220 For of his ordre he was licentiat.° — *licensed to hear confessions*
Ful swetely herde he confessioun,
And plesaunt was his absolucioun;
He was an esy man to yeve° penaunce — *give*
Ther as he wiste to have a good pitaunce.[3]
225 For unto a povre° ordre for to yive° — *poor / give*
Is signe that a man is wel y-shrive°— — *shriven*
For if he yaf,° he dorste make avaunt,° — *gave / (the Friar) dared assert*
He wiste° that a man was repentaunt. — *knew*
For many a man so hard is of his herte,
230 He may nat wepe al-thogh hym sore smerte:° — *it sorely pain him*
Therfore, in stede of wepinge and preyeres,
Men moot° yeve silver to the povre° freres. — *may / poor*
His tipet° was ay farsed° ful of knyves — *scarf / always stuffed*
And pinnes, for to yeven° faire wyves. — *give to*
235 And certeinly he hadde a murye note;° — *pleasant voice*
Wel coude he singe and pleyen on a rote;° — *stringed instrument*
Of yeddinges he bar outrely the prys.[4]
His nekke whyt was as the flour-de-lys;° — *lily*

---

7. That gleamed like a furnace (a fire) under a cauldron.
8. One licensed to beg within a certain region or limit.
9. The four orders of friars (Franciscan, Dominican, Carmelite, and Augustinian).

1. I.e., he gave them dowries out of his own funds, perhaps after having first seduced them himself.
2. With rich landholders everywhere in his region.
3. Wherever he knew (that he could expect) to have a good gift in return.
4. At narrative songs, he absolutely took the prize.

Therto° he strong was as a champioun.   *Moreover*

240 He knew the tavernes wel in every toun,
And everich hostiler° and tappestere°   *innkeeper / barmaid*
Bet than a lazar or a beggestere,[5]
For unto swich° a worthy man as he   *such*
Acorded nat, as by his facultee,[6]

245 To have with seke lazars° aqueyntaunce: *sick lepers*
It is nat honest,° it may nat avaunce°   *respectable / be profitable*
For to delen with no swich poraille,°   *such poor people*
But al with riche and selleres of vitaille.°   *victuals*
And over al,° ther as° profit sholde aryse,   *everywhere / wherever*

250 Curteys he was, and lowely of° servyse.   *humble in*
Ther nas° no man nowher so vertuous.°   *was not / capable*
He was the beste beggere in his hous,

252a [And yaf° a certeyn ferme° for the graunt: *gave / payment*
252b Noon of his bretheren cam ther in his haunt.]°   *area of begging*
For thogh a widwe° hadde noght a sho,°   *widow / shoe*
So plesaunt was his *In principio*,°   *"In the beginning"*

255 Yet wolde he have a ferthing,° er he wente.   *farthing*
His purchas was wel bettre than his rente.[7]
And rage he coude, as it were right a whelpe;[8]
In love-dayes° ther coude he muchel° helpe,   *legal arbitrations / much*
For there he was nat lyk a cloisterer,[9]

260 With a thredbare cope,° as is a povre scoler.   *cape*
But he was lyk a maister° or a pope: *Master of Arts*
Of double worsted was his semi-cope,°   *half-cape*
That rounded as a belle out of the presse.°   *mould*
Somwhat he lipsed, for his wantownesse,[1]

265 To make his English swete upon his tonge;
And in his harping, whan that he hadde songe,
His eyen° twinkled in his heed aright   *eyes*
As doon° the sterres° in the frosty night.   *do / stars*
This worthy limitour was cleped° Huberd.   *called*

270   A MARCHANT was ther with a forked berd,°   *beard*
In mottelee,° and hye[2] on horse he sat;   *figured cloth*
Upon his heed a Flaundrish° bever° hat,   *Flemish / beaver fur*
His bootes clasped° faire and fetisly.°   *tied / neatly*
His resons° he spak ful solempnely,°   *opinions / impressively*

275 Souninge° alway th'encrees° of his winning.° *Proclaiming / increase / profit*
He wolde the see were kept for any thing[3]

---

5. Better than a leper or beggar woman.
6. It was not fitting, considering his position.
7. His profit from begging was much greater than "his regular income," or "the fee he paid for his exclusive begging rights." (Meaning uncertain.)
8. And he knew how to play and flirt, as if he were a puppy.
9. A religious who knows only the enclosed life of the cloister.
1. He lisped a little, out of affectation.
2. On a high saddle.
3. He wanted the sea to be guarded (against pirates) at any cost. (His profits depended on it.)

Bitwixe Middelburgh° and Orewelle.°   *(in Holland) / (in England)*
Wel coude he in eschaunge° sheeldes° selle.   *foreign exchange / French coins*
This worthy man ful wel his wit bisette:°   *used*
280 Ther wiste no wight° that he was in dette,   *no person knew*
So estatly° was he of his governaunce,°   *dignified / conduct*
With his bargaynes and with his chevisaunce.°   *(possibly illegal) lending*
For sothe he was a worthy man with alle,
But sooth to seyn, I noot° how men him calle.   *know not*
285   A CLERK° ther was of Oxenford° also,   *student / Oxford*
That unto logik hadde longe y-go.[4]
As leene° was his hors as is a rake,   *lean*
And he nas° nat right fat, I undertake,°   *was not / declare*
But loked holwe,° and therto° soberly.   *hollow / also*
290 Ful thredbar was his overest courtepy,°   *outer short cloak*
For he hadde geten him° yet no benefyce,   *obtained for himself*
Ne was so worldly for to have offyce;°   *secular employment*
For him was levere° have at his beddes heed   *he would rather*
Twenty bokes, clad° in blak or reed,   *bound*
295 Of Aristotle and his philosophye,
Than robes riche, or fithele,° or gay sautrye.°   *fiddle / psaltery, harp*
But al be that° he was a philosophre,[5]   *although*
Yet hadde he but litel gold in cofre;°   *coffer*
But al that he mighte of his freendes hente,°   *get*
300 On bokes and on lerninge he it spente,
And bisily gan for the soules preye[6]
Of hem that yaf him wherwith[7] to scoleye.°   *study*
Of studie took he most cure° and most hede.°   *care / heed*
Noght o° word spak he more than was nede,   *Not one*
305 And that was seyd in forme° and reverence,°   *properly / respectfully*
And short and quik, and ful of hy sentence.°   *serious meaning*
Souninge° in moral vertu was his speche,   *Resounding*
And gladly wolde he lerne, and gladly teche.
  A SERGEANT OF THE LAWE,° war° and wys,   *eminent lawyer / alert*
310 That often hadde been at the Parvys,[8]
Ther was also, ful riche of excellence.
Discreet he was and of greet reverence:[9]
He semed swich,° his wordes weren so wyse.   *such*
Justyce° he was ful often in assyse,°   *Judge / local courts*
315 By patente° and by pleyn° commissioun;   *letter of appointment / full*
For his science° and for his heigh renoun,   *knowledge*
Of fees and robes hadde he many oon.°   *a one*

4. Who had long since proceeded to (the study of) logic in the university curriculum.
5. With a pun on alchemist, another meaning of the word.
6. And busily did pray for the souls.
7. I.e., the means.
8. The porch of St. Paul's Cathedral, a favorite gathering place for lawyers.
9. Worthy of great respect.

So greet a purchasour° was nowher noon:°   *speculator in land / none*
Al was fee simple to him in effect;[1]
320 His purchasing mighte nat been infect.°   *invalidated*
Nowher so bisy a man as he ther nas;
And yet he semed bisier than he was.
In termes hadde he caas and domes alle,[2]
That from the tyme of King William[3] more falle,°   *had taken place*
325 Therto he coude endyte,° and make a thing;°   *write / draw up papers*
Ther coude no wight pinche at° his wryting,   *no one find fault with*
And every statut coude° he pleyn by rote.°   *knew / completely by heart*
He rood but hoomly° in a medlee° cote,   *informally / figured*
Girt with a ceint° of silk, with barres° smale;   *girdle / metal bars*
330 Of his array telle I no lenger tale.
    A FRANKELEYN° was in his companye.   *wealthy landowner*
Whyt was his berd as is the dayesye;°   *daisy*
Of his complexioun° he was sangwyn.°   *temperament / sanguine*
Wel loved he by the morwe a sop in wyn.[4]
335 To liven in delyt was everc his wone,°   *custom*
For he was Epicurus[5] owene sone,
That heeld opinioun that pleyn° delyt   *complete*
Was verray° felicitee parfyt.°   *true / perfect*
An housholdere, and that a greet,° was he;   *a great one*
340 Seint Julian[6] he was in his contree.°   *region*
His breed, his ale, was alweys after oon;°   *of uniform good quality*
A bettre cnvyned° man was nowher noon.   *stocked with wine*
Withoute bake mete° was nevere his hous,   *meat pies*
Of fish and flesh,° and that so plentevous°   *meat / plentiful*
345 It snewed° in his hous of mete° and drinke.   *snowed / food*
Of alle deyntees° that men coude thinke,   *delicacies*
After° the sondry sesons of the yeer,   *According to*
So chaunged° he his mete° and his soper.   *varied / dinner*
Ful many a fat partrich° hadde he in mewe,°   *partridge / coop*
350 And many a breem° and many a luce° in stewe.°   *carp / pike / fishpond*
Wo° was his cook, but if° his sauce were   *(Made) sorry / unless*
Poynaunt° and sharp, and redy al his gere.°   *Pungent / utensils*
His table dormant[7] in his halle° alway   *main room*
Stood redy covered° al the longe day.   *set*
355 At sessiouns ther was he lord and sire;[8]
Ful ofte tyme he was knight of the shire.[9]

---

1. I.e., he always got unrestricted possession ("fee simple") of the property.
2. He knew the exact terms (details) of all the cases and decisions.
3. I.e., since the Norman Conquest (1066).
4. In the morning he dearly loved a sop (a piece of bread or cake) in wine.
5. A Greek philosopher who held that pleasure was the highest good.
6. The patron saint of hospitality.
7. Most tables were made of boards laid on trestles and were taken down after each meal; this one seems to have been permanent.
8. I.e., he presided over meetings of local justices of the peace, when they gathered to hear cases.
9. Member of Parliament for his county.

An anlas° and a gipser° al of silk — *dagger / purse*
Heng° at his girdel, whyt as morne° milk. — *Hung / morning*
A shirreve° hadde he been, and a countour;° — *sheriff / auditor*
360 Was nowher such a worthy vavasour.° — *landholder*
    An HABERDASSHER and a CARPENTER,
A WEBBE,° a DYERE, and a TAPICER,° — *weaver / tapestry-maker*
Were with us eek, clothed in o liveree° — *one livery (uniform)*
Of a solempne° and greet fraternitee.° — *distinguished / (parish) guild*
365 Ful fresh and newe hir gere° apyked° was; — *equipment / adorned*
Hir knyves were chaped° noght with bras, — *mounted*
But al with silver; wroght ful clene and weel
Hire girdles° and hire pouches° everydeel.° — *belts / purses / altogether*
Wel semed ech of hem a fair burgeys° — *citizen, burgher*
370 To sitten in a yeldhalle° on a deys.[1] — *guildhall*
Everich,° for the wisdom that he can,° — *Each one / knows*
Was shaply° for to been an alderman. — *fit*
For catel° hadde they ynogh and rente,° — *property / income*
And eek° hir wyves wolde it wel assente;° — *also / assent to*
375 And elles° certein were they to blame.° — *otherwise / deserving of blame*
It is ful fair to been y-clept° "Madame,"° — *called / "my lady"*
And goon to vigilyës al bifore,[2]
And have a mantel royalliche y-bore.° — *royally carried*
    A COOK they hadde with hem for the nones,° — *occasion*
380 To boille the chiknes° with the mary-bones° — *chickens / marrowbones*
And poudre-marchant tart and galingale.[3]
Wel coude he knowe° a draughte of London ale. — *recognize*
He coude° roste, and sethe,° and broille, and frye, — *knew how to / boil*
Maken mortreux,° and wel bake a pye. — *stews*
385 But greet harm° was it, as it thoughte° me, — *misfortune / seemed to*
That on his shine° a mormal° hadde he. — *shin / ulcerous sore*
For blankmanger,[4] that made he with the beste.
    A SHIPMAN was ther, woninge fer by weste:[5]
For aught I woot,° he was of Dertemouthe.° — *know / Dartmouth (in Devon)*
390 He rood upon a rouncy, as he couthe,[6]
In a gowne of falding° to the knee. — *heavy wool*
A daggere hanginge on a laas° hadde he — *cord*
Aboute his nekke, under his arm adoun.
The hote somer° hadde maad his hewe al broun; — *summer*
395 And certeinly he was a good felawe.° — *cheerful companion*
Ful many a draughte of wyn had he y-drawe° — *drawn off*

---

1. The dais (a raised platform) on which the mayor or alderman of a city sat.
2. And go to church vigils at the head of the procession.
3. Both are spices, one tart and one sweet.
4. An elaborate dish of chicken in a sweet milk-and-rice sauce.
5. There was a shipmaster, dwelling far off to the west.
6. He rode on a small sturdy horse, as (well as) he knew how. (A man more used to ships than horses.)

Fro Burdeux-ward, whyl that the chapman sleep.[7]
Of nyce° conscience took he no keep:°   *scrupulous / heed*
If that he faught, and hadde the hyer hond,°   *upper hand*
400 By water he sente hem hoom[8] to every lond.
But of his craft, to rekene wel his tydes,[9]
His stremes° and his daungers him bisydes,°   *currents / close to him*
His herberwe° and his mone,° his lodemenage,°   *harbor / moon / pilotage*
Ther nas noon swich° from Hulle to Cartage.[1]   *such*
405 Hardy he was, and wys to undertake;[2]
With many a tempest hadde his berd been shake.
He knew wel alle the havenes,° as they were,   *harbors*
From Gootlond to the cape of Finistere,[3]
And every cryke° in Britayne° and in Spayne;   *creek / Brittany*
410 His barge y-cleped° was the Maudelayne.°   *called / Magdalen*
     With us ther was a DOCTOUR OF PHISYK;°   *a physician*
In al this world ne was ther noon him lyk
To speke of phisik° and of surgerye,   *In regard to medicine*
For he was grounded in astronomye.°   *astrology*
415 He kepte° his pacient a ful greet deel   *watched*
In houres, by his magik naturel.[4]
Wel coude he fortunen the ascendent
Of his images for his pacient.[5]
He knew the cause of everich maladye,
420 Were it of hoot or cold, or moiste, or drye,[6]
And where engendred,° and of what humour;   *originated*
He was a verrey° parfit practisour.°   *true / practitioner*
The cause y-knowe,° and of his harm° the roote,°   *known / malady / cause*
Anon° he yaf° the seke man his boote.°   *Quickly / gave / remedy*
425 Ful redy hadde he his apothecaries,[7]
To sende him drogges and his letuaries,°   *medicinal syrups*
For ech of hem made other for to winne;°   *profit*
Hir° frendschipe nas nat newe to biginne.°   *Their / recently begun*
Wel knew he the olde Esculapius,
430 And Deiscorides, and eek Rufus,
Old Ypocras, Haly, and Galien,
Serapion, Razis, and Avicen,
Averrois, Damascien, and Constantyn,

---

7. On the way from Bordeaux, while the (wine-)
merchant slept.
8. I.e., drowned them.
9. But at his craft, in calculating well the tides.
1. From Hull (in England) to Carthage (in northern
Africa) or possibly Cartagena (in Spain).
2. Prudent in the risks he undertook.
3. From Gotland (an island in the Baltic Sea) to
Cape Finisterre (in Spain).
4. During those hours (best for treatment), through

his knowledge of natural magic (i.e., astrology).
5. He knew well how to determine the most favorable position of the stars for (making astrological)
images for his patient.
6. The four fundamental qualities, which were
thought to combine in pairs to form the four elements and the four humors (melancholia, cholera,
phlegm, and blood); bodily health depended upon
the existence of a proper equilibrium between them.
7. I.e., pharmacists.

Bernard, and Gatesden, and Gilbertyn.[8]

435 Of his diete mesurable° was he,   *moderate*
For it was of no superfluitee,
But of greet norissing° and digestible.   *nourishment*
His studie was but litel on the Bible.[9]
In sangwin° and in pers° he clad was al,   *bloodred / blue*
440 Lyned with taffata and with sendal;[1]
And yet he was but esy of dispence.°   *slow to spend*
He kepte that he wan in pestilence,
For gold in phisik is a cordial;[2]
Therefore he lovede gold in special.°   *particularly*
     A good WYF was ther of bisyde BATHE,°   *from near Bath*
445 But she was somdel° deef, and that was scathe.°   *somewhat / a pity*
Of clooth-making she hadde swiche an haunt,°   *such practiced skill*
She passed° hem of Ypres and of Gaunt.[3]   *surpassed*
In al the parisshe wyf ne was ther noon
450 That to the offringe° bifore hir sholde goon;°   *offering in church / go*
And if ther dide, certeyn so wrooth° was she,   *angry*
That she was out of alle charitee.
Hir coverchiefs° ful fyne were of ground;°   *kerchiefs / texture*
I dorste° swere they weyeden° ten pound   *would dare / weighed*
455 That on a Sonday weren upon hir heed.
Hir hosen° weren of fyn scarlet reed,   *hose*
Ful streite y-teyd,° and shoos ful moiste° and newe.   *tightly tied / soft*
Bold was hir face, and fair, and reed of hewe.°   *hue*
She was a worthy womman al hir lyve:
460 Housbondes at chirche dore[4] she hadde fyve,
Withouten° other companye in youthe—   *Not to mention*
But therof nedeth nat to speke as nouthe°—   *at present*
And thryes° hadde she been at Jerusalem.   *thrice*
She hadde passed many a straunge streem:[5]
465 At Rome she hadde been, and at Boloigne,°   *Boulogne (France)*
In Galice at Seint Jame, and at Coloigne;[6]
She coude° muchel of wandringe by the weye.°   *knew / along the road(s)*
Gat-tothed° was she, soothly for to seye.   *Gap-toothed*
Upon an amblere° esily° she sat,   *saddle-horse / comfortably*
470 Y-wimpled° wel, and on hir heed an hat   *Covered with a wimple*
As brood as is a bokeler or a targe;[7]

8. A list of the best medical authorities, ancient and modern (e.g., John of Gaddesden, an Englishman, died ca. 1349).
9. Doctors were often held to be skeptical in religious matters.
1. With linings of taffeta and fine silk.
2. He kept what he had earned during time of plague, for gold in medicine is good for the heart. (An ironic reference to *aurum potabile*, a liquid medicine compounded of gold and held to be a sovereign remedy for disease.)

3. Cloth-making in the Low Countries (here represented by Ypres and Ghent) was of high repute.
4. The medieval marriage ceremony was customarily performed by the priest on the church porch. Afterward the company entered the church to hear the nuptial mass.
5. She had crossed many a foreign river.
6. In Galicia (in Spain) at (the shrine of) St. James of Compostella, and at Cologne.
7. Both buckler and targe are shields.

A foot-mantel° aboute hir hipes large,   *outer skirt*
And on hir feet a paire of spores° sharpe.   *spurs*
In felawschipe wel coude she laughe and carpe.°   *talk*
475 Of remedyes of love she knew per chaunce,°   *as it happened*
For she coude° of that art the olde daunce.°   *knew / (steps of the) dance*
   A good man was ther of religioun,
And was a povre PERSOUN° of a toun   *poor parson*
But riche he was of holy thoght and werk.
480 He was also a lerned man, a clerk,°   *scholar*
That Cristes gospel trewely wolde preche;
His parisshens° devoutly wolde he teche.   *parishioners*
Benigne° he was, and wonder° diligent,   *Kindly / very*
And in adversitee ful pacient,
485 And swich he was y-preved ofte sythes.[8]
Ful looth° were him to cursen° for his tithes,   *loath / excommunicate*
But rather wolde he yeven,° out of doute,°   *give / there is no doubt*
Unto his povre parisshens aboute
Of° his offring, and eek of his substaunce.°   *From / income*
490 He coude in litel thing han suffisaunce.[9]
Wyd was his parisshe, and houses fer asonder,
But he ne lafte° nat, for reyn ne° thonder,   *ceased / nor*
In siknes nor in meschief,° to visyte   *misfortune*
The ferreste in his parisshe, muche and lyte,[1]
495 Upon his feet, and in his hand a staf.
This noble ensample° to his sheep he yaf,°   *example / gave*
That first he wroghte,° and afterward he taughte.   *did (what was right)*
Out of the gospel he tho° wordes caughte,°   *those / took*
And this figure° he added eek therto,   *metaphor, image*
500 That if gold ruste, what shal iren° do?   *iron*
For if a preest be foul,° on whom we truste,   *corrupted*
No wonder is a lewed man to ruste;[2]
And shame it is, if a preest take keep,°   *heed (it)*
A shiten[3] shepherde and a clene sheep.
505 Wel oghte a preest ensample for to yive,°   *give*
By his clennesse, how that his sheep sholde live.
He sette nat his benefice to hyre,[4]
And leet° his sheep encombred in the myre,   *left*
And ran to London unto Seynte Poules°   *St. Paul's cathedral*
510 To seken him a chaunterie for soules,
Or with a bretherhed to been withholde,[5]

8. And he was proved (to be) such many times.
9. He knew how to have enough in very little.
1. The furthest (members) of his parish, great and humble.
2. It is no wonder that an unlearned man (should go) to rust.
3. I.e., covered with excrement.
4. He did not hire out (i.e., engage a substitute for)
his benefice (church appointment).
5. To seek for himself an appointment as a chantry-priest singing masses for the souls of the dead, or to be retained (as a chaplain) by a guild. (Both sorts of position were relatively undemanding, and paid enough for such a priest to retain a curate at home and have money to spare.)

But dwelte at hoom, and kepte° wel his folde,   *took care of*
So that the wolf ne made it nat miscarie;°   *come to harm*
He was a shepherde and noght a mercenarie.
515 And though he holy were, and vertuous,
He was to sinful men nat despitous,°   *scornful*
Ne of his speche daungerous ne digne,°   *haughty nor disdainful*
But in his teching discreet and benigne.
To drawen folk to heven by fairnesse,
520 By good ensample, this was his bisinesse;°   *endeavor*
But it were° any persone obstinat,   *were there*
What so° he were, of heigh or lough estat,°   *Whatever / condition, class*
Him wolde he snibben° sharply for the nones.°   *rebuke / on such an occasion*
A bettre preest I trowe° that nowher noon is.   *believe*
525 He wayted after° no pompe and reverence,   *looked for*
Ne maked him a spyced conscience,[6]
But Cristes lore,° and his apostles twelve,   *teaching*
He taughte, and first he folwed it himselve.
    With him ther was a PLOWMAN, was his brother,
530 That hadde y-lad° of dong° ful many a fother.°   *hauled / dung / cartload*
A trewe swinkere° and a good was he,   *worker*
Livinge in pees° and parfit charitee.   *peace*
God loved he best with al his hole° herte   *whole*
At alle tymes, thogh him gamed or smerte,[7]
535 And thanne his neighebour right as himselve.
He wolde thresshe, and therto dyke° and delve,°   *make ditches / dig*
For Cristes sake, for every povre wight,°   *poor man*
Withouten hyre,° if it lay in his might.°   *wages / power*
His tythes° payed he ful faire and wel,   *tithes*
540 Bothe of his propre swink° and his catel.°   *own work / possessions*
In a tabard° he rood upon a mere.°   *smock / mare*
    Ther was also a Reve° and a Millere,   *Reeve*
A Somnour° and a Pardoner also,   *Summoner*
A Maunciple,° and myself—ther were namo.°   *Manciple / no more*
    The MILLERE was a stout carl° for the nones;[8]   *exceedingly strong man*
546 Ful big he was of brawn, and eek of bones—
That proved wel, for over al ther he cam,
At wrastling he wolde have alwey the ram.[9]
He was short-sholdred, brood, a thikke knarre:°   *knotty fellow*
550 Ther nas no dore that he nolde heve of harre,[1]
Or breke it at a renning° with his heed.   *(by butting it)*
His berd as any sowe or fox was reed,

---

6. Nor affected an overly scrupulous nature.
7. At all times, whether he was glad or in distress.
8. A tag-ending, useful to fill out the line metrically, but almost wholly devoid of meaning (cf. 1. 523).

9. That (was) well proved, for everywhere he went, at wrestling contests he would always win the ram (a usual prize).
1. There was no door he wasn't willing to heave off (its) hinges.

And therto brood, as though it were a spade.
Upon the cop right° of his nose he hade   *very top*
555 A werte,° and theron stood a tuft of herys,   *wart*
Reed as the bristles of a sowes erys;°   *ears*
His nosethirles° blake were and wyde.   *nostrils*
A swerd and a bokeler° bar he by his syde.   *small shield*
His mouth as greet° was as a greet forneys;°   *large / furnace*
560 He was a janglere° and a goliardeys,°   *chatterer / teller of jests*
And that was most of sinne and harlotryes.°   *vulgarities*
Wel coude he stelen corn, and tollen thryes,[2]
And yet he hadde a thombe of gold, pardee.[3]
A whyt cote and a blew hood wered° he.   *wore*
565 A baggepype wel coude he blowe and sowne,°   *play*
And therwithal° he broghte us out of towne.   *with it*
        A gentil° MAUNCIPLE was ther of a temple,[4]   *worthy, proper*
Of which° achatours° mighte take exemple   *From whom / buyers*
For to be wyse in bying of vitaille,°   *provisions*
570 For whether that he payde, or took by taille,°   *on account*
Algate he wayted so in his achat[5]
That he was ay biforn° and in good stat.   *always ahead*
Now is nat that of God a ful fair grace,
That swich a lewed° mannes wit shal pace°   *unlearned / surpass*
575 The wisdom of an heep of lerned men?
Of maistres hadde he mo° than thryes ten   *more*
That weren of° lawe expert and curious,°   *in / skillful*
Of which° ther were a doseyn° in that hous   *Among whom / dozen*
Worthy to been stiwardes of rente° and lond   *income*
580 Of any lord that is in Engelond,
To make him live by his propre good[6]
In honour, dettelees,° but° he were wood,°   *debtless / unless / mad*
Or live as scarsly as him list desire,[7]
And[8] able for to helpen al a shire°   *an entire county*
585 In any cas° that mighte falle° or happe;   *eventuality / befall*
And yit this maunciple sette hir aller cappe.°   *made fools of them all*
        The REVE was a sclendre colerik man.[9]
His berd was shave as ny° as ever he can;   *close*
His heer was by his eres° ful round y-shorn;°   *ears / cut off*
590 His top was dokked° lyk a preest biforn.°   *cut short / in front*

2. He knew well how to steal corn and take his toll
(his percentage for grinding it) three times over.
3. The proverb "An honest miller hath a golden
thumb" implies there are no honest millers; "pardee"
is a weak form of "by God," perhaps best translated
simply as "I swear."
4. A manciple was in charge of purchasing provisions for a college or (as here) for an inn of court,
where law was studied.
5. He was always so watchful in his purchasing.

6. Within his own income.
7. Or live as frugally as it pleases him to wish.
8. The subject is again the "doseyn" men of l. 578
worthy to be stewards.
9. A reeve was manager and accountant on an estate
or manor and chosen from among the serfs. This
one is choleric, i.e., dominated by the humor called
choler (or yellow bile), and thus hot-tempered by
nature.

Ful longe were his legges, and ful lene,
Y-lyk° a staf; ther was no calf y-sene.°   *Like / to be seen*
Wel coude he kepe a gerner° and a binne—   *granary*
Ther was noon auditour coude on him winne.°   *catch him short*
595 Wel wiste° he by the droghte and by the reyn   *knew*
The yeldinge of his seed and of his greyn.
His lordes sheep, his neet,° his dayerye,°   *cattle / dairy cows*
His swyn, his hors, his stoor,° and his pultrye,°   *livestock / poultry*
Was hoolly° in this reves governinge,   *wholly*
600 And by his covenaunt° yaf° the rekeninge,   *contract / (he) gave*
Sin that° his lord was twenty yeer of age.   *Since*
Ther coude no man bringe him in arrerage.°   *arrears*
Ther nas baillif, ne herde, ne other hyne,¹
That he ne knew his sleighte° and his covyne;°   *cunning / deceit*
605 They were adrad° of him as of the deeth.²   *afraid*
His woning° was ful fair upon an heeth;   *dwelling*
With grene trees shadwed was his place.
He coude bettre than his lord purchace.³
Ful riche he was astored prively;°   *privately stocked*
610 His lord wel coude he plesen subtilly,
To yeve and lene him of his owne good,
And have a thank, and yet a cote and hood.⁴
In youthe he hadde lerned a good mister:°   *trade*
He was a wel good wrighte,° a carpenter.   *craftsman*
615 This reve sat upon a ful good stot°   *farm horse*
That was al pomely° grey and highte° Scot.   *dappled / named*
A long surcote° of pers° upon he hade,   *outer coat / blue cloth*
And by his syde he bar° a rusty blade.   *bore*
Of Northfolk° was this reve of which I tell,   *Norfolk*
620 Bisyde° a toun men clepen° Baldeswelle.   *(From) near / call*
Tukked° he was as is a frere° aboute;   *Belted / friar*
And evere he rood the hindreste° of oure route.°   *hindmost / company*
    A SOMONOUR⁵ was ther with us in that place,
That hadde a fyr-reed cherubinnes face,⁶
625 For saucefleem° he was, with eyen° narwe.   *pimpled / eyes*
As hoot° he was and lecherous as a sparwe,°   *passionate / sparrow*
With scalled° browes blake, and piled berd;°   *scabby / scraggy beard*
Of his visage° children were aferd.°   *face / afraid*

---

1. There was no overseer, nor herdsman, nor (any) other servant.
2. Death in general, or perhaps the Black Death (plague).
3. He knew, better than his lord, how to increase one's possessions.
4. He knew well how to please his lord in sly ways, giving and lending to him from his (the lord's) own resources, and earn thanks (for it), and a coat and hood besides.

5. A summoner was an officer who cited ("summoned") malefactors to appear before an ecclesiastical court: in this case, an archdeacon's, having jurisdiction over matrimonial cases, adultery, and fornication.
6. Cherubim, the second order of angels, were sometimes painted brilliant red ("fire-red") in medieval art. The summoner resembles them, not through beatitude, but through a skin disease.

Ther nas quik-silver, litarge,° ne brimstoon,   *lead oxide*
630 Boras,° ceruce,° ne oille° of tartre noon,   *Borax / white lead / cream*
Ne oynement that wolde clense and byte,°   *sting*
That him mighte helpen of° his whelkes° whyte,   *cure / pimples*
Nor of the knobbes° sittinge on his chekes.   *lumps*
Wel loved he garleek, oynons, and eek lekes,°   *leeks*
635 And for to drinken stronge wyn, reed as blood
Thanne wolde he speke, and crye° as° he were wood;°   *shout / as if / mad*
And whan that he wel dronken hadde the wyn,
Thanne wolde he speke no word but Latyn.°   *(in) Latin*
A fewe termes° hadde he, two or three,   *technical phrases*
640 That he had lerned out of som decree—
No wonder is,° he herde it al the day;   *it is*
And eek ye knowen wel, how that a jay°   *a chattering bird*
Can clepen "Watte" as well as can the Pope.[7]
But whoso coude in other thing him grope,°   *question*
645 Thanne hadde he spent° al his philosophye;   *exhausted*
Ay "*Questio quid iuris*" wolde he crye.[8]
He was a gentil° harlot° and a kinde;°   *worthy / rascal / natural one*
A bettre felawe° sholde men noght finde: *companion*
He wolde suffre,° for a quart of wyn,   *allow*
650 A good felawe to have his concubyn
A° twelf-month, and excuse him atte fulle;°   *(For) a / fully*
Ful prively a finch eek coude he pulle.[9]
And if he fond° owher° a good felawe,   *found / anywhere*
He wolde techen him to have non awe°   *fear*
655 In swich cas of the erchedeknes curs,[1]
But-if° a mannes soule were in his purs,   *Unless*
For in his purs he sholde y-punisshed be.
"Purs is the erchedeknes helle," seyde he.
But wel I woot° he lyed right in dede: *know*
660 Of cursing oghte ech gilty man him drede—
For curs wol slee, right as assoilling saveth—
And also war him of a *significavit*.[2]
In daunger° hadde he at° his owene gyse°   *his power / in / way*
The yonge girles° of the diocyse,   *wenches*
665 And knew hir counseil,° and was al hir reed.°   *their secrets / adviser to them all*
A gerland° hadde he set upon his heed,   *garland*
As greet as it were for an ale-stake;°   *tavern sign*
A bokeler° hadde he maad him of a cake.°   *shield / round bread*

7. Knows how to say "Walter" as well as does the Pope.
8. He would always cry "The question is what point of law applies?"
9. He was skilled in secretly seducing girls. ("To pull a finch," i.e., to pluck a bird, was an obscene expression.)
1. Curse, the power of excommunication.
2. Every guilty man ought to be fearful of excommunication, for it will slay (the soul eternally), just as absolution (the forgiveness granted through the sacrament of penance) saves—and (he ought) also beware a *significavit* (a writ of arrest).

With him ther rood a gentil PARDONER [3]
670 Of Rouncival, [4] his freend and his compeer,° companion
That streight was comen fro the court of Rome.
Ful loude he song,° "Com hider,° love, to me." sang / hither
This somnour bar to° him a stif burdoun,° accompanied / sturdy bass
Was nevere trompe° of half so greet a soun.° trumpet / sound
675 This pardoner hadde heer° as yelow as wex,° hair / wax
But smothe it heng,° as dooth a strike of flex;° hung / bunch of flax
By ounces° henge his lokkes that he hadde, In thin strands
And therwith° he his shuldres overspradde;° with it / covered
But thinne it lay, by colpons° oon and oon; in small bunches
680 But hood, for jolitee,° wered° he noon, sportiveness / wore
For it was trussed° up in his walet.° packed / pouch
Him thoughte he rood al of the newe jet;
Dischevele, save his cappe, he rood al bare. [5]
Swiche glaringe eyen° hadde he as an hare. staring eyes
685 A vernicle [6] hadde he sowed on his cappe.
His walet lay biforn° him in his lappe, in front of
Bretful of pardoun comen from Rome al hoot. [7]
A voys he hadde as smal as hath a goot.° goat
No berd hadde he, ne nevere sholde have,
690 As smothe it was as it were late shave:° recently shaved
I trowe° he were a gelding or a mare. believe
But of his craft, fro Berwik into Ware, [8]
Ne was ther swich another pardoner.
For in his male° he hadde a pilwe-beer,° bag / pillowcase
695 Which that he seyde was Oure Lady veyl.° Our Lady's veil
He seyde he hadde a gobet° of the seyl° piece / sail
That seynt Peter hadde, whan that he wente° walked
Upon the see, til Jesu Crist him hente.° took hold of
He hadde a croys° of latoun,° ful of stones,° cross / metal / gems
700 And in a glas° he hadde pigges bones. glass container
But with thise relikes,° whan that he fond relics
A povre person dwellinge upon lond, [9]
Upon a° day he gat him more moneye In one
Than that the person gat in monthes tweye.° two
705 And thus, with feyned flaterye and japes,° tricks
He made the person and the peple his apes.° fools
But trewely to tellen, atte laste,° after all

3. A pardoner was a seller of papal indulgences (remissions of punishment for sin), whose proceeds were often intended to build or support a religious house. Many pardoners were fraudulent, and their abuses were much criticized.
4. Near Charing Cross in London.
5. It seemed to him he rode in the very latest fashion; (his hair) loose, he rode bareheaded except for his cap.
6. A copy of the veil St. Veronica gave to Christ when He was carrying the cross, that He might wipe His brow; it received the imprint of Christ's face.
7. Brimful of pardons, come all hot (fresh) from Rome.
8. I.e., from north to south.
9. A poor parson living in the country.

He was in chirche a noble ecclesiaste.°   *preacher*
Wel coude he rede a lessoun or a storie,°   *religious tale*
710 But alderbest° he song° an offertorie;   *best of all / sang*
For wel he wiste,° whan that song was songe,   *knew*
He moste preche, and wel affyle° his tonge   *make smooth*
To winne silver, as he ful wel coude—
Therefore he song the murierly° and leude.   *more merrily*
715   Now have I told you soothly, in a clause,°   *briefly*
Th'estaat, th'array, the nombre, and eek the cause
Why that assembled was this compaignye
In Southwerk, at this gentil° hostelrye,   *worthy*
That highte° the Tabard, faste° by the Belle.°   *was called / close / Bell Inn*
720 But now is tyme to yow for to telle
How that we baren us° that ilke° night,   *conducted ourselves / same*
Whan we were in that hostelryc alight;°   *alighted*
And after wol I telle of our viage,°   *journey*
And al the remenaunt° of oure pilgrimage.   *remainder*
725 But first I pray yow, of youre curteisye,
That ye n'arette it nat my vileinye,[1]
Thogh that° I pleynly speke in this matere,   *Even though*
To tell yow hir° wordes and hir chere,°   *their / behavior*
Ne thogh I speke hir wordes properly.°   *exactly*
730 For this ye knowen al so wel as I:
Whoso shal telle a tale after a man,[2]
He moot reherce° as ny° as evere he can   *must repeat / closely*
Everich a word, if it be in his charge,
Al speke he never so rudeliche and large;[3]
735 Or elles° he moot° telle his tale untrewe,   *else / must*
Or feyne thing,° or finde wordes newe.   *invent something*
He may nat spare, althogh he[4] were his brother;
He moot° as wel seye o° word as another.   *must / one*
Crist spak himself ful brode° in Holy Writ,   *broadly*
740 And wel ye woot,° no vileinye° is it.   *know / churlishness*
Eek Plato seith, whoso can him rede,
The wordes mote be cosin° to the dede.   *cousin*
Also I prey yow to foryeve° it me,   *forgive*
Al have I nat set folk in hir degree[5]
745 Here in this tale, as that they sholde stonde;
My wit is short, ye may wel understonde.
   Greet chere made oure Hoste us everichon,[6]
And to the soper sette he us anon;°   *immediately*

---

1. That you do not attribute it to my churlishness.
2. I.e., repeats another man's story.
3. Each and every word, if that be the responsibility
he's charged with, however roughly and broadly he
(may) speak.

4. I.e., the original teller.
5. Although I haven't described (these) people in
(the order of) their social rank.
6. Our host made great welcome to every one of us.

He served us with vitaille° at the beste.   *victuals*
750 Strong was the wyn, and wel to drinke us leste.°   *it pleased us*
A semely° man oure hoste was withalle   *suitable*
For to been a marshal in an halle;[7]
A large man he was with eyen stepe°—   *protruding eyes*
A fairer burgeys° was ther noon in Chepe.°   *citizen / Cheapside (in London)*
755 Bold of his speche, and wys, and wel y-taught,
And of manhod him lakkede° right naught.   *he lacked*
Eek therto he was right° a mery man,   *truly*
And after soper pleyen° he bigan,   *to jest*
And spak of mirthe amonges othere thinges—
760 Whan that we hadde maad oure rekeninges°—   *paid our bills*
And seyde thus: "Now, lordinges, trewely,
Ye been° to me right welcome hertely.°   *are / heartily*
For by my trouthe, if that I shal nat lye,
I saugh nat this yeer so mery a compaignye
765 Atones° in this herberwe° as is now.   *At one time / inn*
Fayn wolde I doon yow mirthe, wiste I how,
And of a mirthe I am right now bithoght,[8]
To doon yow ese,° and it shal coste noght.   *give you pleasure*
    Ye goon° to Caunterbury—God yow spede;   *are going*
770 The blisful martir quyte° yow your mede.°   *pay / reward*
And wel I woot, as ye goon by the weye,
Ye shapen yow to talen and to pleye;[9]
For trewely, confort° ne mirthe is noon°   *pleasure / (there) is none*
To ryde by the weye doumb as a stoon;
775 And therfore wol I maken yow disport,°   *amusement*
As I seyde erst,° and doon yow som confort.   *before*
And if yow lyketh° alle, by oon° assent,   *it pleases you / one*
Now for to stonden at° my jugement,   *abide by*
And for to werken° as I shal yow seye,   *do*
780 To-morwe, whan ye ryden by the weye—
Now by my fader° soule that is deed—   *father's*
But° ye be merye, I wol yeve° yow myn heed.°   *Unless / give / head*
Hold up youre hondes, withouten more speche."
    Oure counseil° was nat longe for to seche;°   *decision / seek*
785 Us thoughte it was noght worth to make it wys,[1]
And graunted him withouten more avys,°   *further consideration*
And bad him seye his voirdit° as him leste.°   *verdict / it pleased him*
"Lordinges," quod° he, "now herkneth° for the beste,   *said / listen*
But tak it nought, I prey yow, in desdeyn.°   *disdain*
790 This is the poynt, to speken short and pleyn:

---

7. I.e., the officer in charge of the serving of meals and banquets in a great hall.
8. I would gladly make you (some) amusement, if I knew how, and I have just now thought of some fun.
9. You plan to tell tales and to play.
1. It seemed to us (that) it was not worth pondering over.

That ech of yow, to shorte with° oure weye,   *with which to shorten*
In this viage° shal telle tales tweye,°   *journey / two*
To Caunterbury-ward,° I mene° it so,   *toward Canterbury / intend*
And homward he shal tellen othere two,
795 Of aventures that whylom° han bifalle.   *once upon a time*
And which° of yow that bereth° him best of alle,   *whichever / conducts*
That is to seyn, that telleth in this cas°   *on this occasion*
Tales of best sentence° and most solas,°   *wisdom, instruction / delight*
Shal have a soper at oure aller cost°   *the expense of us all*
800 Here in this place, sittinge by this post,°   *column*
Whan that we come agayn fro Caunterbury.
And for to make yow the more mery,°   *merry*
I wol myselven goodly° with yow ryde,   *gladly*
Right at myn owne cost, and be youre gyde.
805 And whoso wole my jugement withseye°   *oppose*
Shal paye al that we spenden by the weye.
And if ye vouchesauf° that it be so,   *grant*
Tel me anon,° withouten wordes mo,°   *immediately / more*
And I wol erly shape me° therfore."   *prepare myself*
810   This thing was graunted, and oure othes° swore°   *oaths / sworn*
With ful glad herte, and preyden° him also   *we begged*
That he wolde vouchesauf for° to do so,   *grant*
And that he wolde been oure governour
And of oure tales juge and reportour,°   *referee(?)*
815 And sette a soper at a certeyn prys;°   *price*
And we wol reuled been at his devys°   *desire, will*
In heigh and lowe,°and thus, by oon assent,   *In all respects*
We been acorded to his jugement.
And therupon the wyn was fet° anon;°   *fetched / at once*
820 We dronken, and to reste wente echon,°   *each one*
Withouten any lenger taryinge.
        Amorwe,° whan that day bigan to springe,   *In the morning*
Up roos oure Host and was oure aller cok,²
And gadrede° us togidre,° alle in a flok;   *gathered / together*
825 And forth we riden,° a° litel more than pas,°   *rode / at a / walking speed*
Unto the watering of Seint Thomas,³
And there oure Host bigan his hors areste,°   *stopped his horse*
And seyde, "Lordinges, herkneth, if yow leste.°   *it may please*
Ye woot° youre forward,° and I it yow recorde.°   *know / agreement / recall*
830 If even-song and morwe-song° acorde,   *morning-song*
Lat se° now who shal telle the firste tale.   *Let us see*
As evere mote° I drinke wyn or ale,   *may*
Whoso be rebel to my jugement

2. The rooster who wakened us all.
3. St. Thomas a Watering was a brook two miles from London on the Canterbury road.

Shal paye for al that by the weye is spent.
835 Now draweth cut,° er that we ferrer twinne;°   *lots, cut straws / go farther*
He which that hath the shortest shal biginne.
Sire Knight," quod he, "my maister and my lord,
Now draweth cut, for that is myn acord.°   *decision*
Cometh neer,"° quod he, "my lady Prioresse;   *nearer*
840 And ye, sire Clerk, lat be° youre shamfastnesse,°   *leave off / shyness*
Ne studieth° noght. Ley hond to, every man!"   *deliberate*
Anon° to drawen every wight° bigan,   *At once / person*
And shortly for to tellen as it was,
Were it by aventure,° or sort,° or cas,°   *chance / fate / fortune*
845 The sothe° is this, the cut fil° to the Knight,   *truth / fell*
Of which ful blythe and glad was every wight;
And telle he moste° his tale, as was resoun,°   *must / right*
By forward° and by composicioun,°   *agreement / arrangement*
As ye han herd. What nedeth wordes mo?°   *more*
850 And whan this gode man saugh it was so,
As he that wys was and obedient
To kepe his forward by his free assent,
He seyde: "Sin° I shal biginne the game,   *Since*
What,° welcome be the cut, a Goddes° name!   *Why / in God's*
855 Now lat us ryde, and herkneth what I seye."
And with that word we riden° forth oure weye;   *rode*
And he bigan with right a mery chere[4]
His tale anon, and seyde as ye may heere.

The Knight's Tale

PART ONE

Whylom,° as olde stories tellen us,   *Once, formerly*
Ther was a duk that highte° Theseus;   *was called*
Of Athenes he was lord and governour,
And in his tyme swich° a conquerour,   *such*
5 That gretter was ther noon under the sonne.
Ful many a riche contree hadde he wonne;
What with his wisdom and his chivalrye,°   *knightly prowess*
He conquered al the regne° of Femenye,[1]   *kingdom, realm*
That whylom was y-cleped° Scithia,   *called*
10 And weddede the quene Ipolita,°   *Hippolyta*
And broghte hire hoom with him in his contree
With muchel glorie and greet solempnitee,°   *pomp, ceremony*
And eek hire yonge suster Emelye.

---

4. In a very merry mood.   1. The country of the Amazons.

And thus with victorie and with melodye
15 Lete I this noble duk to Athenes ryde,
And al his hoost, in armes, him bisyde.
    And certes,° if it nere° to long to here,   *certainly / were not*
I wolde have told yow fully the manere
How wonnen was the regne of Femenye
20 By Theseus, and by his chivalrye,°   *host of knights*
And of the grete bataille for the nones°   *occasion, purpose*
Bitwixen Athenës and Amazones;
And how asseged° was Ipolita,   *besieged*
The faire hardy quene of Scithia;
25 And of the feste that was at hir° weddinge,   *their*
And of the tempest at hir hoomcominge;
But al that thing I moot° as now° forbere.   *must / at this time*
I have, God woot,° a large feeld to ere,°   *knows / harrow, plough*
And wayke° been the oxen in my plough.   *weak*
30 The remenant of the tale is long ynough.
I wol nat letten° eek noon of this route;°   *hinder / company*
Lat every felawe telle his tale aboute,°   *in turn*
And lat see now who shal the soper winne;
And ther° I lefte, I wol ageyn biginne.   *where*
35   This duk, of whom I make mencioun,
When he was come almost unto the toun,
In al his wele° and in his moste pryde,   *success, happiness*
He was war,° as he caste his eye asyde,   *aware*
Where that ther kneled in the hye weye
40 A companye of ladies, tweye and tweye,°   *two by two*
Ech after other, clad in clothes blake;
But swich a cry and swich a wo they make,
That in this world nis° creature livinge,   *(there) is not*
That herde swich another weymentinge;°   *lamenting*
45 And of this cry they nolde° nevere stenten,°   *would not / cease*
Til they the reynes of his brydel henten.°   *seized*
    "What folk ben ye, that at myn hoomcominge
Perturben so my feste with cryinge?"
Quod Theseus. "Have ye so greet envye
50 Of myn honour, that° thus compleyne and crye?   *that ye*
Or who hath yow misboden° or offended?   *insulted, harmed*
And telleth me if it may been amended,
And why that ye ben clothed thus in blak."
    The eldeste lady of hem alle spak,
55 When she hadde swowned° with a deedly chere°   *fainted / deathly appearance*
That it was routhe° for to seen and here.   *a pity*
She seyde: "Lord, to whom Fortune hath yiven°   *given*
Victorie, and as a conquerour to liven,
Noght greveth us° youre glorie and youre honour;   *We do not resent*

60 But we biseken° mercy and socour.°   *beseech / aid, comfort*
    Have mercy on oure wo and oure distresse.
    Som drope of pitee, thurgh thy gentillesse,
    Upon us wrecched wommen lat thou falle.
    For certes, lord, ther nis noon of us alle,
65 That she ne hath been a duchesse or a quene;
    Now be we caitifs,° as it is wel sene,   *wretches*
    Thanked be Fortune and hire false wheel,
    That noon estat assureth to be weel.[2]
    And certes, lord, to abyden° your presence,   *await*
70 Here in this temple of the goddesse Clemence°   *Mercy*
    We han ben waytinge al this fourtenight;°   *fourteen nights*
    Now help us, lord, sith° it is in thy might.   *since*
        I, wrecche, which that wepe and waille thus,
    Was whylom° wyf to king Capaneus,   *once*
75 That starf° at Thebes—cursed be that day!   *died*
    And alle we that been in this array°   *condition*
    And maken al this lamentacioun,
    We losten alle oure housbondes at that toun,
    Whyl that the sege° theraboute lay.   *siege*
80 And yet now the olde Creon, weylaway,°   *alas*
    That lord is now of Thebes the citee,
    Fulfild° of ire and of iniquitee,   *filled full*
    He, for despyt° and for his tirannye,   *malice, spite*
    To do the dede bodyes vileinye,°   *outrage*
85 Of alle oure lordes whiche that ben y-slawe,°   *slain*
    Hath alle the bodyes on an heep y-drawe,°   *dragged*
    And wol nat suffren° hem, by noon assent,°   *allow / on any terms*
    Neither to been y-buried nor y-brent,°   *burned*
    But maketh houndes ete hem in despyt."
90 And with that word, withouten more respyt,°   *further delay*
    They fillen gruf° and cryden pitously,   *fell face downward*
    "Have on us wrecched wommen som mercy,
    And lat oure sorwe sinken in thyn herte."
        This gentil duk doun from his courser sterte°   *leaped*
95 With herte pitous,° whan he herde hem speke.   *pitying, merciful*
    Him thoughte° that his herte wolde breke,   *It seemed to him*
    Whan he saugh hem so pitous° and so mat,°   *pitiable / dejected*
    That whylom° weren of so greet estat.   *formerly*
    And in his armes he hem alle up hente,°   *took*
100 And hem conforteth in ful good entente;
    And swoor his ooth, as he was trewe knight,
    He wolde doon so ferforthly° his might   *exert to such an extent*
    Upon the tyraunt Creon hem to wreke,°   *avenge*

2. Who ensures that no estate will be (permanently) in prosperity.

That al the peple of Grece sholde speke
105 How Creon was of° Theseus y-served,°   *by / treated*
As he that hadde his deeth ful wel deserved.
And right anoon, withouten more abood,°   *delay*
His baner he desplayeth, and forth rood
To Thebes-ward,° and al his host bisyde.°   *Toward Thebes / with him*
110 No neer° Athenës wolde he go° ne ryde,   *nearer / go*
Ne take his ese fully half a day,
But onward on his wey that night he lay,°   *lodged*
And sente anoon° Ipolita the quene   *at once*
And Emelye, hir yonge suster shene,°   *bright, fair*
115 Unto the toun of Athenës to dwelle;
And forth he rit;° ther is namore to telle.   *rides*
    The rede statue° of Mars, with spere and targe,°   *red image / shield*
So shyneth in his whyte baner large,
That alle the feeldes gliteren up and doun;
120 And by his baner born is his penoun°   *pennant*
Of gold ful riche, in which ther was y-bete°   *embroidered*
The Minotaur, which that he slough° in Crete.   *slew*
Thus rit this duk, thus rit this conquerour,
And in his host of chivalrye the flour,°   *the flower of knighthood*
125 Til that he cam to Thebes, and alighte°   *alighted*
Faire in a feeld, ther as° he thoghte to fighte.   *where*
But shortly for to speken of this thing,
With Creon, which that was of Thebes king,
He faught, and slough him manly° as a knight *in a manly fashion, boldly*
130 In pleyn° bataille, and putte the folk to flight;   *open*
And by assaut° he wan° the citee after,   *assault / conquered*
And rente° adoun bothe wal and sparre° and rafter;   *tore / beam*
And to the ladyes he restored agayn
The bones of hir housbondes that were slayn,
135 To doon obsequies, as was tho° the gyse.°   *then / custom*
But it were al to longe for to devyse°   *tell, describe*
The grete clamour and the waymentinge°   *lamentation*
That the ladyes made at the brenninge°   *burning*
Of the bodyes, and the grete honour
140 That Theseus, the noble conquerour,
Doth to the ladyes, whan they from him wente;
But shortly for to telle is myn entente.
Whan that this worthy duk, this Theseus,
Hath Creon slayn and wonne Thebes thus,
145 Stille in that feeld he took al night his reste,
And dide with al the contree as him leste.°   *as it pleased him*
    To ransake in the tas° of bodyes dede,   *pile, heap*
Hem for to strepe° of harneys° and of wede,°   *strip / armor / clothing*
The pilours° diden bisinesse and cure°   *pillagers / worked busily and carefully*

150 After the bataille and disconfiture.°   *defeat*
     And so bifel,° that in the tas they founde,   *it happened*
     Thurgh-girt° with many a grevous blody wounde,   *Pierced through*
     Two yonge knightes ligginge° by and by,°   *lying / side by side*
     Bothe in oon armes,[3] wroght° ful richely,   *made*
155 Of whiche two, Arcita highte that oon,
     And that other knight highte Palamon.
     Nat fully quike° ne fully dede they were,   *alive*
     But by hir cote-armures[4] and by hir gere°   *accoutrements*
     The heraudes° knew hem best in special°   *heralds / especially well*
160 As they that weren of the blood royal
     Of Thebes, and of sustren° two y-born.   *sisters*
     Out of the tas the pilours han hem torn,
     And han hem caried softe° unto the tente   *gently*
     Of Theseus, and he ful sone hem sente
165 To Athenës, to dwellen in prisoun
     Perpetuelly: he nolde no raunsoun.°   *would not (accept) ransom*
     And whan this worthy duk hath thus y-don,
     He took his host, and hoom he rit anon
     With laurer° crowned as a conquerour;   *laurel*
170 And there he liveth in joye and in honour
     Terme° of his lyf; what nedeth wordes mo?°   *The remainder / more*
     And in a tour,° in angwish and in wo,   *tower*
     Dwellen this Palamoun and eek Arcite
     For everemore; ther may no gold hem quyte.°   *ransom*
175   This passeth yeer by yeer and day by day,
     Til it fil° ones, in a morwe° of May,   *befell, happened / morning*
     That Emelye, that fairer was to sene°   *see*
     Than is the lilie upon his° stalke grene,   *its*
     And fressher than the May with floures newe—
180 For with the rose colour stroof° hire hewe,°   *strove / hue, complexion*
     I noot° which was the fairer of hem two—   *know not*
     Er° it were day, as was hir wone° to do,   *Before / wont, custom*
     She was arisen and al redy dight;°   *promptly dressed*
     For May wole have no slogardye° a-night.°   *laziness / at night*
185 The sesoun priketh° every gentil herte,   *incites, rouses*
     And maketh him out of his sleep to sterte,°   *start, wake up*
     And seith "Arys, and do thyn observaunce."
     This maked Emelye have remembraunce
     To doon honour to May, and for to ryse.
190 Y-clothed was she fresh, for to devyse:°   *as I may tell*
     Hir yelow heer was broyded° in a tresse   *braided*
     Bihinde hir bak, a yerde long, I gesse.

3. Having the same coat of arms.
4. Coat-armor—a vest displaying a knight's heraldic emblems that is worn over armor.

And in the gardin, at the sonne upriste,°   sun's uprising
She walketh up and doun, and as hire liste°   it pleased her
195 She gadereth floures, party° whyte and rede,   particolored
To make a sotil° gerland for hire hede,   skillfully woven
And as an aungel hevenysshly she song.
    The grete tour, that was so thikke and strong,
Which of the castel was the chief dongooun,
200 (Theras the knightes weren in prisoun,
Of whiche I tolde yow and tellen shal)
Was evene joynant to° the gardin-wal   directly adjoining
Ther as this Emelye hadde hir pleyinge.°   amusement
Bright was the sonne and cleer that morweninge,
205 And Palamon, this woful prisoner,
As was his wone, by leve° of his gayler,°   permission, leave / jailer
Was risen and romed in a chambre on heigh,
In which he al the noble citee seigh,°   saw
And eek the gardin, ful of braunches grene,
210 Theras this fresshe Emelye the shene
Was in hire walk, and romed up and doun.
This sorweful prisoner, this Palamoun,
Goth in the chambre rominge to and fro,
And to himself compleyninge of his wo.
215 That he was born, ful ofte he seyde, "Alas!"
And so bifel, by aventure° or cas,°   chance / accident
That thurgh a window, thikke of° many a barre   thickset with
Of yren greet and square° as any sparre,°   sturdy / beam
He caste his eye upon Emelya,
220 And therwithal he bleynte° and cryde "A!"   flinched
As though he stongen were unto the herte.
And with that cry Arcite anon up sterte
And seyde, "Cosin myn, what eyleth° thee,   ails
That art so pale and deedly° on to see?°   deathly / to look at
225 Why crydestow?° Who hath thee doon offence?   didst thou cry
For Goddes love, tak al in pacience
Oure prisoun, for it may non other be;°   may not be otherwise
Fortune hath yeven° us this adversitee.   given
Som wikke aspect or disposicioun
230 Of Saturne, by sum constellacioun,
Hath yeven us this, although we hadde it sworn: [5]
So stood the hevene whan that we were born.
We moste endure it; this is the short and pleyn."
    This Palamon answerde and seyde ageyn,°   in reply
235 "Cosyn, for sothe,° of this opinioun   in truth

5. Some ill-omened aspect or disposition of Saturn, in relation to the other stars, has given us this (adversity), no matter what we might have done.

Thou hast a veyn imaginacioun.°   *foolish, mistaken idea*
This prison caused me nat for to crye,
But I was hurt right now thurghout myn yë°   *eye*
Into myn herte, that wol my bane° be.   *destruction*
240 The fairnesse of that lady that I see
Yond° in the gardin romen to and fro   *Yonder*
Is cause of al my crying and my wo.
I noot wher° she be womman or goddesse,   *do not know whether*
But Venus is it soothly, as I gesse."
245 And therwithal on kneës doun he fil,°   *fell*
And seyde: "Venus, if it be thy wil
Yow° in this gardin thus to transfigure   *Yourself*
Bifore me, sorweful wrecched creature,
Out of this prisoun help that we may scapen.°   *escape*
250 And if so be my destinee be shapen°   *shaped, determined*
By eterne° word to dyen in prisoun,   *eternal*
Of oure linage have som compassioun,
That is so lowe y-broght by tirannye."
And with that word Arcite gan° espye   *did*
255 Wher as this lady romed to and fro;
And with that sighte hir beautee hurte him so,
That, if that Palamon was wounded sore,
Arcite is hurt as muche as he, or more.
And with a sigh he seyde pitously:
260 "The fresshe beautee sleeth° me sodeynly   *slays*
Of hire that rometh in the yonder place;
And, but° I have hir mercy and hir grace,   *unless*
That I may seen hire atte leeste weye,°   *at least*
I nam but deed;° ther nis namore to seye."   *I am (not) but dead*
265   This Palamon, whan he tho° wordes herde,   *those*
Dispitously° he loked and answerde: *Angrily*
"Whether seistow° this in ernest or in pley?"   *sayest thou*
"Nay," quod Arcite, "in ernest, by my fey!°   *faith*
God help me so, me list ful yvele pleye."°   *I have no desire to jest*
270   This Palamon gan knitte his browes tweye:
"It nere,"° quod he, "to thee no greet honour   *were not*
For to be fals, ne for to be traytour
To me, that am thy cosin and thy brother
Y-sworn ful depe,[6] and ech of us til° other,   *to*
275 That nevere, for to dyen in the peyne,[7]
Til that the deeth departe° shal us tweyne,°   *part / two*
Neither of us in love to hindre other,
Ne in non other cas, my leve° brother;   *dear*
But that thou sholdest trewely forthren° me   *assist*

---

6. I.e., deeply sworn to you in blood brotherhood.   7. Even should it mean death by torture.

280 In every cas, as I shal forthren thee.
This was thyn ooth, and myn also, certeyn;
I wot right wel, thou darst° it nat withseyn.°   *darest / deny*
Thus artow of my counseil,° out of doute,°   *in on my secrets / beyond doubt*
And now thou woldest falsly been aboute°   *set about*
285 To love my lady, whom I love and serve,
And evere shal, til that myn herte sterve °   *die*
Now certes,° false Arcite, thou shalt nat so.   *surely*
I loved hire first, and tolde thee my wo
As to my counseil° and my brother sworn   *confidant*
290 To forthre me, as I have told biforn.
For which thou art y-bounden as a knight
To helpen me, if it lay in thy might,
Or elles artow fals, I dar wel seyn."
    This Arcite ful proudly spak ageyn:°   *in reply*
295 "Thou shalt," quod he, "be rather° fals than I;   *sooner*
But thou art fals, I telle thee outrely;°   *plainly*
For paramour° I loved hire first er thow.   *With passionate love*
What wiltow seyn? Thou woost° nat yet now   *knowest*
Whether she be a womman or goddesse!
300 Thyn is affeccioun of° holinesse,   *pertaining to*
And myn is love, as to a creature;
For which I tolde thee myn aventure
As to my cosin and my brother sworn.
I pose° that thou lovedest hire biforn:°   *I put the case (hypothetically) / first*
305 Wostow° nat wel the olde clerkes sawe,°   *Knowest thou / saying*
That 'who shal yeve° a lovere any lawe?'   *give*
Love is a gretter lawe, by my pan,°   *brainpan, skull*
Than may be yeve to any erthly man.
And therefore positif lawe[8] and swich decree
310 Is broken al day° for love in ech degree.°   *every day / every social rank*
A man moot nedes love, maugree his heed.[9]
He may nat fleen° it, thogh he sholde be deed,   *flee, escape*
Al be she° mayde or widwe or elles wyf.   *Whether she be*
And eek it is nat lykly al° thy lyf   *during*
315 To stonden in hir grace; namore shal I;
For wel thou woost° thy-selven, verraily,   *knowest*
That thou and I be dampned° to prisoun   *condemned*
Perpetuelly; us gayneth° no raunsoun.   *we shall gain*
We stryve as dide the houndes for the boon:°   *bone*
320 They foughte al day, and yet hir part° was noon;   *their share*
Ther cam a kyte,° whyl that they were so wrothe,   *kite (bird)*
And bar awey the boon bitwixe hem bothe.

8. Laws made by man, rather than natural law.
9. A man must necessarily love, despite his intention (not to).

And therfore, at the kinges court, my brother,
Ech man for himself: ther is non other.°   *no other way*
325 Love if thee list;° for I love and ay° shal;   *if it please you / always*
And soothly, leve° brother, this is al.   *dear*
Here in this prisoun mote° we endure,°   *must / remain*
And everich° of us take his aventure."°   *each / what befalls him*
      Greet was the stryf and long bitwixe hem tweye,
330 If that I hadde leyser° for to seye,   *leisure, opportunity*
But to th'effect.° It happed on a day,   *outcome*
To telle it yow as shortly as I may,
A worthy duk that highte Perotheus,
That felawe° was unto duk Theseus   *fellow, friend*
335 Sin° thilke day that they were children lyte,°   *Since / little*
Was come to Athenes his felawe to visyte,
And for to pleye as he was wont to do;
For in this world he loved no man so,
And he loved him as tendrely ageyn.
340 So wel they lovede, as olde bokes seyn,
That whan that oon was deed, sothly to telle,
His felawe wente and soghte him doun in helle;
But of that story list me nat to wryte.
Duk Perotheus loved wel Arcite,
345 And hadde him knowe° at Thebes yeer by° yere;   *known / after*
And fynally, at requeste and preyere
Of Perotheus, withouten any raunsoun,
Duk Theseus him leet out of prisoun
Freely to goon wher that him liste over al,°   *anywhere it pleased him*
350 In swich a gyse° as I you tellen shal.   *manner*
      This was the forward,° pleynly for t'endyte,°   *agreement / write*
Bitwixen Theseus and him Arcite:
That if so were, that Arcite were y-founde
Evere in his lyf, by day or night, o stounde°   *one moment*
355 In any contree of this Theseus,
And he were caught, it was acorded° thus,   *agreed*
That with a swerd he sholde lese° his heed;   *lose*
Ther nas non other remedye ne reed;°   *option*
But taketh his leve, and homward he him spedde;
360 Let him be war, his nekke lyth to wedde.°   *lies as a pledge*
      How greet a sorwe suffreth now Arcite!
The deeth he feleth thurgh his herte smyte;°   *smite, strike*
He wepeth, wayleth, cryeth pitously;
To sleen himself he wayteth prively.[1]
365 He seyde, "Allas that day that I was born!
Now is my prison worse than biforn;

---

1. He secretly looks for a chance to slay himself.

Now is me shape° eternally to dwelle   *it is destined for me*
Noght in purgatorie but in helle.
Allas, that evere knew I Perotheus!
370 For elles hadde I dwelled with Theseus
Y-fetered° in his prisoun everemo.   *Fettered, confined*
Than hadde I been in blisse, and nat in wo.
Only the sighte of hire whom that I serve,
Though that I nevere hir grace may deserve,
375 Wolde han suffised right ynough for me.
O dere cosin Palamon," quod he,
"Thyn is the victorie of this aventure:
Ful blisfully in prison maistow dure.°   *endure, remain*
In prison? certes nay, but in paradys!
380 Wel hath Fortune y-turned thee the dys,°   *dice*
That hast the sighte of hire, and I th'absence.
For possible is, sin° thou hast hire presence,   *since*
And art a knight, a worthy and an able,
That by som cas,° sin Fortune is chaungeable,   *case, chance*
385 Thou mayst to thy desyr somtyme atteyne.°   *attain*
But I, that am exyled and bareyne°   *barren*
Of alle grace, and in so greet despeir
That ther nis erthe, water, fyr, ne eir,°   *air*
Ne creature that of hem maked is
390 That may me helpe or doon confort in this,
Wel oughte I sterve° in wanhope° and distresse.   *die / despair*
Farwel my lyf, my lust,° and my gladnesse!   *joy*
    Allas, why pleynen° folk so in commune°   *complain / commonly*
On purveyaunce° of God, or of Fortune,   *About the providence*
395 That yeveth° hem ful ofte in many a gyse   *gives*
Wel bettre than they can hemself devyse?
Som man desyreth for to han° richesse,   *have*
That cause is of his mordre° or greet siknesse.   *murder*
And som man wolde° out of his prison fayn,°   *would be / gladly*
400 That in his hous is of his meynee° slayn.   *household, retinue*
Infinite harmes been in this matere;
We witen° nat what thing we preyen° here.   *know / pray for*
We faren° as he that dronke° is as a mous: *fare, behave / drunk*
A dronke man wot° wel he hath an hous,   *knows*
405 But he noot° which the righte wey is thider;   *does not know*
And to a dronke man the wey is slider.°   *slippery*
And certes, in this world so faren we;
We seken faste° after felicitee,   *seek steadily*
But we goon wrong ful often, trewely.
410 Thus may we seyen alle, and namely° I,   *especially*
That wende° and hadde a greet opinioun   *thought*
That if I mighte escapen from prisoun,

Than hadde I been in joye and perfit hele,°   *perfect well-being*
Ther° now I am exyled fro my wele.°   *Whereas / happiness*
415   Sin that I may nat seen yow, Emelye,
I nam but deed; ther nis no remedye."
    Upon that other syde Palamon,
Whan that he wiste° Arcite was agon,°   *knew / gone*
Swich sorwe he maketh that the grete tour
420   Resouneth° of his youling° and clamour.   *Resounds / howling*
The pure° fettres on his shines grete°   *very / swollen shins*
Weren of his bittre salte teres wete.
"Allas!" quod he, "Arcita, cosin myn,
Of al our stryf, God woot, the fruyt is thyn.
425   Thow walkest now in Thebes at thy large,°   *freely, at large*
And of my wo thou yevest litel charge.°   *care, consideration*
Thou mayst, sin thou hast wisdom and manhede,°   *manliness*
Assemblen alle the folk of our kinrede,°   *kindred*
And make a werre° so sharp on this citee,   *war*
430   That by som aventure, or some tretee,°   *treaty, agreement*
Thou mayst have hir to lady and to wyf,
For whom that I moste nedes lese° my lyf.   *lose*
For, as by wey of possibilitee,
Sith° thou art at thy large,° of prison free,   *Since / at large*
435   And art a lord, greet is thyn avauntage
More than is myn, that sterve° here in a cage.°   *die / prison*
For I mot wepe and wayle, whyl I live,
With al the wo that prison may me yive,
And eek with peyne that love me yiveth also,
440   That doubleth al my torment and my wo."
Therwith the fyr of jalousye up sterte
Withinne his brest, and hente° him by the herte   *seized*
So woodly,° that he lyk was to biholde   *madly*
The boxtree or the asshen° dede and colde.   *ashes*
445   Thanne seyde he: "O cruel goddes, that governe
This world with binding of youre word eterne,
And wryten in the table of athamaunt°   *adamant, hardest stone*
Your parlement° and youre eterne graunt,°   *decision / grant, decree*
What is mankinde more unto yow holde
450   Than is the sheep that rouketh in the folde?²
For slayn is man right as another beste,
And dwelleth eek in prison and areste,°   *arrest, detention*
And hath siknesse and greet adversitee,
And ofte tymes giltelees, pardee!°   *certainly*
455   What governaunce is in this prescience³

2. In what way is mankind more highly valued by you than is the sheep that cowers in the fold?   3. What sort of governing purpose is there in such foreknowledge.

That giltelees tormenteth innocence?
And yet encreseth° this al my penaunce,°   *increases / suffering*
That man is bounden to his observaunce,°   *bound to the obligation*
For Goddes sake, to letten of° his wille,   *restrain*
460 Ther as° a beest may al his lust° fulfille.   *Whereas / desire*
And whan a beest is deed, he hath no peyne;
But man after his deeth moot wepe and pleyne,°   *lament, complain*
Though in this world he have care and wo.
Withouten doute it may stonden so.
465 The answere of this I lete° to divynis,°   *leave / theologians*
But wel I woot, that in this world gret pyne° is.   *suffering*
Allas! I see a serpent or a theef,
That many a trewe man hath doon mescheef,°   *harm*
Goon at his large, and where him list may turne.
470 But I mot° been in prison thurgh Saturne,   *must*
And eek thurgh Juno,[4] jalous and eek wood,°   *mad, angry*
That hath destroyed wel ny° al the blood   *near*
Of Thebes, with his waste° walles wyde.   *its wasted, destroyed*
And Venus sleeth° me on that other syde   *slays*
475 For jalousye, and fere of him Arcite."
    Now wol I stinte° of Palamon a lyte,°   *cease (to tell) / little*
And lete him to his prison stille dwelle,
And of Arcita forth I wol yow telle.
    The somer passeth, and the nightes longe
480 Encresen double wyse° the peynes stronge   *twofold*
Bothe of the lovere and the prisoner.
I noot° which hath the wofullere mester.°   *do not know / sadder situation*
For, shortly for to seyn, this Palamoun
Perpetuelly is dampned° to prisoun,   *condemned*
485 In cheynes and in fettres to ben deed;
And Arcite is exyled upon his heed°   *on pain of losing his head*
For evermo as out of that contree,
Ne neveremo ne shal his lady see.
    Yow loveres axe° I now this questioun: *ask*
490 Who hath the worse, Arcite or Palamoun?
That oon may seen his lady day by day,
But in prison he moot dwelle alway.
That other wher him list may ryde or go,°   *walk*
But seen his lady shal he neveremo.
495 Now demeth° as yow liste, ye that can,°   *judge, decide / know how*
For I wol telle forth as I bigan.

4. Through the influence of the planet Saturn,   of the goddess Juno, occasioned by Jove's several
whose characteristic workings are enumerated in ll.   infidelities with Theban women.
1598–1611, and through the hostility toward Thebes

PART TWO

Whan that Arcite to Thebes comen was,
Ful ofte a day he swelte° and seyde "allas,"   *fainted*
For seen his lady shal he neveremo.
500 And shortly to concluden° al his wo,   *briefly to sum up*
So muche sorwe hadde nevere creature
That is, or shal,° whyl that the world may dure.°   *shall (be) / endure*
His sleep, his mete,° his drink is him biraft,°   *(appetite for) food / bereft*
That lene he wex and drye as is a shaft.[5]
505 His eyen holwe,° and grisly° to biholde;   *hollow / horrible*
His hewe falow° and pale as asshen colde;   *faded*
And solitarie he was and evere allone,
And waillinge al the night, makinge his mone.°   *moan, lament*
And if he herde song or instrument,
510 Thanne wolde he wepe, he mighte nat be stent.°   *stopped*
So feble eek were his spirits, and so lowe,
And chaunged so, that no man coude knowe
His speche nor his vois, though men it herde.
And in his gere° for al the world he ferde°   *erratic behavior / fared*
515 Nat oonly lyk° the loveres maladye   *like (one afflicted with)*
Of Hereos,[6] but rather lyk manye°   *mania*
Engendred of humour malencolyk°   *Born of the melancholic humor*
Biforen,° in his celle fantastyk.[7]   *In the front (of the brain)*
And shortly, turned was al up so doun°   *upside down*
520 Bothe habit° and eek disposicioun   *outward form*
Of him, this woful lovere daun° Arcite.   *sir, lord*
What sholde I al day of his wo endyte?°   *write*
Whan he endured hadde a yeer or two
This cruel torment and this peyne and wo,
525 At Thebes, in his contree, as I seyde,
Upon a night, in sleep as he him leyde,°   *laid*
Him thoughte how that the winged god Mercurie
Biforn him stood and bad° him to be murye.°   *bade, requested / merry*
His slepy yerde° in hond he bar uprighte;   *sleep-bringing wand*
530 An hat he werede° upon his heres° brighte.   *wore / hair*
Arrayed was this god, as he took keep,°   *as (Arcite) took note*
As he was whan that Argus[8] took his sleep;
And seyde him thus: "To Athenes shaltou° wende: *shalt thou*
Ther is thee shapen° of thy wo an ende."   *destined, determined*
535 And with that word Arcite wook° and sterte.°   *woke / gave a start*

---

5. So that he became as thin and dry as the shaft of an arrow.
6. An illness caused by passionate love. Its symptoms, according to medieval medical authorities, are those attributed to Arcite in ll. 498–513.
7. Medieval medicine divided the brain into three cells, the front one containing the imagination (fantasy), the middle cell judgment, the back cell memory. Mania was a disease of the imagination.
8. Argus, the monster with a hundred eyes, had likewise been put to sleep by Mercury.

"Now trewely, how° sore that me smerte,"°   *however / it may hurt me*
Quod he, "to Athenes right now wol I fare;
Ne for the drede of deeth shal I nat spare°   *refrain*
To see my lady, that I love and serve.
540 In hire presence I recche° nat to sterve."°   *care / if I die*
    And with that word he caughte° a greet mirour,   *seized*
And saugh° that chaunged was al his colour,   *saw*
And saugh his visage al in another kinde.°   *totally altered*
And right anoon it ran him in his minde,
545 That, sith his face was so disfigured
Of maladye,° the which he hadde endured,   *By illness*
He mighte wel, if that he bar him lowe,°   *behaved humbly*
Live in Athenes everemore unknowe,°   *unknown*
And seen his lady wel ny° day by day.   *nearly*
550 And right anon he chaunged his array,
And cladde him as a povre° laborer,   *poor*
And al allone, save° oonly a squyer   *except for*
That knew his privetee° and al his cas,°   *private affairs / condition*
Which° was disgysed povrely as he was,   *Who*
555 To Athenes is he goon the nexte° way.   *nearest*
And to the court he wente upon a day,
And at the gate he profreth his servyse
To drugge° and drawe,° what so men wol devyse.°   *drudge / carry / require*
And shortly of this matere for to seyn,
560 He fil in office° with a chamberleyn,   *got a job*
The which that dwellinge was with Emelye;
For he was wys, and coude soone aspye°   *discover*
Of every servaunt, which that serveth here.°   *her*
Wel coude he hewen° wode and water bere,   *cut*
565 For he was yong and mighty for the nones,°   *occasion, purpose*
And therto he was strong and big of bones
To doon that° any wight can him devyse.   *what*
A yeer or two he was in this servyse,
Page of the chambre of Emelye the brighte;
570 And Philostrate he seide that he highte.°   *was named*
But half so wel biloved a man as he
Ne was ther nevere in court of his degree;°   *social position*
He was so gentil of condicioun°   *disposition*
That thurghout al the court was his renoun.
575 They seyden that it were° a charitee   *would be*
That Theseus wolde enhauncen his degree°   *improve his rank*
And putten him in worshipful° servyse,   *honorable*
Ther as he mighte his vertu° excercyse.   *natural ability*
And thus withinne a whyle his name is spronge,°   *sprung up, become well-known*
580 Bothe of his dedes and his goode tonge,
That Theseus hath taken him so neer°   *so near (to himself)*

That of his chambre he made him a squyer,
And gaf him gold to mayntene his degree;
And eek men broghte him out of his contree
585 From yeer to yeer, ful prively, his rente;°   income
But honestly° and slyly° he it spente,   fittingly / discreetly
That no man wondred how that he it hadde.
And three yeer in this wyse° his lyf he ladde,°   manner / led
And bar him so in pees and eek in werre,
590 Ther was no man that Theseus hath derre.°   holds more dear
And in this blisse lete° I now Arcite,   leave
And speke I wol of Palamon a lyte.
      In derknesse and horrible and strong prisoun
Thise seven yeer hath seten° Palamoun,   dwelt
595 Forpyned,° what for wo and for distresse;   Wasted away
Who feleth double soor° and hevinesse   sorrow
But Palamon, that love destreyneth° so   distresses
That wood° out of his wit he gooth for wo?   mad
And eek therto he is a prisoner
600 Perpetuelly, noght oonly for a yeer.
Who coude ryme in English proprely
His martirdom? For sothe, it am nat I;
Therefore I passe as lightly° as I may.   quickly
It fel° that in the seventhe yeer, of May   befell
605 The thridde night, as olde bokes seyn,
That al this storie tellen more pleyn,°   fully
Were it by aventure° or destinee—   chance
As, whan a thing is shapen,° it shal be—   determined (in advance)
That sone after the midnight Palamoun,
610 By helping of a freend, brak° his prisoun   escaped from
And fleeth the citee faste as he may go;
For he hadde yive his gayler° drinke so   jailor
Of a clarree° maad of a certeyn wyn,   spiced wine
With nercotikes and opie of Thebes fyn,⁹
615 That al that night, thogh that men° wolde him shake,   one
The gayler sleep,° he mighte nat awake;   slept
And thus he fleeth as faste as evere he may.
The night was short and faste by the day,°   near daybreak
That nedes cost° he moot° himselven hyde,   of necessity / must
620 And til° a grove, faste ther bisyde,   to
With dredful° foot thanne stalketh Palamoun.   fearful
For, shortly, this was his opinioun:
That in that grove he wolde him hyde al day,
And in the night thanne wolde he take his way
625 To Thebes-ward,° his freendes for to preye   Toward Thebes

9. Fine opium from Thebes (in Egypt).

On Theseus to helpe him to werreye;°   *make war*
And shortly, outher° he wolde lese° his lyf   *either / lose*
Or winnen Emelye unto his wyf.
This is th'effect° and his entente pleyn.°   *substance / complete intent*
630   Now wol I turne to Arcite ageyn,
That litel wiste° how ny° that was his care,   *knew / near*
Til that Fortune had broght him in the snare
   The bisy larke, messager of day,
Salueth° in hir song the morwe° gray;   *Salutes, greets / morning*
635 And fyry Phebus ryseth up so brighte
That al the orient° laugheth of the lighte,   *eastern sky*
And with his stremes° dryeth in the greves°   *beams / bushes*
The silver dropes hanginge on the leves.
And Arcite, that in the court royal
640 With Theseus is squyer principal,
Is risen and loketh on the myrie day.
And for to doon his observaunce to May,
Remembringe on° the poynt° of his desyr,   *Holding in mind / object*
He on a courser, startlinge° as the fyr,°   *leaping / fire*
645 Is riden into the feeldes him to pleye,
Out of the court, were it a myle or tweye;
And to the grove of which that I yow tolde,
By aventure his wey he gan to holde,
To maken him a gerland of the greves,°   *branches*
650 Were it of wodebinde or hawethorn-leves,
And loude he song ageyn° the sonne shene:°   *in response to / bright*
"May, with alle thy floures and thy grene,
Welcome be thou, faire fresshe May,
In hope that I som grene° gete may."   *something green*
655 And from his courser, with a lusty herte,
Into the grove ful hastily he sterte,°   *leaped*
And in a path he rometh up and doun,
Theras,° by aventure, this Palamoun   *Where*
Was in a bush, that no man mighte him see,
660 For sore afered° of his deeth was he.   *afraid*
Nothing° ne knew he that it was Arcite;   *Not at all*
God wot he wolde have trowed° it ful lyte.   *believed*
But sooth is seyd, go sithen many yeres,°   *since many years ago*
That "feeld hath eyen° and the wode hath eres."   *the field has eyes*
665 It is ful fair° a man to bere him evene,°   *desirable (for) / with restraint*
For al day° meeteth men at unset stevene.[1]   *every day*
Ful litel woot Arcite of his felawe,
That was so ny° to herknen al his sawe,°   *near / speech*
For in the bush he sitteth now ful stille.

1. For people are always meeting at unexpected moments.

670 Whan that Arcite hadde romed al his fille,
And songen al the roundel° lustily,   *song*
Into a studie² he fil sodeynly,
As doon thise loveres in hir queynte geres,°   *strange behaviors*
Now in the croppe,° now doun in the breres,°   *treetop / briars*
675 Now up, now doun, as boket in a welle.
Right as° the Friday, soothly for to telle,   *Just as*
Now it shyneth, now it reyneth faste,
Right so can gery° Venus overcaste°   *changeable / cloud over, darken*
The hertes of hir folk; right as hir day
680 Is gereful, right so chaungeth she array.°   *the order, disposition of things*
Selde is the Friday al the wyke ylyke.³
    Whan that Arcite had songe, he gan to syke,°   *sigh*
And sette him doun withouten any more.°   *without further delay*
"Alas!" quod he, "that day that I was bore!
685 How longe, Juno, thurgh thy crueltee,
Woltow° werreyen° Thebes the citee?   *Wilt thou / make war on*
Allas! y-broght is to confusioun
The blood royal of Cadme° and Amphioun—   *Cadmus*
Of Cadmus, which that was the firste man
690 That Thebes bulte,° or first the toun bigan,   *built*
And of the citee first was crouned king.
Of his lynage° am I, and his ofspring   *lineage*
By verray ligne,° as of the stok royal;   *true descent*
And now I am so caitif° and so thral°   *wretched / enslaved*
695 That he that is my mortal enemy,
I serve him as his squyer povrely.°   *in a lowly manner*
And yet doth Juno me wel more shame,
For I dar noght biknowe° myn owne name;   *acknowledge*
But ther as I was wont to highte° Arcite,   *be called*
700 Now highte I Philostrate, noght worth a myte.
Allas, thou felle° Mars! allas, Juno!   *cruel, deadly*
Thus hath youre ire our lynage al fordo,°   *destroyed*
Save only me and wrecched Palamoun,
That Theseus martyreth in prisoun.
705 And over al this, to sleen me outrely,°   *utterly*
Love hath his fyry dart so brenningly°   *burningly*
Y-stiked° thurgh my trewe careful° herte,   *stabbed / woeful*
That shapen was my deeth erst than° my sherte.°   *before / shirt*
Ye sleen° me with youre eyen, Emelye!   *slay*
710 Ye been the cause wherfore that I dye.
Of all the remenant of myn other care°   *woe*
Ne sette I nat the mountaunce° of a tare,°   *amount / weed*
So° that I coude don aught to your plesaunce!"   *If*

---

2. I.e., deep thought.   3. Seldom is Friday like the other days of the week.

And with that word he fil doun in a traunce
715 A longe tyme; and after he up sterte.
    This Palamoun, that thoughte that thurgh his herte
He felte a cold swerd sodeynliche° glyde,   *suddenly*
For ire he quook,° no lenger wolde he byde.   *quaked*
And whan that he had herd Arcites tale,
720 As he were wood,° with face deed° and pale,   *mad / deathly*
He sterte him up out of the buskes° thikke,   *bushes*
And seyde: "Arcite, false traitour wikke,°   *wicked*
Now artow hent,° that lovest my lady so,   *art thou caught*
For whom that I have al this peyne and wo,
725 And art my blood, and to my counseil° sworn,   *secret counsel*
As I ful ofte have told thee heerbiforn,
And hast byjaped° here duk Theseus,   *tricked*
And falsly chaunged hast thy name thus!
I wol be deed, or elles° thou shalt dye.   *else*
730 Thou shalt nat love my lady Emelye,
But I wol love hire only, and namo;°   *no one else*
For I am Palamoun, thy mortal fo.
And though that I no wepne° have in this place,   *weapon*
But out of prison am astert° by grace,   *escaped*
735 I drede noght° that outher° thou shalt dye   *doubt not / either*
Or thou ne shalt nat loven Emelye.
Chees° which thou wolt,° for thou shalt nat asterte."   *Choose / wish*
    This Arcitë, with ful despitous° herte,   *scornful*
Whan he him knew, and hadde his tale herd,
740 As fiers as leoun pulled out his swerd
And seyde thus: "By God that sit° above,   *sits*
Nere it° that thou art sik and wood for love,   *Were it not*
And eek that thou no wepne hast in this place,
Thou sholdest nevere out of this grove pace,°   *pass, leave*
745 That thou ne sholdest dyen of myn hond.
For I defye° the seuretee° and the bond   *scorn, disclaim / pledge*
Which that thou seyst that I have maad to thee.
What, verray° fool, think wel that love is free,   *true*
And I wol love hire maugre° al thy might!   *in spite of*
750 But, for as muche thou art a worthy knight,
And wilnest° to darreyne hire° by batayle,   *wish / decide the claim to her*
Have heer my trouthe:° tomorwe I wol nat fayle,   *troth, promise*
Withoute witing° of any other wight,°   *knowledge / person*
That here I wol be founden as° a knight,   *(on my honor) as*
755 And bringen harneys° right ynough for thee;   *armor*
And chees° the beste, and leve the worste for me.   *(you may) choose*
And mete and drinke this night wol I bringe
Ynough for thee, and clothes for thy beddinge.
And if so be that thou my lady winne,

760 And slee° me in this wode ther° I am inne,   *slay / where*
    Thou mayst wel have thy lady, as for me."°   *as far as I am concerned*
    This Palamon answerde: "I graunte it thee."
    And thus they been departed° til amorwe,°   *parted / the next morning*
    Whan ech of hem had leyd his feith to borwe.°   *as a pledge*
765   O Cupide, out of° alle charitee!°   *devoid of / unselfish love*
    O regne,° that wolt no felawe° have with thee!   *sovereign rule / associate*
    Ful sooth is seyd that love ne lordshipe
    Wol noght, his thankes,° have no felaweshipe;   *willingly*
    Wel finden that Arcite and Palamoun.
770 Arcite is riden anon unto the toun,
    And on the morwe, er it were dayes light,
    Ful prively two harneys hath he dight,°   *prepared*
    Bothe suffisaunt° and mete° to darreyne°   *sufficient / suitable / decide*
    The bataille in the feeld bitwix hem tweyne.°   *two*
775 And on his hors, allone as he was born,
    He carieth al this harneys him biforn;
    And in the grove, at tyme and place y-set,
    This Arcite and this Palamon ben met.
      To chaungen gan the colour in hir face,
780 Right as the hunters° in the regne° of Trace,°   *hunter's / kingdom / Thrace*
    That stondeth at the gappe° with a spere,   *gap (in the forest)*
    Whan hunted is the leoun or the bere,°   *bear*
    And hereth him come russhing in the greves,°   *bushes*
    And breketh bothe bowes° and the leves,   *boughs*
785 And thinketh, "Heere cometh my mortel enemy!
    Withoute faile, he moot° be deed or I;   *must*
    For outher° I mot sleen him at the gappe,   *either*
    Or he mot sleen me, if that me mishappe,"°—   *if it should go ill for me*
    So ferden° they in chaunging of hir hewe.   *acted*
790   As fer as° everich° of hem other knewe,   *Although / each*
    Ther nas no "good day," ne no saluing;°   *saluting, greeting*
    But streight, withouten word or rehersing,°   *restating (their pact)*
    Everich of hem heelp° for to armen other   *helped*
    As freendly as he were his owne brother;
795 And after that, with sharpe speres stronge
    They foynen° ech at other wonder longe.   *thrust*
    Thou mightest wene° that this Palamoun   *suppose*
    In his fighting were a wood leoun,
    And as a cruel tygre was Arcite;
800 As wilde bores gonne they to° smyte,   *they did*
    That frothen whyte as foom for ire wood.°   *mad anger*
    Up to the ancle° foghte they in hir blood.   *ankle*
    And in this wyse I lete° hem fighting dwelle;°   *leave / continuing to fight*
    And forth I wole of Theseus yow telle.
805   The destinee, ministre° general,   *agent*

That executeth in the world over al°   *everywhere*
The purveyaunce° that God hath seyn biforn,°   *providential plan / foreseen*
So strong it is that, though the world had sworn
The contrarie of a thing by ye or nay,
810 Yet somtyme it shal fallen° on a day   *befall, happen*
That falleth nat eft° withinne a thousand yere.   *again*
For certeinly, oure appetytes° here   *desires*
Be it of werre, or pees, or hate, or love,
Al is this reuled by the sighte° above.   *foresight*
815 This mene I now by° mighty Theseus,   *in relation to*
That for to hunten is so desirous,
And namely° at the grete hert° in May,   *especially / hart*
That in his bed ther daweth him° no day,   *dawns for him*
That he nis clad and redy for to ryde
820 With hunte° and horn and houndes him bisyde.   *huntsman*
For in his hunting hath he swich delyt
That it is al his joye and appetyt
To been himself the grete hertes bane;°   *slayer*
For after Mars° he serveth now Diane.°   *god of war / goddess of the hunt*
825   Cleer was the day, as I have told er this,
And Theseus, with alle joye and blis,
With his Ipolita, the fayre quene,
And Emelye, clothed al in grene,
On hunting be they riden royally.
830 And to the grove that stood ful faste by,
In which ther was an hert, as men him tolde,
Duk Theseus the streighte wey hath holde.°   *has taken*
And to the launde he rydeth him ful right,[4]
For thider was the hert wont have his flight,
835 And over a brook, and so forth on his weye.
This duk wol han a cours° at him or tweye,   *chase*
With houndes swiche as that him list° comaunde.   *it pleases him*
    And whan this duk was come unto the launde,
Under the sonne he loketh, and anon
840 He was war of Arcite and Palamon,
That foughten breme° as it were bores two.   *furiously*
The brighte swerdes wenten to and fro
So hidously that with the leeste strook
It seemed as it wolde felle an ook;
845 But what° they were, no thing he ne woot.   *who*
This duk his courser with his spores° smoot,°   *spurs / struck*
And at a stert° he was bitwix hem two,   *in an instant*
And pulled out a swerd and cryed, "Ho!
Namore, up° peyne of lesinge° of youre heed!   *upon / losing*

---

4. And he rides directly to a clearing in the forest.

850 By mighty Mars, he shal anon be deed
That smyteth° any strook that I may seen.   *strikes*
But telleth me what mister men° ye been,   *what kind of men*
That been so hardy° for to fighten here   *audacious*
Withouten juge or other officere,
855 As it were in a listes° royally?"   *lists (of a tournament)*
     This Palamon answerde hastily,
And seyde: "Sire, what nedeth wordes mo?
We have the deeth deserved bothe two.
Two woful wrecches been we, two caytyves,°   *captives*
860 That been encombred° of our owne lyves;   *weary*
And as thou art a rightful lord and juge,
Ne yeve° us neither mercy ne refuge,°   *give / protection*
But slee° me first, for seynte° charitee.   *slay / holy*
But slee my felawe eek as wel as me,
865 Or slee him first: for though thou knowest it lyte,°   *little*
This is thy mortal fo, this is Arcite,
That fro thy lond is banished on his heed,°   *on pain of losing his head*
For which he hath deserved to be deed.
For this is he that cam unto thy gate
870 And seyde that he highte Philostrate.
Thus hath he japed° thee ful many a yeer,   *tricked*
And thou hast maked him thy chief squyer;
And this is he that loveth Emelye.
For sith° the day is come that I shal dye,   *since*
875 I make pleynly° my confessioun   *frankly, fully*
That I am thilke° woful Palamoun   *that*
That hath thy prison broken wikkedly.
I am thy mortal fo, and it am I
That loveth so hote° Emelye the brighte   *fervently*
880 That I wol dye present° in hir sighte.   *at once*
Wherfore I axe° deeth and my juwyse;°   *ask (for) / just sentence*
But slee my felawe in the same wyse,°   *way*
For bothe han we deserved to be slayn."
     This worthy duk answerde anon agayn,
885 And seyde, "This is a short conclusioun.°   *quick decision*
Youre owne mouth, by your confessioun,
Hath dampned you, and I wol it recorde;°   *declare it as my verdict*
It nedeth noght to pyne° yow with the corde.°   *torture / rope*
Ye shul be deed, by mighty Mars the rede!"
890   The quene anon, for verray° wommanhede,   *true*
Gan for to wepe, and so dide Emelye,
And alle the ladies in the companye.
Gret pitee was it, as it thoughte hem° alle,   *it seemed to them*
That ever swich a chaunce sholde falle;°   *befall, occur*
895 For gentil° men they were of greet estat,   *well-born, courteous*

And no thing but for love was this debat;°   conflict
And sawe hir blody woundes wyde and sore,
And alle cryden, bothe lasse and more,°   the lesser and the greater
"Have mercy, lord, upon us wommen alle!"
900 And on hir bare knees adoun they falle,
And wolde have kist his feet ther as he stood,
Til at the laste aslaked° was his mood·°   diminished
For pitee renneth° sone in gentil herte.   runs
And though he first for ire quook° and sterte,°   quaked / started
905 He hath considered shortly, in a clause,°   a brief while
The trespas of hem bothe, and eek the cause,
And although that his ire hir gilt accused,°   blamed their offense
Yet in his resoun he hem bothe excused,
As thus: he thoghte wel that every man
910 Wol helpe himself in love, if that he can,
And eek delivere himself out of prisoun.
And eek his herte had compassioun
Of wommen, for they wepen evere in oon.[5]
And in his gentil herte he thoghte anoon,
915 And softe unto himself he seyde: "Fy
Upon a lord that wol have no mercy,
But been a leoun, bothe in word and dede,
To hem that been in repentaunce and drede
As wel as to a proud despitous° man   scornful
920 That wol maynteyne that° he first bigan!   what
That lord hath litel of discrecioun°   discernment
That in swich cas can° no divisioun,°   knows (how to make) / distinction
But weyeth° pryde and humblesse after oon."°   weighs, judges / alike
And shortly, whan his ire is thus agoon,°   passed away
925 He gan to loken up with eyen lighte,°   cheerful
And spak thise same wordes al on highte:°   aloud
"The god of love, a, *benedicite*,°   bless us
How mighty and how greet a lord is he!
Ayeins° his might ther gayneth° none obstacles.   Against / prevails
930 He may be cleped° a god for his miracles,   called
For he can maken at his owne gyse°   as he chooses
Of everich herte as that him list devyse.°   whatever it pleases him to contrive
Lo heere, this Arcite and this Palamoun,
That quitly° weren out of my prisoun,   freely, entirely
935 And mighte han lived in Thebes royally,
And witen° I am hir mortal enemy   know
And that hir deeth lyth in my might also;
And yet hath love, maugree hir eyen two,[6]
Broght hem hider bothe for to dye!

5. I.e., continued to weep.
6. Despite their two eyes (i.e., despite anything they can do).

940 Now loketh, is nat that an heigh° folye?   great
Who may been a fool but if° he love?   unless
Bihold, for Goddes sake that sit° above,   sits
Se how they blede! be they noght wel arrayed?
Thus hath hir lord, the god of love, y-payed
945 Hir wages and hir fees for hir servyse!
And yet they wenen° for to been ful wyse   think (themselves)
That serven love, for aught that may bifalle.
But this is yet the beste game° of alle: joke
That she, for whom they han this jolitee,°   frolic, diversion
950 Can hem therfore as muche thank as me;[7]
She woot° namore of al this hote fare,°   knows / frantic business
By God, than woot a cokkow° or an hare!   cuckoo
But al mot been assayed,° hoot and cold;   tried, experienced
A man mot been a fool, or yong or old;
955 I woot it by myself ful yore agoon,°   long ago
For in my tyme a servant[8] was I oon.
And therfore, sin° I knowe of loves peyne,   since
And woot how sore it can a man distreyne,°   distress, torment
As he that° hath ben caught ofte in his las,°   one who / net
960 I yow foryeve al hoolly° this trespas,   wholly
At requeste of the quene that kneleth here,
And eek of Emelye, my suster dere.
And ye shul bothe anon unto me swere
That neveremo ye shul my contree dere,°   harm
965 Ne make werre upon me night ne day,
But been my freendes in al that ye may.
I yow foryeve this trespas every del.'"°   in every respect
And they him swore his axing° fayre and wel,   request
And him of lordshipe° and of mercy preyde,   his protection as their overlord
970 And he hem graunteth grace, and thus he seyde:
    "To speke of royal linage and richesse,
Though that she were a quene or a princesse,
Ech of yow bothe is worthy, doutelees,
To wedden whan tyme is, but nathelees°—   nevertheless
975 I speke as for my suster Emelye,
For whom ye have this stryf and jalousye—
Ye woot yourself she may not wedden two
Atones,° though ye fighten everemo: At one time
That oon of yow, al be him looth or leef,°   whether he like it or not
980 He moot go pypen° in an ivy leef;   go whistle
This is to seyn, she may nat now han bothe,
Al be ye never so jalous ne so wrothe.
And forthy° I yow putte in this degree,°   therefore / condition, position

7. I.e., has no more to thank them for than I do.   8. I.e., of love.

That ech of yow shal have his destinee
985 As him is shape,° and herkneth in what wyse;   *determined*
Lo heer your ende° of that I shal devyse.   *fate*
  My wil is this, for plat° conclusioun,   *blunt, plain*
Withouten any replicacioun°—   *reply*
If that yow lyketh, tak it for the beste:
990 That everich of yow shal gon wher him leste
Frely, withouten raunson° or daunger;°   *ransom / control*
And this day fifty wykes, fer ne ner,°   *neither later nor sooner*
Everich of yow shal bringe an hundred knightes
Armed for listes° up at alle rightes,°   *tournament / points*
995 Al redy to darreyne hire° by bataille.   *to settle claim to her*
And this bihote° I yow withouten faille,   *promise*
Upon my trouthe, and as I am a knight,
That whether° of yow bothe that hath might—   *whichever*
This is to seyn, that whether he or thou
1000 May with his hundred, as I spak of now,
Sleen° his contrarie° or out of listes dryve—   *Slay / opponent*
Thanne shal I yeve Emelya to wyve°   *as wife*
To whom that Fortune yeveth so fair a grace.
The listes° shal I maken in this place,   *tournament arena*
1005 And God so wisly° on my soule rewe,°   *surely / have pity*
As I shal even° juge been and trewe.   *impartial*
Ye shul non other ende° with me maken,   *agreement*
That oon of yow ne shal be deed or taken.
And if yow thinketh this is wel y-sayd,
1010 Seyeth your avys,° and holdeth yow apayd.°   *opinion / content*
This is your ende and youre conclusioun."
  Who loketh lightly now but Palamoun?
Who springeth up for joye but Arcite?
Who couthe telle, or who couthe it endyte,°   *write*
1015 The joye that is maked in the place
Whan Theseus hath doon so fair a grace?
But doun on knees wente every maner wight,
And thanked him with al hir herte and might,
And namely° the Thebans often sythe.°   *especially / many times*
1020 And thus with good hope and with herte blythe°   *glad*
They take hir leve, and homward gonne° they ryde   *did*
To Thebes, with his° olde walles wyde.   *its*

PART THREE

I trowe° men wolde deme it necligence   *believe*
If I foryete° to tellen the dispence°   *forget / spending*
1025 Of Theseus, that goth so bisily
To maken up the listes royally,

That swich a noble theatre° as it was, *amphitheater*
I dar wel seyn that in this world ther nas.
The circuit a myle was aboute,
1030 Walled of stoon, and diched° al withoute. *ditched*
Round was the shap, in manere of compas,° *circle*
Ful of degrees,° the heighte of sixty pas,° *steps / paces*
That whan a man was set on o° degree, *one*
He letted° nat his felawe for to see. *hindered*
1035   Estward ther stood a gate of marbel whyt,
Westward right swich another in the opposit.
And shortly to concluden, swich a place
Was noon in erthe, as in so litel space;° *(built) in such a short time*
For in the lond ther was no crafty° man *skilled*
1040 That geometrie or ars-metrike° can,° *arithmetic / knows*
Ne purtreyour,° ne kervere° of images, *painter / carver*
That Theseus ne yaf° him mete and wages *gave*
The theatre for to maken and devyse.
And for to doon his ryte and sacrifyse,
1045 He estward hath, upon the gate above,
In worshipe of Venus, goddesse of love,
Don make° an auter° and an oratorie; *Had made / altar*
And on the gate westward, in memorie
Of Mars, he maked hath right swich another,
1050 That coste largely of gold a fother.° *load, large quantity*
And northward, in a touret° on the wal, *turret*
Of alabastre whyt and reed° coral, *red*
An oratorie riche for to see,
In worshipe of Dyane° of chastitee, *Diana*
1055 Hath Theseus don wroght° in noble wyse. *had constructed*
    But yet hadde I foryeten to devyse
The noble kerving and the portreitures,° *representations*
The shap, the countenaunce, and the figures,
That weren in thise oratories three.
1060   First in the temple of Venus maystow° see *mayest thou*
Wroght on the wal, ful pitous to biholde,
The broken slepes and the sykes° colde,° *sighs / chilling, fatal*
The sacred teres and the waymentinge,° *lamenting*
The fyry strokes of the desiringe
1065 That loves servaunts in this lyf enduren;
The othes that hir covenants assuren;° *bind their vows*
Plesaunce and Hope, Desyr, Foolhardinesse,
Beautee and Youthe, Bauderie,° Richesse, *Pandering*
Charmes and Force, Lesinges,° Flaterye, *Deceits*
1070 Dispense,° Bisynesse, and Jalousye, *Expense*
That wered of yelwe goldes° a gerland, *marigolds*
And a cokkow sittinge on hir hand;

Festes,° instruments, caroles,° daunces,   *Feasts / songs sung dancing*
Lust° and array, and alle the circumstaunces   *Pleasure*
1075 Of love, whiche that I rekned° and rekne shal,   *reckoned, considered*
By ordre weren peynted on the wal,
And mo than I can make of mencioun.⁹
For soothly, al the mount of Citheroun,°   *Cithaeron*
Ther° Venus hath hir principal dwellinge,   *Where*
1080 Was shewed on the wal in portreyinge,
With al the gardin and the lustinesse.
Nat was foryeten the porter, Ydelnesse,
Ne Narcisus the faire of yore agon,°   *long ago*
Ne yet the folye of king Salamon,
1085 Ne yet the grete strengthe of Hercules,
Th'enchauntements of Medea and Circes,
Ne of Turnus, with the hardy fiers corage,°   *proud heart*
The riche Cresus, caytif in servage.°   *wretched in bondage*
Thus may ye seen that wisdom ne richesse,
1090 Beautee ne sleighte,° strengthe ne hardinesse,°   *cleverness / boldness*
Ne may with Venus holde champartye,°   *equal power*
For as hir list the world than may she gye.°   *guide, govern*
Lo, alle thise folk so caught were in hir las,°   *net*
Til they for wo ful ofte seyde "Allas!"
1095 Suffyceth heer ensamples oon or two,
And though° I coude rekne a thousand mo.   *Although*
     The statue of Venus, glorious for to see,
Was naked fletinge° in the large see,   *floating*
And fro the navele doun all covered was
1100 With wawes° grene, and brighte as any glas.   *waves*
A citole° in hir right hand hadde she,   *cithara (a stringed instrument)*
And on hir heed, ful semely° for to see,   *seemly, comely*
A rose gerland, fresh and wel smellinge;
Above hir heed hir dowves flikeringe.°   *doves fluttering*
1105 Biforn hir stood hir sone Cupido,
Upon his shuldres winges hadde he two,
And blind he was, as it is ofte sene.
A bowe he bar° and arwes brighte and kene.   *carried*
     Why sholde I noght as wel eek telle yow al
1110 The portreiture that was upon the wal
Withinne the temple of mighty Mars the rede?
Al peynted was the wal, in lengthe and brede,°   *breadth*
Lyk to the estres° of the grisly place   *like the interior*
That highte° the grete temple of Mars in Trace,°   *is called / Thrace*
1115 In thilke° colde frosty regioun   *that*
Ther as° Mars hath his sovereyn mansioun.   *Where*

9. I.e., make mention of.

　　　First on the wal was peynted a foreste,
　　In which ther dwelleth neither man ne beste,
　　With knotty knarry° bareyne° treës olde,　　　　　　　　*gnarled / barren*
1120　Of stubbes° sharpe and hidouse to biholde,　　　　　　*With stublike branches*
　　In° which ther ran a rumbel in a swough,°　　　*Through / sough, noise (of wind)*
　　As though a storm sholde bresten° every bough.　　　　　　*break*
　　And downward from an hille, under a bente,°　　　　*below a grassy slope*
　　Ther stood the temple of Mars armipotente,°　　　　　*powerful in arms*
1125　Wroght al of burned° steel, of which the entree°　　*burnished / entrance*
　　Was long and streit,° and gastly for to see.　　　　　　　*narrow*
　　And therout cam a rage° and such a vese°　　　　*roar (of wind) / blast*
　　That it made al the gate for to rese.°　　　　　　　　　*shake*
　　The northren light in at the dores shoon,°　　　　　　　*shone*
1130　For windowe on the wal ne was ther noon,
　　Thurgh which men mighten any light discerne.
　　The dore was al of adamant eterne,
　　Y-clenched° overthwart° and endelong°　　　*Braced / crosswise / lengthwise*
　　With iren tough; and for to make it strong,
1135　Every piler,° the temple to sustene,　　　　　　　　　　*pillar*
　　Was tonne-greet,° of iren bright and shene.°　　*big as a cask /shiny*
　　　　Ther saugh I first the derke imagining
　　Of Felonye,° and al the compassing;°　　　　*Crime, Treachery / plotting*
　　The cruel Ire, reed as any glede;°　　　　　　　　　　*live coal*
1140　The pykepurs,° and eek the pale Drede;　　　　　　　　*pick-purse*
　　The smylere with the knyf under the cloke;
　　The shepne° brenning° with the blake smoke;　　　*stable, shed / burning*
　　The treson of the mordring° in the bedde;　　　　　　　*murdering*
　　The open werre, with woundes al bibledde;°　　　　　*blood-stained*
1145　Contek,° with blody knyf and sharp manace.°　　*Strife / menace, threat*
　　Al ful of chirking° was that sory place.　　　　　　　*harsh noises*
　　The sleere of himself[1] yet saugh I ther:
　　His herte-blood hath bathed al his heer;°　　　　　　　*hair*
　　The nayl y-driven in the shode[2] a-night;
1150　The colde deeth, with mouth gaping upright.
　　Amiddes of° the temple sat Meschaunce,°　　*In the middle of / Misfortune*
　　With disconfort° and sory contenaunce.　　　　　*discouragement*
　　Yet saugh I Woodnesse° laughing in his rage,　　　　　*Madness*
　　Armed Compleint, Outhees,° and fiers Outrage;　　　　*Outcry*
1155　The careyne° in the bush, with throte y-corve;°　　　*corpse / cut*
　　A thousand slayn, and nat of qualm y-storve;°　　*dead by plague*
　　The tiraunt, with the prey° by force y-raft;°　　　*plunder / seized*
　　The toun destroyed, ther was nothing laft.
　　Yet saugh I brent the shippes hoppesteres;°　　*dancing, bobbing*
1160　The hunte° strangled with° the wilde beres;　　　*hunter / killed by*

---

1. I.e., the suicide (self-slayer).　　　　2. The top of the head, where the hair parts.

The sowe freten° the child right in the cradel;   *devour*
The cook yscalded, for al his longe ladel—
Noght was foryeten by the infortune of Marte³—
The carter overriden with° his carte,   *run over by*
1165 Under the wheel ful lowe he lay adoun.
Ther were also, of Martes divisioun,°   *company, category*
The barbour and the bocher° and the smith,   *butcher*
That forgeth sharpe swerdes on his stith.°   *anvil*
And al above, depeynted° in a tour,   *depicted*
1170 Saw I Conquest, sitting in greet honour,
With the sharpe swerde over his heed
Hanginge by a sotil twynes threed.°   *thin thread of twine*
Depeynted was the slaughtre of Julius,°   *Julius Caesar*
Of grete Nero, and of Antonius;°   *Mark Antony*
1175 Al be that thilke tyme they were unborn,
Yet was hir deeth depeynted ther-biforn
By manasinge of Mars, right by figure.⁴
So was it shewed in that portreiture,
As is depeynted in the sterres° above   *stars*
1180 Who shal be slayn or elles deed for love.
Sufficeth oon ensample in° stories olde: *from*
I may not rekene hem alle, thogh I wolde.
     The statue of Mars upon a carte stood
Armed, and loked grim as he were wood;
1185 And over his heed ther shynen° two figures   *shine*
Of sterres, that been cleped° in scriptures°   *called / writings*
•That oon Puella, that other Rubeus:⁵
This god of armes was arrayed thus.
A wolf ther stood biforn him at his feet
1190 With eyen rede, and of a man he eet.°   *ate*
With sotil° pencel was depeynted this storie   *subtle*
In redoutinge° of Mars and of his glorie.   *fearful reverence*
     Now to the temple of Diane the chaste,
As shortly as I can, I wol me haste
1195 To telle yow al the descripcioun.
Depeynted been the walles up and doun
Of hunting and of shamfast° chastitee.   *modest*
Ther saugh° I how woful Calistopee,°   *saw / Callisto*
Whan that Diane agreved° was with here,°   *aggrieved, angry / her*
1200 Was turned from a womman til° a bere,°   *into / bear*
And after was she maad the lode-sterre;°   *lodestar (North Star)*
Thus was it peynted, I can say yow no ferre;°   *further*

---

3. Nothing was forgotten concerning the evil influence of Mars.
4. Yet their death through the menacing influence
of Mars was depicted beforehand, in an image.

5. Puella and Rubeus are the names of two patterns
of dots (not stars) used in geomancy—a form of
divination—to determine astrological influences.

Hir sone is eek a sterre, as men may see.
Ther saugh I Dane,° y-turned til a tree—   *Daphne*
1205 I mene nat the goddesse Diane,
But Penneus doughter, which that highte Dane.
Ther saugh I Attheon° an hert° y-maked,   *Actaeon / hart*
For vengeaunce that he saugh Diane al naked;
I saugh how that his houndes have him caught
1210 And freten° him, for that they knewe him naught.   *devoured*
Yet° peynted was a litel forther moor,°   *In addition / along*
How Atthalante° hunted the wilde boor,   *Atalanta*
And Meleagre,° and many another mo,   *Meleager*
For which Diane wroghte him care and wo.
1215 Ther saugh I many another wonder storie,
The whiche me list nat drawen to memorie.°   *remember*
    This goddesse on an hert ful hye° seet,°   *high / sat*
With smale houndes al aboute hir feet;
And undernethe hir feet she hadde a mone,°   *moon*
1220 Wexinge it was, and sholde wanie° sone.   *wane*
In gaude° grene hir statue clothed was,   *yellowish*
With bowe in honde, and arwes in a cas.°   *quiver*
Hir eyen caste she ful lowe adoun,
Ther Pluto hath his derke regioun.
1225 A womman travailinge° was hir biforn,   *in labor*
But for° hir child so longe was unborn,   *because*
Ful pitously Lucyna[6] gan she calle,
And seyde, "Help, for thou mayst best of alle."
Wel koude he peynten lyfly° that it wroghte;   *in a lifelike way*
1230 With many a florin he the hewes° boghte.   *colors, pigments*
    Now been thise listes maad, and Theseus,
That at his grete cost arrayed° thus   *adorned*
The temples and the theatre every del,°   *in every part*
Whan it was doon, him lyked° wonder wel.   *it pleased him*
1235 But stinte° I wole of Theseus a lyte,   *stop (talking)*
And speke of Palamon and of Arcite.
    The day approcheth of hir retourninge,
That everich° sholde an hundred knightes bringe   *each*
The bataille to darreyne,° as I yow tolde;   *decide*
1240 And til Athenes, hir covenant for to holde,
Hath everich of hem broght an hundred knightes
Wel armed for the werre at alle rightes.°   *points*
And sikerly,° ther trowed° many a man   *surely / believed, thought*
That never, sithen that the world bigan,
1245 As for to speke of knighthod of hir hond,[7]
As fer as God hath maked see or lond,

6. Lucina, goddess of childbirth, a role attributed to   7. I.e., the deeds of knighthood.
Diana.

Nas of so fewe so noble a companye.
For every wight that lovede chivalrye,
And wolde, his thankes,° han a passant° name,   *gladly / outstanding*
1250 Hath preyed that he mighte ben of that game;
And wel was him that therto chosen was.
For if ther fille° tomorwe swich a cas,°   *befell / case, situation*
Ye knowen wel that every lusty knight
That loveth paramours° and hath his might,°   *passionately / the power*
1255 Were it in Engelond or elleswhere,
They wolde, hir thankes, wilnen° to be there.   *wish*
To fighte for a lady, *benedicite!*°   *bless us*
It were° a lusty° sighte for to see.   *would be / joyful*
And right so ferden° they with Palamon.   *fared, did*
1260 With him ther wenten knightes many oon;°   *a one*
Som° wol ben armed in an habergeoun,°   *One / hauberk, coat of mail*
And in a brest plate and a light gipoun;°   *tunic (worn under hauberk)*
And som wol have a peyre° plates large;   *pair, suit of*
And som wol have a Pruce° sheeld or a targe;°   *Prussian / light shield*
1265 Som wol ben armed on his legges weel,°   *well*
And have an ax, and som a mace of steel.
Ther nis no newe gyse that it nas old.⁸
Armed were they, as I have you told,
Everich after his opinioun.
1270 Ther maistow° seen, coming with Palamoun,   *mayest thou*
Ligurge° himself, the grete king of Trace.°   *Lycurgus / Thrace*
Blak was his berd, and manly was his face.
The cercles° of his eyen in his heed,   *irises*
They gloweden bitwixen yelow and reed;
1275 And lyk a griffon loked he aboute,
With kempe° heres on his browes stoute;°   *shaggy / large*
His limes° grete, his braunes° harde and stronge,   *limbs / muscles*
His shuldres brode, his armes rounde and longe;
And as the gyse was in his contree,
1280 Ful hye upon a char° of gold stood he,   *chariot*
With foure whyte boles° in the trays.°   *bulls / traces*
In stede of cote-armure⁹ over his harnays,°   *armor*
With nayles° yelewe and brighte as any gold   *claws*
He hadde a beres skin, col-blak for old.°   *because of age*
1285 His longe heer was kembd° bihinde his bak—   *combed*
As any ravenes fethere it shoon° for° blak;   *shone / very*
A wrethe of gold arm-greet,° of huge wighte,°   *thick as an arm / weight*
Upon his heed, set ful of stones brighte,
Of fyne rubies and of dyamaunts.°   *diamonds*
1290 Aboute his char ther wenten whyte alaunts,°   *wolfhounds*

8. There is no new fashion (in arms) that did not   9. See n. 4, p. 28.
exist long ago.

Twenty and mo, as grete as any steer,
To hunten at the leoun or the deer,
And folwed him with mosel° faste y-bounde,   *muzzle*
Colered° of gold, and tourettes¹ fyled° rounde.   *Wearing collars / filed*
1295 An hundred lordes hadde he in his route,°   *retinue*
Armed ful wel, with hertes sterne and stoute.
    With Arcita, in stories as men finde,
The grete Emetreus, the king of Inde,°   *India*
Upon a steede bay° trapped in steel,°   *bay-colored / with steel trappings*
1300 Covered in cloth of gold diapred weel,°   *finely patterned*
Cam ryding lyk the god of armes, Mars.
His cote-armure was of cloth of Tars,°   *Tarsia, in Turkestan*
Couched° with perles whyte and rounde and grete.   *Set, overlaid*
His sadel was of brend° gold newe y-bete;°   *burnished / hammered, crafted*
1305 A mantelet° upon his shuldre hanginge   *short cloak*
Bret-ful° of rubies rede as fyr sparklinge.   *Brimful*
His crispe° heer lyk ringes was y-ronne,²   *curly*
And that was yelow, and glitered as the sonne.
His nose was heigh, his eyen bright citryn,°   *lemon-colored*
1310 His lippes rounde, his colour was sangwyn;°   *bloodred*
A fewe frakenes° in his face y-spreynd,°   *freckles / scattered*
Betwixen yelow and somdel blak y-meynd;°   *mingled*
And as a leoun he his loking caste.
Of fyve and twenty yeer his age I caste:°   *estimate*
1315 His berd was wel bigonne for to springe.
His voys was as a trompe° thunderinge.   *trumpet*
Upon his heed he wered of laurer° grene   *laurel*
A gerland fresh and lusty for to sene.
Upon his hand he bar for his deduyt°   *delight*
1320 An egle tame, as any lilie whyt.
An hundred lordes hadde he with him there,
Al armed, sauf° hir heddes, in al hir gere,°   *except / gear, armor*
Ful richely in alle maner thinges.
For trusteth wel that dukes, erles, kinges
1325 Were gadered° in this noble companye   *gathered*
For love and for encrees° of chivalrye.   *increase*
Aboute this king ther ran on every part°   *side*
Ful many a tame leoun and leopart.
And in this wyse° thise lordes, alle and some,°   *way / one and all*
1330 Ben on the Sonday to the citee come
Aboute pryme,° and in the toun alight.   *9 A.M.*
    This Theseus, this duk, this worthy knight,
Whan he had broght hem into his citee,
And inned° hem, everich in his degree,°   *housed / each according to his rank*

---

1. Rings on the collar for attaching a leash.   2. I.e., hung down.

1335 He festeth hem, and dooth so greet labour
      To esen° hem and doon hem al honour,   *set at ease*
      That yet men wenen° that no mannes wit   *think*
      Of noon estat ne coude amenden° it.   *improve on*
      The minstralcye, the service at the feste,
1340 The grete yiftes° to the moste and leste,°   *gifts / highest and lowest (in rank)*
      The riche array of Theseus paleys,
      Ne who sat first ne last upon the deys,°   *dais, platform*
      What ladies fairest been or best daunsinge,
      Or which of hem can daunce best and singe,
1345 Ne who most felingly° speketh of love;   *sensitively*
      What haukes sitten on the perche above,
      What houndes liggen° on the floor adoun—   *lie*
      Of al this make I now no mencioun;
      But al° th'effect, that thinketh me° the beste.   *only / seems to me*
1350 Now comth the poynt, and herkneth if yow leste.° *it please you*
        The Sonday night, er day bigan to springe,
      When Palamon the larke herde singe
      (Although it nere° nat day by houres two,   *were*
      Yet song the larke) and Palamon right tho
1355 With holy herte and with an heigh corage,°   *spirit*
      He roos° to wenden on his pilgrimage   *arose*
      Unto the blisful Citherea benigne—
      I mene Venus, honurable and digne.°   *worthy*
      And in hir houre [3] he walketh forth a pas° *slowly, at a footpace*
1360 Unto the listes ther° hir temple was,   *where*
      And doun he kneleth, and with humble chere
      And herte soor,° he seyde as ye shul here: *sore (with love)*
      "Faireste of faire, O lady myn, Venus,
      Doughter to Jove and spouse of Vulcanus,
1365 Thou gladere° of the mount of Citheroun,   *gladdener*
      For thilke love thou haddest to Adoun,°   *Adonis*
      Have pitee of my bittre teres smerte,
      And tak myn humble preyere at thyn herte.
      Allas! I ne have no langage to telle
1370 Th'effectes ne the torments of myn helle;
      Myn herte may myne harmes nat biwreye;°   *reveal*
      I am so confus° that I can noght seye   *bewildered*
      But mercy, lady bright, that knowest weele
      My thought, and seest what harmes that I feele.
1375 Considere al this, and rewe° upon my sore,°   *have pity / pain*

---

3. An hour of the day assigned astrologically to Venus. The hours were assigned to the planets in rotation, beginning at sunrise with the planet specially associated with that day. All three characters pray to their deities at the appropriate hours: Palamon to Venus two hours before Monday's sunrise; Emily to Diana during the first hour of Monday, the moon's day (ll. 1413–16); and Arcite to Mars during the fourth hour (ll. 1509–11).

As wisly° as I shal for everemore,   *surely*
Emforth° my might, thy trewe servant be,   *To the extent of*
And holden werre° alwey with chastitee.   *war*
That make I myn avow,° so ye me helpe.   *vow*
1380 I kepe° noght of armes for to yelpe,°   *dare / boast*
Ne I ne axe nat tomorwe to have victorie,
Ne renoun in this cas,° ne veyne glorie   *event*
Of pris° of armes blowen up and doun,   *reputation, praise*
But I wolde have fully possessioun
1385 Of Emelye, and dye in thy servyse.
Find thou the manere how, and in what wyse:
I recche° nat but° it may bettre be   *care / whether*
To have victorie of hem, or they of me,
So that I have my lady in myne armes. \
1390 For though so be that Mars is god of armes,
Youre vertu is so greet in hevene above,
That if yow list, I shal wel have my love.
Thy temple wol I worshipe everemo,
And on thyn auter,° where° I ryde or go,°   *altar / whether / walk*
1395 I wol don sacrifice and fyres bete.°   *kindle*
And if ye wol nat so, my lady swete,
Than preye I thee, tomorwe with a spere
That Arcita me thurgh the herte bere.°   *pierce*
Thanne rekke I noght, whan I have lost my lyf,
1400 Though that Arcita winne hire to his wyf.
This is th'effect° and ende of my preyere: *essence*
Yif° me my love, thou blisful lady dere."   *Give*
    Whan the orison° was doon of Palamon,   *prayer*
His sacrifice he dide, and that anon,°   *promptly*
1405 Ful pitously, with alle circumstaunces,°   *attendant details*
Al° telle I noght as now his observaunces.   *Although*
But atte laste the statue of Venus shook,
And made a signe, wherby that he took
That his preyere accepted was that day.
1410 For thogh the signe shewed a delay,
Yet wiste° he wel that graunted was his bone;°   *knew / boon, request*
And with glad herte he wente him hoom ful sone.
    The thridde houre inequal[4] that° Palamon   *after*
Bigan to Venus temple for to goon,
1415 Up roos the sonne, and up roos Emelye,
And to the temple of Diane gan hye.°   *hastened*
Hir maydens, that she thider with hir ladde,°   *led*
Ful redily with hem the fyr they hadde,

---

4. The hours assigned to the planets (see n. 3, p. 55) were based on a system that divided them into twelve each of daylight and darkness. Hence they would almost always be unequal in duration, since day and night are the same length only at the equinoxes.

Th'encens,° the clothes,° and the remenant al   *incense / cloths, hangings*
1420 That to the sacrifyce longen shal;°   *should belong*
The hornes fulle of meth,° as was the gyse;°   *mead / fashion*
Ther lakked noght to doon hir sacrifyse.
Smokinge the temple, full of clothes faire,[5]
This Emelye, with herte debonaire,°   *gracious, humble*
1425 Hir body wessh° with water of a welle;°   *washed / spring*
But how she dide hir ryte I dar nat telle,
But° it be any thing in general;   *Unless*
And yet it were a game° to heren al;   *pleasure*
To him that meneth wel it were no charge,°   *it wouldn't matter*
1430 But it is good a man ben at his large.°   *at liberty (to speak or not)*
Hir brighte heer was kembd,° untressed° al;   *combed / loose*
A coroune° of a grene ook cerial°   *garland / a species of oak*
Upon hir heed was set ful fair and mete.°   *fitting*
Two fyres on the auter gan she bete,
1435 And dide hir thinges, as men may biholde
In Stace° of Thebes and thise bokes olde.   *Statius*
Whan kindled was the fyr, with pitous chere°   *countenance*
Unto Diane she spak as ye may here:
   "O chaste goddesse of the wodes grene,
1440 To whom bothe hevene and erthe and see is sene,°   *visible*
Quene of the regne° of Pluto derk and lowe,   *realm*
Goddesse of maydens, that myn herte hast knowe
Ful many a yeer, and woost° what I desire,   *knowest*
As keepe me fro thy vengeaunce and thyn ire,
1445 That Attheon° aboughte° cruelly.   *Actaeon / suffered for*
Chaste goddesse, wel wostow° that I   *knowest thou*
Desire to been a mayden al my lyf,
Ne never wol I be° no love° ne wyf.   *do I wish to be / lover*
I am, thou woost, yet of thy companye,
1450 A mayde, and love hunting and venerye,°   *hunting, the chase*
And for to walken in the wodes wilde,
And noght to been a wyf and be with childe.
Noght wol I knowe companye of man.
Now help me, lady, sith ye may and can,
1455 For tho° thre formes[6] that thou hast in thee.   *those*
And Palamon, that hath swich love to me,
And eek Arcite, that loveth me so sore,
This grace I preye thee withoute more:
As sende love and pees° bitwixe hem two,   *peace*
1460 And fro me turne awey hir hertes so
That al hir hote love and hir desyr,

5. Censing the temple, full of beautiful cloth hangings.
6. The goddess appears as Diana on earth, Luna in heaven, and Proserpina in the underworld (the "regne of Pluto" referred to in l. 1441).

And al hir bisy° torment and hir fyr,   *intense*
Be queynt° or turned in another place.°   *quenched / direction*
And if so be thou wolt° not do me grace,   *will*
1465 Or if my destinee be shapen° so,   *shaped, determined*
That I shal nedes° have oon of hem two,   *must necessarily*
As sende me him that most desireth me.
Bihold, goddesse of clene chastitee,
The bittre teres that on my chekes falle.
1470 Sin° thou are mayde° and kepere° of us alle,   *Since / a virgin / guardian*
My maydenhede thou kepe and wel conserve,
And whyl I live a mayde, I wol thee serve."
    The fyres brenne° upon the auter° clere,°   *burn / altar / brightly*
Whyl Emelye was thus in hir preyere.
1475 But sodeinly she saugh a sighte queynte,°   *strange*
For right anon oon of the fyres queynte,°   *died out*
And quiked° agayn, and after that anon   *became alive, flamed up*
That other fyr was queynt, and al agon;°   *gone*
And as it queynte, it made a whistelinge,
1480 As doon thise wete brondes° in hir brenninge,   *pieces of burning wood*
And at the brondes ende out ran anoon
As it were° blody dropes many oon;   *What seemed like*
For which so sore agast was Emelye
That she was wel ny° mad, and gan to crye,   *near*
1485 For she ne wiste what it signifyed;
But only for the fere° thus hath she cryed,   *fear*
And weep,° that it was pitee for to here.   *wept*
And therwithal Diane gan appere,
With bowe in hond, right as an hunteresse,
1490 And seyde: "Doghter, stint° thyn hevinesse.°   *stop / sorrow*
Among the goddes hye° it is affermed,   *high*
And by eterne word writen and confermed,
Thou shalt ben wedded unto oon of tho°   *those*
That han° for thee so muchel care and wo;   *have*
1495 But unto which of hem I may nat telle.
Farwel, for I ne may no lenger dwelle.
The fyres which that on myn auter brenne
Shulle thee declaren, er that thou go henne,°   *hence*
Thyn aventure° of love, as in this cas."   *What will befall thee*
1500 And with that word, the arwes in the cas°   *quiver*
Of the goddesse clateren faste and ringe,
And forth she wente, and made a vanisshinge;
For which this Emelye astoned° was,   *stunned, astonished*
And seyde, "What amounteth° this, allas!   *means*
1505 I putte me in thy proteccioun,
Diane, and in° thy disposicioun."°   *at / disposing*
And hoom she gooth anon the nexte° weye.   *nearest*

This is th'effect, ther is namore to seye.
   The nexte houre of Mars folwinge this,
1510 Arcite unto the temple walked is°   *has walked*
Of fierse Mars, to doon his sacrifyse,
With alle the rytes of his payen wyse.°   *pagan customs*
With pitous herte and heigh devocioun,
Right thus to Mars he gynde his orisoun:[†]   *prayer*
1515   "O stronge god, that in the regnes° colde   *realms*
Of Trace° honoured art and lord y-holde,°   *Thrace / considered*
And hast in every regne and every lond
Of armes al the brydel[7] in thyn hond,
And hem fortunest as thee list devyse,[8]
1520 Accepte of me my pitous sacrifyse.
If so be that my youthe may deserve,
And that my might be worthy for to serve
Thy godhede, that I may been oon of thyne,
Thanne preye I thee to rewe° upon my pyne.° *take pity / suffering*
1525 For thilke° peyne and thilke hote fyr   *that same*
In which thou whylom° brendest° for desyr, *once / burned*
Whan that thou usedest° the beautee   *enjoyed*
Of fayre yonge fresshe Venus free,°   *noble, generous*
And haddest hir in armes at thy wille—
1530 Although thee ones° on a tyme misfille° *once / it went wrong with*
Whan Vulcanus hadde caught thee in his las,°   *net*
And fond° thee ligginge° by thy wyf, allas!— *found / lying*
For thilke sorwe that was in thyn herte,
Have routhe° as wel upon my peynes smerte.°   *pity / sharp*
1535 I am yong and unkonning,° as thou wost,° *ignorant / knowest*
And, as I trowe,° with love offended° most *believe / assailed*
That evere was any lyves° creature;   *living*
For she that dooth° me al this wo endure,   *makes*
Ne reccheth° nevere wher° I sinke or flete.° *cares / whether / float*
1540 And wel I woot, er she me mercy hete,°   *promise*
I moot with strengthe winne hire in the place;[9]
And wel I woot, withouten help or grace
Of thee, ne may my strengthe noght availle.
Than help me, lord, tomorwe in my bataille,
1545 For thilke fyr that whylom brente° thee,   *burned*
As wel as thilke fyr now brenneth me;
And do° that I tomorwe have victorie.   *bring it about*
Myn be the travaille,° and thyn be the glorie!   *labor*
Thy soverein temple wol I most honouren
1550 Of any place, and alwey most labouren
In° thy plesaunce° and in thy craftes° stronge, *For / pleasure / activities*

---

7. I.e., control.   to devise.
8. And give them (whatever) fortune it pleases you   9. I.e., the tournament lists.

And in thy temple I wol my baner honge,°   *hang*
And alle the armes of my companye;
And everemo, unto that day I dye,
1555 Eterne fyr I wol biforn thee finde.°   *provide*
And eek° to this avow I wol me binde: *also*
My berd, myn heer, that hongeth long adoun,
That never yet ne felte offensioun°   *damage*
Of rasour nor of shere,° I wol thee yive,   *shears*
1560 And ben thy trewe servant whyl I live.
Now lord, have routhe upon my sorwes sore:
Yif° me the victorie, I aske thee namore."   *Give*
      The preyere stinte° of Arcita the stronge,   *being ended*
The ringes on the temple dore that honge,
1565 And eek the dores, clatereden ful faste,
Of which Arcita somwhat him agaste.°   *took fright*
The fyres brenden up on the auter brighte,
That it gan al the temple for to lighte;
And swete smel the ground anon up yaf,°   *gave*
1570 And Arcita anon his hand up haf,°   *lifted*
And more encens° into the fyr he caste,   *incense*
With othere rytes mo; and atte laste
The statue of Mars bigan his hauberk° ringe.   *coat of mail*
And with that soun he herde a murmuringe
1575 Ful lowe and dim, that sayde thus, "Victorie,"
For which he yaf to Mars honour and glorie.
And thus with joye and hope wel to fare,
Arcite anon unto his in° is fare,°   *dwelling / gone*
As fayn° as fowel° is of the brighte sonne.   *glad / fowl, bird*
1580   And right anon swich stryf ther is bigonne,
For thilke graunting, in the hevene above,
Bitwixe Venus, the goddesse of love,
And Mars, the sterne god armipotente,°   *strong in arms*
That Jupiter was bisy it to stente;°   *stop*
1585 Til that the pale Saturnus the colde,[1]
That knew so manye of aventures olde,
Fond° in his olde experience an art   *Found*
That he ful sone hath plesed every part.°   *side*
As sooth is sayd, elde° hath greet avantage;   *old age*
1590 In elde is bothe wisdom and usage;°   *experience*
Men may the olde atrenne° and noght atrede.°   *outrun / outwit*
Saturne anon, to stinten stryf and drede,
Al be it that it is agayn° his kynde,°   *against / nature*
Of al this stryf he gan remedie fynde.
1595   "My dere doghter Venus," quod Saturne,

1. In describing Saturn, the word not only indicates his imbalance of humors but also means ominous, baleful.

"My cours,° that hath so wyde for to turne,   *orbit*
Hath more power than wot° any man.   *knows*
Myn is the drenching° in the see so wan;°   *drowning / pale, colorless*
Myn is the prison° in the derke cote;°   *imprisonment / hut, cell*
1600 Myn is the strangling and hanging by the throte;
The murmure and the cherles° rebelling,   *churls', peasants'*
The groyninge° and the pryvee° empoysoning.   *grumbling / secret*
I do vengeance and pleyn° correccioun°   *full / punishment*
Whyl I dwelle in the signe of the leoun.[2]
1605 Myn is the ruine of the hye halles,
The falling of the toures and of the walles
Upon the mynour° or the carpenter.   *miner*
I slow° Sampsoun, shakinge the piler;   *slew*
And myne be the maladyes colde,
1610 The derke tresons, and the castes° olde;   *plots, deceits*
My loking° is the fader of pestilence.   *aspect*
Now weep namore, I shal doon diligence
That Palamon, that is thyn owne knight,
Shal have his lady, as thou hast him hight.°   *promised*
1615 Though Mars shal helpe his knight, yet nathelees
Bitwixe yow ther moot be som tyme pees,°   *peace*
Al be ye noght of o complexioun,°   *the same temperament*
That causeth al day swich divisioun.
I am thin aycl,° redy at thy wille;   *grandfather*
1620 Weep now namore, I wol thy lust° fulfille."   *desire*
Now wol I stinten° of the goddes above,   *cease (to tell)*
Of Mars and of Venus, goddesse of love,
And telle yow as pleynly as I can
The grete effect° for which that I bigan.   *outcome*

PART FOUR

1625   Greet was the feste in Athenes that day,
And eek the lusty seson of that May
Made every wight to been in swich plesaunce,°   *pleasure*
That al that Monday justen° they and daunce,   *joust*
And spenden it in Venus heigh servyse.
1630 But by the cause that[3] they sholde ryse
Erly, for to seen the grete fight,
Unto hir reste wenten they at night.
And on the morwe, whan that day gan springe,
Of hors and harneys° noyse and clateringe   *equipment*
1635 Ther was in hostelryes al aboute;
And to the paleys rood ther many a route°   *company*

2. Saturn is most malign while in the astrological   3. I.e., because.
house of Leo.

Of lordes upon stedes and palfreys.
Ther maystow seen devysing° of harneys   *fashioning, preparation*
So uncouth° and so riche, and wroght so weel°   *curious, unusual / well*
1640 Of goldsmithrie, of browdinge,° and of steel;   *embroidery*
The sheeldes brighte, testeres,° and trappures;°   *headpieces / trappings*
Gold-hewen helmes, hauberkes, cote-armures;
Lordes in paraments° on hir courseres,°   *decorated robes / coursers, chargers*
Knightes of retenue,° and eek squyeres   *in service*
1645 Nailinge the speres,[4] and helmes bokelinge;
Gigginge of° sheeldes with layneres° lacinge—   *Putting straps on / thongs*
Ther as° need is, they weren no thing ydel;   *Wherever*
The fomy steedes on the golden brydel
Gnawinge, and faste the armurers also
1650 With fyle and hamer prikinge° to and fro;   *riding*
Yemen° on foote and communes° many oon   *Yeomen / common people*
With shorte staves, thikke as they may goon;
Pypes, trompes,° nakers,° clariounes   *trumpets / kettledrums*
That in the bataille blowen blody sounes;°   *warlike sounds*
1655 The paleys ful of peple up and doun,
Heer three, ther ten, holding hir questioun,
Divyninge of° thise Thebane knightes two.   *Speculating about*
Somme seyden thus, somme seyde it shal be so;
Somme helden with° him with the blake berd,   *sided with*
1660 Somme with the balled,° somme with the thikke herd;°   *bald / haired*
Somme sayde he° loked grim, and he wolde fighte—   *that one*
"He hath a sparth° of twenty pound of wighte."°   *battle-ax / weight*
Thus was the halle ful of divyninge,
Longe after that the sonne gan to springe.
1665   The grete Theseus, that of° his sleep awaked   *out of*
With minstralcye and noyse that was maked,
Held yet the chambre of his paleys riche,
Til that the Thebane knightes, bothe yliche°   *equally*
Honoured, were into the paleys fet.°   *summoned*
1670 Duk Theseus was at a window set,
Arrayed right as he were a god in trone.°   *throne*
The peple preesseth thiderward ful sone
Him for to seen, and doon heigh reverence,
And eek to herkne° his heste° and his sentence.°   *hear / command / decision*
1675   An heraud on a scaffold made an "Oo!"
Til al the noyse of peple was ydo;°   *done, finished*
And whan he saugh the peple of noyse al stille,
Thus showed he the mighty dukes wille:
   "The lord hath of his heigh discrecioun°   *acumen*
1680 Considered that it were destruccioun

---

4. I.e., nailing the head to the shaft.

To gentil blood to fighten in the gyse°   manner
Of mortal bataille now in this empryse.°   undertaking
Wherfore, to shapen° that they shal not dye,   arrange things so
He wol his firste purpos modifye.
1685 No man therfore, up° peyne of los of lyf,   upon
No maner shot,° ne polax,° ne short knyf   arrow, missile / battle-ax
Into the listes sende ° or thider bringe,   may send
Ne short swerd, for to stoke° with poynt bytinge,°   stab / piercing
No man ne drawe ne bere it by his syde.
1690 Ne no man shal unto his felawe° ryde   against his opponent
But o cours° with a sharp y-grounde spere;   one charge
Foyne,° if him list, on fote, himself to were.°   He may parry / defend
And he that is at meschief° shal be take,°   in trouble / taken, captured
And noght slayn, but be broght unto the stake
1695 That shal ben ordeyned° on either syde;   set up
But thider he shal by force, and ther abyde.⁵
And if so falle° the chieftayn be take   befall, happen
On either syde, or elles° sleen° his make,⁶   else / slay
No lenger shal the turneyinge laste.
1700 God spede yow! goth forth, and ley on faste.
With long swerd and with mace fighteth youre fille.
Goth now youre wey—this is the lordes wille."
     The voys of peple touchede the hevene,
So loude cryde they with mery stevene:°   voice
1705 "God save swich a lord, that is so good,
He wilneth° no destruccioun of blood!"   desires
     Up goon the trompes° and the melodye,   trumpets
And to the listes rit° the companye,   rides
By ordinaunce,° thurghout the citee large,   In order
1710 Hanged with cloth of gold and nat with sarge.°   serge
Ful lyk a lord this noble duk gan ryde,
Thise two Thebans upon either syde;
And after rood the quene and Emelye,
And after that another companye
1715 Of oon and other, after hir degree.°   according to their rank
And thus they passen thurghout the citee,
And to the listes come they bytyme.°   promptly
It nas° not of the day yet fully pryme°   was / 9 A.M.
Whan set was Theseus ful riche and hye,
1720 Ipolita the quene and Emelye,
And othere ladies in degrees° aboute.   tiers
Unto the seetes preesseth al the route.°   crowd
     And westward, thurgh the gates under Marte,°   Mars
Arcite, and eek the hundred of his parte,°   on his side

5. But there he must be brought by force, and there   6. I.e., the opposing leader.
remain.

1725 With baner° reed is entred right anon;   *banner*
And in that selve° moment Palamon   *same*
Is under Venus, estward in the place,
With baner whyt, and hardy chere° and face.   *countenance*
In al the world, to seken up and doun,
1730 So evene° withouten variacioun,   *equal*
Ther nere° swiche companyes tweye.   *were not*
For ther was noon so wys that coude seye
That any hadde of other avauntage
Of° worthinesse, ne of estaat ne age,   *In*
1735 So evene were they chosen, for to gesse.°   *one would guess*
And in two renges° faire they hem dresse.°   *rows / place themselves*
Whan that hir names rad° were everichoon,°   *read / every one*
That° in hir nombre gyle° were ther noon,   *So that / deception*
Tho° were the gates shet,° and cryed was loude: *Then / shut*
1740 "Do now your devoir,° yonge knightes proude!"   *duty*
   The heraudes lefte hir priking° up and doun;   *their riding*
Now ringen trompes loude and clarioun.
Ther is namore to seyn, but west and est
In goon the speres ful sadly° in th'arest;°   *firmly / into the spear rests*
1745 In goth the sharpe spore° into the syde.   *spur*
Ther seen men who can juste° and who can ryde;   *joust*
Ther shiveren shaftes upon sheeldes thikke;
He° feleth thurgh the herte-spoon° the prikke.   *One / breastbone*
Up springen speres twenty foot on highte;°   *on high*
1750 Out goon the swerdes as the silver brighte.
The helmes they tohewen and toshrede;°   *hew and shred to pieces*
Out brest° the blood, with sterne° stremes rede.   *bursts / powerful, violent*
With mighty maces the bones they tobreste.°   *smash to bits*
He thurgh the thikkeste of the throng gan threste;°   *thrust*
1755 Ther stomblen stedes stronge, and doun goth al;
He rolleth under foot as dooth a bal.
He foyneth° on his feet with his tronchoun,°   *parries / truncheon, shattered spear*
And he him hurtleth° with his hors adoun.   *strikes*
He thurgh the body is hurt and sithen° y-take,   *then*
1760 Maugree his heed,° and broght unto the stake.   *In spite of all he could do*
As forward° was, right ther he moste abyde;   *agreement*
Another lad° is on that other syde.   *led, carried off*
And som tyme dooth° hem Theseus to reste,   *causes*
Hem to refresshe and drinken, if hem leste.°   *if it please them*
1765   Ful ofte a day° han thise Thebanes two   *during this day*
Togidre y-met, and wroght his felawe wo;°   *done harm to each other*
Unhorsed hath ech other of hem tweye.°   *twice*
Ther nas no tygre° in the vale of Galgopheye,[7]   *tigress*

---

7. Probably the valley of Gargaphie, where according to Ovid's *Metamorphoses* Actaeon was killed by his
hounds. Chaucer describes the event in ll. 1207–10. For Belmarye (l. 1772), see *General Prologue*, l. 57.

Whan that hir whelp is stole whan it is lyte,°   *little*
1770 So cruel on the hunte° as is Arcite   *toward the hunter*
For jelous herte upon° this Palamoun.   *toward*
Ne in Belmarye ther nis so fel° leoun   *fierce*
That hunted is, or for° his hunger wood,°   *because of / enraged*
Ne of his praye desireth so the blood,
1775 As Palamon to sleen° his foo Arcite   *slay*
The jelous strokes on hir helmes byte;
Out renneth° blood on bothe hir sydes rede.   *runs*
    Som tyme an ende ther is of every dede.
For er the sonne unto the reste wente,
1780 The stronge king Emetreus gan hente°   *seize*
This Palamon, as he faught with Arcite,
And made his swerd depe in his flesh to byte;
And by the force of twenty is he take
Unyolden,° and y-drawe° unto the stake.   *Not having yielded / drawn, dragged*
1785 And in the rescus° of this Palamoun   *(attempted) rescue*
The stronge king Ligurge is born adoun;
And king Emetreus, for al his strengthe,
Is born° out of his sadel a swerdes lengthe,   *carried, knocked*
So hitte him Palamon er he were take.
1790 But al for noght: he was broght to the stake.
His hardy herte mighte him helpe naught;
He moste abyde, whan that he was caught,
By force° and eek by composicioun.°   *necessity / agreement*
Who sorweth now but woful Palamoun,
1795 That moot° namore goon agayn to fighte?   *may*
    And whan that Theseus had seyn this sighte,
Unto the folk that foghten thus echoon
He cryde, "Ho! namore, for it is doon!
I wol be trewe juge, and nat partye.°   *partisan*
1800 Arcite of Thebes shal have Emelye,
That by his fortune hath hir faire° y-wonne."   *fairly*
Anon ther is a noyse of peple bigonne
For joye of this, so loude and heighe° withalle,   *great*
It semed that the listes sholde falle.
1805   What can now faire Venus doon above?
What seith she now? what dooth this quene of love
But wepeth so, for wanting° of hir wille,   *lacking*
Til that hir teres in the listes fille?°   *fell*
She seyde, "I am ashamed,° doutelees."   *shamed, disgraced*
1810   Saturnus seyde, "Doghter, hold thy pees.°   *peace*
Mars hath his wille: his knight hath al his bone;°   *request*
And, by myn heed,° thou shalt ben esed° sone."   *head / eased, satisfied*
    The trompours° with the loude minstralcye,°   *trumpeters / music*
The heraudes that ful loude yelle and crye,

1815 Been in hir wele° for joye of daun° Arcite.　　　　　*happiness / sir, master*
　　　But herkneth me, and stinteth° noyse a lyte,°　　　*cease / little*
　　　Which° a miracle ther bifel anon.　　　　　　　　*What*
　　　　　This fierse° Arcite hath of° his helm y-don,°　*bold / off / taken*
　　　And on a courser, for to shewe his face,
1820 He priketh endelong° the large place,　　　　　　*the length of*
　　　Loking upward upon this Emelye;
　　　And she agayn° him caste a freendlich yë　　　　*toward*
　　　(For wommen, as to speken in comune,°　　　　　*generally*
　　　They folwen alle the favour of fortune)
1825 And she was al his chere,° as in his herte.　　　　*happiness*
　　　　　Out of the ground a furie infernal sterte,°　*started, leaped*
　　　From Pluto sent at requeste of Saturne,
　　　For which his hors for fere° gan to turne　　　　*fear*
　　　And leep° asyde, and foundred° as he leep;　　*leaped / foundered, stumbled*
1830 And er that Arcite may taken keep,°　　　　　　　*heed*
　　　He pighte° him on the pomel° of his heed,　　　*pitched / crown, top*
　　　That in the place he lay as he were deed,
　　　His brest tobrosten° with° his sadel-bowe.⁸　　*broken, shattered / by*
　　　As blak he lay as any cole° or crowe,　　　　　*coal*
1835 So was the blood y-ronnen in° his face.　　　　　*into*
　　　Anon he was y-born out of the place,
　　　With herte soor, to Theseus paleys.
　　　Tho° was he corven° out of his harneys,°　　　*Then / cut / armor*
　　　And in a bed y-brought ful faire and blyve,°　*quickly*
1840 For he was yet in memorie° and alyve,　　　　　*conscious*
　　　And alway crying after Emelye.
　　　　　Duk Theseus, with al his companye,
　　　Is comen hoom to Athenes his citee,
　　　With alle blisse and greet solempnitee.
1845 Al be it that this aventure° was falle,°　　　　*accident / had occurred*
　　　He nolde noght disconforten° hem alle.　　　　*dishearten*
　　　Men seyde eek that Arcite shal nat dye;
　　　He shal ben heled of his maladye.
　　　And of another thing they were as fayn:°　　　*glad*
1850 That of hem alle was ther noon y-slayn,
　　　Al° were they sore y-hurt, and namely° oon,　*Although / especially*
　　　That with a spere was thirled° his brest-boon.　*pierced*
　　　To° othere woundes and to broken armes　　　*For*
　　　Some hadden salves, and some hadden charmes;
1855 Fermacies° of herbes, and eek save°　　*Medicines / a drink made of herbs*
　　　They dronken, for they wolde hir limes° have.°　*limbs / keep, preserve*
　　　For which this noble duk, as he wel can,°　　　*knows how*
　　　Conforteth and honoureth every man,

---

8. The high arched front of a saddle. Arcite's horse, after rearing and pitching him off, falls backward on top of him.

And made revel al the longe night
1860 Unto the straunge° lordes, as was right.   *foreign*
Ne ther was holden no disconfitinge
But as a justes or a tourneyinge;
For soothly ther was no disconfiture,
For falling nis nat but an aventure.[9]
1865 Ne to be lad° with fors unto the stake   *led, carried*
Unyolden,° and with twenty knightes take,   *Not having yielded*
O° persone allone, withouten mo,   *One*
And haried° forth by arme, foot, and to,°   *dragged / toe*
And eek his steede driven forth with staves
1870 With° footmen, bothe yemen and eek knaves°—   *By / servants*
It nas aretted° him no vileinye;°   *attributed to / disgrace*
Ther may no man clepen° it cowardye.°   *call / cowardice*
For which anon duk Theseus leet crye,°   *caused to be proclaimed*
To stinten° alle rancour and envye,°   *stop / bad will*
1875 The gree° as wel of o syde as of other,   *worthiness*
And either syde ylyk° as otheres brother;   *alike*
And yaf hem yiftes after hir degree,
And fully heeld a feste dayes three;
And conveyed the kinges worthily
1880 Out of his toun a journee° largely.°   *a day's journey / fully*
And hoom wente every man the righte way.
Ther was namore but "Farewel, have good day!"
Of this bataille I wol namore endyte,°   *tell, make verses*
But speke of Palamon and of Arcite.
1885   Swelleth the brest of Arcite, and the sore
Encreesseth at his herte more and more.
The clothered° blood, for° any lechecraft,°   *clotted / despite / medical care*
Corrupteth and is in his bouk° y-laft,°   *body / left*
That neither veyne-blood,° ne ventusinge,°   *bloodletting / cupping*
1890 Ne drinke of herbes may ben his helpinge.
The vertu expulsif, or animal,
Fro thilke vertu cleped natural[1]
Ne may the venim voyden° ne expelle.   *void, remove*
The pypes° of his longes° gonne to swelle,   *tubes / lungs*
1895 And every lacerte° in his brest adoun   *muscle*
Is shent° with venim and corrupcioun.°   *damaged / decay*
Him gayneth° neither, for to gete° his lyf,   *It helps him / save*
Vomyt upward ne dounward laxatif;
Al is tobrosten° thilke regioun.   *shattered*

9. Nor was anything accounted a defeat except as is proper to a jousting or a tournament; for truly there was no dishonor, since falling (in a joust) is nothing but an accident.

1. Medieval medicine thought three powers ("virtues") controlled the functions of the body. Here the animal virtue, located in the brain, is unable to force the muscles to expel the corrupted blood from the natural virtue, located in the liver. Hence the natural virtue is powerless to perform one of its normal tasks, cleansing the lungs of corrupt substances.

1900 Nature hath now no dominacioun;°   *dominion, power*
     And certeinly, ther nature wol nat wirche,°   *work*
     Farewel, phisyk;° go ber the man to chirche.   *medicine*
     This al and som,° that Arcita mot° dye;   *This is the entire matter / must*
     For which he sendeth after Emelye
1905 And Palamon, that was his cosin dere.
     Than seyde he thus, as ye shul after here:
          "Naught may the woful spirit in myn herte
     Declare o poynt° of alle my sorwes smerte°   *one part / painful*
     To yow, my lady, that I love most;
1910 But I biquethe° the service of my gost°   *bequeath / spirit, soul*
     To yow aboven every creature,
     Sin° that my lyf may no lenger dure.°   *Since / last*
     Allas, the wo! allas, the peynes stronge,
     That I for yow have suffred, and so longe!
1915 Allas, the deeth! allas, myn Emelye!
     Allas, departinge° of oure companye!   *separation*
     Allas, myn hertes quene! allas, my wyf!
     Myn hertes lady, endere of my lyf!
     What is this world? what asketh men° to have?   *does one ask*
1920 Now with his love, now in his colde grave
     Allone, withouten any companye.
     Farewel, my swete fo, myn Emelye!
     And softe tak me in your armes tweye,
     For love of God, and herkneth what I seye:
1925   I have heer with my cosin Palamon
     Had stryf and rancour many a day agon,°   *past*
     For love of yow and for my jalousye.
     And Jupiter so wis° my soule gye,°   *wise / guide*
     To speken of° a servant° proprely,   *about / servant (of love)*
1930 With alle circumstaunces° trewely—   *necessary qualities*
     That is to seyn, trouthe,° honour, knighthede,   *fidelity*
     Wisdom, humblesse,° estaat,° and heigh kinrede,°   *humility / position / kindred*
     Fredom,° and al that longeth° to that art—   *Generosity / belongs*
     So Jupiter have of my soule part,[2]
1935 As in this world right now ne knowe I non
     So worthy to ben loved as Palamon,
     That serveth yow and wol don al his lyf.
     And if that evere ye shul been a wyf,
     Foryet nat Palamon, the gentil° man."   *noble, virtuous*
1940 And with that word his speche faille gan,°   *began to*
     For from his feet up to his brest was come
     The cold of deeth, that hadde him overcome,
     And yet moreover, in his armes two

2. I.e., receive after death.

The vital strengthe is lost and al ago.
1945 Only° the intellect, withouten more,°   *Only then / without delay*
That dwelled in his herte syk and sore,
Gan faillen when the herte felte deeth.
Dusked° his eyen two, and failled breeth,   *Became dim*
But on his lady yet caste he his yë;
1950 His laste word was, "Mercy, Emelye!"
His spirit chaunged hous and wente ther
As° I cam never, I can nat tellen wher.   *Where*
Therfor I stinte,° I nam no divinistre;°   *stop / diviner, theologian*
Of soules finde I nat in this registre,°   *register, list*
1955 Ne me ne list° thilke° opiniouns to telle   *It does not please me / those*
Of hem, though that they wryten wher they dwelle.
Arcite is cold, ther° Mars his soule gye.°   *wherefore may / guide*
Now wol I speken forth of Emelye.
     Shrighte° Emelye and howleth Palamon,   *Shrieked*
1960 And Theseus his suster took anon
Swowninge, and bar° hire fro the corps away.   *bore, carried*
What helpeth it to tarien forth the day³
To tellen how she weep° bothe eve and morwe?   *wept*
For in swich cas wommen have swich sorwe,
1965 Whan that hir housbondes been from hem ago,°   *gone*
That for the more part they sorwen so,°   *thus, in that manner*
Or elles fallen in swich a maladye
That at the laste certeinly they dye.
     Infinite been the sorwes and the teres
1970 Of olde folk and folk of tendre yeres
In al the toun, for deeth of this Theban;
For him ther wepeth bothe child and man.
So greet weping was ther noon, certayn,
Whan Ector° was y-broght, al fresh y-slayn,   *Hector*
1975 To Troye. Allas, the pitee that was ther:
Cracchinge° of chekes, renting° eek of heer.   *Scratching / rending, tearing*
"Why woldestow° be deed," thise wommen crye,   *didst thou wish to*
"And haddest gold ynough, and Emelye?"
     No man mighte gladen Theseus
1980 Savinge° his olde fader Egeus,   *Except*
That knew this worldes transmutacioun,°   *mutability*
As he had seyn it chaunge bothe up and doun—
Joye after wo, and wo after gladnesse—
And shewed hem ensamples and lyknesse.⁴
1985   "Right as ther deyed° nevere man," quod he,   *died*
"That he ne livede in erthe in some degree,
Right so ther livede never man," he seyde,

---

3. What does it serve to while away the day.   4. I.e., analogies.

"In al this world, that som tyme he ne deyde.
This world nis but a thurghfare° ful of wo,   *thoroughfare, roadway*
1990 And we ben pilgrimes, passinge to and fro;
Deeth is an ende of every worldly sore."°   *pain, sorrow*
And over° al this yet seyde he muchel more   *beyond*
To this effect, ful wysely to enhorte°   *exhort*
The peple that they sholde hem reconforte.°   *be comforted*
1995   Duk Theseus, with al his bisy cure,°   *diligent concern*
Caste° now wher that the sepulture°   *Considered / burial*
Of goode Arcite may best y-maked be,
And eek most honurable in° his degree.°   *according to / rank*
And at the laste he took conclusioun,
2000 That ther as° first Arcite and Palamoun   *where*
Hadden for love the bataille hem bitwene,
That in that selve° grove, swote° and grene,   *same / sweet*
Ther as he hadde his amorouse desires,
His compleynte,° and for love his hote fires,   *lament*
2005 He wolde make a fyr, in which the office°   *duties, rites*
Funeral he mighte al accomplice;
And leet comaunde° anon to hakke and hewe   *had commands given*
The okes olde, and leye hem on a rewe°   *row*
In colpons° wel arrayed° for to brenne.°   *pieces / arranged / burn*
2010 His officers with swifte feet they renne°   *run*
And ryde anon at his comaundement.
And after this, Theseus hath y-sent
After a bere,° and it al overspradde°   *bier / covered*
With cloth of gold, the richeste that he hadde;
2015 And of the same suyte° he cladde Arcite.   *material*
Upon his hondes hadde he gloves whyte,
Eek on his heed a croune of laurer° grene,   *laurel*
And in his hond a swerd ful bright and kene.
He leyde him, bare the visage,° on the bere;   *with face uncovered*
2020 Therwith he weep° that pitee was to here.   *wept*
And for° the peple sholde seen him alle,   *so that*
Whan it was day he broghte him to the halle,
That roreth of the crying and the soun.
   Tho cam this woful Theban Palamoun,
2025 With flotery° berd and ruggy,° asshy° heres,   *fluttering / unkempt / ash-covered*
In clothes blake, y-dropped° al with teres;   *wet*
And, passinge othere of° weping, Emelye,   *surpassing others in*
The rewfulleste° of al the companye.   *most rueful, sorrowful*
In as muche as the service sholde be
2030 The more noble and riche in° his degree,   *according to*
Duk Theseus leet° forth three stedes bringe,°   *caused / to be brought*
That trapped° were in steel al gliteringe   *outfitted*
And covered with the armes° of daun Arcite.   *coat of arms*

Upon thise stedes, that weren grete and whyte,
2035 Ther seten° folk, of which oon bar° his sheeld,   *sat / bore*
Another his spere up in his hondes heeld,
The thridde bar with him his bowe Turkeys°—   *Turkish*
Of brend° gold was the cas° and eek the harneys;°   *refined / quiver / fittings*
And riden° forth a pas° with sorweful chere°   *(they) rode / at a walk / countenance*
2040 Toward the grove, as ye shul after here
         The nobleste of the Grekes that ther were
Upon hir shuldres carieden the bere,
With slakke pas° and eyen rede and wete,   *slow pace*
Thurghout the citee by the maister° strete,   *principal*
2045 That sprad° was al with blak; and wonder hye°   *spread / wondrously high*
Right of the same is the strete y-wrye.⁵
Upon the right hond wente old Egeus,
And on that other syde duk Theseus,
With vessels in hir hand of gold ful fyn,
2050 Al ful of hony, milk, and blood, and wyn;
Eek Palamon, with ful greet companye;
And after that cam woful Emelye,
With fyr in honde, as was that tyme the gyse,°   *custom*
To do the office of funeral servyse.
2055   Heigh° labour and ful greet apparaillinge°   *Great / preparation*
Was at the service and the fyr-makinge,
That with his° grene top the hevene raughte,°   *its / reached*
And twenty fadme of brede the armes straughte⁶—
This is to seyn, the bowes° were so brode.   *boughs*
2060 Of stree° first ther was leyd ful many a lode;   *straw*
But how the fyr was maked upon highte,°   *in height*
Ne eek the names how the treës highte°—   *were called*
As ook, firre, birch, aspe,° alder, holm,° popler,   *aspen / holm-oak (holly)*
Wilow, elm, plane, ash, box, chasteyn,° lind,° laurer,   *chestnut / linden*
2065 Mapul, thorn, beech, hasel, ew,° whippeltree°—   *yew / dogwood*
How they weren feld shal nat be told for me;
Ne how the goddes⁷ ronnen° up and doun,   *ran*
Disherited° of hire habitacioun,   *Disinherited*
In which they woneden° in reste and pees—   *dwelled*
2070 Nymphes, faunes, and amadrides;°   *hamadryads*
Ne how the bestes and the briddes alle
Fledden for fere whan the wode was falle;°   *felled*
Ne how the ground agast was of the light,
That was nat wont° to seen the sonne bright;   *accustomed*
2075 Ne how the fyr was couched° first with stree,°   *laid / straw*
And thanne with drye stikkes cloven a° three,   *in*
And thanne with grene wode and spycerye,°   *spices*

5. With the same material the street fronts were   6. And twenty fathoms in breadth the sides stretched.
draped.   7. I.e., tree spirits.

And thanne with cloth of gold and with perrye,°   *jewels*
And gerlandes hanginge with ful many a flour,
2080 The mirre,° th'encens,° with al so greet odour;   *myrrh / incense*
Ne how Arcite lay among al this,
Ne what richesse aboute his body is;
Ne how that Emelye, as was the gyse,°   *custom*
Putte in[8] the fyr of funeral servyse;
2085 Ne how she swowned whan men made the fyr,
Ne what she spak, ne what was hir desyr;
Ne what jeweles men in the fyr caste,
Whan that the fyr was greet and brente° faste;   *burned*
Ne how som caste hir sheeld, and som hir spere,
2090 And of hire° vestiments whiche that they were,° *part of their / were wearing*
And cuppes ful of milk and wyn and blood,
Into the fyr that brente as it were wood;°   *mad*
Ne how the Grekes with an huge route°   *company*
Thryës° riden al the fyr aboute   *Thrice*
2095 Upon the left hand, with a loud shoutinge,
And thryës with hir speres clateringe;
And thryës how the ladies gonne crye;°   *cried out*
Ne how that lad° was homward Emelye;   *led*
Ne how Arcite is brent to asshen colde;
2100 Ne how that liche-wake° was y-holde°   *funeral wake / held*
Al thilke night; ne how the Grekes pleye
The wake-pleyes,° ne kepe° I nat to seye—   *funeral games / care*
Who wrastleth best naked with oille enoynt,°   *anointed*
Ne who that bar him best in no disjoynt.°   *in any difficulty*
2105 I wol nat tellen eek how that they goon
Hoom til° Athenes whan the pley is doon;   *to*
But shortly to the poynt than wol I wende,°   *proceed*
And maken of my longe tale an ende.
    By processe° and by lengthe of certeyn° yeres *In course / a certain number of*
2110 Al stinted° is the moorninge and the teres   *ceased*
Of Grekes, by oon general assent.
Thanne semed me ther was a parlement
At Athenes, upon certeyn poynts and cas;°   *matters*
Among the whiche poynts y-spoken was
2115 To have with certeyn contrees alliaunce,
And have fully of Thebans obeisaunce.°   *submission*
For which this noble Theseus anon
Leet° senden after gentil Palamon,   *Caused*
Unwist of° him what was the cause and why;   *Unknown to*
2120 But in his blake clothes sorwefully
He cam at his comaundement in hye.°   *haste*

8. I.e., lit.

Tho sente Theseus for Emelye.
Whan they were set, and hust° was al the place, — *hushed*
And Theseus abiden hadde a space° — *space of time*
2125 Er any word cam from his wyse brest,
His eyen sette he ther as was his lest,° — *pleasure*
And with a sad visage he syked stille,° — *sighed quietly*
And after that right thus he seyde his wille·
    "The Firste Moevere of the cause above,
2130 Whan he first made the faire cheyne of love,
Greet was th'effect, and heigh° was his entente. — *noble*
Wel wiste he why, and what thereof he mente;° — *intended*
For with that faire cheyne of love he bond° — *bound*
The fyr, the eyr, the water, and the lond
2135 In certeyn boundes, that they may nat flee.
That same Prince and that Moevere," quod he,
"Hath stablissed° in this wrecched world adoun° — *established / below*
Certeyne[9] dayes and duracioun
To al that is engendred in this place,
2140 Over° the whiche day they may nat pace,° — *Beyond / pass*
Al mowe they° yet tho dayes wel abregge.° — *Although they may / abridge, shorten*
Ther needeth non auctoritee to allegge,° — *cite*
For it is preved° by experience, — *proved*
But that me list° declaren my sentence.° — *it pleases me / thought*
2145 Than may men by this ordre wel discerne
That thilke Moevere stable is and eterne.° — *eternal*
Wel may men knowe, but it be a fool,
That every part deryveth° from his hool.° — *derives, descends / its own whole*
For nature hath nat taken his beginning
2150 Of no partye° or cantel° of a thing, — *part / portion*
But of° a thing that parfit is and stable, — *from*
Descendinge so[1] til it be corrumpable.° — *corruptible*
And therfore, of his wyse purveyaunce,° — *providence, foresight*
He hath so wel biset° his ordinaunce° — *arranged / plan*
2155 That speces° of thinges and progressiouns° — *species / natural changes*
Shullen enduren by successiouns° — *succession of generations*
And nat eterne,° withouten any lye. — *by being eternal*
    This maistow° understonde and seen at eye:° — *mayest thou / by looking*
Lo, the ook that hath so long a norisshinge° — *growth*
2160 From tyme that it first biginneth springe,
And hath so long a lyf, as we may see,
Yet at the laste wasted is the tree.
Considereth eek, how that the harde stoon
Under oure feet, on which we trede and goon,
2165 Yet wasteth it, as it lyth by the weye.

9. I.e., a certain number of.   1. I.e., from heaven.

The brode river somtyme wexeth dreye;°   *becomes dry*
The grete tounes see we wane and wende.°   *pass away*
Than may ye see that al this thing hath ende.
    Of man and womman seen we wel also
2170 That nedes,° in oon of thise termes° two,   *by necessity / times*
This is to seyn, in youthe or elles age,
He moot be deed, the king as shal a page;
Som° in his bed, som in the depe see,   *One*
Som in the large feeld, as men may see.
2175 Ther helpeth noght: al goth that ilke° weye.   *same*
Thanne may I seyn that al this thing moot deye.°   *must die*
    What° maketh this but Jupiter the king,   *Who*
That is prince and cause of alle thing,
Convertinge al unto his° propre welle°   *its / source*
2180 From which it is deryved, sooth to telle?
And here-agayns no creature on lyve,°   *alive*
Of no degree, availleth° for to stryve.   *it avails*
    Thanne is it wisdom, as it thinketh° me,   *seems to*
To maken vertu of necessitee,
2185 And take it wel that° we may nat eschue,°   *what / eschew, avoid*
And namely° that to us alle is due.   *especially*
And whoso gruccheth° ought,° he dooth folye, *grouches, complains / in any way*
And rebel is to him that al may gye.°   *govern*
And certeinly a man hath most honour
2190 To dyen in his excellence and flour,
Whan he is siker° of his gode name;   *sure*
Than hath he doon his freend ne him° no shame. *himself*
And gladder oghte his freend ben of his deeth
Whan with honour up yolden° is his breeth,   *yielded*
2195 Than whan his name apalled° is for age,   *faded, dimmed*
For al forgeten is his vasselage.°   *prowess*
Than is it best, as for a worthy fame,
To dyen whan that he is best of name.
    The contrarie of al this is wilfulnesse.
2200 Why grucchen we, why have we hevinesse,°   *sorrow*
That goode Arcite, of chivalrye flour,°   *the flower*
Departed is with duetee° and honour   *due respect*
Out of this foule prison of this lyf?
Why grucchen heer his cosin and his wyf
2205 Of his welfare, that loveth hem so weel?
Can he hem thank? Nay, God wot, never a deel,°   *not a bit*
That° bothe his soule and eek hemself° offende,° *Who / themselves / hurt*
And yet they mowe° hir lustes° nat amende.° *can / happiness / advance*
    What may I conclude of this longe serie,°   *sequence of arguments*
2210 But after wo I rede° us to be merie,   *advise*
And thanken Jupiter of al his grace;
And er that we departen from this place,

I rede that we make of sorwes two
O° parfyt joye, lastinge everemo;   *One*
2215 And loketh now, wher most sorwe is herinne,
Ther wol we first amenden and biginne.
    Suster," quod he, "this is my fulle assent,°   *desire*
With al th'avys° heer of my parlement: *advice*
That gentil Palamon, your owne knight,
2220 That serveth yow with wille, herte, and might,
And ever hath doon sin° ye first him knewe,   *since*
That ye shul of your grace upon him rewe,°   *take pity*
And taken him for housbonde and for lord.
Leene° me your hond, for this is our acord.°   *Give / agreement*
2225 Lat see now of youre wommanly pitee.
He is a kinges brother° sone, pardee;°   *brother's / indeed (Fr. par Dieu)*
And though he were a povre bacheler,°   *young knight*
Sin he hath served yow so many a yeer,
And had for yow so greet adversitee,
2230 It moste been considered, leveth° me;   *believe*
For gentil mercy oghte to passen° right."°   *surpass, prevail over / justice*
    Than seyde he thus to Palamon the knyght:
"I trowe° ther nedeth litel sermoning°   *believe / preaching, persuading*
To make yow assente to this thing.
2235 Com neer, and tak your lady by the hond."
Bitwixen hem was maad anon° the bond   *at once*
That highte matrimoigne° or mariage,   *matrimony*
By al the counseil° and the baronage.   *council*
And thus with alle blisse and melodye
2240 Hath Palamon y-wedded Emelye.
And God, that al this wyde world hath wroght,
Sende him his love that hath it dere aboght.°   *who has paid dearly for it*
For now is Palamon in alle wele,°   *happiness*
Livinge in blisse, in richesse, and in hele;°   *health, well-being*
2245 And Emelye him loveth so tendrely,
And he hir serveth so gentilly
That nevere was ther no word hem bitwene
Of jalousye or any other tene.°   *trouble, vexation*
Thus endeth Palamon and Emelye;
2250 And God save al this faire companye! Amen.

The Miller's Prologue and Tale

The Prologue

    Whan that the Knight had thus his tale y-told,
In al the route° nas° ther yong ne old   *company / was not*
That he ne seyde it was a noble storie,

And worthy for to drawen to° memorie,   *hold in*
5 And namely the gentils everichoon.[1]
Oure Hoste lough° and swoor, "So moot I goon,[2]   *laughed*
This gooth aright;° unbokeled° is the male.°   *well / opened / bag*
Lat see now who shal telle another tale,
For trewely, the game is wel bigonne.
10 Now telleth ye, sir Monk, if that ye conne,°   *know how*
Sumwhat° to quyte with° the Knightes tale."   *Something / match*
The Miller, that fordronken° was al pale,   *totally drunk*
So that unnethe° upon his hors he sat,   *with difficulty*
He nolde avalen° neither hood ne hat,   *take off*
15 Ne abyde° no man for his° curteisye,   *wait for / out of*
But in Pilates vois he gan to crye,[3]
And swoor, "By armes° and by blood and bones,   *(Christ's) arms*
I can° a noble tale for the nones,°   *know / occasion*
With which I wol now quyte° the Knightes tale."   *repay*
20 Oure Hoste saugh that he was dronke of° ale,   *drunken from*
And seyde, "Abyd,° Robin, my leve° brother,   *wait / dear*
Som bettre man shal telle us first another:
Abyd, and lat us werken thriftily."°   *proceed properly*
"By Goddes soul," quod° he, "that wol nat I;   *said*
25 For I wol speke or elles° go my wey."   *else*
Oure Hoste answerde, "Tel on, a devel wey!°   *what the devil*
Thou art a fool, thy wit is overcome."
"Now herkneth,"° quod the Miller, "alle and some!°   *listen / one and all*
But first I make a protestacioun
30 That I am dronke, I knowe it by my soun.°   *the sound of my voice*
And therfore, if that I misspeke or seye,°   *speak or talk amiss*
Wyte it° the ale of Southwerk, I yow preye;°   *Blame it on / beseech*
For I wol telle a legende and a lyf
Bothe of a carpenter and of his wyf,
35 How that a clerk hath set the wrightes cappe."[4]
The Reve[5] answerde and seyde, "Stint thy clappe!°   *Stop your chatter*
Lat be thy lewed° dronken harlotrye.°   *coarse / ribaldry*
It is a sinne and eek° a greet folye°   *also / folly*
To apeiren° any man, or him diffame,   *injure*
40 And eek to bringen wyves in swich fame.°   *into such (bad) repute*
Thou mayst y-nogh of othere thinges seyn."°   *speak*
This dronken Miller spak ful sone ageyn,°   *in response*
And seyde, "Leve brother Osewold,
Who hath no wyf, he is no cokewold.°   *cuckold*
45 But I sey nat therfore that thou art oon;

1. And particularly the well-born (pilgrims), each and every one.
2. Roughly, "As I may hope to live."
3. He cried aloud in a voice like Pilate's (familiar from the mystery plays—a ranting voice conventionally high and hoarse).
4. How a student made a fool of the carpenter.
5. The Reeve is the general manager of an estate; see the *General Prologue*, ll. 587–622.

Ther been ful gode wyves many oon,°	*a one*
And ever a thousand gode ayeyns° oon badde.	*(to set) against*
That knowestow wel thyself, but if thou madde.[6]	
Why artow° angry with my tale now?	*art thou*
50 I have a wyf, pardee,° as well as thou,	*by God*
Yet nolde° I, for the oxen in my plogh,°	*would not / plow*
Take upon me more° than y-nogh,°	*more (enough) (enough)*
As demen of myself that I were oon;[7]	
I wol beleve wel that I am noon.	
55 An housbond shal nat been inquisitif	
Of Goddes privetee,° nor of his wyf.	*secrets*
So he may finde Goddes foyson° there,	*plenty*
Of the remenant nedeth nat enquere."[8]	
What sholde I more seyn, but this Millere	
60 He nolde° his wordes for no man forbere,°	*would not / spare*
But tolde his cherles° tale in his manere.	*churl's*
M'athynketh° that I shal° reherce it here.	*I regret / must*
And therfore every gentil wight° I preye,°	*person / beg*
For Goddes love, demeth° nat that I seye°	*judge / speak*
65 Of° evel entente, but that I moot° reherce	*From / must*
Hir° tales alle, be they bettre or werse,	*Their*
Or elles falsen° som of my matere.	*falsify*
And therfore, whoso list° it nat y-here,°	*desires / to hear*
Turne over the leef,° and chese° another tale;	*page / choose*
70 For he shal finde y-nowe,° grete and smale,	*enough*
Of storial° thing that toucheth° gentillesse,	*historical / treats of*
And eek° moralitee and holinesse.	*also*
Blameth nat me if that ye chese amis.	
The Millere is a cherl,° ye knowe wel this;	*churl, rude fellow*
75 So was the Reve eek and othere mo,°	*more*
And harlotrye° they tolden bothe two.	*ribaldry*
Avyseth yow° and putte me out of blame;	*think (before you choose)*
And eek men shal nat maken ernest of game.[9]	

The Tale

Whylom° ther was dwellinge at Oxenford°	*Once / Oxford*
80 A riche gnof,° that gestes heeld to bord,°	*churl / took in lodgers*
And of his craft° he was a carpenter.	*by trade*
With him ther was dwellinge a povre scoler,°	*poor student*
Hadde lerned art, but al his fantasye[1]	
Was turned for to lerne astrologye,	

---

6. Thou knowest that well thyself, unless thou art mad.
7. As to think that I am one (i.e., a cuckold).
8. There is no need to inquire about the rest.

9. And furthermore one should not treat game as something serious.
1. Who had studied the liberal arts, but all his fancy.

85 And coude a certeyn of conclusiouns
   To demen by interrogaciouns,[2]
   If that men asked him in certein houres
   Whan that men sholde have droghte or elles shoures,°   *else showers*
   Or if men asked him what sholde bifalle
90 Of every thing, I may nat rekene hem° alle.   *count them*
     This clerk was cleped hende Nicholas.[3]
   Of derne° love he coude° and of solas;°   *secret / knew / pleasure*
   And therto he was sleigh° and ful privee,°   *sly / secretive*
   And lyk a mayden meke for to see.°   *meek to look at*
95 A chambre hadde he in that hostelrye°   *lodging house*
   Allone, withouten any companye,
   Ful fetisly y-dight° with herbes swote;°   *neatly arrayed / sweet*
   And he himself as swete as is the rote°   *root*
   Of licorys, or any cetewale.[4]
100 His Almageste[5] and bokes grete and smale,
   His astrelabie,° longinge for° his art,   *astrolabe / belonging to*
   His augrim-stones[6] layen faire apart
   On shelves couched° at his beddes heed;   *placed*
   His presse y-covered with a falding reed.[7]
105 And al above ther lay a gay sautrye,[8]
   On which he made a-nightes° melodye   *by night*
   So swetely, that al the chambre rong,°   *rang*
   And *Angelus ad virginem*° he song,   *(an Annunciation hymn)*
   And after that he song the kinges note;°   *(an unidentified song)*
110 Ful often blessed was his mery throte.
   And thus this swete clerk his tyme spente
   After his freendes finding and his rente.[9]
     This carpenter hadde wedded newe° a wyf   *recently*
   Which that he lovede more than his lyf;
115 Of eightetene yeer she was of age.
   Jalous he was, and heeld hire narwe in cage,°   *confined, as in a cage*
   For she was wilde and yong, and he was old
   And demed himself ben lyk° a cokewold.°   *likely to be / cuckold*
   He knew nat Catoun, for his wit was rude,[1]
120 That bad° man sholde wedde his similitude.°   *bade / his like*
   Men sholde wedden after hire estaat,°   *according to their condition*
   For youthe and elde° is often at debaat.°   *old age / strife*
   But sith that° he was fallen in the snare,   *since*
   He moste° endure, as other folk, his care.   *must*

2. And he knew a certain (number) of propositions
by which to arrive at an opinion on questions.
3. This scholar was called gentle (pleasant) Nicholas.
4. A spice of the ginger family.
5. An astronomical treatise by Ptolemy.
6. Counters for doing arithmetic.

7. His clothes chest covered with red wool cloth.
8. Psaltery, a flat, stringed instrument.
9. In accordance with the money found (for him)
by his friends, and his income.
1. He didn't know Cato (the *Distichs*, a Latin reader
used in the schools), for his intelligence was untutored.

125 Fair was this yonge wyf, and therwithal
      As any wesele° hir body gent° and smal.   *weasel / graceful*
      A ceynt° she werede° barred° al of silk;   *belt / wore / striped*
      A barmclooth eek as whyt as morne milk²
      Upon hir lendes,° ful of many a gore.°   *loins / very fully cut*
130 Whyt was hir smok,° and broyden° al bifore   *dress / embroidered*
      And eek bihinde, on hir coler° aboute   *collar*
      Of col-blak silk, withinne and eek withoute.
      The tapes° of hir whyte voluper°   *strings / bonnet*
      Were of the same suyte of° hir coler;°   *kind as / collar*
135 Hir filet° brood of silk, and set ful hye.°   *headband / high*
      And sikerly° she hadde a likerous yë:°   *certainly / lecherous eye*
      Ful smale y-pulled° were hire browes° two,   *plucked / eyebrows*
      And tho° were bent, and blake as any sloo.³   *they*
      She was ful more blisful on to see°   *to look on*
140 Than is the newe pere-jonette° tree;   *newly (blossomed) pear*
      And softer than the wolle° is of a wether.°   *wool / sheep*
      And by hir girdel heeng° a purs of lether   *hung*
      Tasseled with silk, and perled with latoun.°   *studded with metal*
      In al this world, to seken up and doun,
150 There nis° no man so wys° that coude thenche°   *is not / wise / imagine*
      So gay a popelote,° or swich° a wenche.   *plaything (puppet-doll) / such*
      Ful brighter was the shyning of hir hewe°   *complexion*
      Than in the Tour° the noble° y-forged° newe.   *Tower of London / gold coin / minted*
      But of° hir song, it was as loude and yerne°   *in regard to / lively*
155 As any swalwe° sittinge on a berne.°   *swallow / barn*
      Therto she coude skippe and make game,°   *play*
      As any kide or calf folwinge his dame.°   *mother*
      Hir mouth was swete as bragot or the meeth,⁴
      Or hord of apples leyd in hey or heeth.°   *heather*
160 Winsinge° she was, as is a joly colt,   *Skittish*
      Long as a mast, and upright° as a bolt.°   *straight / crossbow bolt*
      A brooch she baar° upon hir lowe coler,°   *wore / collar*
      As brood as is the bos of a bocler;⁵
      Hir shoes were laced on hir legges hye.°   *high*
165 She was a prymerole,° a piggesnye,°   *primrose / cuckooflower*
      For any lord to leggen° in his bedde,   *lay*
      Or yet for any good yeman° to wedde.   *yeoman*
           Now sire, and eft° sire, so bifel the cas,°   *again / affair*
      That on a day this hende° Nicholas   *gracious, gentle, clever*
170 Fil with this yonge wyf to rage° and pleye,   *dally*
      Whyl that hir housbond was at Oseneye,°   *Osney (a town near Oxford)*
      As clerkes ben ful subtile and ful queynte.°   *sly*

2. An apron also, as white as morning milk.   ale and honey.
3. Sloeberry, a purple-black fruit.   5. And broad as is the boss (the central fitting) of a
4. "Bragot" and "meeth" (mead) are drinks made of   shield.

And prively he caughte hire by the queynte,[6]
And seyde, "Y-wis, but if ich° have my wille,   *Surely, unless I*
175 For derne° love of thee, lemman,° I spille,"° *hidden / sweetheart / perish*
And heeld hire harde° by the haunche-bones,°   *firmly / hips*
And seyde, "Lemman, love me al atones,°   *immediately*
Or I wol dyen, also° God me save!"   *as*
And she sprong as a colt doth in the trave,[7]
180 And with hir heed she wryed° faste awey,   *twisted*
And seyde, "I wol nat kisse thee, by my fey.°   *faith*
Why, lat be,"° quod° she, "lat be, Nicholas, *leave off / said*
Or I wol crye 'out, harrow'° and 'allas.'   *help*
Do wey your handes° for your curteisye!" *Take your hands away*
185 This Nicholas gan° mercy for to crye,   *began*
And spak so faire, and profred him° so faste,° *offered himself / eagerly*
That she hir love him graunted atte laste,°   *at (the) last*
And swoor hir ooth, by Seint Thomas of Kent,° *Thomas à Becket*
That she wol been at his comandement,
190 Whan that she may hir leyser° wel espye.° *chance, opportunity / perceive*
"Myn housbond is so ful of jalousye,
That but ye wayte° wel and been privee,° *watch out / secretive*
I woot° right wel I nam but° deed," quod she. *know / I'm as good as*
"Ye moste been ful derne,° as in this cas."   *secret*
195 "Nay, therof care thee noght," quod Nicholas.
"A clerk had litherly biset his whyle,° *poorly used his time*
But if° he coude a carpenter bigyle."°   *Unless / trick*
And thus they been acorded and y-sworn
To wayte a tyme, as I have told biforn.
200 Whan Nicholas had doon thus everydeel,°   *all this so*
And thakked° hire aboute the lendes° weel, *stroked / loins*
He kiste° hire swete, and taketh his sautrye,° *kissed / psaltery*
And pleyeth faste, and maketh melodye.
 Thanne fil° it thus, that to the parish chirche, *befell*
205 Cristes owene werkes for to wirche,°   *perform*
This gode wyf wente on an haliday;°   *holy day*
Hir forheed shoon as bright as any day,
So was it wasshen whan she leet° hir werk.   *left*
 Now was ther of that chirche a parish clerk,[8]
210 The which that was y-cleped° Absolon.   *called*
Crul° was his heer, and as the gold it shoon, *Curly*
And strouted° as a fanne large and brode; *spread out*
Ful streight and evene lay his joly shode.° *the part in his hair*
His rode° was reed, his eyen greye as goos;° *complexion / a goose*
215 With Powles window corven on his shoos,[9]

---

6. And when they were alone he grabbed her between her legs.
7. A stall for shoeing unruly horses.
8. Assistant to the parish priest.
9. With (a design like) the window of St. Paul's (Cathedral) cut into the leather of his shoes.

In hoses rede° he wente fetisly.°   *red stockings / neatly*
Y-clad he was ful smal° and properly,   *tightly*
Al in a kirtel° of a light waget°—   *coat / blue*
Ful faire and thikke° been the poyntes° set—   *close together / laces*
220 And therupon he hadde a gay surplys°   *loose robe*
As whyt as is the blosme upon the rys.°   *twig*
A mery child° he was, so God me save   *jolly man*
Wel coude he laten° blood and clippe° and shave,   *let / cut hair*
And make a chartre° of lond or acquitaunce.°   *charter / deed of release*
225 In twenty mancre° coude he trippe and daunce   *ways*
After the scole° of Oxenforde° tho,°   *fashion / Oxford / then*
And with his legges casten to and fro,
And pleyen songes on a small rubible;°   *fiddle*
Therto he song som tyme a loud quinible;°   *high treble*
230 And as wel coude he pleye on a giterne.°   *guitar*
In al the toun nas° brewhous ne taverne   *there was no*
That he ne visited with his solas,°   *entertainment*
Ther° any gaylard tappestere° was.   *Where / gay barmaid*
But sooth to seyn, he was somdel squaymous°   *somewhat squeamish*
235 Of farting, and of speche daungerous.°   *fastidious*
   This Absolon, that jolif° was and gay,   *jolly, amorous*
Gooth with a sencer° on the haliday,°   *(incense) censer / holy day*
Sensinge the wyves of the parish faste,°   *diligently*
And many a lovely look on hem° he caste,   *them*
240 And namely° on this carpenteres wyf: *especially*
To loke on hire him thoughte a mery lyf.
She was so propre° and swete and likerous,°   *comely / flirtatious*
I dar wel seyn, if she had been a mous,
And he a cat, he wolde hire hente anon.°   *seize immediately*
245 This parish clerk, this joly Absolon,
Hath in his herte swich° a love-longinge,   *such*
That of° no wyf ne took he noon offringe;   *from*
For curteisye, he seyde, he wolde noon.°   *wanted none*
   The mone, whan it was night, ful brighte shoon,
250 And Absolon his giterne hath y-take;
For paramours he thoghte for to wake.¹
And forth he gooth; jolif and amorous,
Til he cam to the carpenteres hous
A litel after cokkes° hadde y-crowe,°   *cocks / crowed*
255 And dressed him up by a shot-windowe²
That was upon the carpenteres wal.°   *wall*
He singeth in his vois gentil and smal,°   *high, thin*
"Now, dere lady, if thy wille be,
I preye yow that ye wol rewe° on me,"   *have pity*

1. For love's sake, he intended to stay awake.
2. And took a place up near a casement window, one that opens and closes.

260 Ful wel acordaunt to his giterninge.[3]
    This carpenter awook and herde him singe,
    And spak unto his wyf, and seyde anon,
    "What, Alison, herestow° nat Absolon   *hearest thou*
    That chaunteth° thus under oure boures° wal?"   *sings / bedroom's*
265 And she answerde hir housbond therwithal,
    "Yis, God wot,° John, I here it every deel."°   *knows / every bit*
    This passeth forth; what wol ye bet than wel?°   *what more do you want?*
    Fro day to day this joly Absolon
    So woweth hire, that him is wo bigon.[4]
270 He waketh° al the night and al the day;   *remains awake*
    He kembeth° hise lokkes brode, and made him gay;   *combs*
    He woweth hire by menes and brocage,[5]
    And swoor he wolde been hir owene page;
    He singeth, brokkinge° as a nightingale;   *quavering*
275 He sente hire piment,° meeth,° and spyced ale,   *spiced wine / mead*
    And wafres,° pyping hote out of the glede;°   *wafer cakes / embers*
    And for° she was of toune, he profred mede.°   *because / money, bribes*
    For som folk wol ben wonnen for° richesse,   *by*
    And som for strokes,° and som for gentillesse.   *blows*
280   Somtyme, to shewe his lightnesse° and maistrye,°   *agility / skill*
    He pleyeth Herodes on a scaffold hye.[6]
    But what availleth him as in this cas?
    She loveth so this hende Nicholas,
    That Absolon may blowe the bukkes horn;[7]
285 He ne hadde for his labour but a scorn.
    And thus she maketh Absolon hire ape,°   *monkey*
    And al his ernest turneth til° a jape.°   *into / joke*
    Ful sooth is this proverbe, it is no lye,°   *lie*
    Men seyn right thus, "Alwey the nye slye°   *nearby sly (one)*
290 Maketh the ferre leve to be looth."[8]
    For though that Absolon be wood° or wrooth,°   *mad / angry*
    By cause that he fer° was from hir sighte,   *far*
    This nye° Nicholas stood in his lighte.   *nearby*
    Now bere thee wel, thou hende Nicholas!
295 For Absolon may waille and singe "allas."
    And so bifel it on a Saterday,
    This carpenter was goon til° Osenay,°   *gone to / Osney*
    And hende Nicholas and Alisoun
    Acorded been to° this conclusioun,   *Were agreed on*
300 That Nicholas shal shapen him a wyle°   *prepare a stratagem*

---

3. In fine harmony with his guitar-playing.
4. Woos her so that he is utterly wretched (woe-begone).
5. Through (the use of) go-betweens and agents, intermediaries.

6. He plays Herod (in a mystery play), high on a scaffold (stage).
7. I.e., doesn't have a chance.
8. Makes the far-off dear (one) to be hated.

This sely° jalous housbond to bigyle;°   *foolish, simple / trick*
And if so be the game wente aright,
She sholde slepen in his arm al night,
For this was his desyr and hire° also.   *hers*
305 And right anon,° withouten wordes mo,°   *at once / more*
This Nicholas no lenger wolde tarie,
But doth ful softe° unto his chambre carie°   *quietly / carry*
Bothe mete and drinke for a day or tweye,°   *two*
And to hire housbonde bad° hire for to seye,   *bade*
310 If that he axed after° Nicholas,   *asked about*
She sholde seye she niste° where he was,   *did not know*
Of° al that day she saugh him nat with yë;   *During*
She trowed° that he was in maladye,°   *believed / sickness*
For for no cry hir mayde coude him calle
315 He nolde° answere, for thing° that mighte falle.°   *wouldn't / anything / befall*
    This passeth forth° al thilke° Saterday,   *goes on / that same*
That Nicholas stille in his chambre lay,
And eet° and sleep, or dide what him leste,°   *ate / pleased*
Til Sonday, that° the sonne gooth to reste.   *when*
320 This sely carpenter hath greet merveyle°   *marveled greatly*
Of Nicholas, or what thing mighte him eyle,°   *ail*
And seyde, "I am adrad,° by Seint Thomas,   *afraid*
It stondeth nat aright with Nicholas.
God shilde° that he deyde° sodeynly!   *forbid / should die*
325 This world is now ful tikel,° sikerly:°   *unstable / surely*
I saugh to-day a cors° y-born° to chirche   *corpse / carried*
That now, on Monday last, I saugh him wirche.°   *work*
Go up," quod he unto his knave° anoon,°   *servant / at once*
"'Clepe° at his dore, or knokke with a stoon,   *Call*
330 Loke how it is, and tel me boldely."°   *straightway*
    This knave gooth him up ful sturdily,
And at the chambre dore, whyl that he stood,
He cryde and knokked as that° he were wood:°   *as if / insane*
"What! how! what do ye, maister Nicholay?
335 How may° ye slepen al the longe day?"   *can*
But al for noght, he herde nat a word.
    An hole he fond, ful lowe upon a bord,
Ther as the cat was wont in for to crepe;[9]
And at that hole he looked in ful depe,
340 And at the laste he hadde of him a sighte.
This Nicholas sat evere caping uprighte,°   *staring upward*
As he had kyked on the newe mone.[1]
Adoun° he gooth, and tolde his maister sone°   *Down / at once*
In what array° he saugh this ilke° man.   *state / same*

9. There where the cat was accustomed to creep in.
1. As if he were gazing (half-crazed) at the new moon.

345   This carpenter to blessen him° bigan,   *cross himself*
    And seyde, "Help us, Seinte Frideswyde!²
    A man woot° litel what him shal bityde.°   *knows / happen to*
    This man is falle, with his astromye,³
    In som woodnesse° or in som agonye;°   *madness / fit*
350 I thoghte ay° wel how that it sholde be!°   *ever / might happen*
    Men sholde nat knowe of Goddes privetee.°   *secrets*
    Ye, blessed be alwey a lewed° man   *unlearned*
    That noght but oonly his bileve° can!°   *creed / knows*
    So ferde° another clerk° with astromye: *fared / scholar*
355 He walked in the feeldes for to prye°   *spy*
    Upon the sterres, what ther sholde bifalle,
    Til he was in a marle-pit⁴ y-falle—
    He saugh nat that. But yet, by Seint Thomas,
    Me reweth sore of° hende Nicholas.   *I pity greatly*
360 He shal be rated of° his studying,   *berated for*
    If that I may, by Jesus, hevene° king!   *heaven's*
    Get me a staf, that I may underspore,°   *pry up*
    Whyl that thou, Robin, hevest up° the dore.   *push on*
    He shal° out of his studying, as I gesse."   *shall (come)*
365 And to the chambre dore he gan him dresse.°   *directed his attentions*
    His knave was a strong carl° for the nones,°   *fellow / for this purpose*
    And by the haspe he haf it up atones;°   *heaved it off at once*
    Into° the floor the dore fil anon.°   *On to / straightway*
    This Nicholas sat ay° as stille as stoon,   *ever*
370 And ever caped° upward into the eir.°   *stared / air*
    This carpenter wende° he were in despeir,   *thought*
    And hente° him by the sholdres mightily,   *seized*
    And shook him harde, and cryde spitously,°   *violently*
    "What, Nicholay! what, how! what, loke adoun!
375 Awake, and thenk on Cristes passioun!
    I crouche thee from elves and fro wightes!"⁵
    Therwith the night-spel⁶ seyde he anon-rightes°   *at once*
    On foure halves° of the hous aboute,   *sides*
    And on the threshfold° of the dore withoute:°   *threshold / outside*
380 "Jesu Crist, and Seynte Benedight,°   *Benedict*
    Blesse this hous from every wikked wight,°   *creature*
    For nightes verye, the white *pater-noster!*⁷
    Where wentestow, seynt Petres soster?"⁸
    And atte laste° this hende Nicholas   *finally*

---

2. Patron saint of Oxford.
3. This man has fallen, because of his astronomy (John mispronounces "astronomye").
4. A pit from which clay is dug.
5. I make the sign of the cross over thee (to protect thee) from elves and from (other such) creatures.
6. A charm against evil spirits, said at night.

7. A bedtime blessing, "white" because black magic plays no part in it.
8. The sense of these lines is confused and comically intended: they represent a carpenter's version of "white" magic. Line 383 means literally "Where didst thou go, St. Peter's sister?"

385 Gan for to syke° sore,° and seyde, "Allas!   *began to sigh / deeply*
    Shal al the world be lost eftsones° now?"   *so soon again*
        This carpenter answerde, "What seystow?°   *sayest thou*
    What! thenk on God, as we don, men that swinke!"°   *labor*
    This Nicholas answerde, "Fecche me drinke;
390 And after wol I speke in privitee°   *secretly*
    Of certeyn thing that toucheth me and thee;
    I wol telle it non other man, certeyn."
        This carpenter goth doun and comth ageyn,
    And broghte of mighty ale a large quart;
395 And whan that ech of hem° had dronke his part,   *them*
    This Nicholas his dore faste shette,°   *shut*
    And doun the carpenter by him he sette.
        He seyde, "John, myn hoste lief° and dere,   *beloved*
    Thou shalt upon thy trouthe° swere me here,   *honor*
400 That to no wight° thou shalt this conseil° wreye;°   *person / secret / betray*
    For it is Cristes conseil that I seye,
    And if thou telle it man,° thou art forlore;°   *to anyone / lost*
    For this vengeaunce thou shalt han therfore,
    That if thou wreye° me, thou shalt be wood!"°   *betray / go mad*
405 "Nay, Crist forbede it, for° his holy blood!"   *by*
    Quod tho this sely man, "I nam no labbe,
    Ne, though I seye, I nam nat lief to gabbe.⁹
    Sey what thou wolt, I shal it nevere telle
    To child ne wyf, by him¹ that harwed° helle!"   *harrowed*
410 "Now John," quod Nicholas, "I wol nat lye.
    I have y-founde in myn astrologye,
    As I have loked in the mone bright,
    That now, a Monday next, at quarter night,°   *about 9 P.M.*
    Shal falle a reyn° and that so wilde and wood,°   *rain / furious*
415 That half so greet was nevere Noës° flood.   *Noah's*
    This world," he seyde, "in lasse° than in an hour   *less*
    Shal al be dreynt,° so hidous is the shour;°   *drowned / shower, storm*
    Thus shal mankynde drenche° and lese° hir lyf."   *drown / lose*
        This carpenter answerde, "Allas, my wyf!
420 And shal she drenche?° allas, myn Alisoun!"   *drown*
    For sorwe of this he fil almost adoun,
    And seyde, "Is ther no remedie in this cas?"
        "Why, yis, for° Gode," quod hende Nicholas,   *before*
    "If thou wolt werken after lore and reed;²
425 Thou mayst nat werken after thyn owene heed;°   *head, wits*
    For thus seith Salomon, that was ful trewe,°   *trustworthy*
    'Werk al by conseil,° and thou shalt nat rewe.'°   *advice / be sorry*

9. This foolish man said then, "I am no blabber-   1. I.e., Christ.
mouth, nor, though I say (it myself), am I fond of   2. If thou wilt work according to learning and good
chattering."   counsel.

And if thou werken wolt by good conseil,
I undertake,° withouten mast and seyl,°   *promise / sail*
430 Yet shal I saven hire and thee and me.
Hastow° nat herd° how saved was Noë,°   *Hast thou / heard / Noah*
Whan that Oure Lord hadde warned him biforn
That al the world with water sholde be lorn?"°   *lost*
"Yis," quod this carpenter, "ful yore° ago."   *long*
435 "Hastow nat herd," quod Nicholas, "also
The sorwe of Noë with his felawshipe?³
Er that° he mighte gete his wyf to shipe,   *Before*
Him hadde be levere, I dar wel undertake,⁴
At thilke° tyme than alle hise wetheres° blake   *that same / sheep*
440 That she hadde had a ship hirself allone.
And therfore, wostou° what is best to done?°   *knowest thou / do*
This asketh° haste, and of an hastif° thing   *requires / urgent*
Men may nat preche or maken tarying.
Anon° go gete us faste into this in°   *At once / dwelling*
445 A kneding trogh° or elles a kymelyn°   *kneading trough / shallow tub*
For ech of us, but loke that they be large,
In whiche we mowe swimme° as in a barge,   *may float*
And han therinne vitaille suffisant°   *provisions sufficient*
But for a day; fy on the remenant!
450 The water shal aslake° and goon away   *diminish*
Aboute pryme° upon the nexte day.   *9 A.M.*
But Robin may nat wite° of this, thy knave,°   *know / servant*
Ne eek° thy mayde° Gille I may nat save.   *Nor / maid*
Axe° nat why, for though thou aske me,   *Ask*
455 I wol nat tellen Goddes privetee.°   *secret things*
Suffiseth thee, but if° thy wittes madde,°   *unless / are gone (insane)*
To han as greet a grace as Noë hadde.
Thy wyf shal I wel saven, out of° doute.   *without*
Go now thy wey, and speed thee heer-aboute.
460 But whan thou hast, for hire and thee and me,
Y-geten us thise kneding tubbes three,
Than shaltow° hange hem in the roof ful hye,°   *must thou / high*
That no man of oure purveyaunce° espye.°   *provision / catch sight*
And whan thou thus hast doon, as I have seyd,
465 And hast oure vitaille faire in hem y-leyd,°   *laid*
And eek an ax, to smyte the corde atwo°   *in two*
When that the water comth, that we may go,
And breke an hole an heigh° upon the gable   *on high*
Unto the gardin-ward,° over the stable,   *Toward the garden*
470 That we may frely passen forth our way
Whan that the grete shour° is goon away—   *shower, storm*

3. The trouble(s) of Noah and his companions (as   4. He would have rather, I dare declare.
portrayed in the mystery plays).

Than shaltow swimme as myrie, I undertake,[5]
As doth the whyte doke° after hire° drake.   *duck / its*
Thanne wol I clepe,° 'How, Alison! how, John!   *call*
475 Be myrie, for the flood wol passe anon!'°   *at once*
And thou wolt seyn, 'Hayl, maister Nicholay!
Good morwe, I se thee wel, for it is day.'
And thanne shul we be lordes al oure lyf
Of al the world, as° Noë and his wyf.   *as (were)*
480   But of o thyng I warne thee ful right:
Be wel avysed° on that ilke° night   *forewarned / same*
That we ben entred into shippes bord°   *on board the ship*
That noon of us ne speke nat a word,
Ne clepe, ne crye, but been in his preyere;[6]
485 For it is Goddes owene heste° dere.   *commandment*
    Thy wyf and thou mote° hange fer a-twinne,°   *must / far apart*
For that° bitwixe yow shal be no sinne   *So that*
No more in looking than ther shal° in dede;   *shall (be)*
This ordinance is seyd, go, God thee spede!°   *give thee success*
490 Tomorwe at night, whan men ben alle aslepe,
Into oure kneding-tubbes wol we crepe,
And sitten ther, abyding° Goddes grace.   *awaiting*
Go now thy wey, I have no lenger space°   *no more time*
To make of this no lenger sermoning.
495 Men seyn thus, 'Send the wyse, and sey no thing.'
Thou art so wys, it nedeth thee nat teche;[7]
Go, save oure lyf, and that I thee biseche."
    This sely carpenter goth forth his wey.
Ful ofte he seith "allas" and "weylawey,"
500 And to his wyf he tolde his privetee;°   *secret*
And she was war,° and knew it bet° than he,   *aware / better*
What al this queynte cast was for to seye.[8]
But nathelees she ferde as° she wolde deye,°   *acted as if / die*
And seyde, "Allas! go forth thy wey anon,°   *immediately*
505 Help us to scape,° or we ben dede echon.°   *escape / each one*
I am thy trewe verray° wedded wyf;   *real*
Go, dere spouse, and help to save oure lyf."
    Lo, which° a greet thyng is affeccioun!°   *what / emotion*
Men may dyen° of imaginacioun,   *die*
510 So depe may impressioun be take.°   *taken*
This sely° carpenter biginneth quake;   *foolish, simple*
Him thinketh verraily° that he may see   *truly*
Noës flood come walwing° as the see°   *rolling / sea*
To drenchen° Alisoun, his hony dere.   *drown*
515 He wepeth, weyleth, maketh sory chere,°   *a long face*

---

5. Then shalt thou swim as merrily, I declare.   7. It's not necessary to teach thee.
6. Nor call, nor cry out, but be at his prayer(s). 8. What all this elaborate stratagem meant.

He syketh° with ful many a sory swogh.°   *sighs / groan*
He gooth and geteth him a kneding trogh,°   *(dough-)kneading trough*
And after that a tubbe and a kymelyn,°   *a shallow tub*
And prively° he sente hem to his in,°   *secretly / inn*
520 And heng° hem in the roof in privetee.°   *hung / secret*
His owene° hand he made laddres three,   *(With) his own*
To climben by the ronges° and the stalkes°   *rungs / shafts*
Unto the tubbes hanginge in the balkes,°   *beams*
And hem vitailled,° bothe trogh and tubbe,   *provisioned*
525 With breed and chese, and good ale in a jubbe,°   *jug*
Suffysinge right y-nogh as for a day.
But er that° he had maad al this array,°   *before / preparation*
He sente his knave° and eek his wench° also   *servant / maid*
Upon his nede° to London for to go.   *business*
530 And on the Monday, whan it drow° to night,   *drew near*
He shette° his dore withoute candel-light,   *shut*
And dressed° al thing as it sholde be.   *arranged*
And shortly, up they clomben° alle three;   *climbed*
They sitten stille wel a furlong-way.°   *short time*
535 "Now, *Pater-noster*, clom!" seyde Nicholay,[9]
And "clom," quod John, and "clom," seyde Alisoun.
This carpenter seyde his devocioun,
And stille he sit,° and biddeth° his preyere,   *sits / offers*
Awaytinge on° the reyn,° if he it here.   *Waiting for / rain*
540 The dede sleep, for wery bisinesse,[1]
Fil° on this carpenter right as I gesse   *Fell*
Aboute corfew°-tyme, or litel more;   *curfew (8 P.M.)*
For travail of his goost° he groneth sore,   *spirit*
And eft he routeth, for his heed mislay.[2]
545 Doun of° the laddre stalketh° Nicholay,   *from / creeps*
And Alisoun, ful softe adoun she spedde;°   *hastened*
Withouten wordes mo,° they goon to bedde   *more*
Ther-as° the carpenter is wont to lye.   *Where*
Ther was the revel and the melodye;
550 And thus lyth° Alison and Nicholas   *lie*
In bisinesse of mirthe and of solas,°   *pleasure*
Til that the belle of Laudes gan to ringe,[3]
And freres° in the chauncel° gonne° singe.   *friars / chancel / began to*
This parish clerk, this amorous Absolon,
555 That is for love alwey so wo bigon,
Upon the Monday was at Oseneye
With compaignye him to disporte° and pleye,   *to amuse himself*

---

9. "Now, (an) 'Our Father' (and then) 'mum!' " said Nicholas.
1. A dead sleep, because of (his) tiring labor.
2. And also he snores, for his head lay uncomfort- ably.
3. Till the chapel bell began to ring Lauds (a canonical hour, about 4 A.M.).

And axed upon cas a cloisterer[4]
Ful prively after John the carpenter;
560 And he drough° him apart° out of the chirche,   *drew / aside*
And seyde, "I noot,° I saugh him here nat wirche°   *don't know / work*
Sin° Saterday. I trow° that he be went   *Since / believe*
For timber, ther° oure abbot hath him sent,   *where*
For he is wont for timber for to go
565 And dwellen at the grange° a day or two;   *monastery's farmhouse*
Or elles° he is at his hous, certeyn.°   *else / for sure*
Wher that he be, I can nat sothly° seyn."   *truly*
    This Absolon ful joly was and light,°   *joyous*
And thoghte, "Now is tyme to wake° al night;   *to stay awake*
570 For sikirly° I saugh him nat stiringe   *surely*
Aboute his dore sin° day bigan to springe.   *since*
So moot I thryve,° I shal, at cokkes° crowe,   *So may I thrive / cock's*
Ful prively° knokken at his windowe   *secretly*
That stant° ful lowe upon his boures° wal.   *stands / bedroom's*
575 To Alison now wol I tellen al
My love-longing, for yet I shal nat misse
That at the leste wey° I shal hire kisse.   *at least*
Som maner° confort shal I have, parfay.°   *kind of / by my faith*
My mouth hath icched al this longe day;
580 That is a signe of kissing atte leste.°   *at the least*
Al night me mette eek, I was at a feste.[5]
Therfore I wol gon slepe an houre or tweye,°   *two*
And al the night than wol I wake and pleye."
    Whan that the firste cok hath crowe, anon°   *immediately*
585 Up rist° this joly lovere Absolon,   *rises*
And him arrayeth gay, at point-devys.°   *to perfection*
But first he cheweth greyn° and lycorys,   *an aromatic spice*
To smellen swete, er° he had kembd° his heer.   *before / combed*
Under his tonge a trewe-love he beer,[6]
590 For therby wende° he to ben gracious.   *thought*
He rometh to the carpenteres hous,
And stille he stant° under the shot-windowe—   *stood*
Unto his brest it raughte,° it was so lowe—   *reached*
And softe he cougheth with a semi-soun:°   *small sound*
595 "What do ye, hony-comb, swete Alisoun,
My faire brid,° my swete cinamome?°   *bird / cinnamon*
Awaketh, lemman° myn, and speketh to me!   *sweetheart*
Wel litel thenken ye upon my wo,
That for youre love I swete° ther° I go.   *sweat / wherever*
600 No wonder is thogh that I swelte° and swete;   *swelter*

4. And asked by chance a resident of the cloister.   thought to bring good fortune in love) under his
5. Also I dreamt all night (that) I was at a feast.   tongue.
6. He bore a true-love (the leaf of a plant evidently

I moorne° as doth a lamb after the tete.°   *yearn / teat*
Y-wis,° lemman, I have swich° love-longinge,   *Truly / such*
That lyk a turtel° trewe is my moorninge;°   *turtledove / mourning*
I may nat ete na more than a mayde."
605   "Go fro the window, Jakke fool,"° she sayde,   *you Jack-fool*
"As help me God, it wol nat be 'com pa me.'°   *come kiss me*
I love another, and elles° I were to blame,   *otherwise*
Wel bet° than thee, by Jesu, Absolon!   *much better*
Go forth thy wey or I wol caste a ston,
610 And lat me slepe, a twenty devel wey!"°   *in the devil's name*
    "Allas," quod Absolon, "and weylawey,
That trewe love was evere so yvel biset!°   *ill-bestowed*
Thanne kisse me, sin° it may be no bet,°   *since / better*
For Jesus love and for the love of me."
615   "Wiltow thanne go thy wey therwith?" quod she.
"Ye, certes,° lemman,"° quod this Absolon.   *truly / lover*
"Thanne make thee redy," quod she, "I come anon;"°   *at once*
And unto Nicholas she seyde stille,°   *quietly*
"Now hust,° and thou shalt laughen al thy fille."   *hush*
620 This Absolon doun sette him on his knees,
And seyde, "I am a lord at alle degrees;[7]
For after this I hope ther cometh more.
Lemman, thy grace, and swete brid, thyn ore!"°   *mercy*
The window she undoth,° and that in haste,   *opens*
625 "Have do,"° quod she, "com of,° and speed thee faste,   *done / on*
Lest that oure neighebores thee espye."
    This Absolon gan° wype his mouth ful drye: *did*
Derk was the night as pich,° or as the cole,°   *pitch / coal*
And at the window out she putte hir hole,
630 And Absolon, him fil no bet ne wers,[8]
But with his mouth he kiste hir naked ers°   *arse*
Ful savourly, er° he was war° of this.   *before / aware*
    Abak he stirte,° and thoghte it was amis,   *leaped*
For wel he wiste a womman hath no berd;°   *beard*
635 He felte a thing al rough and long y-herd,°   *haired*
And seyde, "Fy! allas, what have I do?"°   *done*
    "Tehee!" quod she, and clapte the window to;°   *shut*
And Absolon goth forth a sory pas.°   *with a sad step*
    "A berd,° a berd!" quod hende Nicholas,   *trick, joke*
640 "By Goddes *corpus*,° this goth faire and weel!"   *body*
    This sely° Absolon herde every deel,°   *poor / bit*
And on his lippe he gan° for anger byte;   *began*
And to himself he seyde, "I shal thee quyte."°   *repay*
    Who rubbeth now, who froteth° now his lippes   *chafes*

---

7. I am (equal to) a lord, in every way.
8. And Absolom, it befell him neither better nor worse.

645 With dust,° with sond,° with straw, with clooth, with
      chippes,°   *dirt / sand / bark*
But Absolon, that seith ful ofte, "Allas!
My soule bitake° I unto Sathanas,°   *commit / Satan*
But me wer levere° than al this toun," quod he,   *If I would not rather*
"Of this despyt° awroken° for to be.   *insult / avenged*
650 Allas!" quod he, "allas, I ne hadde y-bleynt!"° *that I did not abstain*
His hote love was cold and al y-queynt;°   *quenched*
For fro that tyme that he had kiste hir ers,
Of paramours he sette nat a keis,[9]
For he was heeled° of his maladye.   *cured*
655 Ful ofte paramours he gan deffye,°   *denounce*
And weep° as dooth a child that is y-bete.° *wept / beaten*
A softe paas° he wente over the strete   *(With) a soft step*
Until° a smith men cleped daun° Gerveys,   *To / sir, mister*
That in his forge smithed plough harneys:°   *parts*
660 He sharpeth shaar and culter[1] bisily.
This Absolon knokketh al esily,°   *quietly*
And seyde, "Undo,° Gerveys, and that anon." *Open up*
      "What, who artow?"° "It am I, Absolon." *art thou*
"What, Absolon! for Cristes swete tree,°   *cross*
665 Why ryse ye so rathe,° ey, *benedicite!*° *early / bless us all*
What eyleth° yow? som gay gerl, God it woot,° *ails / knows*
Hath broght yow thus upon the viritoot;°   *astir(?)*
By Seynt Note,° ye woot wel what I mene." *St. Neot*
      This Absolon ne roghte° nat a bene° *cared / bean*
670 Of° al his pley. No word agayn° he yaf;° *For / in response / gave*
He hadde more tow on his distaf[2]
Than Gerveys knew, and seyde, "Freend so dere,
That hote culter in the chimenee° here,   *forge*
As lene° it me: I have therwith to done,   *Do lend*
675 And I wol bringe it thee agayn ful sone."
      Gerveys answerde, "Certes,° were it gold, *Truly*
Or in a poke° nobles alle untold,° *sack / coins uncounted*
Thou sholdest have,° as I am trewe smith. *have (it)*
Ey, Cristes foo![3] what wol ye do therwith?"
680 "Therof," quod Absolon, "be as be may:
I shal wel telle it thee to-morwe day,"
And caughte the culter by the colde stele.° *handle*
Ful softe out at the dore he gan to stele,° *stole away*
And wente unto the carpenteres wal.
685 He cogheth first, and knokketh therwithal
Upon the windowe, right as° he dide er.° *just as / before*

9. For stylish love affairs he didn't care a cress (a common waterweed).
1. A plowshare and colter (the front part of a plow).
2. I.e., more business in hand.
3. I.e., the devil.

This Alison answerde, "Who is ther
That knokketh so? I warante it° a theef."   *believe it (is)*
"Why, nay," quod he, "God woot, my swete leef,°   *dear one*
690 I am thyn Absolon, my dereling.°   *darling*
Of gold," quod he, "I have thee brought a ring—
My moder yaf° it me, so God me save—   *gave*
Ful fyn it is, and therto wel y-grave.°   *engraved*
This wol I yeve° thee, if thou me kisse!"   *give*
695 This Nicholas was risen for to pisse,
And thoghte he wolde amenden° al the jape;°   *improve / joke*
He sholde kisse his ers° er that° he scape.°   *arse / before / escape*
And up the windowe dide° he hastily,   *put*
And out his ers he putteth prively
700 Over the buttok, to the haunche-bon;
And therwith spak this clerk, this Absolon,
"Spek, swete brid,° I noot° nat wher thou art."   *bird / know not*
This Nicholas anon° leet fle° a fart,   *at once / fly*
As greet as it had been a thonder-dent,°   *thunderclap*
705 That with the strook he was almost y-blent;°   *blinded*
And he was redy with his iren hoot,
And Nicholas amidde the ers he smoot.°   *struck*
Of gooth the skin an hande-brede aboute,[4]
The hote culter brende° so his toute,°   *burned / rump*
710 And for the smert he wende° for to dye.   *expected*
As° he were wood,° for wo he gan to crye°—   *As if / mad / cried out*
"Help! water! water! help, for Goddes herte!"
This carpenter out of his slomber sterte,
And herde oon° cryen 'water' as° he were wood,°   *someone / as if / mad*
715 And thoghte, "Allas! now comth Nowelis flood!"[5]
He sit° him up withouten wordes mo,°   *sits / more*
And with his ax he smoot the corde atwo,°   *in two*
And doun goth al; he fond° neither to selle   *found time*
Ne breed ne ale, til he cam to the celle°   *floorboards*
720 Upon the floor; and ther aswowne° he lay.   *in a faint*
Up sterte hire° Alison and Nicholay,   *leaped*
And cryden "out" and "harrow"° in the strete.   *help*
The neighebores, bothe smale and grete,
In ronnen° for to gauren° on this man,   *ran / stare*
725 That yet° aswowne lay, bothe pale and wan;   *still*
For with the fal he brosten° hadde his arm.   *broken*
But stonde he moste unto his owene harm.[6]
For whan he spak, he was anon° bore doun°   *at once / shouted down*
With° hende Nicholas and Alisoun.   *By*

---

4. Off goes the skin (from an area) a hand's-breadth around.
5. John confuses "Noah" with "Nowell" (Noel, or Christmas).
6. But he must accept responsibility for his own misfortune.

730 They tolden every man that he was wood,°   *crazy*
He was agast so of "Nowelis flood"
Thurgh fantasye,° that of his vanitee°   *delusion / foolish pride*
He hadde y-boght him kneding-tubbes three,
And hadde hem hanged in the roof above;
735 And that he preyed hem, for Goddes love,
To sitten in the roof, *par° compaignye,*   *for the sake of*
    The folk gan laughen° at his fantasye;   *laughed heartily*
Into the roof they kyken° and they cape,°   *gaze / gape*
And turned al his harm° unto a jape.°   *misfortune / joke*
740 For what so that this carpenter answerde,
It was for noght; no man his reson° herde.   *explanation*
With othes° grete he was so sworn adoun,   *oaths*
That he was holden° wood° in al the toun.   *considered / mad*
For every clerk° anonright° heeld° with other: *scholar / at once / agreed*
745 They seyde, "The man is wood, my leve° brother;"   *dear*
And every wight° gan laughen at this stryf.   *person*
    Thus swyved° was this carpenteres wyf   *made love to*
For al his keping° and his jalousye;   *watchfulness*
And Absolon hath kist hir nether yë;°   *lower eye*
750 And Nicholas is scalded in the toute.°   *rump*
This tale is doon, and God save al the route!°   *company*

The Reeve's Prologue and Tale

The Prologue

    Whan folk had laughen at this nyce cas°   *foolish matter*
Of Absolon and hende° Nicholas,   *courteous, gentle*
Diverse folk diversely they seyde,
But, for the more° part, they loughe° and pleyde;°   *greater / laughed / jested*
5 Ne at this tale I saugh no man him greve,°   *become vexed*
But° it were only Osewold the Reve.   *Except*
By cause he was of carpenteres craft,
A litel ire° is in his herte y-laft:°   *anger / left*
He gan° to grucche° and blamed it a lyte.°   *began / grumble / little*
10 "So theek," quod he, "ful wel coude I thee quyte
With blering of a proud milleres yë,[1]
If that me liste° speke of ribaudye.°   *it pleased me / ribaldry*
But ik° am old; me list not pley for° age;   *I / because of*
Gras-tyme is doon, my fodder° is now forage;[2]   *food*
15 This whyte top wryteth° myne olde yeres.   *declares*
Myn herte is also mowled° as myne heres,°   *as moldy / hair(s)*

1. "So may I thrive," said he, "I could very well pay   miller" (*lit.*, "the blearing of his eye").
you back with (a story of) the deceiving of a proud   2. Hay laid up for winter.

But if° I fare as dooth an open-ers;[3]   *Unless*
That ilke° fruit is ever lenger the wers,°   *same / the older the worse*
Til it be roten in mullok° or in stree.°   *muck / straw*
20 We olde men, I drede,° so fare we: *fear*
Til we be roten, can we nat be rype;
We hoppen alwey whyl that the world wol pype.
For in oure wil ther stiketh evere a nayl,[4]
To have an hoor° heed and a grene tayl,   *hoary*
25 As hath a leek;[5] for thogh our might° be goon,°   *power, force / gone*
Oure wil desireth folie evere in oon.°   *always the same*
For whan we may nat doon,° than wol we speke;   *act*
Yet in oure asshen° olde is fyr y-reke.°   *ashes / raked up*
     Foure gledes° han we, whiche I shal devyse:°   *burning coals / mention*
30 Avaunting,° lying, anger, coveityse.°   *Boasting / avarice*
Thise foure sparkles° longen° unto elde.°   *sparks / belong / old age*
Our olde lemes° mowe° wel been unwelde,°   *limbs / may / weak*
But wil ne shal nat faillen, that is sooth.
And yet ik have alwey a coltes tooth,[6]
35 As many a yeer as it is passed henne°   *hence*
Sin that my tappe of lyf bigan to renne.[7]
For sikerly,° whan I was bore,° anon°   *truly / born / at once*
Deeth drogh the tappe° of lyf and leet it gon;°   *drew the tap / run*
And ever sithe° hath so the tappe y-ronne,   *afterward*
40 Til that almost al empty is the tonne.°   *tun, cask*
The streem of lyf now droppeth on the chimbe.°   *rim of the cask*
The sely° tonge° may wel ringe and chimbe°   *foolish / tongue / chime*
Of wrecchednesse that passed is ful yore;°   *long ago*
With olde folk, save° dotage, is° namore."   *except for / there is*
45   Whan that oure Host hadde herd this sermoning,°   *preaching*
He gan to speke as lordly as a king.
He seide, "What amounteth al this wit?[8]
What shul° we speke alday of Holy Writ?   *Why must*
The devel made a reve for to preche,
50 Or of a soutere° a shipman or a leche.°   *shoemaker / doctor*
Sey forth thy tale, and tarie° nat the tyme,   *delay*
Lo, Depeford, and it is half-way pryme!
Lo, Grenewich, ther many a shrewe is inne![9]
It were al tyme thy tale to biginne."
55   "Now, sires," quod this Osewold the Reve,

3. The medlar fruit, inedible until it is mushy and decayed.
4. We dance on always, as long as the world will pipe. For in our will (desire), there is always an obstruction (*lit.*, a nail sticking up).
5. A kind of onion.
6. And even now I have in every way the desire of youth (*lit.*, a colt's tooth).

7. Since my tap of life began to run. (The figure is that of a wine cask.)
8. He said, "What does all this wisdom amount to?"
9. Lo, Deptford, and it's half past seven in the morning! Lo, Greenwich, wherein there is many a rascal! (Both are suburbs of London; Chaucer lived in Greenwich for a time.)

"I pray yow alle that ye nat yow greve,°   *take (it) amiss*
Thogh I answere and somdel sette his howve;[1]
For leveful is with force force of-showve.[2]
   This dronke millere hath y-told us heer
60 How that bigyled° was a carpenteer,   *deceived*
Peraventure° in scorn, for I am oon.   *Perhaps*
And, by youre leve,° I shal him quyte° anoon;   *permission / pay back*
Right in his cherles° termes wol I speke.   *churl's*
I pray to God his nekke mote tobreke°—   *may break*
65 He can wel in myn yë seen a stalke,°   *straw*
But in his owne he can nat seen a balke."°   *beam*

The Tale

   At Trumpyngtoun,° nat fer° fro Cantebriggc,°   *Trumpington / far / Cambridge*
Ther goth a brook and over that a brigge,°   *bridge*
Upon the whiche brook ther stant a melle;°   *mill*
70 And this is verray soth° that I yow telle.   *the real truth*
A millere was ther dwelling many a day;
As eny pecok° he was proud and gay.   *peacock*
Pypen he coude and fisshe, and nettes bete,
And turne coppes, and wel wrastle and shete;[3]
75 Ay by his belt he baar a long panade,°   *cutlass*
And of a swerd ful trenchant° was the blade.   *sharp*
A joly popper° baar he in his pouche—   *dagger*
Ther was no man for peril dorste° him touche—   *dared*
A Sheffeld thwitel° baar he in his hose.   *knife*
80 Round was his face, and camus° was his nosc;   *flat, pug*
As piled° as an ape was his skulle.   *bald*
He was a market-betere atte fulle.[4]
Ther dorste no wight hand upon him legge,°   *lay*
That he ne swoor he sholde anon abegge.°   *pay for it*
85 A theef he was for sothe° of corn° and mele,°   *truly / grain / meal*
And that a sly,° and usaunt for° to stele.   *sly one / accustomed*
His name was hote° deynous° Simkin.   *called / scornful, proud*
A wyf he hadde, y-comen of noble kin:
The person of the toun hir fader was.[5]
90 With hire he yaf° ful many a panne° of bras,   *gave / pan (as dowry)*
For that Simkin sholde in his blood allye.[6]
She was y-fostred° in a nonnerye   *raised*
For Simkin wolde° no wyf, as he sayde,   *desired*

---

1. Somewhat adjust his hood (i.e., make a fool of him).
2. For it is lawful to repel force with force.
3. He knew how to play bagpipes, and fish, and mend (fishing) nets, and turn (wooden) cups on a lathe, and wrestle well, and shoot.
4. He was a great swaggerer at markets.
5. The parson of the town was her father. (She was therefore born out of wedlock.)
6. I.e., marry her (with a pun on "alloy").

But° she were wel y-norissed° and a mayde,° *Unless / brought up / virgin*
95 To saven his estaat of yomanrye.[7]
And she was proud, and pert as is a pye.° *magpie*
A ful fair sighte was it upon hem two;[8]
On halydayes° biforn hire wolde he go *holy days*
With his tipet° wounde about his heed, *scarf*
100 And she cam after in a gyte of reed;° *red gown*
And Simkin hadde hosen° of the same. *stockings*
Ther dorste no wight clepen° hire but "Dame."° *call / Lady*
Was noon so hardy that wente by the weye
That with hir dorste rage° or ones° pleye, *dally / once*
105 But if° he wolde° be slayn of Simkin *Unless / wished (to)*
With panade,° or with knyf, or boydekin,° *cutlass / dagger*
For jalous folk ben perilous° everemo— *dangerous*
Algate they wolde hire wyves wenden so.[9]
And eek, for she was somdel smoterlich,[1]
110 She was as digne° as water in a dich, *dignified, worthy*
And ful of hoker° and of bisemare.° *scorn / disdain*
Hir thoughte that a lady sholde hire spare,[2]
What for hire kinrede° and hir nortelrye° *family / education*
That she had lerned in the nonnerye.
115   A doghter hadde they bitwixe hem two
Of twenty yeer, withouten any mo,° *more*
Savinge° a child that was of half-yeer age; *Except for*
In cradel it lay and was a propre page.° *fine boy*
This wenche thikke° and wel y-growen was, *stout*
120 With camuse° nose and eyen greye as glas, *pug*
With buttokes brode and brestes rounde and hye;
But right fair was hire heer,° I wol nat lye. *hair*
    The person° of the toun, for° she was feir, *parson / because*
In purpos was to maken hire his heir
125 Bothe of his catel° and his messuage,° *property / house*
And straunge he made it of hir mariage.[3]
His purpos was for to bistowe hire hye° *in a high place*
Into som worthy blood of auncetrye;° *old lineage*
For holy chirches good° moot° been despended° *goods / must / spent*
130 On holy chirches blood, that is descended.
Therfore he wolde his holy blood honoure,
Though that he holy chirche sholde devoure.
    Gret soken° hath this miller, out of doute,° *monopoly / doubtless*
With° whete and malt of al the land aboute; *On*

---

7. To preserve his rank as a freeman.
8. It was a handsome sight (to look) upon the two of them.
9. At any rate, they would like their wives to believe so.
1. And also, because she was somewhat besmirched

(i.e., by her illegitimate birth).
2. It seemed to her that a lady ought to treat her with respect.
3. And he made (the question of) her marriage difficult.

135 And nameliche ther was a greet collegge
     Men clepen° the Soler Halle° at Cantebregge;°   *call / Solar Hall / Cambridge*
     Ther was hir whete and eek° hir malt y-grounde.   *also*
     And on a day it happed, in a stounde,°   *at one time*
     Sik lay the maunciple on a maladye:[4]
140 Men wenden wisly° that he sholde dye,   *expected for certain*
     For which this millere stal° bothe mele and corn   *stole*
     An hundred tyme more than biforn;
     For ther-biforn he stal but curteisly,[5]
     But now he was a theef outrageously.
145 For which the wardeyn chidde and made fare,[6]
     But ther-of sette° the millere nat a tare;°   *cared / whit*
     He craketh boost,° and swoor it was nat so.   *talks loudly*
         Than were ther yonge povre scolers° two   *poor scholars*
     That dwelten in this halle of which I seye.°   *speak*
150 Testif° they were, and lusty for to pleye,   *Headstrong*
     And, only for hire mirthe and revelrye,
     Upon the wardeyn bisily they crye
     To yeve° hem leve° but a litel stounde°   *give / permission / while*
     To goon to mille and seen hir corn° y-grounde;   *grain*
155 And hardily,° they dorste leye° hir nekke,   *boldly / wager*
     The millere shold nat stele hem° half a pekke°   *from them / peck*
     Of corn by sleighte, ne by force hem reve;°   *rob*
     And at the laste the wardeyn yaf hem leve.°   *gave them permission*
     John highte° that oon, and Aleyn highte that other;   *was named*
160 Of o° toun were they born, that highte Strother,   *one*
     Fer in the north—I can nat telle where.[7]
         This Alcyn maketh redy al his gere,°   *gear, equipment*
     And on an hors the sak° he caste anon.°   *sack (of grain) / at once*
     Forth goth Aleyn the clerk,° and also John,   *scholar*
165 With good swerd and with bokeler° by hir syde.   *buckler, shield*
     John knew the wey, hem nedede° no gyde,   *they needed*
     And at the mille the sak adoun he layth.
     Aleyn spak first, "Al hayl, Symond, y-fayth!°   *in faith*
     How fares thy faire doghter and thy wyf?"
170 "Aleyn, welcome," quod° Simkin, "by my lyf!   *said*
     And John also, how now, what do ye heer?"°   *here*
         "Symond," quod John, "by God, nede has na peer.°   *need has no equal*
     Him boes serve himselve that has na swayn,[8]
     Or elles he is a fool, as clerkes sayn.

4. The college steward lay sick with an illness.
5. For previously he stole only in a polite fashion.
6. On account of which the warden (the college head) chided (him) and made a fuss.
7. The town has not been identified, though there was a Strother castle in Northumberland. The speech of the students firmly characterizes them as North-

erners: words such as "boes," "lathe," "fonne," "hethyng," "taa"; the substitution of long *a* for normal long *o* (as in "gas," "swa," "ham"); present indicative verbs in *-es* or *-s*, and so on, are used to create a distinct and slightly comic dialect.
8. It behooves him who has no servant to serve himself.

175 Oure manciple, I hope° he wil be deed,   *expect*
    Swa werkes ay the wanges in his heed.[9]
    And forthy° is I come, and eek° Alayn,   *therefore / also*
    To grinde our corn and carie it ham° agayn;   *home*
    I pray yow spede us hethen° that° ye may."   *hence / as much as*
180   "It shal be doon," quod Simkin, "by my fay.°   *faith*
    What wol ye doon whyl that it is in hande?"°   *being processed*
      "By God, right by the hopur° wil I stande,"   *hopper*
    Quod John, "and se how that the corn gas° in.   *goes*
    Yet saugh I never, by my fader° kin,   *father's*
185 How that the hopur° wagges til and fra."°   *hopper / to and fro*
      Aleyn answerde, "John, and wiltow swa?°   *wilt thou (do) so*
    Than wil I be bynethe, by my croun,°   *head*
    And se how that the mele° falles doun   *meal*
    Into the trough; that sal° be my disport.   *shall*
190 For John, in faith, I may° been of youre sort: *must*
    I is as ille° a millere as are ye."   *bad*
      This miller smyled of° hir nycetee,°   *at / foolishness*
    And thoghte, "Al this nis doon but for a wyle.°   *only as a trick*
    They wene° that no man may hem bigyle,°   *think / beguile, trick*
195 But, by my thrift, yet shal I blere hire yë°   *blur their eye(s)*
    For al the sleighte° in hir philosophye.   *craftiness*
    The more queynte crekes° that they make,   *sly tricks*
    The more wol I stele whan I take.
    In stide of flour, yet wol I yeve° hem bren.°   *give / bran*
200 'The gretteste clerkes been noght wysest men,'
    As whylom° to the wolf thus spak the mare;[1]   *once*
    Of al hir° art counte I noght a tare."°   *their / whit*
      Out at the dore he gooth ful prively,°   *secretly*
    Whan that he saugh his tyme, softely;
205 He loketh up and doun til he hath founde
    The clerkes hors, ther as° it stood y-bounde   *where*
    Bihinde the mille, under a levesel.°   *leafy arbor*
    And to the hors he gooth him faire and wel;
    He strepeth of° the brydel right anon.   *strips off*
210 And whan the hors was laus,° he ginneth gon°   *loose / dashes off*
    Toward the fen,° ther° wilde mares renne,°   *marsh / where / run*
    Forth with "wehee,"° thurgh thikke and thurgh thenne.°   *a whinny / thin*
      This miller gooth agayn, no word he seyde,
    But dooth his note,° and with the clerkes pleyde,°   *job / jested*
215 Til that hir corn° was faire and wel y-grounde.   *grain*
    And whan the mele° is sakked° and y-bounde,°   *flour / sacked / tied*
    This John goth out and fynt° his hors away,   *finds*
    And gan to crye "harrow" and "weylaway!"[2]

---

9. The molars in his head keep aching so.
1. Refers to a fable in which the wolf, very hungry,
is kicked by a mare while trying to read on her hind
foot the price of her foal.
2. And cried out "help" and "alas-alack."

Oure hors is lorn!° Alayn, for goddes banes,°   *lost / bones*
220 Step on thy feet! com of, man, al atanes!°   *right now*
     Allas, our wardeyn has his palfrey° lorn!"°   *riding horse / lost*
     This Aleyn al forgat bothe mele and corn;
     Al was out of his mynde his housbondrye.°   *shrewd management*
     "What, whilk° way is he geen?"° he gan to crye.°   *which / gone / cried out*
225   The wyf cam lepinge inward with a ren·°   *run*
     She seyde, "Allas! youre hors goth to the fen
     With wilde mares, as faste as he may go.
     Unthank° come on his hand that bound him so,   *Bad luck*
     And he that bettre sholde han knit the reyne."°   *tied the reins*
230   "Allas," quod John, "Aleyn, for Cristes peyne,°   *pain*
     Lay doun thy swerd, and I wil myn alswa.°   *also*
     I is ful wight,° God waat,° as is a raa;°   *swift / knows / roe*
     By Goddes herte he sal° nat scape° us bathe!°   *shall / escape / both*
     Why ne had thou pit° the capul° in the lathe?°   *put / horse / barn*
235 Il-hayl,° by God, Aleyn, thou is a fonne!"°   *Bad luck / fool*
         This sely clerkes° han ful faste y-ronne   *These poor scholars*
     Toward the fen, bothe Aleyn and eek John.
         And whan the millere saugh° that they were gon,   *saw*
     He half a busshel of hir flour hath take,
240 And bad his wyf go knede it in a cake.[3]
     He seyde, "I trowe° the clerkes were aferd,°   *believe / afraid, suspicious*
     Yet can a millere make a clerkes berd[4]
     For al his art; now lat hem goon hir weye.
     Lo, wher he gooth! ye, lat the children pleye.
245 They gete him nat so lightly, by my croun!"[5]
         Thise sely clerkes rennen up and doun
     With "Keep! keep! stand! stand! jossa! warderere![6]
     Ga° whistle thou, and I shal kepe him here!"   *Go*
     But shortly,° til that it was verray° night,   *in short / real*
250 They coude nat, though they dide al hir might,°   *their best*
     Hir capul cacche,° he ran alwey so faste,   *Catch their horse*
     Til in a dich they caughte him atte laste.
         Wery and weet,° as beest° is in the reyn,° *wet / animal / rain*
     Comth sely John, and with him comth Aleyn.
255 "Allas," quod John, "the day that I was born!
     Now are we drive til hething° and til scorn.   *driven into derision*
     Oure corn° is stole, men wil us foles° calle,   *grain / fools*
     Bathe° the wardeyn and our felawes° alle,   *Both / companions*
     And namely° the millere, weylaway!"°   *especially / alas*
260   Thus pleyneth° John as he goth by° the way   *complains / on*
     Toward the mille, and Bayard[7] in his hond.
     The millere sitting by the fyr he fond,

---

3. And told his wife to go knead it into a loaf.   6. Down here! look out behind!
4. Outwit a scholar.   7. The horse's name.
5. They won't catch him so easily, by my head!

For it was night, and forther° mighte they noght. — *go farther*
But for the love of God they him bisoght
265　Of herberwe° and of ese,° as for hir peny.° — *lodging / rest / money*
　　　The millere seyde agayn,° "If ther be eny, — *in response*
Swich° as it is, yet shal ye have youre part. — *Such*
Myn hous is streit,° but ye han lerned art: — *narrow, small*
Ye conne° by argumentes make a place — *know how to*
270　A myle brood of° twenty foot of space. — *out of*
Lat see now if this place may suffyse—
Or make it roum° with speche, as is youre gyse."° — *roomy / way*
　　　"Now, Symond," seyde John, "by Seint Cutberd,° — *Cuthbert*
Ay° is thou mery, and this is faire answerd. — *Ever*
275　I have herd seyd, 'man sal taa of twa thinges:
Slyk as he fyndes, or taa slyk as he bringes.'[8]
But specially, I pray thee, hoste dere,
Get us som mete and drinke and make us chere,° — *good cheer*
And we wil payen trewely atte fulle;
280　With empty hand men may na haukes tulle.° — *lure no hawks*
Lo, here oure silver, redy for to spende."
　　　This millere into toun his doghter sende° — *sent*
For ale and breed, and rosted hem° a goos, — *roasted for them*
And bond hir hors, it sholde namoore go loos;
285　And in his owene chambre hem made a bed
With shetes and with chalons° faire y-spred, — *bedspreads*
Noght from his owene bed ten foot or twelve.
His doghter hadde a bed, al by hirselve,
Right in the same chambre, by and by.° — *side by side*
290　It mighte be no bet, and cause why,[9] —
Ther was no roumer° herberwe° in the place. — *larger / lodgings*
They soupen° and they speke, hem to solace,° — *sup / for amusement*
And drinken evere strong ale atte beste.° — *of the best*
Aboute midnight wente they to rest.
300　　　Wel hath this millere vernisshed his heed:[1]
Ful pale he was fordronken,° and nat reed; — *very drunk*
He yexeth,° and he speketh thurgh the nose — *hiccups*
As he were on the quakke,° or on the pose.° — *hoarse / had a cold*
To bedde he gooth, and with him goth his wyf—
305　As any jay she light° was and jolyf,° — *cheerful / jolly*
So was hir joly whistle wel y-wet.
The cradel at hir beddes feet is set,
To rokken,° and to yeve° the child to souke.° — *rock / give / suck*
And whan that dronken al was in the crouke,° — *jug*
310　To bedde went the doghter right anon;

---

8. I have heard said, "a man must take one of two
things; such as he finds, or take such as he brings."　reason why.
9. No better could be (arranged), and (this is the)　1. *Lit.*, varnished his head (with ale).

To bedde gooth Aleyn and also John;
Ther nas na more, hem nedede no dwale.°   *sleeping potion*
This millere hath so wisly° bibbed° ale,   *deeply / imbibed*
That as° an hors he fnorteth° in his sleep,   *like / snores*
315 Ne of his tayl bihinde he took no keep.°   *heed*
His wyf bar him a burdon,° a ful strong: *bass accompaniment*
Men mighte hir routing° here two furlong;   *snoring*
I he wenche routeth eek *par compaignye.*°   *to keep (them) company*
     Aleyn the clerk, that herd this melodye,
320 He poked John, and seyde, "Slepestow?°   *Art thou asleep?*
Herdestow evere slyk° a sang° er° now?   *such / song / before*
Lo, swilk° a compline° is y-mel° hem alle!   *such / evening song / among*
A wilde fyr[2] upon thair bodyes falle!
Wha herkned° ever slyk° a ferly° thing?   *Who heard / such / weird*
325 Ye, they sal have the flour of il ending.[3]
This lange° night ther tydes° me na° reste;   *long / comes to / no*
But yet, na fors,° al sal° be for the beste.   *no matter / shall*
For John," seyde he, "als evere moot I thryve,°   *may I thrive*
If that I may, yon wenche wil I swyve.°   *lie with*
330 Som esement° has lawe y-shapen° us.   *redress / provided*
For John, ther is a lawe that says thus,
That gif° a man in a° point be agreved,°   *if / one / aggrieved*
That in another he sal be releved.°   *relieved*
Oure corn is stoln, sothly, it is na nay,°   *there is no denial*
335 And we han had an il fit° al this day.   *sorry time of it*
And sin° I sal have neen amendement°   *since / no amends*
Agayn my los,° I wil have esement.°   *loss / redress*
By Goddes saule, it sal neen other be!"[4]
     This John answerde, "Alayn, avyse thee,°   *consider*
340 The miller is a perilous° man," he seyde,   *dangerous*
"And gif° that he out of his sleep abreyde,°   *if / awake*
He mighte doon us bathe° a vileinye."°   *both / harm*
     Aleyn answerde, "I count him nat a flye."
And up he rist,° and by the wenche he crepte.   *rises*
345 This wenche lay upright,° and faste° slepte   *face up / soundly*
Til he so ny° was, er° she mighte espye,°   *near / before / see (him)*
That it had been to° late for to crye,   *too*
And shortly for to seyn, they were aton;°   *at one, united*
Now pley, Aleyn! for I wol speke of John.
350   This John lyth stille a furlong-wey or two,[5]
And to himself he maketh routhe° and wo: *lamentation*
"Allas!" quod he, "this is a wikked jape.°   *joke*
Now may I seyn° that I is but an ape.   *say*

2. A painful skin disease.
3. The best of bad ending(s).
4. By God's soul, it shall not be otherwise!

5. This John lies still for a moment or two (*lit.*, the length of time it takes to walk a furlong or two. A furlong is an eighth of a mile).

Yet has my felawe° somwhat° for his harm: *companion / something*
355 He has the milleris° doghter in his arm.   *miller's*
He auntred him,° and has his nedes sped,°   *took a chance / satisfied*
And I lye as a draf-sak° in my bed.   *bag of straw or refuse*
And when this jape is tald° another day,   *told*
I sal been halde° a daf,° a cokenay!°   *held / fool / milksop*
360 I wil aryse and auntre° it, by my fayth!   *chance*
Unhardy is unsely,[6] thus men sayth."
And up he roos° and softely he wente   *arose*
Unto the cradel, and in his hand it hente,°   *took*
And baar° it softe unto his beddes feet.   *bore*
365   Sone after this the wyf hir routing leet,°   *ceased snoring*
And gan awake,° and wente hir out to pisse,   *woke up*
And cam agayn, and gan hir cradel misse,
And groped heer and ther, but she fond noon.
"Allas!" quod she, "I hadde almost misgoon;°   *gone amiss*
370 I hadde almost gon to the clerkes bed—
Ey, *benedicite*, thanne hadde I foule y-sped!"[7]
And forth she gooth til she the cradel fond;
She gropeth alwey° forther with hir hond,   *ever*
And fond the bed, and thoghte noght but good,°   *everything was well*
375 By cause that the cradel by it stood,
And niste° wher she was, for it was derk;   *knew not*
But faire and wel she creep° in to the clerk,°   *crept / scholar*
And lyth° ful stille, and wolde han caught a sleep.°   *lies / fallen asleep*
Withinne a whyl this John the clerk up leep,°   *leapt*
380 And on this gode wyf he leyth on sore.°   *sets to it vigorously*
So mery a fit ne hadde she nat ful yore;[8]
He priketh harde and depe as he were mad.
This joly lyf han thise two clerkes lad°   *led*
Til that the thridde cok[9] bigan to singe.
385   Aleyn wex° wery in the daweninge,°   *grew / at dawn*
For he had swonken° al the longe night,   *labored*
And seyde, "Fare weel, Malyne, swete wight!
The day is come; I may no lenger byde;°   *remain*
But everemo, wher so° I go° or ryde,   *wherever / walk*
390 I is thyn awen clerk, swa have I seel!"[1]
"Now, dere lemman,"° quod she, "go, far weel!   *sweetheart*
But er° thou go, o° thing I wol thee telle: *before / one*
Whan that thou wendest homward by the melle,°   *mill*
Right at the entree of the dore bihinde,
395 Thou shalt a cake° of half a busshel finde   *loaf*
That was y-maked of thyn owene mele,°   *meal*

6. (He who is) not bold is unlucky.
7. Aye, bless me! then I would have fared badly.
8. She hadn't had so merry a bout for a long time.
9. The third crow of the cock that heralds dawn.
1. I'm your very own scholar, as I hope to have bliss.

Which that I heelp° my sire for to stele.   *helped*
And, gode lemman, God thee save and kepe!"
And with that word almost she gan to wepe.°   *fell to weeping*
400 Aleyn up rist,° and thoughte, "Er° that it dawe,°   *rises / Before / dawns*
I wol go crepen in by my felawe,"
And fond the cradel with his hand anon.°   *at once*
"By God," thoghte he, "al wrang° I have misgon °   *wrong / gone amiss*
Myn heed is toty° of° my swink° to-night: *dizzy / from / labor*
405 That maketh me that I go nat aright.
I woot° wel by the cradel I have misgo—   *know*
Heere lyth the miller and his wyf also."
And forth he goth, a twenty devel way,°   *straight to the devil*
Unto the bed ther as° the miller lay—   *there where*
410 He wende have cropen by his felawe John²—
And by the millere in he creep° anon,   *crept*
And caughte hym by the nekke, and softe he spak.
He seyde, "Thou, John, thou swynes-heed,° awak   *swine's-head*
For Cristes saule, and heer a noble game.°   *great joke*
415 For by that lord that called is Seint Jame,°   *James*
As° I have thryes° in this shorte night   *So / thrice*
Swyved the milleres doghter bolt upright,³
Whyl thow hast as a coward been agast."°   *afraid*
    "Ye, false harlot,"° quod the millere, "hast?   *rascal*
420 A! false traitour! false clerk!" quod he,
"Thou shalt be deed, by Goddes dignitee!
Who dorste° be so bold to disparage°   *would dare / dishonor*
My doghter, that is come of swich linage?"°   *such (high) birth*
And by the throte-bolle° he caughte Alayn;   *Adam's apple*
425 And he hente hym despitously agayn,⁴
And on the nose he smoot him with his fest°—   *fist*
Doun ran the blody streem upon his brest.
And in° the floor, with nose and mouth tobroke,°   *on / smashed*
They walwe° as doon two pigges in a poke.   *wallow*
430 And up they goon, and doun agayn anon,°   *immediately*
Til that the miller sporned at a stoon,⁵
And doun he fil bakward upon his wyf,
That wiste° no thing of this nyce° stryf,   *Who knew / foolish*
For she was falle aslepe a lyte wight°   *little bit*
435 With John the clerk, that waked hadde al night;
And with the fal, out of hir sleep she breyde.°   *started*
"Help, holy croys of Bromeholm," she seyde,⁶

---

2. He thought to have crept in alongside his friend
John.
3. Made love to the miller's daughter (as she lay)
flat on her back.
4. And he (Alan) grabbed him fiercely in return.

5. Until the miller tripped on a stone.
6. "Help, holy cross of Bromholm," she said (a
famous relic, supposed to be a piece of the true cross
of Christ, brought to Bromholm in Norfolk in 1223).

"*In manus tuas!*° Lord, to thee I calle!   *Into thy hands*
Awak, Symond! the feend° is on me falle,°   *fiend / fallen*
440 Myn herte is broken, help, I nam but° deed: *am just about*
There lyth oon upon my wombe° and on myn heed.   *belly*
Help, Simkin, for the false clerkes fighte."
    This John sterte° up as faste as ever he mighte,   *leaped*
And graspeth by° the walles to and fro,   *gropes along*
445 To finde a staf; and she sterte° up also,   *leaped*
And knew the estres° bet° than dide this John,   *interior / better*
And by the wal a staf she fond anon,
And saugh° a litel shimering of a light—   *saw*
For at an hole in shoon the mone bright—
450 And by that light she saugh hem bothe two,
But sikerly° she niste° who was who,   *truly / knew not*
But as° she saugh a whyt° thing in hir yë.   *Except that / white*
And whan she gan° this whyte thing espye,   *did*
She wende the clerk hadde wered a volupeer,[7]
455 And with the staf she drough° ay neer° and neer,   *drew / ever nearer*
And wende han hit this Aleyn at the fulle,[8]
And smoot the millere on the pyled° skulle   *bald*
That° doun he gooth and cryde, "Harrow!° I dye!"   *So that / Help!*
Thise clerkes bete° him weel and lete him lye,   *beat*
460 And greythen hem,° and toke hir hors anon,   *get themselves ready*
And eek hire mele,° and on hir wey they gon.   *meal*
And at the mille yet they toke hir cake
Of half a busshel flour, ful wel y-bake.°   *baked*
    Thus is the proude millere wel y-bete,°   *beaten*
465 And hath y-lost the grinding of the whete,
And payed for the soper everideel°   *completely*
Of Aleyn and of John, that bette° him weel;   *beat*
His wyf is swyved, and his doghter als.[9]
Lo, swich it is° a millere to be fals!   *thus it is for*
470 And therfore this proverbe is seyd ful sooth,
"Him thar nat wene wel that yvel dooth;[1]
A gylour° shal himself bigyled° be."   *beguiler, deceiver / deceived*
And God, that sitteth heighe in magestee,
Save al this compaignye grete and smale!
Thus have I quit° the Millere in my tale.   *repaid*

From The Cook's Prologue

    The Cook of London, whyl the Reve spak,
For joye him thoughte he clawed him on the bak.[1]

---

7. She thought the scholar had worn a nightcap.
8. And thought to have hit this Alan square-on.
9. His wife's been made love to, and his daughter as well.

1. He need not expect good who does evil.
1. For the joy (he felt), it seemed to him the Reeve was scratching him on the back.

"Ha! ha!" quod he, "for Cristes passioun,
This millere hadde a sharp conclusioun
5 Upon° his argument of herbergage!°   *To / concerning lodging(s)*
Wel seyde Salomon in his langage,
'Ne bringe nat every man into thyn hous;'
For herberwinge° by nighte is perilous.   *lodging*
Wel oghte a man avysed° for to be   *cautious*
10 Whom that he broughte into his privetee.°   *privacy*
I pray to God, so yeve° me sorwe and care,   *give*
If ever, sith I highte Hogge of Ware,[2]
Herde I a millere bettre y-set a-werk:°   *set to work, tricked*
He hadde a jape° of malice in the derk.   *joke*
15 But God forbede that we stinten° here;   *leave off*
And therfore, if ye vouche-sauf° to here   *agree*
A tale of me, that am a povre man,
I wol yow telle as wel as evere I can
A litel jape° that fil° in our citee."   *joke / befell*

                    *   *   *

The Wife of Bath's Prologue and Tale

The Prologue

"Experience, though noon auctoritee[1]
Were in this world, is right y-nough° for me   *certainly enough*
To speke of wo that is in mariage:
For, lordinges, sith° I twelf yeer was of age,   *since*
5 Thonked be God that is eterne on lyve,°   *alive eternally*
Housbondes at chirche-dore I have had fyve[2]
(If I so ofte myghte have y-wedded be)
And alle were worthy men in hir degree.°   *within their station*
But me was told, certeyn,° nat longe agon is,°   *truly / not long ago*
10 That sith that Crist ne wente nevere but onis°   *once*
To wedding in the Cane° of Galilee,   *Cana*
That by the same ensample° taughte he me   *example*
That I ne sholde wedded be but ones.°   *once*
Herkne eek, lo, which a sharp word for the nones[3]
15 Besyde a welle, Jesus, God and man,
Spak in repreve° of the Samaritan: *reproof*
'Thou hast y-had fyve housbondes,' quod he,
'And that ilke° man that now hath thee   *that same*

---

2. If ever, since I (first) was called Hodge (Roger) of
Ware (in Hertfordshire).
1. The authoritative truths of learned tradition, preserved in writings from the past.
2. Medieval marriages were performed at the church
door, and only the nuptial mass within the church.

3. (And) lo, hear also what a sharp word on the
matter ("for the nones" is a tag-ending: "for the
occasion," "to the purpose," but often nearly mean-
ingless). The incident referred to can be found in
John 4.5–42.

Is noght thyn housbond;' thus seyde he certeyn.
20 What that he mente therby, I can nat seyn,°   *say*
But that° I axe,° why that the fifthe man   *Except / ask*
Was noon housbond to the Samaritan?
How manye mighte she have in mariage?
Yet herde I nevere tellen in myn age°   *in all my days*
25 Upon° this nombre diffinicioun.°   *Of / definition, explanation*
Men may devyne° and glosen° up and doun,   *guess / interpret, comment upon*
But wel I woot expres,° withoute lye,°   *know particularly / lie*
God bad us for to wexe° and multiplye: *wax, increase*
That gentil° text can I wel understonde.   *noble*
30 Eek° wel I woot° he seyde, myn housbonde   *Also / know*
Sholde lete° fader and moder, and take to me;   *leave*
But of no nombre mencioun made he,
Of bigamye or of octogamye.[4]
Why sholde men thanne speke of it vileinye?°   *rude things, reproach*
35   Lo, here the wyse king, daun Salomon;[5]
I trowe° he hadde wyves mo than oon.   *believe*
As wolde° God it leveful° were unto me   *Would to / lawful*
To be refresshed[6] half so ofte as he!
Which yifte° of God hadde he for alle his wyvis!   *What a gift*
40 No man hath swich,° that in this world alyve is.   *such*
God woot° this noble king, as to my wit,°   *knows / understanding*
The firste night had many a mery fit°   *bout, turn*
With ech of hem, so wel was him on lyve![7]
Blessed be God that I have wedded fyve,
44a Of whiche I have pyked out° the beste,[8]   *extracted*
Bothe of here nether purs and of here cheste.[9]
Diverse scoles° maken parfyt clerkes,°   *schools / perfect scholars*
And diverse practyk° in many sondry° werkes   *practice / sundry, varied*
Maketh the werkman parfyt sekirly:°   *assuredly*
44f Of fyve husbondes scoleiyng° am I.   *schooling*
45 Welcome the sixte, whan that evere he shall!°   *shall (come along)*
For sothe I wol nat kepe me chast in al.°   *entirely chaste*
Whan myn housbond is fro the world y-gon,
Som Cristen man shal wedde me anon;°   *at once*
For thanne th'Apostle° seith that I am free   *St. Paul*
50 To wedde, a Goddes half,° where it lyketh° me.   *on God's behalf / pleases*
He seith that to be wedded is no sinne:
Bet° is to be wedded than to brinne.°   *Better / burn*
What rekketh me° thogh folk seye vileinye°   *do I care / speak ill*
Of shrewed Lameth° and his bigamye?   *accursed Lamech*

---

4. Here, marriages in succession.
5. Consider the wise king, lord Solomon. (According to 1 Kings 11.3, he had seven hundred wives and three hundred concubines.)
6. I.e., sexually.

7. With each of them, so fortunate was his life.
8. Lines 44a–44f are probably a late addition; the best manuscripts exclude them.
9. Both from their lower purse (i.e., testicles) and from their (money-)chest.

55	I woot° wel Abraham was an holy man,	*know*
	And Jacob eek, as ferforth° as I can;°	*far / know*
	And ech of hem° hadde wyves mo° than two,	*each of them / more*
	And many another holy man also.	
	Wher can ye seye,° in any manere age,°	*say / any age whatever*
60	That hye° God defended° mariage	*high / forbade*
	By expres word? I pray you telleth me	
	Or where comanded he virginitee?	
	I woot as wel as ye, it is no drede,°	*no doubt about it*
	Th'Apostel,° whan he speketh of maydenhede,	*St. Paul*
65	He seyde that precept¹ therof hadde he noon.	
	Men may conseille° a womman to been oon,	*advise*
	But conseilling is no comandement:	
	He putte it in oure owene° jugement.	*own*
	For hadde God comanded maydenhede,	
70	Thanne hadde he dampned° wedding with the° dede.	*damned / in that*
	And certes, if ther were no seed y-sowe,°	*sown*
	Virginitee, thanne wherof sholde it growe?	
	Poul dorste nat comanden, atte leste,²	
	A thing of which his maister yaf noon heste.°	*gave no order*
75	The dart° is set up for virginitee:	*dart (given as prize)*
	Cacche who so may: who renneth best lat see.³	
	But this word is nat take of every wight,	
	But ther as God list give it of his might.⁴	
	I woot° wel that th'Apostel was a mayde;°	*know / virgin*
80	But natheless,° thogh that he wroot° and sayde	*nevertheless / wrote*
	He wolde° that every wight° were swich° as he,	*wished / person / such*
	Al nis° but conseil to virginitee,	*All (this) is nothing*
	And for to been a wyf, he yaf° me leve°	*gave / leave, permission*
	Of° indulgence. So nis it no repreve°	*By / reproach*
85	To wedde me, if that my make dye,	
	Withoute excepcioun of bigamye,⁵	
	Al° were it good no womman for to touche—	*Although*
	He mente as in his bed or in his couche—	
	For peril is bothe fyr and tow t'assemble;⁶	
90	Ye knowe what this ensample° may resemble.	*example*
	This al and som: he heeld virginitee	
	More parfit than wedding in freletee.	
	Freletee clepe I, but if that he and she⁷	
	Wolde leden° al hir lyf in chastitee.	*Should wish to lead*
95	I graunte it wel, I have noon envye	

1. I.e., commandment.
2. (St.) Paul did not dare in the least command.
3. Catch (win) it whoever may: let's see who runs the best.
4. But this counsel (i.e., the preference for virginity) is not required of every person, but (only) there where God is pleased to impose it, by His might.
5. To wed (again), if my mate die, without being criticized for bigamy.
6. For it is perilous to bring together both fire and flax.
7. "Frailty" I call it, unless he and she.

Thogh maydenhede preferre° bigamye.   *be preferred over*
Hem lyketh° to be clene, body and goost.°   *They wish / soul, spirit*
Of myn estaat° I nil nat° make no boost: *condition / will not*
For wel ye knowe, a lord in his houshold
100 He hath nat every vessel al of gold;
Somme been of tree,° and doon hir lord servyse.   *wood*
God clepeth° folk to him in sondry wyse,°   *calls / various ways*
And everich hath of God a propre yifte,°   *his own special gift*
Som this, som that, as Him lyketh shifte.°   *it pleases Him to ordain*
105   Virginitee is greet perfeccioun,
And continence eek with devocioun.⁸
But Crist, that of perfeccioun is welle,°   *the well, the source*
Bad° nat every wight° he sholde go selle   *Commanded / person*
All that he hadde and give it to the pore,°   *poor*
110 And in swich wyse° folwe him and his fore.°   *such a way / footsteps*
He spak to hem that wolde live parfitly,
And lordinges, by youre leve,° that am nat I.   *leave*
I wol bistowe the flour° of al myn age   *the flower, the best part*
In the actes and in fruit of mariage.
115   Telle me also, to what conclusioun°   *end, purpose*
Were membres maad of generacioun
And of so parfit wys a wright y-wroght?⁹
Trusteth right wel, they were nat maad for noght.
Glose° whoso wole,° and seye bothe up and doun   *Interpret / will*
120 That they were maked for purgacioun
Of urine, and oure bothe° thinges smale   *both our*
Were eek to knowe° a femele from a male,   *to distinguish*
And for noon other cause: sey ye no?
The experience° woot° wel it is noght so.   *experience (in general) / knows*
125 So that the clerkes be nat with me wrothe,°   *wroth, angry*
I sey this, that they maked been for bothe—
This is to seye, for office,° and for ese°   *natural duty / pleasure*
Of engendrure,° ther° we nat God displese.   *In procreation / there where*
Why sholde men elles° in hir bokes sette   *otherwise*
130 That man shal yelde° to his wyf hire dette?°   *pay / what is owing her*
Now wherwith° sholde he make his payement   *by what means*
If he ne used his sely° instrument?   *simple, blessed*
Thanne° were they maad upon a creature   *Therefore*
To purge uryne, and eek for engendrure.
135   But I seye noght that every wight is holde,°   *beholden, bound*
That hath swich harneys° as I to yow tolde,   *such equipment*
To goon and usen hem in engendrure:
Thanne sholde men take of chastitee no cure.¹

---

8. And continence also (when) accompanied by   God).
devotion.   1. Then people wouldn't be concerned about chas-
9. And by so perfect and wise a workman? (i.e., tity.

Crist was a mayde° and shapen as° a man,   *virgin / formed like*
140 And many a seint, sith that° the world bigan,   *since*
Yet lived they evere in parfit chastitee.
I nil° envye no virginitee: *will not*
Lat hem be breed° of pured whete-seed,°   *bread / finest wheat*
And lat us wyves hoten° barly-breed.°   *be called / barley bread*
145 And yet with barly-breed, Mark° telle can   *Oh Mark*
Oure Lord Jesu refresshed² many a man.
In swich estaat° as God hath cleped° us   *condition / called*
I wol persevere, I nam nat precious.³
In wyfhode I wol use myn instrument
150 As frely° as my Makere hath it sent.   *generously*
If I be daungerous,° God yeve° me sorwe!   *standoffish / give*
Myn housbond shal it have bothe eve and morwe,°   *morning*
Whan that him list° com forth and paye his dette.   *it pleases him to*
An housbonde I wol have, I wol nat lette,°   *will not leave off*
155 Which shal be bothe my dettour and my thral,°   *thrall, slave*
And have his tribulacioun withal°   *besides*
Upon his flessh, whyl that I am his wyf.
I have the power duringe al my lyf
Upon° his propre° body, and noght he: *Over / own*
160 Right thus th' Apostel° tolde it unto me,   *St. Paul*
And bad oure housbondes for to love us weel.
Al this sentence me lyketh every deel."⁴
     Up sterte the Pardoner, and that anon:⁵
"Now dame," quod he, "by God and by Seint John,
165 Ye been a noble prechour° in this cas!°   *preacher / matter*
I was aboute to wedde a wyf. Allas,
What° sholde I bye° it on my flesh so dere?   *Why / pay for*
Yet hadde I levere° wedde no wyf to-yere!"°   *rather / this year*
     "Abyde!"° quod° she, "my tale is nat bigonne.   *Wait / said*
170 Nay, thou shalt drinken of another tonne°   *tun, cask*
Er that I go, shal savoure wors than ale.⁶
And whan that I have told thee forth my tale
Of tribulacioun in mariage,
Of which I am expert in al myn age—⁷
175 This° to seyn, myself° have been the whippe—   *This is / (I) myself*
Than maystow chese° whether thou wolt sippe°   *mayst thou choose / sip*
Of thilke° tonne that I shal abroche.°   *that same / open*
Be war° of it, er thou to ny° approche,   *wary / too near*
For I shall telle ensamples° mo° than ten.   *examples / more*
180 'Whoso that nil be war° by othere men,   *Whoever will not be warned*
By him shul othere men corrected be.'

2. I.e., fed.   5. The Pardoner broke in (*lit.*, started up) at once.
3. I will continue; I'm not overly fastidious.   6. Before I go, (which) shall taste worse than ale.
4. All this lesson pleases me, every bit (of it). 7. About which I have been expert all my life.

The same wordes wryteth Ptholomee:°   *Ptolemy*
Rede in his Almageste,[8] and take it there."
    "Dame, I wolde praye yow, if youre wil it were,"
185 Seyde this Pardoner, "as ye bigan,
Telle forth youre tale, spareth° for no man,   *hold back*
And teche us yonge men of youre praktike."°   *practice*
    "Gladly," quod she, "sith it may yow lyke.°   *please*
But yet I praye to al this companye,
190 If that I speke after my fantasye,°   *according to my fancy*
As taketh not agrief of that I seye;[9]
For myn entente° nis° but for to pleye.   *intention / is not*
    Now sires, now wol I telle forth my tale.
As evere mote° I drinken wyn or ale,   *might*
195 I shal seye sooth,° tho° housbondes that I hadde,   *tell the truth / (of) those*
As three of hem were gode and two were badde.
The three men were gode, and riche, and olde;
Unnethe mighte they the statut holde [1]
In° which that they were bounden unto me.   *By*
200 Ye woot° wel what I mene of this, pardee!°   *know / by God*
As help me God, I laughe whan I thinke
How pitously° a-night° I made hem swinke;°   *pitiably / at night / labor*
And by my fey, I tolde of it no stoor.[2]
They had me yeven° hir lond and hir tresoor;°   *given / wealth*
205 Me neded nat do lenger diligence[3]
To winne hir love, or doon hem reverence.°   *to honor them*
They loved me so wel, by God above,
That I ne tolde no deyntee of° hir love!   *took no pleasure in*
A wys womman wol bisye hire evere in oon[4]
210 To gete hire love, ye, ther as° she hath noon.   *there where*
But sith I hadde hem hoolly° in myn hond,   *wholly*
And sith they hadde me yeven° all hir lond,   *given*
What° sholde I taken keep° hem for to plese,   *Why / heed*
But° it were for my profit and myn ese?°   *Unless / comfort*
215 I sette hem so a-werke,° by my fey,°   *working / faith*
That many a night they songen° 'weilawey!'°   *sang / woe is me*
The bacoun was nat fet for hem, I trowe,[5]
That som men han in Essex at Dunmowe.
I governed hem so wel after° my lawe   *according to*
220 That ech° of hem ful blisful° was and fawe°   *each / happy / fain, eager*
To bringe me gaye thinges fro the fayre.°   *fair*
They were ful glad whan I spak to hem fayre,°   *nicely*

8. An astronomical treatise.
9. Not to take amiss that (which) I say.
1. They could scarcely observe the statute (law).
2. And by my faith, I set no store by it.
3. It wasn't necessary that I be diligent any longer.
4. A prudent woman will exert herself constantly.

5. The bacon wasn't fetched for them I'm sure. (A side of bacon was awarded annually at Dunmow in Essex to couples who could claim they had not quarreled or been unhappy in their marriage that year.)

For God it woot, I chidde° hem spitously.°   chided, scolded / spitefully
  Now herkneth° how I bar me° proprely: listen / conducted myself
225 Ye wyse° wyves, that can understonde,   prudent
Thus shul ye speke and bere hem wrong on honde,°   put them in the wrong
For half so boldely can ther no man
Swere and lyen as a womman can.
I sey nat this by° wyves that ben wyse,
230 But it° it be whan they hem misavyse.°   Unless / act ill-advisedly
A wys wyf, if that she can hir good,
Shal beren him on hond the cow is wood,[6]
And take witnesse of° hir owene mayde   take as witness
Of° hir assent.° But herkneth° how I sayde: With / consent / listen
235   'Sire olde kaynard, is this thyn array?[7]
Why is my neighebores wyf so gay?°   gaily dressed
She is honoured over al ther° she goth:°   everywhere / goes
I sitte at hoom, I have no thrifty cloth.°   suitable clothing
What dostow° at my neighebores hous?   dost thou
240 Is she so fair?° artow° so amorous?   beautiful / art thou
What rowne° ye with oure mayde? benedicite!°   whisper / God bless us
Sire olde lechour, lat thy japes be!°   leave off thy pranks
And if I have a gossib° or a freend,   gossip, confidante
Withouten gilt, thou chydest as a feend,[8]
245 If that I walke or pleye unto his hous!
Thou comest hoom as dronken as a mous,°   mouse
And prechest on thy bench, with yvel preef![9]
Thou seist° to me, it is a greet meschief°   sayst / misfortune
To wedde a povre womman, for costage.°   because of expense
250 And if that she be riche, of heigh parage,°   parentage, blood
Thanne seistow° that it is a tormentrye°   sayst thou / torment
To suffre° hire pryde and hire malencolye.°   endure / melancholy, moodiness
And if that she be fair,° thou verray knave,°   pretty / true rascal
Thou seyst that every holour° wol hire have: lecher
255 She may no whyle in chastitee abyde°   abide, remain
That° is assailled upon ech a syde.°   Who / on every side
  Thou seyst som folk desyren us for richesse,°   (our) money
Somme for oure shap,° and somme for oure fairnesse,°   figure / beauty
And som for° she can outher° singe or daunce,   because / either
260 And som for gentillesse° and daliaunce,°   good breeding / flirtatiousness
Som for hir handes and hir armes smale;°   slender
Thus goth al to the devel, by thy tale.°   according to thy account
Thou seyst men may nat kepe° a castel-wal,   hold
It may so longe assailled been over al.°   everywhere

6. A prudent (skillful) wife, if she knows her (own) good, shall trick him into believing the chough is mad (refers to common stories—Chaucer's own Manciple's Tale is an example—in which a speaking bird tells tales to the husband of a wife's infidelity).
7. Old dotard, sir, is this how you dress me?
8. Without guilt (on our part), thou scoldest like a devil.
9. And preachest (sermons, sitting) on thy bench—bad luck to you!

265 And if that she be foul,° thou seist that she   *ugly*
    Coveiteth° every man that she may se;   *Desires*
    For as a spaynel° she wol on him lepe,   *spaniel*
    Til that she finde som man hire to chepe.°   *to buy her wares*
    Ne noon so grey goos goth ther in the lake[1]
270 As, seistow,° that wol been withoute make.°   *sayst thou / a mate*
    And seyst, it is an hard thing for to welde°   *control*
    A thing that no man wol, his thankes,° helde.°   *willingly / hold*
    Thus seistow, lorel,° whan thow goost to bedde,   *you wretch*
    And that no wys man nedeth for to wedde,
275 Ne no man that entendeth unto° hevene.   *aims to get to*
    With wilde thonder-dint° and firy levene°   *thunderclap / fiery lightning*
    Mote° thy welked° nekke be to-broke!°   *May / withered / broken*
        Thow seyst that dropping° houses and eek smoke   *leaking*
    And chyding wyves maken men to flee
280 Out of hir owene hous; a, *benedicite!*°   *God bless us*
    What eyleth° swich an old man for to chyde?   *ails*
    Thow seyst we wyves wol oure vyces° hyde   *vices*
    Til we be fast,° and thanne we wol hem shewe°—   *secure (married) / show*
    Wel may that be a proverbe of a shrewe!°   *(fit) for a villain*
285   Thou seist that oxen, asses, hors,° and houndes,   *horses*
    They been assayed° at diverse stoundes;°   *tested / various times*
    Bacins,° lavours,° er° that men hem bye,°   *Basins / washbowls / before / buy*
    Spones° and stoles,° and al swich
        housbondrye,°   *Spoons / stools / all such housewares*
    And so been pottes, clothes, and array;°   *ornament(s)*
290 But folk of wyves maken noon assay°   *test*
    Til they be wedded. Olde dotard shrewe!°   *wretched rascal*
    And thanne, seistow,° we wol oure vices shewe.   *sayst thou*
        Thou seist also that it displeseth me
    But if that° thou wolt preyse° my beautee,   *Unless / praise*
295 And but° thou poure° alwey upon my face,   *unless / gaze intently*
    And clepe° me "faire dame" in every place;   *call*
    And but thou make a feste° on thilke° day   *feast / that same*
    That I was born, and make me fresh and gay,
    And but thou do to my norice° honour,   *nurse*
300 And to my chamberere° withinne my bour,°   *chambermaid / bower, bedroom*
    And to my fadres folk° and his allyes°—   *relatives / connections*
    Thus seistow, olde barel ful of lyes!°   *lies (pun on lees)*
        And yet of oure apprentice Janekyn,
    For his crispe heer,° shyninge as gold so fyn,   *curly hair*
305 And for° he squiereth° me bothe up and doun,   *because / escorts*
    Yet hastow caught a fals suspicioun.[2]
    I wol hym noght,° thogh thou were deed to-morwe.   *I don't want him*

---

1. There swims in the lake no goose so gray.   2. I.e., become wrongly suspicious.

But tel me this, why hydestow, with sorwe,[3]
The keyes of thy cheste[4] awey fro me?
310 It is my good° as wel as thyn, pardee.°   property / by God
What, wenestow make an idiot of oure dame?[5]
Now by that lord that called is Seint Jame,°   St. James
Thou shalt nat bothe, thogh that thou were wood,°   mad (with rage)
Be maister of my body and of my good;°   goode, possessions
315 I hat oon thou shalt forgo, maugree thyne yën.[6]
What helpith thee of me to enquere° or spyën?   inquire
I trowe,° thou woldest loke° me in thy chiste!°   believe / lock / chest
Thou sholdest seye, "Wyf, go wher thee liste;°   it pleases thee
Tak your disport,° I wol nat leve no talis.°   pleasure / believe any tales
320 I knowe yow for a trewe wyf, dame Alis."°   Alice
We love no man that taketh kepe or charge°   takes heed or cares
Wher that we goon; we wol ben at oure large.°   liberty
    Of alle men y-blessed moot° he be,   may
The wyse astrologien° Daun Ptholome,°   astrologer / Lord Ptolemy
325 That seith this proverbe in his Almageste:
"Of alle men his wisdom is the hyeste,°   greatest
That rekketh° nevere who hath the world in honde."°   cares / in (his) control
By this proverbe thou shalt understonde,
Have thou y-nogh, what thar thee recche or care[7]
330 How merily that othere folkes fare?°   get along
For certeyn, olde dotard, by youre leve,°   leave
Ye shul have queyntc° right y-nough at eve.   sex, pudendum
He is to° greet a nigard that wol werne°   too / refuse
A man to lighte a candle at his lanterne;
335 He shal have never the lasse° light, pardee.   less
Have thou y-nough, thee thar nat pleyne thee.°   thou needst not complain
    Thou seyst also that if we make us gay
With clothing and with precious array,°   ornaments
That it is peril of° oure chastitee;   a danger of
340 And yet, with sorwe, thou most enforce thee,[8]
And seye thise wordes in th'Apostles° name: St. Paul
"In habit° maad with chastitee and shame,   garment(s)
Ye wommen shul apparaille yow,"° quod he,   dress yourselves
"And noght in tressed heer° and gay perree,°   braided hair / precious stones
345 As° perles, ne with gold, ne clothes riche."   Such as
After thy text, ne after thy rubriche
I wol nat wirche as muchel as a gnat.[9]

3. But tell me this, why dost thou hide (may you
have sorrow).
4. For storing valuables.
5. What, do you think to make an idiot of our
mistress? (She here uses a kind of royal plural: she
means herself.)
6. Thou shalt give up one (of them), despite thy
eyes (i.e., despite anything you can do).

7. As long as thou hast enough, what need for thee
to take heed or care.
8. And further—sorrow beset thee!—thou must
strengthen thyself (in the argument).
9. I will not behave according to thy text or thy
rubric (i.e., interpretation) as much as (would) a
gnat.

Thou seydest this, that I was lyk a cat:
For whoso wolde senge° a cattes skin,[1]   *singe*
350 Thanne wolde the cat wel dwellen in his in;°   *lodgings*
And if the cattes skin be slyk° and gay,   *sleek*
She wol nat dwelle in house half a day,
But forth she wole, er° any day be dawed,°   *before / has dawned*
To shewe hir skin and goon a-caterwawed.°   *caterwauling*
355 This is to seye, if I be gay, sire shrewe,°   *wretch*
I wol renne out,° my borel° for to shewe.   *run about / clothing*
    Sire olde fool, what helpeth thee to spyën?
Thogh thou preye° Argus, with his hundred yën,°   *beg / eyes*
To be my warde-cors,° as he can° best,   *bodyguard / knows how*
360 In feith, he shal nat kepe me but me lest;°   *unless I wish*
Yet coude I make his berd, so moot I thee.[2]
    Thou seydest eek that ther ben thinges three,
The whiche thinges troublen al this erthe,
And that no wight ne may endure the ferthe.°   *fourth*
365 O leve° sire shrewe, Jesu shorte° thy lyf!   *dear / may Jesus shorten*
Yet prechestow° and seyst an hateful wyf   *Still thou preachest*
Y-rekened° is for° oon of thise meschances.°   *Counted / as / misfortunes*
Been ther none othere maner° resemblances   *kind of*
That ye may lykne° youre parables to,   *liken*
370 But if° a sely° wyf be oon of tho?°   *Unless / innocent / those*
    Thou lykenest eek wommanes love to helle,
To bareyne° lond, ther° water may not dwelle;   *barren / where*
Thou lyknest it also to wilde fyr:[3]
The more it brenneth,° the more it hath desyr   *burns*
375 To consume every thing that brent wol be.°   *can be burned*
Thou seyst that right° as wormes shende° a tree,   *just / damage*
Right so a wyf destroyeth hire housbonde;
This knowe they that been to wyves bonde.'°   *bound*
    Lordinges, right thus, as ye have understonde,
380 Bar I stifly myne olde housbondes on honde[4]
That thus they seyden in hir dronkenesse;
And al was fals, but that° I took witnesse   *and yet*
On° Janekin and on my nece° also.   *From / niece*
O Lord, the peyne I dide° hem and the wo,   *suffering I caused*
385 Ful giltelees, by Goddes swete pyne!°   *suffering*
For as° an hors I coude byte° and whyne.°   *like / bite / whinny*
I coude pleyne,° thogh I were in the gilt,°   *complain / wrong*
Or elles° often tyme hadde I ben spilt.°   *otherwise / ruined*
Whoso that first to mille comth, first grint.°   *grinds (his grain)*
390 I pleyned first: so was oure werre° y-stint.°   *strife / concluded*

---

1. I.e., fur.
2. I could still trick him, as I hope to thrive.
3. "Greek fire," a highly inflammable compound

used in sea warfare.
4. I firmly got the better of my old husbands.

They were ful glad to excusen hem° ful blyve°   *themselves / quickly*
Of thing of which they nevere agilte° hir lyve.   *were guilty (in)*
Of wenches wolde I beren hem on honde,°   *accuse him (falsely)*
Whan that for syk° unnethes° mighte they stonde.   *illness / scarcely*
395   Yet tikled° I his herte, for that he   *tickled, pleased*
Wende° that I hadde of him so greet chiertee.°   *Thought / affection*
I swoor that al my walkinge out by nighte
Was for t'espye° wenches that he dighte.°   *to spy out / lay with*
Under that colour° hadde I many a mirthe,°   *pretense / merry time*
400 For al swich wit° is yeven° us in oure birthe.   *such cleverness / given*
Deceite, weping, spinning God hath yive°   *given*
To wommen kindely° whyl they may live.   *by nature*
And thus of o° thing I avaunte° me: *one / boast*
Atte° ende I hadde the bettre in ech degree,°   *At the / in every way*
405 By sleighte,° or force, or by som maner° thing,   *trick / kind of*
As by continuel murmur or grucching.°   *grumbling*
Namely abedde° hadden they meschaunce:°   *Especially in bed / misfortune*
Ther wolde I chyde° and do° hem no plesaunce;°   *scold / give / pleasure*
I wolde no lenger in the bed abyde,
410 If that I felte his arm over my syde,
Til he had maad his raunson° unto me;   *paid his ransom*
Thanne wolde I suffre° him do his nycetee.°   *endure, allow / foolishness, lust*
And therfore every man this tale I telle,
Winne whoso may, for al is for to selle.[5]
415 With empty hand men may none haukes° lure.   *hawks*
For winning° wolde I al his lust endure,   *profit*
And make me a feyned° appetyt—   *feigned*
And yet in bacon° hadde I nevere delyt.   *old meat (aged men)*
That made me that evere I wolde hem chyde.
420 For thogh the Pope hadde seten hem biside,°   *sat next to them*
I wolde nat spare hem at hir owene bord.°   *table*
For by my trouthe,° I quitte° hem word for word.   *troth / requited, paid back*
As° help me verray° God omnipotent,   *So / true*
Thogh I right now sholde make my testament,°   *will*
425 I ne owe hem nat a word that it nis quit.°   *is not paid back*
I broghte it so aboute, by my wit,°   *cleverness*
That they moste yeve it up,° as for the beste,   *give up*
Or elles° hadde we nevere been in reste.   *else*
For thogh he loked as a wood leoun,°   *like a mad lion*
430 Yet sholde he faille of his conclusioun.°   *fail in the end*
      Thanne wolde I seye, 'Godelief,° tak keep°   *Sweetheart / heed*
How mekely loketh Wilkin oure sheep!
Com neer, my spouse, lat me ba° thy cheke!   *kiss*
Ye sholde been al pacient and meke,

5. Profit whoever may, for all is for sale.

435 And han a swete spyced conscience,°   *sweetly seasoned disposition*
Sith° ye so preche of Jobes° pacience.   *Since / Job's*
Suffreth° alwey, sin° ye so wel can preche;   *Endure / since*
And but° ye do, certein we shal yow teche   *unless*
That it is fair° to have a wyf in pees.°   *good / peace*
440 Oon of us two moste bowen,° doutelees,   *bow (to the other's will)*
And sith° a man is more resonable   *since*
Than womman is, ye moste been suffrable.°   *patient*
What eyleth° yow to grucche° thus and grone?°   *ails / grumble / groan*
Is it for ye wolde have my queynte° allone?   *pudendum*
445 Why taak it al! lo, have it every-deel!°   *every bit of it*
Peter!° I shrewe° yow but ye love it weel!   *(By St.) Peter / curse*
For if I wolde° selle my *bele chose,*°   *wished to / pretty thing*
I coude walke as fresh as is a rose;
But I wol kepe it for your owene tooth.[6]
450 Ye be to blame. By God, I sey yow sooth.'°   *tell you the truth*
Swiche manere° wordes hadde we on honde.   *kind of*
Now wol I speken of my fourthe housbonde.

    My fourthe housebonde was a revelour°—   *reveler, rioter*
This is to seyn, he hadde a paramour°—   *mistress*
455 And I was yong and ful of ragerye,°   *wantonness, passion*
Stiborn° and strong, and joly as a pye.°   *Stubborn / magpie*
Wel coude I daunce to an harpe smale,
And singe, y-wis,° as any nightingale,   *truly*
Whan I had dronke a draughte of swete wyn.
460 Metellius, the foule cherl, the swyn,°   *swine*
That with a staf birafte° his wyf hir lyf   *bereft*
For she drank wyn, thogh° I hadde been his wyf,   *if*
He sholde nat han daunted° me fro drinke!   *frightened*
And after wyn on Venus moste° I thinke,   *must*
465 For al so siker° as cold engendreth° hayl,°   *surely / engenders / hail*
A likerous mouth moste han a likerous tayl.[7]
In wommen vinolent° is no defence°—   *full of wine / resistance*
This knowen lechours by experience.
    But, Lord Crist! whan that it remembreth me°   *I think*
470 Upon my yowthe, and on my jolitee,°   *gaiety*
It tikleth° me aboute myn herte rote.°   *tickles / heart's root*
Unto this day it dooth myn herte bote°   *good*
That I have had my world as in my tyme.
But age, allas! that al wol envenyme,°   *poison*
475 Hath me biraft° my beautee and my pith.°   *bereft of / vigor*
Lat go,° farewel! the devel go therwith!   *Let it go*
The flour is goon, ther is namore to telle:
The bren,° as I best can, now moste I selle;   *bran, husks*

6. I.e., your own sexual appetite.
7. A gluttonous mouth must have (i.e., necessarily implies) a lecherous tail.

But yet to be right mery wol I fonde.°   *try*
480 Now wol I tellen of my fourthe housbonde.
      I seye, I hadde in herte greet despyt°   *malice*
That he of any other° had delyt.   *other woman*
But he was quit,° by God and by Seint Joce!⁸   *repaid*
I made him of the same wode° a croce°—   *wood / cross*
485 Nat of my body in no foul° manere,   *unclean*
But certeinly, I made folk swich chere°   *such good cheer*
That in his owene grece° I made him frye   *grease*
For angre and for verray° jalousye.   *pure*
By God, in erthe° I was his purgatorie,   *on earth*
490 For which I hope his soule be in glorie.
For God it woot,° he sat ful ofte and song°   *knows / sang*
Whan that his shoo° ful bitterly him wrong.°   *shoe / hurt*
Ther was no wight,° save° God and he, that wiste°   *person / except / knew*
In many wyse° how sore° I him twiste.°   *ways / sorely / tormented*
495 He deyde whan I cam fro° Jerusalem,   *from (a pilgrimage to)*
And lyth y-grave under the rode-beem,⁹
Al° is his tombe noght so curious°   *Although / elaborate*
As was the sepulcre¹ of him Darius,
Which that Appelles wroghte subtilly;°   *made skillfully*
500 It nis but wast to burie him preciously.²
Lat him° farewel, God yeve his soule reste!   *May he*
He is now in the grave and in his cheste.°   *coffin*
      Now of my fifthe housbond wol I telle—
God lete his soule nevere come in helle!
505 And yet was he to me the moste shrewe.°   *worst rascal*
That fele° I on my ribbes al by rewe,°   *feel / in a row*
And evere shal unto myn ending-day.³
But in oure bed he was so fresh and gay,
And therwithal so wel coude he me glose°   *cajole, flatter*
510 Whan that he wolde han my *bele chose*,°   *pretty thing*
That thogh he hadde me bet° on every boon,°   *beaten / bone*
He coude winne agayn my love anoon.°   *at once*
I trowe° I loved him beste for that he   *believe*
Was of his love daungerous° to me.   *standoffish, grudging*
515 We wommen han, if that I shal nat lye,
In this matere a queynte fantasye:°   *an odd fancy*
Wayte what° thing we may nat lightly have,   *Whatever*
Therafter wol we crye al day and crave.
Forbede us thing,° and that desyren we;   *something*
520 Prees on° us faste,° and thanne wol we flee.   *Crowd, pursue / hard*

8. A Breton saint.   2. It is (i.e., would have been) nothing but a waste
9. And lies buried under the rood-beam (a timber   to bury him expensively.
separating the nave from the chancel in a church). 3. I.e., dying day.
1. A very famous tomb.

With daunger° oute° we al oure chaffare:°   *haughtiness / set out / wares*
Greet prees° at market maketh dere° ware,   *press, crowd / expensive*
And to° greet cheep° is holde at litel prys.°   *too / a bargain / worth*
This knoweth every womman that is wys.
525   My fifthe housbonde, God his soule blesse!
Which that I took for love and no richesse,
He som tyme° was a clerk° of Oxenford,°   *once / scholar / Oxford*
And had left scole, and wente at hoom to bord°   *to board at home*
With my gossib,° dwellinge in oure toun—   *gossip, intimate friend*
530   God have hir soule! hir name was Alisoun.
She knew myn herte and eek° my privetee°   *also / secrets*
Bet° than oure parisshe preest, so moot I thee!°   *Better / as I may thrive*
To hire biwreyed° I my conseil° al,   *disclosed / thoughts*
For had myn housebonde pissed on a wal,
535   Or doon a thing that sholde han cost his lyf,
To hire and to another worthy wyf,
And to my nece,° which that I loved weel,   *niece*
I wolde han told his conseil° every deel.°   *secrets / (in) every detail*
And so I dide ful often, God it woot,°   *knows*
540   That made his face ful often reed and hoot
For verray° shame, and blamed himself for° he   *pure / because*
Had told to me so greet a privetee.°   *secret*
    And so bifel° that ones° in a Lente°—   *it happened / once / at Lent*
So often tymes I to my gossib wente,
545   For evere yet I lovede to be gay,
And for to walke in March, Averille,° and May,   *April*
Fro hous to hous, to here° sondry talis°—   *hear / various tales*
That Jankin clerk° and my gossib dame Alis   *Jankin (the) clerk*
And I myself into the feldes° wente.   *fields*
550   Myn housbond was at London al that Lente:
I hadde the bettre leyser° for to pleye,   *leisure, opportunity*
And for to see, and eek° for to be seye°   *also / seen*
Of lusty folk. What wiste I wher my grace
Was shapen for to be, or in what place?[4]
555   Therefore I made my visitaciouns,°   *visits*
To vigilies and to processiouns,[5]
To preching eek and to thise pilgrimages,
To pleyes° of miracles, and mariages,   *(stage-)plays*
And wered upon° my gaye scarlet gytes.°   *wore / gowns*
560   Thise wormes, ne thise motthes,° ne thise mytes,°   *moths / mites*
Upon my peril, frete hem never a deel;[6]
And wostow° why? for° they were used weel.   *knowest thou / because*
    Now wol I tellen forth what happed° me.   *befell*

---

4. By pleasure-loving folk. How could I know where grace was destined to befall me, or in what place?
5. "Vigilies": vigils (services on the eve of a feast day); "processiouns": ceremonial processions within a church service.
6. On peril (of my soul), ate into them not at all.

I seye that in the feeldes walked we,
565 Til trewely we hadde swich daliance,[7]
This clerk and I, that of my purveyance°   *by my foresight*
I spak to him and seyde him how that he,
If I were widwe,° sholde wedde me.   *a widow*
For certeinly, I sey for no bobance,°   *not as a boast*
570 Yet was I nevere withouten purveyance°   *(future) ...*
Of° mariage, n'of° othere thinges eek.   *Concerning / nor concerning*
I holde a mouses herte nat worth a leek°   *leek, onion*
That hath but oon hole for to sterte° to,   *run*
And if that faille,° thanne is al y-do.°   *fails / done for*
575 I bar him on honde° he hadde enchanted me—   *made him believe*
My dame° taughte me that soutiltee°—   *mother / subtlety, trick*
And eek I seyde I mette° of him al night: *dreamed*
He wolde han slayn° me as I lay up-right,°   *wanted to slay / face-up*
And al my bed was ful of verray° blood;   *real*
580 But yet I hope that he shal do me good,
For blood bitokeneth gold, as me was taught.
And al was fals—I dremed of it right naught,
But as° I folwed ay° my dames lore°   *But / ever / teaching*
As wel of° this as of othere thinges more.   *concerning*
585 But now sire, lat me see, what I shal seyn?
Aha! by God, I have my tale ageyn.
Whan that my fourthe housbond was on bere,°   *(his) bier*
I weep algate, and made sory chere[8]
As wyves moten,° for it is usage,°   *must / the custom*
590 And with my coverchief° covered my visage;°   *kerchief / face*
But for that° I was purveyed of° a make,°   *because / provided with / mate*
I wepte but smal,° and that I undertake.°   *little / declare*
To chirche was myn housbond born° a-morwe°   *borne / in the morning*
With° neighebores, that for him maden sorwe;   *By*
595 And Jankin oure clerk was oon of tho.°   *them*
As° help me God! whan that I saugh° him go°   *So / saw / walk*
After the bere, me thoughte he hadde a paire
Of legges and of feet so clene° and faire,   *neat*
That al myn herte I yaf° unto his hold.°   *gave / possession*
600 He was, I trowe,° twenty winter old,   *believe*
And I was fourty, if I shal seye sooth;°   *tell the truth*
But yet I hadde alwey a coltes tooth.[9]
Gat-tothed I was, and that bicam me weel;[1]
I hadde the prente of Seynte Venus seel.[2]

---

7. I.e., were getting along so well.
8. I wept, of course, and put on a sad look.
9. I.e., youthful appetites.
1. I was gap-toothed, and that suited me well. (In medieval handbooks of physiognomy, gap teeth are said to indicate a bold and lascivious nature.)
2. I had the print of St. Venus's seal—i.e., Venus had given me a birthmark (again indicative of amorousness).

605 As help me God, I was a lusty° oon,   *vigorous*
   And faire, and riche, and yong, and wel bigoon;°   *well-off*
   And trewely, as myne housbondes tolde me,
   I had the beste *quoniam*[3] mighte be.
   For certes, I am al Venerien
610 In felinge, and myn herte is Marcien:[4]
   Venus me yaf° my lust, my likerousnesse,°   *gave / lecherousness*
   And Mars yaf me my sturdy hardinesse;°   *boldness*
   Myn ascendent was Taur, and Mars therinne.[5]
   Allas! allas! that evere love was sinne!
615 I folwed ay° myn inclinacioun   *ever*
   By vertu of my constellacioun;[6]
   That made me I coude noght withdrawe°   *withhold*
   My chambre of Venus from a good felawe.°   *companion*
   Yet have I Martes° mark upon my face,   *Mars's*
620 And also in another privee° place.   *secret*
   For, God so wis be my savacioun,°   *salvation*
   I ne loved nevere by no discrecioun,°   *with any wisdom*
   But evere folwede myn appetyt:
   Al° were he short or long,° or blak or whyt,   *Whether / tall*
625 I took no kepe, so that he lyked me,[7]
   How pore he was, ne eek° of what degree.°   *nor / social rank*
       What sholde I seye but, at the monthes ende,
   This joly clerk Jankin, that was so hende,°   *pleasant*
   Hath wedded me with greet solempnitee,°   *ceremony*
630 And to him yaf° I al the lond° and fee°   *gave / land / property*
   That evere was me yeven° therbifore.   *given (by earlier husbands)*
   But afterward repented me° ful sore;°   *I regretted it / deeply*
   He nolde suffre nothing of my list.[8]
   By God, he smoot° me ones° on the list°   *hit / once / ear*
635 For that° I rente° out of his book a leef,°   *Because / tore / leaf, page*
   That of the strook myn ere wex al deef.[9]
   Stiborn° I was as is a leonesse,°   *Stubborn / lionness*
   And of my tonge a verray jangleresse,°   *real ranter*
   And walke I wolde, as I had doon biforn,
640 From hous to hous, although he had it sworn.[1]
   For which he often tymes wolde preche,
   And me of° olde Romayn gestes° teche,   *from / Roman stories*
   How he Simplicius Gallus lefte his wyf,
   And hire forsook for terme° of al his lyf,   *the duration*
645 Noght but for open-heveded he hir say[2]

---

3. I.e., pudendum.
4. "Venerien": under the influence of the planet Venus; "Marcien": under the influence of the planet Mars. Together they determine her appetites for love and marital strife.
5. (When I was born) the sign of Taurus was ascendant, and Mars was in it.

6. Through the influence of my horoscope (the planets reigning over my birth).
7. I took no heed, as long as he was pleasing to me.
8. He wouldn't allow (me) anything I wanted.
9. So that from the blow my ear grew wholly deaf.
1. I.e., he had sworn I shouldn't.
2. Only because he saw her bareheaded.

Lokinge out at his dore upon a day.
   Another Romayn tolde he me by name,
That, for° his wyf was at a someres game°   *because / summer's revel*
Withoute his witing,° he forsook hire eke.°   *knowledge / also*
650 And thanne wolde he upon° his Bible seke   *in*
That ilke° proverbe of Ecclesiaste°   *same / Ecclesiasticus*
Wher he comandeth and forbedeth faste°   *firmly*
Man shal nat suffre° his wyf go roule° aboute;   *allow / to go roaming*
Thanne wolde he seye right thus, withouten doute:
655 'Whoso that° buildeth his hous al of salwes,°   *Whoever / willow twigs*
And priketh° his blinde hors over the falwes,°   *spurs / fallow (ploughed) land*
And suffreth° his wyf to go seken halwes,°   *allows / shrines*
Is worthy to been hanged on the galwes!'°   *gallows*
But al for noght; I sette noght an hawe°   *haw (hawthorn berry)*
660 Of his proverbes n'of his olde sawe,°   *saw, proverb*
Ne I wolde nat of° him corrected be.   *by*
I hate him that° my vices telleth me,   *the one who*
And so do mo,° God woot,° of us than I.   *more / knows*
This made him with me wood° al outrely:°   *mad / completely*
665 I nolde noght forbere him in no cas.[3]
    Now wol I seye yow sooth,° by Seint Thomas,   *tell you the truth*
Why that I rente° out of his book a leef,°   *tore / leaf*
For which he smoot° me so that I was deef.   *struck*
He hadde a book that gladly, night and day,
670 For his desport° he wolde rede alway.   *amusement*
He cleped it Valerie and Theofraste,[4]
At which book he lough° alwey ful faste.°   *laughed / strongly*
And eek ther was somtyme° a clerk° at Rome,   *once / scholar*
A cardinal, that highte° Seint Jerome,   *was called*
675 That made a book agayn Jovinian;
In which book eek ther was Tertulan,
Crisippus, Trotula, and Helowys,[5]
That was abbesse nat fer fro Parys;°   *Paris*
And eek the Parables° of Salomon,   *Proverbs*
680 Ovydes Art,° and bokes many on,°   *Ovid's Art (of Love) / a one*
And alle thise were bounden in o° volume.   *one*
And every night and day was his custume,
Whan he hadde leyser° and vacacioun°   *leisure / free time*
From other worldly occupacioun,
685 To reden on this book of wikked° wyves.   *wicked*
He knew of hem mo° legendes and lyves   *more*

3. I wouldn't give way to him on any occasion.
4. Jankyn's "book of wikked wyves" includes several antifeminist works: Walter Map's *Letter of Valerius*, Theophrastus's *On Marriage*; and St. Jerome's *Against Jovinian*; they quote other authorities in turn (Tertullian, Chrysippus, etc.). For these texts, see the Sources and Backgrounds section on the *Wife*

of Bath's Tale.
5. "Trotula": the supposed woman-author of a well-known medieval treatise on the diseases of women; "Helowys": Eloise, who loved the great scholar Abelard, but argued in her letters against marrying him; she later became a nun and abbess.

Than been° of gode wyves in the Bible.   *there are*
For trusteth wel, it is an impossible°   *impossibility*
That any clerk wol speke good of wyves,
690 But if° it be of holy seintes lyves,   *Unless*
Ne of noon other womman never the mo.°   *in any way*
Who peyntede the leoun, tel me, who?[6]
By God, if wommen hadde writen stories,
As clerkes han withinne hir oratories,°   *chapels, studies*
695 They wolde han writen of men more wikkednesse
Than all the mark° of Adam may redresse.   *sex*
The children[7] of Mercurie and of Venus
Been in hir wirking° ful contrarious:°   *actions / contrary*
Mercurie loveth wisdom and science,°   *knowledge*
700 And Venus loveth ryot° and dispence;°   *revelry / spending*
And, for° hire diverse disposicioun,   *because of*
Ech° falleth in otheres exaltacioun,°   *Each / moment of highest ascent*
And thus, God woot, Mercurie is desolat°   *without influence*
In Pisces wher Venus is exaltat,°   *in her greatest influence*
705 And Venus falleth ther° Mercurie is reysed;°   *there where / has risen*
Therfore no womman of° no clerk is preysed.   *by*
The clerk, whan he is old, and may noght do
Of Venus werkes worth° his olde sho°—   *to the value of / shoe*
Thanne sit he doun and writ in his dotage
710 That wommen can nat kepe[8] hir mariage!
   But now to purpos why I tolde thee
That I was beten° for a book, pardee.°   *beaten / by God*
Upon a night Jankin, that was our syre,°   *lord, husband*
Redde on his book as he sat by the fyre
715 Of Eva° first, that for hir wikkednesse   *Eve*
Was al mankinde broght to wrecchednesse,
For which that Jesu Crist himself was slayn,
That boghte us with his herteblood agayn.
Lo, here expres° of womman may ye finde   *specifically*
720 That womman was the los° of all mankinde.   *destruction*
   Tho° redde he me how Sampson loste his heres:°   *Then / hair(s)*
Slepinge, his lemman° kitte° hem° with hir sheres,   *lover / cut / it (them)*
Thurgh whiche tresoun loste he bothe his yën.°   *eyes*
   Tho° redde he me, if that I shal nat lyen,   *Then*
725 Of Hercules and of his Dianyre,°   *Deianira*
That caused him to sette himself afyre.°   *on fire*
   Nothing forgat he the sorwe and the wo
That Socrates had with hise wyves two—

---

6. In the *Fables* of Avianus, a man and a lion come upon a sculpture (here spoken of as a painting) in which a lion bows in submission before a man; the lion suggests that if such a work were made by a creature of his race, it would show the man being eaten by the lion.
7. Those born under the sign.
8. I.e., be faithful in.

How Xantippa caste pisse upon his heed:
730 This sely° man sat stille, as° he were deed;   *poor / as if*
He wyped his heed; namore dorste° he seyn   *dared*
But 'Er° that thonder stinte,° comth a reyn.'°   *Before / ceases / rain, shower*
    Of Phasipha⁹ that was the quene of Crete—
For shrewednesse° him thoughte the tale swete—   *Out of cursedness*
735 Fy! spek namore, it is a grisly thing
    Of hire horrible lust and hir lyking.°   *desire*
    Of Clitermistra,¹ for hire lecherye,
That falsly made hire housbond for to dye,
He redde it with ful good devocioun.
740 He tolde me eek for what occasioun
Amphiorax² at Thebes loste his lyf.
Myn housbond hadde a legende of his wyf,
Eriphilem, that° for an ouche° of gold   *Eryphile, who / brooch*
Hath prively° unto the Grekes told   *secretly*
745 Wher that hir housbonde hidde him in a place,
For which he hadde at Thebes sory grace.°   *ill fortune*
    Of Lyvia tolde he me, and of Lucye.³
They bothe made hir housbondes for to dye,
That oon for love, that other was for hate.
750 Lyvia hir housbond, on an even° late,   *evening*
Empoysoned° hath, for that she was his fo.°   *Poisoned / foe*
Lucya, likerous,° loved hire housbond so,   *lecherous*
That, for° he sholde alwey upon hire thinke,   *so that*
She yaf° him swich a manere° love-drinke,   *gave / such a kind of*
755 That he was deed er° it were by the morwe;°   *before / morning*
And thus algates° housbondes han sorwe.   *in every way*
    Thanne tolde he me how oon Latumius
Compleyned unto his felawe° Arrius,   *companion*
That in his gardin growed swich a° tree   *a certain*
760 On which he seyde how that his wyves three
Hanged hemself° for herte despitous.°   *themselves / spiteful*
'O leve° brother,' quod this Arrius,   *dear*
'Yif° me a plante° of thilke° blissed tree,   *Give / slip / that same*
And in my gardin planted shal it be!'
765 Of latter date, of wyves hath he red
That somme han slayn hir housbondes in hir bed,
And lete hir lechour° dighte° hire al the night   *lecher, lover / lie with*
Whyl that the corps lay in° the floor up-right.°   *on / face-up*
And somme han drive° nayles° in hir brayn°   *driven / nails / brain*

---

9. Pasiphaë, who loved a bull and gave birth to the Minotaur.
1. Clytemnestra, who murdered her husband Agamemnon, in order to keep Aegisthus her lover.
2. Amphiaraus, a soothsayer who prophesied his own death if he fought at Thebes; he was persuaded into battle by his wife.
3. Livia poisoned her husband, Drusus, at Sejanus's instigation; Lucilia, wife to the poet Lucretius, poisoned him with a love potion meant to increase his amorousness.

770 Whyl that they slepte, and thus they han hem slayn.
Somme han hem yeve° poysoun in hire drinke.   *given*
He spak more harm than herte may bithinke,°   *imagine*
And therwithal° he knew of mo° proverbes   *in addition / more*
Than in this world ther growen gras or herbes.°   *plants*
775 'Bet is,'° quod he, 'thyn habitacioun   *Better it is (that)*
Be with a leoun or a foul dragoun,
Than with a womman usinge for° to chyde.   *accustomed*
Bet is,' quod he, 'hye in° the roof abyde°   *high on / to stay*
Than with an angry wyf doun in the hous;
780 They been so wikked and contrarious°   *contradictory*
They haten that° hir housbondes loveth ay.'°   *what / ever*
He seyde, 'A womman cast° hir shame away,   *casts*
Whan she cast of° hir smok;'° and forthermo,°   *off / smock, underdress / furthermore*
'A fair° womman, but° she be chaast also,   *beautiful / unless*
785 Is lyk a gold ring in a sowes° nose.'   *sow's*
Who wolde wene,° or who wolde suppose°   *think / imagine*
The wo that in myn herte was, and pyne?°   *suffering*
    And whan I saugh° he wolde nevere fyne°   *saw / finish*
To reden on this cursed book al night,
790 Al sodeynly° three leves° have I plight°   *suddenly / pages / plucked*
Out of his book, right° as he radde,° and eke°   *just / read / also*
I with my fist so took° him on the cheke   *hit*
That in oure fyr he fil° bakward adoun.   *fell*
And he upstirte° as dooth a wood leoun,°   *jumped up / mad lion*
795 And with his fist he smoot° me on the heed   *struck*
That in° the floor I lay as° I were deed.   *(So) that on / as if*
And when he saugh° how stille that I lay,   *saw*
He was agast,° and wolde han fled his way,   *frightened*
Til atte laste out of my swogh° I breyde:°   *swoon, faint / started up*
800 'O! hastow° slayn me, false theef?'° I seyde,   *hast thou / criminal*
'And for my land thus hastow mordred° me?   *murdered*
Er° I be deed, yet wol I kisse thee.'   *Before*
    And neer he cam, and kneled faire° adoun,   *courteously*
And seyde, 'Dere suster Alisoun,
805 As° help me God, I shall thee nevere smyte;°   *So / strike*
That I have doon, it is thyself to wyte.[4]
Foryeve° it me, and that I thee biseke'°—   *Forgive / beseech*
And yet eftsones° I hitte him on the cheke   *again*
And seyde, 'Theef! thus muchel° am I wreke.°   *much / avenged*
810 Now wol I dye: I may no lenger speke.'
But atte laste, with muchel care and wo,
We fille acorded° by us selven two.   *came to an agreement*
He yaf me al° the brydel° in myn hond,   *completely / bridle*

---

4. For what I've done, it's thyself (who is) to blame.

To han the governance° of hous and lond,   *direction*
815 And of his tonge and of his hond also;
And made him brenne his book anon right tho.⁵
And whan that I hadde geten unto me,°   *gotten for myself*
By maistrie,° al the soveraynetee,°   *mastery / supremacy, sovereignty*
And that he seyde, 'Myn owene trewe wyf,
820 Do as thee lust° the terme° of al thy lyf;   *please / (to the) end*
Keep thyn honour, and keep eek myn estaat'°—   *Preserve / public position*
After that day we hadden never debaat.°   *contention*
God help me so, I was to him as kinde
As any wyf from Denmark unto Inde,°   *India*
825 And also° trewe, and so was he to me.   *equally as*
I prey to God that sit° in magestee,°   *who sits / majesty*
So blesse his soule for his° mercy dere!   *by his*
Now wol I seye my tale, if ye wol here."

Biholde the wordes bitween the Somonour and the Frere.

The Frere° lough° whan he hadde herd al this.   *Friar / laughed*
830 "Now, dame," quod° he, "so have I° joye or blis,   *said / as I may have*
This is a long preamble of⁶ a tale!"
And whan the Somnour herde the Frere gale,°   *exclaim aloud*
"Lo,"° quod the Somnour, "Goddes armes two,°   *Behold / by God's two arms*
A frere wol entremette hiim° everemo!   *intrude himself*
835 Lo, gode men, a flye and eek a frere
Wol falle in every dish and eek matere.°   *subject*
What spekestow° of preambulacioun?°   *Why speakest thou / preambling*
What!° amble, or trotte, or [pace,]° or go sit doun!   *Lo / walk*
Thou lettest° oure disport° in this manere."   *hinderest / pleasure*
840 "Ye, woltow so,° sire Somnour?" quod the Frere;   *wouldst thou (have it) so*
"Now by my feith, I shal, er that I go,
Telle of a somnour swich° a tale or two   *such*
That alle the folk shal laughen in this place."
"Now elles,° Frere, I wol bishrewe° thy face,"   *otherwise / curse*
845 Quod this Somnour, "and I bishrewe me
But if° I telle tales two or thre   *Unless*
Of freres, er I come to Sidingborne,⁷
That° I shal make thyn herte for to morne°—   *So that / mourn*
For wel I woot° thy pacience is goon."   *know*
850 Oure Hoste cryde "Pees!° and that anoon!"°   *Peace / at once*
And seyde, "Lat the womman telle hire tale.
Ye fare° as folk that dronken been of ale.   *act*
Do, dame, tel forth youre tale, and that is best."
"Al redy, sire," quod she, "right as yow lest,⁸

5. And (I) made him burn his book then at once.   way to Canterbury.
6. I.e., introduction to.   8. "(I am) all ready, sir," she said, "just as you
7. Sittingbourne, a town roughly two-thirds of the wish."

855 If I have licence° of this worthy Frere."   *the permission*
     "Yis, dame," quod he, "tel forth, and I wol here."°   *listen*

The Tale

In th'olde dayes of the King Arthour,
Of which that Britons speken greet honour,
All was this land fulfild of fayerye.°   *filled with fairy people*
860 The elf-queen with hir joly companye
Daunced ful ofte in many a grene mede.°   *meadow*
This was the olde opinion, as I rede—
I speke of manye hundred yeres ago—
But now can no man see none elves mo.°   *more*
865 For now the grete charitee and prayeres
Of limitours[9] and othere holy freres,
That serchen° every lond and every streem,   *visit*
As thikke° as motes in the sonne-beem,°   *thick / sunbeam*
Blessinge halles, chambres, kichenes, boures,°   *bowers, sleeping rooms*
870 Citees, burghes,° castels, hye toures,°   *towns / high towers*
Thropes, bernes, shipnes, dayeryes[1]—
This maketh° that ther been no fayeryes.   *is the cause*
For ther as wont to walken was an elf,[2]
Ther walketh now the limitour himself
875 In undermeles° and in morweninges,°   *afternoons / mornings*
And seyth his Matins° and his holy thinges   *morning service*
As he goth in his limitacioun.[3]
Wommen may go now saufly° up and doun: *safely*
In every bush or under every tree[4]
880 Ther is noon other incubus[5] but he,
And he ne wol doon hem but dishonour.[6]

And so bifel° that this King Arthour   *it happened*
Hadde in his hous a lusty bacheler,°   *young knight*
That on a day cam rydinge fro river;[7]
885 And happed that, allone as he was born,
He saugh° a mayde walkinge him biforn,   *saw*
Of whiche mayde anon, maugree hir heed,[8]
By verray force° he rafte° hire maydenheed.   *force itself / took*
For which oppressioun° was swich° clamour   *wrong / such*
890 And swich pursute° unto the King Arthour,   *suing (for justice)*
That dampned° was this knight for to be deed   *condemned*

9. Friars given exclusive rights by license to beg within a certain area, or "limits."
1. Villages, barns, sheds, dairies.
2. For there where an elf was accustomed to walk.
3. Licensed begging area.
4. Places popularly thought to be haunted by fairies.
5. An evil spirit supposed to lie upon women in their sleep and have intercourse with them.
6. Shame, dishonor; as opposed to the begetting of devils upon them.
7. From hawking; riverbanks were favorite places for the sport.
8. (And) from this maid at once, in spite of anything she could do.

By cours of lawe, and sholde han° lost his heed—   *was to have*
Paraventure° swich was the statut° tho°—   *By chance / statute, law / then*
But that° the quene and othere ladies mo°   *Except / besides*
895 So longe preyeden° the king of° grace   *begged / for*
Til he his lyf him graunted in the place,
And yaf° him to the quene al at hir wille,   *gave*
To chese whether she wolde him save or spille °   *destroy*
   The quene thanketh the king with al hir might,
900 And after this thus spak she to the knight
Whan that she saugh hir tyme, upon a day:
"Thou standest yet," quod she, "in swich array°   *such a condition*
That of thy lyf yet hastow° no suretee.°   *hast thou / security, guarantee*
I grante thee lyf, if thou canst tellen me
905 What thing is it that wommen most desyren.
Be war, and keep thy nekke-boon from yren.⁹
And if thou canst nat tellen it anon,°   *right away*
Yet wol I yeve° thee leve° for to gon   *give / leave*
A twelf-month and a day, to seche° and lere°   *seek out / learn*
910 An answere suffisant° in this matere.°   *sufficient / subject*
And suretee° wol I han, er that thou pace,°   *a pledge, security / walk off*
Thy body for to yelden° in this place."   *yield up, return*
   Wo° was this knight and sorwefully he syketh.°   *Woeful / sighs*
But what! he may nat do al as him lyketh,¹
915 And at the laste he chees him for to wende,°   *decided to go off*
And come agayn, right° at the yeres ende,   *exactly*
With swich answere as God wolde him purveye;°   *provide for him*
And taketh his leve and wendeth forth his weye.
   He seketh every hous and every place
920 Wheras° he hopeth for to finde grace,°   *Where / good fortune*
To lerne what thing wommen loven most;
But he ne coude arryven in no cost°   *coast, country*
Wheras he mighte finde in this matere°   *subject*
Two creatures accordinge in-fere.°   *agreeing together*
925   Somme seyde wommen loven best richesse,
Somme seyde honour, somme seyde jolynesse;
Somme riche array,° somme seyden lust abedde,°   *adornment / pleasure in bed*
And ofte tyme to be widwe° and wedde.°   *widowed / (re-)married*
   Somme seyde that oure hertes been most esed
930 Whan that we been y-flatered and y-plesed.
He gooth ful ny the sothe,° I wol nat lye: *very near the truth*
A man shal winne us best with flaterye;
And with attendance° and with bisinesse°   *attention / diligence*
Been we y-lymed, bothe more and lesse.²

9. Be wary, and keep thy neck from the ax (*lit.*,   2. We are ensnared (caught, as with birdlime), both
iron).   great and small.
1. But lo! he cannot do everything just as he pleases.

935   And somme seyn how that we loven best
For to be free and do right as us lest,°   *just as we please*
And that no man repreve us of° oure vyce,   *reproach us for*
But seye that we be wyse, and no thing nyce.°   *not at all foolish*
For trewely, ther is noon of us alle,
940 If any wight wol clawe° us on the galle,°   *scratch / sore spot*
That we nil kike for he seith us sooth:³
Assay,° and he shal finde it that so dooth.   *Try*
For be we never so vicious withinne,
We wol been holden° wyse, and clene of sinne.   *wish to be considered*
945   And somme seyn that greet delyt han we
For to ben holden stable° and eek secree,°   *steadfast / discreet*
And in o° purpos stedefastly to dwelle,   *one*
And nat biwreye° thing that men us telle—   *reveal*
But that tale is nat worth a rake-stele.°   *rake handle*
950 Pardee, we wommen conne no-thing hele:⁴
Witnesse on Myda°—wol ye here the tale?   *Midas*
    Ovyde,° amonges othere thinges smale,   *Ovid*
Seyde Myda hadde under his longe heres,°   *hair*
Growinge upon his heed two asses eres,°   *ears*
955 The whiche vyce° he hidde as he best mighte°   *deformity / could*
Ful subtilly° from every mannes sighte,   *cleverly*
That, save his wyf, ther wiste of it namo.⁵
He loved hire most, and trusted hire also;
He preyede° hire that to no creature   *begged*
960 She sholde tellen of his disfigure.°   *disfigurement*
    She swoor him nay, for al this world to winne,
She nolde° do that vileinye° or sinne,   *would not / bad deed*
To make hir housbond han so foul a name.
She nolde nat telle it for⁶ hir owene shame.
965 But nathelees, hir thoughte that she dyde⁷
That° she so longe sholde a conseil° hyde.   *If / secret*
Hir thoughte it swal° so sore° aboute hir herte   *swelled / painfully*
That nedely som word hire moste asterte,⁸
And sith° she dorste° telle it to no man,   *since / dared*
970 Doun to a mareys° faste by° she ran.   *marsh / close by*
Til she came there hir herte was a-fyre,°   *on fire*
And as a bitore bombleth in the myre,⁹
She leyde° hir mouth unto the water doun: *laid*
"Biwreye° me nat, thou water, with thy soun,"°   *Betray / sound*
975 Quod she, "to thee I telle it, and namo;°   *no one else*

3. Who will not kick back, because he tells us the truth. (The metaphor is of horses.)
4. By heaven, we women don't know how to conceal anything.
5. So that no one else knew about it except his wife.
6. I.e., to spare.

7. But nonetheless, it seemed to her that she would die.
8. That of necessity some word must burst out of her.
9. And as a bittern (a marsh bird) booms in the mire.

Myn housbond hath longe asses eres° two!   *ears*
Now is myn herte all hool,° now is it oute.   *whole (again)*
I mighte no lenger kepe it, out of doute."
Heer° may ye se, thogh we a tyme abyde,°   *Here / wait for a time*
980 Yet out it moot,° we can no conseil° hyde.   *must / secret*
The remenant of the tale[1] if ye wol here,
Redeth Ovyde,° and ther ye may it lere[°]   *Read Ovid / learn*
   This knight of which my tale is specially,
Whan that he saugh he mighte nat come therby,[2]
985 This is to seye, what wommen loven moost,
Withinne his brest ful sorweful was the goost,°   *spirit*
But hoom he gooth, he mighte nat sojourne.°   *linger*
The day was come that hoomward moste° he tourne,   *must*
And in his wey it happed him to ryde
990 In al this care under a forest-syde,°   *on the edge of a forest*
Wheras he saugh° upon a daunce go°   *saw / moving in a dance*
Of ladies foure and twenty and yet mo;
Toward the whiche daunce he drow° ful yerne,°   *drew / eagerly*
In hope that som wisdom sholde he lerne.
995 But certeinly, er° he came fully there,   *before*
Vanisshed was this daunce, he niste° where.   *knew not*
No creature saugh he that bar° lyf,   *bore*
Save on the grene° he saugh sittinge a wyf°—   *grass / woman*
A fouler wight° ther may no man devyse.°   *An uglier being / imagine*
1000 Agayn[3] the knight this olde wyf gan ryse,°   *rose up*
And seyde, "Sire knight, heerforth° ne lyth no wey.   *through here*
Tel me what that ye seken,° by youre fey!°   *seek / faith*
Paraventure° it may the bettre be: *By chance*
Thise olde folk can muchel thing," quod she.[4]
1005 "My leve° mooder," quod this knight, "certeyn°   *dear / certainly*
I nam but deed, but if that I can seyn[5]
What thing it is that wommen most desyre.
Coude ye me wisse,° I wolde wel quyte your hyre."°   *inform / repay your trouble*
   "Plighte° me thy trouthe,° heer in myn hand," quod she,   *Pledge / promise*
1010 "The nexte thing that I requere° thee,   *request of*
Thou shalt it do, if it lye in thy might,°   *power*
And I wol telle it yow er it be night."
   "Have heer my trouthe,"° quod the knight, "I grante."°   *pledge / grant (it)*
   "Thanne," quod she, "I dar me wel avante°   *dare well boast*
1015 Thy lyf is sauf,° for I wol stonde therby.   *safe*
Upon my lyf, the queen wol seye as I.
Lat see which is the proudeste of hem alle,

---

1. In Ovid's conclusion—his version differs in several ways from the Wife of Bath's—the marsh reeds whisper the secret aloud whenever the wind blows.
2. I.e., learn the answer.
3. I.e., to meet.
4. "These old folk (i.e., *we* old folk) know many things," said she.
5. I'm as good as dead, unless I can say.

That wereth° on a coverchief° or a calle,°   *wears / kerchief / hairnet*
That dar° seye nay of that° I shal thee teche.   *dares to / to that which*
1020 Lat us go forth withouten lenger speche."
Tho rouned° she a pistel° in his ere,°   *Then whispered / message / ear*
And bad him to be glad and have no fere.
    Whan they be comen to the court, this knight
Seyde he had holde° his day, as he hadde hight,°   *kept to / promised*
1025 And redy was his answere, as he sayde.
Ful many a noble wyf, and many a mayde,
And many a widwe°—for that° they ben wyse—   *widow / because*
The quene hirself sittinge as a justyse,°   *judge*
Assembled been, his answere for to here;
1030 And afterward this knight was bode appere.°   *bidden to appear*
    To every wight° comanded was silence,   *person*
And that the knight sholde telle in audience°   *in open hearing*
What thing that worldly wommen loven best.
This knight ne stood nat stille as doth a best,°   *beast*
1035 But to his questioun anon° answerde   *at once*
With manly voys,° that° al the court it herde: *voice / so that*
    "My lige° lady, generally," quod he,   *liege*
"Wommen desyren to have sovereyntee°   *sovereignty, domination*
As wel over hir housbond as hir love,⁶
1040 And for to been in maistrie° him above.   *mastery, control*
This is youre moste° desyr, thogh ye me kille.   *greatest*
Doth as yow list°—I am heer at youre wille."   *it please you*
In al the court ne was ther wyf, ne mayde,
Ne widwe that contraried° that° he sayde,   *opposed / what*
1045 But seyden he was worthy han° his lyf.   *to have*
And with that word up stirte° the olde wyf,   *started up*
Which that the knight saugh° sittinge in the grene: *saw (had seen)*
"Mercy," quod she, "my sovereyn lady quene!
Er that youre court departe, do me right.°   *give me justice*
1050 I taughte this answere unto the knight;
For which he plighte me his trouthe there,
The firste thing I wolde of him requere°   *request*
He wolde it do, if it lay in his might.°   *power*
Bifore the court thanne preye I thee, sir knight,"
1055 Quod she, "that thou me take unto thy wyf,
For wel thou wost° that I have kept° thy lyf.   *knowest / preserved*
If I sey fals, sey nay, upon thy fey!"°   *faith*
    This knight answerde, "Allas and weylawey!°   *woe is me*
I woot° right wel that swich° was my biheste.°   *know / such / promise*
1060 For Goddes love, as chees° a newe requeste: *choose*
Tak al my good,° and lat my body go."   *goods, property*

6. Over their husband(s) as well as over their lover(s).

"Nay thanne," quod she, "'I shrewe° us bothe two!   *curse*
For thogh that I be foul° and old and pore,   *ugly*
I nolde° for al the metal ne for ore   *would not*
1065 That under erthe is grave° or lyth° above   *buried / lies*
But if° thy wyf I were, and eek thy love."   *(Have anything) except*
   "My love?" quod he, "Nay, my dampnacioun!°   *damnation*
Allas! that any of my nacioun°   *birth, lineage*
Sholde evere so foule disparaged° be!"   *disgracefully degraded*
1070 But al for noght, the ende° is this, that he   *outcome*
Constreyned was: he nedes moste° hire wedde,   *needs must*
And taketh his olde wyf and gooth to bedde.
   Now wolden som men seye, paraventure,°   *perchance*
That for° my necligence I do no cure°   *out of / omit*
1075 To tellen yow the joye and al th'array°   *the pomp*
That at the feste° was that ilke° day.   *feast / same*
To whiche thing shortly° answere I shal: *in brief*
I seye ther nas° no joye ne feste at al;   *was not*
Ther nas but° hevinesse and muche sorwe,   *was only*
1080 For prively° he wedded hire on morwe,°   *privately / in the morning*
And al day after hidde him as an oule,°   *like an owl*
So wo was him, his wyf looked so foule.[7]
   Greet was the wo the knight hadde in his thoght,
Whan he was with his wyf abedde° y-broght;   *to bed*
1085 He walweth,° and he turneth to and fro.   *tosses about*
His olde wyf lay smylinge everemo,°   *all the while*
And seyde, "O dere housbond, *benedicite!*°   *bless us*
Fareth° every knight thus with his wyf as ye?   *Acts, behaves*
Is this the lawe of King Arthures hous?
1090 Is every knight of his so dangerous?°   *haughty, reluctant*
I am youre owene love and eek youre wyf;
I am she which that saved hath youre lyf;
And certes yet dide I yow nevere unright.°   *wrong*
Why fare° ye thus with me this firste night?   *act*
1095 Ye faren lyk a man had° lost his wit!   *(who) had*
What is my gilt?° for Goddes love, tel me it,   *error*
And it shal been amended, if I may."°   *can*
   "Amended?" quod this knight, "allas! nay, nay!
It wol nat been amended nevere mo!°   *more*
1100 Thou art so loothly,° and so old also,   *loathsome, ugly*
And therto comen of so lowe a kinde,°   *such low birth*
That litel wonder is° thogh I walwe and winde.°   *it is / toss and turn*
So wolde God myn herte wolde breste!"°   *burst*
   "Is this," quod she, "the cause of youre unreste?"
1105 "Ye, certainly," quod he, "no wonder is."°   *it is*

7. So woeful was he, (because) his wife looked so ugly.

"Now, sire," quod she, "I coude amende al this,
If that me liste, er it were dayes three,
So wel ye mighte bere yow unto me.[8]
        But for ye speken of swich gentillesse[9]
1110 As is descended out of old richesse°—   *wealth*
That therfore sholden ye be gentil men[1]—
Swich° arrogance is nat worth an hen.   *Such*
Loke who that° is most vertuous alway,   *See who*
Privee and apert, and most entendeth ay[2]
1115 To do the gentil dedes that he can,
And tak him for the grettest gentil man.
Crist wol° we clayme of° him oure gentillesse,   *desires (that) / from*
Nat of oure eldres° for hire old richesse.   *elders, ancestors*
For thogh they yeve° us al hir heritage—   *give*
1120 For which we clayme to been of heigh parage°—   *parentage, birth*
Yet may they nat biquethe,° for no thing,°   *bestow / by any means*
To noon of us hir vertuous living
That made hem gentil men y-called be,
And bad us folwen hem in swich degree.°   *in a similar condition*
1125   Wel can the wyse poete of Florence,
That highte Dant, speken in this sentence;[3]
Lo, in swich maner rym° is Dantes tale: *this sort of rhyme*
'Ful selde° up ryseth by his branches[4] smale   *seldom*
Prowesse° of man, for God of° his goodnesse   *The excellence / out of*
1130 Wol° that of° him we clayme oure gentillesse;'   *Desires / from*
For of oure eldres may we no thing clayme
But temporel thing, that man may hurte and mayme.[5]
        Eek° every wight° wot° this as wel as I,   *Also / being / knows*
If gentillesse were planted naturelly°   *by nature*
1135 Unto a certeyn linage doun the lyne,
Privee and apert, than wolde they nevere fyne°   *cease*
To doon of gentillesse the faire offyce°—   *function(s)*
They mighte° do no vileinye or vyce.°   *could / vicious act*
        Tak fyr, and ber it in° the derkeste hous   *bear it into*
1140 Bitwix this° and the Mount of Caucasus,   *here*
And lat men shette° the dores and go thenne,°   *shut / away*
Yet wol the fyr as faire lye and brenne,°   *burn*
As° twenty thousand men mighte it biholde: *As when*
His office° naturel ay° wol it holde,°   *Its function / ever / perform*
1145 Up° peril of my lyf, til that it dye.°   *Upon / die out*

8. If it pleased me, before three days were past, if
you could behave well toward me.
9. "Gentillesse" implies the kind of behavior and
sensibility proper to good ("gentil") birth—openness,
generosity, compassion, courtesy—but as the Wife
points out (with learned authority to support her), a
high ancestry is no guarantee of these things, nor
does low birth necessarily preclude them.

1. That because of this, you must necessarily be
"gentle"-men.
2. In private and in public, and always seeks most
diligently.
3. Who is called Dante, speak on this theme.
4. I.e., of the family tree.
5. But temporal (worldly) things, that can harm and
maim man.

Heer may ye see wel how that genterye°   *nobility*
Is nat annexed° to possessioun,   *attached*
Sith° folk ne doon hir operacioun°   *Since / perform their function*
Alwey, as dooth the fyr, lo, in his kinde.°   *according to its nature*
1150 For, God it woot, men may wel often finde
A lordes sone° do° shame and vileinye;   *son / doing*
And he that wol han prys of° his gentrye   *have praise (esteem) for*
For he was boren° of a gentil hous,   *Because / born*
And hadde his eldres noble and vertuous,
1155 And nil° himselven do no gentil dedis,   *will not*
Ne folwe his gentil auncestre° that deed is,°   *ancestry / which is dead*
He nis nat° gentil, be he duk or erl;   *is not*
For vileyns° sinful dedes make a cherl.°   *villainous / churl*
For gentillesse nis° but renomee°   *is nothing / the renown*
1160 Of thyne auncestres, for hire heigh bountee,°   *their great goodness*
Which is a straunge thing° to thy persone.   *a thing foreign*
Thy gentillesse cometh fro God allone.
Thanne comth oure verray gentillesse of grace:
It was nothing biquethe us with oure place.[6]
1165 Thenketh how noble, as seith Valerius,°   *Valerius Maximus*
Was thilke Tullius Hostilius,[7]
That out of povert° roos° to heigh noblesse.   *poverty / rose*
Redeth Senek,° and redeth eek° Boëcc:°   *Seneca / also / Boethius*
Ther shul ye seen expres° that it no drede° is   *explicitly / doubt*
1170 That he is gentil that doth gentil dedis.°   *deeds*
And therfore, leve° housbond, I thus conclude: *dear*
Al were it that° myne auncestres were rude,°   *Even though / humble*
Yet may the hye° God, and so hope I,   *high*
Grante me grace to liven vertuously.
1175 Thanne am I gentil, whan that I biginne
To liven vertuously and weyve° sinne.   *put aside*
And ther as ye of povert° me repreve,°   *poverty / reproach*
The hye God, on° whom that we bileve,   *in*
In wilful° povert chees° to live his lyf.   *voluntary / chose*
1180 And certes every man, mayden, or wyf,
May understonde that Jesus, hevene king,
Ne wolde nat chese a vicious living.°   *way of living*
Glad° povert is an honest thing, certeyn;°   *Contented / certainly*
This wol Senek and othere clerkes seyn.
1185 Whoso that halt him payd of his poverte,[8]
I holde him riche, al° hadde he nat a sherte.°   *although / shirt*
He that coveyteth° is a povre wight,°   *covets / poor creature*
For he wolde han that° is nat in his might.°   *what / power*

---

6. Then our real *gentillesse* comes from (God's) grace; it was in no way bestowed upon us with our social position.

7. Third legendary king of Rome.

8. Whosoever considers himself satisfied with his poverty.

But he that noght hath, ne coveyteth have,°   *desires (to) have*
1190 Is riche, although ye holde him but a knave.°   *one of low estate*
Verray° povert, it singeth proprely.[9]   *True*
Juvenal seith of povert merily:
'The povre man, whan he goth by the weye,
Bifore the theves he may singe and pleye.'
1195 Poverte is hateful good,° and as I gesse,   *a hated good*
A ful greet bringere out of bisinesse;°   *anxiety, care*
A greet amendere eek of sapience°   *wisdom*
To him that taketh it in° pacience.   *accepts it with*
Poverte is this, although it seme elenge,°   *miserable*
1200 Possessioun that no wight wol chalenge;°   *claim (as his own)*
Poverte ful ofte, whan a man is lowe,
Maketh° his God and eek himself to knowe;   *Makes (him)*
Poverte a spectacle° is, as thinketh me,   *eyeglass*
Thurgh which he may his verray frendes see.
1205 And therfore, sire, sin that I noght yow greve,[1]
Of° my povert namore ye me repreve.°   *For / reproach*
    Now, sire, of elde° ye repreve me: *old age*
And certes, sire, thogh° noon auctoritee   *even if*
Were in no book, ye gentils of honour°   *who are honorable*
1210 Seyn that men sholde an old wight° doon favour   *(to) an old person*
And clepe° him fader, for° youre gentillesse;   *call / out of*
And auctours° shal I finden, as I gesse.   *authorities (for this opinion)*
    Now ther ye seye that I am foul° and old,   *ugly*
Than drede° you noght to been a cokewold,°   *fear / cuckold*
1215 For filthe and elde, also moot I thee,°   *as I may prosper*
Been grete wardeyns upon° chastitee.   *guardians of*
But nathelees, sin° I knowe youre delyt,°   *since / pleasure, wish*
I shal fulfille youre worldly appetyt.°   *appetite, lust*
    Chese° now," quod she, "oon of thise thinges tweye:°   *Choose / two*
1220 To han me foul and old til that I deye°   *die*
And be to yow a trewe° humble wyf,   *faithful*
And nevere yow displese in al my lyf,
Or elles° ye wol han me yong and fair,   *else*
And take youre aventure of° the repair[2]   *chance with*
1225 That shal be to youre hous, by cause of me,
Or in som other place, may wel be.°   *(it) may well be*
Now chese yourselven whether that yow lyketh."°   *whichever pleases you*
    This knight avyseth him and sore syketh,[3]
But atte laste he seyde in this manere:
1230 "My lady and my love, and wyf so dere,
I put me in youre wyse governance:°   *under your wise control*

---

9. By its nature.
1. And therefore, sir, since I don't trouble you (with
it).

2. I.e., the crowd.
3. This knight thinks it over and sorrowfully sighs.

Cheseth° youreself which may be most plesance°   *Choose / the greatest pleasure*
And most honour to yow and me also.
I do no fors the whether of the two,
1235 For as yow lyketh, it suffiseth me."[4]
    "Thanne have I gete of° yow maistrye,"° quod she,   *gotten from / mastery*
"Sin° I may chese and governe as me lest?"°   *Since / I please*
    "Ye, certes,° wyf," quod he, "I holde° it best "   *certainly / consider*
    "Kis me," quod she. "We be no lenger wrothe,°   *longer wroth (angry)*
1240 For by my trouthe,[5] I wol be to yow bothe,
This is to seyn, ye,° bothe fair and good.   *yes*
I prey to God that I mot sterven wood,°   *may die mad*
But° I to yow be also° good and trewe   *Unless / just as*
As evere was wyf, sin° that the world was newe.   *since*
1245 And but I be to-morn as fair to sene[6]
As any lady, emperyce,° or quene,   *empress*
That is bitwixe the est and eke the west,
Doth with my lyf and deeth right as yow lest.°   *just as you please*
Cast° up the curtin:° loke how that it is."   *Lift / (bed-)curtain*
1250 And whan the knight saugh° verraily° al this,   *saw / in truth*
That she so fair was and so yong therto,
For joye he hente° hire in his armes two;   *clasped*
His herte bathed in a bath of blisse.
A thousand tyme a-rewe° he gan hire kisse,°   *in a row / did kiss her*
1255 And she obeyed him in every thing
That mighte doon° him plesance° or lyking.°   *give / pleasure / delight*
    And thus they live unto hir lyves ende
In parfit° joye. And Jesu Crist us sende   *perfect*
Housbondes meke,° yonge, and fresshe a-bedde,°   *meek / in bed*
1260 And grace t'overbyde hem that we wedde.[7]
And eek I preye Jesu shorte hir lyves°   *to shorten their lives*
That° noght wol be governed by hir wyves;   *Who*
And olde and angry nigardes of dispence,°   *niggards with their money*
God sende hem sone° verray° pestilence.   *soon / a real*

From The Friar's Prologue

This worthy limitour,[1] this noble Frere,
He made alwey a maner louring chere°   *a kind of glowering face*
Upon the Somnour, but for honestee[2]

---

4. I don't care which of the two (it be), for as it is pleasing to you, (so) it suffices me.
5. I.e., I swear.
6. And unless I am in the morning as fair to look upon.
7. And the grace to outlive them that we wed.
1. See n.9, p. 126.
2. Toward the Summoner, but for propriety's sake.

No vileyns° word as yet to him spak he.   *rude*
5 But atte laste° he seyde unto the Wyf,   *at (the) last*
"Dame," quod he, "God yeve° yow right good lyf!"   *give*
Ye han heer touched, also moot I thee,°   *as I may thrive*
In scole-matere greet difficultee.[3]
Ye han seyd muchel thing° right wel, I seye.   *many things*
10 But dame, here as we ryden by the weye,
Us nedeth nat to speken but of game,°   *sport, fun*
And lete auctoritees,° on° Goddes name,   *leave the authorities / in*
To preching and to scole of clergye.°   *to the learned schools*
But if it lyke to° this companye,   *please*
15 I wol yow of a somnour telle a game."°   *joke, funny story*

*   *   *

The Clerk's Prologue and Tale

The Prologue

"Sir Clerk of Oxenford,"° our Hoste sayde,   *scholar from Oxford*
"Ye ryde as coy° and stille as dooth a mayde   *shy*
Were newe spoused, sittinge at the bord.[1]
This day ne herde I of° your tonge a word.   *from*
5 I trowe ye studie aboute som sophyme,[2]
But Salomon seith, 'every thing hath tyme.'
   For Goddes sake, as beth° of bettre chere.   *be*
It is no tyme for to studien here.
Telle us som mery tale, by youre fey!°   *faith*
10 For what man that is entred in a pley,[3]
He nedes moot° unto the pley assente.   *needs must*
But precheth nat,° as freres° doon in Lente,   *don't preach / friars*
To make us for our olde sinnes wepe,
Ne that thy tale make us nat to slepe.
15   Telle us som mery thing of aventures.
Youre termes, youre colours, and youre figures,[4]
Kepe hem in stoor til so be ye endyte[5]
Heigh° style, as whan that men to kinges wryte.   *High*
Speketh so pleyn° at this time, we yow preye,°   *plain / beseech*
20 That we may understonde what ye seye."
   This worthy Clerk benignely° answerde: *graciously*
"Hoste," quod he, "I am under your yerde;°   *rod, rule*
Ye han° of us as now the governaunce,°   *have / the governing*

---

3. Upon scholastic questions of great difficulty.
1. (Who) is newly wed, sitting at the (wedding) table.
2. I believe you're pondering over some sophism (i.e., clever, specious argument).

3. For whoever has entered into a game.
4. Various learned devices of rhetoric.
5. Keep them in store until you (have occasion to) compose in.

And therfor wol I do yow obeisaunce°   *obey you*
25 As fer° as reson axeth,° hardily.°   *far / demands / certainly*
I wol yow telle a tale which that I
Lerned at Padowe° of a worthy clerk,   *Padua*
As preved° by his wordes and his werk.   *(was) proved*
He is now deed° and nayled° in his cheste,°   *dead / nailed / coffin*
30 I prey to God so yeve° his soule reste!   *give*
Fraunceys Petrark,° the laureat poete,   *Francis Petrarch*
Highte° this clerk, whos rethoryke° sweete   *Was called / rhetoric*
Enlumincd° al Itaille° of° poetrye,   *Illumined / Italy / with*
As Linian° dide of philosophye   *(Giovanni da) Legnano*
35 Or lawe, or other art° particuler;   *field of knowledge*
But deeth, that wol nat suffre° us dwellen heer°   *allow / here*
But as it were a twinkling of an yë,°   *eye*
Hem° bothe hath slayn, and alle shul we dye.°   *Them / shall die*
But forth to tellen of this worthy man
40 That taughte me this tale, as I bigan,
I seye that first with heigh style he endyteth,°   *composes*
Er° he the body° of his tale wryteth,   *Before / main part*
A proheme, in the which discryveth he[6]
Pemond,° and of Saluces° the contree,   *Piedmont / Saluzzo*
45 And speketh of Apennyn,° the hilles hye,°   *the Apennines / high*
That been the boundes° of West Lumbardye,°   *boundaries / Lombardy*
And of Mount Vesulus° in special,   *Viso*
Where as the Poo,° out of a welle° smal,   *Po River / spring*
Taketh his firste springing and his sours,°   *source*
50 That estward ay encresseth in his cours
To Emelward, to Ferrare, and Venyse:[7]
The which a long thing were to devyse,°   *relate*
And trewely, as to my jugement,
Me thinketh it a thing impertinent,°   *irrelevant*
55 Save that he wol conveyen his matere.[8]
But this° his tale, which that ye may here."°   *this is / hear*

The Tale

PART ONE

Ther is, at the west syde of Itaille,
Doun at the rote° of Vesulus° the colde,   *base / Mount Viso*
A lusty playne, habundant of vitaille,[9]
60 Wher many a tour° and toun thou mayst biholde   *tower*
That founded were in tyme of fadres olde,°   *forefathers*

6. A proem (introduction) in which he describes.
7. That eastward ever grows larger in its course, toward Emilia, Ferrara, and Venice.
8. Except that he wishes to introduce his (main) subject.
9. A pleasant plain, abounding in food.

And many another delitable° sighte,   *delightful*
And Saluces° this noble contree highte.°   *Saluzzo / was called*

A markis° whylom° lord was of that londe,   *marquis / at one time*
65 As were his worthy eldres° him bifore;   *elders*
And obeisant,° ay° redy to his honde   *obedient / ever*
Were alle his liges, bothe lasse and more.[1]
Thus in delyt he liveth, and hath don yore,°   *for a long time*
Biloved and drad,° thurgh° favour of Fortune,   *feared / through*
70 Bothe of° his lordes and of his commune.°   *by / common people*

Therwith° he was, to speke as of linage,°   *In addition / lineage*
The gentilleste[2] y-born of Lumbardye,
A fair° persone, and strong, and yong of age,   *handsome*
And ful of honour and of curteisye;°   *courtesy*
75 Discreet y-nogh his contree for to gye[3]—
Save in somme thinges that° he was to blame°—   *wherein / at fault*
And Walter was this yonge lordes name.

I blame him thus, that he considered noght
In tyme cominge° what mighte him bityde,   *In future time*
80 But on his lust present° was al his thoght,   *immediate pleasure*
As for to hauke° and hunte on every syde;   *hawk*
Wel ny alle othere cures leet he slyde,[4]
And eek° he nolde°—and that was worst of alle—   *also / would not*
Wedde no wyf, for noght° that may bifalle.   *whatever*

85 Only that point his peple bar so sore°   *took so hard*
That flokmele° on a day they to him wente,   *in flocks, droves*
And oon of hem, that wysest was of lore,°   *in learning*
Or elles that° the lord best wolde assente   *Or because*
That he sholde telle him what his peple mente,
90 Or elles coude he shewe wel swich matere,[5]
He to the markis seyde as ye shul here.

"O noble markis, your humanitee
Assureth us and yeveth° us hardinesse,°   *giveth / the boldness*
As ofte as tyme is of necessitee,°   *it is necessary*
95 That we to yow mowe° telle our hevinesse.   *may*
Accepteth, lord, now of youre gentillesse,
That we with pitous° herte unto yow pleyne,°   *sorrowful / make plaint*
And lete youre eres nat my voys disdeyne.[6]

1. Were all his vassals, both small and great.
2. I.e., the highest.
3. Wise enough to guide (govern) his country.
4. He let slide almost all other responsibilities.

5. Or else (because) he knew well how to put forward such a subject.
6. And let your ears not disdain (to hear) my voice.

Al° have I noght to done in this matere   *Although*
100 More than another man hath in this place,
Yet for as muche as ye, my lord so dere,
Han alwey shewed me favour and grace,
I dar the better aske of yow a space°   *opportunity*
Of audience, to shewen° our requeste,   *put forward*
105 And ye, my lord, to doon right as yow leste [7]

For certes, lord, so wel us lyketh yow [8]
And al your werk, and ever han doon, that we
Ne coude nat us self° devysen° how   *ourselves / imagine*
We mighte liven in more felicitee,°   *happiness*
110 Save o° thing, lord, if it youre wille be,   *one*
That for to been a wedded man yow leste: [9]
Than° were your peple in sovereyn hertes reste.°   *Then / supreme happiness*

Boweth youre nekke under that blisful yok
Of soveraynetee, noght of servyse,
115 Which that men clepeth spousaille° or wedlok;   *call marriage*
And thenketh, lord, among your thoghtes wyse,
How that oure dayes passe in sondry wyse;°   *various ways*
For though we slepe or wake, or rome,° or ryde,   *wander about*
Ay fleeth the tyme, it nil no man abyde. [1]

120 And though youre grene youthe floure° as yit,°   *flower / yet*
In crepeth age alwey, as stille as stoon, [2]
And deeth manaceth° every age, and smit°   *threatens / smites*
In ech estaat,° for ther escapeth noon:°   *every rank / no one*
And al so° certein as we knowe echoon°   *even as / each one*
125 That we shul deye,° as uncerteyn we alle   *die*
Been of that day whan deeth shal on us falle.

Accepteth than of us the trewe entente,°   *loyal intention*
That never yet refuseden youre heste,°   *command*
And we wol, lord, if that ye wol assente,
130 Chese yow a wyf in short tyme, atte leste,°   *at (the) least*
Born of the gentilleste and of the meste°   *greatest*
Of al this lond, so that it oghte seme
Honour to God and yow, as we can deme.°   *judge*

Delivere us out of al this bisy drede°   *anxious fear*
135 And tak a wyf, for hye° Goddes sake;   *high*
For if it so bifelle, as God forbede, [3]

---

7. And you, my lord, to do just as you please.
8. For truly, lord, you please us so well.
9. That it pleases you to become a married man.

1. Time always flees, it will not wait for any man.
2. Age creeps in steadily, as quietly as (a) stone.
3. I.e., may God forbid.

That thurgh your deeth your lyne sholde slake,°   *cease*
And that a straunge° successour sholde take   *unknown*
Youre heritage, O, wo were us alyve!
140 Wherfor we pray you hastily to wyve."°   *take a wife*

Hir° meke preyere and hir pitous chere°   *Their / appearance*
Made the markis herte° han pitee.   *marquis's heart*
"Ye wol,"° quod he, "myn owene peple dere,   *wish*
To that° I never erst° thoghte streyne° me.   *what / before / constrain*
145 I me rejoysed of my libertee
That selde tyme° is founde in mariage;   *seldom*
Ther I was free, I moot been in servage.[4]

But nathelees° I see your trewe entente,   *nevertheless*
And truste upon youre wit,° and have don ay;   *judgment*
150 Wherfore of my free wil I wole assente
To wedde me, as sone as evere I may.
But theras° ye han profred° me to-day   *where / offered*
To chese° me a wyf, I yow relesse°   *choose / release*
That choys, and prey yow of that profre cesse.[5]

155 For God it woot,° that children ofte been   *knows*
Unlyk hir worthy eldres° hem bifore;°   *ancestors / before them*
Bountee° comth al of God, nat of the streen°   *Goodness / strain, lineage*
Of which they been engendred and y-bore.°   *born*
I truste in Goddes bountee, and therfore
160 My mariage and myn estaat° and reste°   *noble station / quiet peace*
I him bitake; he may don as him leste.[6]

Lat me alone in chesinge° of my wyf—   *the choosing*
That charge° upon my bak I wol endure;   *load*
But I yow preye, and charge upon youre lyf,
165 That what° wyf that I take, ye me assure   *whatever*
To worshipe hire° whyl that hir lyf may dure,°   *revere her / last*
In word and werk,° bothe here and everywhere,   *deed*
As° she an emperoures doghter were.   *As if*

And forthermore this shal ye swere,° that ye   *swear*
170 Agayn my choys shul neither grucche° ne stryve;°   *grumble / oppose*
For sith° I shal forgoon° my libertee   *since / forgo*
At your requeste, as ever moot I thryve,°   *I may prosper*
Ther as° myn herte is set, ther wol I wyve.°   *There where / marry*
And but° ye wole assente in swich manere,   *unless*
175 I prey yow, speketh namore of this matere."

---

4. Where I (once) was free, I must be in servitude.   offer.
5. (From) that choice, and ask you to withdraw that   6. I entrust to Him; He may do as it pleases Him.

With hertely° wil they sworen and assenten   sincere, good
To al this thing—ther seyde no wight° nay—   person
Bisekinge him of grace, er that they wenten,[7]
That he wolde graunten hem° a certein day   grant (to name) them
180 Of° his spousaille, as sone as evere he may;   For
For yet alwey° the peple somwhat dredde°   still / feared
Lest that this markis no wyf wolde wedde

He graunted hem a day, swich as him leste,[8]
On which he wolde be wedded sikerly,°   certainly
185 And seyde he dide al this at hir° requeste.   their
And they, with humble entente, buxomly,°   submissively
Knelinge upon hir knees ful reverently,
Him thanken alle; and thus they han an ende
Of hire entente,° and hoom agayn they wende.   purpose

190 And heerupon he to his officeres°   household officials
Comaundeth for the feste° to purveye,°   feast / provide
And to his privee° knightes and squyeres   personal
Swich charge yaf as him liste on hem leye;[9]
And they to his comandement obeye,
195 And ech of them doth al his diligence
To doon unto the feste reverence.°   honor

PART TWO

Noght fer fro thilke paleys honurable
Wheras this markis shoop his mariage,[1]
Ther stood a throp,° of site delitable,°   village / pleasant
200 In which that povre° folk of that village   poor
Hadden hir bestes° and hir herbergage,°   animals / lodgings
And of° hire labour took hir sustenance   by
After that the erthe yaf hem habundance.[2]

Amonges thise povre folk ther dwelte a man
205 Which that was holden° povrest of hem alle;   Who was held to be
But hye° God somtyme senden can   high
His grace into a litel oxes stalle.
Janicula men of that throp him calle;
A doghter hadde he, fair y-nogh to sighte,°   to the eye
210 And Grisildis this yonge mayden highte.°   was named

---

7. Beseeching him of (his) grace, before they departed.
8. Such as it pleased him.
9. (He) gave such responsibility as it pleased him to lay on them.

1. Not far from that same worthy place where this marquis prepared for his marriage.
2. In whatever abundance the earth yielded them.

But for to speke of vertuous beautee,
Than was she oon the faireste° under sonne;   *one of the loveliest*
For povreliche y-fostred up was she,
No likerous lust was thurgh hire herte y-ronne.[3]
215 Wel ofter of the welle° than of the tonne°   *spring / (wine) cask*
She drank; and for she wolde vertu plese,
She knew wel labour, but non ydel ese.°   *no idle ease*

But thogh this mayde tendre were of age,[4]
Yet in the brest of hir virginitee
220 Ther was enclosed rype and sad corage;°   *a mature and firm heart*
And in greet reverence and charitee
Hir° olde povre fader fostred° she.   *Her / cared for*
A fewe sheep, spinninge, on feeld she kepte;[5]
She wolde noght been ydel til she slepte.

225 And whan she hoomward cam, she wolde bringe
Wortes° or othere herbes tymes ofte,   *Plants*
The whiche she shredde and seeth° for hir° livinge,   *boiled / their*
And made hir° bed ful harde and nothing softe;   *her*
And ay she kepte hir fadres lyf on lofte°   *sustained her father's life*
230 With everich° obeisaunce and diligence   *every*
That child may doon to fadres reverence.

Upon Grisilde, this povre creature,
Ful ofte sythe° this markis sette his yë   *oftentimes*
As he on hunting rood paraventure;°   *rode by chance*
235 And whan it fil° that he mighte hire espye,°   *befell / see*
He noght with wantoun loking of folye[6]
His eyen° caste on hire, but in sad° wyse   *eyes / serious*
Upon hir chere° he wolde him ofte avyse,°   *countenance / often ponder*

Commendinge in his herte hir wommanhede,
240 And eek hir vertu, passinge° any wight°   *surpassing / person*
Of so yong age, as wel in chere° as dede.   *appearance*
For thogh the peple have no greet insight
In vertu, he considered ful right
Hir bountee,° and disposed° that he wolde   *goodness / decided*
245 Wedde hire only, if ever he wedde sholde.

The day of wedding cam, but no wight° can   *nobody*
Telle what womman that it sholde be;
For which merveille wondred many a man,
And seyden, whan they were in privetee,°   *private*

---

3. Because she was raised in poverty, no wanton
desire had run through her heart.
4. I.e., young in years.
5. (While) spinning, she watched over a few sheep
in the field.
6. He did not with wanton, foolish looks.

250 "Wol nat our lord yet leve his vanitee?°   *foolishness*
    Wol he nat wedde? allas, allas the whyle!
    Why wol he thus himself and us bigyle?"°   *deceive*

    But natheles this markis hath don make°   *has had made*
    Of gemmes, set in gold and in asure,°   *azure, blue*
255 Broches and ringes, for Grisildis sake,
    And of hir clothing took he the mesure
    By a mayde, lyk to hire stature,
    And eek of othere ornamentes° alle   *adornments*
    That unto swich° a wedding sholde falle.   *such*

260 The tyme of undern° of the same day   *mid-morning*
    Approcheth, that this wedding sholde be;
    And al the paleys° put was in array,°   *palace / order*
    Bothe halle and chambres, ech in his° degree;   *its*
    Houses of office[7] stuffed with plentee
265 Ther maystow° seen, of deyntevous vitaille°   *mayest thou / dainty foods*
    That may be founde as fer as last Itaille.°   *Italy extends*

    This royal markis, richely arrayed,
    Lordes and ladyes in his companye,
    The whiche unto the feste were y-prayed,°   *asked*
270 And of his retenue the bachelrye,°   *young knights*
    With many a soun° of sondry° melodye,   *sound / various*
    Unto the village of the which I tolde,
    In this array the righte wey° han holde.°   *direct way / taken*

    Grisilde of this, God woot,° ful innocent°   *knows / entirely unaware*
275 That for hire shapen° was al this array,   *prepared*
    To fecchen water at a welle is went,°   *has gone*
    And cometh hoom as sone as ever she may.
    For wel she hadde herd seyd that thilke° day   *that same*
    The markis sholde wedde, and, if she mighte,
280 She wolde fayn° han seyn some of that sighte.   *gladly*

    She thoghte, "I wol with othere maydens stonde,
    That been my felawes,° in our dore and see   *companions*
    The markisesse,° and therfor wol I fonde°   *marchioness / try*
    To doon[8] at hoom as sone as it may be
285 The labour which that longeth° unto me;   *belongs*
    And than I may at leyser° hire biholde,   *leisure*
    If she this wey unto the castel holde."°   *takes*

    And as she wolde over hir threshfold° goon,   *threshold*
    The markis cam and gan hire for to calle;°   *did call her*

---

7. Service buildings (storerooms, kitchens, etc.).   8. I.e., to finish.

290 And she sette doun hir water-pot anoon°　　　　　*at once*
　　Bisyde the threshfold, in an oxes stalle,
　　And doun upon hir knees she gan to falle,°　　　　*fell*
　　And with sad° contenance kneleth stille　　　　　*earnest*
　　Til she had herd what was the lordes wille.

295 This thoghtful° markis spak unto this mayde　　　*pensive*
　　Ful sobrely,° and seyde in this manere:　　　　　*gravely*
　　"Wher is your fader, Grisildis?" he sayde,
　　And she with reverence, in humble chere,°　　　　*manner*
　　Answerde, "Lord, he is al redy° here."　　　　*right at hand*
300 And in she gooth withouten lenger lette,°　　　　*delay*
　　And to the markis she hir fader fette.°　　　　*fetched*

　　He by the hond than took this olde man,
　　And seyde thus whan he him hadde asyde,°　　　*off to the side*
　　"Janicula, I neither may ne can
305 Lenger the plesance° of myn herte hyde.　　　*pleasure, desire*
　　If that thou vouche sauf, what so bityde,⁹
　　Thy doghter wol I take er that° I wende°　　　*before / depart*
　　As for my wyf, unto hir lyves,ende.

　　Thou lovest me, I woot it wel, certeyn,
310 And art my feithful lige man y-bore;¹
　　And al that lyketh° me, I dar wel seyn　　　*all that which pleases*
　　It lyketh thee; and specially therfore
　　Tel me that poynt that I have seyd bifore:²
　　If that thou wolt unto that purpos drawe°　　　*incline*
315 To take me as for thy sone-in-lawe."

　　This sodeyn cas this man astoned so
　　That reed he wex; abayst and al quaking
　　He stood.³ Unnethes° seyde he wordes mo,°　　*Scarcely / more*
　　But only thus: "Lord," quod he, "my willinge
320 Is as ye wole, ne ayeines° your lykinge　　　*contrary to*
　　I wol° no thing, ye be my lord so dere.　　　*wish*
　　Right as yow lust° governeth this matere."　　　*Just as you please*

　　"Yet wol I," quod this markis softely,
　　"That in thy chambre I and thou and she
325 Have a collacion,° and wostow° why?　　　*conference / knowest thou*
　　For I wol axe° if it hire wille be　　　*ask*

9. If thou wilt permit (it), whatever may happen.
1. And were born my faithful vassal.
2. Answer me in that particular that I have named
before.

3. This sudden event astonished this man so much
that he grew red; he stood abashed and trembling all
over.

To be my wyf, and reule hire after me.⁴
And al this shal be doon in thy presence—
I wol noght speke out of thyn audience."°   *hearing*

330 And in the chambre whyl they were aboute
Hir tretis,° which as ye shal after here,   *Their contract*
The peple cam unto the hous withoute,°   *outside*
And wondred hem in how honest manere
And tentifly she kepte hir fader dere.⁵
335 But outerly° Grisildis wondre mighte,   *truly*
For never erst° ne saugh° she swich° a sighte.   *before / saw / such*

No wonder is thogh that she were astoned°   *bewildered*
To seen so greet a gest° come in that place;   *guest*
She never was to swiche gestes woned,°   *accustomed*
340 For° which she loked with ful pale face.   *On account of*
But shortly forth this matere for to chace,°   *pursue*
Thise arn° the wordes that the markis sayde   *are*
To this benigne,° verray,° feithful mayde.   *gracious / true*

"Grisilde," he seyde, "ye shul wel understonde
345 It lyketh to° your fader and to me   *It pleases*
That I yow wedde, and eek° it may so stonde,°   *also / be the case*
As I suppose, ye wol that it so be.
But thise demandes axe I first," quod he,
"That sith° it shal be doon in hastif wyse,°   *since / hastily*
350 Wol ye assente, or elles yow avyse?°   *deliberate*

I seye this, be ye redy with good herte
To al my lust,⁶ and that I frely may,
As me best thinketh, do yow laughe or smerte,⁷
And never ye to grucche° it, night ne day?   *grumble about*
355 And eek° whan I sey 'ye,'° ne sey nat 'nay,'   *also / yes*
Neither by word ne frowning contenance?
Swere this, and here I swere our alliance."

Wondringe upon this word,° quakinge for drede,   *speech*
She seyde, "Lord, undigne° and unworthy   *undeserving*
360 Am I to thilke° honour that ye me bede;°   *that same / offer*
But as ye wol yourself, right so wol I.
And heer I swere that nevere willingly
In werk° ne thoght I nil° yow disobeye,   *deed / will not*
For to be deed, though me were looth to deye."⁸

---

4. To be my wife, and govern herself according to   6. To (honor) my every wish.
my will.   7. As it seems best to me, make you laugh or suffer.
5. And they marveled at how decently and atten-   8. Even to die, though I would be loath to die.
tively she cared for her dear father.

365 "This is y-nogh, Grisilde myn!" quod he.
    And forth he gooth with a ful sobre chere
    Out at the dore, and after that cam she,
    And to the peple he seyde in this manere:
    "This is my wyf," quod he, "that standeth here.
370 Honoureth hire and loveth hire I preye
    Whoso° me loveth; ther is namore to seye."   *Whosoever*

    And for that° nothing of hir olde gere°   *in order that / apparel*
    She sholde bringe into his hous, he bad
    That wommen sholde dispoilen° hire right there;   *strip*
375 Of which thise ladyes were nat right glad
    To handle hir clothes wherinne she was clad.
    But natheles,° this mayde bright of hewe°   *nevertheless / hue*
    Fro foot to heed they clothed han al newe.

    Hir heres° han they kembd,° that lay untressed°   *hair / combed / all loose*
380 Ful rudely,° and with hir° fingres smale   *Artlessly / their*
    A corone° on hire heed they han y-dressed,°   *crown / set*
    And sette° hire ful of nowches° grete and smale.   *adorned / jewels*
    Of hire array what sholde I make a tale?
    Unnethe° the peple hir knew for hire fairnesse,   *Scarcely*
385 Whan she translated° was in swich richesse.   *transformed, elevated*

    This markis hath hire spoused° with a ring   *married*
    Broght for the same cause, and thanne hire sette
    Upon an hors, snow-whyt and wel ambling,°   *paced*
    And to his paleys,° er° he lenger lette,°   *palace / before / delayed*
390 With joyful peple that hire ladde° and mette,   *led*
    Conveyed hire; and thus the day they spende
    In revel, til the sonne gan descende.°   *did set*

    And shortly forth this tale for to chace,°   *pursue*
    I seye that to this newe markisesse°   *marchioness*
395 God hath swich° favour sent hire of his grace,   *such*
    That it ne semed nat by lyklinesse°   *likely*
    That she was born and fed in rudenesse,°   *lowliness*
    As in a cote° or in an oxe-stalle,   *cottage*
    But norished in an emperoures halle.

400 To every wight° she woxen is° so dere   *person / has grown*
    And worshipful, that folk ther she was bore[9]
    And from hire birthe knewe hire yeer by yere,
    Unnethe trowed they—but dorste han swore—[1]
    That to Janicle, of which I spak bifore,

9. And worthy of honor, that people where she was   1. They could scarcely believe—though they'd have
born.   dared to swear it.

405 She doghter were, for, as by conjecture,
Hem thoughte° she was another creature.   *It seemed to them*

For thogh that evere vertuous was she,
She was encressed in swich excellence
Of thewes° gode, y-set in heigh bountee,°   *qualities / goodness*
410 And so discreet° and fair of eloquence,°   *wise / speech*
So benigne° and so digne° of reverence,°   *gracious / worthy / honor*
And coude so the peples herte embrace,[2]
That ech hire lovede that loked on hir face.

Noght only of Saluces° in the toun   *Saluzzo*
415 Publiced° was the bountee° of hir name,   *Made known / goodness*
But eek° bisyde in many a regioun: *also*
If oon° seyde wel, another seyde the same.   *one*
So spraddc° of hire heighe bountee the fame   *spread*
That men and wommen, as wel yonge as olde,
420 Gon to Saluce upon hire to biholde.

Thus Walter lowly—nay but royally—
Wedded with fortunat honestetee,°   *honor*
In Goddes pees° liveth ful esily   *God's peace*
At hoom, and outward grace y-nogh had he;
425 And for° he saugh° that under low degree   *because / saw*
Was ofte vertu hid, the peple him helde
A prudent man, and that is seyn° ful selde.°   *seen / seldom*

Nat only this Grisildis thurgh hir wit
Coude al the feet of wyfly hoomlinesse,[3]
430 But eek,° whan that the cas requyred it,   *also*
The commune profit° coude she redresse.°   *general welfare / amend*
Ther nas° discord, rancour, ne hevinesse[4]   *was not*
In al that lond that she ne coude apese,°   *appease*
And wysly bringe hem alle in reste and ese.

435 Though that hire housbonde absent were, anoon°   *at once*
If gentil men or othere of hire contree
Were wrothe,° she wolde bringen hem atoon;°   *angered / into accord*
So wyse and rype° wordes hadde she,   *mature*
And jugements of so greet equitee,°   *fairness*
440 That she from heven sent was, as men wende,°   *they supposed*
Peple to save and every wrong t'amende.°   *to amend*

Nat longe tyme after that this Grisild
Was wedded, she a doughter hath y-bore.°   *borne*

2. And so (well) knew how to hold fast the hearts of   duties.
the people.   4. I.e., of heart.
3. Knew all the feats (skills) of a wife's household

Al had hire levere have born a knave child,[5]
445 Glad was this markis and the folk therfore;
For though a mayde child come al bifore,
She may unto a knave child atteyne
By lyklihed, sin she nis nat bareyne.[6]

PART THREE

Ther fil, as it bifalleth tymes mo,[7]
450 Whan that this child had souked° but a throwe,°   *nursed / short time*
This markis° in his herte longeth so   *marquis*
To tempte his wyf, hir sadnesse° for to knowe,   *steadfastness*
That he ne mighte out of his herte throwe
This merveillous° desyr, his wyf t'assaye;°   *strange / to test*
455 Needless,° God woot,° he thoughte hire
          for t'affraye.°   *Needlessly / knows / to frighten*

He hadde assayed hire y-nogh bifore
And fond hire evere good. What needed it
Hire for to tempte and alwey° more and more,   *continually*
Though som men preise for it for a subtil wit?
460 But as for me, I seye that yvel it sit[8]
T'assaye a wyf whan that it is no nede,
And putten hire in anguish and in drede.

For which this markis wroghte in this manere:
He cam alone a-night,° ther as° she lay,   *by night / there where*
465 With sterne face and with ful trouble chere,°   *troubled countenance*
And seyde thus: "Grisilde," quod he, "that day
That I yow took out of your povre array°   *condition of poverty*
And putte yow in estaat of heigh noblesse,
Ye have nat that forgeten, as I gesse.

470 I seye, Grisild, this present dignitee,
In which that I have put yow, as I trowe,°   *believe*
Maketh yow nat foryetful° for to be   *forgetful*
That I yow took in povre estaat ful lowe.
For any wele° ye moot° your-selven knowe,   *happiness / may*
475 Take hede of every word that I yow seye:
Ther is no wight° that hereth it but we tweye.°   *no one / two*

Ye woot° youreself wel how that ye cam here   *know*
Into this hous, it is nat longe ago,
And though to me that ye be lief° and dere,   *beloved*

5. Although she had rather have borne a male child.   7. It happened, as it often happens.
6. Quite probably, since she is not barren.   8. It ill becomes (a man), i.e., is evil.

480 Unto my gentils° ye be no-thing so;   *gentlefolk*
They seyn, to hem it is greet shame and wo
For to be subgets° and ben in servage°   *subjects / waiting, servitude*
To thee, that born art of a smal village.

And namely sith thy doghter was y-bore°   *born*
485 Thise wordes han they spoken, douteles·
But I desyre, as I have doon bifore,
To life my lyf with hem in reste and pees;°   *peace*
I may nat in this caas° be recchelees.°   *matter / heedless*
I moot° don with thy doghter for the beste,   *must*
490 Nat as I wolde, but as my peple leste.⁹

And yet, God wot,° this is ful looth° to me.   *knows / hateful*
But nathelees° withoute your witing°   *nevertheless / knowledge*
I wol nat doon;° but this wol I," quod he,   *act*
"That ye to me assente as in this thing.
495 Shewe now youre pacience in youre werking°   *deeds*
That ye me highte° and swore in your village   *promised*
That day that maked was oure mariage."

Whan she had herd al this, she noght ameved°   *made no motion*
Neither in word or chere° or countenaunce;   *manner*
500 For as it semed, she was nat agreved.
She seyde, "Lord, al lyth° in youre plesaunce;   *lies*
My child and I with hertely° obeisaunce   *sincere*
Ben youres al,° and ye mowe° save or spille°   *wholly / may / destroy*
Youre owene thing: werketh after° youre wille.   *according to*

505 Ther may no thing, God so my soule save,
Lyken to yow° that may displese me;   *Please you*
Ne I desyre no thing for to have,
Ne drede for to lese, save only ye;
This wil is in myn herte and ay° shal be.   *ever*
510 No lengthe of tyme or deeth may this deface,
Ne chaunge my corage° to another place."   *heart*

Glad was this markis of° hire answering,   *for*
But yet he feyned° as he were nat so;   *feigned*
Al drery° was his chere° and his loking   *sad / face*
515 Whan that he sholde out of the chambre go.
Sone after this, a furlong wey or two,¹
He prively° hath told al his entente°   *secretly / plan, intention*
Unto a man, and to his wyf him sente.

9. Not as I would wish, but as my people desire.   takes to walk a furlong—one-eighth of a mile—or
1. I.e., within a little while (the length of time it   two).

A maner sergeant was this privee man,[2]
520 The which that feithful ofte he founden hadde
In thinges grete, and eek° swich° folk wel can   *also / such*
Don execucioun in° thinges badde.   *Perform*
The lord knew wel that he him loved and dradde;°   *feared*
And whan this sergeant wiste° his lordes wille,   *knew*
525 Into the chambre he stalked him ful stille.°   *crept very quietly*

"Madame," he seyde, "ye mote foryeve° it me,   *must forgive*
Thogh I do thing to which I am constreyned.
Ye ben so wys that ful wel knowe ye
That lordes hestes° mowe° nat been y-feyned;°   *commands / may / avoided*
530 They mowe wel been biwailled or compleyned,°   *lamented*
But men mot nede° unto hire lust° obeye,   *needs must / their will*
And so wol I; ther is na more to seye.

This child I am comanded for to take"—
And spak na more, but out the child he hente°   *seized*
535 Despitously,° and gan a chere make[3]   *Cruelly*
As though he wolde han slayn it er° he wente.°   *before / left*
Grisildis mot° al suffren and al consente;   *must*
And as a lamb she sitteth meke and stille,
And leet this cruel sergeant doon his wille.

540 Suspecious was the diffame° of this man,   *bad reputation*
Suspect[4] his face, suspect his word also;
Suspect the tyme in which he this bigan.
Allas! hir doghter that she lovede so,
She wende° he wolde han slawen° it right tho.°   *thought / slain / then*
545 But natheles she neither weep ne syked,°   *wept nor sighed*
Conforminge hire to that the markis lyked.[5]

But atte laste° speken she bigan,   *finally*
And mekely she to the sergeant preyde,°   *begged*
So as he was a worthy gentil man,
550 That she moste° kisse hire child er° that it deyde;°   *might / before / died*
And in hir barm° this litel child she leyde°   *lap / laid*
With ful sad face, and gan the child to blisse[6]
And lulled it, and after gan it kisse.

And thus she seyde in hire benigne voys,°   *gracious voice*
555 "Far weel, my child; I shal thee nevere see.
But, sith° I thee have marked with the croys°   *since / cross*
Of thilke° Fader, blessed mote he be,   *that same*

---

2. This trusted man was a kind of sergeant-at-law.
3. I.e., acted.
4. I.e., ominous, foreboding (causing suspicion).

5. Conforming her (conduct) to what was pleasing to the marquis.
6. With a most somber face, and blessed the child.

That for us deyde upon a croys of tree,°   *wood*
Thy soule, litel child, I him bitake,°   *entrust to Him*
560 For this night shaltow° dyen for my sake."   *shalt thou*

I trowe° that to a norice° in this cas   *believe / nurse*
It had ben hard this rewthe° for to se;   *pitiful sight*
Wel⁷ mighte a mooder than han cryed "allas!"
But natheless so sad° stedfast was she   *firmly*
565 That she endured all adversitee,
And to the sergeant mekely she sayde,
"Have heer agayn your litel yonge mayde.

Goth now," quod she, "and dooth my lordes heste.°   *command*
But o° thing wol I preye yow of youre grace,   *one*
570 That, but° my lord forbad yow, atte leste°   *unless / at (the) least*
Burieth this litel body in som place
That bestes ne no briddes it torace."⁸
But he no word wol to that purpos seye,
But took the child and wente upon his weye.

575 This sergeant cam unto his lord ageyn,
And of Grisildis wordes and hire chere°   *behavior*
He tolde him point for point, in short and playn,°   *briefly and clearly*
And him presenteth with his doghter dere.
Somwhat this lord hath rewthe in his manere,⁹
580 But nathelees his purpos heeld he stille,
As lordes doon whan they wol han hir wille.

And bad this sergeant that he prively°   *in secret*
Sholde this child softe winde and wrappe¹
With alle circumstances° tendrely,   *In every detail*
585 And carie it in a cofre° or in a lappe;°   *box / cloth*
But, upon peyne his heed of for to swappe,²
That no man sholde knowe of his entente,°   *purpose*
Ne whenne° he cam, ne whider° that he wente;   *whence / whither*

But at Boloigne° to his suster° dere,   *Bologna / sister*
590 That thilke° tyme of Panik³ was countesse,   *(at) that same*
He sholde it take, and shewe hire° this matere,   *explain*
Bisekinge hire to don hire bisinesse
This child to fostre in alle gentilesse;⁴

---

7. I.e., well more.
8. (So) that no beasts or birds tear it to pieces.
9. This lord showed something of pity in his behavior.
1. I.e., cover with clothing.

2. But on pain of having his head struck off.
3. Panico, near Bologna.
4. Beseeching her to give her careful attention to the raising of this child, in all things proper to gentle birth.

And whos child that it was he bad hire hyde°   *hide*
595 From every wight, for oght that may bityde.⁵

The sergeant gooth, and hath fulfild this thing;
But to this markis now retourne we.
For now goth he ful faste imagining°   *intently wondering*
If by his wyves chere° he mighte see,   *countenance*
600 Or by hire word aperceyve,° that she   *perceive*
Were chaunged; but he never hire coude finde
But ever in oon y-lyke° sad° and kinde.   *consistently / steadfast*

As glad, as humble, as bisy in servyse,
And eek° in love as she was wont° to be,   *also / accustomed*
605 Was she to him in every manner wyse;°   *sort of way*
Ne of hir doghter noght a word spak she.
Non accident° for noon adversitee   *outward sign*
Was seyn in hire, ne never hir doghter° name   *daughter's*
Ne nempned° she, in ernest nor in game.°   *named / play*

PART FOUR

610 In this estaat° ther passed been foure yeer   *condition*
Er° she with childe was; but, as God wolde,   *Before*
A knave° child she bar° by this Walter,   *male / bore*
Ful gracious and fair° for to biholde.   *handsome*
And whan that folk it to his fader tolde,
615 Nat only he, but al his contree, merie
Was for this child, and God they thanke and herie.°   *praise*

When it was two yeer old and fro the brest
Departed of his norice,° on a day   *nurse*
This markis caughte° yet another lest°   *conceived / desire*
620 To tempte his wyf yet ofter,° if he may.   *more often*
O needles was she tempted in assay!°   *trial*
But wedded men ne knowe no mesure°   *moderation*
Whan that they finde a pacient creature.

"Wyf," quod this markis, "ye han herd er° this,   *before*
625 My peple sikly berth° oure mariage,   *bear ill, dislike*
And namely, sith° my sone y-boren° is,   *since / born*
Now is it worse than ever in al our age.°   *time*
The murmur sleeth° myn herte and my corage,°   *slays / spirit*
For to myne eres° comth the voys so smerte°   *ears / sharply*
630 That it wel ny° destroyed hath myn herte.   *well nigh, almost*

5. From every man, no matter what might happen.

Now sey they thus, 'Whan Walter is agoon,°   gone, dead
Thanne shal the blood of Janicle succede
And been our Lord, for other have we noon;'
Swiche wordes seith my peple, out of drede.°   there is no doubt
635 Wel oughte I of swich° murmur taken hede,   such
For certeinly, I drede swich sentence,°   opinion
Though they nat pleyn° spoke in myn audience.°   plainly / hearing

I wolde live in pees° if that I mighte;   peace
Wherfor I am disposed outerly,°   entirely
640 As I his suster servede° by nighte,   dealt with
Right so thenke I to serve him prively.°   in secret
This warne I yow, that ye nat sodeynly
Out of youreself for no wo sholde outraye:[6]
Beth pacient, and therof I yow preye."

645 "I have," quod she, "seyd thus, and ever shal,
I wol no thing ne nil° no thing, certayn,   desire not
But as yow list; noght greveth me at al,[7]
Thogh that my doghter and my sone be slayn—
At your comandement, this is to sayn.
650 I have noght had no part of children tweyne°   the two children
But first siknesse,[8] and after wo and peyne.

Ye been oure lord, doth with youre owene thing
Right as yow list; axeth no reed at me.[9]
For as I lefte at hoom° al my clothing   home
655 Whan I first cam to yow, right so," quod she,
"Left I my wil and al my libertee,
And took your clothing. Wherfore I yow preye,
Doth your plesaunce; I wol youre lust° obeye.   desire

And certes,° if I hadde prescience°   certainly / foreknowledge
660 Your wil to knowe er° ye youre lust° me tolde,   before / pleasure, will
I wolde it doon withouten necligence.
But now I woot° youre lust and what ye wolde,   know
Al youre plesaunce ferme° and stable° I holde;   firmly / steadfastly
For wiste I° that my deeth wolde do yow ese,°   if I knew / give you pleasure
665 Right gladly wolde I dyen, yow to plese.

Deth may noght make no comparisoun
Unto youre love." And whan this markis sey°   saw
The constance° of his wyf, he caste adoun   constancy
His eyen two,° and wondreth that she may   two eyes

---

6. Should lose control of yourself for any sorrow.   8. I.e., in childbearing.
7. But as it pleases you; it doesn't grieve me at all.   9. Just as you please; ask no advice from me.

670 In pacience suffre al this array.°   *all these things*
And forth he gooth with drery° contenaunce,   *doleful*
But to his herte it was ful greet plesaunce.

This ugly° sergeant, in the same wyse°   *fearsome / way*
That he hire doghter caughte,° right so he—   *took away*
675 Or worse, if men worse can devyse—
Hath hent° hire sone that ful was of beautee.   *seized*
And evere in oon° so pacient was she   *always*
That she no chere° made of hevinesse,[1]   *appearance*
But kiste° hir sone, and after gan it blesse.°   *kissed / blessed him*

680 Save this:° she preyede him that if he mighte   *Except for this*
Hir litel sone he wolde in erthe grave,°   *bury*
His tendre limes,° delicat to sighte,   *limbs*
Fro foules° and fro bestes for to save.   *birds*
But she non answer of him mighte have.
685 He wente his wey, as him nothing ne roghte,[2]
But to Boloigne he tendrely it broghte.

This markis wondreth evere lenger the more[3]
Upon hir pacience, and if that he
Ne hadde soothly° knowen ther-bifore   *truly*
690 That parfitly hir children loved she,
He wolde have wend° that of° som subtiltee,°   *thought / out of / trick*
And of malice or for cruel corage,°   *heart*
That she had suffred this with sad visage.°   *unchanged countenance*

But wel he knew that next himself, certayn,°   *certainly*
695 She loved hir children best in every wyse.
But now of wommen wolde I axen fayn,[4]
If thise assayes° mighte nat suffyse?   *trials*
What coude a sturdy° housbond more devyse   *cruel*
To preve° hir wyfhod and hir stedfastnesse,   *prove, test*
700 And he continuinge evere in sturdinesse?°   *cruelty*

But ther ben folk of swich condicioun°   *such disposition*
That, whan they have a certein purpos take,°   *decided on*
They can nat stinte° of hire entencioun;°   *stop short / intention*
But right as° they were bounden to a stake,   *just as if*
705 They wol nat of that firste purpos slake.°   *leave off*
Right so this markis fulliche° hath purposed°   *fully / intended*
To tempte his wyf as he was first disposed.

---

1. I.e., of a heavy heart.
2. He went on his way, as though he didn't care at all.
3. I.e., increasingly.
4. But now I would like to ask of (you) women.

He waiteth° if by word or contenance   *watched*
That she to him was changed of corage,°   *in her heart*
710 But never coude he finde variance:
She was ay° oon in herte and in visage.   *ever*
And ay the forther⁵ that she was in age,
The more trewe, if that it were possible,
She was to him in love, and more penible,°   *painstaking*

715 For which it semed thus, that of hem two°   *for them both*
Ther nas° but o° wil; for, as Walter leste,°   *was not / one / wished*
The same lust° was hire plesance also;   *desire*
And, God be thanked, al fil° for the beste.   *turned out*
She shewed wel for no worldly unreste⁶
720 A wyf, as of hirself,° no thing ne sholde   *for her own sake*
Wille in effect° but as hir housbond wolde.   *Wish in fact*

The sclaundre° of Walter ofte and wyde spradde°   *scandalous report / spread*
That of a cruel herte he wikkedly,
For° he a povre womman wedded hadde,   *Because*
725 Hath mordred° bothe his children prively.°   *murdered / secretly*
Swich° murmur was among hem comunly.°   *Such / them generally*
No wonder is, for to the peples ere°   *ear*
Ther cam no word but that they mordred were.

For which, wher as his peple therbifore
730 Had loved him wel, the sclaundre of his diffame°   *ill repute*
Made hem that they him hatede therfore:°   *for it*
To been a mordrer is an hateful name.
But natheles, for ernest nc for game,
He of his cruel purpos nolde stente.°   *would not desist*
735 To tempte his wyf was set al his entente.

Whan that his doghter twelf yeer was of age,
He to the court of Rome, in subtil wyse°   *secretly*
Enformed of his wil, sente his message,°   *messenger(s)*
Comaundinge hem swiche bulles to devyse⁷
740 As to his cruel purpos may suffyse:
How that the Pope, as for his peples reste,
Bad° him to wedde another if him leste.°   *Bid / if he wished*

I seye, he bad they sholde countrefete°   *counterfeit*
The Popes bulles, makinge mencioun
745 That he hath leve° his firste wyf to lete,°   *permission / to leave*
As by the Popes dispensacioun,

---

5. I.e., older.   7. Commanding them (i.e., those at the court of
6. (That) for no earthly distress.   Rome) to contrive such (papal) bulls.

To stinte° rancour and dissencioun   stop
Bitwixe his peple and him—thus seyde the bulle,
The which they han publiced atte fulle.°   published widely

750 The rude° peple, as it no wonder is,   ignorant
Wenden° ful wel that it had been right so;   Thought
But whan thise tydinges cam to Grisildis,
I deme[8] that hire herte was ful wo.
But she, y-lyke sad° for evermo,   uniformly steadfast
755 Disposed was, this humble creature,
Th'adversitee of Fortune al t'endure,°   wholly to endure

Abydinge evere° his lust and his plesaunce,   Waiting ever upon
To whom that she was yeven° herte and al,   given
As to hire verray worldly suffisaunce.[9]
760 But shortly if this storie I tellen shal,
This markis writen hath in special
A lettre in which he sheweth° his entente,   reveals
And secrely he to Boloigne it sente.

To the Erl° of Panik,° which that hadde tho°   Earl / Panico / then
765 Wedded his suster, preyde° he specially   requested
To bringen hoom agayn his children two
In honurable estaat° al openly.   state
But o° thing he him preyede outerly,°   one / above all
That he to no wight,° though men wolde enquere,°   nobody / inquire
770 Sholde nat telle whos° children that they were,   whose

But seye the mayden sholde y-wedded be°   was to be wed
Unto the Markis of Saluce° anon.°   Saluzzo / immediately
And as this erl was preyed, so dide he,
For at day set° he on his wey is goon   on the day appointed
775 Toward Saluce, and lordes many oon°   many a lord
In riche array, this mayden for to gyde,°   conduct
Hir yonge brother rydinge hire bisyde.

Arrayed was toward° hir mariage   for
This fresshe mayde, ful of gemmes clere;°   shining jewels
780 Hir brother, which that seven yeer was of age,
Arrayed eek° ful fresh in his manere.   also
And thus in greet noblesse° and with glad chere,°   magnificence / aspect
Toward Saluces shapinge° hir journey,   making
Fro day to day they ryden in hir° wey.   on their

8. I.e., am certain.
9. As (being) her true, earthly contentment (refers back to "his lust and his plesaunce" in l. 757).

PART FIVE

785 Among al this, after his wikke usage,°   *wicked custom*
      This markis yet his wyf to tempte more
      To the uttereste preve° of hir corage,°   *utmost proof / heart, spirit*
      Fully to han experience and lore°   *knowledge*
      If that she were as stedfast as bifore,
790 He on a day in open audience°   *assembly*
      Ful boistously° hath seyd hire this sentence:° *roughly / decision*

      "Certes,° Grisilde, I hadde y-nough plesaunce   *Truly*
      To han yow to my wyf for youre goodnesse—
      As for youre trouthe and for youre obeisaunce—
795 Nought for youre linage ne for your richesse.
      But now knowe I in verray soothfastnesse°   *certain truth*
      That in gret lordshipe, if I wel avyse,°   *discern*
      Ther is gret servitute in sondry wyse.°   *in sundry ways*

      I may nat don as every° plowman may.   *any*
800 My peple me constreyneth° for to take   *constrain*
      Another wyf, and cryen° day by day;   *call (for it)*
      And eek the Pope, rancour for to slake,°   *appease*
      Consenteth it,° that dar I undertake;°   *Consents to it / declare*
      And trewcliche thus muche I wol yow seye,
805 My newe wyf is coming by° the weye.   *along*

      Be strong of herte, and voyde anon° hir place; *vacate at once*
      And thilke° dowere that ye broghten me   *that same*
      Tak it agayn, I graunte it of my grace.
      Retourneth to your fadres hous," quod he.
810 "No man may alwey han prosperitee;
      With evene° herte I rede° yow t'endure   *steady / advise*
      The strook° of Fortune or of aventure."°   *stroke / chance*

      And she agayn answerde in pacience,
      "My lord," quod she, "I woot,° and wiste° alway, *know / knew*
815 How that bitwixen° youre magnificence   *between*
      And my poverte no wight° can ne may   *no one*
      Maken comparison; it is no nay.°   *it cannot be denied*
      I ne heeld me nevere digne° in no manere   *worthy*
      To be youre wyf, no, ne youre chamberere.°   *chambermaid*

820 And in this hous ther° ye me lady made—   *where*
      The heighe God take I for my witnesse,
      And also wisly° he my soule glade°—   *as surely / may gladden*
      I nevere heeld me° lady ne maistresse,   *considered myself*
      But humble servant to youre worthinesse,

825 And ever shal, whyl that my lyf may dure,°   *last*
    Aboven every worldly creature.

    That ye so longe of youre benignitee°   *graciousness*
    Han holden me in honour and nobleye,°   *nobleness*
    Wher as I was noght worthy for to be,
830 That thonke I God and yow, to whom I preye
    Foryelde° it yow. There is namore to seye.   *Repay*
    Unto my fader gladly wol I wende,°   *go*
    And with him dwelle unto my lyves ende.

    Ther I was fostred of° a child ful smal,   *raised from*
835 Til I be deed, my lyf ther wol I lede:
    A widwe clene,° in body, herte, and al.   *widow pure*
    For sith I yaf° to yow my maydenhede,   *gave*
    And am youre trewe wyf, it is no drede,°   *without doubt*
    God shilde° swich a lordes wyf to take   *forbid*
840 Another man to housbonde or to make.°   *as mate*

    And of youre newe wyf, God of his grace
    So graunte yow wele° and prosperitee!   *happiness*
    For I wol gladly yelden hire° my place,   *yield to her*
    In which that I was blisful wont° to be.   *accustomed*
845 For sith it lyketh yow,° my lord," quod she,   *since it pleases you*
    "That° whylom° weren al myn hertes reste,   *Who / formerly*
    That I shal goon,° I wol gon whan yow leste.   *must go*

    But ther as ye me profre swich dowaire°   *such a dowry*
    As I first broghte, it is wel in my minde
850 It were my wrecched clothes, nothing° faire,   *in no way*
    The which to me were hard now for to finde.
    O gode God! how gentil and how kynde
    Ye semed by youre speche and youre visage°   *face, appearance*
    The day that maked was oure mariage!

855 But sooth is seyd—algate I finde it trewe,[1]
    For in effect it preved is on° me—   *is proven in*
    Love is noght° old as whan that it is newe.   *not (the same)*
    But certes, lord, for noon adversitee,
    To dyen in the cas, it shal nat be[2]
860 That evere in word or werk° I shal repente   *deed*
    That I yow yaf° myn herte in hool entente.°   *gave / wholeheartedly*

    My lord, ye woot° that in my fadres place   *know*
    Ye dide me strepe out of my povre wede,[3]

---

1. But it is truly said—in any case, I find it true.   be.
2. (Even) if I should die in this affair, it shall not   3. You had me stripped out of my poor clothing.

And richely me cladden, of° youre grace.   *by*
865 To yow broghte I noght elles, out of drede,°   *there is no doubt*
But feyth° and nakednesse and maydenhede.   *loyalty*
And here agayn your clothing I restore,
And eek° your wedding-ring, for everemore.   *also*

The remenant of your jewels redy be°   *in prepared*
870 Inwith your chambre, dar I saufly° sayn.   *Within / safely*
Naked out of my fadres hous," quod she,
"I cam, and naked moot° I turne° agayn.   *must / return*
Al youre plesaunce wol I folwen fayn.°   *follow willingly*
But yet I hope it be nat youre entente
875 That I smoklees⁴ out of youre paleys wente.°   *should go*

Ye coude nat doon so dishoneste a thing
That thilke wombe in which youre children leye°   *lay*
Sholde biforn the peple, in my walking,
Be seyn al bare;° wherfore I yow preye,   *naked*
880 Lat me nat lyk a worm go by° the weye.   *along*
Remembre yow, myn owene lord so dere,
I was youre wyf, thogh I unworthy were.

Wherfore in guerdon° of my maydenhede,   *recompense*
Which that I broghte, and noght agayn I bere,°   *bear*
885 As voucheth sauf to yeve me to my mede⁵
But swich° a smok as I was wont° to were,   *Only such / used*
That I therwith may wrye° the wombe of here°   *hide / her*
That was youre wyf. And heer take I my leve°   *leave*
Of yow, myn owene lord, lest I yow greve."°   *vex*

890 "The smok," quod he, "that thou hast on thy bak,
Lat it be° stille, and bere° it forth with thee."   *remain / bear*
But wel unnethes° thilke° word he spak   *hardly / that same*
But wente his wey for rewthe° and for pitee.   *compassion*
Biforn the folk hirselven strepeth° she,   *strips*
895 And in hir smok, with heed and foot al bare,
Toward hir fader hous forth is she fare.⁶

The folk hire folwe wepinge in hir weye,°   *on their way*
And Fortune ay they cursen as they goon.
But she fro weping kepte hire eyen dreye,°   *eyes dry*
900 Ne in this tyme word ne spak she noon.
Hir fader, that this tydinge° herde anoon,   *news*
Curseth the day and tyme that nature
Shoop° him to been a lyves° creature.   *Created / living*

---

4. Smockless, without even an undergarment.   6. She has journeyed forth toward her father's house.
5. Just allow me to be given as my reward (my pay).

For out of doute° this olde povre man   certainly
105 Was evere in suspect° of hir mariage;   doubtful
For evere he demed,° sith° that it bigan,   thought / since
That whan the lord fulfild hadde his corage,°   desire
Him wolde thinke it were a disparage⁷
To his estaat° so lowe for t'alighte,°   rank / to settle
910 And voyden° hire as sone as ever he mighte.   (would) get rid of

Agayns° his doghter hastilich° goth he,   Toward / hastily
For he by noyse of folk knew hire cominge,
And with hire old cote, as it mighte be,⁸
He covered hire ful sorwefully wepinge.
915 But on° hire body mighte he it nat bringe,   around
For rude was the cloth and she more of age
By dayes fele° than at hire mariage.   many

Thus with hire fader for a certeyn space°   space of time
Dwelleth this flour° of wyfly pacience,   flower
920 That neither by hire wordes ne hire face
Biforn° the folk, ne eek in hire° absence,   In front of / their
Ne shewed she that hire° was doon offence;   to her
Ne of hire heighe estaat no remembraunce
Ne hadde she, as by° hire countenaunce.   to judge by

925 No wonder is, for in hire grete° estaat   high
Hire goost° was evere in pleyn° humylitee: spirit / perfect
No tendre mouth, noon herte delicaat,
No pompe, no semblant° of royaltee,   semblance
But ful of pacient benignitee,°   graciousness
930 Discreet and prydeles,° ay° honurable,   without pride / ever
And to hire housbonde evere meke and stable.°   constant

Men speke of Job and most° for his humblesse,° above all / humbleness
As clerkes, whan hem list, can wel endyte,°   write
Namely of men; but as in soothfastnesse,°   with regard to truth
935 Thogh clerkes preyse wommen but a lyte,°   very little
Ther can no man in humblesse him acquyte°   acquit himself
As womman can, ne can ben half so trewe
As wommen been, but it be falle of newe.⁹

PART SIX

Fro Boloigne is this Erl of Panik come,
940 Of which the fame up sprang° to more and lesse,° arose / great and small

7. It would seem to him that it was a disgrace.   9. Unless it has happened just recently.
8. And with her old cloak, as well as he could.

And in the peples eres° alle and some[1]   *ears*
Was couth eek° that a newe markisesse   *It was known also*
He with him broghte, in swich pompe and richesse,
That never was ther seyn with mannes yë°   *eye*
945 So noble array in al West Lumbardye.

The markis, which that shoop° and knew al this,   *planned*
Er that' this er was come sente his message°   *Before / had / messenger*
For thilke° sely° povre Grisildis;   *that same / good*
And she with humble herte and glad visage,
950 Nat with no swollen[2] thoght in hire corage,°   *heart*
Cam at his heste,° and on hire knees hire sette,   *command*
And reverently and wysly° she him grette.°   *discreetly / greeted*

"Grisild," quod he, "my wille is outrely°   *completely*
This mayden, that shal wedded been to me,
955 Receyved be to-morwe as royally
As it possible is in myn hous to be,
And eek that every wight° in his degree   *person*
Have his estaat in sitting° and servyse   *proper place at table*
And heigh plesaunce, as I can best devyse.

960 I have no wommen suffisaunt,° certayn,   *not women enough*
The chambres for t'arraye in ordinaunce°   *to put in order*
After my lust, and therfor wolde I fayn[3]
That thyn° were al swich maner governaunce;   *thine*
Thou knowest eek of old al my plesaunce.
965 Though thyn array° be badde and yvel biseye,°   *apparel / poor to see*
Do thou thy devoir° at the leeste weye."°   *duty / all the same*

"Nat only, lord, that I am glad," quod she,
"To doon youre lust, but I desyre also
970 Yow for to serve and plese in my degree°   *according to my station*
Withouten feynting,° and shal everemo.   *weariness*
Ne nevere, for no wele ne no wo,
Ne shal the gost° withinne myn herte stente°   *spirit / cease*
To love yow best with al my trewe entente."

And with that word she gan° the hous to dighte,°   *began / to make ready*
975 And tables for to sette and beddes make;
And peyned hir° to doon al that she mighte,   *she took pains*
Preying the chambereres,° for Goddes sake,   *Urging the chambermaids*
To hasten hem,° and faste swepe and shake.   *To hurry*
And she, the most servisable° of alle,   *diligent*
980 Hath every chambre arrayed and his halle.

1. I.e., one and all.   3. According to my desire, and therefore I would be
2. I.e., prideful.   pleased.

Abouten undern gan this erl alighte, [4]
That with him broghte thise noble children tweye,
For which the peple ran to seen the sighte
Of hire° array, so richely biseye;°   *their / rich to see*
985 And thanne at erst amonges hem they seye [5]
That Walter was no fool thogh that him leste°   *it pleased him*
To chaunge his wyf, for it was for the beste.

For she is fairer, as they demen° alle,   *judge*
Than is Grisild, and more tendre° of age,   *young*
990 And fairer fruit° bitwene hem sholde falle,   *offspring*
And more plesant, for hire heigh linage; [6]
Hir brother eek so fair was of visage
That hem° to seen the peple hath caught° plesaunce,   *them / taken*
Commendinge now the markis governaunce.°   *conduct*

995 "O stormy peple! unsad and evere untrewe!
Ay undiscreet and chaunging as a vane! [7]
Delytinge evere in rumbel° that is newe,   *rumor*
For lyk the mone ay wexe° ye and wane!   *wax, grow larger*
Ay ful of clapping, dere y-nogh a jane! [8]
1000 Youre doom is fals, youre constance yvel preveth, [9]
A ful greet fool is he that on yow leveth!"°   *believes in you*

Thus seyden sadde° folk in that citee,   *steadfast*
Whan that the peple gazed up and doun,
For they were glad, right° for the noveltee,   *just*
1005 To han a newe lady of hir toun.
Namore of this make I now mencioun,
But to Grisilde agayn wol I me dresse,°   *address myself*
And telle hir constance and hir bisinesse.

Ful bisy was Grisilde in every thing
1010 That to the feste was apertinent;°   *appertained*
Right noght was she abayst° of hire clothing,   *ashamed*
Though it were rude and somdel eek torent.°   *also somewhat torn*
But with glad chere to the yate° is went°   *gate / has gone*
With other folk, to grete the markisesse,
1015 And after that doth forth° hire bisinesse.   *continues*

With so glad chere his gestes she receyveth,
And so conningly, everich in his degree,

---

4. About mid-morning this earl arrived (*lit.*, dismounted).
5. And then for the first time they say amongst themselves.
6. Because of her noble birth (lineage).

7. Ever unwise, and changeable as a weather vane.
8. Ever full of chatter, not worth a penny (a "jane").
9. Your judgment is false, your constancy proves poor.

That no defaute no man aperceyveth; [1]
But ay they wondren what she mighte be
1020 That in so povre array was for to see,
And coude° swich honour and reverence;   *understood*
And worthily they preisen° hire prudence.   *praise*

In al this mene whyle she ne stente°   *did not ssase*
This mayde and eek hir brother to commende
1025 With al hir herte, in ful benigne entente,
So wel that no man coude hir prys° amende.°   *praise / improve*
But atte laste,° whan that thise lordes wende°   *at (the) last / thought*
To sitten doun to mete,° he gan to calle   *to the meal*
Grisilde, as she was bisy in his halle.

1030 "Grisilde," quod he, as° it were in his pley,   *as if*
"How lyketh thee my wyf and hire beautee?"
"Right wel," quod she, "my lord, for in good fey,°   *faith*
A fairer say° I nevere noon than she.   *saw*
I prey to God yeve° hire prosperitee,   *give*
1035 And so hope I that he wol to yow sende
Plesance y-nogh unto youre lyves ende.

O° thing biseke° I yow, and warne also,   *One / beseech*
That ye ne prikke° with no tormentinge   *goad*
This tendre mayden, as ye han don mo.°   *others*
1040 For she is fostred° in hire norishinge°   *raised / upbringing*
More tendrely, and to my supposinge,
She coude nat adversitee endure
As coude a povre fostred° creature."   *raised in poverty*

And whan this Walter say° hire pacience,   *saw*
1045 Hir glade chere and no malice at al—
And he so ofte had doon to hire offence,
And she ay sad° and constant as a wal,   *ever firm*
Continuinge evere hire innocence overal°—   *in every respect*
This sturdy markis gan his herte dresse [2]
1050 To rewen° upon hire wyfly stedfastnesse.   *take pity*

"This is y-nogh,° Grisilde myn," quod he,   *enough*
"Be now namore agast° ne yvel apayed;°   *afraid / ill-pleased*
I have thy feith° and thy benignitee,   *faithfulness*
As wel as ever womman was, assayed.°   *tested*
1055 In greet° estaat, and povreliche° arrayed,   *high / poorly*
Now knowe I, dere wyf, thy stedfastnesse,"
And hire in armes took and gan hire kesse.°   *kissed her*

1. She receives his guests in so happy a mood and (so) skillfully—each and every one according to his rank—that no one (could) discover anything lacking.
2. This cruel (stern) marquis did turn his heart.

And she for wonder took of it no keep;°   *heed*
She herde nat what thing he to hire seyde;
1060 She ferde as° she had stert° out of a sleep,   *acted as if / started*
Til she out of hir masednesse° abreyde.°   *bewilderment / awoke*
"Grisilde," quod he, "by God that for us deyde,
Thou art my wyf, ne noon other I have,
Ne never hadde, as God my soule save!

1065 This is thy doghter which thou hast supposed
To be my wyf; that other feithfully
Shal be myn heir, as I have ay disposed;°   *ever intended*
Thou bare° him in thy body trewely.   *bore*
At Boloigne have I kept hem prively;°   *secretly*
1070 Tak hem agayn, for now maystow° nat seye   *mayest thou*
That thou hast lorn° non of thy children tweye.   *lost*

And folk that otherweyes° han seyd of me,   *otherwise*
I warne hem wel that I have doon this dede
For no malice ne for no crueltee,
1075 But for t'assaye in thee thy wommanhede,
And nat to sleen° my children, God forbede!   *slay*
But for to kepe hem prively and stille,°   *quietly*
Til I thy purpos knewe and al thy wille."

Whan she this herde, aswowne° doun she falleth   *in a faint*
1080 For pitous joye, and after hire swowninge
She bothe hire yonge children to hire calleth,
And in hire armes, pitously wepinge,
Embraceth hem, and tendrely kissinge,
Ful lyk a mooder, with hire salte teres
1085 She batheth bothe hire visage° and hire heres.°   *their faces / hair*

O, which a° pitous thing it was to see   *what a*
Hir swowning, and hire humble voys° to here!   *voice*
"Grauntmercy,° lord, God thanke° it yow," quod she,   *Great thanks / reward*
"That ye han saved me my children dere!
1090 Now rekke I never to ben deed right here;³
Sith° I stonde in youre love and in youre grace,   *Since*
No fors of deeth, ne whan my spirit pace!⁴

O tendre, o dere, o yonge children myne,
Your woful mooder wende° stedfastly   *thought*
1095 That cruel houndes or som foul vermyne°   *low animal*
Hadde eten yow; but God of his mercy,
And youre benigne° fader, tendrely   *gracious*

3. Now I do not care if I should die right here.
4. Death is of no consequence, nor (the time) when my spirit (shall) go hence.

Hath doon yow kept;" and in that same stounde⁵

Al sodeynly she swapte° adoun to grounde.   *fell*

1100 And in her swough° so sadly° holdeth she   *faint / firmly*

Hire children two, whan she gan hem t'embrace,°   *embraced them*

That with greet sleighte° and greet difficultee   *skill*

The children from hire arm they gonne arace,°   *torn away*

U many a teer on many a pitous face

1105 Doun ran of hem that stoden hire bisyde;

Unnethe° abouten hire mighte thcy abyde.°   *Scarcely / remain*

Walter hire gladeth° and hire sorwe slaketh;°   *cheers her / eases*

She ryseth up, abaysed,° from hire traunce,   *embarrassed*

And every wight hire joye and feste maketh⁶

1110 Til she hath caught° agayn hire contenaunce.°   *got / composure*

Walter hire dooth so feithfully plesaunce

That it was deyntee° for to seen the chere°   *delight / happiness*

Bitwixe hem two, now they ben met y-fere.°   *together*

Thise ladyes, whan that they hir° tyme say,°   *their / saw*

1115 Han taken hire and into chambre goon,

And strepen° hire out of hire rude array,   *undress*

And in a cloth of gold that brighte shoon,

With a coroune° of many a riche stoon°   *crown / stone, jewel*

Upon hire heed, they into halle hire broghte,

1120 And ther she was honoured as hire oghte.°   *was due her*

Thus hath this pitous day a blisful ende,

For every man and womman dooth his might

This day in murthe and revel to dispende°   *spend*

Til on the welkne° shoon the sterres light.   *in the sky*

1125 For more solempne° in every mannes sight   *splendid*

This feste was, and gretter of costage,°   *cost*

Than was the revel of hire mariage.

Ful many a yeer in heigh prosperitee

Liven thise two in concord and in reste,

1130 And richely his doghter maried he

Unto a lord, oon of the worthieste

Of al Itaille; and than in pees° and reste   *peace*

His wyves fader in his court he kepeth,

Til that the soule out of his body crepeth.

1135 His sone succedeth in his heritage,

In reste and pees, after his fader° day,   *father's*

5. Have had you cared for;" and in that same   6. And every person makes joy for her, and good
moment.   cheer.

And fortunat was eek in mariage,
Al° putte he nat his wyf in greet assay.   *Although*
This world is nat so strong, it is no nay,°   *it cannot be denied*
1140 As it hath been in olde tymes yore.°   *long ago*
And herkneth° what this auctour° seith therfore: *listen to / Petrarch*

This storie is seyd, nat for that wyves sholde
Folwen Grisilde as in humilitee,
For it were importable, though they wolde;[7]
1145 But for that every wight° in his degree   *person*
Sholde be constant in adversitee
As was Grisilde. Therfore Petrark wryteth
This storie, which with heigh style he endyteth.°   *composes*

For sith° a womman was so pacient   *since*
1150 Unto a mortal man, wel more us oghte
Receyven al in gree° that God us sent.   *good will*
For greet skile is he preve that he wroghte,[8]
But he ne tempteth° no man that he boghte°—   *tempts / redeemed*
As seith Seint Jame,° if ye his pistel° rede.   *James / epistle*
1155 He preveth folk al day, it is no drede,°   *doubtless*

And suffreth° us, as for our excercyse,°   *allows / discipline*
With sharpe scourges of adversitee
Ful ofte to be bete° in sondry wyse,°   *beaten / ways*
Nat for to knowe oure wil; for certes he,
1160 Er we were born, knew al oure freletee.°   *frailty*
And for our beste is al his governaunce:
Lat us than live in vertuous suffraunce.°   *patience*

But o word, lordinges, herkneth° er I go: *listen to*
It were ful hard to finde now-a-dayes
1165 In al a° toun Grisildes three or two;   *In an entire*
For if that they were put to swiche assayes,
The gold of hem hath now so° badde alayes°   *such / alloys*
With bras, that thogh the coyne be fair at yë,°   *to the eye*
It wolde rather breste a-two° than plye.°   *break in two / bend*

1170 For which heer, for the Wyves love of Bathe[9]—
Whos lyf and al hire secte° God mayntene   *sect*
In heigh maistrye,° and elles were it scathe°—   *mastery / a pity*
I wol with lusty° herte fresshe and grene   *vigorous*
Seyn yow a song to glade° yow, I wene,°   *gladden / think*

7. For it would be intolerable (*lit.*, unbearable),
even if they should wish to.
8. For there is good reason why He (should) test

what He created.
9. For which right now, for love of the Wife of
Bath.

1175 And lat us stinte of ernestful matere.[1]
     Herkneth my song, that seith in this manere:

THE ENVOY

Grisilde is deed, and eek° hire pacience,   also
And bothe atones° buried in Itaille.   togethan
For which I crye in open audience: hearing
1180 No wedded man so hardy° be t'assaille   bold
His wyves pacience, in hope to finde
Grisildes, for in certein he shall faille!

O noble wyves, ful of heigh prudence,
Lat noon humilitee your tonge naille,°   nail down
1185 Ne lat no clerk have cause or diligence
To wryte of yow a storie of swich mervaille
As of Grisildis, pacient and kinde,
Lest Chichevache yow swelwe in hire entraille![2]

Folweth Ekko,° that holdeth no silence,   Echo
1190 But evere answereth at the countretaille;°   in counterreply
Beth nat bidaffed for youre innocence,[3]
But sharply tak on yow the governaille.°   control
Emprinteth wel this lesson in youre minde
For commune profit, sith it may availle.

1195 Ye archewyves, stondeth at defence[4]—
Sin° ye be stronge as is a greet camaille°—   Since / camel
Ne suffreth° nat that men yow doon offence.   allow
And sclendre° wyves, feble as in bataille,   slender
Beth egre° as is a tygre yond° in Inde;°   fierce / yonder / India
1200 Ay clappeth as a mille, I yow consaille.[5]

Ne dreed° hem nat, doth hem no reverence;°   fear / honor
For though thyn housbonde armed be in maille,°   mail
The arwes° of thy crabbed eloquence   arrows
Shal perce his brest, and eek his aventaille.°   helmet's faceplate
1205 In jalousye I rede eek° thou him binde,   advise also
And thou shalt make him couche° as dooth a quaille.   cower

If thou be fair, ther° folk ben in presence°   where / present
Shew thou thy visage and thyn apparaille;°   clothing

---

1. And let's stop (talking) of serious matters.
2. Lest Chichevache swallow you into her entrails. (Chichevache was a fabled cow who fed only on patient wives, and hence was very lean.)
3. Don't be made a fool of because of (your) sim-
plemindedness.
4. You archwives, stand up in self-defense.
5. Always be noisy (clatter, chatter), I advise you, like a mill.

If thou be foul, be free of thy dispence;°   *spending*
1210 To gete thee freendes ay do thy travaille.°   *take thy pains*
Be ay of chere as light as leef on linde,[6]
And lat him care,° and wepe, and wringe, and waille!   *worry*

[THE WORDS OF THE HOST

1212a This worthy Clerk, whan ended was his tale,
Our Hoste seyde and swoor, "By Goddes bones,
Me were lever than a barel ale[7]
My wyf at hoom had herd this legende ones.°   *once*
This is a gentil tale for the nones,°   *occasion*
As to my purpos, wiste ye° my wille;   *if you know*
1212g But thing that wol nat be, lat it be stille."][8]

The Merchant's Prologue

"Weping and wayling, care, and other sorwe
I know y-nogh, on even and a-morwe,"[1]
Quod the Marchant, "and so doon othere mo°   *many others*
That wedded been, I trowe° that it be so.   *believe*
5 For wel I woot it fareth so with me.
I have a wyf, the worste that may be:
For thogh the feend° to hir y-coupled were,   *devil*
She wolde him overmacche,° I dar wel swere.   *overmatch, master*
What° sholde I yow reherce° in special°   *Why / rehearse / in detail*
10 Hir hye° malice? She is a shrewe at al.°   *proud / in every respect*
Ther is a long and large difference
Bitwix° Grisildis grete pacience   *Between*
And of my wyf the passing° crueltee.   *surpassing*
Were I unbounden, also moot I thee,[2]
15 I wolde nevere eft° comen in the snare.   *again*
We wedded men live in sorwe and care:
Assaye° whoso wol, and he shal finde   *Test (it)*
That I seye sooth, by Seint Thomas of Inde,[3]
As for the more part[4]—I sey nat alle.
20 God shilde° that it sholde so bifalle!   *forbid*
A! goode sire Hoost, I have y-wedded be
Thise monthes two, and more nat,° pardee;   *no more*

6. In behavior, always be as light as a leaf of the linden tree.
7. I'd sooner than a barrel of ale (that).
8. This stanza appears in some manuscripts and seems to have been an earlier draft canceled when Chaucer chose to have the Merchant respond directly to the Clerk's tale.

1. I.e., by night and day.
2. Were I freed of the marriage bond, so may I thrive.
3. St. Thomas of India ("Doubting Thomas," who tested Christ's wounds).
4. I.e., the majority.

And yet, I trowe, he that all his lyve
Wyflees[5] hath been, though that men wolde him ryve°   stab
25 Unto the herte, ne coude in no manere
Tellen so muchel sorwe as I now heere
Coude tellen of my wyves cursednesse!"°   shrewishness
     "Now," quod our Hoost, "Marchaunt, so God yow blesse,
Sin° ye so muchel knowen of that art   since
30 Ful hertely I pray yow telle us part."   heartily
     "Gladly," quod he, "but of myn owene sore,°   misery
For sory° herte, I telle may namore."   (a) vexed

The Franklin's Prologue and Tale

The Introduction

     "In feith, Squier, thou hast thee wel y-quit°   acquitted
And gentilly.[1] I preise wel thy wit,"
Quod the Frankeleyn. "Consideringe thy youthe,
So feelingly thou spekest, sire, I allow the:°   commend thee
5 As to my doom,° there is non that is here   judgment
Of cloquence that shal be thy pere,°   peer, equal
If that thou live. God yeve° thee good chaunce,°   give / fortune
And in vertu sende thee continuaunce,
For of thy speche I have greet deyntee.°   pleasure
10 I have a sone, and by the Trinitee,
I hadde levere than twenty pound worth lond—[2]
Though it right now were fallen in myn hond—
He were a man of swich discrecioun
As that ye been. Fy on possessioun,°   property, wealth
15 But if° a man be vertuous withal!   Unless
I have my sone snibbed,° and yet shal,   rebuked
For he to vertu listeth nat entende;[3]
But for to pleye at dees,° and to despende,°   dice / spend freely
And lese° al that he hath, is his usage.°   lose / custom
20 And he hath levere° talken with a page°   rather / young servant
Than to comune° with any gentil wight°   talk / gentlemanly person
Where he mighte lerne gentillesse° aright."   gentility
     "Straw for your gentillesse!" quod our Host.
"What, Frankeleyn! pardee,° sire, wel thou wost°   by God / knowest
25 That eche of yow mot° tellen atte leste°   must / at (the) least
A tale or two, or breken his biheste."°   promise

5. I.e., a bachelor.
1. I.e., like a gentleman.
2. I would rather than land worth twenty pounds a
year.

3. Because he does not care to concern himself with
(the development of his) capacities. ("Vertu" involves
notions of power, strength, and efficacy, as well as
moral goodness.)

"That knowe I wel, sire," quod the Frankeleyn;
"I prey yow, haveth me nat in desdeyn°   *don't disdain me*
Though to this man I speke a word or two."
30   "Telle on thy tale withouten wordes mo."°   *more*
"Gladly, sire Host," quod he, "I wol obeye
Unto your wil; now herkneth° what I seye.   *listen to*
I wol yow nat contrarien° in no wyse   *oppose*
As fer as that my wittes wol suffyse.
35   I prey to God that it may plesen yow:
Thanne woot I wel that it is good y-now."°   *enough*

The Prologue

Thise olde gentil Britons° in hir° dayes   *Bretons / their*
Of diverse aventures maden layes,°   *lays, poems*
Rymeyed° in hir firste° Briton tonge;   *Rhymed / original*
40   Which layes with hir instruments they songe,
Or elles redden hem° for hir plesaunce;°   *else read them / pleasure*
And oon of hem have I in remembraunce,
Which I shal seyn with good wil as I can:
But, sires, by cause° I am a burel° man,   *because / plain, untutored*
45   At my biginning first I yow biseche
Have me excused of my rude° speche.   *crude, inartistic*
I lerned nevere rethoryk,° certeyn:°   *rhetoric / in truth*
Thing that I speke, it moot° be bare and pleyn.°   *must / plain*
I sleep° nevere on the Mount of Pernaso,°   *slept / Parnassus*
50   Ne lerned Marcus Tullius Cithero.°   *Cicero*
Colours ne knowe I none, withouten drede,[4]
But swiche° colours as growen in the mede,°   *Only such / meadow*
Or elles swiche as men dye or peynte.°   *paint*
Colours of rethoryk ben to me queynte:°   *too abstruse for me*
55   My spirit feleth noght of° swich matere.   *has no feeling for*
But if yow list,° my tale shul ye here.   *it pleases you*

The Tale

In Armorik,° that called is Britayne,°   *Armorica / Brittany*
Ther was a knight that loved and dide his payne°   *took pains*
To serve a lady in his beste wyse;
60   And many a labour, many a greet empryse°   *undertaking, exploit*
He for his lady wroghte,° er° she were wonne.   *performed / before*
For she was oon the faireste° under sonne,   *one of the loveliest*
And eek° therto come of so heigh kinrede,°   *also / high lineage*
That wel unnethes dorste° this knight, for drede,°   *scarcely dared / fear*

---

4. I don't know any rhetorical "colors" (devices)—no fear of that. (The Franklin's modest apology is of a traditional kind, recommended by the very art he claims not to know.)

65 Telle hire his wo, his peyne, and his distresse.
But atte laste° she, for his worthinesse,   *at (the) last*
And namely° for his meke obeysaunce,°   *especially / obedience*
Hath swich° a pitee caught of° his penaunce°   *such / felt for / suffering*
That prively° she fil of his accord⁵   *secretly*
70 To take him for hir housbonde and hir lord,
Of swich lordshipe as men han over hir wyves,
And for to lede° the more in blisse hir° lyves,   *lead / their*
Of his free wil he swoor hire° as a knight   *swore to her*
That nevere in al his lyf he, day ne night,
75 Ne sholde upon him take no maistrye°   *mastery, domination*
Agayn hir wil, ne kythe hire° jalousye,   *display to her*
But hire obeye and folwe hir wil in al
As any lovere to his lady shal°—   *must*
Save that the name° of soveraynetee,   *title, appearance*
80 That wolde he have for shame of his degree.⁶
     She thanked him, and with ful greet humblesse
She seyde, "Sire, sith° of youre gentillesse   *since*
Ye profre me to have so large° a reyne,°   *free / rein*
Ne wolde nevere God bitwixe us tweyne,
85 As in my gilt, were outher werre or stryf.⁷
Sire, I wol be youre humble trewe wyf:
Have heer my trouthe,° til that myn herte breste."°   *loyal pledge / burst*
Thus been they bothe in quiete and in° reste.   *at*
     For o° thing, sires, saufly° dar I seye,   *one / safely*
90 That frendes everich other° moot° obeye,   *each other / must*
If they wol longe holden companye.
Love wol nat ben constreyned by maistrye.⁸
When maistrie comth, the God of Love anon°   *at once*
Beteth° hise winges, and farewel, he is gon!   *Beats*
95 Love is a thing as° any spirit free.   *like*
Wommen of kinde° desiren libertee,   *by nature*
And nat to ben constreyned as a thral;°   *thrall, slave*
And so don men, if I soth° seyen shal.   *truth*
Loke who that° is most pacient in love: *Consider the man who*
100 He is at his avantage al above.°   *above all others*
Pacience is an heigh vertu, certeyn,
For it venquisseth,° as thise clerkes° seyn,   *vanquishes / scholars*
Thinges that rigour° sholde° never atteyne.   *harshness, strictness / could*
For every word men may nat chyde or pleyne:°   *complain*
105 Lerneth to suffre, or elles, so moot I goon,°   *as I may live*
Ye shul it lerne, wher so ye wole or noon.°   *whether you wish to or not*

5. I.e., consented.
6. That would he retain, lest it reflect on his rank.
7. God would not wish that there should ever be either war or strife between us two, for any fault

(guilt) of mine.
8. Love will not be constrained by mastery (i.e., by one partner exercising absolute power over the other).

For in this world, certein, ther no wight° is   *person*
That he ne dooth or seith somtyme amis.°   *wrongly*
Ire,° siknesse, or constellacioun,°   *Anger / fate, his stars*
110 Wyn, wo, or chaunginge of complexioun[9]
Causeth ful ofte to doon amis or speken.
On every wrong a man may nat be wreken:°   *avenged*
After° the tyme moste be temperaunce°   *According to / moderation*
To every wight that can on governaunce.°   *understands self-control*
115 And therfore hath this wyse worthy knight,
To live in ese, suffrance hire bihight,°   *promised her (his) forbearance*
And she to him ful wisly gan to swere°   *truly did swear*
That nevere sholde ther be defaute in here.°   *a lacking in her*
Heere may men seen an humble wys accord:°   *agreeing*
120 Thus hath she take hir servant and hir lord,
Servant in love, and lord in mariage;
Thanne was he bothe in lordship and servage.°   *servitude*
Servage? Nay, but in lordshipe above,
Sith he hath bothe his lady and his love;
125 His lady, certes,° and his wyf also,   *certainly*
The which that lawe of love acordeth to.
And whan he was in this prosperitee,
Hoom with his wyf he gooth to his contree,°   *region*
Nat fer fro Pedmark, ther his dwelling was,[1]
130 Where as he liveth in blisse and in solas.°   *solace, joy*
Who coude telle, but he hadde wedded be,°   *unless he'd been married*
The joye, the ese, and the prosperitee
That is bitwixe an housbonde and his wyf?
A yeer and more lasted this blisful lyf,
135 Til that the knight of which I speke of thus,
That of Kayrrud° was cleped° Arveragus,   *from Kerru / called*
Shoop him° to goon and dwelle a yeer or tweyne°   *Prepared himself / two*
In Engelond, that cleped was eek° Briteyne,°   *also / Britain*
To seke in armes worshipe and honour—
140 For al his lust° he sette° in swich° labour—   *pleasure / took / such*
And dwelled ther two yeer; the book seith thus.
Now wol I stinten of° this Arveragus,   *cease concerning*
And speken I wole of Dorigene his wyf.
That loveth hire housbonde as hire hertes lyf.
145 For his absence wepeth she and syketh,°   *sighs*
As doon thise noble wyves whan hem lyketh.°   *it pleases them*
She moorneth, waketh,° wayleth, fasteth, pleyneth;°   *stays awake / laments*
Desyr of his presence hire so distreyneth°   *afflicts*
That al this wyde world she sette at noght.°   *holds to be nothing*

9. Wine, woe, or a change in the balances of humors ("complexioun") that determine a man's temperament.

1. Not far from Penmarch (on the coast of Finistère, in Brittany), where his dwelling was.

150 Hire frendes, whiche that knewe hir hevy thoght,
    Conforten hire in al that ever they may:
    They prechen° hire, they telle hire night and day,   *preach to*
    That causelees she sleeth° hirself, allas!   *is killing*
    And every confort possible in this cas
155 They doon to hire with al hire bisinesse,°   *their diligence*
    Al for to make hire leve hire hevinesse.
        By proces,° as ye knowen everichoon,°   *In course of time / each and every one*
    Men may so longe graven in° a stoon   *engrave*
    Til som figure therinne emprented be.
160 So longe han° they conforted hire til she   *have*
    Receyved hath, by hope and by resoun,
    The emprenting° of hire° consolacioun,   *imprint / their*
    Thurgh which hir grete sorwe gan aswage:°   *was assuaged*
    She may nat alwey duren° in swich rage.°   *continue / passion*
165   And eek° Arveragus, in al this care,   *also*
    Hath sent hire lettres hoom of his welfare,°   *well-being*
    And that he wol come hastily agayn;
    Or elles hadde this sorwe hir herte slayn.
        Hire freendes sawe hir sorwe gan to slake,°   *was abating*
170 And preyde hire on knees, for Goddes sake,
    To come and romen hire° in companye,   *walk about*
    Awey to dryve hire derke fantasye.°   *dark imagining(s)*
    And finally, she graunted that requeste,
    For wel she saugh° that it was for the beste.   *saw*
175   Now stood hire castel faste° by the see,   *close*
    And often with hire freendes walketh she
    Hire to disporte° upon the bank an heigh,°   *amuse / on high*
    Where as she many a ship and barge seigh°   *saw*
    Seilinge hir° cours, where as hem liste go.   *their*
180 But thanne was that a parcel° of hire wo,   *portion*
    For to hirself ful ofte "Allas!" seith she,
    "Is ther no ship, of so manye as I see,
    Wol bringen hom my lord? Thanne were myn herte
    Al warisshed° of his bittre peynes smerte."°   *cured / smart, sharp*
185   Another tyme ther wolde she sitte and thinke,
    And caste hir eyen dounward fro the brinke.°   *edge*
    But whan she saugh the grisly rokkes blake,°   *black rocks*
    For verray fere° so wolde hir herte quake   *Out of real fear*
    That on hire feet she mighte hire noght sustene.
190 Than wolde she sitte adoun upon the grene,°   *grass*
    And pitously into the see biholde,
    And seyn right thus, with sorweful sykes° colde: *sighs*
        "Eterne God, that thurgh thy purveyaunce°   *foresight, providence*
    Ledest° the world by certein governaunce,°   *Guidest / rule*
195 In ydel,° as men seyn, ye no thing make.   *vain*

But Lord, thise grisly feendly° rokkes blake,   *hostile, devilish*
That semen° rather a foul confusioun   *seem (to be)*
Of werk, than any fair creacioun
Of swich a parfit wys° God and a stable,°   *wise / steadfast*
200 Why han ye wroght this werk unresonable?²
For by this werk, south, north, ne west, ne eest,
Ther nis y-fostred° man, ne brid, ne beest.   *is not served, supported*
It dooth no good, to my wit,° but anoyeth.°   *understanding / injures*
See ye nat, Lord, how mankinde it destroyeth?
205 An hundred thousand bodies of mankinde
Han rokkes slayn, al be they nat in minde:°   *although they be unremembered*
Which mankinde is so fair part of thy werk
That thou it madest lyk to thyn owene merk.°   *image*
Thanne semed it ye hadde a greet chiertee°   *affection*
210 Toward mankinde; but how thanne may it be
That ye swiche meenes° make it to destroyen,   *such means*
Which meenes do no good, but evere anoyen?
I woot wel clerkes° wol seyn as hem leste,°   *scholars / they please*
By arguments,³ that al is for the beste,
215 Though I ne can the causes nat y-knowe.
But thilke° God that made wind to blowe,   *that same*
As kepe° my lord! This° my conclusioun.   *May He protect / This is*
To clerkes lete° I al disputisoun,°   *leave / debate*
But wolde° God that alle thise rokkes blake   *would (to)*
220 Were sonken° into helle for his sake!   *sunken*
Thise rokkes sleen° myn herte for the fere."°   *slay / fear*
Thus wolde she seyn, with many a pitous tere.

Hire freendes sawe that it was no disport°   *pleasure (for her)*
To romen by the see, but disconfort,
225 And shopen° for to pleyen somewher elles.°   *arranged / else*
They leden hire by riveres and by welles,°   *springs*
And eek in othere places delitables;°   *pleasant*
They dauncen, and they pleyen at ches° and tables.°   *chess / backgammon*
So on a day, right in the morwe-tyde,°   *morning*
230 Unto a gardin that was ther bisyde,
In which that they hadde maad hir ordinaunce°   *their arrangements*
Of vitaille° and of other purveyaunce,°   *For food / provisions*
They goon and pleye hem al the longe day.
And this was on the sixte morwe° of May,   *morning*
235 Which May had peynted° with his softe shoures°   *painted / showers*
This gardin ful of leves and of floures;
And craft of mannes hand so curiously°   *skillfully*
Arrayed° hadde this gardin, trewely,   *Adorned*
That nevere was ther gardin of swich prys,°   *so priceless*

---

2. I.e., that confounds reason.   3. I.e., of philosophy.

240 But if° it were the verray Paradys.°   *Unless / Paradise itself*
     The odour of floures and the fresshe sighte
     Wolde han maked any herte lighte
     That evere was born, but if to gret° siknesse   *too great*
     Or to gret sorwe helde it in distresse,
245 So ful it was of beautee with plesaunce.°   *delight*
     At after-diner gonne they to daunce,⁴
     And singe also, save° Dorigen allone,   *except*
     Which made alwey hir compleint° and hir mone,°   *lament / moan*
     For she ne saugh° him on the daunce go,   *saw*
250 That was hir housbonde and hir love also.
     But nathelees° she moste° a tyme abyde,   *nevertheless / must*
     And with good hope lete hir sorwe slyde.°   *pass*
        Upon° this daunce, amonges othere men,   *In*
     Daunced a squyer biforen Dorigen,
255 That fressher was and jolyer of array,°   *dress*
     As to my doom,° than is the monthe of May.   *judgment*
     He singeth, daunceth, passinge° any man   *surpassing*
     That is, or was, sith° that the world bigan.   *since*
     Therwith he was, if men sholde him discryve,°   *describe*
260 Oon of the beste faringe° man on lyve:°   *handsomest / alive*
     Yong, strong, right vertuous, and riche and wys,
     And wel biloved, and holden in gret prys.°   *held in great esteem*
     And shortly, if the sothe° I tellen shal,   *truth*
     Unwiting of° this Dorigen at al,   *Unknown to*
265 This lusty° squyer, servant to Venus,   *vigorous, joyful*
     Which that y-cleped° was Aurelius,   *called*
     Hadde loved hire best of any creature
     Two yeer and more, as was his aventure,°   *lot*
     But never dorste° he telle hire his grevaunce:°   *dared / sorrow*
270 Withouten coppe he drank al his penaunce.⁵
     He was despeyred;° no thing dorste° he seye,   *in despair / dared*
     Save in his songes somwhat wolde he wreye°   *disclose*
     His wo, as in a general compleyning;°   *lamentation*
     He seyde he lovede, and was biloved no thing.°   *not at all*
275 Of swich matere° made he manye layes,   *such substance*
     Songes, compleintes, roundels, virelayes,⁶
     How that he dorste nat his sorwe telle,
     But languissheth as a furie dooth in helle;
     And dye he moste, he seyde, as dide Ekko
280 For Narcisus, that dorste nat telle hir wo.⁷

---

4. After dinner (i.e., in the late forenoon), they
began to dance.
5. Literally, "He drank all his penance without
cup," but the exact meaning is unclear: perhaps "He
endured his sorrow in the most difficult of ways,"

i.e., not even being able to speak of it to her.
6. Various forms of lyric.
7. Echo, unable to speak in her own right, could
not tell Narcissus of her love for him; she died in
despair, ever faithful to that love.

In other manere than ye here me seye,
Ne dorste he nat to hire his wo biwreye,°   *reveal*
Save that, paraventure,° somtyme at daunces,   *by chance*
Ther° yonge folk kepen hir observaunces,°   *Where / perform their devotions*
285 It may wel be he loked on hir face
In swich a wyse as man that asketh grace,
But nothing wiste° she of his entente.°   *knew / purpose(s)*
Nathelees, it happed, er they thennes wente,°   *before they departed thence*
By cause that he was hire neighebour,
290 And was a man of worshipe and honour,
And hadde y-knowen him of tyme yore,[8]
They fille in speche;° and forth more and more   *fell into conversation*
Unto his purpos drough° Aurelius,   *drew*
And when he saugh° his tyme, he seyde thus: *saw*
295   "Madame," quod he, "by God that this world made,
So that° I wiste° it mighte youre herte glade,°   *If only / knew / gladden*
I wolde that day that youre Arveragus
Wente over the see, that I, Aurelius,
Had went ther° nevere I sholde have come agayn.   *there where*
300 For wel I woot° my service is in vayn: *know*
My guerdon° is but bresting° of myn herte.   *reward / breaking*
Madame, reweth° upon my peynes smerte,°   *take pity / sharp*
For with a word ye may me sleen° or save.   *slay*
Heere at your feet God wolde that I were grave!°   *buried*
305 I ne have as now no leyser° more to seye: *leisure, opportunity*
Have mercy, swete, or ye wol do me deye!"°   *make me die*
    She gan to loke upon° Aurelius: *stared at*
"Is this youre wil," quod she, "and sey ye thus?
Nevere erst,"°, quod she, "ne wiste° I what ye mente.   *before / knew*
310 But now, Aurelie, I knowe youre entente,
By thilke° God that yaf° me soule and lyf,   *that same / gave*
Ne shal I nevere been untrewe° wyf,   *unfaithful*
In word ne werk,° as fer as I have wit.   *deed*
I wol ben his to whom that I am knit:[9]
315 Tak this for fynal answere as of me."
But after that in pley thus seyde she:
    "Aurelie," quod she, "by heighe God above,
Yet wolde I graunte yow to been youre love,
Sin° I yow see so pitously complayne.   *Since*
320 Loke what° day that, endelong° Britayne,   *Whatever / along the edge of*
Ye remoeve alle the rokkes, stoon by stoon,
That they ne lette° ship ne boot to goon°—   *prevent / from passing*
I seye, whan ye han maad the coost so clene
Of rokkes, that ther nis° no stoon y-sene—   *is not*

8. The subject "she" must be supplied; "of tyme   9. I.e., in matrimony.
yore": for a long time past.

325 Thanne wol I love yow best of any man;
    Have heer my trouthe,° in al that evere I can."   *pledge*
        "Is ther non other grace° in yow?" quod he.   *mercy*
        "No, by that Lord," quod she, "that maked me!
    For wel I woot° that it shal never bityde.°   *know / happen*
330 Lat swiche° folies out of youre herte slyde.°   *such / pass*
    What deyntee° sholde a man han in his lyf   *delight*
    For to go love another mannes wyf,
    That hath hir body whan so that him lyketh?"[1]
        Aurelius ful ofte sore sykcth,°   *painfully sighs*
335 Wo was Aurelie, whan that he this herde,
    And with a sorweful herte he thus answerde:
        "Madame," quod he, "this were an inpossible!°   *impossibility*
    Than° moot° I dye of sodein deth horrible."   *Then / must*
    And with that word he turned him anoon.°   *at once*
340 Tho° come hir othere freendes many oon,   *Then*
    And in the aleyes° romeden° up and doun,   *garden walks / strolled*
    And nothing wiste° of this conclusioun;°   *knew / outcome*
    But sodeinly bigonne revel newe°   *began new revelry*
    Til that the brighte sonne loste his hewe,°   *hue*
345 For th'orisonte° hath reft° the sonne his light—   *the horizon / taken from*
    This is as muche to seye as it was night—
    And hoom they goon in joye and in solas,
    Save only wrecche° Aurelius, allas!   *wretched*
    He to his hous is goon with sorweful herte.
350 He secth° he may nat fro his deeth asterte:°   *sees / escape*
    Him semed that he felte his herte colde.[2]
    Up to the hevene° his handes he gan holde,°   *heavens / did raise*
    And on his knowes° bare he sette him doun,   *knees*
    And in his raving seyde his orisoun.°   *prayer*
355 For verray wo out of his wit he breyde.[3]
    He niste° what he spak, but thus he seyde;   *knew not*
    With pitous herte his pleynt° hath he bigonne   *complaint*
    Unto the goddes, and first unto the sonne:°   *sun*
        He seyde, "Appollo, god and governour
360 Of every plaunte,° herbe, tree and flour,   *plant*
    That yevest, after thy declinacioun,[4]
    To ech of hem° his tyme and his sesoun,   *each of them*
    As thyn herberwe° chaungeth lowe or hye,   *lodging, zodiacal position*
    Lord Phebus, cast thy merciable yë°   *merciful eye*
365 On wrecche Aurelie, which that am but lorn.°   *lost*
    Lo, lord! my lady hath my deeth y-sworn
    Withoute gilt, but° thy benignitee°   *unless / kindness*

---

1. Who possesses her body (in the act of love) whensoever it pleases him.
2. It seemed to him that he felt his heart grow cold.
3. For sheer grief he went out of his mind.
4. That givest, according to thy distance from the equator ("declinacioun").

Upon my dedly° herte have som pitee!　　　　　　　　　　*dying*
For wel I woot,° lord Phebus, if yow lest,°　　　*know / if it please you*
370　Ye may me helpen, save° my lady, best.　　　　　　*except for*
Now voucheth sauf° that I may yow devyse°　　　*grant / describe*
How that I may been holpe° and in what wyse.°　　*helped / way*
　　Youre blisful suster, Lucina the shene,°　　　　　　*bright*
That of the see° is chief goddesse and quene⁵—　　　*sea*
375　Though Neptunus have deitee in the see,
Yet emperesse aboven him is she—
Ye knowen wel, lord, that right as hir desyr
Is to be quiked and lighted of youre fyr,⁶
For which she folweth yow ful bisily,
380　Right° so the see desyreth naturelly　　　　　　　　*Just*
To folwen hire, as she that is goddesse
Bothe in⁷ the see and riveres more and lesse.
Wherfore, lord Phebus, this is my requeste:
Do this miracle—or do° myn herte breste°—　　*make / burst*
385　That now, next at this opposicioun,°　　*opposition (of the sun and moon)*
Which in the signe° shal be of the Leoun,°　　*(zodiacal) sign / Lion (Leo)*
As preyeth hire so greet a flood to bringe
That fyve fadme° at the leeste it overspringe°　　*fathoms / tower over*
The hyeste rokke in Armorik Briteyne;
390　And lat this flood endure yeres tweyne.°　　　　　　*two*
Thanne certes to my lady may I seye:
'Holdeth youre heste,° the rokkes been aweye.'　　*promise*
　　Lord Phebus, dooth this miracle for me!
Preye hire she go no faster cours than ye;
395　I seye, preyeth your suster° that she go　　　　　　*sister*
No faster cours than ye thise yeres two.⁸
Than shal she been evene atte fulle° alway,　　*just at the full*
And spring-flood laste bothe night and day.
And but° she vouche sauf° in swiche manere°　　*unless / grant / such a way*
400　To graunte me my sovereyn lady dere,
Prey hire to sinken every rok adoun
Into hir owene derke regioun⁹
Under the ground, ther° Pluto dwelleth inne,　　　　*where*
Or nevere mo shal I my lady winne.
405　Thy temple in Delphos wol I barefoot seke.°　　*seek (visit)*
Lord Phebus, see the teres on my cheke,
And of my peyne have som compassioun."
And with that word in swowne° he fil adoun,　　　　*a faint*

---

5. Lucina is the goddess of light, here identified
with Diana, the moon.
6. "Quiked": given life; "lighted of": illumined by.
The simple fact referred to here is that the moon
depends on the sun for its light. (Cf. the explanation
of tides in ll. 380–82).

7. I.e., goddess of.
8. The miracle requested would keep the sun and
moon in perfect opposition for two years, so that the
high tide covering the rocks might not wane.
9. Lucina is here also identified with Proserpina,
Pluto's queen in the underworld.

And longe tyme he lay forth° in a traunce.   *thereafter*
410   His brother, which that knew of his penaunce,°   *suffering*
Up caughte him and to bedde he hath him broght.
Dispeyred° in this torment and this thoght   *Filled with despair*
Lete I this woful creature lye:
Chese he, for me, wher he wol live or dye.[1]
415   Arveragus, with hele° and greet honour   *in health*
As he that was of chivalrye the flour,
Is comen hoom, and othere worthy men.
O blisful artow° now, thou Dorigen,   *art thou*
That hast thy lusty° housbonde in thyne armes,   *vigorous, merry*
420 The fresshe° knight, the worthy man of armes,   *lively*
That loveth thee as his owene hertes lyf.
No thing list him to been imaginatyf[2]
If any wight° hadde spoke, whyl he was oute,°   *person / away*
To hire of love; he hadde of it no doute.°   *fear*
425 He noght entendeth° to no swich matere,   *paid no attention*
But daunceth, justeth,° maketh hire good chere;   *jousts*
And thus in joye and blisse I lete hem dwelle,
And of the syke° Aurelius wol I telle.   *sick*
In langour° and in torment furious   *sickness*
430 Two yeer and more lay wrecche Aurelius,
Er° any foot he mighte on erthe goon.°   *Before / walk*
Ne confort in this tyme hadde he noon,
Save of his brother, which that was a clerk:°   *scholar*
He knew of al this wo and al this werk,°   *affair*
435 For to non other creature, certeyn,°   *certainly*
Of this matere he dorste° no word seyn.   *dared*
Under° his brest he bar it more secree   *Within*
Than evere dide Pamphilus for Galathee.[3]
His brest was hool° withoute for to sene,°   *whole / seen from outside*
440 But in his herte ay was the arwe° kene;   *arrow*
And wel ye knowe that of a sursanure[4]
In surgerye is perilous the cure,
But° men mighte touche the arwe, or come therby.°   *Unless / near to it*
His brother weep° and wayled prively,°   *wept / secretly*
445 Til atte laste him fil in remembraunce,°   *it occurred to him*
That whiles he was at Orliens° in Fraunce,   *Orléans (university)*
As yonge clerkes that been likerous°   *desirous*
To reden artes that been curious°   *recondite, subtle*
Seken in every halke° and every herne°   *nook / corner*
450 Particuler° sciences for to lerne—   *Little-known*

---

1. Let *him* choose, for my part, whether he will live   3. Pamphilus and Galatea were lovers in a widely
or die.   circulated twelfth-century dialogue, *Pamphilus de*
2. He has no wish at all to be suspicious (full of   *Amore.*
imaginings).   4. A wound healed only on the surface.

He him remembred that, upon a day,
At Orliens in studie a book he say°   *saw*
Of magik naturel,[5] which his felawe,°   *companion*
That was that tyme a bacheler of lawe—
455 Al° were he ther to lerne another craft—   *Although*
Had prively° upon his desk y-laft:°   *secretly / left*
Which book spak muchel of the operaciouns
Touchinge the eighte and twenty mansiouns°   *positions in the heavens*
That longen° to the mone°—and swich folye   *belong / moon (in a month)*
460 As in oure dayes is nat worth a flye;°   *fly*
For holy chirches feith in our bileve
Ne suffreth noon illusion° us to greve.°   *deception / vex*
And whan this book was in his remembraunce,
Anon° for joye his herte gan° to daunce,   *Immediately / began*
465 And to himself he seyde prively:°   *secretly*
"My brother shal be warisshed° hastily;   *cured*
For I am siker° that ther be sciences°   *certain / kinds of knowledge*
By whiche men make diverse apparences°   *apparitions*
Swiche as thise subtile tregetoures° pleye.°   *magicians / perform*
470 For ofte at festes° have I wel herd seye   *feasts*
That tregetours withinne an halle° large   *(dining) hall*
Have maad come in a water° and a barge,   *some water*
And in the halle rowen° up and doun;   *rowed*
Somtyme hath semed come a grim leoun;°   *lion*
475 And somtyme floures springe as in a mede;°   *meadow*
Somtyme a vyne, and grapes whyte and rede;
Somtyme a castel,° al of lym° and stoon—   *castle / lime*
And whan hem lyked, voyded it anoon.[6]
Thus semed it to every mannes sighte.
480   Now thanne conclude I thus, that if I mighte
At Orliens som old felawe° y-find   *companion*
That hadde this° mones mansions in minde,   *these*
Or other magik naturel above,[7]
He sholde wel make my brother han his love.
485 For with an apparence° a clerk° may make   *illusion / scholar*
To mannes sighte, that alle the rokkes blake
Of Britaigne weren y-voyded° everichon,°   *removed / every one*
And shippes by the brinke° comen and gon,   *coast*
And in swich forme endure a wowke° or two.   *week*
490 Than were my brother warisshed° of his wo;   *cured*
Than moste she nedes holden hir biheste,[8]
Or elles he shal shame hire atte leste."

---

5. I.e., employing astronomy.
6. And when it pleased them, caused it at once to disappear. (The "tregetours" are as much artisans as magicians, working the kind of "magic" ordinarily associated with stage sets and properties. A feast given for Charles V in Paris in 1378 included an entertainment much like this.)
7. I.e., even higher.
8. Then she needs must keep her promise.

What° sholde I make a lenger tale of this?   *Why*
Unto his brotheres bed he comen is,
495 And swich confort he yaf° him for to gon   *gave*
To Orliens, that he up stirte anon,°   *jumped up at once*
And on his wey forthward thanne is he fare,°   *has he traveled*
In hope for to ben lissed° of his care.   *eased*
     Whan they were come almost to that citee,
500 But it it were a two furlong or three,⁹
A yong clerk rominge° by himself they mette,   *strolling*
Which that in Latin thriftily hem grette,°   *suitably greeted them*
And after that he seyde a wonder° thing: *wondrous*
"I knowe," quod he, "the cause of youre coming."
505 And er° they ferther any fote° wente,   *before / a foot further*
He tolde hem al that was in hire entente.
     This Briton clerk him asked of felawes
The whiche that he had knowe in olde dawes;°   *days*
And he answerde him that they dede were,
510 For which he weep° ful ofte many a tere.   *wept*
     Doun of his hors Aurelius lighte° anon,   *alighted*
And forth with this magicien is he gon
Hoom to his hous, and maden hem° wel at ese.   *made themselves*
Hem lakked° no vitaille° that mighte hem plese;   *they lacked / food*
515 So wel arrayed° hous as ther was oon   *furnished (a)*
Aurelius in his lyf saugh nevere noon.
     He shewed him, er° he wente to sopeer,°   *before / supper*
Forestes, parkes ful of wilde deer;
Ther saugh he hertes° with hir hornes hye,°   *harts / tall*
520 The gretteste° that evere were seyn with yë;°   *largest / eye*
He saugh of hem an hondred slayn with houndes,
And somme with arwes° blede of° bittre woundes.   *arrows / bled from*
He saugh, whan voided° were thise wilde deer,   *departed*
Thise fauconers° upon a fair river,°   *Some falconers / riverbank*
525 That with hir haukes han the heron slayn.
     Tho saugh° he knightes justing° in a playn;   *Then saw / jousting*
And after this he dide him swich plesaunce
That he him shewed his lady on° a daunce   *in*
On which himself he daunced, as him thoughte.°   *so it seemed to him*
530 And whan this maister° that this magik wroughte   *Master of Arts*
Saugh it was tyme, he clapte his handes two,
And farewel! al oure revel was ago.°   *gone*
And yet remoeved° they nevere out of the hous   *moved*
Whyl they saugh al this sighte merveillous,
535 But in his studie, ther as° his bookes be,   *where*
They seten stille, and no wight but they three.

9. Unless it was two or three furlongs before. (A furlong is one-eighth of a mile.)

To him this maister called his squyer,
And seyde him thus: "Is redy oure soper?
Almost an houre it is, I undertake,° *declare*
540 Sith° I yow bad° oure soper for to make, *Since / ordered*
Whan that thise worthy men wenten with me
Into my studie, ther as my bookes be."
"Sire," quod this squyer, "whan it lyketh yow,° *it pleases*
It is al redy, though ye wol° right now." *wish (it)*
545 "Go we than soupe,"° quod he, "as for the beste: *to eat supper*
This° amorous folk somtyme mote° han reste." *These / must*
At after-soper fille° they in tretee° *fell / negotiations*
What somme° sholde this maistres guerdon° be, *sum / reward*
To remoeven alle the rokkes of Britayne,
550 And eek from Gerounde to the mouth of Sayne.[1]
He made it straunge,° and swoor,° so God him save, *difficult / swore*
Lasse° than a thousand pound he wolde nat have, *Less*
Ne gladly for that somme he wolde nat goon.[2]
Aurelius with blisful herte anoon° *at once*
555 Answerde thus, "Fy on a thousand pound!
This wyde world, which that men seye is round,
I wolde it yeve,° if I were lord of it. *give*
This bargayn is ful drive,° for we ben knit.° *driven, concluded / agreed*
Ye shal be payed trewely, by my trouthe!° *loyalty, fidelity*
560 But loketh now, for no necligence or slouthe,° *sloth*
Ye tarie us heer° no lenger than to-morwe." *delay us here*
"Nay," quod this clerk, "have heer my feith to borwe."[3]
To bedde is goon Aurelius whan him leste,° *it pleased him*
And wel ny° al that night he hadde his reste: *well nigh, almost*
565 What for his labour and his hope of blisse,
His woful herte of penaunce° hadde a lisse.° *suffering / relief*
Upon the morwe,° whan that it was day, *morning*
To Britaigne toke they the righte° way, *direct*
Aurelius and this magicien bisyde,° *at his side*
570 And been descended° ther° they wolde abyde;° *have dismounted / where / stay*
And this was, as thise bokes me remembre,° *remind me*
The colde frosty seson of Decembre.
Phebus wex old, and hewed lyk latoun,[4]
That in his hote declinacioun[5]
575 Shoon as the burned° gold with stremes° brighte; *burnished / beams*
But now in Capricorn adoun he lighte,° *alighted*
Where as he shoon ful pale, I dar wel seyn.
The bittre frostes, with the sleet and reyn,° *rain*

---

1. And also from the Gironde River to the mouth of the Seine.
2. I.e., the price is his absolute minimum, nothing to cause him delight.
3. I.e., as pledge.
4. Phoebus (the sun) grew old, and colored like brass.
5. I.e., in the Tropic of Cancer.

Destroyed hath the grene in every yerd.° _garden, yard_
580 Janus[6] sit by the fyr with double berd,
And drinketh of his bugle-horn° the wyn; _goblet made of ox horn_
Biforn him stant° brawen° of the tusked swyn,° _stands / brawn, meat / boar_
And "Nowel"° cryeth every lusty man. _Noel, Christmas_
    Aurelius, in al that evere he can,
585 Doth' to this maister cheie° and reverence, _Makes / good cheer_
And preyeth him to doon his diligence
To bringen him out of his peynes smerte,
Or with a swerd that he wolde slitte his herte.
    This subtil° clerk swich routhe° had of this man _skillful / compassion_
590 That night and day he spedde him that° he can, _hurried as much as_
To wayten a tyme of his conclusioun;[7]
This is to seye, to maken illusioun,
By swich an apparence° or jogelrye°— _apparition / magic, jugglery_
I ne can° no termes of astrologye— _do not know_
595 That she and every wight° sholde wene° and seye _person / suppose_
That of Britaigne the rokkes were aweye,
Or elles they were sonken under grounde.
So atte laste he hath his tyme y-founde
To maken his japes° and his wrecchednesse° _tricks / miserable actions_
600 Of swich° a supersticious cursednesse. _From such_
His tables Toletanes[8] forth he broght,
Ful wel corrected, ne ther lakked noght,
Neither his collect ne his expans yeres,[9]
Ne his rotes° ne his othere geres,° _statistics / gear_
605 As been his centres and his arguments,
And his proporcionels convenients
For his equacions in every thing.[1]
And by his eighte spere[2] in his wirking
He knew ful wel how fer Alnath° was shove° _the star / advanced_
610 Fro the heed° of thilke fixe° Aries above _head / that same fixed (constellation)_
That in the ninthe speere considered is:[3]
Ful subtilly he calculed at this.
    Whan he had founde his firste mansioun,° _position (of the moon)_
He knew the remenant° by proporcioun, _remainder_
615 And knew the arysing° of his mone° weel, _rising / moon_
And in whos face, and terme,[4] and everydeel;
And knew ful weel the mones mansioun,

---

6. The two-headed Roman god (hence double-bearded), who looks both forward and backward, to the future and the past. The month of January is named for him, and medieval calendars (in the Books of Hours) often show him feasting, in the character of a medieval prince or rich landowner.
7. To watch for a time to conclude the matter.
8. Astronomical tables, calculated for the city of Toledo, which gives them their name.

9. The "collect" recorded movements of the planets over long periods of years; the "expans yeres" for shorter periods of up to twenty years.
1. Astronomical instruments and formulae used to determine astrological positions.
2. The eighth sphere, of the fixed stars.
3. That is held to be in the ninth sphere (the Primum Mobile).
4. Divisions, even and uneven, of zodiacal signs.

Acordaunt to his operacioun,
And knew also his othere observaunces°   *ceremonies*
620 For swiche illusiouns and swiche meschaunces°   *mischief*
As hethen° folk used in thilke° days.   *heathen / those same*
For which no lenger maked he delayes,
But thurgh his magik, for a wyke or tweye,°   *week or two*
It semed that alle the rokkes were aweye.
625   Aurelius, which that yet despeired° is   *despairing*
Wher° he shal han his love or fare amis,   *Whether*
Awaiteth night and day on this miracle;
And whan he knew that ther was noon obstacle—
That voided° were thise rokkes everichon°—   *removed / each and every one*
630 Doun to his maistres feet he fil anon°   *fell at once*
And seyde, "I woful wrecche, Aurelius,
Thanke yow, lord, and lady myn Venus,
That me han holpen fro my cares colde."°   *bitter, fatal*
And to the temple his wey forth hath he holde,
635 Where as he knew he sholde his lady see.
And whan he saugh° his tyme, anon-right° he,   *saw / right away*
With dredful° herte and with ful humble chere,°   *fearful / appearance*
Salewed° hath his sovereyn lady dere: *Greeted*
    "My righte° lady," quod this woful man,   *own true*
640 "Whom I most drede° and love as I best can,   *fear*
And lothest° were of al this world displese,   *most loath*
Nere it° that I for yow have swich disese°   *Were it not / misery*
That I moste° dyen heer at youre foot anon,   *must*
Noght wolde I telle how me is wo bigon.°   *woebegone I am*
645 But certes outher° moste I dye or pleyne;°   *either / speak my grief*
Ye slee° me, giltelees, for verray° peyne.   *slay / real*
But of my deeth, thogh that ye have no routhe,°   *compassion*
Avyseth yow,° er° that ye breke your trouthe.°   *Take heed / before / pledge*
Repenteth yow, for thilke God above,⁵
650 Er ye me sleen° by cause that I yow love.   *slay*
For, madame, wel ye woot what ye han hight°—   *promised*
Nat that I chalange° any thing of right°   *claim / by rights*
Of yow, my sovereyn lady, but youre grace°—   *mercy, favor*
But in a gardin yond,° at swich a place,   *yonder*
655 Ye woot right wel° what ye bihighten° me;   *know full well / promised*
And in myn hand youre trouthe plighten° ye   *pledged*
To love me best. God woot, ye seyde so,
Al be° that I unworthy be therto.   *Although*
Madame, I speke it for the honour of yow
660 More than to save myn hertes lyf right now.
I have do° so as ye comanded me;   *done*

5. Repent you, for (the sake of) that same God on high.

And if ye vouche-sauf,° ye may go see.   (will) grant (it)
Doth as yow list, have youre biheste in minde,
For, quik° or deed, right there ye shul me finde.   living
665 In yow lyth al to do° me live or deye: make
But wel I woot the rokkes been aweye!"
      He taketh his leve, and she astonied° stood;   astonished
In al hir face nas° a drope of blood.   was not
She wende° never han come in swich a trappe.   thought
670 "Allas!" quod she, "that evere this sholde happe!°   occur
For wende I nevere, by possibilitee,
That swich a monstre° or merveille mighte be!   strange thing
It is agayns the proces° of nature."   course
And hoom she gooth a sorweful creature.
675 For verray fere° unnethe° may she go.°   deep fear / scarcely / walk
She wepeth, wailleth, al a day° or two,   a whole day
And swowneth,° that it routhe° was to see;   faints / pity
But why it was, to no wight° tolde she,   person
For out of toune was goon Arveragus.
680 But to hirself she spak, and seyde thus,
With face pale and with ful sorweful chere,°   countenance
In hire compleynt,° as ye shul after here: lament
      "Allas," quod she, "on thee, Fortune, I pleyne,°   make complaint
That unwar° wrapped hast me in thy cheyne,°   unawares / chain
685 Fro which t'escape woot° I no socour°   know / help
Save only deeth or elles° dishonour;   else
Oon of thise two bihoveth me° to chese.   it's necessary for me
But nathelees yet have I lever to lese°   would I rather lose
My lyf, than of my body to have a shame,
690 Or knowe° myselven fals, or lese my name;   acknowledge
And with my deth I may be quit,° y-wis.   freed (from the debt)
Hath ther nat many a noble wyf er this,°   before now
And many a mayde, y-slayn hirself, allas!
Rather than with hir body doon trepas?°   commit a sin
695   Yis, certes, lo, thise stories[6] beren witnesse;
Whan thretty° tyraunts, ful of cursednesse,   thirty
Hadde slayn Phidoun in Athenes atte feste,°   at (the) feasting
They comanded his doghtres for t'areste,°   to be seized
And bringen hem biforn hem in despyt°   scorn
700 Al naked, to fulfille hir foul delyt,°   pleasure
And in hir fadres blood they made hem daunce
Upon the pavement, God yeve hem mischaunce!°   give them misfortune
For which thise woful maydens, ful of drede,°   fear
Rather than they wolde lese hir maydenhede,
705 They prively° ben stirt° into a welle,   secretly / have leaped

6. The examples of virtuous women she brings to mind, from Phidon's daughters on, are all found in St. Jerome's treatise against Jovinian.

And dreynte° hemselven, as the bokes telle.   *drowned*
  They of Messene lete enquere and seke [7]
Of Lacedomie° fifty maydens eke,°   *From Sparta / also*
On whiche they wolden doon° hir lecherye;   *perform*
710 But was ther noon of al that compaignye
That she nas° slayn, and with a good entente°   *was not / will, purpose*
Chees° rather for to dye than assente   *Chose*
To been oppressed° of hir maydenhede.   *ravished*
Why sholde I thanne to dye been in drede?
715 Lo eek the tiraunt Aristoclides [8]
That loved a mayden, heet° Stimphalides,   *named*
Whan that hir fader slayn was on a night,
Unto Dianes temple goth she right,°   *directly*
And hente° the image [9] in hir handes two,   *clasped*
720 Fro which image wolde she nevere go.
No wight° ne mighte hir handes of it arace,°   *person / tear away*
Til she was slayn right in the selve place.
  Now sith that° maydens hadden swich despyt°   *since / disdain, scorn*
To been defouled with mannes foul delyt,
725 Wel oghte a wyf rather hirselven slee
Than be defouled,° as it thinketh me.°   *defiled / it seems to me*
What shal I seyn of Hasdrubales° wyf,   *Hasdrubal's*
That at Cartage° birafte° hirself hir lyf?   *Carthage / took from*
For whan she saugh° that Romayns wan° the toun,   *saw / won*
730 She took hir children alle, and skipte° adoun   *jumped*
Into the fyr, and chees rather to dye
Than any Romayn dide° hire vileinye.   *should do*
Hath nat Lucresse° y-slayn hirself, allas!   *Lucretia*
At Rome, whanne she oppressed° was   *violated*
735 Of° Tarquin, for hire thoughte° it was a shame   *By / it seemed to her*
To liven whan she hadde lost hir name?
The sevene maydens of Milesie [1] also
Han slayn hemself,° for verray° drede and wo,   *themselves / great*
Rather than folk of Gaule° hem sholde oppresse.   *the Galatians*
740 Mo than a thousand stories, as I gesse,
Coude I now telle as touchinge this matere.
When Habradate [2] was slayn, his wyf so dere
Hirselven slow,° and leet hir blood to glyde   *slew*
In Habradates woundes depe and wyde,
745 And seyde, 'My body, at the leeste way,°   *at least*
Ther shal no wight defoulen, if I may.'°   *if I can help it*
  What sholde I mo ensamples heerof sayn,
Sith that so manye han hemselven slayn

---

7. The men of Messene (in the Peloponnesus) had
inquiries made and sought.
8. A tyrant of Arcadia.

9. Of the goddess.
1. Miletus, in Asia Minor.
2. Abradates, king of the Susi.

Wel rather than they wolde defouled be?
750 I wol conclude that it is bet° for me   *better*
To sleen myself than been defouled thus.
I wol be trewe unto Arveragus,
Or rather sleen myself in som manere—
As dide Demociones° doghter dere   *Demotion's*
755 By cause that she wolde nat defouled be.
O Cedasus!³ it is ful greet pitee
To reden how thy doghtren° deyde, allas!   *daughters*
That slowe hemself for swich manere cas.°   *such a kind of occurrence*
As greet a pitee was it, or wel more,
760 The Theban mayden that for Nichanore⁴
Hirselven slow° right for swich manere wo.   *slew*
Another Theban mayden dide right so:
For° oon of Macedoine° hadde hire oppressed,°   *Because / Macedonia / violated*
She with hire deeth hir maydenhede redressed.°   *made amends for*
765 What shal I seye of Nicerates⁵ wyf
That for swich cas birafte hirself hir lyf?
How trewe eek was to Alcebiades⁶
His love, that rather for to dyen chees°   *chose*
Than for to suffre his body unburied be!
770 Lo, which a⁷ wyf was Alceste," quod she.
"What seith Omer° of gode Penalopee?⁸   *Homer*
Al Grece knoweth of hire chastitee.
Pardee, of Laodomya° is writen thus,   *Laodamia*
That whan at Troye was slayn Prothesclaus,°   *Protesilaus*
775 No lenger wolde she live after his day.
The same of noble Porcia° telle I may: *Portia*
Withoute Brutus coude she nat live,
To whom she hadde al hool° hir herte yive.°   *completely / given*
The parfit wyfhod of Arthemesye⁹
780 Honoured is thurgh al the Barbarye.°   *heathendom*
O Teuta,¹ queen! thy wyfly chastitee
To alle wyves may a mirour be.
The same thing I seye of Bilia,²
Of Rodogone, and eek Valeria."³
785   Thus pleyned° Dorigene a day or tweye,   *lamented*
Purposinge evere that she wolde deye.°   *die*
But nathelees, upon the thridde night,
Hom cam Arveragus, this worthy knight,

3. Scedasus, of Boeotia.
4. Nichanor, an Alexandrian.
5. Niceratus's, an Athenian.
6. Alcibiades, friend of Socrates.
7. What a. Alcestis, wife of Admetus, died his death
for him.
8. Penelope, Ulysses's wife.

9. Artemesia, queen of Caria, built a famous tomb
for her husband.
1. Queen of Illirica.
2. Wife of Gaius Duillius.
3. Rhodogune, wife of Darius; Valeria, daughter of
Diocletian.

And asked hire why that she weep° so sore;°   wept / painfully
790 And she gan wepen ever lenger the more.°   ever more and more
"Allas!" quod she, "that ever was I born!
Thus have I seyd," quod she, "thus have I sworn,"
And told him al as ye han herd bifore;
It nedeth nat reherce° it yow namore.   be recited
795 This housbonde, with glade chere,° in freendly wyse, expression, countenance
Answerde and seyde as I shal yow devyse:°   relate
"Is ther oght elles, Dorigen, but this?"
    "Nay, nay," quod she, "God help me so as wis;°   indeed
This is to° muche, and° it were Goddes wille."   too / if
800   "Ye, wyf," quod he, "lat slepen that° is stille.°   what / quiet
It may be wel, paraventure,° yet to-day.   by chance
Ye shul youre trouthe holden,° by my fay!   keep your pledge
For God so wisly° have mercy on me,   surely
I hadde wel levere° y-stiked° for to be,   rather / stabbed
805 For verray° love which that I to yow have,   true
But if ye sholde youre trouthe kepe and save.°   guard and preserve
Trouthe is the hyeste thing that man may kepe."[4]
But with that word he brast anon to wepe,[5]
And seyde, "I yow forbede, up° peyne of deeth,   on
810 That nevere, whyl thee lasteth lyf ne breeth,
To no wight° tel thou of this aventure—   person
As I may best, I wol my wo endure—
Ne make no contenance of hevinesse,[6]
That folk of yow may demen° harm or gesse."°   suppose / guess (at it)
815   And forth he cleped° a squyer and a mayde: called
"Goth forth anon° with Dorigen," he sayde,   at once
"And bringeth hire to swich a° place anon."   a certain
They take hir° leve, and on hir wey they gon,   their
But they ne wiste° why she thider° wente: knew / thither
820 He nolde° no wight tellen his entente.   would not
    Paraventure° an heep° of yow, y-wis,°   Perhaps / many / certainly
Wol holden him a lewed° man in this,   thoughtless, foolish
That he wol putte his wyf in jupartye.°   jeopardy
Herkneth the tale, er ye upon hire crye.[7]
825 She may have bettre fortune than yow semeth,[8]
And whan that ye han herd the tale, demeth.°   judge
    This squyer, which that highte° Aurelius,   was called
On Dorigen that was so amorous,

---

4. "Trouthe" is a central concept in this poem, for
which no single modern equivalent can be found.
In certain idioms, it can be defined as "pledge" or
"promise"; but its larger sense (as here) is fidelity,
steadfastness, integrity—the capacity to embody a
single "entente" without variance, whatever the circumstances. The keeping of a promise is only symp-

tomatic of the presence of this deeper, pervasive
moral quality.
5. But with that word, he burst at once into tears.
6. I.e., look sorrowful.
7. Hear the (whole) tale, before you complain about
her.
8. I.e., expect.

Of aventure° happed hire to mete   *By chance*
830 Amidde the toun, right in the quikkest° strete,   *busiest*
As she was boun° to goon the wey forth right°   *ready / directly*
Toward the gardin ther as she had hight;°   *promised*
And he was to the gardinward° also,   *(going) toward the garden*
For wel he spyed whan she wolde go   *he watched closely*
835 Out of hir hous to any maner° place.   *kind of*
But thus they mette, of aventure or grace;°   *by chance or good fortune*
And he saleweth° hire with glad entente,°   *greets / cheerfully*
And asked of hire whiderward she wente;
And she answerde, half as she were mad,
840 "Unto the gardin, as myn housbond bad,
My trouthe for to holde, allas! allas!"
    Aurelius gan wondren° on this cas,°   *fell to wondering / event*
And in his herte hadde greet compassioun
Of° hire and of hire lamentacioun,   *For*
845 And of Arveragus, the worthy knight,
That bad hire holden° al that she had hight,°   *keep / promised*
So looth him was⁹ his wyf sholde breke hir trouthe.
And in his herte he caughte of this greet routhe,°   *took great pity on this*
Consideringe the beste on every syde,
850 That fro his lust yet were him levere abyde¹
Than doon so heigh° a cherlish wrecchednesse°   *great / churlish miserable act*
Agayns franchyse° and alle gentillesse;°   *Against generosity / nobleness*
For which in fewe wordes seyde he thus:
"Madame, seyth to youre lord Arveragus,
855 That sith° I see his grete gentillesse   *since*
To yow, and eek° I see wel youre distresse,   *also*
That him were levere han shame (and that were routhe)°   *would be a pity*
Than ye to me sholde breke thus youre trouthe,
I have wel levere° evere to suffre wo   *would much rather*
860 Than I departe° the love bitwix yow two.   *(that) I divide*
I yow relesse,° madame, into youre hond,   *release*
Quit° every serement° and every bond   *Discharged of / oath*
That ye han maad to me as heerbiforn,
Sith thilke tyme which that ye were born.²
865 My trouthe I plighte, I shal yow never repreve°   *reproach*
Of no biheste,° and here I take my leve,   *promise*
As of the treweste and the beste wyf
That evere yet I knew in al my lyf.
But every wyf be war° of hire biheste!   *be careful*
870 On Dorigene remembreth atte leste.°   *at (the) least*
Thus can a squyer doon a gentil dede
As well as can a knight, withouten drede."°   *doubt*

9. So hateful to him was (the notion that).   desire.
1. (So) that he thought it better to abstain from his   2. Since that same time (in) which.

She thonketh him upon hir knees al bare,
And hoom unto hir housbond is she fare,°   *has she gone*
875 And tolde him al as ye han herd me sayd;
And be ye siker,° he was so weel apayd°   *sure / pleased*
That it were inpossible me to wryte.
What° sholde I lenger of this cas endyte?°   *Why / relate*
Arveragus and Dorigene his wyf
880 In sovereyn° blisse leden forth° hir lyf.   *supreme / lead on*
Never eft° ne was ther angre hem bitwene: *again*
He cherisseth hire as though she were a quene,
And she was to him trewe for everemore.
Of° thise two folk ye gete of³ me namore.   *Concerning*
885   Aurelius, that his cost° hath al forlorn,°   *expense / lost*
Curseth the tyme that evere he was born:
"Allas," quod he, "allas! that I bihighte°   *promised*
Of pured° gold a thousand pound of wighte°   *refined / by weight*
Unto this philosophre!° How shal I do?   *philosopher (alchemist?)*
890 I see namore but that I am fordo.°   *done in, ruined*
Myn heritage° moot I nedes° selle   *inheritance / I needs must*
And been a beggere; heer may I nat dwelle,
And shamen al my kinrede° in this place,   *kindred, family*
But° I of him may gete bettre grace.⁴   *Unless*
895 But nathelees, I wol of him assaye°   *try (to arrange with) him*
At certeyn dayes, yeer by yeer, to paye,
And thanke him of his grete curteisye;
My trouthe wol I kepe, I wol nat lye."
With herte soor° he gooth unto his cofre,°   *painful / money chest*
900 And broghte gold unto this philosophre
The value of fyve hundred pound, I gesse,°   *guess*
And him bisecheth of° his gentillesse   *(out) of*
To graunte him dayes of the remenaunt,⁵
And seyde, "Maister, I dar wel make avaunt,°   *boast*
905 I failled nevere of my trouthe as yit;
For sikerly° my dette shal be quit°   *surely / repaid*
Towardes yow, howevere that I fare°   *although I may go off*
To goon a-begged° in my kirtle° bare.   *begging / shirt*
But wolde ye vouche sauf,° upon seuretee,°   *grant / surety, pledge*
910 Two yeer or three for to respyten me,°   *to give me a delay*
Than were I wel; for elles° moot° I selle   *otherwise / must*
Myn heritage; ther is namore to telle."
This philosophre sobrely° answerde,   *gravely*
And seyde thus, whan he thise wordes herde:
915 "Have I nat holden° covenant unto thee?"   *kept*
    "Yes, certes,° wel and trewely," quod° he.   *certainly / said*
    "Hastow° nat had thy lady as thee lyketh?"   *Hast thou*

3. I.e., hear from.
4. I.e., better terms.

5. To grant him days (i.e., some time) in which to
pay the remainder.

"No, no," quod he, and sorwefully he syketh.°   *sighs*
"What was the cause? tel me if thou can."
920 Aurelius his tale anon bigan,
And tolde him al, as ye han herd bifore:
It nedeth nat to yow reherce it more.°   *recite it again*
He seide, "Arveragus, of gentillesse,
Hadde levere° dye in sorwe and in distresse   *rather*
925 Than that his wyf were of hir trouthe fals."
The sorwe of Dorigen he tolde him als,°   *also*
How looth° hire was to been a wikked wyf,   *loath*
And that she levere had lost that day hir lyf,
And that hir trouthe° she swoor° thurgh innocence: *pledge / swore*
930 She nevere erst° herde speke of apparence.°   *before / illusion, magic*
"That made me han of hire so greet pitee;
And right as frely° as he sente hire me,   *generously*
As frely sente I hire to him ageyn.
This al and som,° ther is namore to seyn."   *This is the whole*
935 This philosophre answerde, "Leve° brother,   *Dear*
Everich° of yow dide gentilly til other.°   *Everyone / toward the other*
Thou art a squyer, and he is a knight;
But God forbede, for his blisful might,
But if° a clerk° coude doon a gentil dede   *Unless / scholar*
940 As wel as any of yow, it is no drede!°   *doubt*
Sire, I relesse thee thy thousand pound,
As° thou right now were cropen° out of the ground,   *As if / had crept*
Ne nevere er° now ne haddest knowen me.   *before*
For sire, I wol nat take a peny of thee
945 For al my craft, ne noght for my travaille.°   *labor*
Thou hast y-payed wel for my vitaille;°   *food, entertainment*
It is y-nogh.° And farewel, have good day."   *enough*
And took his hors, and forth he gooth his way.
Lordinges, this question thanne wolde I aske now:
950 Which was the moste free,° as thinketh yow?[6]   *generous*
Now telleth me, er that° ye ferther wende.°   *before / travel*
I can namore:° my tale is at an ende.   *know no more*

The Pardoner's Prologue and Tale

The Introduction

* * *

"By corpus bones![1] but° I have triacle,°   *unless / medicine*
Or elles a draught of moyste° and corny° ale,   *fresh / malty*
Or but° I here anon° a mery tale,   *unless / at once*

---

6. I.e., in your judgment.   1. I.e., Christ's bones.

Myn herte is lost for pitee of this mayde.[2]
5 Thou bel amy,° thou Pardoner," he seyde,   *sweet friend*
"Tel us som mirthe or japes° right anon."   *jokes*
    "It shall be doon," quod° he, "by Seint Ronyon![3]   *said*
But first," quod he, "heer at this ale-stake°   *tavern sign*
I wol both drinke and eten° of a cake."   *eat*
10   But right anon thise gentils gonne to crye,[4]
"Nay! lat him telle us of no ribaudye;°   *ribaldry*
Tel us som moral thing, that we may lere°   *learn*
Som wit,° and thanne wol we gladly here."°   *Something instructive / listen*
"I graunte,° y-wis,"° quod he, "but I mot° thinke   *agree / certainly / must*
15 Upon som honest° thing whyl that I drinke."   *decent, decorous*

The Prologue

    "Lordinges," quod he, "in chirches whan I preche,
I peyne me° to han an hauteyn° speche,   *take pains / elevated*
And ringe it out as round as gooth° a belle,   *sounds*
For I can al by rote° that I telle.   *know all by memory*
20 My theme° is alwey oon,° and evere was—   *text / always the same*
Radix malorum est Cupiditas.[5]
    First I pronounce° whennes° that I come,   *proclaim / whence, from where*
And thanne my bulles[6] shewe I, alle and somme.°   *one and all*
Oure lige lordes seel[7] on my patente,°   *license*
25 That shewe I first, my body° to warente,°   *person / authorize*
That no man be so bold, ne preest ne clerk,°   *neither priest nor scholar*
Me to destourbe of Cristes holy werk;
And after that thanne telle I forth my tales.
Bulles of popes and of cardinales,
30 Of patriarkes,° and bishoppes I shewe,   *heads of churches*
And in Latyn I speke a wordes fewe,
To saffron with my predicacioun,[8]
And for to stire° hem to devocioun.   *stir*
Thanne shewe I forth my longe cristal stones,°   *glass cases*
35 Y-crammed ful of cloutes° and of bones—   *rags*
Reliks been they, as wenen they echoon.[9]
Thanne have I in latoun[1] a sholder-boon
Which that was of an holy Jewes shepe.
'Goode men,' seye I, 'tak of my wordes kepe:°   *heed*

2. The Host is speaking to the Physician, who has just concluded his sad tale of a young Roman girl who allows her father to kill her, rather than submit to the lust of a corrupt judge.
3. St. Ronan or St. Ninian, with a possible pun on "runnion," meaning loins (including the sexual organs).
4. But immediately these gentlefolk raised a cry.
5. Avarice (the love of money) is the root of all evil

(1 Timothy 6.10).
6. Bulls—writs of indulgence for sin, purchasable in lieu of other forms of penance.
7. I.e., bishop's seal.
8. With which to season my preaching. (Saffron is a yellow spice.)
9. They are (saints') relics, or so they all suppose.
1. Latten, a metal like brass.

40 If that this boon be wasshe° in any welle,	*washed, dunked*
If cow, or calf, or sheep, or oxe swelle,°	*swell (up)*
That any worm hath ete, or worm y-stonge,[2]	
Tak water of that welle, and wash his tonge,	
And it is hool° anon;° and forthermore,	*healed / at once*
45 Of pokkes° and of scabbe and every sore	*pox*
Shal every sheep be hool,° that of this welle	*healed*
Drinketh a draughte. Tak kepe° eek° what I telle:	*heed / also*
If that the good-man that the bestes° oweth°	*animals / owns*
Wol every wike,° er° that the cok him croweth,	*week / before*
50 Fastinge,° drinken of this welle a draughte—	*(While) fasting*
As thilke° holy Jewe[3] oure eldres taughte—	*that same*
His bestes and his stoor° shal multiplye.	*stock*
And, sires, also it hcleth° jalousye:	*heals*
For though a man be falle in jalous rage,	
55 Let maken with this water his potage,[4]	
And nevere shal he more his wyf mistriste,°	*mistrust*
Though he the sooth° of hir defaute° wiste°—	*truth / erring / should know*
Al° had she taken° preestes two or three.	*Even if / taken (as lovers)*
Heer is a miteyn° eek, that ye may see:	*mitten*
60 He that his hond wol putte in this miteyn,	
He shal have multiplying of his greyn°	*grain*
Whan he hath sowen, be it whete° or otes,°	*wheat / oats*
So that he offre pens, or elles grotes.[5]	
Goode men and wommen, o° thing warne° I yow:	*one / tell*
65 If any wight° be in this chirche now,	*person*
That hath doon sinne horrible, that he	
Dar° nat for shame of it y-shriven[6] be,	*Dare*
Or any womman, be she yong or old,	
That hath y-maked hir housbonde cokewold,°	*a cuckold*
70 Swich° folk shul have no power ne no grace	*Such*
To offren° to my reliks in this place.	*To offer (money)*
And whoso findeth him out of swich blame,°	*not deserving such blame*
He wol com up and offre a° Goddes name,	*make an offering in*
And I assoille° him by the auctoritee°	*(will) absolve / authority*
75 Which that by bulle y-graunted was to me.'	
By this gaude° have I wonne,° yeer° by yeer,	*trick / earned / year*
An hundred mark sith I was pardoner.[7]	
I stonde lyk a clerk° in my pulpet,	*scholar*
And whan the lewed° peple is doun y-set,	*ignorant, unlearned*
80 I preche, so as ye han herd bifore,	
And telle an hundred false japes° more.	*tricks, stories*

2. Who has eaten any (poisonous) worm, or whom a snake has stung (bitten).
3. I.e., Jacob.
4. Have his soup made with this water.
5. Provided that he offers (to me) pennies or else groats (coins worth fourpence).
6. I.e., confessed and absolved.
7. A hundred marks (coins worth thirteen shillings fourpence) since I became a pardoner.

Thanne peyne I me° to strecche forth the nekke,   *I take pains*
And est and west upon the peple I bekke°   *nod*
As doth a dowve,° sittinge on a berne.°   *dove / in a barn*
85 Myn hondes and my tonge goon so yerne°   *rapidly*
That it is joye to see my bisinesse.
Of avaryce and of swich° cursednesse   *such*
Is al my preching, for° to make hem free°   *in order / generous*
To yeven hir pens, and namely unto me.⁸
90 For myn entente° is nat but for to winne,°   *intention / profit*
And nothing° for correccioun of sinne: *not at all*
I rekke° nevere, whan that they ben beried,°   *care / buried*
Though that hir soules goon a-blakeberied!⁹
For certes,° many a predicacioun°   *certainly / sermon*
95 Comth ofte tyme of yvel° entencioun: *evil*
Som for plesaunce° of folk and flaterye,   *the entertainment*
To been avaunced by ypocrisye,¹
And som for veyne glorie,° and som for hate.   *vainglory*
For whan I dar non other weyes debate,²
100 Than wol I stinge him³ with my tonge smerte°   *sharp*
In preching, so that he shal nat asterte°   *leap up (to protest)*
To been° defamed falsly, if that he   *At being*
Hath trespased to° my brethren⁴ or to me.   *wronged*
For, though I telle noght his propre° name,   *own*
105 Men shal wel knowe that it is the same
By signes and by othere circumstances.
Thus quyte° I folk that doon us displesances;°   *requite / offenses*
Thus spitte I out my venim under hewe°   *hue, coloring*
Of holynesse, to semen° holy and trewe.   *seem*
110   But shortly° myn entente I wol devyse:°   *briefly / describe*
I preche of no thing but for coveityse.°   *out of covetousness*
Therfore my theme is yet, and evere was,
Radix malorum est cupiditas.
Thus can I preche agayn° that same vyce   *against*
115 Which that I use,° and that is avaryce.   *practice*
But though myself be gilty in that sinne,
Yet can I maken other folk to twinne°   *part*
From avaryce, and sore° to repente.   *ardently*
But that is nat my principal entente:
120 I preche nothing but for coveityse.
Of this matere° it oughte y-nogh suffyse.   *subject*
    Than telle I hem ensamples many oon°   *examples many a one*
Of olde stories longe tyme agoon,°   *past*

---

8. In giving their pence, and particularly to me.   other way.
9. Blackberrying, i.e., wandering.   3. I.e., some enemy.
1. (Thus) to seek advancement through hypocrisy.   4. I.e., fellow pardoners.
2. For when I dare enter into contest (argument) no

For lewed° peple loven tales olde;   *unlearned*
125 Swich° thinges can they wel reporte° and holde.°   *Such / repeat / remember*
    What, trowe ye, the whyles I may preche⁵
    And winne° gold and silver for° I teche,   *obtain / because*
    That I wol live in povert° wilfully?°   *poverty / willingly*
    Nay, nay, I thoghte° it nevere trewely!   *considered*
130 For I wol preche and begge in sondry° londes;   *various*
    I wol nat do no labour with myn hondes,
    Ne make baskettes,⁶ and live therby,
    By cause I wol nat beggen ydelly.°   *without profit*
    I wol non of the Apostles counterfete:°   *imitate*
135 I wol have money, wolle,° chese, and whete,   *wool*
    Al° were it yeven of° the povereste page,°   *Even if / given by / servant*
    Or of° the povercste widwe° in a village,   *by / poorest widow*
    Al sholde hir children sterve for famyne.⁷
    Nay! I wol drinke licour° of the vyne,   *liquor, wine*
140 And have a joly wenche in every toun.
    But herkneth,° lordinges, in conclusioun: *listen*
    Youre lyking is that I shall telle a tale.
    Now have I dronke a draughte of corny° ale,   *malty*
    By God, I hope I shal yow telle a thing
145 That shal by resoun° been at° youre lyking.   *with reason / to*
    For though myself be a ful vicious° man,   *evil, vice-ridden*
    A moral tale yet I yow telle can,
    Which I am wont to preche for to winne.⁸
    Now holde youre pees,° my tale I wol beginne."   *peace*

The Tale

150   In Flaundres whylom was° a compaignye   *once (there) was*
    Of yonge folk, that haunteden folye—
    As ryot, hasard, stewes, and tavernes,⁹
    Where as° with harpes, lutes, and giternes,°   *There where / guitars*
    They daunce and pleyen at dees° bothe day and night,   *dice*
155 And eten also and drinken over hir might,°   *beyond their capacity*
    Thurgh which they doon the devel sacrifyse°   *make sacrifice to the devil*
    Withinne that develes temple,¹ in cursed wyse,°   *way*
    By superfluitee° abhominable.   *excess*
    Hir othes° been so grete and so dampnable,°   *oaths, curses / condemnable*
160 That it is grisly for to here hem swere.
    Our blissed Lordes body they totere°—   *tear apart*
    Hem thoughte° Jewes rente° him noght y-nough—   *It seemed to them / tore*

5. What? do you believe (that) as long as I can   to make some money.
preach.   9. Of young folk who gave themselves up to folly—
6. St. Paul was said to have been a basket-maker.   (such) as excessive revelry, gambling with dice, (vis-
7. Even though her children should die of hunger.   iting) brothels and taverns.
8. Which I am in the habit of preaching, in order   1. I.e., the tavern.

And ech° of hem at otheres sinne lough.°   *each / laughed*
And right anon thanne comen tombesteres°   *female tumblers, dancers*
165 Fetys and smale, and yonge fruytesteres,[2]
Singeres with harpes, baudes,° wafereres,°   *bawds / girls selling cakes*
Whiche been the verray° develes officeres   *the very*
To kindle and blowe the fyr of lecherye
That is annexed° unto glotonye: *joined (as a sin)*
170 The Holy Writ take I to my witnesse
That luxurie° is in wyn and dronkenesse.   *lechery*
    Lo, how that dronken Loth° unkindely°   *Lot / unnaturally*
Lay by his doghtres two, unwitingly;°   *unknowingly*
So dronke he was, he niste° what he wroghte.°   *knew not / did*
175 Herodes,° whoso wel the stories soghte,°   *Herod / should seek out*
Whan he of wyn was repleet° at his feste,   *replete, full*
Right at his owene table he yaf° his heste°   *gave / command*
To sleen the Baptist John ful giltelees.°   *guiltless (innocent)*
    Senek° seith a good word doutelees: *Seneca*
180 He seith, he can no difference finde
Bitwix a man that is out of his minde
And a man which that is dronkelewe,°   *drunken*
But that woodnesse, y-fallen in a shrewe,[3]
Persevereth lenger° than doth dronkenesse.   *Continues longer*
185 O glotonye,° ful of cursednesse!   *gluttony*
O cause first° of oure confusioun!°   *first cause / ruin*
O original° of oure dampnacioun,   *origin*
Til Crist had boght us with his blood agayn!
Lo, how dere,° shortly for to sayn,°   *costly / to speak briefly*
190 Aboght was thilke cursed vileinye;[4]
Corrupt° was al this world for glotonye!   *Corrupted*
Adam oure fader and his wyf also
Fro Paradys to labour and to wo
Were driven for that vyce, it is no drede.°   *doubt*
195 For whyl that Adam fasted, as I rede,°   *read*
He was in Paradys; and whan that he
Eet of the fruyt defended° on the tree,   *forbidden*
Anon° he was outcast to wo and peyne.°   *Immediately / pain*
O glotonye, on thee wel oghte us pleyne![5]
200   O, wiste a man° how manye maladyes   *(if) a man knew*
Folwen of° excesse and of glotonyes,   *Follow on*
He wolde been the more mesurable°   *measured, temperate*
Of his diete, sittinge at his table.
Allas! the shorte throte, the tendre mouth,[6]

2. Shapely and slender, and young girls selling fruit.
3. Except that madness, having afflicted a miserable
man.
4. Bought was that same cursed, evil deed.

5. Oh, gluttony, we certainly ought to complain
against you.
6. I.e., the brief pleasure of swallowing, the mouth
accustomed to delicacies.

205 Maketh that,° est and west, and north and south,   *Causes*
In erthe, in eir,° in water, men to swinke°   *air / labor*
To gete a glotoun deyntee° mete and drinke!   *dainty*
Of this matere,° O Paul, wel canstow trete:°   *subject / canst thou treat*
"Mete° unto wombe,° and wombe eek unto mete,   *Meat / belly*
210 Shal God destroyen bothe." as Paulus seith.[7]
Allas! a foul thing is it, by my feith,
To seye this word, and fouler is the dede,
Whan man so drinketh of the whyte and rede[8]
That of his throte he maketh his privee,°   *privy (toilet)*
215 Thurgh thilke° cursed superfluitee.°   *that same / excess*
     The apostle,[9] weping, seith ful pitously,
"Ther walken manye of whiche yow told have I"—
I seye it now weping with pitous voys—
"They been enemys of Cristes croys,°   *cross*
220 Of which the ende is deeth: wombe° is her° god!"   *belly / their*
O wombe! O bely! O stinking cod,[1]
Fulfild of donge and of corrupcioun![2]
At either ende of thee foul is the soun.°   *sound*
How° greet labour and cost is thee to finde!°   *What / to provide for*
225 Thise cookes, how they stampe,° and streyne,° and grinde,   *pound / strain*
And turnen substaunce into accident,[3]
To fulfille al thy likerous talent!°   *lecherous (here, gluttonous) appetite*
Out of the harde bones knokke they
The mary,° for they caste noght° awey   *marrow / nothing*
230 That may go thurgh the golet° softe and swote;°   *gullet / sweet*
Of spicerye° of leef, and bark, and rote°   *spices / root(s)*
Shal been his sauce y-maked by delyt,°   *to give pleasure*
To make him yet a newer° appetyt.   *renewed*
But certes, he that haunteth swich delyces[4]
235 Is deed, whyl that° he liveth in tho° vyces.   *while / those*
     A lecherous thing is wyn, and dronkenesse
Is ful of stryving° and of wrecchednesse.   *quarreling*
O dronke man, disfigured is thy face,
Sour is thy breeth, foul artow° to embrace,   *art thou*
240 And thurgh thy dronke nose semeth the soun°   *sound*
As though thou seydest ay° "Sampsoun, Sampsoun";[5]   *ever*
And yet, God wot,° Sampsoun drank nevere no wyn.   *knows*
Thou fallest,[6] as it were a stiked swyn;°   *stuck pig*
Thy tonge is lost, and al thyn honest cure,°   *care for decency*

---

7. 1 Corinthians 6.13.
8. I.e., wines.
9. St. Paul. See Philippians 3.18–19.
1. Bag, i.e., the stomach.
2. Filled up with dung and with decaying matter.
3. And turn substance into accident (a scholastic joke: "substaunce" means essence, essential quali-

ties; "accident," external appearances).
4. But truly, he that gives himself up to such pleasures.
5. A witty kind of onomatopoeia—the snoring sound seems to say "Samson," who was betrayed (see *Wife of Bath's Prologue*, ll. 721–23).
6. I.e., down.

245 For dronkenesse is verray sepulture°   *the true tomb*
     Of mannes wit° and his discrecioun.°   *understanding / discretion*
     In whom that° drinke hath dominacioun,   *In him whom*
     He can no conseil° kepe, it is no drede.°   *secrets / doubt*
     Now kepe yow fro the whyte and fro the rede—
250 And namely° fro the whyte wyn of Lepe[7]   *especially*
     That is to selle° in Fishstrete° or in Chepe.° *for sale / Fish Street / Cheapside*
     This wyn of Spaigne crepeth subtilly
     In othere wynes growinge faste by,[8]
     Of° which ther ryseth swich fumositee,°   *From / vapor*
255 That whan a man hath dronken draughtes three
     And weneth° that he be at hoom in Chepe,   *thinks*
     He is in Spaigne, right at the toune of Lepe,
     Nat at The Rochel,° ne at Burdeux toun;°   *La Rochelle / Bordeaux*
     And thanne wol he seye, "Sampsoun, Sampsoun."
260   But herkneth,° lordinges, o° word I yow preye,   *listen / one*
     That alle the sovereyn actes,° dar I seye,   *supreme deeds*
     Of victories in the Olde Testament,
     Thurgh verray° God, that is omnipotent,   *true*
     Were doon in abstinence and in preyere:
265 Loketh the Bible, and ther ye may it lere.°   *learn*
       Loke Attila,[9] the grete conquerour,
     Deyde° in his sleep, with shame and dishonour,   *Died*
     Bledinge ay° at his nose in dronkenesse: *continually*
     A capitayn shoulde live in sobrenesse.
270 And over al this, avyseth yow right wel°   *be well advised*
     What was comaunded unto Lamuel°—   *Lemuel*
     Nat Samuel, but Lamuel, seye I—
     Redeth the Bible, and finde it expresly
     Of wyn-yeving to hem that han justyse.[1]
275 Namore of this, for it may wel suffyse.
       And now that I have spoke of glotonye,
     Now wol I yow defenden° hasardrye.°   *forbid / gambling at dice*
     Hasard is verray moder° of lesinges,°   *the true mother / lies*
     And of deceite and cursed forsweringes,°   *perjuries*
280 Blaspheme of Crist, manslaughtre, and wast° also   *waste*
     Of catel° and of tyme; and forthermo,   *goods*
     It is repreve° and contrarie of honour   *a reproach*
     For to ben holde a commune hasardour.°   *gambler*
     And ever the hyer° he is of estaat°   *higher / in social rank*
285 The more is he y-holden desolaat:°   *considered debased*
     If that a prince useth° hasardrye,   *practices*
     In alle governaunce and policye

---

7. Near Cadiz.
8. That is, the wines sold as French are often mixed with the cheaper wines of Spain.
9. The Hun.
1. Concerning the giving of wine to those responsible for the law (see Proverbs 31.4–5).

	He is, as by commune opinioun,	
	Y-holde the lasse in reputacioun.	
290	Stilbon, that was a wys° embassadour,	*wise*
	Was sent to Corinthe in ful greet honour,	
	For Lacidomie° to make hire alliaunce.°	*Lacedaemon (Sparta) / their alliance*
	And whan he cam, him happede par chaunce°	*it happened by chance*
	That alle the grettest° that were of that lond,	*greatest (men)*
295	Pleyinge atte° hasard he hem fond.	*at (the)*
	For which, as sone as it mighte be,°	*could be*
	He stal him° hoom agayn to his contree,	*stole away*
	And seyde, "Ther wol I nat lese° my name,°	*lose / (good) name*
	Ne I wol nat take on me so greet defame,°	*dishonor*
300	Yow for to allye° unto none hasardours.°	*to ally / gamblers*
	Sendeth othere wyse embassadours—	
	For by my trouthe, me were levere dye°	*I would rather die*
	Than I yow sholde to hasardours allye.	
	For ye that been so glorious in honours	
305	Shul nat allyen yow with hasardours	
	As by my wil, ne as by my tretee."°	*negotiations*
	This wyse philosophre, thus seyde he.	
	Loke eek° that to the king Demetrius	*also*
	The king of Parthes,° as the book seith us,[2]	*Parthia*
310	Sente him a paire of dees° of gold in scorn,	*dice*
	For he hadde used hasard ther-biforn;	
	For which he heeld his glorie or his renoun°	*renown*
	At no value or reputacioun.	
	Lordes may finden other maner pley	
315	Honeste° y-nough to dryve the day awey.	*Honorable*
	Now wol I speke of othes° false and grete	*oaths, curses*
	A word or two, as olde bokes trete.	
	Gret swering° is a thing abhominable,	*cursing*
	And false swering[3] is yet more reprevable.°	*reproachable*
320	The heighe° God forbad swering at al—	*high*
	Witnesse on Mathew—but in special	
	Of swering seith the holy Jeremye,°	*Jeremiah*
	"Thou shalt swere sooth° thyn othes° and nat lye,	*truly / oaths*
	And swere in dome,° and eek in rightwisnesse;"°	*(good) judgment / righteousness*
325	But ydel° swering is a cursednesse.°	*vain / wickedness*
	Bihold and see, that in the first table°	*tablet (of Moses)*
	Of heighe Goddes hestes° honurable,	*commandments*
	How that the seconde heste of him is this:	
	"Tak nat my name in ydel° or amis."°	*in vain / amiss (wrongly)*
330	Lo, rather° he forbedeth swich° swering	*earlier (in the list) / such*
	Than homicyde or many a cursed thing—	

2. The *Policraticus* of John of Salisbury, which also   3. I.e., of oaths.
contains the preceding story.

I seye that, as by ordre,° thus it stondeth—   *in terms of the order*
This knoweth, that his hestes understondeth,[4]
How that the second heste of God is that.
335 And forther over,° I wol thee telle al plat°   *moreover / flatly*
That vengeance shal nat parten° from his hous   *depart*
That° of his othes is to° outrageous.   *Who / too*
"By Goddes precious herte," and "By his nayles,"
And "By the blode of Crist that is in Hayles,[5]
340 Seven is my chaunce,[6] and thyn is cink° and treye;"°   *five / three*
"By Goddes armes, if thou falsly pleye,
This dagger shal thurghout thyn herte go!"
This fruyt cometh of the bicched bones two—[7]
Forswering,° ire,° falsnesse, homicyde.   *Perjury / anger*
345 Now for the love of Crist that for us dyde,
Lete° youre othes, bothe grete and smale.   *Cease*
But, sires, now wol I telle forth my tale.
        Thise ryotoures° three of which I telle,   *rioters, revelers*
Longe erst er° pryme° rong of any belle,   *before / 9 A.M.*
350 Were set hem° in a taverne for to drinke;   *Had set themselves down*
And as they sat, they herde a belle clinke
Biforn a cors° was° caried to his grave.   *corpse / (which) was (being)*
That oon of hem gan callen to his knave,
"Go bet," quod he, "and axe redily,[8]
355 What cors is this that passeth heer forby;°   *by here*
And looke that thou reporte his name wel."[9]
        "Sire," quod this boy, "it nedeth never-a-del.°   *it isn't at all necessary*
It was me told, er° ye cam heer two houres.   *before*
He was, pardee,[1] an old felawe° of youres;   *companion*
360 And sodeynly he was y-slayn to-night,
For-dronke,° as he sat on his bench upright.   *Dead drunk*
Ther cam a privee° theef men clepeth° Deeth,   *secret / call*
That in this contree° al the peple sleeth,°   *region / kills*
And with his spere he smoot his herte atwo,[2]
365 And wente his wey withouten wordes mo.°   *more*
He hath a thousand slayn this pestilence.°   *(during) this plague*
And maister, er° ye come in his presence,   *before*
Me thinketh° that it were necessarie   *It seems to me*
For to be war° of swich an adversarie: *aware, careful*
370 Beth redy for to mete him everemore.°   *always*
Thus taughte me my dame,° I sey namore."   *mother*

---

4. (He) knows this, who understands His commandments.
5. An abbey in Gloucestershire supposed to possess
(as a high relic) some of Christ's blood.
6. I.e., throw.
7. This fruit, i.e., result, comes from the two cursed
dice. (Dice were made of bone; hence "bones" here.)
8. The one of them proceeded to call to his servant-

boy, "Go quickly," he said, "and ask straightway."
9. I.e., correctly.
1. A weak form of the oath "by God," based on the
French *par dieu.*
2. And with his spear he struck his heart in two.
(Death was often shown in the visual arts as a
hideous skeleton menacing men with a spear or
arrow.)

"By Seinte Marie," seyde this taverner,°   *tavernkeeper*
"The child seith sooth, for he hath slayn this yeer,
Henne° over a myle, withinne a greet village,   *Hence, from here*
375 Bothe man and womman, child, and hyne,° and page;°   *laborer / servant*
I trowe° his habitacioun be there.   *believe*
To been avysed° greet wisdom it were,   *forewarned*
Er that° he dide a man a dishonour."   *Before*
      "Ye,° Goddes armes," quod° this ryotour,°   *Aye, yes / said / reveler*
380 "Is it swich peril with him for to mete?
I shal him seke by wey° and eek° by strete,   *road / also*
I make avow to° Goddes digne° bones!   *avow (it) by / worthy*
Herkneth, felawes, we three been al ones:°   *all of one mind*
Lat ech° of us holde up his hond til other,°   *each / to the other*
385 And ech of us bicomen otheres° brother,   *the others'*
And we wol sleen° this false traytour Deeth.   *slay*
He shal be slayn, he that so manye sleeth,
By Goddes dignitee,° er it be night."   *worthiness*
      Togidres° han thise three hir trouthes plight°   *Together / plighted their troth*
390 To live and dyen ech of hem for other,°   *one another*
As though he were his owene y-boren° brother.   *born*
And up they sterte,° al dronken in this rage,°   *leaped / passion*
And forth they goon towardes that village
Of which the taverner hadde spoke biforn,
395 And many a grisly ooth thanne han they sworn,
And Cristes blessed body they to-rente°—   *tore apart*
Deeth shal be deed, if that they may him hente.°   *seize*
      Whan they han goon nat fully half a myle,
Right° as they wolde han troden° over a style,°   *Just / stepped / stile*
400 An old man and a povre° with hem mette.   *poor (one)*
This olde man ful mekely° hem grette,°   *meekly / greeted them*
And seyde thus, "Now, lordes, God yow see!"°   *may God protect you*
      The proudest of thise ryotoures three
Answerde agayn, "What, carl,° with sory grace!°   *Hey, fellow / confound you*
405 Why artow al forwrapped save thy face?³
Why livestow° so longe in so greet age?"   *livest thou*
      This olde man gan loke in° his visage,   *scrutinized*
And seyde thus, "For° I ne can nat finde   *Because*
A man, though that I walked into Inde,°   *India*
410 Neither in citee nor in no village,
That wolde chaunge his youthe for myn age;
And therfore moot° I han myn age stille,   *must*
As longe time as it is Goddes wille.
Ne Deeth, allas! ne wol nat han my lyf.
415 Thus walke I, lyk° a restelees caityf,°   *like / captive*

3. Why art thou all wrapped up, except for thy face?

And on the ground, which is my modres° gate,   *mother's*
I knokke with my staf bothe erly and late,
And seye, 'Leve° moder, leet me in!   *Dear*
Lo, how I vanish,° flesh, and blood, and skin!   *waste away*
420 Allas! whan shul my bones been at reste?
Moder, with yow wolde I chaunge° my cheste°   *exchange / chest (of clothes)*
That in my chambre longe tyme hath be,°   *been*
Ye, for an heyre clout° to wrappe me!'   *haircloth (for burial)*
But yet to me she wol nat do that grace,
425 For which ful pale and welked° is my face.   *withered*
     But sires, to yow it is no curteisye⁴
To speken to an old man vileinye,°   *rudeness*
But° he trespasse° in worde or elles° in dede.   *Unless / offend / else*
In Holy Writ ye may yourself wel rede,°   *read*
430 'Agayns° an old man, hoor° upon his heed,   *Before / hoary, white*
Ye sholde aryse.' Wherfor I yeve yow reed:⁵
Ne dooth unto an old man noon harm now,
Namore than that ye wolde men did to yow
In age, if that ye so longe abyde.°   *remain (alive)*
435 And God be with yow, wher ye go° or ryde;   *walk*
I moot° go thider as° I have to go."   *must / thither where*
     "Nay, olde cherl, by God, thou shalt nat so,"
Seyde this other hasardour° anon;°   *gambler / at once*
"Thou partest° nat so lightly, by Seint John!   *departest*
440 Thou spak right now of thilke° traitour Deeth   *that same*
That in this contree alle oure frendes sleeth.
Have heer my trouthe,° as° thou art his espye,°   *pledge / since / spy*
Telle wher he is, or thou shalt it abye,°   *pay for*
By God, and by the holy sacrament!
445 For soothly thou art oon of his assent°   *in league with him*
To sleen us yonge folk, thou false theef!"
     "Now, sires," quod he, "if that yow be so leef°   *desirous*
To finde Deeth, turne up this croked° wey,   *crooked*
For in that grove I lafte° him, by my fey,°   *left / faith*
450 Under a tree, and there he wol abyde:°   *stay*
Nat for youre boost he wole him nothing hyde.⁶
See ye that ook?° right ther ye shul him finde.   *oak*
God save yow, that boghte agayn° mankinde,   *redeemed*
And yow amende!"° Thus seyde this olde man.   *make you better*
455   And everich° of thise ryotoures° ran,   *each / revelers*
Til he cam to that tree, and ther they founde
Of florins° fyne of golde y-coyned° rounde   *florins, coins / coined*
Wel ny an° eighte busshels, as hem thoughte.°   *nearly / it seemed to them*

---

4. But, sirs, it is not courteous of you.
5. "You should stand up (in respect)." Therefore I give you (this) advice.

6. He won't conceal himself at all because of your boasting.

No lenger thanne° after Deeth they soughte,   *No longer then*
460 But ech° of hem so glad was of that sighte—   *each*
For that the florins been so faire and brighte—
That doun they sette hem by this precious hord.
The worste of hem he spake the firste word.
      "Brethren," quod he, "take kepe° what that I seye: *heed*
465 My wit° is greet, though that I bourde and pleye.   *mind / trifling / jest*
This tresor° hath Fortune unto us yiven°   *treasure / given*
In mirthe and jolitee° our lyf to liven,   *merriment*
And lightly as it comth, so wol we spende.
Ey! Goddes precious dignitee!° who wende°   *worthiness / would have supposed*
470 To-day that we sholde han so fair a grace?°   *favor*
But° mighte this gold be caried fro this place   *If only*
Hoom to myn hous—or elles unto youres—
For wel ye woot° that al this gold is oures—   *know*
Thanne were we in heigh felicitee.°   *supreme happiness*
475 But trewely, by daye it may nat be:°   *be (done)*
Men wolde seyn that we were theves stronge,°   *flagrant*
And for oure owene tresor doon us honge.°   *have us hanged*
This tresor moste y-caried be by nighte,
As wysly° and as slyly° as it mighte.°   *prudently / craftily / can (be)*
480 Wherfore I rede° that cut° among us alle   *advise / lots, straws*
Be drawe,° and lat se wher the cut wol falle;   *drawn, pulled*
And he that hath the cut with herte blythe
Shal renne° to the toune, and that ful swythe,°   *run / quickly*
And bringe us breed and wyn ful prively.°   *secretly*
485 And two of us shul kepen° subtilly°   *guard / carefully*
This tresor wel; and if he wol nat tarie,°   *tarry*
Whan it is night we wol this tresor carie,
By oon assent, where as us thinketh best."[7]
That oon of hem the cut broughte in his fest,°   *fist*
490 And bad hem drawe, and loke wher it wol falle;
And it fil on the yongeste of hem alle,
And forth toward the toun he wente anon.
And also sone as° that he was agon,   *as soon as*
That oon of hem° spak thus unto that other: *The one of them*
495 "Thou knowest wel thou art my sworne brother;
Thy profit° wol I telle thee anon.   *Something to thy advantage*
Thou woost° wel that oure felawe is agon,°   *knowest / gone*
And heer is gold, and that° ful greet plentee,   *that (in)*
That shal departed° been among us three.   *divided*
500 But natheles,° if I can shape° it so   *nonetheless / arrange*
That it departed were among us two,
Hadde I nat doon a freendes torn° to thee?"   *turn*

7. By common assent, wherever seems to us best.

That other answerde, "I noot° how that may be: know not
He woot how that the gold is with us tweye.
505 What shal we doon? what shal we to him seye?"
    "Shal it be conseil?"° seyde the firste shrewe;°   a secret / wretch
"And I shal tellen in a wordes fewe
What we shal doon, and bringe it wel aboute."
"I graunte,"° quod that other, "out of doute,[8]   grant (it)
510 That, by my trouthe, I wol thee nat biwreye."°   betray
    "Now," quod the firste, "thou woost° wel we be tweye,°   knowest / two
And two of us shul strenger° be than oon.   stronger
Looke whan that he is set,° that right anoon°   has sat down / right away
Arys° as though thou woldest with him pleye;   Arise (get up)
515 And I shal ryve° him thurgh the sydes tweye°   stab / through his two sides
Whyl that thou strogelest° with him as in game,°   strugglest / as if in play
And with thy dagger looke° thou do the same;   take heed
And thanne shall al this gold departed° be,   divided
My dere freend, bitwixen me and thee.
520 Thanne may we bothe oure lustes° al fulfille,   desires
And pleye at dees° right at oure owene wille."   dice
And thus acorded° been thise shrewes° tweye   agreed / cursed fellows
To sleen the thridde, as ye han herd me seye.
    This yongest, which that wente unto the toun,
525 Ful ofte in herte he rolleth up and doun[9]
The beautee of thise florins newe and brighte.
"O Lord!" quod he, "if so were that I mighte
Have al this tresor to myself allone,
Ther is no man that liveth under the trone°   throne
530 Of God that sholde live so mery as I!"
And atte laste° the feend,° our enemy,   at (the) last / devil
Putte in his thought that he shold poyson beye,°   buy poison
With which he mighte sleen his felawes tweye°—   two companions
For-why the feend fond him in swich lyvinge[1]
535 That he had leve° him to sorwe bringe: permission (from God)
For this was outrely° his fulle entente,°   completely / purpose
To sleen hem bothe, and nevere to repente.
And forth he gooth—no lenger wolde he tarie—
Into the toun, unto a pothecarie,°   apothecary, pharmacist
540 And preyed° him that he him wolde selle   asked
Som poyson, that° he mighte his rattes quelle,°   so that / kill his rats
And eek° ther was a polcat° in his hawe,°   also / weasel / yard
That, as he seyde, his capouns° hadde y-slawe,°   capons / killed
And fayn° he wolde wreke him,° if he mighte,   gladly / avenge himself
545 On vermin, that destroyed° him by nighte.   were ruining
    The pothecarie answerde, "And thou shalt have

8. I.e., you can be sure.   1. Because the fiend (the devil) found him living in
9. I.e., thinks on.   such a way.

A thing that, also° God my soule save,   so (may)
In al this world ther nis no° creature,   is not any
That ete or dronke hath of this confiture°   mixture
550 Noght but the mountance of a corn of whete,[2]
That he ne shal his lyf anon° forlete.°   at once / lose
Ye,° sterve° he shal, and that in lasse whyle°   Yes / die / shorter time
Than thou wolt goon a paas° nat but° a myle,   walk at normal pace / only
This poyson is so strong and violent."
555   This cursed man hath in his hond y-hent°   grasped
This poyson in a box, and sith° he ran   afterward
Into the nexte strete unto a man
And borwed [of] him large botels° three,   bottles (probably of leather)
And in the two his poyson poured he—
560 The thridde he kepte clene for his° drinke—   his (own)
For al the night he shoop him° for to swinke°   was preparing himself / work
In caryinge of the gold out of that place.
And whan this ryotour, with sory grace,[3]
Hadde filled with wyn his grete botels three,
565 To his felawes agayn repaireth° he.   returns
What nedeth it to sermone° of it more?   speak
For right as they hadde cast° his deeth bifore,   planned
Right so they han him slayn, and that anon.°   immediately
And whan that this was doon, thus spak that oon:
570 "Now lat us sitte and drinke, and make us merie,
And afterward we wol his body berie."°   bury
And with that word it happed° him, par cas,°   befell / by chance
To take the botel ther° the poyson was,   where
And drank, and yaf° his felawe drink also,   gave
575 For which anon they storven° bothe two.   died
But certes, I suppose that Avicen
Wroot nevere in no canon, ne in no fen,
Mo wonder signes of empoisoning[4]
Than hadde thise wrecches two, er° hir° ending.   before / their
580 Thus ended been thise homicydes two,
And eek° the false empoysoner° also.°   also / poisoner / as well
O cursed sinne of alle cursednesse!
O traytours° homicyde, O wikkednesse!   traitorous
O glotonye, luxurie,° and hasardrye!   lechery
585 Thou blasphemour of Crist with vileinye°   vile speech
And othes grete, of usage° and of pryde!   out of habit
Allas! mankinde, how may it bityde°   happen
That to thy Creatour which that thee wroghte,
And with his precious herte-blood thee boghte,°   redeemed

2. No more than the quantity of a grain of wheat.   physician and author—never described, in any trea-
3. I.e., blessed by evil.   tise or chapter, more terrible symptoms of poisoning.
4. But truly, I would guess that Avicenna—an Arab

590 Thou art so fals and so unkinde,° allas!   *unnatural*
    Now, goode men, God forgeve° yow youre trespas,   *may God forgive*
And ware yow fro° the sinne of avaryce.   *make you beware of*
Myn holy pardoun may yow alle waryce°—   *cure*
So that ye offre nobles or sterlinges,⁵
595 Or elles silver broches, spones,° ringes.   *spoons*
Boweth youre heed° under this holy bulle!   *head*
Cometh up, ye wyves, offreth of youre wolle!°   *wool*
Youre names I entre heer in my rolle° anon:°   *roll, list / at once*
Into the blisse of hevene shul ye gon.
600 I yow assoile,° by myn heigh power—   *absolve*
Yow that wol offre°—as clene and eek as cleer°   *make an offering / pure*
As ye were born.—And, lo, sires, thus I preche.
And Jesu Crist, that is our soules leche,°   *healer, doctor*
So graunte° yow his pardon to receyve,   *May He grant*
605 For that is best; I wol yow nat deceyve.
    But sires, o° word forgat I in my tale: *a, one*
I have relikes and pardon in my male°   *pouch*
As faire as any man in Engelond,
Whiche were me yeven° by the Popes hond.   *given*
610 If any of yow wol of devocioun°   *out of devotion*
Offren and han myn absolucioun,
Cometh forth anon, and kneleth heer adoun,
And mekely receyveth my pardoun;
Or elles, taketh pardon as ye wende,°   *travel*
615 Al newe and fresh, at every myles ende—
So that ye offren alwey newe and newe⁶
Nobles or pens,° which that be gode and trewe.   *pence*
It is an honour to everich° that is heer   *every one*
That ye mowe° have a suffisant° pardoneer   *may / capable*
620 T'assoille° yow, in contree as ye ryde,   *To absolve*
For aventures whiche that may bityde.⁷
Peraventure° ther may falle oon or two   *By chance*
Doun of his hors, and breke his nekke atwo.°   *in two*
Look which a seuretee° is it to you alle   *what a security*
625 That I am in youre felaweship y-falle,
That may assoille yow, bothe more and lasse,°   *great and small*
Whan that the soule shal fro the body passe.
I rede° that oure Host heer shal biginne,   *advise*
For he is most envoluped° in sinne.   *enveloped, wrapped up*
630 Com forth, sire Hoste, and offre first anon,°   *first now*
And thou shalt kisse the reliks everichon,°   *every one*
Ye, for a grote:° unbokel° anon thy purs."   *groat (four pence) / unbuckle*

---

5. As long as you offer nobles (gold coins) or silver   6. As long as you make offering anew each time (of).
pennies.   7. In respect to things which may befall.

"Nay, nay," quod° he, "thanne have I Cristes curs!   *said*
Lat be," quod he, "it shal nat be, so theech!°   *as I hope to prosper*
635 Thou woldest make me kisse thyn olde breech°   *breeches*
And swere it were a relik of a seint,
Thogh it were with thy fundement° depeint!°   *fundament (rectum) / stained*
But by the croys° which that Seint Eleyne° fond,   *(true) Cross / St. Helena*
I wolde I hadde thy coillons° in myn hond   *testicles*
640 In stede of relikes or of seintuarie.[8]
Lat cutte hem of! I wol thee helpe hem carie.[9]
Thay shul be shryned° in an hogges tord!"°   *enshrined / turd*
This Pardoner answerde nat a word;
So wrooth° he was, no word ne wolde he seye.   *wroth, angered*
645 "Now," quod our Host, "I wol no lenger pleye
With thee, ne with noon other angry man."
But right anon the worthy Knight bigan,
Whan that he saugh that al the peple lough,°   *laughed*
"Namore of this, for it is right y-nough!°   *quite enough*
650 Sire Pardoner, be glad and mery of chere;°   *mood*
And ye, sire Host, that been to me so dere,
I prey yow that ye kisse the Pardoner.
And Pardoner, I prey thee, drawe thee neer,
And, as we diden, lat us laughe and pleye."
655 Anon° they kiste, and riden forth hir weye.°   *At once / (on) their way*

The Prioress's Prologue and Tale

The Introduction

"Well seyd, by *corpus dominus*,"° quod° oure Hoste, *the Lord's body / said*
"Now longe moot° thou sayle by the coste,°   *may / sail along the coast*
Sire gentil maister, gentil marineer![1]
God yeve this monk a thousand last quad yeer![2]
5 A ha! felawes!° beth ware of swiche° a jape!°   *companions / such / trick*
The monk putte in the mannes hood an ape,[3]
And in his wyves eek,° by Seint Austin!°   *as well / Augustine*
Draweth° no monkes more unto youre in.°   *Take / lodging*
But now passe over,° and lat us seke aboute,   *on*
10 Who shal now telle first, of al this route,°   *company*
Another tale;" and with that word he sayde,
As curteisly as it had been a mayde,[4]

---

8. I.e., holy things.
9. Have them cut off! I'll help thee carry them.
1. The Shipman has just told his tale of a merchant, his wife, and a lecherous monk.
2. God give this monk a thousand cartloads of bad

years.
3. The monk put an ape in the man's hood, i.e., made a fool of him.
4. As courteously as if it had been a maiden (speaking).

"My lady Prioresse, by your leve,
So that I wiste° I sholde yow nat greve,°   *knew / vex*
15 I wolde demen° that ye tellen sholde   *would decide*
  A tale next, if so were that ye wolde.°   *were willing*
  Now wol ye vouche sauf,° my lady dere?"   *agree*
    "Gladly," quod she, and seyde as ye shal here.

The Prologue

Domine, dominus noster.°   *Oh Lord, our lord*

  O Lord, oure Lord, thy name how merveillous°   *marvelously*
20 Is in this large worlde y-sprad°—quod° she—   *spread / said*
  For noght only thy laude° precious   *praise*
  Parfourned° is by men of dignitee,   *celebrated, performed*
  But by the mouth of children thy bountee°   *goodness*
  Parfourned is, for on the brest soukinge°   *sucking*
25 Somtyme shewen° they thyn heryinge.°   *show forth / praise*

  Wherfore in laude,° as I best can or may,   *praise*
  Of thee, and of the whyte lily flour⁵
  Which that thee bar,° and is a mayde° alway,   *Who bore thee / virgin*
  To telle a storie I wol do my labour;
30 Not that I may encresen° hir honour,   *increase*
  For she hirself is honour, and the rote°   *root*
  Of bountee, next° hir sone, and soules bote.°   *next (to) / help*

  O moder mayde! o mayde moder free!°   *gracious, bountiful*
  O bush unbrent, brenninge in Moyses sighte,⁶
35 That ravysedest° doun fro the deitee,   *ravished*
  Thurgh thyn humblesse, the goost° that in
     th'alighte,°   *(Holy) Spirit / alighted in thee*
  Of whos vertu, whan he thyn herte lighte,
  Conceived was the Fadres sapience,⁷
  Help me to telle it in thy reverence!

40 Lady, thy bountee, thy magnificence,
  Thy vertu, and thy grete humilitee,
  Ther may° no tonge expresse in no science;°   *can / whatever its learning*
  For somtyme, lady, er° men praye to thee,   *before*
  Thou goost biforn° of thy benignitee,   *proceedest*

---

5. I.e., the Virgin.
6. Oh, bush unburned, burning in Moses's sight (a common figure for the miracle of Mary's virginity, preserved even in her motherhood of Christ; ultimately based on Exodus 3.1–5).
7. Through whose power, when he illumined thy heart, was conceived the Wisdom of the Father, i.e., Christ, the Logos.

45 And getest us the light, of° thy preyere,   *by means of*
    To gyden° us unto thy Sone so dere.   *guide*

    My conning° is so wayk,° o blisful Quene,   *skill / weak*
    For to declare thy grete worthinesse,
    That I ne may the weighte nat sustene;
50 But as a child of twelf monthe old, or lesse,
    That can unnethes° any word expresse,   *hardly*
    Right so fare I, and therfor I yow preye,
    Gydeth° my song that I shal of yow seye.   *Guide*

The Tale

    Ther was in Asie,° in a greet citee,   *Asia (Minor)*
55 Amonges Cristen folk, a Jewerye,°   *Jews' quarter*
    Sustened by a lord of that contree
    For foule usure° and lucre of vileynye,°   *usury / wicked financial gain*
    Hateful to Crist and to his compaignye;[8]
    And thurgh° the strete men mighte ryde or wende,°   *through / go*
60 For it was free, and open at either ende.

    A litel scole° of Cristen° folk ther stood   *school / Christian*
    Doun at the ferther ende, in which ther were
    Children an heep,° y-comen° of Cristen blood,   *many, a crowd / come*
    That lerned in that scole yeer by yere
65 Swich manere doctrine as men used there—[9]
    This is to seyn,° to singen and to rede,°   *say / read*
    As smale children doon in hire childhede.

    Among thise children was a widwes° sone,   *widow's*
    A litel clergcoun,° seven yeer of age,   *schoolboy*
70 That day by day to[1] scole was his wone,°   *custom*
    And eek also, where as° he saugh° th'ymage   *wherever / saw*
    Of Cristes moder, hadde he in usage,°   *he was accustomed*
    As him was taught, to knele adoun and seye
    His *Ave Marie,*° as he goth by the weye.   *Hail, Mary*

75 Thus hath this widwe hir litel sone y-taught
    Our blisful Lady, Cristes moder dere,
    To worshipe ay;° and he forgat it naught,   *always*
    For sely child wol alday sone lere.[2]
    But ay,° whan I remembre[3] on this matere,   *ever*

---

8. I.e., Christians.   2. For a good child will always learn quickly.
9. Such kinds of subject as were usual there.   3. I.e., think, meditate.
1. I.e., to go.

80 Seint Nicholas[4] stant° evere in my presence,   *stands*
For he so yong to Crist did reverence.°   *honored*

This litel child, his litel book lerninge,
As he sat in the scole at his prymer,[5]
He *Alma redemptoris*[6] herde singe,
85 As children lerned hire antiphoner;°   *their anthem-book*
And, as he dorste, he drough him ner and ner,[7]
And herkned ay° the wordes and the note,°   *ever / music*
Til he the firste vers coude° al by rote.°   *knew / by heart*

Noght wiste° he what this Latin was to seye,°   *knew / meant*
90 For he so yong and tendre was of age;
But on a day his felaw gan he preye[8]
T'expounden him this song in his langage,°   *his own language*
Or telle him why this song was in usage;°   *used*
This preyde he him to construe° and declare   *interpret*
95 Ful ofte tyme upon his knowes° bare.   *knees*

His felawe, which that elder was than he,
Answerde him thus: "This song, I have herd seye,
Was maked of° our blisful Lady free,°   *about / generous*
Hire to salue,° and eek° hire for to preye   *salute, greet / also*
100 To been oure help and socour° whan we dye.°   *succor, aid / die*
I can no more expounde in this matere:
I lerne song, I can° but smal° grammere."   *know / little*

"And is this song maked in reverence
Of Cristes moder?" seyde this innocent.
105 "Now certes,° I wol do my diligence   *certainly*
To conne° it al, er° Cristemasse be went.°   *learn / before / is passed*
Though that I for my prymer[9] shal be shent,°   *scolded*
And shal be beten thryes° in an houre,   *thrice*
I wol it conne, oure Lady for to honoure."

110 His felaw taughte him homward prively,[1]
Fro day to day, til he coude° it by rote,   *knew*
And thanne he song° it wel and boldely°   *sang / forcefully*
Fro word to word, acording with the note;
Twyes° a day it passed thurgh his throte,   *Twice*

---

4. St. Nicholas is said to have fasted even as an infant; he took the breast only once on Wednesdays and Fridays. He is also the patron saint of school-boys.
5. A prayerbook used as an elementary school text.
6. For text and translation of this anthem, see p. 427.

7. And, as (much as) he dared, he drew nearer and nearer.
8. But one day he begged his companion.
9. I.e., for failing to study my primer.
1. His companion taught him (on the way) home-ward, privately.

115 To scoleward° and homward whan he wente.   *Toward school*
On Cristes moder set was his entente.°   *(heart's) intent*

As I have seyd, thurghout the Jewerye
This litel child, as he cam to and fro,
Ful merily than wolde he singe and crye°   *cry out*
120 O *Alma redemptoris* everemo.
The swetnesse his herte perced° so   *pierced*
Of Cristes moder, that, to hire to preye,
He can nat stinte of° singing by° the weye.   *cease from / along*

Oure firste fo,° the serpent Sathanas,°   *foe / Satan*
125 That hath in Jewes herte his waspes nest,
Up swal° and seide, "O Hebraik peple, allas!   *swelled*
Is this to yow a thing that is honest,°   *honorable, seemly*
That swich° a boy shal walken as him lest°   *such / it pleases him*
In youre despyt, and singe of swich sentence,[2]
130 Which is agayn° oure lawes reverence?"[3]   *against*

Fro thennes forth° the Jewes han° conspyred   *thenceforth / have*
This innocent out of this world to chace:°   *drive*
An homicyde° therto han they hyred,°   *murderer / hired*
That in an aley° hadde a privee° place;   *alley / secret*
135 And as the child gan forby for to pace,°   *was walking by*
This cursed Jew him hente° and heeld him faste,   *seized*
And kitte° his throte, and in a pit him caste.   *cut*

I seye that in a wardrobe° they him threwe   *privy*
Where as these Jewes purgen hir entraille.[4]
140 O cursed folk of Herodes° al newe,°   *Herod / always renewed*
What may youre yvel entente° yow availle?   *evil plan*
Mordre° wol out, certein, it wol nat faille,   *Murder*
And namely ther° th'onour of God shal sprede,   *there where*
The blood out cryeth on your cursed dede.

145 O martir souded to° virginitee,   *made fast in*
Now maystou° singen, folwinge evere in oon°   *mayest thou / forever*
The Whyte Lamb celestial—quod she—
Of which the grete evangelist Seint John
In Pathmos[5] wroot, which seith that they that goon°   *walk*
150 Biforn° this Lamb and singe a song al newe,°   *Before / wholly new*
That nevere, fleshly,° wommen they ne knewe.   *carnally*

2. In scorn of you, and sing of such a subject.   4. Where these Jews empty their bowels.
3. The best manuscripts read "oure," as here; some   5. The isle of Patmos in Greece, where St. John
read "youre."   wrote the Book of Revelation.

This povre widwe° awaiteth al that night   *poor widow*
After hir litel child, but he cam noght;
For which, as sone as it was dayes light,
155 With face pale of drede° and bisy thoght,°   *fear / anxiety*
She hath at scole and elleswhere him soght,
Til finally she gan so fer espye°   *found out this much*
That he last seyn° was in the Jewerye.   *seen*

With modres pitee in hir brest enclosed,
160 She gooth, as° she were half out of hir minde,   *as if*
To every place wher she hath supposed
By lyklihede hir litel child to finde.
And evere on Cristes moder meke and kinde
She cryde, and atte laste thus she wroghte:[6]
165 Among the cursed Jewes she him soghte.

She frayneth° and she preyeth° pitously   *inquires / begs*
To every Jew that dwelte in thilke° place,   *that same*
To telle hire if hir child wente oght forby.°   *by at all*
They seyde "Nay"; but Jesu, of° his grace,   *by*
170 Yaf in hir thought, inwith a litel space,[7]
That° in that place after hir sone she cryde°   *So that / called*
Where he was casten in a pit bisyde.°   *nearby*

O grete God, that parfournest thy laude[8]
By mouth of innocents, lo heer° thy might!   *behold here*
175 This gemme of chastitee, this emeraude,°   *emerald*
And eek° of martirdom the ruby bright,   *also*
Ther he with throte y-corven lay upright,[9]
He *Alma redemptoris* gan° to singe   *began*
So loude that al the place gan to ringe.°   *resounded*

180 The Cristen folk, that thurgh the strete wente,
In coomen° for to wondre upon this thing,   *came*
And hastily they for the provost° sente;   *magistrate*
He cam anon withouten tarying,
And herieth° Crist that is of heven king,   *praises*
185 And eek° his moder, honour of mankinde,   *also*
And after that the Jewes leet he binde.°   *he had bound*

This child with pitous lamentacioun
Up taken was, singing his song alway;
And with honour of greet processioun
190 They carien him unto the nexte abbay.°   *nearest abbey*
His moder swowning° by his bere° lay.   *swooning / bier*

6. She called, and in the end she did thus.   8. Oh, great God, that (hast) thy praise performed.
7. Gave her an idea, within a little while.   9. There where he lay face-up, with his throat cut.

Unnethe° might the peple that was there   *Scarcely*
This newe Rachel¹ bringe fro his bere.

With torment° and with shamful deth echon°   *torture / each one*
195 This provost dooth° thise Jewes for to sterve°   *causes / die*
That of this mordre wiste,° and that anon;°   *knew / immediately*
He nolde no swich cursednesse observe.²
"Yvel shal have that yvel wol deserve:"³
Therfore with wilde hors° he dide hem drawe,°   *horses / had them drawn*
200 And after that he heng° hem by the lawe.   *hanged (probably on pikes)*

Upon his bere al lyth° this innocent   *still lies*
Biforn the chief auter,° whyl the masse° laste,   *altar / the mass*
And after that, the abbot with his covent°   *monks*
Han sped hem° for to burien him ful faste;   *have hastened*
205 And whan they holy water on him caste,
Yet spak this child, whan spreynd° was holy water,   *sprinkled*
And song° O *Alma redemptoris mater!*   *sang*

This abbot, which that was an holy man
As monkes been°—or elles oghten° be—   *are / else ought to*
210 This yonge child to conjure° he bigan,   *entreat*
And seyde, "O dere child, I halse° thee,   *beg*
In vertu of the Holy Trinitee,
Tel me what is thy cause for to singe,
Sith that° thy throte is cut, to my seminge?"°   *Since / it seems to me*

215 "My throte is cut unto my nekke-boon,"
Seyde this child, "and, as by wey of kinde,°   *nature*
I sholde have deyed, ye,° longe tyme agoon,°   *yea, yes / ago*
But Jesu Crist, as ye in bokes finde,
Wil° that his glorie laste and be in minde;   *Wills*
220 And for the worship of his moder dere
Yet° may I singe O *Alma* loude and clere.   *Still*

This welle° of mercy, Cristes moder swete,   *spring*
I lovede alwey as after my conninge;°   *as best I could*
And whan that I my lyf sholde forlete,°   *was to leave*
225 To me she cam, and bad me for to singe
This antem° verraily° in my deyinge,   *hymn / truly*
As ye han herd; and whan that I had songe,
Me thoughte she leyde a greyn° upon my tonge.   *seed*

Wherfore I singe, and singe moot certeyn,°   *indeed must*
230 In honour of that blisful mayden free,°   *generous*

1. This second Rachel (a grieving Jewish mother, in   Herod, in Matthew 2.18).
Jeremiah 31.15, who was said to prefigure the griev-   2. He would not tolerate such evil doings.
ing mothers of the innocents slain by command of   3. "He who will deserve evil shall have evil."

Til fro my tonge of° taken is the greyn;   *off*
And afterward thus seyde she to me,
'My litel child, now wol I fecche° thee   *fetch*
Whan that the greyn is fro thy tonge y-take;
235 Be nat agast,° I wol thee nat forsake.' "   *afraid*

This holy monk, this abbot, him mene I,
His tongue out caughte and took a-wey the greyn,
And he yaf° up the goost ful softely.   *gave*
And whan this abbot had this wonder seyn,°   *seen*
240 His salte teres° trikled doun as reyn,°   *tears / like rain*
And gruf° he fil al plat° upon the grounde,   *face downward / flat*
And stille° he lay as° he had been y-bounde.   *(as) quietly / as if*

The covent° eek° lay on the pavement,   *monks / also*
Weping and herying° Cristes moder dere,   *praising*
245 And after that they ryse, and forth ben went,°   *have gone*
And toke awey this martir fro his bere,°   *bier*
And in a tombe of marbulstones clere°   *bright, splendid*
Enclosen they his litel body swete.
Ther° he is now, God leve° us for to mete.°   *Where / grant / meet*

250 O yonge Hugh of Lincoln,⁴ slayn also
With° cursed Jewes, as it is notable°—   *By / well known*
For it nis° but a litel whyle ago—   *is not*
Preye eek° for us, we sinful folk unstable,°   *also / unsteadfast*
That, of his mercy, God so merciable°   *merciful*
255 On us his grete mercy multiplye,
For reverence of his moder Marye. Amen.

The Nun's Priest's Prologue and Tale

The Prologue

"Ho!"° quod° the Knight, "good sir, namore of this: *Stop / said*
That ye han seyd is right y-nough, y-wis,°¹   *indeed*
And mochel more; for litel hevinesse²
Is right y-nough to mochel° folk, I gesse.   *for many*
5 I seye for me it is a greet disese,°   *discomfort*
Where as° men han ben in greet welthe and ese,   *There where*
To heeren° of hire sodeyn° fal, allas!   *hear / sudden*
And the contrarie is joie° and greet solas,°   *joy / comfort*

---

4. Hugh of Lincoln was thought to have been mur-   ones from high fortune into misery.
dered by the Jews in a similar fashion in 1255.   2. And much more (than enough); for a little seri-
1. The Knight here breaks off the Monk's tale, a   ousness.
recital of "tragedies," i.e., stories of the fall of great

As whan a man hath been in povre estaat,° — *a condition of poverty*
10 And clymbeth up, and wexeth° fortunat, — *becomes increasingly*
And ther abydeth in prosperitee—
Swich° thing is gladsom, as it thinketh me, — *Such*
And of swich thing were goodly for to telle."
"Ye," quod our Hoste, "by Seinte Poules° belle, — *St. Paul's (cathedral)*
15 Ye seye right sooth: this Monk, he clappeth louder° — *you say right, he chatters loudly*
He spak 'how Fortune covered with a cloude'—
I noot° never what. And als° of a 'tragedie' — *know not / besides*
Right now ye herde, and pardee!° no remedie — *by God*
It is for to biwaille° ne compleyne — *bewail*
20 That that° is doon, and als° it is a peyne, — *which / besides*
As ye han seyd, to heere° of hevinesse. — *hear*
    Sire Monk, namore of this, so God yow blesse!
Your tale anoyeth al this compaignye.
Swich talking is nat worth a boterflye,° — *butterfly*
25 For therinne is ther no desport° ne game. — *pleasure*
Wherfore sir Monk, or daun° Piers by youre name, — *sir*
I preye yow hertely° telle us somwhat elles,° — *heartily / something else*
For sikerly, nere clinking of youre belles [3]
That on your brydel hange on every syde,
30 By hevene° king that for us alle dyde,° — *heaven's / died*
I sholde er° this han fallen doun for slepe, — *before*
Althogh the slough° had never been so depe. — *mire*
Than had your tale al be° told in vayn; — *been*
For certeinly, as that° thise clerkes seyn, — *just as*
35 'Whereas° a man may have noon audience, — *There where*
Noght helpeth it to tellen his sentence.'° — *meaning*
    And wel I woot the substance is in me,[4]
If any thing shal wel reported be.
Sir, sey somwhat of hunting, I yow preye."
40   "Nay," quod this Monk, "I have no lust° to pleye; — *desire*
Now let another telle, as I have told."
Than spak our Host, with rude speche and bold,
And seyde unto the Nonnes Preest° anon, — *Nun's Priest*
"Com neer,° thou preest, com hider, thou sir John, — *nearer*
45 Tel us swich thing as may oure hertes glade.° — *gladden*
Be blythe,° though thou ryde upon a jade!° — *cheerful / jade, a poor horse*
What though thyn hors be bothe foule and lene?° — *lean*
If he wol serve thee, rekke nat a bene.° — *don't care a bean*
Look that thyn herte be mery evermo."
50   "Yis, sir," quod he, "yis, Host, so mote I go,° — *as I may thrive*
But° I be mery, y-wis,° I wol be blamed." — *Unless / truly*

---

3. For certainly, were it not for the clinking of your bells.
4. Sense uncertain: *either* I know well I have the capacity to understand; *or* I know I've got the meaning (if it's been well told).

And right anon° his tale he hath attamed,°   *right away / begun*
And thus he seyde unto us everichon,°   *every one*
This sweete preest, this goodly man sir John.

The Tale

55   A povre widwe, somdel stape in age,[5]
    Was whylom° dwelling in a narwe° cotage,   *once / small*
    Bisyde a grove, stondinge in a dale.°   *valley*
    This widwe of which I telle yow my tale,
    Sin thilke° day that she was last a wyf,   *Since that same*
60   In pacience ladde° a ful simple lyf,   *led*
    For litel was hir catel° and hir rente.°   *property / income*
    By housbondrye° of such as God hire sente   *careful management*
    She fond° hirself and eek° hir doghtren° two.   *provided for / also / daughters*
    Three large sowes hadde she and namo,°   *no more*
65   Three kyn,° and eek a sheep that highte° Malle.   *cows / was called*
    Ful sooty was hire bour, and eek hir halle,[6]
    In which she eet ful many a sclendre° meel.   *lean*
    Of poynaunt° sauce hir neded never a deel:°   *pungent / portion*
    No deyntee morsel passed thurgh hir throte.
70   Hir diete was accordant° to hir cote°—   *matched / small farm*
    Repleccioun° ne made hir never syk.   *Surfeit*
    Attempree diete was al hir phisyk,[7]
    And exercyse, and hertes suffisaunce.°   *heart's contentment*
    The goute lette° hire nothing for to daunce,°   *hindered / from dancing*
75   N'apoplexye shente° nat hir heed.   *Nor did apoplexy injure*
    No wyn° ne drank she, neither whyt° ne reed;°   *wine / white / red*
    Hir bord° was served most with whyt and blak—   *table*
    Milk and broun breed—in which she fond no lak,°   *found no fault*
    Seynd° bacoun, and somtyme an ey or tweye,°   *Broiled / egg or two*
80   For she was as it were a maner deye.°   *kind of dairymaid*
    A yerd° she hadde, enclosed° al aboute   *yard / fenced*
    With stikkes, and a drye dich° with-oute,   *ditch*
    In which she hadde a cok hight° Chauntecleer: *called*
    In al the land of° crowing nas° his peer.   *at / there was not*
85   His voys was merier than the mery orgon°   *organ*
    On messe-dayes° that in the chirche gon;°   *feast days / plays*
    Wel sikerer° was his crowing in his logge°   *more certain / lodgings*
    Than is a clokke or an abbey orlogge.°   *(great) clock*
    By nature knew he ech ascencioun
90   Of the equinoxial in thilke toun:[8]

5. A poor widow, somewhat advanced in years.
6. Her "bed-chamber" and her "banquet hall" were grimy with soot. (The terms are being used ironically; her humble cottage lacks such rooms, and offers implicit moral criticism of such grandeur.)

7. A temperate diet was her only medicine.
8. By natural instinct he knew each revolution of the equinoctial circle—the celestial equator—in that same town (a complicated astronomical description of how the hours pass and are numbered).

For whan degrees fiftene were ascended,
Thanne crew he, that it mighte nat ben amended.°   *improved*
His comb was redder than the fyn coral,
And batailed° as it were a castel-wal.   *notched (like battlements)*
95 His bile° was blak, and as the jeet° it shoon;   *bill / jet (semiprecious stone)*
Lyk asur° were his legges and his toon;°   *azure / toes*
His nayles° whytter than the lilie flour,   *claws / lily flower*
And lyk the burned° gold was his colour.   *burnished*
This gentil cok hadde in his governaunce°   *under his control*
100 Sevene hennes,° for to doon al his plesaunce,   *hens*
Whiche were his sustres° and his paramours,   *sisters*
And wonder lyk to him, as of colours;
Of whiche the faireste hewed° on hir throte   *hued, colored*
Was cleped° faire damoysele° Pertelote.   *named / (ma)damoiselle*
105 Curteys° she was, discreet, and debonaire,°   *Courteous / gracious*
And compaignable,° and bar hirself so faire,   *sociable*
Sin thilke day that she was seven night old,
That trewely she hath the herte in hold
Of Chauntecleer, loken° in every lith;°   *locked / limb*
110 He loved hire so, that wel was him therwith.
But such a joye was it to here hem° singe,   *them*
Whan that the brighte sonne gan to springe,°   *began to rise*
In swete acord, "my lief is faren in londe."⁹
For thilke tyme,° as I have understonde,   *in those days*
115 Bestes° and briddes° coude speke and singe.   *Beasts / birds*
       And so bifel that in a daweninge,¹
As Chauntecleer among his wyves alle
Sat on his perche that was in the halle,
And next him sat this faire Pertelote,
120 This Chauntecleer gan gronen° in his throte   *did groan*
As man that in his dreem is drecched sore.°   *severely troubled*
And whan that Pertelote thus herde him rore,
She was agast,° and seyde, "Herte dere,   *afraid*
What eyleth° yow to grone in this manere?   *ails*
125 Ye been a verray sleper,° fy for shame!"   *You're a fine sleeper*
       And he answerde and seyde thus, "Madame,
I pray yow, that ye take it nat a-grief:°   *amiss*
By God, me mette° I was in swich meschief°   *I dreamed / trouble*
Right now, that yet myn herte is sore afright.
130 Now God," quod he, "my swevene recche aright,²
And keep my body out of foul prisoun!
Me mette how that I romed° up and doun   *roamed*
Withinne our yerde, wher as I saugh° a beste,   *saw*

9. In sweet harmony, "my love has gone to the   2. "Now God," he said, "(help) interpret my dream
country" (a popular song).   correctly."
1. And so it happened, one morning at dawn.

Was lyk an hound and wolde han maad areste°　　　　*laid hold*
135 Upon my body, and wolde han had me deed.°　　　　*dead*
His colour was bitwixe yelow and reed,°　　　　*red*
And tipped was his tail and bothe his eres°　　　　*ears*
With blak, unlyk the remenant° of his heres;°　　　　*rest / hair(s)*
His snowte° smal, with glowinge eyen tweye.°　　　　*snout / two eyes*
140 Yet° of his look for fere° almost I deye:°　　　　*Still / fear / die*
This caused me my groning, doutelees."
　　　"Avoy!"° quod she, "fy on yow, hertelees!°　　　　*Go on / faint heart*
Allas!" quod she, "for, by that God above,
Now han ye lost myn herte and al my love.
145 I can nat love a coward, by my feith!
For certes, what so any womman seith,
We alle desiren,° if it mighte be,　　　　*desire*
To han housbondes hardy,° wyse, and free,°　　　　*bold / generous*
And secree,° and no nigard, ne no fool,　　　　*discreet*
150 Ne him that is agast° of every tool,°　　　　*afraid / weapon*
Ne noon avauntour.° By that God above,　　　　*boaster*
How dorste° ye seyn for shame unto your love　　　　*dare*
That any thing mighte make yow aferd?°　　　　*afraid*
Have ye no mannes herte, and han a berd?°　　　　*beard*
155 Allas! and conne ye been agast of swevenis?°　　　　*dreams*
Nothing, God wot, but vanitee° in sweven is.　　　　*foolishness, illusion*
Swevenes[3] engendren of replecciouns,°　　　　*are born of surfeits*
And ofte of fume,° and of complecciouns,　　　　*vapor(s)*
Whan humours been to habundant° in a wight.°　　　　*too abundant / person*
160 Certes° this dreem, which ye han met to-night,　　　　*Certainly*
Cometh of the grete superfluitee
Of youre rede *colera*,° pardee,　　　　*choler (a humor)*
Which causeth folk to dreden° in hir° dremes　　　　*fear / their*
Of arwes,° and of fyr with rede lemes,°　　　　*arrows / flames*
165 Of rede bestes, that they wol hem byte,
Of contek,° and of whelpes° grete and lyte;°　　　　*strife / pups, cubs / little*
Right as the humour of malencolye°　　　　*melancholy (black bile)*
Causeth ful many a man in sleep to crye
For fere of blake beres,° or boles° blake,　　　　*bears / bulls*
170 Or elles, blake develes wole hem take.
Of othere humours coude I telle also
That werken° many a man in sleep ful wo;°　　　　*cause / great woe*
But I wol passe as lightly as I can.
　　　Lo Catoun,° which that was so wys a man,　　　　*Cato*
175 Seyde he nat thus, 'Ne do no fors of° dremes?'　　　　*Pay no attention to*

---

3. Pertelote's discussion of the causes of dreams and her insistence that Chauntecleer's dream is of physiological rather than supernatural origin (with the conclusion that it therefore need not be heeded) are learned in medieval dream theory. On the humours, see n. 6, p. 13, in the *General Prologue*: "compleccioun" refers to the existing balance between them.

Now, sire," quod she, "whan we flee° fro the bemes,   *fly*
For Goddes love, as tak some laxatyf.
Up° peril of my soule and of my lyf   *On*
I counseille yow the beste, I wol nat lye,
180 That bothe of colere and of malencolye
   Ye purge yow; and for° ye shul nat tarie,°   *so that / delay*
Though in this toun is noon apothecarie,
I shal myself to herbes techen° yow,   *direct*
That shul ben for yourc hcle° and for youre prow;°   *health / benefit*
185 And in oure yerd tho° herbes shal I finde   *those*
The whiche han of hire propretee by kinde°   *nature*
To purgen yow binethe and eek above.
Forget not this, for Goddes owene love!
Ye been ful colerik of compleccioun.°   *temperamentally dominated by choler*
190 Ware° the sonne in his ascencioun   *Beware*
Ne fynde yow nat repleet° of humours hote;   *full*
And if it do, I dar wel leye° a grote,°   *bet / Dutch coin*
That ye shul have a fevere terciane,[4]
Or an agu,° that may be youre bane.°   *ague / destruction*
195 A day or two ye shul have digestyves
Of wormes, er° ye take your laxatyves,   *before*
Of lauriol,° centaure,° and fumetere,°   *spurge-laurel / centaury / fumitory*
Or elles of ellebor° that groweth there,   *hellebore*
Of catapuce,° or of gaytres beryis,°   *caper-spurge / dogwood's berries*
200 Of erbe yve,° growing in oure yerd, ther mery is.°   *ivy / where it is pleasant*
Pekke hem° up right as they growe, and ete° hem in.   *Peck them / eat*
Be mery, housbond, for youre fader kin!°   *father's kin*
Dredeth no dreem: I can say yow namore."
   "Madame," quod he, "*graunt mercy*° of youre lore.   *many thanks*
205 But natheleces, as touching dann Catoun,
That hath of wisdom swich a greet renoun,°   *such great fame*
Though that he bad° no dremes for to drede,   *commanded*
By God, men may in olde bokes rede
Of many a man, more of auctoritee
210 Than ever Catoun was, so mote I thee,°   *as I may thrive*
That al the revers° seyn of his sentence,   *reverse, opposite*
And han wel founden° by experience,   *established*
That dremes ben significaciouns°   *meaningful signs*
As wel of joye° as tribulaciouns   *joy*
215 That folk enduren in this lyf present.
Ther nedeth make of this noon argument:
The verray preve° sheweth it in dede.   *true proof*
   Oon of the gretteste auctours° that men rede   *authorities, writers*
Seith thus, that whylom° two felawes° wente   *once / companions*

4. A fever recurring every third day.

220 On pilgrimage, in a ful good entente;
And happed so thay come into a toun,
Wher as° ther was swich congregacioun°   *Where / such a gathering*
Of peple, and eek so streit of herbergage,°   *such scarcity of lodgings*
That they ne founde as muche as o° cotage   *one*
225 In which they bothe mighte y-logged° be.   *lodged*
Wherfor thay mosten° of necessitee,   *had to*
As for that night, departen° compaignye;   *part*
And ech of hem goth° to his hostelrye,°   *goes / lodging place*
And took his logging as it wolde falle.
230 That oon of hem° was logged in a stalle,   *The one of them*
Fer° in a yerd, with oxen of the plough;   *Far-off*
That other man was logged wel y-nough,
As was his aventure° or his fortune,   *chance*
That us governeth alle as in commune.°   *in general*
235   And so bifel that, longe er° it were day,   *before*
This man mette° in his bed, ther as he lay,   *dreamed*
How that his felawe gan° upon him calle,   *began*
And seyde, 'Allas! for in an oxes stalle
This night I shal be mordred ther° I lye.   *murdered where*
240 Now help me, dere brother, or I dye;
In alle haste com to me,' he sayde.
This man out of his sleep for fere abrayde,°   *started up*
But whan that he was wakened of his sleep,
He turned him, and took of this no keep:°   *heed*
245 Him thoughte his dreem nas but a vanitee.[5]
Thus twyes° in his sleping dremed he;   *twice*
And atte thridde° tyme yet his felawe   *at the third*
Cam, as him thoughte, and seide, 'I am now slawe.°   *slain*
Bihold my blody woundes, depe and wyde!
250 Arys° up erly in the morwe tyde,°   *Arise / morning*
And at the west gate of the toun,' quod he,
'A carte ful of donge° ther shaltow° see,   *dung / shalt thou*
In which my body is hid ful prively:°   *secretly*
Do thilke carte aresten° boldely.   *Have that cart stopped*
255 My gold caused my mordre, sooth to sayn;'°   *the truth to tell*
And tolde him every poynt how he was slayn,
With a ful pitous face, pale of hewe.
And truste wel, his dreem he fond ful trewe,
For on the morwe, as sone as it was day,
260 To his felawes in° he took the way;   *companion's inn*
And whan that he cam to this oxes stalle,
After his felawe he bigan to calle.
   The hostiler° answered him anon,°   *innkeeper / immediately*

5. It seemed to him his dream was nothing but foolishness.

And seyde, 'Sire, your felawe is agon:°   gone
265 As sone as day he wente out of the toun.'
    This man gan fallen in suspecioun,°   became suspicious
    Remembringe on his dremes that he mette,
    And forth he goth, no lenger wolde he lette,°   delay
    Unto the west gate of the toun, and fond
270 A dong-carte, wente as it were to donge lond,⁶
    That was arrayed in the same wyse°   way
    As ye han herd the dede man devyse.°   describe
    And with an hardy° herte he gan to crye,   bold
    'Vengeaunce and justice of this felonye!
275 My felawe mordred is this same night,
    And in this carte he lyth° gapinge upright.°   lies / face up
    I crye out on the ministres,'° quod he,   officers
    'That sholden kepe and reulen° this citee,   care for and rule
    Harrow!° allas! heer lyth my felawe slayn!'   Help
280 What sholde I more unto this tale sayn?
    The peple out sterte,° and caste the cart to grounde, came forth
    And in the middel of the dong they founde
    The dede man, that mordred was al newe.°   just recently
    O blisful God, that art so just and trewe!
285 Lo, how that thou biwreyest° mordre alway!   revealest
    Mordre wol out, that see we day by day.
    Mordre is so wlatsom° and abhominable   loathsome
    To God, that is so just and resonable,
    That he ne wol nat suffre it heled be.°   to be concealed
290 Though it abyde° a yeer, or two, or three,   remain (hidden)
    Mordre wol out, this my conclusioun.
    And right anoon,° ministres of that toun   right away
    Han hent° the carter and so sore him pyned,°   seized / tortured
    And eek the hostiler so sore engyned,°   racked
295 That thay biknewe° hir wikkednesse anoon,   acknowledged
    And were anhanged by the nekke-boon.°   neck(bone)
    Here may men seen that dremes been to drede.°   are to be feared
    And certes,° in the same book I rede,   certainly
    Right in the nexte chapitre after this—
300 I gabbe° nat, so have I° joye or blis—   lie / as I may have
    Two men that wolde han passed° over see,   wished to travel
    For certeyn cause, in-to a fer° contree,   far-off
    If that the wind ne hadde been contrarie:
    That made hem in a citee for to tarie
305 That stood ful mery upon an haven° syde.   harbor
    But on a day, agayn the even-tyde,°   toward evening
    The wind gan chaunge, and blew right as hem leste.° just as they wished

6. A dung-cart, going out as if to manure the land.

Jolif° and glad they wente unto hir reste,   *Jolly*
And casten hem° ful erly for to saille;   *they planned*
310 But herkneth! To that oo° man fil° a greet mervaille.   *one / befell*
That oon of hem, in sleping as he lay,
Him mette° a wonder dreem, agayn the° day: *He dreamed / toward*
Him thoughte° a man stood by his beddes syde,   *It seemed to him*
And him comaunded that he sholde abyde,°   *wait*
315 And seyde him thus, 'If thou to-morwe wende,°   *travel*
Thou shalt be dreynt:° my tale is at an ende.'   *drowned*
He wook,° and tolde his felawe what he mette,   *awoke*
And preyde him his viage for to lette;[7]
As° for that day, he preyde him to byde.   *Just*
320 His felawe, that lay by his beddes syde,
Gan for° to laughe, and scorned him ful faste.°   *Began / very hard*
'No dreem' quod he, 'may so myn herte agaste°   *frighten*
That I wol lette° for to do my thinges.°   *leave off / business*
I sette not a straw by thy dreminges,
325 For swevenes° been but vanitees and japes.°   *dreams / follies*
Men dreme alday of owles or of apes,
And eke° of many a mase° therwithal;   *also / maze, bewilderment*
Men dreme of thing that nevere was ne shal.°   *nor shall (be)*
But sith° I see that thou wolt heer abyde,   *since*
330 And thus for-sleuthen° wilfully thy tyde,°   *slothfully waste / time*
God woot it reweth me;[8] and have good day.'
And thus he took his leve, and wente his way.
But er that° he hadde halfe his cours y-seyled,°   *before / sailed*
Noot° I nat why, ne what mischaunce it eyled,°   *Know not / ailed*
335 But casuelly° the shippes botme rente,°   *by chance / tore open*
And ship and man under the water wente
In sighte of othere shippes it byside,°   *alongside it*
That with hem seyled at the same tyde.
And therfore faire Pertelote so dere,
340 By swiche ensamples olde maistow lere[9]
That no man sholde been to recchelees°   *heedless*
Of dremes, for I sey thee, doutelees,
That many a dreem ful sore° is for to drede.°   *greatly / to be dreaded*
Lo, in the lyf° of Seint Kenelm I rede,   *life*
345 That was Kenulphus sone,[1] the noble king
Of Mercenrike,° how Kenelm mette° a thing   *Mercia / dreamed*
A lyte er° he was mordred on a day.   *A little before*
His mordre in his avisioun° he say.°   *vision / saw*
His norice° him expouned every del°   *nurse / part of*

---

7. And begged him to put off his voyage.
8. God knows it makes me sorry.
9. By such ancient examples thou mayest learn.
1. When King Cenwulf of Mercia died in 821, his seven-year-old son Kenelm became his heir, but was murdered by agents of his aunt. Shortly before death, Kenelm had a warning dream in which he climbed a tree, was cut down by a friend, and saw himself fly to heaven in the shape of a bird.

350 His sweven, and bad him for to kepe him wel°	*guard himself carefully*
For traisoun;° but he nas but° seven yeer old,	*Against treason / was only*
And therfore litel tale hath he told°	*he took little note*
Of any dreem, so holy was his herte.	
By God, I hadde lever than my sherte	
355 That ye had rad his legende as have I.²	
Dame Pertelote, I sey yow trewely,	
Macrobeus,³ that writ the avisioun°	*vision*
In Affrike° of the worthy Cipioun,°	*Africa / Scipio*
Affermeth° dremes, and seith that they been	*Affirms (the validity of)*
360 Warninge of thinges that men after seen.°	*afterward see*
And forthermore, I pray yow loketh wel	
In the Olde Testament, of Daniel,	
If he held dremes any vanitee.	
Reed eek of Ioseph,⁴ and ther shul ye see	
365 Wher dremes ben somtyme (I sey nat alle)	
Warninge of thinges that shul after falle.°	*occur*
Loke of Egipte the king, daun Pharao,°	*Sir Pharaoh*
His bakere and his boteler° also,	*butler*
Wher° they ne felte noon effect° in dremes.	*Whether / significance*
370 Whoso wol seken actes of sondry remes⁵	
May rede of° dremes many a wonder thing.	*about*
Lo Cresus,° which that was of Lyde° king,	*Croesus / Lydia*
Mette he nat° that he sat upon a tree,	*Did he not dream*
Which signified he sholde anhanged° be?	*hanged*
375 Lo heer Andromacha,° Ectores° wyf,	*Andromache / Hector's*
That day that Ector sholde lese° his lyf,	*was to lose*
She dremed on the same night biforn,	
How that the lyf of Ector sholde be lorn°	*lost*
If thilke° day he wente into bataille;	*that same*
380 She warned him, but it mighte nat availle;	
He wente for to fighte nathelees,°	*nevertheless*
But he was slayn anoon° of Achilles.	*immediately*
But thilke tale is al to long° to telle,	*all too long*
And eek it is ny° day, I may nat dwelle.	*near*
385 Shortly I seye, as for conclusioun,	
That I shal han of this avisioun°	*vision*
Adversitee; and I seye forthermore,	
That I ne telle of laxatyves no store,⁶	
For they ben venimous,° I woot° it wel;	*poisonous / know*
390 I hem defye,° I love hem never a del.°	*defy them / not a bit*

---

2. By God, I'd give my shirt if you had (could have) read his story, as I have. ["Lever:" rather.]

3. At the end of the fourth century, Macrobius wrote a commentary on Cicero's *Dream of Scipio* that became for the Middle Ages a standard authority on the nature of dreams. See pp. 433–35.

4. For the story of Joseph, see Genesis 37, 40, and 41.

5. Whosoever wishes to seek (knowledge of) the histories of various realms.

6. That I set no store by laxatives.

Now let us speke of mirthe and stinte° al this;   *stop*
Madame Pertelote, so have I blis,
Of o° thing God hath sent me large° grace: *one / bounteous*
For whan I see the beautee of your face—
395 Ye ben so scarlet reed about your yën—°   *eyes*
It maketh al my drede° for to dyen.   *fear*
For, also siker° as *In principio*,   *just as sure*
Mulier est hominis confusio.[7]
Madame, the sentence° of this Latin is   *meaning*
400 'Womman is mannes joye and al his blis.'
For whan I fele° a-night° your softe syde,   *feel / at night*
Al be it that I may nat on you ryde,
For that° our perche is maad° so narwe,° alas!   *Because / made / narrow*
I am so ful of joye and of solas°   *comfort*
405 That I defye bothe sweven° and dreem."   *vision*
And with that word he fley° doun fro the beem,   *flew*
For it was day, and eek[8] his hennes alle,
And with a chuk° he gan hem for to calle,°   *cluck / called them*
For he had founde a corn° lay° in the yerd.   *grain / (which) lay*
410 Real° he was, he was namore aferd;°   *Regal / afraid*
He fethered° Pertelote twenty tyme,   *covered with outspread wings*
And trad hir eke as ofte, er it was pryme.[9]
He loketh as it were° a grim leoun,°   *as if he were / lion*
And on his toos° he rometh up and doun—   *toes*
415 Him deyned° not to sette his foot to grounde.   *deigned*
He chukketh whan he hath a corn y-founde,
And to him rennen thanne° his wyves alle.   *run then*
Thus royal, as a prince is in his halle,
Leve I this Chauntecleer in his pasture;°   *feeding*
420 And after wol I telle his aventure.
    Whan that the month in which the world bigan,
That highte° March, whan God first maked man,   *is called*
Was complet, and passed were also,
Sin° March bigan, thritty dayes and two,   *Since*
425 Bifel° that Chauntecleer, in al his pryde,   *It came to pass*
His seven wyves walkinge by his syde,
Caste up his eyen to the brighte sonne,
That in the signe° of Taurus hadde y-ronne°   *zodiacal sign / run*
Twenty degrees and oon, and somwhat more;
430 And knew by kynde,° and by noon° other lore,°   *nature / no / learning*
That it was pryme, and crew with blisful stevene.°   *voice*
"The sonne," he sayde, "is clomben° up on hevene   *has climbed*

---

7. "In the beginning" (the opening of the Gospel of
St. John); "woman is man's ruin" (a much-used
Latin proverb). Chauntecleer tactfully mistranslates
it for Pertelote.

8. I.e., so did.
9. And trod (i.e., copulated with) her just as often,
before it was nine o'clock (the canonical hour of
prime).

Fourty degrees and oon, and more, y-wis.
Madame Pertelote, my worldes blis,
435 Herkneth° thise blisful briddes° how they singe,   *Harken to / birds*
And see the fresshe floures how they springe;
Ful is myn herte of revel and solas."°   *joy*
But sodeinly him fil° a sorweful cas,°   *befell / happening*
For ever the latter ende of joye is wo.
440 God woot° that worldly joye is sone ago;°   *knows / soon gone*
And if a rethor° coude faire endyte,°   *rhetorician / write well*
He in a cronique° saufly° mighte it wryte   *chronicle / safely*
As for a sovereyn notabilitee.°   *supremely noteworthy fact*
Now every wys° man, lat him herkne me: *wise*
445 This storie is also° trewe, I undertake,°   *just as / declare*
As is the book of Launcelot de Lake,[1]
That wommen holde in ful gret reverence.
Now wol I torne agayn° to my sentence.°   *turn again / main subject*
A col-fox,[2] ful of sly iniquitee,
450 That in the grove hadde woned° yeres three,   *dwelt*
By heigh imaginacioun forncast,[3]
The same night thurghout° the hegges brast°   *through / burst*
Into the yerd, ther° Chauntecleer the faire   *where*
Was wont,° and eek his wyves, to repaire;°   *accustomed / to retire to*
455 And in a bed of wortes° stille he lay,   *herbs*
Til it was passed undren° of the day,   *midmorning*
Waytinge° his tyme on Chauntecleer to falle,   *Watching for*
As gladly doon° thise homicydes° alle,   *usually do / murderers*
That in awayt liggen° to mordre men.   *lie in wait*
460 O false mordrour, lurkinge in thy den!
O newe Scariot, newe Genilon![4]
False dissimilour,° O Greek Sinon,[5]   *dissembler*
That broghtest Troye al outrely° to sorwe!   *quite utterly*
O Chauntecleer, acursed be that morwe,°   *morning*
465 That thou into that yerd flough° fro the bemes!   *flew*
Thou were ful wel y-warned by thy dremes
That thilke day was perilous to thee.
But what that God forwoot mot nedes be,°   *that which God foreknows must needs be*
After the opinioun of certeyn clerkis.°   *scholars*
470 Witnesse on him° that any perfit clerk is   *Let him be witness*
That in scole° is gret altercacioun   *in (the) school(s)*
In this matere, and greet disputisoun,°   *disputation*

---

1. Launcelot was the lover of Guinevere, wife to King Arthur—an entirely fictitious story.
2. A coal-fox, i.e., one with black markings (like the animal Chauntecleer saw in his dream).
3. Foreseen (preordained) by a supreme (divine) intelligence (an idea much too grand for the fate of a chicken). It leads to the problem of free will within the context of divine foreknowledge that is worried over in ll. 468–84).
4. Oh, new (Judas) Iscariot, new Ganelon (the traitor in the *Chanson de Roland*).
5. Sinon devised the wooden horse in which the Greeks entered Troy.

And hath ben of an hundred thousand men.
But I ne can not bulte it to the bren,[6]
475 As can the holy doctour Augustyn,°   *St. Augustine*
Or Boece,° or the bishop Bradwardyn,°   *Boethius / Bradwardine (of England)*
Whether that Goddes worthy forwiting°   *excellent foreknowledge*
Streyneth° me nedely° for to doon a thing   *Constrains / necessarily*
("Nedely" clepe° I simple necessitee);   *call*
480 Or elles, if free choys° be graunted me   *choice, will*
To do that same thing or do it noght,
Though God forwoot° it er° that I was wroght;   *foreknows / before*
Or if his witing° streyneth never a del°   *knowing / not at all*
But by necessitee condicionel.[7]
485 I wol not han to do of swich matere;
My tale is of a cok, as ye may here,
That took his counseil of° his wyf, with sorwe,   *advice from*
To walken in the yerd upon that morwe°   *morning*
That he had met° the dreem that I yow tolde.   *dreamt*
490 Wommennes counseils been ful ofte colde;°   *fatal*
Wommannes counseil broghte us first to wo,
And made Adam fro Paradys to go,[8]
Ther as° he was ful mery and wel at ese.   *There where*
But for I noot° to whom it mighte displese,   *since I know not*
495 If I counseil of wommen wolde blame,
Passe over, for I seyde it in my game.
Rede auctours,° wher they trete° of swich matere,   *the authorities / treat*
And what thay seyn of wommen ye may here.
Thise been the cokkes wordes, and nat myne;
500 I can noon harm of no womman divyne.[9]
     Faire in the sond,° to bathe hire merily,   *sand*
Lyth° Pertelote, and alle hire sustres° by,°   *Lies / sisters / nearby*
Agayn° the sonne; and Chauntecleer so free   *In*
Song° merier than the mermayde in the see—   *Sang*
505 For Phisiologus[1] seith sikerly

6. But I cannot sift it down to the bran (i.e., argue the fine points).

7. Except by conditional necessity ("e.g., the sort of 'necessity' found in such a conditional sentence as 'If I see him standing, he must of necessity be standing' "—R. A. Pratt). The perplexity, at its simplest, might be put so: if God is all-knowing (that is, having a perfect knowledge of what *was, is, and will be*), He must know in advance every man's every moral choice. But if He knows how a man will choose, that man is not free to choose the alternative, for then God would be wrong (in a condition of ignorance, not omniscience). Theologians have struggled with the problem for centuries. The Middle Ages, for the most part, agreed to Boethius's resolution of it—that same "conditional necessity" here named: to know is not necessarily to cause, particularly if you postulate a complex difference between the orders of time and eternity. After devot-

ing a considerable time to the question, the Nun's Priest announces with a certain ironic glee (in ll. 485–86): I will not have anything to do with such a subject; my story concerns a rooster.

8. The fall of Adam and Eve was, naturally, the central event in discussions concerning man's free will.

9. I cannot conceive of harm in any woman (with a possible secondary meaning, "I know nothing to the discredit of any holy woman," referring to the Prioress whom he accompanies).

1. Phisiologus was the supposed author of a Greek work on natural history, which was a distant source of the numerous medieval *bestiaries*—popular compilations of lore concerning animals and other creatures, some (as here with the mermaids) imaginary. In the medieval version, almost every description was moralized.

How that they singen wel and merily—
And so bifel that, as he caste his yë°   *eye*
Among the wortes,° on a boterflye,   *herbs*
He was war° of this fox that lay ful lowe.   *became aware*
510 Nothing ne liste him thanne for to crowe,[2]
But cryde anon, "Cok cok!" and up he sterte,°   *leaped*
As man° that was affrayed° in his herte.   *Like someone / frightened*
For naturelly a beest desyreth flee°   *desires to flee*
Fro his contrarie,° if he may it see,   *opposite*
515 Though he never erst° had seyn it with his yë.°   *before / eye*
    This Chauntecleer, whan he gan him espye,°   *caught sight of him*
He wolde han fled, but that the fox anon°   *immediately*
Seyde, "Gentil sire, allas! wher wol ye gon?
Be ye affrayed of me that am your freend?
520 Now certes, I were worse than a feend,°   *devil*
If I to yow wolde° harm or vileinye.°   *wished / wrong*
I am nat come your counseil for t'espye,[3]
But trewely, the cause of my cominge
Was only for to herkne° how that ye singe.   *listen to*
525 For trewely ye have as mery a stevene°   *pleasant a voice*
As eny° aungel hath that is in hevene;   *any*
Therwith ye han in musik more feelinge
Than hadde Boece,[4] or any that can singe.
My lord your fader (God his soule blesse!)
530 And eek your moder, of° hire gentilesse,   *because of*
Han in myn hous y-been, to my gret ese;°   *satisfaction*
And certes, sire, ful fayn° wolde I yow plese.   *very willingly*
But for° men speke of singing, I wol saye,   *since*
So mote I brouke° wel myn eyen tweye,°   *profit by / two eyes*
535 Save° yow, I herde never man so singe   *Except*
As dide your fader in the morweninge.°   *morning*
Certes,° it was of herte,° al that he song.   *Truly / from the heart*
And for to make his voys the more strong,
He wolde so peyne him° that with bothe his yën°   *take such pains / eyes*
540 He moste winke,° so loude he wolde cryen,   *had to shut*
And stonden on his tiptoon therwithal,[5]
And strecche forth his nekke long and smal.°   *thin*
And eek he was of swich discrecioun°   *wisdom*
That ther nas no man° in no regioun   *was no man*
545 That him in song or wisdom mighte passe.
I have wel rad° in 'Daun Burnel the Asse,'[6]   *read*
Among his vers,° how that ther was a cok,   *its (the book's) verses*

2. He had no wish at all to crow then.
3. I've not come to spy on your private affairs.
4. Boethius, in addition to *The Consolation of Philosophy* referred to above, wrote a work on the theory of music that was used as a text in the schools.
5. And stand on (his) tiptoes, at the same time.

6. *Burnellus*, or the *Speculum Stultorum*, a twelfth-century Latin satire in verse by Nigel Wireker: in one episode, a cock takes revenge on a certain Gundulfus, who injured him in his youth, by crowing so late on the morning that Gundulfus is to be ordained that he oversleeps and loses his benefice.

For that° a preestes sone yaf° him a knok°   *Because / gave / blow*
Upon his leg, whyl he was yong and nyce,°   *foolish*
550 He made him for to lese° his benefyce.   *lose*
But certeyn, ther nis no° comparisoun   *is not any*
Bitwix the wisdom and discrecioun
Of youre fader, and of his⁷ subtiltee.
Now singeth, sire, for seinte° charitee!   *holy*
555 Let see, conne ye your fader countrefete?"°   *imitate*
      This Chauntecleer his winges gan to bete,°   *did beat*
As man° that coude his tresoun° nat espye,°   *one / betrayal / perceive*
So was he ravisshed with his flaterye.
      Allas! ye lordes, many a fals flatour°   *flatterer*
560 Is in your courtes, and many a losengeour,°   *liar*
That plesen° yow wel more, by my feith,   *Who please*
Than he that soothfastnesse° unto yow seith.   *truthfulness*
Redeth Ecclesiaste of° flaterye;   *Ecclesiasticus on*
Beth war,° ye lordes, of hir trecherye.   *Beware*
565   This Chauntecleer stood hye° upon his toos,   *high*
Strecching his nekke, and heeld his eyen cloos,°   *closed*
And gan to crowe loude for the nones;°   *for the occasion*
And daun Russel the fox sterte up at ones°   *once*
And by the gargat° hente° Chauntecleer,   *throat / seized*
570 And on his bak toward the wode° him beer,°   *woods / bore*
For yet ne was ther no man that him sewed.°   *pursued*
      O destinee, that mayst nat been eschewed!°   *avoided*
Allas, that Chauntecleer fleigh° fro the bemes!   *flew*
Allas, his wyf ne roghte nat° of dremes!   *took no heed*
575 And on a Friday fil° al this meschaunce.   *befell*
      O Venus, that art goddesse of plesaunce,°   *(amorous) pleasure*
Sin° that thy servant was this Chauntecleer,   *Since*
And in thy service dide al his poweer,°   *expended all his force*
More for delyt than world to multiplye,
580 Why woldestow° suffre him on thy day⁸ to dye?   *wouldst thou*
      O Gaufred,⁹ dere mayster soverayn,
That whan thy worthy king Richard° was slayn   *Richard I*
With shot,° compleynedest his deth so sore,   *an arrow*
Why ne hadde I now thy sentence° and thy lore,   *wisdom*
585 The Friday for to chide, as diden ye?
      (For on a Friday soothly° slayn was he.)   *truly*
Than wolde I shewe yow how that I coude pleyne°   *lament*
For Chauntecleres drede, and for his peyne.
      Certes,° swich cry ne lamentacioun   *Truly*

---

7. I.e., that other rooster's.
8. Friday is Venus's day.
9. Geoffrey de Vinsauf, author of a treatise on the
writing of poetry, the *Poetria Nova* (ca. 1210). Chau-

cer refers to one of Geoffrey's examples of how to
lament in a rhetorically elaborate style, printed on
pp. 435–36.

590 Was never of ladies maad° when Ilioun°   *made by ladies / Ilium (Troy)*
Was wonne, and Pirrus° with his streite° swerd,   *Pyrrhus / drawn*
Whan he hadde hent° king Priam by the berd,   *seized*
And slayn him (as saith us *Eneydos*),°   *the Aeneid*
As maden alle the hennes in the clos,°   *enclosure, yard*
595 Whan they had seyn of Chauntecleer the sighte.
But sovereynly° dame Pertelote shrighte°   *above all / shrieked*
Ful louder than dide Hasdrubales° wyf,   *Hasdrubal's*
Whan that hir housbond hadde lost his lyf,
And that the Romayns hadde brend Cartage:°   *burned Carthage*
600 She was so ful of torment and of rage
That wilfully into the fyr she sterte,°   *leaped*
And brende hirselven¹ with a stedfast herte.
    O woful hennes, right so° cryden ye   *in like manner*
As, whan that Nero brende the citee
605 Of Rome, cryden senatoures wyves,
For that hir° housbondes losten alle hir lyves;   *their*
Withouten gilt this Nero hath hem° slayn.   *them*
Now wol I torne to my tale agayn.
    This sely° widwe and eek hir doghtres two   *good, simple*
610 Herden thise hennes crye and maken wo,
And out at dores sterten they anoon,°   *they leap at once*
And syen° the fox toward the grove goon,°   *saw / go*
And bar° upon his bak the cok away;   *bore, carried*
And cryden, "Out! harrow!° and weylaway!°   *help / alas*
615 Ha, ha, the fox!" and after him they ran,
And eek with staves° many another man;   *sticks*
Ran Colle our dogge, and Talbot, and Gerland,²
And Malkin, with a distaf³ in hir hand;
Ran cow and calf, and eek the verray hogges,
620 So fered° for the berking of the dogges   *frightened*
And shouting of the men and wimmen eke,
They ronne so hem thoughte hir herte breke.⁴
They yelleden as feendes° doon in helle;   *fiends*
The dokes° cryden as° men wolde hem quelle;°   *ducks / as though / kill*
625 The gees for fere° flowen° over the trees;   *fear / flew*
Out of the hyve cam the swarm of bees;
So hidous was the noyse, a! *benedicite!*°   *bless us*
Certes, he Jakke Straw and his meynee⁵
Ne made nevere shoutes half so shrille
630 Whan that they wolden any Fleming kille,
As thilke° day was maad upon the fox.   *that same*

---

1. I.e., to death.
2. All are common names for dogs.
3. For spinning.
4. They ran so (hard), it seemed to them their hearts would burst.

5. Jack Straw was a leader of the Peasants' Revolt ("his meynee" or company) in 1381; many Flemish, most of them weavers, were killed in London in that uprising (see l. 630).

Of bras thay broghten bemes,° and of box,°   *trumpets / boxwood*
Of horn, of boon,° in whiche they blewe and pouped,°   *bone / puffed*
And therwithal thay shryked° and they houped:°   *shrieked / whooped*
635 It semed as that heven sholde falle.
Now, gode men, I pray yow herkneth° alle!   *listen*
    Lo, how Fortune turneth° sodeinly   *overturns*
The hope and pryde eek of hir enemy!
This cok, that lay upon the foxes bak,
640 In al his drede unto the fox he spak,
And seyde, "Sire, if that I were as ye,
Yet sholde I seyn,° as° wis God helpe me,   *say / may*
'Turneth agayn, ye proude cherles° alle!   *churls*
A verray° pestilence upon yow falle!   *real*
645 Now I am come unto this wodes syde,
Maugree your heed,° the cok shal heer abyde;   *Despite your efforts*
I wol him ete° in feith, and that anon.' "   *eat*
    The fox answerde, "In feith, it shal be don,"
And as he spak that word, al sodeinly
650 This cok brak° from his mouth deliverly,°   *broke / nimbly*
And heighe upon a tree he fleigh° anon.   *flew*
And whan the fox saugh that the cok was gon,
"Allas!" quod he, "O Chauntecleer, allas!
I have to yow," quod he, "y-doon trespas,°   *wrong*
655 In as muche as I maked yow aferd
When I yow hente° and broghte out of the yerd.   *seized*
But, sire, I dide it in no wikke entente;°   *with no wicked intent*
Com doun, and I shal telle yow what I mente.
I shal seye sooth° to yow, God help me so."   *tell the truth*
660   "Nay, than," quod he, "I shrewe° us bothe two,   *curse*
And first I shrewe myself, bothe blood and bones,
If thou bigyle° me ofter° than ones.°   *deceive / more / once*
Thou shalt namore, thurgh thy flaterye,
Do° me to singe and winke with myn yë.°   *Cause / shut my eyes*
665 For he that winketh whan he sholde see,
Al wilfully, God lat° him never thee!"°   *let / prosper*
    "Nay," quod the fox, "but God yeve° him meschaunce,   *give*
That is so undiscreet of governaunce°   *self-control*
That jangleth° whan he sholde holde his pees."°   *chatters / peace, silence*
670   Lo, swich it is for to be reccheless°   *reckless*
And necligent, and truste on flaterye.
    But ye that holden this tale a folye,°   *silly thing*
As of a fox, or of a cok and hen,
Taketh the moralitee,° goode men.   *moral (of it)*
675 For Seint Paul seith that al that writen is,
To our doctryne° it is y-write, y-wis.°   *instruction / indeed*

Taketh the fruyt,[6] and lat the chaf° be stille.   *husks*
   Now, gode God, if that it be thy wille,
As seith my lord,° so make us alle good men,   *my bishop*
680 And bringe us to his heighe° bliss. Amen.   *high*

The Epilogue

"Sir Nonnes Preest," our Hoste seyde anoon,[7]
"Y-blessed by thy brechc° and every stoon!°   *breech, thighs / stone, testicles*
This was a mery tale of Chauntecleer.
But by my trouthe, if thou were seculer,°   *a layman*
685 Thou woldest been a trede-foul[8] a-right.
For if thou have corage° as thou hast might,°   *spirit / strength*
Thee were nede of° hennes, as I wene,°   *You would need / suppose*
Ya, mo° than seven tymes seventene.   *more*
See, whiche braunes° hath this gentil preest,   *what brawn, muscles*
690 So greet a nekke, and swich a large breest!
He loketh as a sperhauk° with his yën;°   *sparrowhawk / eyes*
Him nedeth nat his colour° for to dyen°   *complexion / dye*
With brasile, ne with greyn of Portingale.[9]
Now sire, faire falle° yow for youre tale!"   *may good befall*

              *   *   *

---

6. I.e., grain.
7 This epilogue occurs in nine manuscripts only: it is not in Ellesmere, for example, and may have been rejected by Chaucer at some later stage in his work on the *Tales*.
8. "Tread-fowl," a potent rooster.
9. With red powder or red dye from Portugal.

SOURCES AND
BACKGROUNDS

The General Prologue

The *General Prologue* is first of all a framing device for the stories that follow. Among the many story collections in the Middle Ages, Chaucer's is closest to two Italian ones: Giovanni Boccaccio's *Decameron* and Giovanni Sercambi's *Novelle,* written in imitation of Boccaccio. Chaucer probably knew the *Decameron* to at least some extent and might have known the *Novelle.* Both have substantial introductions, which we include here.

Chaucer's decision to tell his stories in the context of a pilgrimage has important consequences. The prologue to the *Parson's Tale* concludes the public storytelling contest and introduces a long devotional treatise on penance and sin, which is followed by Chaucer's personal *Retraction.* The spiritual meaning of pilgrimage invoked by the Parson is discussed in the critical essays by Hoffman and Robertson (pp. 459–71 and pp. 530–35). Pilgrimage was also a social fact as well as a symbol, and by the late fourteenth century reformers argued that its spiritual purposes were being subverted by the worldliness of its participants; the selection from *The Examination of William Thorpe* reveals both Lollard censure and orthodox defense of pilgrimages.

The form of the portraits in the *General Prologue* is indebted to traditional rhetorical modes of character description. For many details of the pilgrims themselves, Chaucer draws heavily on what is known as estates literature: descriptions, usually satiric, of various classes and occupations. Thomas Wimbledon's sermon, probably delivered in London about the time Chaucer was beginning the *Canterbury Tales,* offers a religious perspective on the estates and their purposes. The passages from William Langland and John Gower suggest both what is conventional and what is original in Chaucer's portrait of the Monk. Much social criticism in Chaucer's time came from John Wyclif and his followers in the Lollard movement, some of whom Chaucer doubtless knew; two passages from Wycliffite tracts offer background to Chaucer's portraits of the Merchant, Pardoner, and Parson. For material relevant to the Friar, see the passage from the *Romance of the Rose,* pp. 410–15; for the source of Chaucer's treatment of the Prioress's table manners, see the *Romance* passage on pp. 316–17. On pp. 471–83 Jill Mann discusses Chaucer's portraits in light of the estates tradition.

THE FRAME

GIOVANNI BOCCACCIO

From the *Decameron*, First Day, Introduction†

Here begins the first day of The Decameron, *in which, after the author has explained why certain people (soon to be introduced) have gathered together to tell stories, they speak on any subject that pleases them most, under the direction of Pampinea.*

Whenever, gracious ladies, I consider how compassionate you are by nature, I realize that in your judgment the present work will seem to have had a serious and painful beginning, for it recalls in its opening the unhappy memory of the deadly plague just passed, dreadful and pitiful to all those who saw or heard about it. But I do not wish this to frighten you away from reading any further, as if you were going to pass all of your time sighing and weeping as you read. This horrible beginning will be like the ascent of a steep and rough mountainside, beyond which there lies a most beautiful and delightful plain, which seems more pleasurable to the climbers in proportion to the difficulty of their climb and their descent. And just as pain is the extreme limit of pleasure, so misery ends by unanticipated happiness. This brief pain (I say brief since it contains few words) will be quickly followed by the sweetness and the delight, which I promised you before, and which, had I not promised, might not be expected from such a beginning. To tell the truth, if I could have conveniently led you by any other way than this, which I know is a bitter one, I would have gladly done so; but since it is otherwise impossible to demonstrate how the stories you are about to read came to be told, I am almost obliged by necessity to write about it this way.

Let me say, then, that thirteen hundred and forty-eight years had already passed after the fruitful Incarnation of the Son of God when into the distinguished city of Florence, more noble than any other Italian city, there came the deadly pestilence. It started in the East, either because of the influence of heavenly bodies or because of God's just wrath as a punishment to mortals for our wicked deeds, and it killed an infinite number of people. Without pause it spread from one place and it stretched its miserable length over the West. And against this pestilence no human wisdom or foresight was of any avail; quantities of filth were removed from the city by officials charged with this task; the entry of any sick person into the city was prohibited; and many directives were issued concerning the maintenance of good health. Nor were the humble supplications, rendered not once but many times to God by pious people, through public processions or by other means, effi-

† From *The Decameron*, ed. and trans. Mark Musa and Peter E. Bondanella (New York: W. W. Norton, 1977) 3–17. The translators' notes have been re-numbered. Boccaccio wrote this account of the Black Death in Florence during or shortly after the event, ca. 1348–51.

cacious; for almost at the beginning of springtime of the year in question the plague began to show its sorrowful effects in an extraordinary manner. It did not act as it had done in the East, where bleeding from the nose was a manifest sign of inevitable death, but it began in both men and women with certain swellings either in the groin or under the armpits, some of which grew to the size of a normal apple and others to the size of an egg (more or less), and the people called them *gavoccioli*.[1] And from the two parts of the body already mentioned, within a brief space of time, the said deadly *gavoccioli* began to spread indiscriminately over every part of the body; and after this, the symptoms of the illness changed to black or livid spots appearing on the arms and thighs, and on every part of the body, some large ones and sometimes many little ones scattered all around. And just as the *gavoccioli* were originally, and still are, a very certain indication of impending death, in like manner these spots came to mean the same thing for whoever had them. Neither a doctor's advice nor the strength of medicine could do anything to cure this illness; on the contrary, either the nature of the illness was such that it afforded no cure, or else the doctors were so ignorant that they did not recognize its cause and, as a result, could not prescribe the proper remedy (in fact, the number of doctors, other than the well-trained, was increased by a large number of men and women who had never had any medical training); at any rate, few of the sick were ever cured, and almost all died after the third day of the appearance of the previously described symptoms (some sooner, others later), and most of them died without fever or any other side effects.   *contagious*

This pestilence was so powerful that it was communicated to the healthy by contact with the sick, the way a fire close to dry or oily things will set them aflame. And the evil of the plague went even further: not only did talking to or being around the sick bring infection and a common death, but also touching the clothes of the sick or anything touched or used by them seemed to communicate this very disease to the person involved. What I am about to say is incredible to hear, and if I and others had not witnessed it with our own eyes, I should not dare believe it (let alone write about it), no matter how trustworthy a person I might have heard it from. Let me say, then, that the power of the plague described here was of such virulence in spreading from one person to another that not only did it pass from one man to the next, but, what's more, it was often transmitted from the garments of a sick or dead man to animals that not only became contaminated by the disease, but also died within a brief period of time. My own eyes, as I said earlier, witnessed such a thing one day: when the rags of a poor man who died of this disease were thrown into the public street, two pigs came

1. *Gavoccioli*—or *bubboni*, in modern Italian—are called "buboes" in English, the source of the phrase "bubonic plague." The plague of 1348 is often known as the Black Plague because of the black spots Boccaccio describes. One of the most important casualties of this plague in literature was Laura, the woman who inspired the many sonnets and songs in the *Canzoniere* ("Songbook") by Boccaccio's friend and contemporary, Francesco Petrarca (1304–74). Both *The Decameron* and the *Canzoniere* deal with the experience of human love, and both are set against a stark background of plague, death, and earthly mutability.

upon them, as they are wont to do, and first with their snouts and then with their teeth they took the rags and shook them around; and within a short time, after a number of convulsions, both pigs fell dead upon the ill-fated rags, as if they had been poisoned. From these and many similar or worse occurrences there came about such fear and such fantastic notions among those who remained alive that almost all of them took a very cruel attitude in the matter; that is, they completely avoided the sick and their possessions; and in so doing, each one believed that he was protecting his good health.

There were some people who thought that living moderately and avoiding all superfluity might help a great deal in resisting this disease, and so, they gathered in small groups and lived entirely apart from everyone else. They shut themselves up in those houses where there were no sick people and where one could live well by eating the most delicate of foods and drinking the finest of wines (doing so always in moderation), allowing no one to speak about or listen to anything said about the sick and the dead outside; these people lived, spending their time with music and other pleasures that they could arrange. Others thought the opposite: they believed that drinking too much, enjoying life, going about singing and celebrating, satisfying in every way the appetites as best one could, laughing, and making light of everything that happened was the best medicine for such a disease; so they practiced to the fullest what they believed by going from one tavern to another all day and night, drinking to excess; and often they would make merry in private homes, doing everything that pleased or amused them the most. This they were able to do easily, for everyone felt he was doomed to die and, as a result, abandoned his property, so that most of the houses had become common property, and any stranger who came upon them used them as if he were their rightful owner. In addition to this bestial behavior, they always managed to avoid the sick as best they could. And in this great affliction and misery of our city the revered authority of the laws, both divine and human, had fallen and almost completely disappeared, for, like other men, the ministers and executors of the laws were either dead or sick or so short of help that it was impossible for them to fulfill their duties; as a result, everybody was free to do as he pleased.

Many others adopted a middle course between the two attitudes just described: neither did they restrict their food or drink so much as the first group nor did they fall into such dissoluteness and drunkenness as the second; rather, they satisfied their appetites to a moderate degree. They did not shut themselves up, but went around carrying in their hands flowers, or sweet-smelling herbs, or various kinds of spices; and often they would put these things to their noses, believing that such smells were a wonderful means of purifying the brain, for all the air seemed infected with the stench of dead bodies, sickness, and medicines.

Others were of a crueler opinion (though it was, perhaps, a safer one): they maintained that there was no better medicine against the plague than to flee from it; and convinced of this reasoning, not caring about anything but themselves, men and women in great numbers abandoned their city, their houses, their farms, their relatives, and their possessions and sought other places, and they went at least as far away as the Florentine countryside—as if the wrath of God could not pursue them with this pestilence wherever they went but would only strike those it found within the walls of the city! Or perhaps they thought that Florence's last hour had come and that no one in the city would remain alive.

And not all those who adopted these diverse opinions died, nor did they all escape with their lives; on the contrary, many of those who thought this way were falling sick everywhere, and since they had given, when they were healthy, the bad example of avoiding the sick, they, in turn, were abandoned and left to languish away without care. The fact was that one citizen avoided another, that almost no one cared for his neighbor, and that relatives rarely or hardly ever visited each other—they stayed far apart. This disaster had struck such fear into the hearts of men and women that brother abandoned brother, uncle abandoned nephew, sister left brother, and very often wife abandoned husband, and—even worse, almost unbelievable—fathers and mothers neglected to tend and care for their children, as if they were not their own.

Thus, for the countless multitude of men and women who fell sick, there remained no support except the charity of their friends (and these were few) or the avarice of servants, who worked for inflated salaries and indecent periods of time and who, in spite of this, were few and far between; and those few were men or women of little wit (most of them not trained for such service) who did little else but hand different things to the sick when requested to do so or watch over them while they died, and in this service, they very often lost their own lives and their profits. And since the sick were abandoned by their neighbors, their parents, and their friends and there was a scarcity of servants, a practice that was almost unheard of before spread through the city: when a woman fell sick, no matter how attractive or beautiful or noble she might be, she did not mind having a manservant (whoever he might be, no matter how young or old he was), and she had no shame whatsoever in revealing any part of her body to him—the way she would have done to a woman—when the necessity of her sickness required her to do so. This practice was, perhaps, in the days that followed the pestilence, the cause of looser morals in the women who survived the plague. And so, many people died who, by chance, might have survived if they had been attended to. Between the lack of competent attendants, which the sick were unable to obtain, and the violence of the pestilence, there were so many, many people who died in the city both day and night that it was incredible just to hear this described, not to mention seeing it! Therefore, out of sheer necessity, there arose among those who remained alive customs which were contrary to the established practices of the time.

It was the custom, as it is again today, for the women, relatives, and neighbors to gather together in the house of a dead person and there to mourn with the women who had been dearest to him; on the other hand, in front of the deceased's home, his male relatives would gather together with his male neighbors and other citizens, and the clergy also came (many of them, or sometimes just a few) depending upon the social class of the dead man. Then, upon the shoulders of his equals, he was carried to the church chosen by him before death with the funeral pomp of candles and chants. With the fury of the pestilence increasing, this custom, for the most part, died out and other practices took its place. And so, not only did people die without having a number of women around them, but there were many who passed away without even having a single witness present, and very few were granted the piteous laments and bitter tears of their relatives; on the contrary, most relatives were somewhere else, laughing, joking, and amusing themselves; even the women learned this practice too well, having put aside, for the most part, their womanly compassion for their own safety. Very few were the dead whose bodies were accompanied to the church by more than ten or twelve of their neighbors, and these dead bodies were not even carried on the shoulders of honored and reputable citizens but rather by gravediggers from the lower classes that were called *becchini*. Working for pay, they would pick up the bier and hurry it off, not to the church the dead man had chosen before his death but, in most cases, to the church closest by, accompanied by four or six churchmen with just a few candles, and often none at all. With the help of these *becchini*, the churchmen would place the body as fast as they could in whatever unoccupied grave they could find, without going to the trouble of saying long or solemn burial services.

The plight of the lower class and, perhaps, a large part of the middle class, was even more pathetic: most of them stayed in their homes or neighborhoods either because of their poverty or their hopes for remaining safe, and every day they fell sick by the thousands; and not having servants or attendants of any kind, they almost always died. Many ended their lives in the public streets, during the day or at night, while many others who died in their homes were discovered dead by their neighbors only by the smell of their decomposing bodies. The city was full of corpses. The dead were usually given the same treatment by their neighbors, who were moved more by the fear that the decomposing corpses would contaminate them than by any charity they might have felt towards the deceased: either by themselves or with the assistance of porters (when they were available), they would drag the corpse out of the home and place it in front of the doorstep where, usually in the morning, quantities of dead bodies could be seen by any passerby; then, they were laid out on biers, or for lack of biers, on a plank. Nor did a bier carry only one corpse; sometimes it was used for two or three at a time. More than once, a single bier would serve for a wife and husband, two or three brothers, a father or son, or other relatives, all at the same time. And countless times it happened that two priests, each with a cross, would be on their way to bury someone, when porters carrying three or four biers would just follow along behind them; and where these priests thought they had just one dead man to bury, they had, in fact, six or eight and sometimes more. Moreover, the dead were honored with no tears or candles or funeral mourners but worse: things had reached such a point that the people who died were cared for as we care for goats today. Thus, it became quite obvious that what the wise had not been able to endure with patience through the few calamities of everyday life now became a matter of indifference to even the most simple-minded people as a result of this colossal misfortune.

So many corpses would arrive in front of a church every day and at every hour that the amount of holy ground for burials was certainly insufficient for the ancient custom of giving each body its individual place; when all the graves were full, huge trenches were dug in all of the cemeteries of the churches and into them the new arrivals were dumped by the hundreds; and they were packed in there with dirt, one on top of another, like a ship's cargo, until the trench was filled.

But instead of going over every detail of the past miseries which befell our city, let me say that the same unfriendly weather there did not, because of this, spare the surrounding countryside any evil; there, not to speak of the towns which, on a smaller scale, were like the city, in the scattered villages and in the fields the poor, miserable peasants and their families, without any medical assistance or aid of servants, died on the roads and in their fields and in their homes, as many by day as by night, and they died not like men but more like wild animals. Because of this they, like the city dwellers, became careless in their ways and did not look after their possessions or their businesses; furthermore, when they saw that death was upon them, completely neglecting the future fruits of their past labors, their livestock, their property, they did their best to consume what they already had at hand. So, it came about that oxen, donkeys, sheep, pigs, chickens and even dogs, man's most faithful companion, were driven from their homes into the fields, where the wheat was left not only unharvested but also unreaped, and they were allowed to roam where they wished; and many of these animals, almost as if they were rational beings, returned at night to their homes without any guidance from a shepherd, satiated after a good day's meal.

Leaving the countryside and returning to the city, what more can one say, except that so great was the cruelty of Heaven, and, perhaps, also that of man, that from March to July of the same year, between the fury of the pestiferous sickness and the fact that many of the sick were badly treated or abandoned in need because of the fear that the healthy had, more than one hundred thousand human beings are believed to have lost their lives for certain inside the walls of the city of Florence whereas, before the deadly plague, one would not have estimated that there were actually that many people dwelling in that city.

Oh, how many great palaces, beautiful homes, and noble dwellings, once filled with families, gentlemen, and ladies, were now emptied, down to the last servant! How many notable families, vast domains, and famous fortunes remained without legitimate heir! How many valiant men, beautiful women, and charming young men, who might have been pronounced very healthy by Galen,[2] Hippocrates,[3] and Aesculapius[4] (not to mention lesser physicians), dined in the morning with their relatives, companions, and friends and then in the evening took supper with their ancestors in the other world!

Reflecting upon so many miseries makes me very sad; therefore, since I wish to pass over as many as I can, let me say that as our city was in this condition, almost emptied of inhabitants, it happened (as I heard it later from a person worthy of trust) that one Tuesday morning in the venerable church of Santa Maria Novella[5] there was hardly any congregation there to hear the holy services except for seven young women, all dressed in garments of mourning as the times demanded, each of whom was a friend, neighbor, or relative of the other, and none of whom had passed her twenty-eighth year, nor was any of them younger than eighteen; all were educated and of noble birth and beautiful to look at, well-mannered and gracefully modest. I would tell you their real names, if I did not have a good reason for not doing so, which is this: I do not wish any of them to be embarrassed in the future because of the things that they said to each other and what they listened to—all of which I shall later recount. Today the laws regarding pleasure are again strict, more so than at that time (for the reasons mentioned above when they were very lax), not only for women of their age but even for those who were older; nor would I wish to give an opportunity to the envious, who are always ready to attack every praiseworthy life, to diminish in any way with their indecent talk the dignity of these worthy ladies. But, so that you may understand clearly what each of them had to say, I intend to call them by names which are either completely or in part appropriate to their personalities. We shall call the first and the oldest Pampinea and the second Fiammetta, the third Filomena, and the fourth Emilia, and we shall name the fifth Lauretta and the sixth Neifile, and the last, not without reason, we shall call Elissa.[6] Not by prior agreement, but purely by chance, they gathered together in one part of the church and were seated almost in a circle, saying their rosaries; after many sighs, they began to discuss among themselves various matters concerning the nature of the times, and after a while, as the others fell silent, Pampinea began to speak in this manner:

"My dear ladies, you have often heard, as I have, how a proper use of one's reason does harm to no one. It is only natural for everyone born on this earth to aid, preserve, and defend his own life to the best of his ability; this is a right so taken for granted that it has, at times, permitted men to kill

---

2. Greek anatomist and physician (A.D. 130?–201?).
3. Greek physician (460?–377? B.C.), to whom the Hippocratic oath, administered to new physicians, is attributed.
4. The Roman god of medicine and healing, often identified with Asclepius, Apollo's son, who was the Greek god of medicine.
5. This church, called "novella" or "new" because it replaced a preexisting structure, was begun in 1279 and was completed by Jacopo Talenti in 1348. An excellent example of Italian Gothic style, it is also noted for the Renaissance façade grafted onto its

exterior by Leon Battista Alberti in the fifteenth century and for frescoes in its interior chapels done by various artists.
6. The qualities usually associated by critics with these ladies are as follows: Pampinea (a wise and confident lady, often in love and the most mature of the group); Filomena (wise and discreet and full of desire); Elissa (very young and dominated by a violent passion); Neifile (also young but ingenuous); Emilia (in love with herself); Lauretta (a jealous lover); and Fiammetta (happy to love and to be loved but afraid that she will lose her love).

each other without blame in order to defend their own lives. And if the laws dealing with the welfare of every human being permit such a thing, how much more lawful, and with no harm to anyone, is it for us, or anyone else, to take all possible precautions to preserve our own lives! When I consider what we have been doing this morning and in the past days and what we have spoken about, I understand, and you must understand too, that each one of us is afraid for her life; nor does this surprise me in the least either. I am greatly amazed that since each of us has the natural feelings of a woman, we do not find some remedy for ourselves to cure what each one of us dreads. We live in the city, in my opinion, for no other reason than to bear witness to the number of dead bodies that are carried to burial, or to listen whether the friars (whose number has been reduced to almost nothing) chant their offices at the prescribed hours, or to demonstrate to anyone who comes here the quality and the quantity of our miseries by our garments of mourning. And if we leave the church, either we see dead or sick bodies being carried all about, or we see those who were once condemned to exile for their crimes by the authority of the public laws making sport of these laws, running about wildly through the city, because they know that the executors of these laws are either dead or dying; or we see the scum of our city, avid for our blood, who call themselves *becchini* and who ride about on horseback torturing us by deriding everything, making our losses more bitter with their disgusting songs. Nor do we hear anything but "So-and-so is dead," and "So-and-so is dying"; and if there were anyone left to mourn, we should hear nothing but piteous laments everywhere. I do not know if what happens to me also happens to you in your homes, but when I go home I find no one there except my maid, and I become so afraid that my hair stands on end, and wherever I go or sit in my house, I seem to see the shadows of those who have passed away, not with the faces that I remember, but with horrible expressions that terrify me. For these reasons, I am uncomfortable here, outside, and in my home, and the more so since it appears that no one like ourselves, who is well off and who has some other place to go, has remained here except us. And if there are any who remain, according to what I hear and see, they do whatever their hearts desire, making no distinction between what is proper and what is not, whether they are alone or with others, by day or by night; and not only laymen but also those who are cloistered in convents have broken their vows of obedience and have given themselves over to carnal pleasures, for they have made themselves believe that these things are permissible for them and are improper for others, and thinking that they will escape with their lives in this fashion, they have become wanton and dissolute.

"If this is the case, and plainly it is, what are we doing here? What are we waiting for? What are we dreaming about? Why are we slower to protect our health than all the rest of the citizens? Do we hold ourselves less dear than all the others? Or do we believe that our own lives are tied by stronger chains to our bodies than those of others and, therefore, that we need not worry about anything which might have the power to harm them? We are mistaken and deceived, and we are mad if we believe it. We shall have clear proof of this if we just call to mind how many young men and ladies have been struck down by this cruel pestilence. I do not know if you agree with me, but I think that, in order not to fall prey, out of laziness or presumption, to what we might well avoid, it might be a good idea for all of us to leave this city, just as many others before us have done and are still doing. Let us avoid like death itself the ugly examples of others, and go to live in a more dignified fashion in our country houses (of which we all have several) and there let us take what enjoyment, what happiness, and what pleasure we can, without going beyond the rules of reason in any way. There we can hear the birds sing, and we can see the hills and the pastures turning green, the wheat fields moving like the sea, and a thousand kinds of trees; and we shall be able to see the heavens more clearly which, though they still may be cruel, nonetheless will not deny to us their eternal beauties, which are much more pleasing to look at than the empty walls of our city. Besides all this, there in the country the air is much fresher, and the necessities for living in such times as these are plentiful there, and there are just fewer troubles in general; though the peasants are dying there even as the townspeople here, the displeasure is the less in that there are fewer houses and inhabitants than in the city. Here on the other hand, if I judge correctly, we would not be abandoning anyone; on the contrary, we can honestly say it is we ourselves that have been abandoned, for our loved ones are either dead or have fled and have left us alone in such affliction as though we did not belong to them. No reproach, therefore, can come to us if we follow this course of action, whereas sorrow, worry, and perhaps even death can come if we do not follow this course. So, whenever you like, I think it would be well to take our servants, have all our necessary things sent after us, and go from one place one day to another the next, enjoying what happiness and merriment these times permit; let us live in this manner (unless we are overtaken first by death) until we see what ending Heaven has reserved for these horrible times. And remember that it is no more forbidden for us to go away virtuously than it is for most other women to remain here dishonorably."

When they had listened to what Pampinea had said, the other women not only praised her advice but were so anxious to follow it that they had already begun discussing among themselves the details, as if they were going to leave that very instant. But Filomena, who was most discerning, said:

"Ladies, regardless of how convincing Pampinea's arguments are, that is no reason to rush into things, as you seem to wish to do. Remember that we are all women, and any young girl can tell you that women do not know how to reason in a group when they are without the guidance of some man who knows how to control them. We are changeable, quarrelsome, suspicious, timid, and fearful, because of which I suspect that this company will soon break up without honor to any of us if we do not take a guide other than ourselves. We would do well to resolve this matter before we depart."

Then Elissa said:

"Men are truly the leaders of women, and without their guidance, our actions rarely end successfully. But how are we to find any men? We all know that the majority of our relatives are dead and those who remain alive are scattered here and there in various groups, not knowing where we are (they, too, are fleeing precisely what we seek to avoid), and since taking up with strangers would be unbecoming to us, we must, if we wish to leave for the sake of our health, find a means of arranging it so that while going for our own pleasure and repose, no trouble or scandal follow us."

While the ladies were discussing this, three young men came into the church, none of whom was less than twenty-five years of age. Neither the perversity of the times nor the loss of friends or parents, nor fear for their own lives had been able to cool, much less extinguish, the love those lovers bore in their hearts. One of them was called Panfilo, another Filostrato, and the last Dioneo, each one very charming and well-bred; and in those turbulent times they sought their greatest consolation in the sight of the ladies they loved, all three of whom happened to be among the seven ladies previously mentioned, while the others were close relatives of one or the other of the three men. No sooner had they sighted the ladies than they were seen by them, whereupon Pampinea smiled and said:

"See how Fortune favors our plans and has provided us with these discreet and virtuous young men, who would gladly be our guides and servants if we do not hesitate to accept them for such service."

Then Neifile's face blushed out of embarrassment, for she was one of those who was loved by one of the young men, and she said:

"Pampinea, for the love of God, be careful what you say! I realize very well that nothing but good can be said of any of them, and I believe that they are capable of doing much more than that task and, likewise, that their good and worthy company would be fitting not only for us but for ladies much more beautiful and attractive than we are, but it is quite obvious that some of them are in love with some of us who are here present, and I fear that if we take them with us, slander and disapproval will follow, through no fault of ours or of theirs."

Then Filomena said:

"That does not matter at all; as long as I live with dignity and have no remorse of conscience about anything, let anyone who wishes say what he likes to the contrary: God and Truth will take up arms in my defense. Now, if they were just prepared to come with us, as Pampinea says, we could truly say that Fortune was favorable to our departure."

When the others heard her speak in such a manner, the argument was ended, and they all agreed that the young men should be called over, told about their intentions, and asked if they would be so kind as to accompany the ladies on such a journey. Without further discussion, then, Pampinea, who was related to one of the men, rose to her feet and made her way to where they stood gazing at the ladies, and she greeted them with a cheerful expression, outlined their plan to them, and begged them, in everyone's name, to keep them company in the spirit of pure and brotherly affection.

At first the young men thought they were being mocked, but when they saw that the lady was speaking seriously, they gladly consented; and in order to start without delay and put the plan into action, before leaving the church they agreed upon what preparations must be made for their departure. And when everything had been arranged and word had been sent on to the place they intended to go, the following morning (that is, Wednesday) at the break of dawn the ladies with some of their servants and the three young men with three of their servants left the city and set out on their way; they had traveled no further than two short miles when they arrived at the first stop they had agreed upon.

The place was somewhere on a little mountain, at some distance away from our roads, full of various shrubs and plants with rich, green foliage—most pleasant to look at; at the top there was a country mansion with a beautiful large inner courtyard with open collonades, halls, and bedrooms, all of them beautiful in themselves and decorated with cheerful and interesting paintings; it was surrounded by meadows and marvelous gardens, with wells of fresh water and cellars full of the most precious wines, the likes of which were more suitable for expert drinkers than for sober and dignified ladies. And the group discovered, to their delight, that the entire palace had been cleaned and the beds made in the bedchambers, and that fresh flowers and rushes had been strewn everywhere. Soon after they arrived and were resting, Dioneo, who was more attractive and wittier than either of the other young men, said:

"Ladies, more than our preparations, it was your intelligence that guided us here. I do not know what you intend to do with your thoughts, but I left mine inside the city walls when I passed through them in your company a little while ago; and so, you must either make up your minds to enjoy yourselves and laugh and sing with me (as much, let me say, as your dignity permits), or you must give me leave to return to my worries and to remain in our troubled city."

To this Pampinea, who had driven away her sad thoughts in the same way, replied happily:

"Dioneo, you speak very well: let us live happily, for after all it was unhappiness that made us flee the city. But when things are not organized they cannot long endure, and since I began the discussions which brought this fine company together, and since I desire the continuation of our happiness, I think it is necessary that we choose a leader from among us, whom we shall honor and obey as our superior and whose every thought shall be to keep us living happily. And in order that each one of us may feel the weight of this responsibility together with the pleasure of its authority, so that no one of us who has not experienced it can envy the others, let me say that both the weight and the honor should be granted to each one of us in turn for a day; the first will be chosen by election; the others that follow will be whomever he or she that will have the rule for that day chooses as the hour of vespers[7] approaches; this ruler, as long as his reign endures, will organize and arrange the place and the manner in which we will spend our time."

These words greatly pleased everyone, and they unanimously elected Pampinea queen for the first day; Filomena quickly ran to a laurel bush, whose leaves she had always heard were worthy of praise and bestowed great honor upon those crowned with them, she plucked several branches from it and wove them into a handsome garland of honor. And when it would be placed upon the head of any one of them, it was to be to all in the group a clear symbol of royal rule and authority over the rest of them for as long as their company stayed together.[8]

After she had been chosen queen, Pampinea ordered everyone to refrain from talking; then, she sent for the four servants of the ladies and for those of the three young men, and as they stood before her in silence, she said:

"Since I must set the first example for you all in order that it may be bettered and thus allow our company to live in order and in pleasure, and without any shame, and so that it may last as long as we wish, I first appoint Parmeno, Dioneo's servant, as my steward, and I commit to his care and management all our household and everything which pertains to the services of the dining hall. I wish Sirisco, the servant of Panfilo, to act as our buyer and treasurer and follow the orders of Parmeno. Tindaro, who is in the service of Filostrato, shall wait on Filostrato and Dioneo and Panfilo in their bedchambers when the other two are occupied with their other duties and cannot do so. Misia, my servant, and Licisca, Filomena's, will be occupied in the kitchen and will prepare those dishes which are ordered by Parmeno. Chimera, Lauretta's servant, and Stratilia, Fiammetta's servant, will take care of the bedchambers of the ladies and the cleaning of those places we use. And in general, we desire and command each of you, if you value our favor and good graces, to be sure—no matter where you go or come from, no matter what you hear or see—to bring us back nothing but pleasant news."

And when these orders, praised by all present, were delivered, Pampinea rose happily to her feet and said:

"Here there are gardens and meadows and many other pleasant places, which all of us can wander about in and enjoy as we like; but at the hour of tierce let everyone be here so that we can eat in the cool of the morning."

After the merry group had been given the new queen's permission, the

---

7. According to church practice, special forms of prayers were prescribed by canon law for recitation at specified times during the day. As a result, people often told the time according to these seven canonical hours: matins (dawn); prime (about 6:00 A.M.); tierce (the third hour after sunrise, about 9:00 A.M.); sext (noon); nones (the ninth hour after sunrise, or about 3:00 P.M.); vespers (late afternoon); and compline (in the evening just before retiring).
8. The leaves of the laurel bush were traditionally used in ancient times to fashion crowns or garlands not only for warriors and heroes but also for outstanding poets, musicians, and artists. Laura, the inspiration of Petrarca's *Canzoniere*, was so named because of her association with the laurel and, therefore, with excellence in poetry. Most medieval and Renaissance illustrations of the great Italian poets Dante, Petrarca, and Boccaccio picture them with such laurel crowns, implying that they have equaled and perhaps even excelled the poets of classical antiquity.

young men, together with the beautiful ladies, set off slowly through a garden, discussing pleasant matters, making themselves beautiful garlands of various leaves and singing love songs. After the time granted them by the queen had elapsed, they returned home and found Parmeno busy carrying out the duties of his task; for as they entered a hall on the ground floor, they saw the tables set with the whitest of linens and with glasses that shone like silver and everything decorated with broom blossoms; then, they washed their hands and, at the queen's command, they all sat down in the places assigned them by Parmeno. The delicately cooked foods were brought in and very fine wines were served; the three servants in silence served the tables. Everyone was delighted to see everything so beautiful and well arranged, and they ate merrily and with pleasant conversation. Since all the ladies and young men knew how to dance (and some of them even knew how to play and sing very well), when the tables had been cleared, the queen ordered that instruments be brought, and on her command, Dioneo took a lute and Fiammetta a viola, and they began softly playing a dance tune. After the queen had sent the servants off to eat, she began to dance together with the other ladies and two of the young men; and when that was over, they all began to sing carefree and gay songs. In this manner they continued until the queen felt that it was time to retire; therefore, at the queen's request, the three young men went off to their chambers (which were separate from those of the ladies), where they found their beds pre-pared and the rooms as full of flowers as the halls; the ladies, too, discovered their chambers decorated in like fashion. Then they all undressed and fell asleep.

Not long after the hour of nones, the queen arose and had the other ladies and young men awakened, stating that too much sleep in the daytime was harmful; then they went out onto a lawn of thick, green grass, where no ray of the sun could penetrate; and there, with a gentle breeze caressing them, they all sat in a circle upon the green grass, as was the wish of their queen. Then she spoke to them in this manner:

"As you see, the sun is high, the heat is great, and nothing can be heard except the cicadas in the olive groves; therefore, to wander about at this hour would be, indeed, foolish. Here it is cool and fresh and, as you see, there are games and chessboards with which all of you can amuse your-selves to your liking. But if you take my advice in this matter, I suggest we spend this hot part of the day not in playing games (a pastime which of necessity disturbs the player who loses without providing much pleasure either for his opponents or for those who watch) but rather in telling stories, for this way one person, by telling a story, can provide amusement for the entire company. In the time it takes for the sun to set and the heat to become less oppressive, you will each have told a little story, and then we can go wherever we like to amuse ourselves; so, if what I say pleases you (and in this I am willing to follow your pleasure), then, let us do it; if not, then let everyone do as he pleases until the hour of vespers."

The entire group of men and women liked the idea of telling stories.

"Then," said the queen, "if this is your wish, for this first day I order each of you to tell a story about any subject he likes."

And turning to Panfilo, who sat on her right, she ordered him in a gracious manner to begin with one of his tales; whereupon, hearing her command, Panfilo, while everyone listened, began at once as follows.

* * *

GIOVANNI BOCCACCIO

From the *Decameron*, Tenth Day, Conclusion†

Dioneo's tale had ended, and the ladies, some taking one side and some taking the other, some criticizing one thing about it and some praising another, had discussed the story at great length when the King, looking up at the sky and seeing that the sun had already sunk low toward the hour of vespers, began, without getting up, to speak in this fashion:

"Lovely ladies, as I believe you know, human wisdom does not consist only in remembering past events or in knowing about present ones, but rather in being able, with a knowledge of both one and the other, to predict future events, which wise men consider the highest form of intelligence. As you know, it will be fifteen days tomorrow that we left Florence in order to find some means of amusement, to preserve our health and our lives, and to escape from the melancholy, suffering, and anguish which has existed continuously in our city since the beginning of the plague. This goal, in my opinion, we have virtuously achieved; for, as far as I have been able to observe, even if the stories we have told were amusing, and possibly of the sort conducive to arousing our carnal appetites, and though we have continually eaten and drunk well, played and sung (all things which may well incite weaker minds to less proper behavior), neither in word nor in deed nor in any other way do I feel that either you or ourselves are worthy of criticism. Constant decorum, constant harmony, and constant fraternal friendship are, in fact, what I have seen and felt here—something which, of course, pleases me, for it redounds to both your honor and merit and mine. And therefore, to prevent an overly practiced custom from turning into boredom as well as to prevent anyone from criticizing our having stayed here too long, I now think it proper, since each of us has, with his own day of storytelling, enjoyed his share of the honor that still resides in me, that, with your approval, we return to the place from where we came. Not to mention the fact that, if you consider the matter carefully, since our company is already known to many others in these parts, our numbers could increase in such a way as to destroy all our pleasure. Therefore, if you

† From THE DECAMERON by Giovanni Boccaccio, translated by Mark Musa and Peter Bondanella. Pp. 682–84. Copyright © 1982 by Mark Musa and Peter Bondanella. Reprinted by arrangement with NAL Penguin, Inc., New York, NY.

approve of my suggestion, I shall retain the crown given me until our departure, which I propose should be tomorrow morning; if you decide otherwise, I am already prepared to crown someone else for the next day."

The discussion between the ladies and the young men was long, but
finally, having decided that the King's advice was sensible and proper, they
all decided to do as he had said; and so, having sent for the steward, the
King discussed with him the arrangements that had to be made for the
following morning and then, having given the group their leave until suppertime, he rose to his feet.

The ladies and the other young men got up too, and as they usually did,
some turned their attention to one amusement and others to another; and
when it was time for supper, with the greatest of delight they went to the
table; and after supper they began to sing and play and dance; and while
Lauretta was leading a dance, the King ordered Fiammetta to sing a song,
which she began to sing, most delightfully, in this fashion:

> If there could be Love without jealousy,
> then I know that no woman born,
> no matter who, could have more joy than I.
>
> If it be carefree youth
> that please a lady in her handsome lover,
> or the height of virtuousness,
> or daring prowess, courage,
> intelligence, good manners, eloquence,
> or perfect elegance,
> then I'm the one who's pleased, whose happiness
> in love the way I am,
> rests all within the man who is my hope.
>
> But since I'm well aware
> that other ladies are as wise as I,
> I tremble with my fear
> and dread the worst will happen:
> that others will attempt to take
> the man who took my heart from me.
> And so, the thing that is my greatest fortune
> makes me, in misery,
> sigh deep and lead a wretched life.
>
> If I felt that my lord
> could be as faithful as he's valiant,
> never would I be jealous;
> so many men like this there are—
> who need but one inviting glance—
> I think all men are horrible!
> This grieves my heart, and makes me want to die;

because whenever women look his way,
I dread and fear that I'll be robbed of him.

For God's sake, then, let every single
woman be warned that she dare not
practice such an outrage;
because should any one of them,
with words, or signs, or blandishments
attempt to harm me in this way,
and I should learn of it,
then may I be deformed
if I don't make her weep her bitter folly!

When Fiammetta had finished her song, Dioneo, who was sitting beside her, said with a laugh:

"Madam, you would be doing all the other ladies a great kindness if you would reveal your lover's name to them, so that out of ignorance they would not take from you what is yours, since this would make you so angry!"

After this song, they sang many others; and when it was nearly midnight, they all, at the King's request, went to bed.

By the time they arose at dawn of the new day, the steward had already sent all of their possessions on ahead, and so, under the guidance of their prudent King, they returned to Florence; and having taken their leave of the seven ladies at Santa Maria Novella, from where they had all set out together, the three young men went off to see to their other pleasures, while the ladies, when they felt it was time, returned to their homes.

GIOVANNI SERCAMBI

From the *Novelle* †

[Introduction]

The supreme and powerful God, from whom all good derives, created human nature and made it in His likeness so that this human nature, if it be not filled with sin, may possess the heavenly court. When through its own folly it is deprived of the celestial paradise, nothing is to be blamed but human nature itself; and so too if God sends us varying fortunes because of sins we have committed. For it has often been seen that because of our sins, God has granted to spirits, both angelic and malign, power over many, and

---

† Translated for this volume by Cosimo Corsano from the text edited by Giovanni Sinicropi: Giovanni Sercambi, *Novelle*, 2 vols. (Bari: G. Laterza, 1972). It differs in certain readings from the text established by Robert A. Pratt and Karl Young, included in *Sources and Analogues*, pp. 36–41. Defects in the original manuscript are indicated by asterisks. Most scholars agree that the work as we have it was written ca. 1400; whether an earlier version existed that Chaucer could have seen is a matter of controversy.

to the celestial planets as well, which by means of His power guide and conduct that which is below: mankind, all plants and animals, and all elemental things. And often because of sins committed, fire has come, and floods, and blood from heaven, in order to purge and punish the evil doers. Many cities and countries have been submerged and burned. Yet from the signs which are found written in the ancient scriptures and from those which are seen every day, no one wishes to take warning. They do not wish to abstain from vices, but with all solicitude they endeavor, in as many ways as they know how, to do evil. And he who is himself unable to do it teaches others the way to it. And in this manner that creature whom God made most sublime and whom He created in His semblance, most shamefully departs from God.

There is then no cause for wonder if sometimes human nature suffers afflictions and wars and pestilences, famines, fires, robbery and extortions, for if it abstained from sins, God would give us that good which He promised: in this world every grace, and in that other His glory. But because human nature is drawn to the contrary of good and follows it, God in his power has chosen to send those same signs which He sent to Pharaoh, so that by departing from our vices we might make amends. But we, obstinate and with our hearts hardened like Pharaoh's, awaiting the final judgment, shall be placed in eternal pain. So it is no wonder if now, in 1374, the plague has come and no medicine can cure it. No wealth or high position or any argument one might construct is sufficient to avoid death, except virtue alone, which can free man from all pestilences. That is the medicine which saves the soul and the body, and by not taking the road of such goodness, we necessarily go astray. * * * A person may come close to a sick man and be himself without fever, yet death comes to him. Thus one must not be bold: no position or relations can defend him from such a blow.

So a number of men and women, friars and priests, and others from the city of Lucca, because there was plague and pestilence in that region, decided—God willing—that for some [days they would travel] * * * first to draw nearer to Him in order to do good and abstain from all vices, so that by doing this, God through His pity would put an end to the plague and to other evils among us both present and future. Therefore, men and women, friars and priests, having seen the pestilence increase, first placed themselves in the good grace of God, and then decided, until the air of Lucca was purified and cleansed of pestilence, to pass the time by undertaking a pleasant journey. Having met together, these people decided to depart from Lucca and take their way through Italy in a manner orderly, virtuous and holy.

In the month of February, on a Sunday, having had a mass said and having all taken communion and having made their wills, they met in the church of Santa Maria del Corso, talking about things divine. And there rose to his feet a most worthy and very rich man named Aluizi, who said: "Dear brothers, each more worthy than I, and you, illustrious and worshipful ladies, who are met here out of your various lives in order to flee the

death of the body and this pestilence: before speaking of other matters, I
wish to say that since we are resolved to save our lives and flee the plague,
we must think above all of fleeing the death of the soul, to which more care
is to be given than to that of the body. And in order to flee from both these
perils, it is necessary to follow the way of God and His commandments,
and to guide ourselves in those prudent ways that are necessary. And this
cannot be done unless there first be a person among us to whom all show
reverence, obeying him in all honorable things, and unless he, as a virtuous
man, command for the pleasure of the company only that which is without
sin. And having done this, let him determine the manner and conduct of
our journey, so that without reprimand or evil and without shame we may
safely return to our city and our homes, happy and joyous, having given
good example to all the cities we pass through."

No sooner had Aluizi spoken these words than the company said among
themselves: "Certainly in this group one could not find a better than he."
And immediately they all said in a loud voice: "We wish Aluizi to be the
preposto[1] of this company, and beg him to accept such an office. He may
command us to obey his orders, men and women alike, for in him we sense
such virtue that he will require of us nothing but what is fitting. And through
his great wisdom and foresight, in the name of God he will lead us in good
health back to Lucca."

Aluizi listened to the company and, since he could not do otherwise,
said: "Most illustrious and worthy brothers, and you most honorable ladies,
I know there are in this company those who are wiser, more expert, and of
greater vision than I, who would fulfill such an office in one hour better
than I could in one year. It would be good if you had elected another. But
since it pleases you that I be named your leader, I am content, asking of
you all that whatever shall be commanded shall be obeyed." All said,
"Command, and it shall be done."

The leader then said: "Before we do anything else, we must put our
money together for expenses necessary on the journey." They immediately
got out money, made a pile of three thousand florins and put it into his
hands, saying: "When these have been spent we shall put in more." The
leader, seeing the quantity of money and their willingness to add more,
said: "Now let us be merry, for the company will fare well." With the
money in his hand, he spoke in a loud voice: "Since we go this journey in
order to save ourselves, I command you all, both men and women, that
while we travel you do no unbecoming thing amongst ourselves or with
others. Whoever may have other intentions, let him return to Lucca before
we depart; and if he has paid any money, let him step forward, for it will be
given back to him." The company, at these words, all answered together:
"Oh leader, be assured that we will conduct ourselves with such propriety
(onestà) while we travel that the wife will not be intimate with her husband,

1. Literally "provost" or "vicar," a man put in charge of a group; hereafter translated as "leader": English has
no term exactly comparable.

nor with others: on the contrary, in our journey no one will come close to another in any unchaste way."

The leader being now certain there would be no shameful behavior, chose as treasurer a man so loyal that he would sooner contribute his own money to support the company than take for himself a single coin from the group's treasury. In this manner, the company hoped to be taken care of in its needs. Having made this appointment, the leader next ordained that there should be two stewards, one in the service of the men and the other in the service of the ladies. And because such offices must always be filled by people suited to the task, the leader decided that in the service of the men there should be a young man wise in spending and not given to avarice, and in the service of the ladies a man of mature years, careful with expenses, so that the entire company should have no cause for complaint.

Next he ordered that mass be said every morning by some of the priests among them, which he wished all to hear, and every evening, though the company would not attend, that they say the Hours and Compline so that no negligence might be imputed to them.

He then ordained that at dinner and supper men should joyfully sing songs, both of jousting and of moral truth, and that they should reason with arguments and sometimes fence with swords, to give pleasure to all, and that some among them should dispute upon the liberal arts, this latter group to be selected solely from the company of men and prelates. Others he ordered to perform songs of love and virtue on lutes and delightful instruments, singing with soft, low voices and with treble voices for the pleasure of the ladies (for some were elderly and some betrothed, some wedded and some widowed). He ordered some young people expert on the psalter[2] to play a psalm and a *Gloria;* and whenever mass was heard and at the elevation of Our Lord's Body and Blood, they were to sing a *Sanctus Sanctus Deus.* In this manner he made clear his wish that at morning mass there be music—and at dinner and supper also, if the men and women were feeling like being entertained. He commanded that such instruments and players should make the company happy after dinner and supper, with pleasing songs and without false pride. And all this he established in an orderly manner.

Then the leader turned to the company, and speaking in a deliberately obscure way *(per figura),* said: "That man among us who has sustained so much harm without cause and through no fault of his own, I command in this journey to be the author and maker of this book and to do every day whatever I shall ask of him. And in order that he may not seek excuses from obeying me in all things, and also to prevent him feeling any ill-will toward me, I shall recite a sonnet in which his very name and surname will be found:[3] and by this means, I command that each time I say 'Author of such a thing' he (will) without any excuses (understand) my intention." And he said in a loud voice:

2. A stringed musical instrument, somewhat like a lyre.

3. The sonnet is not very coherent and serves mainly, when the first letter of each line is read downward, to spell out Sercambi's name.

Già trovo che si diè pace Pompeo
Immaginando il grave tradimento,
Omicidio crudele e violento,
Volendo ciò Cesare e Tolomeo.
An' Ecuba quel * * * reo
Nativo d'Antinor (il cui nom sia spento)
Nascose in su l'altare, e con gran pasione
Il converti ringraziando Deo.

Sotto color di pace ancora Giuda
El nostro salvator Cristo tradio
Redendo sé di vita in morte cruda.
Considerando ciò dommi pace io:
Avendo sempre l'anima mia cruda
Mossa a vendetta, cancello il pensier mio.
Ben dico che la lingua colla mente
Insieme non disforma in leal gente.

It seems now that Pompey found peace
In imagining a grave betrayal:
Cruel and violent murder (came after),
Caesar and Ptolomey desiring it.
And Hecuba hid upon the altar
That evil countryman, Antenor
(May his name die out), with great feeling,
Thanking God for the conversion.

And under the guise of peace also, Judas
Betrayed our savior, Christ,
Cutting himself off from life by an ugly death.
Considering this, I find peace,
Though my savage soul is often moved
Toward vengeance, I drive out that thought.
Verily I say that the tongue and the mind
Are not at odds among men of good will.

Everyone in the company heard this pleasing sonnet, but none could understand whom the leader was addressing except he who (comprehending the words and verses of the sonnet) found his name and surname therein. Without saying anything further, he understood that he had to be the author of this book; without saying anything further, he remained like the others, silent.

The leader, having discharged part of his duties and having ordained who was to lead the company. * * *[4]

---

4. The following leaf of the manuscript has been lost. It probably brought this meeting to some conclusion, described the company's departure from Lucca and their journey to a place beyond Pisa; it may also have included a first tale (*novella*). The manuscript as we have it resumes with a love song: the entertainments are underway. Sercambi tells all the tales in his own person and contributes many of the short moral pieces (*moralità*) as well.

THE IDEA OF PILGRIMAGE
GEOFFREY CHAUCER

The Parson's Prologue

By that° the Maunciple hadde his tale al ended,	By the time that
The sonne fro the south lyne° was descended	prime meridian
So lowe, that he nas° nat, to my sighte,	was not
Degrees nyne and twenty as in highte.°	height (above the horizon)
5 Foure of the clokke it was tho,° as I gesse;	then
For elevene foot, or litel more or lesse,	
My shadwe° was at thilke° tyme, as there,°	shadow / that same / at that place
Of swiche° feet as° my lengthe parted° were	such / as if / divided
In six feet equal of proporcioun.[1]	
10 Therwith the mones exaltacioun,°	position of greatest influence
I mene Libra, alwey gan ascende,°	steadily kept ascending
As we were entring° at a thropes ende;°	entering / village's edge
For which oure Host, as he was wont° to gye,°	accustomed / guide
As in this caas,° oure joly companye,	case
15 Seyde in this wyse: "Lordings everichoon,°	every one
Now lakketh us no tales mo than oon.°	one
Fulfild is my sentence and my decree;	
I trowe° that we han herd of ech degree.°	believe / from each (social) rank
Almost fulfild is al myn ordinaunce.	
20 I prey to God, so yeve him° right good chaunce,°	may He give him / fortune
That telleth this tale to us lustily.°	pleasantly
"Sire preest," quod he, "artow° a vicary?°	art thou / vicar
Or art a person?° Sey sooth,° by thy fey!°	parson / tell the truth / faith
Be what thou be,° ne breke thou nat oure pley;°	Whatever thou mayest be / game
25 For every man, save thou,° hath told his tale.	except for thee
Unbokele,° and shewe us what is in thy male.°	Unbuckle / bag
For trewely, me thinketh by thy chere,°	appearance
Thou sholdest knitte up° wel a greet matere.°	bring to conclusion / subject
Telle us a fable anon,° for cokkes° bones!"	immediately / God's
30 This Persone him answerde, al at ones,°	at once
"Thou getest fable noon y-told for° me;	by
For Paul, that wryteth unto Timothee,[2]	
Repreveth hem that weyven° soothfastnesse°	put aside / truthfulness
And tellen fables and swich wrecchednesse.°	such miserable things
35 Why sholde I sowen draf° out of my fest,°	chaff / fist (hand)
Whan I may sowen whete,° if that me lest?°	wheat / it pleases me
For which I seye, if that yow list to here°	it pleases you to listen to

1. I.e., if Chaucer's height were divided into sixths, his shadow would be roughly as long as eleven of those units.
2. Cf. 1 Timothy 1.4 and 4.7; 2 Timothy 4.4.

Moralitee and vertuous matere,
And thanne that ye wol yeve° me audience,°   *give / hearing*
40 I wol ful fayn,° at Cristes reverence,   *willingly*
Do yow pleasaunce leefful, as I can.[3]
But trusteth wel, I am a Southren man:
I can nat geste—rum, ram, ruf—by lettre.[4]
Ne, God wot,° rym° holde I but litel bettre   [[...]
45 And therfore, if yow list, I wol nat glose.°   *be elaborate or subtle*
I wol yow telle a mery tale in prose
To knitte up al this feeste° and make an ende.   *feast, festival*
And Jesu, for his grace, wit° me sende   *wisdom, intelligence*
To shewe yow the wey, in this viage,°   *journey*
50 Of thilke° parfit° glorious pilgrimage   *that same / perfect*
That highte° Jerusalem celestial.   *is called*
And, if ye vouchesauf,° anon I shal   *permit*
Biginne upon my tale, for whiche I preye
Telle youre avys,° I can no bettre seye.   *Make known your wish*
55   But nathelees, this meditacioun
I putte it ay° under correccioun   *ever*
Of clerkes,° for I am nat textuel;°   *scholars / textually learned*
I take but° the sentence,° trusteth wel.   *only / meaning*
Therfor I make protestacioun
60 That I wol stonde to° correccioun."   *submit to*
   Upon this word we han assented sone,°   *at once*
For, as us semed, it was for to done,[5]
To enden in som vertuous sentence,
And for to yeve° him space° and audience,°   *give / the time / a hearing*
65 And bade oure Host he sholde to him seye
That alle we to telle his tale him preye.°   *ask respectfully*
   Oure Host hadde the wordes° for us alle: *was spokesman*
"Sire preest," quod he, "now fayre yow bifalle!°   *may good (chance) befall you*
Sey what yow list, and we wol gladly here."
70 And with that word he seyde in this manere:
"Telleth," quod he, "youre meditacioun.
But hasteth yow,° the sonne wol adoun;°   *hurry along / will set*
Beth fructuous,° and that in litel space,°   *fruitful / a short time*
And to do wel God sende yow his grace!"[6]

---

3. Give you lawful (permissible) pleasure, to the degree that I know how.
4. I do not know how to compose a romance in the alliterative style, "rum, ram, ruf" (nonsense syllables).
5. For, as it seemed to us, it was the thing to do.

6. The Parson's Tale, which follows, is a prose discourse of very great length concerning the Sacrament of Penance and its role in the spiritual life of fallen man; it includes a systematic exposition of the Seven Deadly Sins and their Remedies.

GEOFFREY CHAUCER
Retraction

Here taketh the makere of this book his leve.

Now preye I to hem alle that herkne° this litel
tretis or rede,° that if ther be any thing in it that
lyketh hem,° that therof they thanken oure lord Jesu
Crist, of° whom procedeth al wit° and al goodnesse.
/ And if ther be any thing that displese hem, I preye
hem also that they arrette° it to the defaute° of myn
unconninge,° and nat to my wil, that wolde ful fayn°
have seyd bettre if I hadde had conninge.° / For
oure boke seith, 'al that is writen is writen for oure
doctrine';° and that is myn entente.° / Wherfore I
biseke° yow mekely,° for the mercy of God, that ye
preye for me, that Crist have mercy on me and for-
yeve° me my giltes;° / and namely of° my transla-
cions and endytinges° of° worldly vanitees, the
5 whiche I revoke in my retracciouns: / as is the book
of Troilus; The book also of Fame; The book of the
XXV Ladies;[1] The book of the Duchesse; The book
of seint Valentynes day of the Parlement of Briddes;°
The tales of Caunterbury, thilke° that sounen into°
sinne; / The book of the Leoun;° and many another
book, if they were in my remembrance;° and many
a song and many a lecherous lay; that Crist for his
grete mercy foryeve me the sinne. / But of the trans-
lacion of Boece de Consolacione,[2] and othere bokes
of Legendes of seintes, and omelies,° and moralitee,
and devocioun, / that thanke I oure lord Jesu Crist
and his blisful moder and alle the seintes of hevene;
/ bisekinge hem that they from hennes forth,° unto
my lyves ende, sende me grace to biwayle° my giltes,
and to studie to° the salvacioun of my soule; and
graunte me grace of verray penitence,° confessioun
10 and satisfaccioun to doon° in this present lyf, / thurgh°
the benigne grace of him that is king of kinges and
preest over alle preestes, that boghte° us with the
precious blood of his herte; / so that I may been oon
of hem at the day of dome° that shulle be saved.
Qui cum patre, & c.[3]

**Here is ended the book of the Tales of Caunterbury, com-
piled by Geffrey Chaucer, of° whos soule Iesu Crist have mercy.
Amen.**

Glosses: listen to / read (it) / pleases them / from / understanding / attribute / fault / unskillfulness / very willingly / the skill / instruction / purpose / beseech / meekly / forgive / sins / especially for / compositions / concerning / Birds / those same / tend toward / Lion / memory / homilies / henceforth / bewail / for / true penance / perform / through / redeemed / Doomsday / on

1. I.e., *The Legend of Good Women.*
2. Boethius's *De Consolatione [Philosophiae].*
3. Who (lives) with the Father, etc. (the benedictional close).

SIR WILLIAM THORPE

[On Pilgrimage] †

* * *

And than he [Archbishop Arundel] said to me, "What
saist thou to the thirde poynte that is certified° against   *officially testified*
the: preching openly in Shrewisbery that pilgrimage is
not lefull?° And over this thou saidist that those men   *lawful, permissible*
and women that go on pilgrimagis to Canturbery, to
Beverley, to Karlington, to Walsingame° and to ony   *Walsingham*
soche other placis, ar acursed and made foolisch,
spending their goodes in wastc."

And I said, "Sir, by this certificacion I am accused
to you that I sholde teache that no pilgrimage is lefull.
But I said never thus, for I knowe that ther be trew
pilgrimagis and lefull and full plesaunt to God. And
therfore, sir, how so ever myne enemies have certified
you of me, I tolde at Shrewisbery of two maner of pilgrimagis."

And the Archebisshop said to me, "Whome callest
thou trewe pilgrimes?"

And I said, "Sir, with my protestacion,° I call them   *solemn, public affir-*
trew pilgremis travelyng toward the blisse of heven   *mation*
which—in the state, degre, or ordre that God calleth
them—doo besy them° feithfully for to occupie all their   *themselves*
wittes, bodely and gostely,° to knowe trewly and to keape   *spiritual*
feithfully the biddinges of God, hatyng and fleyng all
the seven dedely synnes and every braunche of them;
reulyng them verteuously, as it is said before, with all
their wittes; doyng discretely, wilfully, and gladly all
the werkis of mercy, bodely and gostely,[1] after° their   *according to*
connyng° and power; ablyng them to° the gyftes of the   *knowledge / preparing*
Holy Goste; disposing them to receyve in their soules   *themselves for*

---

† Text based on *The examinacion of master W.*
Thorpe, preste (Antwerp: J. van Hoochstraten, 1530).
The work is William Thorpe's own account of the
inquiry conducted against him by Thomas Arundel,
archbishop of Canterbury, for preaching Lollard
doctrines in a sermon in Shrewsbury in 1407. The
entire text, in a modernized version, is printed in
A. W. Pollard, *Fifteenth-Century Prose and Verse*
(New York: Cooper Square Publishers, 1964) 97–
167.

1. Thorpe is referring to the traditional categories of
the seven corporal acts of mercy (feeding the hungry,
giving drink to the thirsty, clothing the naked, helping the sick, visiting the prisoner, sheltering the
homeless, burying the dead) and the seven spiritual
acts of mercy (admonishing the sinner, instructing
the ignorant, counseling the doubtful, comforting
the afflicted, bearing wrongs patiently, forgiving
injuries, praying for the living and the dead).

and to holde therin the right blessinges of Christe; beseyng them° to knowe and to kepe the sevene principall vertues. And so than they shall obteyne herethorow° grace for to use thankfully to God all the condicions of charite; and than they shall be moovyd with the good spirite of God for to examyne ofte and diligently their conscience that nother wilfully nor wittingly they erre in ony article of beleve,° havyng continually, as frailte will suffer,° all their besinesse to drede and to flee the offence of God, and to loove over all thing and to seke ever to doo his plesaunt will.

    "Of these pilgremis," I said "what so ever goode thoughte that they ony tyme thinke, what verteuous worde that they speake, and what frutefull worke that they worke: every soche thoughte, worde, and werke is a steppe noumbered of God toward hym into hevene. Thes forsaid pilgremis of God delyte sore° whan they heare of seyntis or of verteuous men and women: how they forsoke wilfully the prosperite of this lyfe; how they withstode the suggestion of the fende; how they restreined their fleschly lustes; how discrete they wer in their penaunce doying; how pacient they wer in all their adversites; how prudent they wer in counseling of men and women, moovyng them to hate all synnes and to flye° them, and to shame ever greatly thereof, and to love all vertues and to drawe to them, ymaginyng how Christe and his folowers—by example of hym—suffered skornis and sclaunders; and how paciently they abode° and toke the wrongfull manasyng° of tyrauntis; how homely° they wer and servisable to poore men to relieve and comforte them, bodely and gostely, after their power and connyng; and how devote they wer in praiers, how fervent they wer in hevenly desyres, and how they absented them fro spectacles of veyne seyngis° and hearingis; and how stable they wer to lett° and to destroye all vices, and how laborious and joifull they wer to sowe and to plante vertues. Thes hevenly condicions and soche other have the pilgremis, or endever them for to have, whose pilgrimagie God acceptith."

    And ageyne I saide, "As their werkis shew, the moste parte of men and women that go now on pilgrimagis have not thes forsaid condicions, nor loveth to besy them feithfully for to have. For as I well know syns I have full ofte assaide:° examyne who so ever will twentie of thes pilgremis, and he shall not fynde thre men or women that knowe surely° a commaundment of God,°

---

busying themselves

through these (actions)

faith
allow

greatly

flee, avoid

endured / hostility
kindly, modest

idle sights
prevent, hinder

tested (it)

correctly / one of the

nor can say their Pater Noster and Ave Maria nor their Credo redely, in ony maner of langage.[2] And as I have learnid and also know somwhat by experience of thes same pilgremis tellyng the cause why that many men and women go hither and thither now on pilgrimagis, it is more for the helthe of their bodies than of their soules, more for to have richenese and prosperite of this worlde than for to be enryched with vertues in their soules, more to have here worldely and fleschely frendship than for to have frendship of God and of his seintis in heven. For what so ever thing man or woman dothe, the frendship of God nor of ony other seynt can not be hadde without keaping of Goddis commaundementis.

"Forther with my protestacion, I say now as I said in Shrewisbery: though they that have fleschely willes travell fer their bodies° and spende mekill° money to seake and to visite the bonys or ymagis (as they say they do) of this seynte or of that, soche pilgrimage-goyng is nother praisable nor thankefull to God nor to ony seinte of God, syns in effect all soche pelgrimes despise God and all his commaundmentis and seyntis. For the commaundmentis of God they will nother knowe nor keape, nor conforme them to lyve verteuosly by example of Christe and of his seyntis. Wherfor, syr, I have prechid and taucht openly—and so I purpose all my lyfetime to do, with Gods helpe—saing that soche fonde° people wast blamefully Gods goods in their veyne pilgrimagis, spending their goodes upon vicious hostelars,° which ar ofte unclene° women of their bodies, and at the leste those goodes with the which thei sholde doo werkis of mercie, after Goddis bidding, to poore nedy men and women.

"Thes poore mennis goodes and their lyvelode° thes runnars about offer to riche priestis, which have mekill more lyvelode than they neade. And thus those goodes they waste wilfully and spende them unjustely, ageinst Goddis bidding, upon straungers, with which thei sholde helpe and releve, after Goddis will, their poore nedy neighbours at home. Ye, and over° this foly, ofte tymes diverse men and women of thes runners thus madly hither and thither in to pilgrimage borowe hereto° other mennis goodes—ye, and some tyme they stele mennis goodes hereto—and they pay them never agein.

"Also, sir, I know well that whan diverse men and

---

2. I.e., either in Latin or in the vernacular.

women will go thus after their own willes, and fynding
out one pilgrimage, they will orden° with them before°   *arrange / in advance*
to have with them bothe men and women that can well
synge wanton songes; and some other pilgremis will have
with them baggepipes, so that every towne that they
come throwe°—what with the noyse of their syngyng,   *through*
and with the sounde of their piping, and with the jan-
gelyng of their Canterbery bellis, and with the barkyng
out of doggis after them—that they make more noyse
than if the kyng came there awaye° with all his clarions°   *along that route /*
and many other menstrelles. And if thes men and   *trumpeters*
women be a monethe out in their pilgrimage, many of
them shall be, an halfe yeare after, greate jangelers,°   *chatterers*
tale tellers, and lyers."

And the Archebishop said to me, "Leude losell,° thou   *Ignorant scoundrel*
seest not ferre ynough in this mater, for thou consider-
est not the great travell° of pilgremys, therfore thou bla-   *travail*
mest that thing that is praisable. I say to the° that it is   *thee*
right well done that pilgremys have with them bothe
syngers and also pipers, that whan one of them that
goeth barfote striketh his too upon a stone and hurteth
hym sore and maketh hym to blede, it is well done that
he or his felow begyn than a songe, or els take out of
his bosome a baggepype, for to dryve away with soche
myrthe the hurte of his felow. For with soche salace°   *solace*
the travell and werinesse off pylgremes is lightely and
merily broughte forthe."°   *relieved*

And I said, "Sir, Seynt Paule teacheth men to wepe
with them that wepe [Romans 12.15]."

And the Archebishoppe saide, "What janglist thou
ageinst mennis devocion? Whatsoever thou or soch other
say, I say that the pilgrimage that now is used° is to   *practiced*
them that doo it a praysable and a good meane to come
the rather° to grace. But I holde the unable to know   *sooner, more readily*
this grace, for thou enforsest the to lett° the devocion   *attemptest to hinder*
of the people, syns by authorite of Holy Scripture men
maye lefully have and use soche solace as thou repro-
vest. For David in his laste psalme teacheth me° to have   *one*
diverse instrumentes of musike for to prayse therwith
God."

And I saide, "Sir, by the sentence° of diverse doc-   *according to the under-*
tours expounding the psalmes of David, the musike and   *standing*
menstrelcy that David and other seyntes of the olde lawe
spake of owe° now nother to be taken nor used by the   *ought*
letter.° But thes instrumentes with theire musike ought   *literally*
to be interpreted gostely, for all those figures are called

vertues and grace, with which vertues men shold please
God and prayse his name.[3] For Saynt Paule saith, 'All
soche thynges befell to them in figure.' Therfore, sir, I
understonde that the letter of this psalme of David, and
of soche other psalmes and sentences, dothe slee them
that take them now letterally. This sentence I understond, sir, Christ approveth him self putting out the
menstrelles or° that he wolde quycken° the deade dam-   *before / bring to life*
sell."

And the Archebishop saide to me, "Leude losell, is
it not lefull to us to have organes in the chirche for to
worship therwithall God?"

And I said, "Ye, syr, by mannys ordynaunce;° but by   *decree*
the ordinaunce of God a goode sermonne to the peo-
ples understondyng were mekill more plesaunt to God."

And the Archebisshoppe sayde that organes and goode
delectable songe quyckened and sharpened more men-
nys wyttes than sholde ony sermonne. But I said, "Sir,
lusty° men and worldly lovers delyte and covete and   *pleasure-loving*
travell to have all theire wittes quickened and sharp-
ened with diverse sensible° solace; but all the feithfull   *sensual*
lovers and folowers of Christe have all their delyte to
heare Goddis worde, and to understond it truely, and
to worke therafter faithfully and continually. For no
doutc, to dreade to offende God and to love to please
him in all thing quyckeneth and sharpeneth all the wittes
of Christes chosen people, and ableth° them so to grace   *aids*
that they joye greatly to withdrawe their eares and all
their wittes and membres frome all worldly delyte and
frome all fleschly solace. For Seynt Jerome, as I thinke,
saith, 'Nobody may joye with this worlde and reigne
with Christe.' "

And the Archebishop, as yf he had ben displeased
with myne answere, said to his clerkes, "What gesse ye
this ydiote will speke ther wher he hath none dreade,
syns he speaketh thus nowe, here in my presence? Well,
well, by God thou shalt be ordened for!"°   *dealt with*

*   *   *

3. By "figures" Thorpe means the details in Psalm
150 that invite an allegorical rather than a literal
reading. His interpretation is consistent with many
medieval "doctours," such as St. Augustine, who in
his *Enarrationes in psalmos* explains that the instruments named in the psalm refer to various aspects of
the human soul or the community of souls that
worship God. They are "figures" of virtues. After
citing 1 Corinthians 10.11, Thorpe alludes to Paul's
famous teaching that "the letter killeth, but the spirit
giveth life" (2 Corinthians 3.6). His allusion to
Christ putting out the minstrels refers to Matthew
9.23–25, part of the story of Jairus's daughter, which
is told more fully, but without the mention of
minstrels, in Mark 5.22–43.

THE PORTRAITS

THOMAS WIMBLEDON

[On the Estates] †

My dere ferendis, ye shullen undirstonde that Crist
Jesus, auctour and doccour° of trewthe, in his book of   *teacher*
the gospel liknyng° the kyngdom of hevene to an   *comparing*
housholdere, seith on this maneres:° "Lik is the kyng-   *in this way*
dom of hevene to an housholdynge man that wente
out first on the morwe° to hire werkemen into his vine.°   *morning / vineyard*
Also aboute the thridde,° sixte, nyenthe, and elevene   *third*
houris he wente out and fond men stondynge ydel°   *idle*
and sey to hem: Go yee into my vyne and that right
is° I wole yeve° yow. Whanne the day was ago, he   *what is just / give*
clepid° his styward and heet° to yeve eche man a peny."   *called / commanded (him)*
To spiritual undirstondyng this housholdere is oure
lord Jesu Crist, that "is heed of the houshold of holi
chirche." [1] And thus he clepith men in diverse houris
of the day, that is in diverse ages of the world; os° in   *as*
tyme of lawe of kynde° he clepide by enspirynge Abel,   *nature*
Ennok, Noe,° and Abraham; in tyme of the olde lawe   *Noah*
Moyses, David, Ysaye,° and Jeremie;° and in tyme of   *Isaiah / Jeremiah*
grace apostelis, martiris, and confessoures,[2] and vir-
gines. Also he clepeth men in diverse ages: summe in
childhod, as Jon Baptist; summe on stat° of wexenge,°   *in the process / maturing*
as Jon the Evangelist; summe in stat of manhod, as
Petir and Andrew; and summe in old age, as Gamaliel
and Josep of Aramathie.° And alle these he clepith to   *Joseph of Arimathea*
travayle on his vyne, that is the chirche, and that on
diverse maneres.

For right as yee seeth that in tilienge° of the mate-   *tilling*
rial vine there beeth diverse laboreris: for summe kut-
tyn awey the voyde° braunchis; summe maken forkes°   *unproductive / forked stakes*
and rayles to beren up the veyne; and summe diggen
awey the olde erthe fro the rote and leyn° there fat-   *put*
tere.° And alle theise offices° ben so nescessarie to the   *richer (soil) / duties*
veyne that yif eny of hem fayle° it schal harme gretly   *are lacking*
or distroye the vyne. For but yif° the vine be kut, he°   *unless / it*

† Text based on *Wimbledon's Sermon "Redde Rationem Villicationis Tue": A Middle-English Sermon of the Fourteenth Century*, ed. Ione Kemp Knight (Pittsburgh: Duquesne UP, 1967), 61–66. Reprinted with permission of the publisher. This opening passage of the sermon is based on the parable of the vineyard (Matthew 20.1–10).
1. Colossians 1.18.
2. Christians who heroically affirm their faith in the face of persecution but escape martyrdom.

schal wexe wilde; but yif she be rayled, she shal be overgoo° [*overrun*] with netles and wedis; and but yif the rote be fettid° [*enriched*] with donge, she for feblenesse shold wexe barayne.

Ryght so in the chirche beeth nedeful° [*necessary*] thes thre offices: presthod, knyghthod, and laboreris. To prestis it fallith° to hatte away the voide braunchis of synnis [*· · / ·*] with the swerd of here tonge. To knyghtis it fallith to lette° wrongis and theftis to be do,° [*stop / from being done*] and to mayntene Goddis lawe and hem that ben techeris ther-of, and also to kepe the lond fro enemyes of other londes. And to laboreris it falleth to travayle bodily and with here sore swet geten out of the erthe bodily liflode° [*sustenance*] for hem and for other parties. And these statis° beth also° [*estates / so*] nedeful to the chirche that non may wel ben withouten other. For yif presthod lackede,° the puple for defaute° [*were missing / lack*] of knowyng of Goddis lawe shulde wexe wilde on vices and deie gostly.° [*spiritually*] And yif the knythod lackid and men to reule the puple by lawe and hardnesse,° [*resoluteness*] theves and enemies shoden so encresse that no man sholde lyven in pes.° [*peace*] And yif the laboreris weren not, bothe prestis and knyghtis mosten bicome acremen° and heerdis,° [*ploughmen / shepherds*] and ellis° [*or otherwise*] they sholde for defaute of bodily sustenaunce deie.

And herfore seith a gret clerk,° [*scholar*] Avycenne,[3] that every unresonable beest, yif he have that that kynde° [*Nature*] hath ordeyned for hym as kynde hath ordeyned it, he is sufficiaunt to lyve by hymself withouten eny other of the same kynde.° [*species / or*] As yif there were but one hors other° oon sheep in the world, yit yif he hadde graas and corn° [*grain*] as kynde hath ordeyned for suche bestes, he shulde lyve wel inow.° [*enough*] But yif ther were but oon man in the world, though he hadde all that good that is ther-in, yit for defaute he scholde die, or his life shulde be worse than yif he were nought.° [*did not exist*] And the cause is this: for thyng that kynde ordeyneth for a mannis sustinaunce, withoutyn other araying° [*preparation*] than it hath of kynde, acordith° [*suits*] nought to hym. As though a man have corn as it cometh fro the erthe, yit it is no mete acordynge to° hym into° [*suitable food for / until*] it be by mannis craft chaungid into bred. And though he have flesche other fissche, yit while it is raw, as kynde ordeyneth it, forto° [*until*] it be by mannis travayle sothen,° [*boiled*] rosted, other bake, it acordith not to mannis liflode. And ryght so wolle° [*wool*] that the sheep ber-

3. This paragraph follows closely the beginning of Avicenna's *Liber de anima seu sextus de naturalibus*, part 5, chapter 1.

ith mot,° by many diverse craftis and travaylis, be   *must*
chaungid er° it be able to clothe eny man. And certis°   *before / certainly*
o° man bi hymsilf shulde nevere don alle thise labouris.   *one*
And therfore seith this clerk, it is nede that summe
beth acremen,° summe bakeris, summe makeris of   *plowmen*
cloth, and summe marchaundis to fecche that that o
lond fauteth° from another ther it is plente.   *lacks*

    And certis this shulde be o cause why every staat
shul love other and men of o craft shulde neither hate
ne despise men of another craft, sith° they beth so   *since*
nedeful everych to other. And ofte thilke° craftis that   *those*
semen most unhonest myghthen worst° be forbore.°   *least well / dispensed with*
And o thyng y dar wel seye: that he that is neither
traveylynge in this world on prayeris and prechynge
for helpe of the puple, as it fallith to prestis; neither°   *nor*
in fyghtinge ayenis tyrauntis and enemyes, as it fallith
to knyghtis; neither travaylynge on the erthe, as it fallith to laboreris—whanne the day of his rekenyng°   *accounting*
cometh (that is, the ende of this lif), ryght as he lyvede
here withoutyn travayle, so he shal there lacke the
reward of the peny (that is, the endeles joye of hev-
ene). And as he was here lyvynge aftir noon° staat ne   *according to no*
ordre, so he shal be put thanne "in that place that
noon ordre is inne, but everelastynge horrour"[4] and
sorwe (that is, in helle).

WILLIAM LANGLAND

[On Monks] †

*   *   *

Amonges rightful° religiouse,° this reule schulde
    be holde: *righteous / members of religious orders*
Gregorie, the grete clerke° and the goed pope,   *scholar*
Of religioun the reule reherseth° in his morales,[1]   *expounds*
And seyth it in ensaumple° for° thei schulde
    do° there-after;   *as an example / so that / act*
5 "Whenne fissches failen° the flode° or the fresche water,   *lack / stream*
Thei deyen for drouthe° whanne thei drie ligge.°   *drought / lie*
Right so," quod Gregorie, "religioun roileth,°   *roams about*

---

4. Job 10.22.
† Text based on *The Vision of William concerning Piers the Plowman*, ed. Walter W. Skeat, 2 vols. (1886; London: Oxford UP, 1965) I.308–10: B-text,

Passus X, 291–320. This version of the poem is thought to have been written ca. 1377–79.
1. The *Moralia*, one of the best-known works of Pope Gregory the Great (d. 604).

Sterveth° and stynketh and steleth lordes almesses,°   *Dies / alms*
That oute of covent° and cloystre coveyten° to libbe."°   *convent / desires / live*
10 For if hevene be on this erthe and ese° to any soule,   *ease, rest*
It is in cloistere or in scole, be° many skilles° I fynde.   *for / reasons*
For in cloistre cometh no man to chide ne to fighte,
But alle is buxumnesse° there and bokes to rede and to lerne.   *obedience*
In scole there is scorne but if° a clerke wil lerne;   *unless*
15 And grete love and lykynge, for eche of hem loveth other.
    Ac° now is Religioun a ryder, a rowmer° bi° stretes,   *But / roamer / through*
A leder of lovedayes² and a lond-bugger,°   *land-buyer*
A priker° on a palfray fro manere° to manere,   *rider / manor*
An heep of houndes at his ers,° as° he a lorde were.   *arse / as if*
20 And but if his knave° knele, that shal his cuppe brynge,   *servant*
He loureth on° hym and axeth him who taughte hym curteisye.   *scowls at*
Litel had lordes to done to gyve londe fram her heires³
To religious, that have no reuthe° though it reyne
    on her auteres.°   *do not care / altars*
In many places ther hii persones ben° be° hemself
    at ese,   *where they are parsons / by*
25 Of the pore have thei no pite—and that is her charite—
Ac thei leten hem as° lordes, her londe lith°
    so brode.°   *behave like / extends / widely*
    Ac there shal come a kyng and confesse° yow religiouses,   *be a confessor to*
And bete° yow, as the Bible telleth, for brekynge of yowre reule,   *chastise*
And amende monyales,° monkes and chanouns,°   *nuns / canons*
30 And putten hem to her penaunce, *ad pristinum statum ire.*⁴
                              * * *

JOHN GOWER

[On Monks] †

                              * * *

We now consider the estate of the religious orders, and first those that
hold property. They should be attentive in praying to the glorious God,

---

2. A judge on lovedays, days when disputes were settled out of court. Cf. *General Prologue*, l. 258.
3. Lords have little reason to transfer property from their heirs.
4. In order to return (them) to their former state (within the Rule).
† Translated by Glending Olson, from *Mirour de l'omme*, lines 20833–92 and 20953–1060, *The Works of John Gower*, ed. G. C. Macaulay (Oxford: Clarendon Press, 1899–1902) I.235–37. These two excerpts contain the closest parallels to Chaucer's portrait of the Monk; they constitute about half of Gower's criticism of the monastic orders. The poem, whose title means *Mirror of Man*, is a didactic poem in French, of which 29,444 lines survive; it was written ca. 1376–78. It begins with an allegory on the origins of sin, treats at length the seven vices and seven virtues, and then offers a critical survey of London life in the 1370s. Chaucer was a close friend of Gower, naming him as one of two persons legally authorized to act on his behalf during his second trip to Italy in 1378 and co-dedicating the *Troilus and Criseyde* to him ("O moral Gower") and the "philosophical Strode."

within their cloisters and monasteries, for us secular people. That is the function of their order, for which they are abundantly endowed with a full measure of goods so that they do not desire to seek elsewhere for money. St. Augustine says in his teaching that just as a fish lives only in water, so Religion must lead its life according to the rule of the convent, fully obedient and cloistered. For if it lives in the world, then it alters the nature of the order that was first established, and consequently respect for the profession is lost.

In following the original order, monks took vows against the pleasures of the flesh and endured the pain of a harsh life. But now those observances have been completely abandoned. Gluttony guards all the doors so that hunger and thirst do not enter in there to make the fat paunches lean. With fur cloaks they have kept out the agonies of cold weather, for they do not wish to make its acquaintance. The old rule regularly ate fish, but this one wants to change that: when meat that has been finely chopped or well pounded in a mortar is prepared and served, the new rule maintains that such ground meat is not flesh. It hopes to deceive God but is itself deceived, for it cherishes the belly so much that rather than lose a single meal, which might make the body grow thinner, it neglects the well-being of the soul. I do not know if the monks dance or joust, but I know well that when one of them takes his large flagon filled with wine, he downs it with great boisterousness and says that is the proper rule. I do not mean St. Augustine's: it is the rule of Robin,[1] who leads the life of a raven, searching first for what he can gulp down to fill himself and giving no thought to his neighbor, just the way a mastiff devours everything down to the crumbs and crust. * * *

The monk who has been made guardian or steward of any outside property is not a good cloisterer, for then he needs a horse and saddle to get around the countryside, and he spends lavishly. He takes the best part of the grain for himself and leaves the chaff for others, such as peasants; and thus the foolish, proud monk behaves like a lord. But an empty barn and a full belly do not yield an even balance. When he is guardian of an estate, the monk says "Everything is ours" out of twisted charity; he speaks the truth in part, but only a little, for with his wicked appetite he wants for himself more than what seven others get. Surely the cloister is better for such a guardian than ownership of property, which only takes income away from others. As St. Bernard says, it is repugnant to see an overseer in a monk's habit. The monk who acts this way is half worldly, and he comes close to apostasy when he has taken possession of the world again and dispossessed himself of the cloister. I do not know how he can justify himself for this failure of rule, nor do I think that his control of land and income can be security for him before God, to whom he first pledged his faith when he became a monk.

St. Jerome tells us that the filthiness of the habit a monk wears is an outward sign that he is without pride and haughtiness, that his inner spirit is of a pure white spotlessness. But our monk of today regularly seeks fancy

---

1. Robin is a standard medieval name for a man of the lower classes and often carries the suggestion of low morals as well. It is the name of Chaucer's Miller and, in the *Miller's Tale*, of John's servant.

adornment for his body and disfigures his soul. Although he wears the habit of suffering, he also has, in his vanity, a coat adorned with fur. There is a story that a great nobleman loved by God dressed himself in wretched hair-cloth when King Manasses married his daughter; even on that occasion he would not sacrifice his simplicity but rather directed his actions more to pleasing God than man. Thus he set an example for others: one should not attend to the body so much that he becomes proud. I do not know how monks will react to this story, but the example should disquiet that monk who behaves luxuriously because of worldliness. He seeks not haircloth but the very best wool he can find, trimmed with gray squirrel fur, for he disdains fleece. Nor does he forget a silver pendant but gaily displays it hanging from his hood on his breast. That is the kind of simplicity we see now in monks and their dress.

A monk should nurture his religion through discretion, humility, and simplicity; but ours does not want to do that. He hates to hear the name of monk, which he vowed to take, even though his mother was a shepherdess and his father without high rank, perhaps a servant. But when those of low status rise to the heights, and poverty becomes wealthy, there is nothing in the world so villainous. The monk who seeks property sins greatly against the rule, but he has nevertheless amassed great sums for himself, wealth which he procured from the world just like a merchant. And moreover, to entertain himself, he goes along the river with game birds, falcon and molted hawk, with swift greyhounds as well, and fine high-spirited horses—all that is missing is a wife. And on the subject of wives, what can I do but wonder, for I have heard about the children that our monk accumulated while he was running around here and there, day after day. But they cannot inherit from him, so he must pass along great sums in order to enrich them. I leave it to you to decide if this is the way charity acts.

* * *

Wycliffite Estates Criticism †

[On Merchants]

* * *

Also marchauntis and riche men of this wikked world fallen in moche ypocrise; for thei traveilen nyght and day, bi watir and lond, in cold and in hete, bi false sotilis° and cautelis° and grete sweringes nedles° and   *tricks / wiles / needless*

† Text based on *The English Works of John Wyclif Hitherto Unprinted*, ed. F. D. Matthew, 2nd ed., EETS o.s. 74 (London, 1902) 24–25, 154. Wyclif (ca. 1329–84) was briefly Master of Balliol College, Oxford (1361), and as philosopher, theologian, and reformer, a most controversial figure in his time. He was first prosecuted for heresy in 1377, and again in 1382, when he was condemned for ten heresies and fourteen errors. But his criticism of corruption in the church and in the estates expressed attitudes shared by many of his contemporaries, including those—a majority—who did not necessarily interest themselves in, or subscribe to, his views on the powers of the Pope, "dominion by Grace," or his denial of the truth of Transubstantiation. He was responsible for the first translation of the Bible into English, a work accomplished in the last quarter of the fourteenth century.

false, for to gete muche drit° or muk of this world, to   *dirt, filth*
gete riche wyves, and purchase° londis and rentis,° and   *acquire / revenues*
dewelle° in pore mennus dette after that thei han des-   *linger*
ceyved hem in byynge of here catel.° And yit ben° so   *goods / they are*
bisi in thought and speche, in goyng and rydyng about-
en this muk, that unnethe° may thei onys° thenke on   *scarcely / once*
God and han mynde of° here false robberie that thei   *reflect on*
usen° bi false wettes° and mesures to amende hem.° Yif *practice / weights / prosper*
alle here° bisinesse and love goo thus wrongly to the   *their*
world and nought or to litel to hevene and hevenely
thingis, thei failen foule of° holy lif; and yit holden   *in*
hem self holy and coveiten to ben holden holy of° other   *by*
men, and ben wode° yif men speken treuly ayenst here   *mad, angry*
cursed synnes. But certes this is ypocrisie.

[On Pardoners and Priests]

Thei [curates, clergymen in charge of a parish]
assenten° to pardoners disceyvynge the peple in feith   *consent*
and charite and worldly goodis for to have part of here
gederynge,° and letten° prestis to preche° the gospel for *winnings / prevent / from*
drede laste° here synne and ypocrisie be knowen and   *preaching / lest*
stoppid. For whanne there cometh a pardoner with
stollen bullis and false relekis,° grauntynge mo yeris of   *relics*
pardon than comen bifore domes day for yevynge° of   *giving*
worldly catel° to riche placis where is no nede, he schal   *goods*
be sped° and resceyved of° curatis for to have part of   *aided / received by*
that° he getith. But a preste that wole telle the trewthe   *what*
to alle men withouten glosynge° and frely withouten   *glossing, distorting*
beggynge of° the pore peple, he schal be lettid by sotil   *from*
cavyllacions° of mannus lawe, for drede last° he touche   *subtle cavils / lest*
the sore of here conscience and cursed lif. And this
pardoner schalle telle of more power than evere Crist
grauntid to Petir or Poul or ony apostle, to drawe the
almes fro pore bedrede° neigheboris that ben knowen   *bedridden*
feble and pore, and to gete it to hem self and wasten it
ful synfulli in ydelnesse and glotonye and lecherie, and
senden gold out of oure lond to riche lordis and housis
where is no nede, and make oure lond pore by many
sotile weies. And here bi° the peple is more bold to   *hereby*
lien° stille in her synne, and weneth° not to have as   *remain / think*
myche thank and reward of Crist for to do° here almes   *give*
to pore feble men—as Crist biddith in the gospel—as
whanne thei don here almes to riche housis aftir graunt°   *following the advice*
of synful foolis. And this is opyn errour ayenst Cristene
feith.

The Knight's Tale

The *Knight's Tale* is an adaptation of Boccaccio's *Teseida* (written ca. 1339–41). At times Chaucer translated it closely; at times he condensed major sections into a few lines. The result is a narrative less than one-fourth as long as Boccaccio's that turns his lengthy story of war and love into a more ritualized, patterned, philosophical romance. The three selections from the *Teseida* printed here correspond to lines 175–328 (the young knights' reactions when they first see Emily), 1109–92 and 1509–79 (the temple of Mars and Arcite's prayer), and 2109–216 (Theseus's speech on Arcite's death). Boccaccio wrote a set of notes to the *Teseida*, mainly to explain his classical references and poetic locutions, but it is uncertain that Chaucer's manuscript included them. We have printed the notes to the section on the temple of Mars, however, since they furnish important evidence of medieval habits of allegorization with which Chaucer was familiar.

In certain speeches of the young knights, and in the final speech of Theseus, Chaucer used material from Boethius's *Consolation of Philosophy*. The passages we print here are from Chaucer's own translation of this immensely influential book; those phrases in italics represent places where he translated glosses to Boethius as well as the original text.

GIOVANNI BOCCACCIO

From *Il Teseida* †

From Book 3

1

When Juno's wrath against ravaged Thebes had somewhat abated, Mars returned with his Furies to the cold regions. Therefore, I shall now sing in gentler tones of Cupid and his battles. I entreat him to be present in what I set down about him.

2

May he imbue my verses with the potency which he instilled into the hearts of the imprisoned Thebans, so that my words may be a match for

† From *The Book of Theseus*, trans. Bernadette Marie McCoy (Sea Cliff: Teesdale Publishing Associates, 1974) 77–85, 171–74, 195–98, 313–16. For the Italian text, see Giovanni Boccaccio, *Teseida delle Nozze d'Emilia*, ed. Alberto Limentani (Verona: Mondadori, 1964).

their mad deeds. They were far removed from salutary suffering, until at last Love made them come to blows and He became displeasing to both of them and for one of them the bitter cause of death.

3

Therefore, the two Thebans, imprisoned in this fashion, in utter sorrow and engaged in little else than weeping, had already despaired of ever having a happy future. They often cursed the evil of their misfortune, and cursed even more the hour when they came into the world.

4

Very often they called on death to slay them, if that might avail. Almost a year had passed in this unhappy state of afffairs, when Venus in her bright heaven chose something else for them to sigh over. No sooner had she thought of it, than action followed on the intention.

First the season and then the manner in which Arcites and Palaemon fell in love with Emilia.

5

Phoebus sallying forth with his steeds was in that part of the heavens which belongs to the lowly beast that carried Europa without stopping to the place where her name still prevails. Venus stepped forth with him and climbed to those lovely mansions, and for this reason all the heaven of Ammon smiled, as he dallied for a time in Pisces.

6

Because of this fortunate position of the stars, the earth enjoyed charming vitality and clothed her lovely form anew with young grass and exquisite little flowers. The new shrubs adorned their limbs with boughs as the trees neared the time of their flowering and fruit-bearing to beautify the world.

7

And all the little birds began to sing about their loves, jubilant and merry among the leaves and the flowers. The animals could not conceal their love, but showed it, rather, in their outward behavior. And happy youths, ripe for love, felt passion glow hotter in their hearts than ever before.

8

Then beautiful young Emilia, as dawn broke each morning, entered alone into the garden which opened out from her room, drawn there by her own nature, not because she was bound by any love. Barefoot and clad in her shift, she entertained herself by singing amorous songs.

9

She led this life for many days, that artless and beautiful maiden, from time to time gathering a new rose from its thorns with her white hand and joining it to other flowers to weave a little garland for her blond head, until a novelty occurred one morning because of the loveliness of this child.

10

One fine morning, after she had arisen and had wound her blond tresses about her head, she descended into the garden as was her custom. There, seated on the grass, singing and taking her delight, blithesome and deftly she wove her garland with many flowers, all the while lightheartedly singing charming love lyrics with her angelic voice.

11

At the sound of that pretty voice, Arcites arose, for he was in the prison adjacent to the amorous garden, without saying anything to Palaemon. Longingly he opened the window to hear that song better. Then to see more easily who was singing, he put his head out a little between the iron bars.

12

The daylight was still somewhat faint, since the horizon still hid part of the sun, but not enough to prevent him with his limited view from discovering to his supreme delight what the young maiden was doing, although he did not know her yet. Looking at her face intently he said to himself: "She is from paradise."

13

As he turned back in he said softly: "O Palaemon, come and see. Venus has truly come down here. Do you not hear her singing? O, if I mean anything to you, come here quickly. I believe for certain that it will please you to see the angelic beauty down there which has descended to us from the sovereign heights."

14

Palaemon arose, for he already heard her with more sweetness than he believed, and he went to the window together with Arcites, and both in silence, to watch the goddess. When he saw her, he said in a bright voice:

"Surely, this is Cytherea. I have never seen anything so beautiful, so charming and so lovely."

15

Meanwhile, they enjoyed themselves, breathless and attentive, keeping their eyes and ears fixed on her, and marveling much over her and over the time they had lost in their grieving, time which had passed before they saw her. Arcites said: "O Palaemon, do you see what I behold in those beautiful immortal eyes?"

16

"What?" answered Palaemon. Arcites said: "I see in them the one who wounded the father of Phaeton because of Daphne, if I am not mistaken. In his hands he holds two golden arrows and now he is placing one on his bowstring as he looks at no one else but me. I do not know if it displeases him that I should look at what gives me so much pleasure."

17

"Indeed," answered Palaemon then, "I do see him. But I do not know if he has shot one arrow, for he does not have more than one in his hand now." Arcites said: "Yes, he has wounded me in such a way that pain will pierce my heart if I am not helped by that goddess." Then Palaemon, utterly astonished, cried out, "Alas, the other has wounded me."

18

At that "Alas!" the beautiful young lady turned around on her right breast and her eyes moved immediately to the little window. Then her face flushed for shame for she did not know who they were. Becoming bold, then, she rose to her feet with the flowers she had gathered and prepared to leave.

19

And as she turned away, she was not oblivious of that "Alas!" and although she was too young for mature love, still she understood what it meant. As it seemed to her that she knew that she was indeed liked, she took pleasure in it, and considered herself more beautiful, and now adorned herself the more every time she returned to the garden.

20

As soon as they saw Emilia leave, the two squires turned back in. They stood there for a while with their new thoughts, when Arcites began to speak first thus: "I do not know what cruel archer has shot an arrow into my heart, for it has taken my life. I feel myself gradually failing, enkindled, alas! by I know not what fire.

21

"And the image of that child will not leave my mind and I have no thought of anything else. Her form is so embedded in my heart and gives so much pleasure to my soul, that I would deem it the greatest good fortune to please her as she pleases me. Without that I do not believe I shall ever have peace."

22

Palaemon said: "The same thing that you are saying has happened to me. I do not want to experience it again ever, for I feel new pangs in my heart such as I do not believe I have ever felt before. I truly believe that that lord holds us in his power, just as I have heard it said many times, and that he is Love, the subtle thief of every noble heart.

23

"I tell you His captivity already weighs on me more heavily than that of Theseus. I feel much more anguish in my mind than I believe this god could inflict. Our great folly made us look out that window when such a lovely creature was singing, for my heart already consumes itself over love for her.

24

"I feel myself seized and bound by her. I do not find any hope for myself. On the contrary, I see myself imprisoned here and stripped of all my strength. Therefore, what can I do to please her? Nothing. Yet I shall die of this without fail. Now would to God I were dead! This would be my dearest and best comfort.

25

"O how good and how soothing would be the Aesculapian treatments for such a wound! It is said that he can bring broken bodies back to life. But what am I saying, for Apollo, who knew all human remedies, could not find a medicine that could help him when he was pierced by just such an arrow."

26

So the two new lovers talked in this fashion and each spoke words of comfort to the other. They did not know if this girl was a goddess of the holy kingdoms come to dwell on earth, or a lady of this world, for her singing and her beauty made them unable to decide. Because they were afflicted by pain and did not know who had taken hold of them, they grieved the more.

27

And the raging winds that pour out of the Siculan caves when Aeolus opens them and that are so furious as they explore now the lower, and now the higher regions, were nothing to the harmonious sighs that these two emitted from their inmost parts, but with small voices, because the wound that pierced them was still fresh.

28

And she continued her walks in the beautiful garden for her recreation, sometimes alone and sometimes in company. She always secretly turned her eyes toward the window from which she had first heard Palaemon's "alas." And she did not do this because she was urged on by love, but to see if others were looking at her.

29

If she saw that she was being observed, she began to sing and to entertain herself in her delightful and clear voice, almost as if she were unaware. She trod the grass among the shrubs with tiny, lady-like steps and clad in modesty, all the while contriving to give more pleasure to whoever was watching her.

30

She was not prompted by any thought or feeling of love, but by vanity, which women have innate in their hearts in making others see their beauty. Almost stripped of any other worth, they are satisfied to be praised for beauty, and by contriving to please by their charm, they enslave others while they keep themselves free.

31

Every morning with the first appearance of dawn, the two lovers arose and looked into the garden to see if she had come whose divine countenance filled them with immeasurable love. As long as she remained in the garden, they could not rise from their places.

32

They thought that if they gazed at her hard enough they would sate the ardent thirst of their yearning and soften their grievous pangs, but they were held the more tightly in the chains of the strong god Cupid. Now they showed a happy countenance and now a pitiful one as they gazed at her, solely to give her as much pleasure as she gave them.

33

As they watched from day to day, the fire of love went on increasing, just as the serpent's tooth wounds someone with a small bite at first, and then the poison spreads rapidly, infecting one member, then another, and still another in succession, until it covers the whole body.

34

They were so completely absorbed that every other thought gave way, and now it began to show in their faces because of their long vigils and the scant food that they ate. They blamed their condition on the fact that they were accustomed to joyous activity and games, whereas now they were prisoners. Thus they concealed the real reasons.

35

Now from sighing they advanced to weeping, and if it were not for the fact that they did not want to reveal their love, they would have frequently cried out in their anguish. This is how Love treats those to whom He is most obliged for service. Whoever has been captured by Him at some time and afflicted with similar pangs knows this.

36

Ancient Thebes and their own high lineage had faded from their memory. Their unhappiness and the injury they had received were also gone; that their life was unpleasant, and that they possessed great heritage had faded. Where these things used to be, they held Emilia only.

37

And it was not at all their greatest desire that Theseus should release them from prison, since they thought that then they would have to go into exile in some other country and would not be able to see or hear the flower of all the Amazon women again. It is true that what they wanted most was to be released and yet remain in Athens.

38

Worn out by love, therefore, they bore their ardor more easily when they saw this lady. Then, when she left, they returned to their earlier madness and often composed measured verse to comfort themselves in singing of her high worth. In this way they took some delight in their misfortune.

39

Because they still did not know who she was, they summoned one of their pages to them one day and Arcites addressed these words to him: "O tell me, for love's sake, dear friend, do you know who she is who showed herself to us the other day as she sang so clearly in the garden? Have you ever seen her elsewhere, or has she come down from heaven?"

40

The valet answered promptly: "She is Emilia, sister of the queen, and more charming than anyone in the world. Because she is very young, she comes safely to the garden without fail every morning. She sings better than Apollo. I have heard her already, and so I know it."

41

They said to one another: "He is telling the truth. It is certainly she who has stolen our hearts and turned our every thought to her. She has made each of us the host of plaints and sighs and severe torment and every other woe, so compellingly does the beauty which shines in her make us desire her."

42

So the two lovers passed the day in sighing and discontent, and when morning came, their martyrdom abated, as long as they beheld the sparkling eyes of Emilia, which made their desires grow more fervent every hour. So they lived while it was summertime, as much in sweetness as in grief.

43

But when Libra stripped the world of the beauty that Aries had bestowed, the two lovers lost the sweetness that used to assuage their fiery thirst; that is, they lost the sight of the sublime splendor which held them in the net of Love. And so they were left in bitter sorrow as they called for death constantly day and night.

44

The weather altered its look and the dew-laden air wept. The grass dried, and the trees were stripped bare, and the stormy tribe of Aeolus raced about, wandering here and there through the unhappy world. And so Emilia with her loving looks left the garden and stayed in her room all the while and took no notice of the weather.

45

Then the martyrdoms and the lamentations, the harsh torments and the painful anguish returned twofold to each of the two lovers, and they did not see or hear anything that pleased them. Thus they were all consumed by grievous pangs. Each one wanted to despair, but then, at the last moment, checked himself.

46

The sighs and sufferings of each were very great. They reached such a point that their imprisonment made them even more unhappy. Every day seemed like a hundred days to them until they might either die or be free. And they called on Emilia for their sole and only comfort and delight.

* * *

From Book 7

* * *

How the Thebans went to temples to pray to the gods to help them in the forthcoming battle. And first, Arcites in the temple of Mars.

22

It was already the day before the one on which the battle was to be fought, when Palaemon and Arcites went humbly and with pious sentiments to pray to the gods. Placing bright fires on their altars, they offered incense, and with fervent desires they prayed that the gods would help each of them in their needs on the following day.

23

But after he had visited the others and placed fire and incense everywhere, Arcites also returned to the temple of Mars and illuminated it much more than any of the others, and having sprinkled the finest distillations with solemn skill, he offered this prayer to Mars with a devout heart and great devotion.

Arcites' prayer to Mars.

24

"O strong God, you maintain your sacred dwelling in the snowy Bistonian realms, in dark places unfriendly to the sun,[1] and brimful of the woes you devised to humble the proud[2] brows of Earth's haughty sons. For they

1. Since they do not see the sun.
2. The poets write that Earth gave birth to the giants. How they were conquered by Jove and by Mars through force of arms is described above.

were left on the ground, every one in mortal cold, under the attacks you and your father Jove made against them.

25

"If by the will of the Most High, my youth and my prowess merit my being called one of yours, by that compassion[3] that Neptune had for you when you passionately enjoyed the beauty of Cytherea and were entrapped by Vulcan and made a spectacle to all the gods, I humbly pray you not to deny my requests.

26

"As you see, I am a young man, and mighty Love so binds me under His lordship for youthful beauty's sake, that I need all my strength and courage if I am to take delight in what my heart most desires. Without you I have little power. In fact, I can do nothing at all.

27

"Therefore, by that holy fire[4] which once burned you as it burns me now, help me. Honor me with your might in this coming palestral game.[5] Such a gift certainly would not seem slight to me, but the greatest good. Perform your task here, therefore. If I am the victor in this contest, I shall have the pleasure and you shall have the honor.

28

"Your everlasting temple will be decorated with the armor of my vanquished comrade and my own will hang there too and the reason for it will be inscribed there. Eternal fires will burn there always. I promise you my beard and those locks of my hair which remain unscathed[6] by the sword, if you allow me to win as I have asked."

How Arcites' Prayer reached Mars, and how and where his temple is built.

---

3. The poets write that when Mars was lying with Venus, whom he loved above everything, the Sun saw them and told Vulcan, god of fire, who was the husband of Venus, about it. On this account Vulcan, who was a clever craftsman, made a very strong net of iron and made it so fine that it could hardly be seen. Then he stretched it around his bed, so that anyone who got into it would be held fast. So it happened that one day, when he was not at home, Venus and Mars, without seeing the net, got into the bed naked. Here Vulcan found them when he returned and so showed them to all the gods, who laughed when they saw this. When Mars wanted to rise, he was not able to do so because of the net in which he found himself caught. Finally Neptune, god of the sea, felt sorry for them. He begged Vulcan so earnestly that Vulcan broke the net and let them go.

4. That is, the fire of love you bore to Venus.

5. What a palestral game is was explained above. Although this should not be done in this way, the author speaks in the poetic manner, for poets do not care if they call different things by the same name, only if they have some similarity in some respect, as they do in this.

6. That is, he had never shaved nor trimmed them.

29

Perhaps Mars was just then[7] engaged in polishing the rusty places in his great and horrible dwelling place when the pious Prayer of Arcites[8] arrived there, all tearful of countenance, to perform her assigned task. As soon as she saw the house of Mars, she became mute from fright.

30

For it is set in the Thracian fields,[9] under wintry skies, storm-tossed by continuous tempest, with hosts of everlasting clouds which are changed,

7. By this the author wants to show that Mars was at his ease when the Prayer of Arcites reached him, since men of arms, when they do not have anything else to do, have their armor furbished, or saddles adjusted, and similar things.

8. When two lords are at a distance from one another, many times there are intermediary ambassadors to make the intention of one known to the other. Prayer between us and God is just like this. Here the author imagines that the Prayer has the shape of a person, so that by making it a person he takes the occasion, consequently, to describe the house of Mars, as something seen by this Prayer.

9. In this part the author describes the house of Mars, concerning which many things must be considered minutely by whoever wants to set them forth in order. However, since it is very superficially touched on hereafter, we shall go over it with a summary explanation. And so that the exposition might be more readily understood, the author says that he intends to show four things here: The first is the kind of place where the house of Mars is situated; the second is how the house of Mars is constructed; the third is who is in the house of Mars; the fourth is with what the house of Mars is adorned. I say, therefore, first of all, that the house of Mars is in Thrace, in cold and cloudy places, full of water and of wind and of ice, wild and thronged with fruitless trees; and in shady places, unfriendly to the sun and full of confusion.

For an understanding of this it should be remarked that in every man there are two principal appetites. One of these is called the concupiscible appetite, whereby man desires and rejoices to have the things which, according to his judgment—whether it be rational or corrupt—are delightful and pleasing. The other is called the irascible appetite, whereby a man is troubled if delightful things are taken away or impeded, or when they cannot be had. This irascible appetite is found very readily in men of much blood, because blood of its nature is hot, and hot things lightly burst into flame for any small provocation. So it happens that men of much blood become angry easily although some, by very strong effort of reason, restrain and conceal their anger.

Since, as we have stated in another place, men in cold regions have more blood than elsewhere, the author says here that the temple of Mars, that is, this irascible appetite, is in Thrace, which is a province situated toward the north and very cold, and in which there are very cruel and warlike men. And

they are irascible because they have much blood. He says that it is cloudy, to show that anger obfuscates the counsel of reason, which he signifies further on by the sun's rays, which he says the house of Mars thrusts away from it. By the ice, he means the coldness of the soul of the angry man, who, overcome by enkindling of his wrath, becomes cruel and intransigent and without any charity. By the water he means the tears which the enraged shed many times out of wrath. He says, likewise, that the house of Mars is in a forest. By this he means the secret schemings to do harm that angry men sometimes harbor. By the barrenness of the forest he means the effects of wrath, which are not only thieves of the fruits of men's labors, but their wasters as well. And that is why it is that in such a forest there is neither shepherd nor beast, since the angry man does not govern himself or others. And therefore the habitation of Mars in such a place has been shown, however briefly.

A look at the second matter, that is, how this habitation or house of Mars is constructed, follows. He says that it is all sparkling with steel, and has gates of diamond and columns of iron. By the steel, he means the hardness of the stubbornness of the angry man, and this shows that it is the covering of the house, because he says that the columns are of iron. And he says that when this steel reflects, it chases away from itself the light of the sun, and deservedly, because if this steel should soften so as to let the light of the sun pass through, that is, the sound advice of reason in the mind of the angry man, it would no longer be the house of Mars, that is of war and tribulation, but of peace.

Not only does this obstinacy make the divine grace which descends upon it fly away, that is, the salutary counsel of reason, but it has doors of diamond, so that no human persuasion may pass within to either bend or soften it. And it is sustained by columns of iron, that is, by unbreakable resolves. And there are many people in this house, which is the third matter that will be expounded.

He says, then, that in this house of Mars there are mad Impulses, which he says emerge through the gate, to show that the first act of the angry man is Impulse, since, as we see, angry men quickly run to take up arms and go against others. He calls these Impulses demented, that is crazy, as we see they are. Next he says there is Blind Sin, which is the effect of Impulse, because he who rushes to do something without reasonable deliberation sins blindly. He says now here, now there, by various winds in various places into spring rain-storms, or are hurled down as globules of water merged together by the cold, as the snow keeps hardening little by little to form ice.

31

It is located in a barren forest of sturdy beech trees, thick-clustering and very tall, gnarled and harsh, unbending and ancient, which cover the face of the sad earth with an eternal shadow. And she heard there among the ancient trunks, a great noise muffled by a thousand Furies; and there was no beast or shepherd there.

32

In this forest she saw the house of the battle-strong god, built entirely of steel, splendid and clean, from which the light of the sun, which shunned that cruel place, was deflected. The narrow entrance[1] was all iron and the gates were re-enforced everywhere with eternal diamond.

---

that there is also every "Alas!" that is, every manner of woe. And that is very reasonable, since woes follow of necessity on things done insanely, either for whoever unjustly receives them or for whoever realizes that he has done them unjustly.

Next he states that there were Wraths, red as fire, whereby he expresses the appearance of the angry man, whom we see generally becomes flushed at first. And he says "Wraths," plural in number, to show that there are two kinds of wrath, and each one causes the angry man to become flushed: one is getting angry without reason, and this is vicious, and is that which is spoken of here. The other can be reasonable, such as becoming troubled when something is done unjustly, and this accepts the advice of reason in reprimanding or in bringing about amends to what has been ill done. And the author wants this Wrath to be in the house of Mars, because from this are born and can be born every day many just wars.

Similarly, he puts Fear there, which is accustomed to being under the lintels of the wrathful since sometimes they grow cold; or let us say the wagers of war grow cold when they do not see things happening as they planned in their undertakings. And he says that this Fear was pale, because we see that the fearful are pale and the reason is that the blood has withdrawn into the heart which is afraid. He also says that there are Betrayals with hidden weapons and Intrigues, that is, ambushes, under a righteous appearance, which belong to the effects that are born of Wrath, that is, wars. And Discord was there, with bloody weapons. She is similar to the effect of Wrath, since many say that Wrath is born of Discord.

He says that there is every Difference, that is, every manner of quarrel and of riot. He also says that there is clamoring, that is, the echoing of harsh

Threats and of Cruel Design, that is, rivalry, which as we all well realize are the acts of the enraged. Besides this, he says that there is unhappy Valor. By this he means bodily strength, which, when it is unjustly employed in the deaths and wounds of the innocents, is a sorry and poor Valor, that is, without any worthy praise. Next he says that there is merry Madness, which we unfailingly detect in every act of the man who is unjustly angered, since all such acts are mad. He calls him merry, because he rushes furiously to his undertakings with an impious soul and with noise and with pomp.

He says next that there are armed Death and Bewilderment, almost always two of the results of the wars born of Wrath, since in arms, one either dies, having been killed by those who are armed, or if one remains alive, there is bewilderment over the stupendous consequences from little beginnings, as we have seen happen many times.

Hence the author proceeds to show the fourth matter, that is, with what the house of Mars is adorned, that is, the temple. And he says that every altar is covered with blood, not that of beasts such as those that were killed when sacrifice was offered to the other gods, but with human blood shed in battle. And he mentions this, and also the other things which follow, to show the cruel endings to which Wrath, unmitigated by reason, leads.

He says, likewise: "Every altar was luminous, etc." What the other ornaments might be appears clear. Nonetheless, I know that many other things could be said on this matter and said better. I leave them to those who still want to examine and write about them with more delight and in detail, since for me it is enough to have said what it seems to me I should, as I write this at the instance of ladies.

1. That is, of the temple.

33

And she saw the iron columns that upheld the building. It seemed to her that she saw mad Impulses coming forth proudly through the door; and Blind Sin and every Alas! appeared there too. Wraths, red as fire, and pale Fear were also to be seen in that place.

34

And she saw Betrayals with their secret weapons, and Intrigues with their fair appearance. Discord was seated there, holding bloody weapons and every Difference in her hand. All the rooms seemed clamorous with harsh Threats and Cruel Design. And in their midst sat unhappy Valor, the least to merit praise.

35

Merry Madness she saw there as well, and behind him, armed Death with his bloody looks, and Bewilderment. Every altar there was covered with blood that had been shed by human bodies only in battles. Every altar was luminous with the fire taken from flame-ravaged lands destroyed by wretched wars.

36

And the temple was all storied by a clever hand, above and roundabout. The first scenes pictured there were the depredations made day and night on ravished lands. And anyone ever subjected to violence was here in somber garb. Enchained peoples, iron gates, and demolished fortresses could be seen here.

37

She also saw warlike ships there, and empty wagons and ravaged[2] countenances, and weeping and unhappy wretches and all Coercions, each with arrogant mien. Every wound was visible there, and blood, mixed with clay. And turbulent, haughty Mars with his proud bearing appeared every-where.

38

And subtle Mulciber[3] had built that retreat with his skill before the sun had shown him by his rays that Cytherea was with Mars. From afar Mars

2. That is, by wounds.
3. That is, Vulcan. The fable of Mars, of Venus, and of Vulcan, has been written down at length a little before this. He is called Vulcan Mulciber because he melts iron, as we see. Vulcan, that is the fire, makes iron, which is hard, so soft by heating it that man can do what he wants with it.

knew what the Prayer wanted and whence she came to entreat him. So he received her and listened to her business.

39

When Mars heard that this Prayer had been sent humbly by Arcites from afar, without waiting for more, he went little by little to where he had been secretly summoned. As soon as the temple heard its sovereign god, it began to tremble and all at once the gates began to roar, so that Arcites was very much afraid.

40

The fires[4] emitted a much brighter glow and the earth a marvelous aroma and the smoke of the incense drew near the image placed in honor of Mars, and the armor[5] moved of its own accord and resounded with a sweet music, and signs were given to wondering Arcites that his prayer had been heard.

41

And so the young man rested content with the thought of achieving victory. He did not leave the temple that night, but instead spent the entire night in prayer. He received other signs that night that assured him of the truth of his experience. As soon as the new day appeared, the elegant youth had himself armed.

* * *

From Book 12

1

Let those who have ever felt sorrow reflect on what the life of Emilia was like while these things were being done in honor of Arcites. She was dressed in black and her cheeks were stained with tears, and refusing to take any comfort, she only wept for her dead Arcites.

2

And the rosy color was fled from her face, which became pale and thin, and the bright splendor of her eyes was clouded over. The cruel sorrow was so strong in her that she could scarcely be recognized, for night and day her only consolation was to call on Arcites in lamentation and tears.

How Theseus, after giving a long speech, commanded Palaemon to marry Emilia and all mourning garb to be laid aside.

---

4. Kindled by Arcites.   5. That is, the statue of Mars.

3

But after many days had passed since the unfortunate occurrence, when the Greeks gathered about Arcites, it seemed to be the consensus of opinion that sad lamentation should be set aside, and that the wish which Arcites had expressed should be carried out: that is, that his beloved Emilia should be wed to Palaemon.

4

For this reason, Theseus summoned Palaemon, and without knowing the reason for the summons, Palaemon obeyed, clad in black and downcast as he was, and accompanied by many kings. With as many as were with him he entered where Emilia, who was still weeping, was seated among many ladies.

5

When everyone had silently sat down there, Theseus stood for a long time without saying anything. When he saw that the ears of all were humbly attentive, he checked the tears of pity that threatened to come to his eyes, and began to speak thus:

6

"Just as anyone who never lived, never came to die, so it can be seen that anyone who has not died, has never lived. And when it shall please Him who sets the limits of the world, we who are living now shall also die. Therefore, we ought to bear up cheerfully under the pleasure of the gods, since we cannot resist it.

7

"As we see, the oak trees that have such a growth span and such vitality also come to an end at some time. We see clearly that even the hard rocks we tread under foot come to fail, through various vicissitudes. We see rivers dry up through the years and other new ones spring forth.

8

"Needless to say, it is very clear that nature draws man to one of two ends: either to an obscure old age full of endless troubles, and this then most certainly ended by death, or else death in the midst of youth and a most joyful life.

9

"And, indeed, I believe that death is better when life is a joy. The valiant man ought not to care how or where it comes, for wherever he might be, fame will preserve the honor he deserves. As for the body that is left behind, one place or another serves, and the soul has neither more nor less its fill of delight.

10

"I say the same for the manner of death. For while some drown in the sea, some die as they lie in their beds, some die with their blood shed in battle, and some for whatever you want to say of how many ways a man can die, yet it is still necessary for each one to come to Acheron, let him die as he will, well or badly.

11

"And it is wisdom, therefore, to make a virtue of necessity when one must. And the opposite is plain vanity, worse in the man who has had experience of this than in one who has never tried it. Certainly, this true maxim of mine can apply to us who live sorrowfully always in the midst of contingencies,

12

"and all the more so in the midst of necessities: such as in this case of the death of someone whose valor was so great and of such a nature, that its flower is followed by the graceful fruit of fame. If we thought deeply about this, we would set aside this wretched grief and turn our efforts toward a valiant life that would win us glorious fame.

13

"It is true that on such occasions sadness and lamentation cannot be kept sealed within us very well, so it ought to be allowed in some measure. But after that it ought to cease, because the desire to exceed the limits so much can hurt the one who indulges, and it is folly, and such a one does not get back what he desires.

14

"And certainly, if ever a brave man was mourned in Greece by many kings and a populous nation, Arcites was deservedly that man. He was also honored with magnificent glory on his splendid pyre, and every respectful office that a dead body could receive was rendered him.

15

"And besides, as we have seen, here in Athens the mourning has continued and everyone has gone on wearing mourning garb, as is especially proper for us who are here, from whom others should take example in every deed and whom they should follow, especially in doing good.

16

"Therefore, whatever is born to us, dies on us as well, no matter what our desire is. And we have paid proper honor to him whom we are mourning now, and with reason I think that it would be better to divest ourselves of this gloomy dress and set sorrow aside, for it is womanish behavior rather than ʌʌʌlʌ.

17

"If I thought that we might have Arcites back by weeping for him, I would say that we should all weep and I would earnestly request it. But it would not avail. Therefore, from now on, let everyone be joyful and set aside the tears and sighs, if you want to please me, for in this great matter you ought to want to do so.

18

"And besides this, let thought be given to carry out his final request. Phoroneus, who first gave us laws, said that the last wish of a dying man with good reason ought to be faithfully carried out; and Arcites prayed that Emilia, whom he loved so much, should be given to Palaemon.

19

"Put aside these black garments, therefore, and when the sorrow and lamentation have ceased, the joyful and bright festivities will begin. Before any lord departs, we shall celebrate with proper splendor and openly the wedding of the couple we have named. So prepare yourselves to do what I want without refusal."

*　*　*

BOETHIUS

From *The Consolation of Philosophy* †

Book 2, Meter 8

"That the world with stable feith varieth° acordable°   *varies in / harmonious*

chaunginges; that the contrarious° qualites of ele-   *contrary*

---

† We print from Chaucer's own translation. The original, written in Latin in 524, was one of the books most central to his thought, as well as to that of the medieval period as a whole. For a lucid modern English translation, see that of Richard Green (Indianapolis: Bobbs-Merrill, 1962). The influence of this work, both in general and in spe- cific detail, is not limited to the passages we print here: they must serve as examples merely. It is customarily assumed that Chaucer translated Boe- thius during the same period in which he wrote the *Knight's Tale*—which existed as an independent nar- rative before the *Canterbury Tales* was begun—and the *Troilus and Criseyde*.

ments holden among hemself aliaunce perdurable;° *enduring*
that Phebus the sonne with his goldene chariet bringeth forth the rosene° day; that the moone hath com- *rosy*
maundement° over the nightes, which nightes *dominion*
Hesperus the eve-sterre° hath brought; that the see, *evening star*
greedy to flowen, constreyneth° with a certein ende° *constrains / limit*
his floodes, so that it is nat leveful° to strecche his *lawful, permissible*
brode termes° or boundes upon the erthes, *that is to* *boundaries*
seyn, to covere al the erthe—al this acordaunce of
thinges is bounden with love, that governeth erthe
and see, and hath also commaundement to the hev-
ene. And yif this love slakede the brydeles,° alle thinges *were to lose control*
that now loven hem togederes wolden maken bataile
continuely° and stryven to fordoon° the fasoun° of *immediately / destroy / order*
this worlde, the whiche they now leden° in acordable *carry out*
feith by faire moevinges. This love halt° togideres *holds*
poeples joyned with an holy bond, and knitteth
sacrement of mariages of chaste loves; and love endy-
teth° lawes to trewe felawes.° O weleful° were man- *prescribes / friends / happy*
kinde, yif thilke love that governeth hevene governed
youre corages!"° *minds, spirits*

From Book 3, Prose 10

"For as moche thanne as thou hast seyn° which is *seen*
the forme of good that nis nat parfit, and which is
the forme of good that is parfit, now trowe° I that it *think*
were good to shewe in what this perfeccioun of blisfulnesse is set. And in° this thing,° I trowe that we *on / topic*
sholden first enquere for to witen° yif that any swiche *know*
maner good as thilke good that thou has diffinisshed° *defined*
a litel heerbiforn, *that is to seyn, soverein good,* may
ben founde[1] in the nature of thinges, for° that veyn *so*
imaginacioun of thought ne deceyve us nat and putte
us out of the sothfastnesse° of thilke thing that is *truth*
summitted° unto us. But it may nat ben deneyed that *submitted*
thilke good ne is and that it nis right as a welle of alle
goodes.[2] For al thing that is cleped° inparfit is proeved° *called / proved, shown*
inparfit by the amenusinge° of perfeccioun or of thing *lack*
that is parfit. And therof comth it, that in every thing
general,° yif that men sen any thing that is inparfit, *(of some) kind, species*
certes° in thilke general ther mot ben som thing that *certainly*
is parfit; for yif so be that perfeccioun is don awey,
men may nat thinke ne seye fro whennes° thilke thing *whence*

1. I.e., exists.
2. But it cannot be denied that this (sovereign) good
exists and that it is exactly like a wellspring of all
goodness.

is that is cleped inparfit. For the nature of thinges ne
took nat hir beginninge of° thinges amenused° and   *from / deficient*
inparfit, but it procedeth of thinges that ben al hoole
and absolut, and descendeth° so doun into outterest°   *falls, diffuses / farthest*
thinges, and into thinges empty and withouten fruyt.°   *fruitfulness*
But, as I have y-shewed° a litel herbiforn, that yif   *shown*
ther be a blisfulnesse that be freele° and veyn and   *frail*
inparfit, ther may no man doute that ther nis som
blisfulnesse that is sad,° stedefast, and parfit."   *trustworthy*

Boece. "This is concluded," quod I, "fermely° and   *firmly*
sothfastly."

Philosophie. "But considere also," quod she, "in
whom this blisfulnesse enhabiteth. The comune
acordaunce° and conceite° of the corages° of men   *agreement / understanding /*
proeveth and graunteth that God, prince of alle   *minds, hearts*
thinges, is good. For, so as° nothing may ben thought   *since*
bettre than God, it may nat ben douted° thanne that   *doubted*
he, that° no thing nis bettre, that he nis³ good. Certes,   *than whom*
resoun sheweth that God is so good, that it proveth
by verray force° that parfit good is in him. For yif   *necessarily*
God ne is swich, he ne may nat ben prince of alle
thinges; for certes somthing possessing in itself parfit
good sholde ben more worthy than God, and it sholde
semen° that thilke thing were first° and elder than   *seem / primary*
God. For we han shewed apertly° that alle thinges   *clearly*
that ben parfit ben first or° thinges that ben inparfit.   *before*
And forthy,° for as moche as that° my resoun or my   *thus / so that*
proces° ne go nat awey withoute an ende,⁴ we owen°   *argument / must*
to graunten that the soverein God is right ful of sov-
erein parfit good. And we han establisshed that the
soverein good is verray° blisfulnesse. Thanne mot it   *true*
nedes° be that verray blisfulnesse is set in soverein   *necessarily*
God."

*   *   *

Book 4, Meter 6

"If thou, wys, wilt demen° in thy pure thought   *consider*
the rightes° or the lawes of the heye thonderer, *that*   *rules*
is to seyn, of God, loke thou and bihold the heightes
of the soverein hevene. There kepen the sterres, by
rightful alliaunce° of thinges, hir olde pees.° The   *harmony / peace*
sonne, y-moeved° by his rody° fyr, ne distorbeth nat   *moved / ruddy*
that colde cercle of the mone. Ne the sterre y-cleped

---

3. I.e., is.   4. I.e., to infinity.

the Bere, that enclyneth his ravisshinge° courses *swirling*
aboute the soverein heighte of the worlde, ne the
same sterre Ursa nis never mo wasshen in the depe
westrene see, ne coveiteth° nat to deyen° his flaumbes° *desires / dye, drench / flames*
in the see of the occian, althogh he see othre sterres
y-plounged in the see. And Hesperus *the sterre* bod-
eth° and telleth alwey the late nightes; and Lucifer *proclaims*
the sterre bringeth ayein the clere day.

And thus maketh Love entrechaungeable the perdurable courses;[5] and thus is discordable bataile y-
put out of the contree of the sterres. This acordaunce
atempreth° by evenelyk° maneres the elements, that *regulates / even*
the moiste thinges, stryvinge with the drye thinges,
yeven° place by stoundes;° and that the colde thinges *give, yield / in time*
joynen hem by feyth° to the hote thinges; and that *in alliance*
the lighte fyr aryseth into heighte, and the hevy erthes
avalen° by hir weightes. By thise same causes the *sink*
floury° yeer yildeth° swote smelles in the firste somer- *flowering / yields*
sesoun° warminge; and the hote somer dryeth the *spring*
cornes;° and autumpne comth ayein, hevy of apples; *crops, grains*
and the fletinge° reyn bideweth° the winter. This *flowing / bedews*
atempraunce° norissheth and bringeth forth al thing *moderated change*
that bretheth° lyf in this world; and thilke same atem- *breathes*
praunce, ravisshinge,° hydeth and binimeth° and *taking away / snatches off*
drencheth° under the laste deeth alle thinges y-born. *drowns*

Amonges thise thinges° sitteth the heye maker, king *During these changes*
and lord, welle° and bigininge, lawe and wys juge, *wellspring, source*
to don equitee;° and governeth and enclyneth the *justice, right*
brydles° of thinges. And tho thinges that he stereth° *holds the reins, controls / stirs*
to gon by moevinge, he withdraweth° and aresteth;° *draws back / restrains*
and affermeth° the moevable or wandringe thinges. *steadies*
For yif that he ne clepede ayein[6] the right goinge of
thinges, and yif that he ne constreinede hem nat eft-
sones° into roundnesses enclynede,° the thinges that *again / circling orbits*
ben now continued by stable ordinaunce,° they shol- *regulation*
den departen from hir welle, *that is to seyn, from hir
biginninge,* and faylen, *that is to seyn, torne into
nought.*

This is the comune love to alle thinges; and alle
thinges axen° to ben holden° by the fyn° of good. For *demand / held / end, goal*
elles ne mighten they nat lasten, yif they ne come
nat eftsones ayein, by love retorned, to the cause that
hath yeven hem beinge, *that is to seyn, to God.*"

---

5. And thus Love makes harmonious the everlasting   6. I.e., did not control.
movements (of the stars).

The Miller's Prologue and Tale

Although there are a number of analogues to individual motifs in the *Miller's Tale*, only one story from Chaucer's age survives that contains all the major plot elements. It is a Flemish fabliau, titled *The Three Guests of Heile of Bersele* in Constance B. Hieatt's translation. Chaucer's source may well have been a French fabliau now lost, but the *Miller's Tale* is rich with detail and nuance usually lacking in the genre, of which *Heile* is a fairly typical representative. Chaucer's apology for the tale in the *Miller's Prologue* shares much of the tone and many of the gambits of Boccaccio's Introduction to the Fourth Day and his Conclusion to the *Decameron*. Whether or not Chaucer was remembering the *Decameron* precisely at this point, both passages offer insight into the defense of nondidactic literature in the later Middle Ages.

The Three Guests of Heile of Bersele †

You have often heard tales of all manner of things, told or sung to the tune of a fiddle or harp; but I think few will have heard of such a strange case as one which happened here in Antwerp some time ago. I will tell you about it at the request of a boon companion of mine; he wouldn't let me off.

Here in the market street in Antwerp, there lived, I recall, a fine wench, and she was called Heile of Bersele. She often made love, for a price, with good fellows to whom she displayed her arts. It fell out once, as I heard the story, that three such fellows came to her on the same day, one after the other, all three asking her that for the sake of friendship she would let them come where she lived: each wanted to speak to her alone, in secret. This was good business for Heile, who determined to satisfy all three.

The first one she made an appointment with was a miller called William Hoeft. She told him to come as soon as evening fell. The second was a priest; she told him to come when the curfew-bell rang. She told the third, a smith who was a neighbor of hers, to come when the clock struck midnight. This satisfied all three, and they all went their way happily, awaiting the proper time.

At twilight, William came promptly. Heile received him graciously and made him quite at home. They played the game of love—she knew that

† From Constance B. Hieatt, ed., *The Miller's Tale, and Analogues*, pp. 112–18. It was written in the by Geoffrey Chaucer (New York: The Odyssey Press, late fourteenth century. 1970) 51–54. The Flemish text is printed in *Sources*

business well—and thus they lay taking their pleasure until it was time for curfew.

As the bell rang out for curfew, the priest came, all eagerness, saying, "Heile, let me in! I am here: you know who."

"Good heavens, Heile," said William, "who is that there?"

"I don't know, William," she answered, "but it seems to me it's the priest. He is supposed to instruct me and mend my faults."

"Oh, dear Heile," William cried, "quick—where can I run so that the priest can't see me?"

Heile said, "Up above there is a trough which I have found useful at various times before. It is tied to the rafters with a good sound rope. You'll be better off there than anywhere else."

William hid himself in the trough and told her to let the priest in. Heile then made her second guest comfortable. After they had done the wide-awake dance three times, the priest began to discourse on the gospels. He said that the time would soon come when God would bring judgment upon the world, coming with water and fire; and that everyone—high and low, young and old—should drown.

William, sitting overhead in the trough, heard all this, and believed that it might well be true: the priests taught it, and the gospel bore witness to it.

But meanwhile Hugh, the smith, came; he thought he had waited quite long enough, and a good deal longer than he had wished. He gave a soft knock at the door. Heile said, "Who is there?"

"Why indeed, Heile, it's me," he replied.

Heile answered, "You can't come in."

"But Heile, my love, are you going to break your promise? I have to speak to you!"

"That you shall not," said Heile, "right now, for I am unwell. You cannot come in at this time."

"Ah, dear Heile, then I beg you, let me at least kiss your mouth right now."

Then Heile said to the priest, "Now, sir, let this fellow kiss your behind: he will certainly think it's me, and nobody else."

"Marvelous!" said the priest. "A splendid jest!" And he jumped right up and quickly put his tail out the window. Hugh, thinking that it was Heile, kissed the priest's arse with such ardour that his nose pushed right inside and he was caught, it seemed to him, like a mouse in a trap. He was thrown into a frenzy of rage: he was not so dull that he could not tell, from the feel and smell of the thing, that he had kissed an arse, for the mouth seemed to be set the wrong way between cheeks above and below.

"By Christ," he said to himself, "I'll come back!"

He ran as though he were mad to his house nearby and quickly picked up a huge iron. He thrust it into the fire until it was so hot that it glowed brightly, then ran with it to Heile's door, crying, "Heile, my love, let me in now, or at least let me kiss your little mouth: one or the other, or I'll stand here all night. The strength of my love for you forces me to it!"

The priest, hearing his cue, again put his hind passage out where it had been before. Without hesitating, the smith struck the glowing iron into his arse. Then the priest sang his verse loud and clear: "Water, water! Oh, I am dead," he cried at length, until the words died out in his mouth.

William, who lay hidden above, was greatly alarmed, for he thought, "What the priest predicted tonight has now come true—surely the water has come and all the earth shall now be drowned! But if I can float away from here, the trough will save my life." Grasping his knife, he cut through the rope by which the trough was hanging, and said, "Now may God and good fortune aid William Hoeft in his voyage!"

Down to the ground came William, trough and all, with such a crash that he was badly hurt—both his arm and his thigh were broken. Now the priest, thinking that the devil had come, scooted off into a corner, where he fell into a privy. They say that he came home covered with filth, burned in the arse, and held up to scorn and shame. It would have been far better for him if he had stayed home and said his prayers!

That was what happened to Heile's guests. The smith had a setback, but he found good consolation for that in burning the priest's hole—he was well revenged.

Saving your dignity, let it be said that whoever keeps company with whores will surely find strife, harm, shame, and sorrow coming upon him. The guests of Heile found this out.

GIOVANNI BOCCACCIO

From the *Decameron*, Fourth Day, Introduction†

Here begins the fourth day of The Decameron, *during which, under the direction of Filostrato, tales are told about those whose love had an unhappy ending.*

Dearest ladies, both from what I heard from wise men and from the things I often saw and read, I used to think that the impetuous and fiery wind of envy would only batter high towers and the topmost part of trees, but I find that I was very much mistaken in my judgment. I flee and have always striven to flee the fiery blast of this angry gale, by trying to proceed quietly and unobtrusively not only through the plains but also through the deepest valleys. This will be clear to whoever reads these short tales which I have written, but not signed, in Florentine vernacular prose, and composed in the most humble and low style possible; yet for all of this, I have not been able to avoid the terrible buffeting of such a wind which has almost uprooted me, and I have been nearly torn to pieces by the fangs of

† From *The Decameron*, ed. and trans. Mark Musa and Peter E. Bondanella (New York: W. W. Norton, 1977) 73–79. The translators' notes have been renumbered and in some cases abridged.

envy. Therefore, I can very easily attest to what wise men say is true: only misery is without envy in this world.

There have been those, discerning ladies, who have read these tales and have said that you please me too much and that it is not fitting for me to take so much pleasure from pleasing and consoling you, and, what seems to be worse, in praising you as I do. Others, speaking more profoundly, have stated that at my age it is not proper to pursue such matters, that is, to discuss women or to try to please them. And many, concerned about my reputation, say that I would be wiser to remain with the Muses[1] on Parnassus[2] than to get myself involved with you and these trifles. And there are those still who, speaking more spitefully than wisely, have said that it would be more practical if I were to consider where my daily bread was coming from rather than to go about "feeding on wind" with this foolishness. And certain others, in order to diminish my labors, try to demonstrate that the things I have related to you did not take place in the manner in which I told you.

Thus, worthy ladies, while I battle in your service, I am buffeted, troubled, and wounded to the quick by such winds and by such fierce, sharp teeth as these. As God knows, I hear and endure these things with a tranquil mind, and however much my defense depends upon you in all of this, I do not, nevertheless, intend to spare my own forces; on the contrary, without replying as much as might be fitting, I shall put forward some simple answer, hoping in this way to shut my ears to their complaints, and I shall do this without delay, for if I have as yet completed only one third of my task, my enemies are numerous and presumptuous and before I reach the end of my labors, they will have multiplied—unless they receive some sort of reply before that time; and if this is not done, then their least effort will be enough to overcome me; and even your power, no matter how great it is, would be unable to resist them.

Before I make my reply to anyone, I should like to recount not an entire tale (for in doing so it might appear that I wished to mix my own tales with those of such a worthy company as I have described to you) but merely a portion of a tale, so that its very incompleteness will separate it from any of the others in my book.

For the benefit of my critics, then, let me tell you about a man named Filippo Balducci, who lived in our city a long time ago. He was of rather modest birth, but he was rich, well-versed, and expert in those matters which were required by his station in life; and he had a wife whom he dearly loved, and she loved him, and together they lived a tranquil life, always trying to please one another. Now it happened, as it must happen to all of us, that the good woman passed from this life and left nothing of herself to

---

1. In Greek mythology, any of the nine daughters of Zeus and Mnemosyne (the goddess of memory) who presided over a different art or science: Calliope (epic poetry); Clio (history); Erato (lyric poetry and mime); Euterpe (lyric poetry and music); Melpomene (tragedy); Polyhymnia (singing, rhetoric, and mime); Terpsichore (dancing and choral singing); Thalia (comedy and pastoral poetry); and Urania (astronomy).

2. A mountain in southern Greece, sacred in Greek mythology to Apollo and to the Muses and, therefore, traditionally linked to poets and poetry.

Filippo except an only child, whom she had conceived with him and who was now almost two years old.

No man was ever more disheartened by the loss of the thing he loved than Filippo was by the loss of his wife; and seeing himself deprived of that companionship which he most cherished, he decided to renounce this world completely and to give himself to serving God, and to do the same for his son. After he had given everything he owned to charity, he immediately went to the top of Mount Asinaio, and there he lived in a small hut with his son, surviving on alms, fasts, and prayers. And with his son, he was careful not to talk about worldly affairs or to expose him to them; with him he would always praise the glory of God and the eternal life, teaching him nothing but holy prayers. They spent many years leading this kind of life, his son restricted to the hut and denied contact with everyone except his father.

The good man was in the habit of coming into Florence from time to time, and he would return to his hut after receiving assistance from the friends of God according to his needs. Now it happened one day, when his son was eighteen years of age, that Filippo told him he was going into the city, and his son replied:

"Father, you are now an old man and can endure hardship very poorly. Why don't you take me with you one time to Florence so that you can introduce me to your friends and to those devoted to God? Since I am young and can endure hardship better than you can, I can, from then on, go to Florence whenever you like for our needs and you can remain here."

This worthy man, realizing that this son of his was now grown up and was already so used to serving God that only with great difficulty could the things of this world have any effect on him, said to himself: "He is right." And since he had to go anyway, he took his son along with him.

When the young man saw the palaces, the houses, the churches, and all the other things that filled the city, he was amazed, for he had never seen such things in his life, and he kept asking his father what many of them were and what they were called. His father told him, and when one question was answered, he would ask about something else. As they went along this way, the son asking and the father explaining, by chance they ran into a group of beautiful and elegantly dressed young women who were returning from a wedding feast; when the young man saw them, he immediately asked his father what they were. To this his father replied:

"My son, lower your eyes and do not look, for they are evil."

Then the son asked: "What are they called?"

In order not to awaken some potential or anything-but-useful desire in the young man's carnal appetite, his father did not want to tell his son their proper name, that is to say "women," so he answered:

"Those are called goslings."

What an amazing thing to behold! The young man, who had never before seen a single gosling, no longer paid any attention to the palaces, oxen, horses, mules, money, or anything else he had seen, and he quickly said:

"Father, I beg you to help me get one of those goslings."

"Alas, my son," said the father, "be silent; they are evil."

To this the young man replied:

"Are evil things put together like that?"

"Yes," his father replied.

And his son answered:

"I do not understand what you are saying or why they are evil. As far as I know, I have never seen anything more beautiful nor more pleasing than they. They are more beautiful than the painted angels which you have pointed out to me so many times. Oh, if you care for me at all, do what you can to take one of these goslings home with us, and I will see to her feeding."

His father replied:

"I will not, for you do not know how to feed them!"

Right then and there the father sensed that Nature had more power than his intelligence, and he was sorry for having brought his son to Florence. But let what I have recounted of this tale up to this point suffice, so that I may return to those for whom it was meant.

Well, young ladies, some of my critics say that I am wrong to try to please you too much, and that I am too fond of you. To these accusations I openly confess, that is, that you do please me and I do try to please you. But why is this so surprising to them? Putting aside the delights of having known your amorous kisses, your pleasurable embraces, and the delicious couplings that one so often enjoys with you, sweet ladies, let us consider merely the pleasure of seeing you constantly: your elegant garments, your enchanting beauty, and the charm with which you adorn yourselves (not to mention your feminine decorum). And so we see that someone who was nourished, raised, and grew up upon a savage and solitary mountain within the confines of a small hut without any other companion but his father, desired only you, asked for only you, gave only you his affection.

Will my critics reproach me, bite and tear me apart if I—whose body heaven made most ready to love you with, and whose soul has been so disposed since my childhood, when I first experienced the power of the light from your eyes, the softness of your honeylike words, and flames kindled by your compassionate sighs—if I strive to please you and if you delight me, when we see how you, more than anything else, pleased a hermit, and what's more, a young man without feeling, much like a wild beast? Of course, those who do not love you and do not desire to be loved by you (people who neither feel nor know the pleasures or the power of natural affection), reprove me for doing this, but I care very little about them. And those who go around talking about my age show that they know nothing about the matter, for though the leek may have a white top, its roots can still be green. But joking aside, I reply by saying to them that I see no reason why I should be ashamed of delighting in these pleasures and in the ladies that give them, before the end of my days, since Guido Cavalcanti[3] and Dante Alighieri[4] (already old men) and Messer Cino da Pistoia[5] (a very old man indeed) considered themselves honored in striving to please the ladies in whose beauty lay their delight. And if it were not a departure from the customary way of arguing, I certainly would cite from history books and show you that they are full of ancient and worthy men who in their most mature years strove with great zeal to please the ladies—if my critics are not familiar with such cases, they should go and look them up! I agree that remaining with the Muses on Parnassus is sound advice, but we cannot always dwell with the Muses any more than they can always dwell with us. If it sometimes happens that a man leaves them, he should not be blamed if he delights in seeing something resembling them: the Muses are women, and although women are not as worthy as the Muses, they do, nevertheless, look like them at first glance; and so for this reason, if for no other, they should please me. What's more, the fact is that women have already been the cause for my composing thousands of verses,[6] while the Muses were in no way the cause of my writing them. They have, of course, assisted me and shown me how to compose these thousands of verses; and it is possible that they have been with me on several occasions while I was writing these tales, no matter how insignificant they be—they came to me perhaps in honor of the likeness that women bear to them. Therefore, if I compose such tales, I am not as far away from Mount Parnassus or the Muses as some people may think.

But what shall we say about those who feel so much compassion for my hunger that they advise me to find myself a bit of bread to eat? I know only this, that if I were to ask myself what their reply would be if I were to ask them for some bread in my need, I imagine that they would tell me—"Go look for it among your fables!" And yet, poets have found more of it in their fables than many rich men have in their treasures, and many more still, by pursuing their fables, have increased the length of their lives while, on the contrary, others have lost them early in the search for more bread than they needed. What more, then? Let these people drive me away if ever I ask bread of them—thanks be to God, as yet I have no such need. And if ever the need arises, I know how to endure both in abundance as well as in poverty, just as the Apostle says.[7] And let no one lose courage on my account more than I myself do!

And as for those who say that these things did not happen the way I have told them here, I should be very happy if they would bring forward the

---

3. Italian lyric poet (c. 1250–1300) and a friend of Dante Alighieri, best known for his *canzone* "Donna mi prega" ("A lady begs me"), a philosophical poem dealing with the nature of love.
4. The greatest of Italian poets (1265–1321) and the author not only of *The Divine Comedy*, a Christian epic poem, but also of *The New Life*, *On Monarchy*, and various sonnets and *canzoni*.
5. Italian lyric poet (1270–1336) from Pistoia, a friend of Dante and a distinguished jurist who taught

at several Italian universities.
6. Although Boccaccio's masterpiece is the prose *Decameron*, many of his works are in verse: the *Caccia di Diana* (a hunting poem in *terza rima*); the *Filostrato* (a verse romance in *ottava rima*); the *Teseida* (an epic poem in *ottava rima*); the *Amorosa visione* (an allegorical work in *terza rima*); and the *Ninfale fiesolano* (an idyll in *ottava rima*).
7. A reference to St. Paul's advice in Philippians 4.12.

original versions, and if these should be different from what I have written, I would call their reproach justified and would try to correct myself; but until something more than words appears, I shall leave them with their opinion and follow my own, saying about them what they say about me.

Most gentle ladies, since I wish this to suffice as my reply for the time being, let me say that armed with the aid of God and that of yourselves, in which I place my trust, and with patience, I shall proceed with my task, turning my back on that wind and letting it blow, for I do not see what more can happen to me than what happens to fine dust in a windstorm—either it does not move from the ground, or it does move from the ground; and if the wind sweeps it up high enough, it will often drop on the heads of men, the crowns of kings and emperors, and sometimes on high palaces and lofty towers; if it falls from there, it cannot go any lower than the spot from which it was lifted up. And if I have ever, with all my strength, striven to please you in any way, I shall now do so even more, for I realize that no one who has the use of his faculty of reason could say that I and the others who love you act in any way but according to Nature, whose laws (that is, Nature's) cannot be resisted without exceptional strength, and they are often resisted not only in vain but with very great damage to the strength of the one who attempts to do so. I confess that I do not possess nor wish to possess such strength, and if I did possess it, I would rather lend it to others than employ it myself. So let my detractors be silent, and if they cannot warm up to my work, let them live numbed with the chill of their pleasures, or rather with corrupted desires, while I go on delighting in my own pleasure during this brief lifetime granted to us. But we have strayed a great deal from where we departed, beautiful ladies, so let us return and follow our established path.

The sun had already driven every star from the sky and the damp shadow of night from the earth, when Filostrato arose and made his whole company stand, and they went into the beautiful garden where they began to amuse themselves; and when it was time to eat, they breakfasted there where they had eaten supper the previous evening. When the sun was at its highest, they took their naps and then arose, and in their usual manner, they sat around the beautiful fountain. Then, Filostrato ordered Fiammetta to tell the first tale of the day; and without waiting to be told again, she began in a graceful fashion as follows.

* * *

GIOVANNI BOCCACCIO

From the *Decameron*, Tenth Day, Author's Conclusion†

Most noble ladies, for whose happiness I have set myself to this lengthy task, I believe that with the assistance of divine grace and your pious pray-

† From *The Decameron*, ed. and trans. Mark Musa and Peter E. Bondanella (New York: W. W. Norton, 1977) 143–47. The translators' notes have been renumbered and in some cases abridged.

ers, rather than my own merits, I have completely fulfilled what I promised to do at the beginning of the present work; now, after rendering thanks first of all to God and then to you, it is time for me to rest my pen and my weary hand. But before I rest, I intend to reply briefly to several objections that perhaps some of you and others might have wished to voice, for one thing seems very clear to me: these tales have no more privileged status than any others; and, indeed, I recall having demonstrated this in the Prologue of the Fourth Day. There will, perhaps, be some among you who will say that I have taken too much license in writing these tales; that is, I have some- times made ladies say things, and more often listen to things, which are not very proper for virtuous ladies to say or hear[1] I deny this, for nothing is so indecent that it cannot be said to another person if the proper words are used to convey it; and this, I believe, I have done very well.

But let us suppose that you are right (I do not intend to argue with you, for you are certain to win); then, let me say that there are many reasons at hand to explain why I have done as I did. First of all, if there are some liberties taken in any of the tales, the nature of the stories themselves required it, as will be clearly understood by any sensitive person who examines them with a reasonable eye, for I could not have told them otherwise, unless I wished to distort their form completely. And if there should be a few expres- sions or little words in them that are somewhat freer than a prude might find proper (ladies of the type who weigh words more than deeds and who strive more to seem good than to be so), let me say that it is no more improper for me to have written these words than for other men and women to have filled their everyday conversation with such words as "hole," "peg," "mortar," "pestle," "sausage," "Bologna sausage," and other similar expres- sions.[2] Moreover, my pen should be granted no less freedom than the brush of a painter, who without any reproach or, at least, any which is justified— not to mention the fact that he will depict Saint Michael wounding the serpent with a sword or a lance and Saint George slaying the dragon wher- ever he wishes—shows Christ as a man and Eve as a woman, and nails to the cross, sometimes with one nail, sometimes with two, the feet of Him who wished to die there for the salvation of the human race.[3]

What is more, one can see quite clearly that these tales were not told in a church, where things must be spoken of with the proper frame of mind and suitable words (despite the fact that even more outrageous stories are to

1. In spite of the fact that Boccaccio received some criticism for his tone, his language, and his satire of various Christian practices and the priesthood in general, no attempt was ever made during the day to censor or suppress his work. Laymen and clergymen alike in the Middle Ages had no difficulty in separat- ing a criticism of a particular institution or office holder (which was considered legitimate) from more basic, and therefore heretical, doctrinal disagree- ments. Dante even condemned popes to hell with impunity. Only when the Protestant Reformation gave rise to serious threats to papal authority and Catholic dogma did the church establish the Index of Prohibited Books, to which list *The Decameron* was added in 1559.

2. The Italian equivalents for these common words were frequently used obscenely. Boccaccio's argu- ments against critics who viewed his work as improper, immoral, and sometimes obscene have a surprisingly contemporary tone.

3. Boccaccio shrewdly shows his critics how an object, or the word which represents the object, has an unlimited number of connotations. His critics see his use of ambiguous expressions, like those used obscenely in conversation which he himself lists, as a proof of his impropriety. Boccaccio, on the other hand, argues that ambiguity is a fact of life—the same pointed objects or phallic symbols appearing in conversations or bawdy literature may also serve different functions in the most sublime religious art.

be found in the church's annals than in my own tales); nor yet in the
schools of the philosophers, where a sense of propriety is required no less
than in other places; nor in any place among churchmen or philosophers.
They were told in gardens, in a place suited for pleasure, in the presence of
young people who were, nevertheless, mature and not easily misled by stories, and at a time when going about with your trousers over your head was
not considered improper if it served to save your life.

But as they stand, these tales, like all other things, may be harmful or
useful, according to whoever listens to them. Who does not recognize wine
as a very good thing for the healthy, according to Cinciglione and Scolaio[4]
and many others, and yet it is harmful to anyone with a fever? Shall we say
because wine harms those with a fever that it is evil? Who does not realize
that fire is most useful, and even more, necessary to mankind? Because it
destroys homes, villages, and cities, shall we say that it is wicked? In like
manner, weapons defend the lives of those who wish to live peacefully, and
they also (on many occasions) kill men, not because of any wickedness
inherent in them but because those who wield them do so in an evil way.

No corrupt mind ever understood a word in a healthy way! And just as
fitting words are of no use to a corrupt mind, so a healthy mind cannot be
contaminated by words which are not so proper, any more than mud can
dirty the rays of the sun or earthly filth can mar the beauties of the skies.
What books, what words, what letters are more holy, more worthy, and
more revered than those of the Holy Scriptures? And yet there are many
who have perversely interpreted them and have dragged themselves and
others down to eternal damnation because of this. Everything is, in itself,
good for some determined goal, but badly used it can also be harmful to
many; and I can say the same of my stories.

Whoever wishes to derive wicked counsel from them or use them for bad
ends will not be prohibited from doing so by the tales themselves if, by
chance, they contain such things and are twisted and distorted in order to
achieve this end; and whoever wishes to derive useful advice and profit from
them will not be prevented from doing so, nor will these stories ever be
described or regarded as anything but useful and proper if they are read at
those times and to those people for whom they have been written. Whoever
has to say "Our Fathers" and make up spicy tales for her confessor should
stay away from these tales. My stories will run after no one asking to be
read, although bigots, too, both say and even do such things as are in my
stories whenever they can!

There will also be those who will say that there are some stories here
which might better have been omitted. This may be true, but I could do
nothing but write down the tales as they were told, and if those people who
had told them had told them more beautifully, I should have written them
more beautifully. But let us suppose that I was both the one who created

4. Boccaccio uses these fictitious characters as representatives of the general class of drunkards and
tavern-crawlers, a form of antonomasia similar to
using the name "Don Juan" or "Casanova" to refer
to a rake or libertine.

these stories as well as the one who wrote them down (which I was not)[5]—then, let me say that I would not be ashamed that they were not all beautiful, since no artisan save God himself creates everything perfect and complete; even Charlemagne, who was the first creator of the Paladins,[6] did not know how to create enough of them to make up an army.

One must be ready to find different characteristics in a multitude of things. No field was ever so well cultivated that it did not contain nettles, brambles, or some other kind of thorny shrub mixed among the better plants. Moreover, in speaking to unassuming young ladies, as most of you are, it would have been foolish to go about trying to find fancy stories and to take great pains speaking in an extremely formal manner. However, whoever goes through these stories can leave aside those he finds offensive and read those he finds pleasing; and in order not to deceive anyone, at the beginning of every story there is a summary of what is contained within.

Also, I suppose there will be people who will say that some of the stories are too long; to them I say once more that for those people who have something better to do with their time, it would be foolish to read any of these tales, no matter how short they might be. And even though much time has passed since I began to write these tales until this moment when my labor is drawing to a close, I have not forgotten that I said I was offering this work of mine to idle ladies and not to others; and for those who read to pass the time of day, no tale can be too long if it serves its purpose. Brevity is much more fitting for the studious who toil not just to pass the time away, but to employ their time to the greatest advantage, but not so for you ladies, who have all that time free which you do not spend on amorous pleasures; besides this, since none of you have been to Athens, Bologna, or Paris to study, it is necessary to speak to you in a more extended fashion than to those who have sharpened their wits with their studies.

There are, without doubt, some others among you who will say that the stories told are too full of nonsense and jokes and that it is not proper for a heavy, serious thinker to have written this way. To them I am obliged to render thanks, and I do so for their zeal and concern for my reputation, but I wish to answer their objections in this way: I confess that I have been heavy (and I have been so many times in my day), so, in speaking to those ladies who have not considered me heavy, let me assure them that I am not heavy—on the contrary, I am so light that I float on water; when you consider that the sermons delivered by friars to reproach men for their sins are,

5. Boccaccio's claim that he only overheard the tales in *The Decameron* but did not invent them is an example of a literary commonplace which is used by such writers as Cervantes and Manzoni. In the sense that Boccaccio made use of the many oral and written sources at his disposal, he did not create *ex nihil* every aspect of every one of his hundred tales. But he did create literary masterpieces out of these many sources, and he did fashion a literary language with them that remained the model of Italian prose style for centuries to come. His claim, in this instance, allows him to assert that whatever is offensive in his work is not his responsibility but rather that of the teller of the tale; the fiction governing *The Decameron* is therefore that the narrator is only the faithful reporter of what he overheard.

6. Here, Boccaccio makes reference to the legendary knights of Charlemagne's army who were sacrificed in a rear-guard action, recounted first in *The Song of Roland*. In Boccaccio's day, this Old French epic poem was unknown, but the legend of Charlemagne, Roland, and the Twelve Peers (Paladins) of France became part of Italian legend and folklore.

for the most part, full of nonsense, jokes, and foolishness, I felt that these same things would not be out of place in my stories, which are, after all, written to drive away a lady's melancholy. However, should they find themselves laughing too much, they can easily remedy this by reading the Lament of Jeremiah, the Passion of Our Savior, or the Lament of Mary Magdalene.

And who would doubt that there are still others who would say that I have an evil and poisonous tongue, because in some places I write the truth about the friars? I plan to forgive those who say this, for it is hard to believe that anything but a good motive moves them, since friars are good people and avoid the discomforts of life for the love of God, and do their grinding when there's water to run the lady's mill and say no more about it; and if it were not for the fact that they all smell a little like goats, it would be most pleasant, indeed, to deal with them.

I must confess, however, that the things of this world have no stability whatsoever—they are constantly changing, and this might have happened with my tongue; I do not trust my own judgment (which, in matters concerning myself I avoid as best I can), but a short time ago, a neighbor lady of mine told me that I had the best and the sweetest tongue in the world— to tell the truth, when this was said, only a few of the above stories remained to be written. But now let what I have just said suffice as a reply to those ladies who have argued so spitefully.

I shall leave it to every lady to say and believe as she pleases, for the time has come to end my words and to humbly thank Him who with his assistance has brought me after so much labor to my desired goal, and may his grace and peace be with you always, lovely ladies, and if, perhaps, reading some of these stories has given any of you some little pleasure, please do remember me.

Here ends the tenth and last day of the book called

Decameron, also known as *Prince Galeotto.*

The Reeve's Prologue and Tale

The cradle-trick story that forms the central episode of the *Reeve's Tale* was popular throughout the later Middle Ages and Renaissance, and a number of analogues survive. *The Miller and the Two Clerics*, a thirteenth-century French fabliau, is close to Chaucer's tale in many ways, but it is not a direct source. In Boccaccio's treatment of the story in the *Decameron*, differences in detail and diction create effects quite unlike those of Chaucer's version.

The Miller and the Two Clerics †

There were once two poor fellows of the minor clergy who were born in the same region and in the same city. They were friends and deacons of a woodland church, where they found a living, until, as happens often and again, they fell on hard times, which is a great pity for poor people. They were heavy at heart when they considered their state of affairs, nor did they see any way out of it. For they did not know how to earn their living, either in their own country or anywhere else, and they were ashamed to beg their bread out of regard for their order, as well as for other reasons. They had no possessions by which they might keep themselves alive, and they didn't know where to turn.

One Sunday they met outside the church, and they went for a walk about the town in order to talk things over. "Listen to me," one of them said to the other, "we are helpless because we cannot earn our livings; and now hunger, which vanquishes everything, has got hold of us. Nobody can defend us against it, and we have nothing to draw upon. Have you put by anything at all by which we might keep ourselves going?" The other one answered: "By Saint Denis, I can't think of anything except that I have a friend to whom I suggest we go and ask for a bushel of wheat at the current price; he will very willingly give me credit, and at long term, until Saint John's Day, to tide us over this bad year." Then the first one said: "That's a piece of luck for us; for I have a brother who owns a fat mare. I'll go get her while you get the wheat, and we'll become bakers. There is no load too shameful

† From *Fabliaux: Ribald Tales from the Old French*, translated by Robert Hellman and Richard O'Gorman (New York: Thomas Y. Crowell Company, 1965) 51–57. English translation copyright © 1965 by Robert Hellman and Richard O'Gorman. Reprinted by permission of Harper & Row, Publishers, Inc. and Weidenfeld & Nicolson Ltd. This version dates from the thirteenth century. A closely related story, "Gombert and the Two Clerks," written by Jean Bodel, ca. 1190–94, may be read in *The Literary Context of Chaucer's Fabliaux*, ed. Larry D. Benson and Theodore M. Andersson (Indianapolis: Bobbs-Merrill, 1971) 88–99.

to bear if it will get us through this bad year." And they did this without further delay.

Then they brought their wheat to the mill, which was at a great distance, more than two leagues away. It was a mill with a millrace near a little wood. There was no town or farm or any house nearby except the house of the miller, who knew his trade only too well. The clerics undid the gate at once and threw their sacks inside. Then they put their mare in a meadow by the millrace. One of them remained outside to keep an eye on things, and the other went in to get the miller started at their work. But the miller had gone into hiding. He had indeed seen the clerics coming, and I think he wanted a part of their wheat.

When the cleric came running into the miller's house, he found his wife at her spinning. "Lady," he said, "by Saint Martin, where is the owner of the mill? He ought to come and help us." "Sir cleric," said she, "it's no trouble at all. You will find him in that wood right near the mill, if you will be so kind as to go there." And the cleric set out quickly to find him. His friend, who was waiting for him, grew impatient that he stayed so long and came running into the house. "Lady," he said, "for the love of God, where has my companion gone?" "Sir," said she, "on my honor, he went in search of my husband who has just left the house." So she sent one cleric after the other, while the miller came around quickly to the mill. With his wife's help he took both sacks and mare and hid them in his barn. Then he returned to the mill.

The two clerics looked everywhere, and finally they also returned to the mill. "Miller," they said, "God be with you! For the love of God, help us out." "My lords," said he, "how may I do so?" "In faith, with the wheat we have here." But, when they went to get the wheat, they found neither sacks nor mare. They looked at one another. "What's this?" said one. "We are robbed!" "Yes," said the other, "so it seems to me. For our sins we are undone!" Then both cried out: "Alas! Alas! Help us, Nicholas!" "What's wrong with you?" said the miller. "Why do you cry so loud?" "Miller, we have surely lost everything. A misfortune has befallen us, for we have neither mare nor anything. And that was our whole fortune." "Lords," said the miller, "I know nothing about this." "Sir," they said, "there's nothing you can do except to tell us where we may go to look for what we have lost." "Lords," he said, "I can't help you very much, but go look in that wood there near the mill." The two clerics set out and at once went into the woods; and the miller went his way.

They looked high and low until the sun had set; and then one of the clerics said to the other: "Surely it is truly said that he's a fool who puts himself out for nothing. Wealth comes and goes like straws blown by the wind. Let's go find a lodging for the night." "And where shall we go?" "To the miller's, in whose mill we were. May God grant us lodging in Saint Martin's name!"

They went straight to the miller's house; but he was not pleased at their coming. At once he asked them: "What has Saint Nicholas done for you?"

"Miller," they said, "not one thing or another." "Then," said he, "you'd better earn other goods. For what you've lost is a long way off; you won't have it for present needs." "Miller," they said, "that may well be. But put us up for Saint Sylvester's sake. We don't know where else to go at this hour." The miller took thought and decided that he would be worse than a dog if he didn't provide something for them out of their own belongings, as he was well able. "My lords," he said, "I have nothing but the floor to offer you; that you shall have and nothing more." "Miller," they said, "that is enough."

The peasant did not have many in his household. With himself there were only four: his daughter, who deserves to be mentioned first, his wife, and a little baby. The daughter was beautiful and charming, and to protect her against her own warmth, the miller put her in a cupboard every night, and there she slept. The miller would lock her in and pass her the key through an opening, and then he would go to bed.

But let us return to our clerics. In the evening at suppertime, the miller brought bread and milk and eggs and cheese, country fare, and he gave each of the clerics a good share. One of them supped with the maiden and the other with the miller and his wife. In the hearth was a little andiron with a ring on it that could be taken off and put back again. The cleric who ate with the maiden took the ring from the andiron and hid it well. That night, when they went to bed, the cleric watched the daughter carefully and saw how the miller locked her in the cupboard and threw her the key.

When they had settled down for the night, the cleric nudged his companion and said: "Friend, I want to go and speak to the miller's daughter, who is locked up in the cupboard." "Do you want to start a quarrel," said the other, "and stir up a tempest in the house? Truth is you are a rogue. Evil can soon come of this." "Even if I die," said the first, "I must go and see if I can make anything of her." He quickly jumped out of bed and went straight to the cupboard. He drew near it and scratched on it a little, and she heard him. "Who is it out there?" she said. "It is he who for your sake is so grieved and so unhappy that, unless you have pity on him, he will never feel joy again. It is he with whom you supped and who brings you a gold ring—you never had such a treasure. It is known and proved that its stone has such power that any woman, no matter how light she may be or how she may wanton about, will remain a virgin if she has it on her finger in the morning. Here, I make you a gift of it." At once she held out the key to him; and he quickly unlocked the chest. He got in and she squeezed over. And so they could take their pleasure, for there was no one to disturb them.

Before daybreak the miller's wife got up from beside her husband and all naked went into the courtyard. And she passed before the cleric where he lay abed. When he saw her go by, he thought of his friend who was taking his pleasure in the cupboard, and he had a great longing for the same kind of pleasure. He thought he would trick the wife on her way back. But then he thought he would not, for fear of what mad consequences might ensue.

And then again he thought of a new stratagem. He jumped out of bed and went straight to the bed where the miller lay. He carried away the child in its cradle; and when the wife came in the door, the cleric pinched the baby's ear, whereupon it awoke and cried out. The wife, who had been going to her own bed, when she heard the cry turned about and went in that direction. When she found the cradle she was reassured, and she lifted the cover and lay down beside the cleric, who hugged her tight. He drew her to him and squeezed her so tight in his pleasure that he quite crushed her. In amazement she allowed him to do what he liked.

Meanwhile, the other cleric, when he heard the cock crow, felt he had been lingering too long. He made himself ready, took his leave of the maiden, and slipped out of the chest. He went straight to his own bed where his companion lay, but when he found the cradle he was dismayed, and no wonder. He was frightened, but nonetheless he felt a little further; and when he came on two heads he knew he must be wrong. So he went quickly to the bed where the miller was lying and lay down beside him. The miller had not yet awakened and noticed nothing. "Comrade," said the cleric, "what are you doing? He who never has anything to say is worth nothing. On my word, I've had a fine night, God save me! She's a warm little girl, the miller's daughter. That kind of pleasure is very wicked indeed, but there is great pleasure in the cupboard. Go, my friend, slip in now yourself and get your share of the bacon. There's plenty left before you get to the rind. I've bent her back seven times tonight, but she still hasn't got her fill. All she got in return was the ring from the andiron. I've done a good job."

When the miller heard this trick, he seized the cleric by the collar; and the cleric, when he saw what was up, grabbed the miller and treated him so roughly that he almost strangled him. The wife began to kick the other cleric who was lying beside her. "Husband," she said, "what's going on? Please, let's get up at once. Those clerics are strangling each other over there." "Never you mind," said the cleric, "let them be, let the fools kill each other." (He knew very well that his companion was the stronger of the two.)

When the miller managed to break loose, he ran at once to light the fire. And when he saw his wife lying with the cleric, he shouted: "Get up, you brazen whore. How did you get in there? Now it's all up with you." "Husband," she said, "it's not quite as you say. For if I am a brazen whore, I was tricked into it. But you're a bold-faced thief, for you have made away with these clerics' sacks of wheat and their mare, for which you will be hanged. It's all stuck away in your barn."

The two clerics took hold of the miller and came little short of milling him like wheat, so hard did they beat and bruise him. They kicked and cuffed him until he gave them back all their wheat. Then they went to another mill to get their wheat ground. They got Saint Martin's lodging, and they worked so well at their new trade that they got through the bad year and gave thanks up and down to God and to Saint Nicholas.

GIOVANNI BOCCACCIO

From the *Decameron*, Ninth Day, Sixth Tale †

[The Story of Pinuccio and Adriano]

Two young men take lodgings at someone's home, where one of them lies with the host's daughter, while his wife inadvertently lies with the other; the man who was with the daughter gets into bed with her father and tells him everything, thinking he is speaking to his companion; they start quarreling; when the wife realizes what has happened, she gets into her daughter's bed and then, with certain remarks, she reconciles everyone.

Calandrino, who had made the company laugh on previous occasions, did so this time as well; and no sooner had the ladies ceased discussing his antics than the Queen commanded Panfilo to tell a story, and he said:

Praiseworthy ladies, the name of Niccolosa, who was loved by Calandrino, calls to mind a tale about another Niccolosa, which I should like to tell you, for in it you will see how a good woman's quick presence of mind prevented a serious scandal.

In the valley of the Mugnone, not long ago, there lived a worthy man who for a charge provided food and drink to travelers; and though he was a poor man and his house was small, he would, from time to time, in cases of extreme emergency, provide lodgings not for strangers but for someone he knew. Now this man had a wife who was a beautiful woman, and by her he had two children: one was a lovely and sprightly girl of about fifteen or sixteen years old, who still had no husband; the other was a small boy who was less than a year old and still nursing at his mother's breasts.

The young girl had caught the eye of a handsome and charming young gentleman from our city, who spent much time in the country, and he fell passionately in love with her; and she, who was very proud of being loved so passionately by such a young man, striving to retain his affection with pleasing glances, fell as much in love with him; and on numerous occasions such a love could have been consummated to the delight of both parties, if Pinuccio (this was the young man's name) had not feared disgracing the young lady and himself. But then, as their ardor increased from day to day, Pinuccio felt that he had to be with the girl and that he had to find a way to take lodgings with her father, for if he could do that, knowing the layout of the girl's house, he might be able to get together with her without anyone's seeing them; and no sooner did this idea come into his head than he immediately put it into effect.

† From THE DECAMERON by Giovanni Boccaccio, translated by Mark Musa and Peter Bondanella. Pp. 581–85. Copyright © 1982 by Mark Musa and Peter Bondanella. Reprinted by arrangement with NAL Penguin Inc., New York, NY.

Late one afternoon, Pinuccio, together with a trusted companion of his named Adriano, who knew all about his love, hired two packhorses, and having loaded them with a couple of saddlebags stuffed probably with straw, they left Florence, and after riding around in a circle, they came to the Mugnone river valley when it was already dark. And from there they turned their horses around to make it seem as though they were returning from Romagna, and rode toward the house of that worthy man and knocked at his door; since the man was a friend of theirs, he immediately opened the door, and Pinuccio said to him:

"Look, you'll have to put us up for the night. We thought we would make it to Florence, but as you can see, we only made it as far as here at this late hour."

To this, the innkeeper replied:

"Pinuccio, you are well aware how poorly equipped I am to lodge such gentlemen as yourselves; however, since this late hour has caught you here and there is not time to go elsewhere, I shall gladly put you up for the night as best I can."

So the two young men, after dismounting and stabling their nags, went into the small house, and since they had brought plenty to eat for supper, they ate supper with their host. Now the host had only one very tiny bedroom, into which he had squeezed three small beds as best he could; nor was there much space left over, what with two of them along one wall of the bedroom and the third on the opposite side against the other wall, and only with great difficulty could you pass between them. The host had the least uncomfortable of the three beds made up for his two friends and then invited them to lie down; then, after a while, when the two of them appeared to be asleep, but neither of them was really asleep, the host had his daughter go to bed in one of the two remaining beds, and he and his wife got into the other bed, by the side of which she placed the cradle in which she kept her infant son.

After things had been arranged in this manner and Pinuccio had observed everything, a little later, when he thought everyone was asleep, he quietly got up and went over to the little bed where his lady love was lying and he lay down beside her; although she was frightened by his appearance she welcomed him joyously, and together they enjoyed that pleasure which they had so much desired. And while Pinuccio was with the girl a cat happened to knock some things over, and the noise woke up the wife, who, fearing it was something else, got out of bed, and in the dark, naked as she was, she went over to where she had heard the noise. Adriano, who had not heard the noise, happened to get up because of a physical need, and as he was going to satisfy it, he discovered the cradle the lady had placed by her bed, and unable to get by it without moving it, he took it, lifted it up from the spot where it was standing, and placed it beside the bed in which he slept; after satisfying the need which had gotten him up, he returned to his bed, and without paying any attention to the cradle, climbed back into it.

After investigating and discovering that what had fallen down was of no importance, the wife yelled at the cat, and without bothering to light a lamp in order to look around, she returned to the bedroom and groped her way straight to the bed where her husband was sleeping; but finding no cradle there, she said to herself: "Oh, how stupid of me. Look what I was about to do! Good God, I was heading straight for the bed of my guests!" Going on a bit farther and finding the cradle, she got into bed with Adriano, thinking she was in bed with her husband. Adriano, who had not yet fallen back to sleep, gave her a happy welcome when he felt her there, and without saying a word, he came hard about on her, to the great delight of the lady.

And while they were thus engaged, Pinuccio, having had the pleasure he desired and now fearing that he might fall asleep with his young lady, arose from her side in order to return to his own bed; when he reached it, discovering the cradle there, he thought it was the bed of his host, and so, going a bit farther ahead, he got into bed with the host, who awakened on Pinuccio's arrival. Believing that he was next to Adriano, Pinuccio said:

"I swear there was nothing sweeter than being in bed with Niccolosa. Jesus, I had the greatest time with her a man could ever have with a woman, and I can tell you, I stopped up her front door at least six times before leaving her."

When the innkeeper heard this bit of news, he was not overly pleased by it, and at first said to himself: "What the hell is he doing here?" Then, more angry than well-advised, he said: "Pinuccio, what you have done is truly foul, and I don't know why you did it to me: but, by the body of Christ, I shall make you pay for it."

Pinuccio, who was not the most intelligent young man in the world, realizing his mistake, did not try to make amends as best he might have, but replied: "How will you pay me back? What could you do to me?"

The innkeeper's wife, who thought she was with her husband, said to Adriano: "Oh, my, listen to our guests, they're quarreling with each other."

Laughing, Adriano said: "Let them alone, and to hell with them—they drank too much last night."

Thinking she heard her husband grumbling over there and now hearing Adriano, the lady immediately realized where she was and whom she was with; so, being a woman of some intelligence, without saying another word, she got out of bed and, picking up her son's cradle, she groped her way across the room, for there was no light at all, and put it beside the bed in which she thought her daughter was sleeping and got in beside her; and pretending she had just been awakened by the racket her husband was making, she called out to him asking him why he was arguing with Pinuccio, and her husband replied: "Didn't you hear what he says he did to Niccolosa tonight?"

His wife said:

"He's lying through his teeth, he never slept with Niccolosa; why, I've been lying here and haven't closed my eyes once, and you're a fool if you believe him. You drink so much in the evening that you dream all night and wander about without knowing it, and you think you've performed all sorts of miracles; it's a great pity you don't all break your necks! But what's Pinuccio doing over there? Why isn't he in his own bed?"

At this point, seeing how cleverly the lady was covering up her own shame and that of her daughter, Adriano said:

"Pinuccio, I've told you a hundred times that you shouldn't wander about at night and that this bad habit of yours of getting up in your sleep and then telling stories that you've dreamed up would get you in trouble one day. Now come back here, damn you!"

When the host heard what his wife and Adriano were saying, he began to believe that Pinuccio was really dreaming; so, taking him by the shoulders, he began shaking him and calling him; he said: "Pinuccio, wake up, go back to your bed."

Having understood everything that they said, Pinuccio, pretending that he was still dreaming, began uttering nonsense, as the host roared with laughter over this. Finally, as he felt himself being shaken, he pretended to awaken, and calling Adriano, he said: "Is it morning already? Why are you calling me?"

Adriano replied: "Yes, it is, come over here."

Continuing his act, and pretending to be very sleepy, Pinuccio finally got up from the host's side and went back to bed with Adriano, and when day came and they got out of bed, the host began to laugh and to make fun of Pinuccio and his dreams. And in this manner, between one joke and another, the two young men got ready, saddled their nags, packed their saddlebags, and after having a drink with the host, they got on their horses and went on to Florence, no less delighted with the adventure than with the way things turned out. And then afterward, Pinuccio found other ways of meeting with Niccolosa, who kept insisting to her mother that Pinuccio really had been dreaming; and thus, remembering Adriano's embraces, the woman was convinced that she alone had been the only one awake.

The Wife of Bath's Prologue and Tale

The Wife of Bath is inimitable, but not unprecedented. Chaucer was indebted to the long speech of the Old Woman in the *Romance of the Rose* for many of the Wife's traits and for some of her lines. As a lusty widow she belongs to a tradition illustrated vividly by *The Widow*, a portrait by a thirteenth-century jongleur, Gautier le Leu.

The Wife's prologue is built up from a vast medieval repertoire of antifeminist literature and debate. We include A. G. Rigg's new translation of sections from the principal sources: Theophrastus, St. Jerome, and Walter Mapes. Various passages from the Bible, used not only by Jerome but by the Wife herself, are the central authorities for medieval ideas on marriage, remarriage, and widowhood. Further commentary may be found in Chaucer's Parson's own treatment of the seven deadly sins and their remedies.

There are a number of analogues to the Wife's tale, the closest being the *Tale of Florent*, one of many *exempla* in the *Confessio Amantis* by Chaucer's friend John Gower. It has been argued that Chaucer based his tale on Gower's treatment alone, but many scholars believe he had a source now lost.

JEAN DE MEUN

From the *Romance of the Rose*†

[*The Old Woman's Speech*]

* * *

"Know then, that if only, when I was your age, I had been as wise about the games of Love as I am now! For then I was a very great beauty, but now I must complain and moan when I look at my face, which has lost its

---

† From Guillaume de Lorris and Jean de Meun, *The Romance of the Rose*, trans. Charles Dahlberg (Princeton: Princeton UP, 1971) 222–33, 241–42, 247–48. Copyright © 1971 by Princeton University Press. Excerpts reprinted by permission of Princeton University Press. The Old Woman is advising a young lady on how to deal with men; the "son" she addresses is Fair Welcoming, a personification of part of the lady's psyche. This episode occurs in Jean de Meun's part of the poem, written in the years around 1275. We know from the prologue to the *Legend of Good Women* that Chaucer had himself "translated the Romaunce of the Rose"; but the surviving Middle English version is in three fragments, not all of them thought to be by Chaucer, and together they amount to only about one-third of the French poem. The Old Woman's speech translated here is not represented in the extant Middle English text, though we may be certain Chaucer knew it in its original French, and nearly as certain he had once translated it himself.

charms; and I see the inevitable wrinkles whenever I remember how my beauty made the young men skip. I made them so struggle that it was nothing if not a marvel. I was very famous then; word of my highly renowned beauty ran everywhere. At my house there was a crowd so big that no man ever saw the like. At night they knocked on my door: I was really very hard on them when I failed to keep my promises to them, and that happened very often, for I had other company. They did many a crazy thing at which I got very angry. Often my door was broken down, and many of them got into such battles as a result of their hatred and envy that before they were separated they lost their members and their lives. If master Algus, the great calculator, had wanted to take the trouble and had come with his ten figures, by which he certifies and numbers everything, he could not, however well he knew how to calculate, have ascertained the number of these great quarrels. Those were the days when my body was strong and active! As I say, if I had been as wise then as I am now, I would possess the value of a thousand pounds of sterling silver more than I do now, but I acted too foolishly.

"I was young and beautiful, foolish and wild, and had never been to a school of love where they read in the theory, but I know everything by practice. Experiments, which I have followed my whole life, have made me wise in love. Now that I know everything about love, right up to the struggle, it would not be right if I were to fail to teach you the delights that I know and have often tested. He who gives advice to a young man does well. Without fail, it is no wonder that you know nothing, for your beak is too yellow. But in the end, I have so much knowledge upon which I can lecture from a chair that I could never finish. One should not avoid or despise everything that is very old; there one finds both good sense and good custom. Men have proved many times that, however much they have acquired, there will remain to them, in the end, at least their sense and their customs. And since I had good sense and manners, not without great harm to me, I have deceived many a worthy man when he fell captive in my nets. But I was deceived by many before I noticed. Then it was too late, and I was miserably unhappy. I was already past my youth. My door, which formerly was often open, both night and day, stayed constantly near its sill.

" 'No one is coming today, no one came yesterday,' I thought, 'unhappy wretch! I must live in sorrow.' My woeful heart should have left me. Then, when I saw my door, and even myself, at such repose, I wanted to leave the country, for I couldn't endure the shame. How could I stand it when those handsome young men came along, those who formerly had held me so dear that they could not tire themselves, and I saw them look at me sideways as they passed by, they who had once been my dear guests? They went by near me, bounding along without counting me worth an egg, even those who had loved me most; they called me a wrinkled old woman and worse before they had passed on by.

"Besides, my pretty child, no one, unless he were very attentive or had experienced great sorrows, would think or know what grief gripped my heart when in my thought I remembered the lovely speeches, the sweet caresses and pleasures, the kisses and the deeply delightful embraces that were so soon stolen away. Stolen? Indeed, and without return. It would have been better for me to be imprisoned forever in a tower than to have been born so soon. God! Into what torment was I put by the fair gifts which had failed me, and how wretched their remnants had made me! Alas! Why was I born so soon? To whom can I complain, to whom except you, my son, whom I hold so dear? I have no other way to avenge myself than by teaching my doctrine. Therefore, fair son, I indoctrinate you so that, when instructed, you will avenge me on those good-for-nothings; for if God pleases, he will remind you of this sermon when he comes. You know that, because of your age, you have a very great advantage in retaining the sermon so that it will remind you. Plato said: 'It is true of any knowledge that one can keep better the memory of what one learns in one's infancy.'

"Certainly, dear son, my tender young one, if my youth were present, as yours is now, the vengeance that I would take on them could not rightly be written. Everywhere I came I would work such wonders with those scoundrels, who valued me so lightly and who vilified and despised me when they so basely passed by near me, that one would never have heard the like. They and others would pay for their pride and spite; I would have no pity on them. For with the intelligence that God has given me—just as I have preached to you—do you know what condition I would put them in? I would so pluck them and seize their possessions, even wrongly and perversely, that I would make them dine on worms and lie naked on dunghills, especially and first of all those who loved me with more loyal heart and who more willingly took trouble to serve and honor me. If I could, I wouldn't leave them anything worth one bud of garlic until I had everything in my purse and had put them all into poverty; I would make them stamp their feet in living rage behind me. But to regret it is worth nothing; what has gone cannot come. I would never be able to hold any man, for my face is so wrinkled that they don't even protect themselves against my threat. A long time ago the scoundrels who despised me told me so, and from that time on I took to weeping. O God! But it still pleases me when I think back on it. I rejoice in my thought and my limbs become lively again when I remember the good times and the gay life for which my heart so strongly yearns. Just to think of it and to remember it all makes my body young again. Remembering all that happened gives me all the blessings of the world, so that however they may have deceived me, at least I have had my fun. A young lady is not idle when she leads a gay life, especially she who thinks about acquiring enough to take care of her expenses.

* * *

"O fair, most sweet son," said the Old Woman, "O beautiful tender flesh, I want to teach you of the games of Love so that when you have learned them you will not be deceived. Shape yourself according to my art, for no one who is not well informed can pass through this course of games without selling his livestock to get enough money. Now give your attention to hearing and understanding, and to remembering everything that I say, for I know the whole story.

"Fair son, whoever wants to enjoy loving and its sweet ills which are so bitter must know the commandments of Love but must beware that he does not know love itself. I would tell you all the commandments here if I did not certainly see that, by nature, you have overflowing measure of those that you should have. Well numbered, there are ten of them that you ought to know. But he who encumbers himself with the last two is a great fool; they are not worth a false penny. I allow you eight of them, but whoever follows Love in the other two wastes his study and becomes mad. One should not study them in a school. He who wants a lover to have a generous heart and to put love in only one place has given too evil a burden to lovers. It is a false text, false in the letter. In it, Love, the son of Venus, lies, and no man should believe him; whoever does will pay dearly, as you will see by the end of my sermon.

"Fair son, never be generous; and keep your heart in several places, never in one. Don't give it, and don't lend it, but sell it very dearly and always to the highest bidder. See that he who buys it can never get a bargain: no matter how much he may give, never let him have anything in return; it were better if he were to burn or hang or maim himself. In all cases keep to these points: have your hands closed to giving and open to taking. Certainly, giving is great folly, except giving a little for attracting men when one plans to make them one's prey or when one expects such a return for the gift that one could not have sold it for more. I certainly allow you such giving. The gift is good where he who gives multiplies his gift and gains; he who is certain of his profit cannot repent of his gift. I can indeed consent to such a gift. * * *

"But I can tell you this much: if you want to choose a lover, I advise you to give your love, but not too firmly, to that fair young man who so prizes you. Love others wisely, and I will seek out for you enough of them so that you can amass great wealth from them. It is good to become acquainted with rich men if their hearts are not mean and miserly and if one knows how to pluck them well. Fair Welcoming may know whomever he wishes, provided that he gives each one to understand that he would not want to take another lover for a thousand marks of fine milled gold. He should swear that if he had wanted to allow his rose, which was in great demand, to be taken by another, he would have been weighed down with gold and jewels. But, he should go on, his pure heart was so loyal that no man would ever stretch out his hand for it except that man alone who was offering his hand at that moment.

"If there are a thousand, he should say to each: 'Fair lord, you alone will have the rose; no one else will ever have a part. May God fail me if I ever divide it.' He may so swear and pledge his faith to them. If he perjures himself, it doesn't matter; God laughs at such an oath and pardons it gladly.

"Jupiter and the gods laughed when lovers perjured themselves; and many times the gods who loved *par amour* perjured themselves. When Jupiter reassured his wife Juno, he swore by the Styx to her in a loud voice and falsely perjured himself. Since the gods give them, such examples should assure pure lovers that they too may swear falsely by all the saints, convents, and temples. But he is a great fool, so help me God, who believes in the oaths of lovers, for their hearts are too fickle. Young men are in no way stable—nor, often times, are the old—and therefore they belie the oaths and faith that they have given.

"Know also another truth: he who is lord of the fair should collect his market toll everywhere; and he who cannot at one mill—Hey! to another for his whole round! The mouse who has but one hole for retreat has a very poor refuge and makes a very dangerous provision for himself. It is just so with a woman: she is the mistress of all the markets, since everyone works to have her. She should take possessions everywhere. If, after she had reflected well, she wanted only one lover, she would have a very foolish idea. For, by Saint Lifard of Meun, whoever gives her love in a single place has a heart neither free nor unencumbered, but basely enslaved. Such a woman, who takes trouble to love one man alone, has indeed deserved to have a full measure of pain and woe. If she lacks comfort from him, she has no one to comfort her, and those who give their hearts in a single place are those who most lack comfort. In the end, when they are bored, or irritated, all these men fly from their women.

❊ ❊ ❊

"Briefly, all men betray and deceive women; all are sensualists, taking their pleasure anywhere. Therefore we should deceive them in return, not fix our hearts on one. Any woman who does so is a fool; she should have several friends and, if possible, act so as to delight them to the point where they are driven to distraction. If she has no graces, let her learn them. Let her be haughtier toward those who, because of her hauteur, will take more trouble to serve her in order to deserve her love, but let her scheme to take from those who make light of her love. She should know games and songs and flee from quarrels and disputes. If she is not beautiful, she should pretty herself; the ugliest should wear the most coquettish adornments.

* * *

"If she has a lovely neck and white chest, she should see that her dressmaker lower her neckline, so that it reveals a half foot, in front and back, of her fine white flesh; thus she may deceive more easily. And if her shoulders are too large to be pleasing at dances and balls, she should wear a dress of fine cloth and thus appear less ungainly. And if, because of insect bites or pimples, she doesn't have beautiful, well-kept hands, she should be careful not to neglect them but should remove the spots with a needle or wear gloves so that the pimples and scabs will not show.

"If her breasts are too heavy she should take a scarf or towel to bind them against her chest and wrap it right around her ribs, securing it with needle and thread or by a knot; thus she can be active at her play.

"And like a good little girl she should keep her chamber of Venus tidy. If she is intelligent and well brought up, she will leave no cobwebs around but will burn or destroy them, tear them down and sweep them up, so that no grime can collect anywhere.

"If her feet are ugly, she should keep them covered and wear fine stockings if her legs are large. In short, unless she's very stupid she should hide any defect she knows of.

"For example, if she knows that her breath is foul she should spare no amount of trouble never to fast, never to speak to others on an empty stomach, and, if possible, to keep her mouth away from people's noses.

"When she has the impulse to laugh, she should laugh discreetly and prettily, so that she shows little dimples at the corners of her mouth. She should avoid puffing her cheeks and screwing her face up in grimaces. Her lips should be kept closed and her teeth covered; a woman should always laugh with her mouth closed, for the sight of a mouth stretched like a gash across the face is not a pretty one. If her teeth are not even, but ugly and quite crooked, she will be thought little of if she shows them when she laughs.

"There is also a proper way to cry. But every woman is adept enough to cry well on any occasion, for, even though the tears are not caused by grief or shame or hurt, they are always ready. All women cry; they are used to crying in whatever way they want. But no man should be disturbed when he sees such tears flowing as fast as rain, for these tears, these sorrows and lamentations flow only to trick him. A woman's weeping is nothing but a ruse; she will overlook no source of grief. But she must be careful not to reveal, in word or deed, what she is thinking of.

"It is also proper to behave suitably at the table. Before sitting down, she should look around the house and let everyone understand that she herself knows how to run a house. Let her come and go, in the front rooms and in back, and be the last to sit down, being sure to wait a little before she finally takes her seat. Then, when she is seated at table, she should serve everyone as well as possible. She should carve in front of the others and pass the bread to those around her. To deserve praise, she should serve food in front of the one who shares her plate. She should put a thigh or wing before him, or, in his presence, carve the beef or pork, meat or fish, depending upon what food there happens to be. She should never be niggardly in her servings as long as there is anyone unsatisfied. Let her guard against getting her fingers wet up to the joint in the sauce, against smearing her lips with soup, garlic, or fat meat, against piling up too large morsels and stuffing her mouth. When she has to moisten a piece in any sauce, either *sauce verte, cameline,* or *jauce,* she should hold the bit with her fingertips and bring it carefully up to her mouth, so that no drop of soup, sauce, or pepper falls on her breast. She must drink so neatly that she doesn't spill anything on herself, for anyone who happened to see her spill would think her either very clumsy or very greedy. Again, she must take care not to touch her drinking cup while she has food in her mouth. She should wipe her mouth so clean that grease will not stick to the cup, and should be particularly careful about her upper lip, for, when there is grease on it, untidy drops of it will show in her wine. She should drink only a little at a time, however great her appetite, and never empty a cup, large or small, in one breath, but rather drink little and often, so that she doesn't go around causing others to say that she gorges or drinks too much while her mouth is full. She should avoid swallowing the rim of her cup, as do many greedy nurses who are so foolish that they pour wine down their hollow throats as if they were casks, who pour it down in such huge gulps that they become completely fuddled and dazed. Now a lady must be careful not to get drunk, for a drunk, man or woman, cannot keep anything secret; and when a woman gets drunk, she has no defenses at all in her, but blurts out whatever she thinks and abandons herself to anyone when she gives herself over to such bad conduct.

"She must also beware of falling asleep at the table, for she would be much less pleasant; many disagreeable things can happen to those who take such naps. There is no sense in napping in places where one should remain awake, and many have been deceived in this way, have many times fallen, either forward or backward or sideways, and broken an arm or head or ribs. Let a woman beware lest such a nap overtake her; let her recall Palinurus, the helmsman of Acneas's ship. While awake, he steered it well, but when sleep conquered him, he fell from the rudder into the sea and drowned within sight of his companions, who afterward mourned greatly for him.

"Further, a lady must be careful not to be too reluctant to play, for she might wait around so long that no one would want to offer her his hand. She should seek the diversion of love as long as youth deflects her in that direction, for, when old age assails a woman, she loses both the joy and the assault of Love. A wise woman will gather the fruit of love in the flower of her age. The unhappy woman loses her time who passes it without enjoying love. And if she disbelieves this advice of mine, which I give for the profit of all, be sure that she will be sorry when age withers her. But I know that women will believe me, particularly those who are sensible, and will stick to our rules and will say many paternosters for my soul, when I am dead who now teach and comfort them. I know that this lesson will be read in many schools.

"O fair sweet son, if you live—for I see well that you are writing down in the book of your heart the whole of my teaching, and that, when you depart from me, you will study more, if it please God, and will become a master like me—if you live I confer on you the license to teach, in spite of all chancellors, in chambers or in cellars, in meadow, garden, or thicket, under a tent or behind the tapestries, and to inform the students in wardrobes, attics, pantries, and stables, if you find no more pleasant places. And may my lesson be well taught when you have learned it well!

"A woman should be careful not to stay shut up too much, for while she remains in the house, she is less seen by everybody, her beauty is less well-known, less desired, and in demand less. She should go often to the principal church and go visiting, to weddings, on trips, at games, feasts, and round dances, for in such places the God and Goddess of Love keep their schools and sing mass to their disciples.

"But of course, if she is to be admired above others, she has to be well-dressed. When she is well turned out and goes through the streets, she should carry herself well, neither too stiffly nor too loosely, not too upright nor too bent over, but easily and graciously in any crowd. She should move her shoulders and sides so elegantly that no one might find anyone with more beautiful movements. And she should walk daintily in her pretty little shoes, so well made that they fit her feet without any wrinkles whatever.

* * *

"And what I say about the black mare, about the sorrel horse and mare and the gray and black horses, I say about the cow and bull and the ewe and ram; for we do not doubt that these males want all females as their wives. Never doubt, fair son, that in the same way all females want all males. All women willingly receive them. By my soul, fair son, it is thus with every man and every woman as far as natural appetite goes. The law restrains them little from exercising it. A little! but too much, it seems to me, for when the law has put them together, it wants either of them, the boy or the girl, to be able to have only the other, at least as long as he or she lives. But at the same time they are tempted to use their free will. I know very well that such a thing does rise up, only some keep themselves from it because of shame, others because they fear trouble; but Nature controls them to that end just as she does the animals that we were just speaking of. I know it from my own experience, for I always took trouble to be loved by all men. And if I had not feared shame, which holds back and subdues many hearts, when I went along the streets where I always wanted to go—so dressed up in adornments that a dressed-up doll would have been nothing in comparison—I would have received all or at least many of those young boys, if I had been able and if it had pleased them, who pleased me so much when they threw me those sweet glances. (Sweet God! What pity for them seized me when those looks came toward me!) I wanted them all one after the other, if I could have satisfied them all. And it seemed to me that, if they could have, they would willingly have received me. I do not except prelates or monks, knights, burgers, or canons, clerical or lay, fool-ish or wise, as long as they were at the height of their powers. They would have jumped out of their orders if they had not thought that they might fail when they asked for my love; but if they had known my thought and the whole of our situations they would not have been in such doubt. And I think that several, if they had dared, would have broken their marriages. If one of them had had me in private he would not have remembered to be faithful. No man would have kept his situation, his faith, vows, or religion unless he were some demented fool who was smitten by love and loved his sweetheart loyally. Such a man, perhaps, would have called me paid and thought about his own possessions, which he would not have given up at any price. But there are very few such lovers, so help me God and Saint Amand; I certainly think so. If he spoke to me for a long time, no matter what he said, lies or truth, I could have made him move everything. What-ever he was, secular, or in an order, with a belt of red leather or of cord, no matter what headdress he wore, I think that he would have carried on with me if he thought that I wanted him or even if I had allowed him. Thus Nature regulates us by inciting our hearts to pleasure. For this reason Venus deserves less blame for loving Mars.

* * *

"By my soul, if I had been wise, I would have been a very rich lady, for I was acquainted with very great people when I was already a coy darling, and I certainly was held in considerable value by them, but when I got something of value from one of them, then, by the faith that I owe God or Saint Thibaut, I would give it all to a rascal who brought me great shame but pleased me more. I called all the others lover, but it was he alone that I loved. Understand, he didn't value me at one pea, and in fact told me so. He was bad—I never saw anyone worse—and he never ceased despising me. This scoundrel, who didn't love me at all, would call me a common whore. A woman has very poor judgment, and I was truly a woman. I never loved a man who loved me, but, do you know, if that scoundrel had laid open my shoulder or broken my head, I would have thanked him for it. He wouldn't have known how to beat me so much that I would not have had him throw himself upon me, for he knew very well how to make his peace, however much he had done against me. He would never have treated me so badly, beaten me or dragged me or wounded my face or bruised it black, that he would not have begged my favor before he moved from the place. He would never have said so many shameful things to me that he would not have counseled peace to me and then made me happy in bed, so that we had peace and concord again. Thus he had me caught in his snare, for this false, treacherous thief was a very hard rider in bed. I couldn't live without him; I wanted to follow him always. If he had fled, I would certainly have gone as far as London in England to seek him, so much did he please me and make me happy. He put me to shame and I him, for he led a life of great gaiety with the lovely gifts that he had received from me. He put none of them into saving, but played everything at dice in the taverns. He never learned any other trade, and there was no need then for him to do so, for I gave him a great deal to spend, and I certainly had it for the taking. Everybody was my source of income, while he spent it willingly and always on ribaldry; he burned everything in his lechery. He had his mouth stretched so wide that he did not want to hear anything good. Living never pleased him except when it was passed in idleness and pleasure. In the end I saw him in a bad situation as a result, when gifts were lacking for us. He became poor and begged his bread, while I had nothing worth two carding combs and had never married a lord. Then, as I have told you, I came through these woods, scratching my temples. May this situation of mine be an example to you, fair sweet son; remember it. Act so wisely that it may be better with you because of my instruction. For when your rose is withered and white hairs assail you, gifts will certainly fail."

* * *

GAUTIER LE LEU

The Widow†

My lords, I should like to instruct you. We all of us must go off to the wars, on that expedition from which no man returns. And do you know how they dispose of someone who has been convoked to that army? They carry him to the church on a litter, toes up and with great speed; and his wife follows after him. Those who are closest to the wife lay hands and arms on her to keep her from, at the very least, beating her palms together. For she cries out in a loud voice: "Holy Mother Mary, fair lady! It is a wonder I can keep going, I am so full of grief and affliction! I have more pain than I can bear! How grieved I am that I live on! How hard and bitter is this life! May it not be God's will that I travel much farther on this road, but let me be laid with my husband, to whom I swore my faith!"

So she carries on, acting her part, in which there is scarcely a word of truth. At the entrance of the church she begins again her business of shrieking and wailing. The priest, who would like to get on with the collection, quickly orders the candles to be lit; and when he has asked God's pardon for the dead man, he says the mass in a great hurry. When the service is finished and the corpse has been laid on his back in the black earth among the worms, then the good wife wants to jump into the open grave. Whoever should see her then, trembling and blinking her eyes open and shut and beating her fists together, would say: "That woman could very well lose her mind." And so they pull her back, and two of them hold her from behind and bring her all the way home. There her neighbors make her drink cold water to cool off her grief.

At the door of her house she begins all over again: "My husband, what has become of you? You have not come back to me. My God, why have you been taken from me? When I think how your wealth had increased, how your business prospered, how well everything was going for you! How well your workaday clothes fit you and how becoming was your Sunday suit, which we had made on New Year's Day! Oh, Magpie, you told me the truth! And you, Heron, how I cursed you for squawking so much this year! You, Dog, how often you howled! And you, Chicken, you sang me a warning! Oh, Devil, how have you bewitched me so that I cannot conjure my love in God's name to return to me! If it were possible to raise a dead man, I would pay any tribute to do so. God, how I dreamed this year— although I have said nothing about it—base, shameful dreams! May God

† From *Fabliaux: Ribald Tales from the Old French,* trans. Robert Hellman and Richard O'Gorman (New York: Thomas Y. Crowell Company, 1965) 145–56. English translation copyright © 1965 by Robert Hellman and Richard O'Gorman. Reprinted by permission of Harper and Row, Publishers, Inc. and Weidenfeld & Nicolson Ltd. Nothing is known of Gautier le Leu except for the ten surviving works that bear his name or can be confidently attributed to him. In his youth he may have been a student at Orleans. "The Widow," which is more a satirical portrait than a fabliau, can be dated ca. 1248 on the basis of internal evidence.

turn them to my advantage! Husband, the day before yesterday I dreamt
that you were in the church, and both the doors were locked. And now you
are locked in the earth! And then, immediately after that, I dreamt that you
had a black cloak and a pair of great leaden boots, and dressed so you dived
into the water and never came up again. You died only a short time after.
Those dreams really came true.

"I dreamt that you were dressed in a coat with a great hood. In your
hands you held a stone with which you beat down the wall of the house.
Lord, what a hole you left me there! No one mourned for you, but I do so
again and again! Then it seemed to me—but I am very loth to speak of it—
that in my dream a dove, white and beautiful, descended into my breast
and made the wall whole again. I do not know what this last dream means."

Then begin the buzzings, the counsels, the parliaments of relatives and
neighbors, of nieces and cousins: "In all charity, my good lady, you must
find a good man, someone who is neither a fool nor a rascal, to take over
this property and maintain this house." Upon which the wife may be seen
to make a sad face and answer sharply: "Ladies, I have no inclination that
way. Henceforth may God curse those who make such proposals to me, for
they do not please me at all." Then she curses all her pretty clothes.

So let us leave the lady to tell over her sorrows and misfortunes, and
speak of her husband, who in all his life had never contented her. He is led
to the great judgment seat up above, where he will be given short shrift if
he cannot account for all his actions here below, and he is held accountable
for the smallest things. He cries out and calls on his household, for whom
he has provided so well, and on his relatives and friends, on whom he has
bestowed his wealth, to come and help him, for the love of God. But this
is something that no man may hope for. Then with a sad face he calls on
his wife, who was so dear to him; but that lady has other concerns. A sweet
sensation pricks her heart and lifts up her spirit, and arouses in the bearded
counselor under her skirts an appetite for meat, neither peacock nor crane,
but that dangling sausage for which so many are eager.

The lady is no longer concerned with the dead; so she washes herself and
dresses up and dyes her frock yellow and tucks up her furbelows and does
over her jabots, her ruffles, and her lace cuffs. She puts on her best things,
and as a new-molted falcon goes flapping through the air, so does the lady
go sporting and showing herself off from street to street. She greets people
with great ingenuousness, bowing right down to the ground. Repeatedly
she closes her mouth tight and purses her lips. She is neither lazy nor bitter
nor sour nor quarrelsome, but sweeter than cinnamon, quicker turning and
more agile than a tambourine or a weather vane. Her heart flies on wings.
She is not inclined to grow angry or to complain or to scold, but rather
seeks to appear both good and full of humility. And she often pulls her
wimple forward to hide her hollow cheeks, which look like open eggshells.

And now that I have told you of her manner and in what style she was
dressed, let me say briefly what sort of life she leads, both on Sundays and
weekdays. On Monday she sets out on her way; and whoever she meets, be

she blond or brunette, she lets her understand what is on her mind. So she comes and goes the entire day. She has many things to remember and when she goes to bed at night, then does she begin to make her rounds. Her heart opens wide and she sends it forth to the many places where people have hardly any use for her. No night is so dark as to keep her heart from voyaging. Then she says over and over again: "It's my opinion that I would suit this one well; he is a fine young man. But that one wouldn't be interested in me at all if my friends should bring up the subject. And there is nothing for me in that other one; he's not worth two eggs." So she goes on all night, for there is no one to keep her from it. And, when morning comes, she says to herself: "I was born lucky! For there is no one who can order me about. I need fear nobody, neither friend nor stranger, neither brown nor blond nor redheaded. My halter is broken." She has no one to answer to. There is no feast or wedding but she makes part of the company, and she needs no invitation. She has plenty to eat and to drink. She lacks only one thing: that rod to chase away the pain in her bottom. And this she searches for and runs after.

She cannot bear the sight of her children and pecks at them the way a hen pecks at her chicks when she is kneeling before the cock. She puts them away from her, becomes a sort of bogeyman for them. Often she makes wax candles and she habitually offers great numbers of them so that God may rid her of her children or that the plague may take them. "Because of them," she says, "I cannot find anyone who will have me. No one would get mixed up in this." And she takes to beating them and knocking them about; she slaps them and scratches them and bites them and calls down the plague on them. <u>Because she does not have the love of a man, the children must pay</u>.

This she does and a great deal more. If she has scraped some money together, she carries it about with her and says that this very morning a man came to her door to pay it to her. Then she speaks of Robert or Martin, who still owe her money, seven times what she has just collected, and who will pay her soon, perhaps in two weeks. To hear her tell it, she is very rich.

If she meets a gossip, someone who likes to go about repeating what she hears, she sidles up to her and says: "There is something bothering me. I'm a very good friend of yours—for you're not stupid or proud—I've always liked you, and for a long time I've been meaning to ask you to come for a walk with me. I know you won't mind if I chat with you a little, because I'm sure we must be related, or so my mother used to say. But my heart is full of grief for my husband whom I have lost. My friends have forbidden me to put off my mourning, because I couldn't gain anything by doing so. And certainly my husband was very good to me. He gave me a great many things, both shoes and dresses. He made me mistress of himself and of his property. He was a very decent sort, but he wasn't much good in bed. As soon as he got into bed, he would turn his behind on me; and he would sleep that way all night. That was all the pleasure I had. It used to make me very unhappy.

"Of course, I can't deny that he was a very wealthy man before I married him. But he was already quite bald when he came my way, and I was just a little girl with a dirty little face. You were only a baby then, running about like a little chick after your mother, who was a good friend of my mother's—they were close relatives. I swear by Our Savior, I am so grieved at his death! But one thing about my husband, he was a good provider; he knew how to rake in the money and how to save it, may his soul rest in peace! I have plenty of kettles and pots and white quilts and good beds and chests and chairs; and bonnets and coats and furs, which he had made in great quantity. Also I have plenty of sheets, both linen and woolen, and two kinds of firewood, the large and the small. My house is not exactly bare; I certainly have lovely kitchen equipment; I still have two caldrons, one made in the old style with the edges turned all around it—my husband set great value on it. But I don't care to brag about what God has given me.

"You know Dieudonné very well? And you know Herbert well and Baudouin, Gombert's son? Do you know anything about their situations? I'm being pushed to marry again. But it's amazing about people: you imagine there is wealth where there is scarcely enough to eat. Many people are deep in debt, but I am truly rich. You can see the bark of the tree, but you can't tell what lies underneath. A great deal so-called wealth is mostly wind, but mine is there to see. I make lots of sheets every year. I'm an honest woman and well brought up. The best people hereabouts often come calling on me. Some of them are relatives of yours. But I don't want to drop names. Are you related to Gomer? But as for Gomer, well, I won't say any more about him.

"But let me tell you something, my dear friend. Last year I went to a fortune teller, and he made me lie down flat in the middle of a circle, and he looked me over, and he said I would yet have a young man. Do you know of any worthy men in your neighborhood? The one who lives next door to you seems like a very intelligent fellow. He gave me such a look the other day! But I was on my guard and took good care not to look back. A man who lives at Tournai and who is related to me on my father's side spoke to me of a friend of his, a very rich, propertied gentleman, who lives close by him. But he's old, they tell me, and I've come to despise him of late. I swear by Saint Leonard I will never take an old man! Because when it comes to getting a little bed exercise, I've no mind to go without seed and take the chaff. I have enough property to get a handsome young man.

"Dear friend, think of me if there is any honest, sensible fellow among your acquaintance; he would be well matched with me. Now be nice and smart, and if you can find something for me, so may God pardon me, you will have a good reward. I don't like making promises or getting involved, but of one thing you can be sure: if this business turns out well, you will be a very well-dressed woman. Look around in the Chausée and Neufbourg sections of Valenciennes or at Anzin. Who is this son of Dame Wiborc and of Geoffrey? The day before yesterday when they proposed Isabel to him, he gave them the cold shoulder. But if you don't mind, perhaps you might speak to him secretly.

"But I've been here such a long time! I would stay the night, but I'm afraid of putting you out. Let's make an appointment for Sunday. Clemence will come too, and we'll have some apples and nuts and some of that wine from Laenois; and I'll tell you about that relative of mine—he doesn't live far from here—who wants to make a nun of me." Then she gives her a tap with the back of her hand and turns away and goes home. The other one goes her way and repeats what she has heard everywhere.

Meanwhile, this is how the widow fares: her hairy Goliath so pricks and excites her and the fire burns so high in her that at last she succeeds in getting a man. And when she has caught him in her trap, he can really complain of being worn out. Though he may know his way about those tender netherparts, though he be lively and quick and can well strike and plunge, he will still be despised in the morning. No one can help him there; he will get rough treatment.

As soon as the lady gets out of bed, she kicks the cat off the hearth. Then all sorts of ill feelings come out, scoldings, reproaches: "What have I got under my roof?—a poor thing, a wretch, a softling. Aie! God must hate me! That I, who disdained proper young men, gallants and gentlemen, that I should take up with such a born weakling! May all who deal in such deceits have bad luck! And after putting me to such torments! All he wants to do is eat and sleep. All night long he snores like a pig. That's his delight and his pastime. Am I not ill treated then? When I stretch out next to him all naked and he turns away from me, it almost tears the heart out of me. My husband, my lord, you never treated me that way. You called me your sweet beloved, and so I called you too, because you turned toward me and kissed me sweetly and said to begin with: 'My beautiful wife and lady, what a sweet breath you have!' Husband, those were your very words. May your soul rest in heaven! And this vagabond treats me like the dung in his barnyard. But I well know, by Saint Loy, that his morals are no better than those of an Albigensian heretic. He doesn't care about loving women."

To which the man replies: "Lady, you are mistaken. You have such a wry face that I find it hard to touch you. And I cannot keep my agreements with you. Goliath gapes too often. I can't satisfy him; I'm likely to die before I do."

"Lying coward!" says the lady. "You ought to be a monk and enter a monastery. You have served me badly. Oh, it is easy to see that I was not in my right mind when I gave up John, with his property, good tillable land, and Geoffrey and Gilbert and Baudouin and Foucuin, and took the worst man from here to Beauvais. Oh, husband, you are ill replaced! You deserve to be deeply mourned, for never was there a better man than you. Alas! that all your good qualities should be gone with you: your wisdom and your knowledge, your good manners and your kindness! You were always kind and submissive. Never did you curse me or beat me or give me an ill word. Whereas this whelp threatens me. It's only right that I hate him."

The young man answers angrily: "Lady, you have a greedy mouth in you

that too often demands to be fed. It has tired my poor old war-horse out.
I've just withdrawn him all shrunken and sore. One cannot work so much
without getting weary and limp. The peasant may be a good worker, but
not every day is a working day. You can drive the mare so hard as not to
leave a drop of blood or saliva in her. You have so milked and drained me
that I am half dead, and half mad too. I'll tell you straight out: a man must
have a tough skin indeed to let the devil trick him into taking a widow with
children, for he will never have a moment's peace thereafter. Come on
then, my sour old girl, give me the thirty marks you promised me on Tuesday or I won't do any more of this back-humping work. But by Saint Richier,
if I don't get them, you'll pay dearly."

When she hears her young man ask for money, the good woman is furious.
She sends him to all the devils in hell. She would sooner he beat her or
killed her than that she should hand over that sum; he'll not have a single
mark of her money. She begins once more to curse him and to quarrel and
say foul things. "Ah, wastrel!" she cries. "All my goods are wasted. You
have so bled me and robbed me that I no longer have a stick of firewood
nor a grain of wheat. My house has been swept clean. You're a heavy
burden to bear. And we know your family well—the stinking wretches—
and your sisters and your aunts, who are all dirty whores. . . ."

At these words the young man leaps up, and without so much as a by-
your-leave he grabs her by the haunches and gives her such a thrashing,
more than she bargined for, that he soon pays her in full for her foul words.
Then he leaps on her again and beats and pounds her with his fists until he
is all in a sweat and worn out. When she has had enough, the widow runs
and hides in her chamber, without hat or headdress. She has been so roughly
handled in the fray that her hair is all disheveled. She goes to bed and
covers up, forbids anyone to come in, and lies there licking her wounds.

But in the end she calls out: "Oh, you thief, how you have hurt me! Now
may God grant me a quick death and bring me where I can be with my
husband. May my soul follow his and may I abide with him. For there is
nothing I want more, dear husband, than to be with you." And she speaks
in an affectedly weak voice as though she were really dying; for she knows
how to make the most of her wounds. Then after a while, she begins to
speak up a little; she calls for hot broth, for cheese tarts, for little cakes. Also
she takes a great many baths, morning and even, early and late, until she
is all healed and cured. Then, the quarrel over, the two of them come back
together again.

For one thing I have learned is that if a man knows how to swing his
balls he can overcome all ills. Where such a man lives, there the cat is
commended to God—no one beats it or lays a hand on it; there the cush-
ions are plumped up and the benches pushed against the wall, so that the
man may not hurt himself on them; there not a log remains on the hearth;
there is he loved and served and given everything he wants—chicken and
other fowl; there is he lord and master; there is he washed and combed and
his hair parted. For I tell you once again, according to the proverb: she who

would have her husband soothe her tail must pile endearments on his head.

You who despise women, think of those endearments in that hour when she is under you and you on top. He who would experience that joy must give up to his beloved a great part of his will, no matter how much it grieves him to do so. A man who is not distressed from time to time is neither kind nor honest. For if my wife scolds and says nasty things to me, all I need do is leave and she stops. Anyone who tried to answer her would be reasoning with madness. And it is better for me to go away than to hit her with a piece of wood. Lords, you who are submissive, deceitful, and blusterers, do not be dismayed in any way: submissive men have more joy than do those quarrelsome rascals who are always looking for a fight. And finally, Gautier le Leu says that he who will oppress his wife or quarrel with her only because she wants what all her neighbors want does not have a gentle heart. But I do not choose to go any deeper into this question. A woman only does what she must. The tale is done. Set up the drinks.

THEOPHRASTUS

From *The Golden Book on Marriage*†

[Theophrastus was a Greek philosopher (371–287 B.C.), who succeeded Aristotle as head of the Peripatetic school. He wrote many works on philosophy, but is best known for his *Characters*, brief sketches of types of men. His work *On Marriage* has not survived in the original, but has been preserved in translation into Latin in Jerome's treatise *Against Jovinian* (see pp. 328–42). It is better to treat it as a separate work from Jerome's in that it presents a purely pagan attitude toward the subject of marriage. The introductory words are by Jerome.]

* * *

[JEROME] I feel that in my catalogue of women [see p. 339], I have exceeded the customary space given to examples, and may rightly be censured by a critical reader. But what else can I do, when women of our own time attack the authority of Paul, and, when the funeral of their first husband is not yet over, start to recite arguments for a second marriage?[1] As they despise belief in Christian chastity, let them at any rate learn chastity from the pagans. There is a book by Theophrastus on the subject of marriage, called *The Golden Book*, in which he discusses whether the wise man should take a wife. After concluding that if the woman is beautiful and virtuous, her parents noble, and the husband healthy and rich, then a wise man may sometimes marry, he immediately adds:

[THEOPHRASTUS] However, it is very unusual for all these conditions to

---

†This excerpt and the ones from St. Jerome and Walter Map following were prepared for this volume by A. G. Rigg. Because of the length and complexity of these texts, Professor Rigg has used a combination of summary, translation, and annotation to present

them to the reader.

1. Cf. the *Wife of Bath's Prologue* 587 ff. (hereafter cited as *WBP*), and Deschamps, *Miroir de Mariage* (cited in *Sources and Analogues* p. 220).

be present in a marriage, and therefore the philosopher[2] ought not to take a wife. Firstly, the pursuit of Philosophy is impeded: no one can serve both books and a wife at the same time.[3] There are many things which women require—fine clothes, gold, jewels, money, maid-servants, all kinds of furniture, litters, and gilded coaches. And then there is the ceaseless chatter and grumbling all through the night—"So-and-so has smarter clothes to go out in than I do. Everyone admires *her*, but when I meet other women they all look down on me, poor thing. Why were you looking at the girl next door? What were you saying to our serving girl? What did you bring me from the market?"[4]

We are not allowed a friend or companion, for she suspects that friendship for another means hatred of her.[5] If a learned lecturer is at some nearby city, we can neither leave our wives behind nor burden ourselves with them. It is difficult to look after a poor wife, but torture to put up with a rich one.[6]

Moreover, there is no choice in the matter of a wife: one has to take whatever comes along. If she's nagging, stupid, ugly, proud, smelly—whatever fault she has, we find out *after* marriage. Now a horse, an ass, a cow, a dog, the cheapest slaves, clothes, kettles, a wooden chair, a cup, a clay pot—all these are tested first, and *then* purchased. Only a wife is not put on display—in case her faults are discovered before we take her.[7]

We always have to be noticing her appearance and praising her beauty, in case she thinks that we don't like her if we ever look at another woman. She has to be called "Madam"; we have to celebrate her birthday and make oaths by her health, saying "Long may you live!" We have to honor her nurse, her old nanny, her father's servant, her foster son, her elegant follower, her curly-haired go-between, some eunuch (cut short for the sake of a long and carefree pleasure!)—all of them are adulterers under another name. Whoever has her favors, you have to love them, like it or not.[8]

If you give the whole management of the house to her, she complains "I'm just a servant"; if you keep any part of it to yourself, "You don't trust me!"[9] She begins to hate you and quarrel with you, and if you don't watch out she'll be mixing poison. If you allow into the house old dames, soothsayers, fortune-tellers, and gem-setters and silkworkers, she says, "You're endangering my virtue!"; but if you don't, "Why are you so suspicious?" But what good is it to keep a careful watch over her?—if a wife is unchaste, she can't be guarded, and if she isn't she doesn't need guarding. In any case, the compulsion to be chaste is an untrustworthy guard—the woman really to be called "chaste" is the one who could sin if she wanted to. Men are quick to desire a beautiful woman: an ugly one is herself lecherous. <u>It is difficult to guard what everyone is after: it is misery to possess what no one thinks worth having</u>. However, there's less misery in having an ugly wife than in trying to keep a beautiful one. Nothing is safe which the whole

2. In all these discussions, "wise man, philosopher," etc. (Lat. *sapiens*) are equivalent to the Middle English *clerk* (i.e., Jankyn, the Wife's fifth husband).
3. The remark is echoed by Cicero, cited by both Jerome and Walter Map (below pp. 339, 345).
4. WBP, 235–42.

5. Chaucer seems to have taken this as part of the woman's speech.
6. WBP, 248–52.
7. WBP, 282–92.
8. WBP, 293–306.
9. WBP, 308–10.

population has set its heart on—one man uses his handsome figure to court her, another his intellect, another his witticisms, another his generosity: some day, in some way, the castle besieged on all sides must surrender.[1]

Now some people marry in order to have someone to run the home, or to cheer them up, or to avoid loneliness: but (i) a faithful servant, obedient to his master's authority and conforming to his wishes, is a better major-domo than a wife, who only considers herself mistress of the house if she goes against her husband's wishes; that is, she does what she pleases, not what she's told. (ii) At the side of a sick man friends, and servants bound by ties of old benefits, do more good than a wife: she puts her tears on our charge sheet, and sells her flood of tears in the hope of the inheritance: by her show of solicitude she upsets the sick man's temper by her despair. On the other hand, if our wife herself is sick, we have to be sick in sympathy and are never allowed to leave her bedside. Or, if she is a good and gentle wife (a rare bird!), then we suffer agony with her in her birthpangs, and are in anguish when she is in danger. (iii) The philosopher can never be alone: he has with him all men who are or ever were good, and can send his free mind where he wishes. What he cannot reach in the flesh, he embraces in contemplation. And if there is a shortage of men, he speaks with God. He will never be less lonely than when he is alone.

Further, to take a wife in order to have children, either to make sure that our name survives, or to have supports in our old age and be sure of having heirs—this is the most stupid of all. For what does it matter to us as we leave this world if someone else has the same name as we did? The son does not immediately assume his father's name (?),[2] and there are countless people who are called by the same name. Why bring up at home aids for your old age, who may either die before you, or may turn out to have bad characters (or at the least, when your son reaches maturity, he will certainly think you are taking a long time to die)? Better and more certain heirs are your friends and neighbors whom you can choose judiciously, than heirs whom you have to have, whether you like it or not. Even if your heredity is sufficiently secure, it is better to use up your wealth while you still live, rather than to abandon to uncertain uses what you have collected by your own hard work.

ST. JEROME

From *Against Jovinian*†

[This treatise, written ca. A.D. 393, was the principal source for the medieval Church in its arguments for clerical celibacy. It is referred to by the Wife of Bath thus:

1. *WBP*, 253–72 (with the arguments in a different order).
2. Translation doubtful.

† Prepared for this volume by A. G. Rigg; see head-note, p. 326.

And eek ther was somtyme a clerk at Rome,
A cardinal, that highte Seint Jerome,
That made a book agayn Jovinian.

(673–75)

It is, however, primarily a refutation of heresy rather than an antifeminist tract: in two books (ed. J. P. Migne, *Patrologia Latina* 23, cols. 211–338), Jerome answers the following points made by the monk Jovinian:

(i) that virgins, widows, and married women, once they have been baptized, are of the same merit, as long as they do not differ because of other actions; (ii) those who are purified by baptism cannot be overcome by the devil; (iii) there is no distinction between fasting and the grateful receiving of food; (iv) all who have been baptized and have kept the Faith obtain the same reward in heaven.

The first of these heresies is dealt with in the first book and is the only one that concerns us here. Quotations are selected below only insofar as they contribute to the general antifeminist debate, the arguments of the Wife of Bath, and the status of the Wife in the eyes of the Church. Omissions are indicated by * * * where the argument is irrelevant for the present purpose. Translations of biblical quotations (in Jerome's Latin) sometimes follow the wording of the King James Bible of 1611; often, however, the Latin presents a different sense from the original Hebrew on which the 1611 version was based—for instance, 1 Corinthians 7.3, the King James version has "Let the husband render unto the wife due benevolence," but the Latin here reads *Uxori vir debitum reddat*, "man shal yelde to his wyf hire dette" (*Wife of Bath's Prologue* 130). In all such cases I have translated Jerome's Latin.]

After some introductory remarks, Jerome presents Jovinian's arguments:

[i, 5: col. 215-] First he says that it is God's decree that "for this reason a man shall leave his father and his mother, and shall cleave unto his wife, and the two shall be in one flesh" (Gen. 2.24). In case we object that this is only an Old Testament saying, he adds that it was confirmed by God himself in the Gospels, "What God has joined together, let no man put asunder" (Matt. 19.5–6).[1] He then adds the quotation, "Be fruitful, and multiply, and replenish the earth" (Gen. 1.28), and lists in order Seth, Enos, Cainam, Malaleel, Jared, Enoch, Mathusalem, Lamech, and Noah, all of whom had wives and produced children according to God's decree. * * * "There was Enoch, who walked with God and was snatched up into Heaven. There was Noah, who, despite all those who must have been virgins by their age, went into the ark alone with his sons and wives, and was saved in the shipwreck of the world. Again, after the flood, pairs of men and women were joined together in, as it were, a second beginning of the human race, and the blessing 'Be fruitful, and multiply, and replenish the earth' was renewed (Gen. 8.17, etc.)." * * * He runs to Abraham, Isaac,

1. For the whole of this section, cf. the *Wife of Bath's Prologue*, (hereafter cited as WBP) 27–29.

and Jacob, of whom the first had three wives, the second one, and the third four. * * * He says that because of his faith Abraham received a blessing in the birth of a son. * * * [His examples include, among others] Rebecca, * * * Jacob, * * * Rachel, * * * Joseph (the most holy and chaste), * * * and all the patriarchs who had wives and were equally blessed by God. * * * [He continues with many more, e.g.] Sampson, * * * he says that there was no difference between Jephta and his daughter who was sacrificed to God. * * * Samuel, he says, produced children, and his priestly honor was not diminished by his embracing a wife. * * * Need I mention Solomon[2] whom he places in his catalogue of married men, asserting that he was a figure of the Savior? * * *

Passing on to the New Testament, he gives us Zacharias, Elizabeth, Peter and his mother-in-law, and the rest of the Apostles, and then adds, "In case my opponents hope to put up a vain defense, and claim that all this was because the early world needed populating, let them hear what Paul has to say!" [From Paul he quotes:] "Therefore my wish is that the younger widows marry and produce children" (1 Tim. 5.14), "Marriage is honorable in all, and the bed undefiled" (Heb. 13.4), "The wife is bound to her husband as long as he lives, but if he dies, let her marry whom she wishes, only in the Lord" (1 Cor. 7.39). * * *

Finally he makes an apostrophe to a virgin, and says, "I wish no harm to you, virgin: you chose chastity because of the present necessity (cf. 1 Cor. 7.26); it pleased you to be holy in body and spirit, but do not be proud—you are a member of the same Church as married women."

> [i, 6, col. 217-]: Jerome now begins his reply. His main authority is St. Paul, 1 Cor. 7, on which his argument depends. The Christians of Corinth have written to Paul asking, among other things, whether they should remain celibate after becoming Christians and, for the sake of continence, leave their wives. Jerome begins by quoting the opening of Paul's reply, 1 Cor. 7.1–9, and then continues:]

[i, 7, col. 218-] Let us go back to the beginning of the quotation: "It is better for a man not to touch a woman." Now if it is good not to touch a woman, it is bad to do so, for the only opposite to "good" is "bad." Now if it is bad and yet pardoned, it is allowed only lest anything worse than bad results. Now what kind of "good" is that which is only allowed because of the risk of something worse? Paul would never have said "let each one have his wife" (1 Cor. 7.2) if he had not first made the premise "because of (the danger of) fornication." Remove this last phrase, and he will not then say "let each one have his wife." It is as though one were to say, "It is good to be fed on the purest wheat and to eat the finest bread, but in case anyone is forced by starvation to eat cow-dung I concede the eating of barley-bread."[3] Now does wheat lose its purity if barley is preferred to cow-dung? That thing

---

2. *WBP*, 35–43.   3. Cf. *WBP*, 143–46.

is good by nature which does not have to be compared with evil, and which is not overshadowed by merely being preferred to something else.

Note also the wisdom of the Apostle: he did not say that it is good not to have a wife, but "it is good not to touch a woman," implying that the danger is in the act of touching: whoever touches her cannot escape, for "she snatches the precious souls of men" (cf. Prov. 6.26) and makes the hearts of young men fly. "Can a man take fire in his bosom, and not be burned? Can one go upon hot coals, and not be burned?" (Prov. 6.27–28). Just as anyone is burnt if they touch a fire, so the touch of a man and a woman senses their nature, and realizes the difference between the sexes.
* * *

He did not say, "On account of fornication let each one *take* a wife"; otherwise he would by this excuse have given a free rein to lust—whenever a wife died, one would take another to avoid fornication! He said, "let each man *have* his wife." * * *[4]

> [Jerome comments on the instruction that wives taken before conversion to Christianity should not be set aside and goes on to elaborate on the implications of 1 Cor. 7.5 and 1 Peter 3.7, that prayer is impeded by sexual activities.]

Do you want to know what the Apostle favors? Then take his remark, "I would that all men were even as I myself" (1 Cor. 7.7).[5] Blessed is the man who is like Paul. Fortunate is the man who listens to Paul not when he is pardoning but when he is giving instruction. "This I want," he said, "this I long for, that you should be imitators of me, just as I am an imitator of Christ." * * *

[i, 9, col. 222-] Having conceded to married people the practice of intercourse, and having shown them what he wants (or rather, what he allows), Paul passes on to the unmarried and the widows; he sets himself as an example, and says that they are blessed if they remain in their present state. * * * He gives the reason why he said "if they cannot contain themselves, let them marry"—namely "for it is better to marry than to burn." This is why is it better to marry—because burning is worse; if you remove the fervence of passion, he will not then say "it is better to marry." He considers it better only by comparison with the worse, not because it is inherently good. It is as though one were to say, "it is better to have one eye than none; it is better to go on one foot supported by a stick, than to crawl with both one's legs broken." * * *

> [(i, 10–11, cols. 223–26): Jerome here expounds the doctrines in 1 Cor. 7.10–24. Most of this is not relevant to our purpose, but in cols. 223–24 he prophetically says:]

"I know that many women will be furious with me, and that with the same lack of shame that they showed in their contempt for Christ they will

---

4. Cf. *WBP*, 47–52 (ignoring Jerome's argument).   5. Cf. *WBP*, 80 ff.

rave against me, a miserable flea, the lowest Christian. Nevertheless, I shall say what the Apostle taught me, that they are on the side of iniquity, not of justice, of the dark rather than the light, of Belial rather than Christ; they are not temples of the living God, but idols and empty shrines of the dead! * * * [i, 12, cols. 226–29] After the discussion of the married and the continent, Paul finally comes to the subject of virgins: "On virgins, I have no order from God, but I give advice, having obtained the mercy of the Lord to be faithful. I think, therefore, that this is good, because of the present need, for it is good for man to be so (virgin)" (1 Cor. 7.25–26).[6] At this our adversary [Jovinian] goes wild with rejoicing, shattering open the wall of virginity with this powerful battering-ram: "You see," he says, "the Apostle says that he has no order from God about virgins; he who made orders with authority about married men and wives, dare not command what God did not order, and rightly: what is ordered, is commanded; what is commanded must be done; what must be done must carry some penalty if it is not done. For a command which is left within the authority of the person to whom it is given is a useless command."

[Jerome's answer:] If God had commanded virginity, he would have seemed to condemn marriage, and to take away the human seedbed from which virginity itself grows.[7] If he cut away the root, how would he get the fruit? If he did not first lay the foundations, how could he raise up the building and set a roof over everything? Mountains are brought down by great labor of ditch-digging: the depths of the earth are penetrated with difficulty in the search for gold. When a necklace is made from the finest pebbles, first in the blast of the furnace, and then set by the skillful hand of the craftsman, it is not the man who refined the gold from the mud who is called beautiful, but the person who uses the beauty of the gold.

Do not be surprised if, amid all the titillations of the flesh and the incentives to sin, we are not commanded to follow the life of the angels but merely recommended to do so. For when advice is given, the decision is left with the person who is freely making the offering to God [or: it is merely the authority of the suggestor],[8] but a command is an obligation imposed on a servant. Paul said, "I do not have an order from God, but I give advice, having obtained the mercy of the Lord." If you do not have a command from God, [one might ask,] why do you dare to give advice? The Apostle will answer, "Do you think I should order what God did not command, but merely suggested? He is the creator, the potter who knows how fragile is the vessel which he made; he left virginity in the power of the person who hears his words. Should I, teacher of peoples, 'made all things to all men,' (1 Cor. 9.22) attempt to win everyone, and right from the start impose a burden of perpetual chastity on the necks of weak believers? Let them enjoy for a while the holiday of marriage, and give some time to prayer; so that having had a taste of chastity they may continue to long for that which they have only delighted in for a short while."

6. WBP, 63–70, 82–86, and frequently.
7. WBP, 69–72.

8. Either is possible: the Latin is *offerentis arbitrium est.*

When Christ was tempted by the Pharisees who asked if it was right according to the Law of Moses to put aside one's wife, he forbade it entirely. His disciples, considering this, said, "If this is the case of a man and his wife, it is advisable not to marry." He replied, "All men cannot receive this saying, save they to whom it is given. For there are some eunuchs which were born this way from their mothers' wombs, some who were castrated by men, and some who castrated themselves for the sake of the kingdom of heaven. He that is able to receive it, let him receive it" (Matt. 19.2–12). This is why the Apostle says he has no command, because God had said "All men cannot receive this saying, save they to whom it is given," and "He that is able to receive it, let him receive it." He sets out the reward for the contest, he invites to the race, he holds in his hand the prize for virginity;[9] he shows the purest fountain, and says, "If any man thirst, let him come and drink (John 7.37); He who can receive, let him receive." He does not say that you *must* drink, and run the race, whether you want to or not, but that he who wishes to, and can, run and drink, will win the race and will be sated. For this reason Christ loves virgins the more, because they pay voluntarily what they were not ordered to pay. It is of greater grace to offer what you do not owe than to hand over what you are forced to pay. The Apostles considered the burdens of a wife and said, "If this is the case of a man and his wife, it is advisable not to marry." God approved their decision, and said, "You are right: marriage is not expedient for a man reaching for heaven, but it is a difficult matter, and not all receive this word, only those to whom it is given." * * *

What is the "immediate necessity" (1 Cor. 7.26) for rejecting the ties of marriage and pursuing the freedom of virginity?—"Woe on those who are pregnant and giving suck on that day!" (Matt. 24.19). Here it is not the prostitute or whore who is condemned (their damnation is not in doubt), but those whose wombs swell, the squalling children, the fruits and works of marriage. * * *

[Jerome argues that virgins who have consecrated themselves to God are guilty of incest if they marry. Marriage is a short-term prospect, for it ends with death. He demonstrates the spiritual distinction between a virgin who thinks only of God and a wife whose thought is on how to please her husband.]

[i, 14, col. 233-] In the same way that Paul allowed virgins to marry because of the danger of fornication, excusing that which is not sought after for its own sake, so, for the same reason (the avoidance of fornication), he allowed widows to marry again, for it is better to have knowledge of one man, even if he is the second or third, than of many: that is, it is more tolerable to be prostituted to one man than to many. The Samaritan woman in the Gospel of John said that her present husband was her sixth, but Christ told her that he was not her husband (John 4.17–18), for where

9. *WBP*, 75–76.

there was a succession of spouses, this one ceased to be her husband, for properly speaking only one man can be the husband.[1] In the beginning one rib was turned into one wife, "and the two will be in one flesh" (Gen. 2.24)—not three, not four, for otherwise there are not two of them, if there are more.

First of all Lamech,[2] who was a man of blood and a homicide, divided one flesh into two wives; the same punishment of the flood destroyed both homicide and bigamy [Jerome means by this marrying a second time]. * * * The holiness of monogamy is illustrated by the fact that a bigamist cannot be chosen as a priest. It is for this reason that Paul writes "let a widow be chosen if she is not less than sixty years old, and has been the wife of one husband only" (1 Tim. 5.9): this instruction concerns those widows who are fed on the charity of the Church—an age limit is prescribed, so that the food of the poor can only be given to those who can no longer work. At the same time, note that a woman who has had two husbands, even if she is old and decrepit and starving, does not deserve to receive the alms of the Church. Now if she is refused the bread of alms, how much more will she lack the bread which comes from heaven—anyone who eats this unworthily is guilty of violating the body and blood of Christ! * * *

[(i, 16, col. 234-) Jerome moves away from a discussion of Paul's teachings, and demonstrates that chastity has *always* been preferred to marriage; he proceeds to take each of the figures of the Old Testament cited by Jovinian, and to show how they are variously to be interpreted. He begins with Adam:]

It should be said of Adam and Eve, that in Paradise, before their offense, they were virgins; it was after their sin, and outside the garden, that marriage took place. * * *[3]

[The Biblical instruction "Be fruitful, and multiply, and replenish the earth" (Gen. 1.28) is explained by Jerome thus:]

It was necessary first to plant trees and to increase, so that there would be something which could be cut away later. Also, consider the meaning of "replenish the earth"—marriage fills the earth, but paradise is filled by virginity.

[Jerome notes that the phrase "God saw that it was good" was not applied to the second day of Creation (Gen. 1.6–8), indicating a disapproval of the number 2, a symbol of marriage. The various married figures proposed by Jovinian are each dealt with in turn: some of them are interpreted typologically (Isaac, for instance, is a figure of the Church rather than a physical reward given to Sarah, Moses signifies the Law, etc.). Of Solomon (i, 24, col. 243) he notes that it was his wives and concubines that turned his heart from God—he built the Temple in

1. WBP, 14–25.
2. WBP, 53–54.

3. Note that Map (below, p. 344) cites Eve as an example of disobedience *within* the garden.

his youth, at the beginning of the reign. Jerome asks the reader not to criticize those who lived under the Old Law—"they served their own times and conditions, and fulfilled the injunction of the Lord to increase and multiply and fill the earth; more than this, they gave us figures of the future. * * *" Further, he notes (i, 26, col. 245) that the married Apostles, etc., all married *before* the arrival of the New Law.

At i, 28 (col. 249) Jerome moves into the attack with quotations from the Proverbs of Solomon:

Above, when my adversary mentioned the many-wived Solomon, the builder of the Temple, I replied specifically to his arguments, so that I could quickly go through the remaining questions. Now, in case he shouts that Solomon and the other patriarchs, prophets and holy men who lived under the Old Law have been insulted by me, I will set out Solomon's sentiments on marriage—the very man who himself had so many wives and concubines—for no one can know better what a woman or wife is really like than someone who has suffered one. In Proverbs (9.13)[4] he says, "A woman is foolish and bold, and is made lacking in bread." What bread is this?—The bread of heaven! He immediately adds, "The people of earth perish in her, and rush into the depths of hell." Who are these "people of earth"?—Those who follow the first Adam, who was of earth, not the second Adam, who was from heaven. Again, in another place Solomon says, "Just as a worm in wood, so does an evil woman destroy her husband" (25.20).[5] If you argue that this was said only of *evil* women, I will reply shortly, "Why should I be compelled to wonder whether my bride is going to turn out good or bad?"

"It is better," Solomon says, "to live in the desert than with a nagging and angry woman" (21.9).[6] As to how rare it is to find a wife who lacks these vices—he knows who is married. As that fine orator Varius Geminus neatly puts it, "The man who doesn't quarrel is the single man."

"It is better to live in the corner of the roof than in a house shared with an evil-tongued woman" (Prov. 25.24). If a house shared by man and wife makes the wife proud and brings shame on her husband, how much more so if the woman is the richer, and the husband lives in *her* house! For rather than behaving as a wife, she begins to have the mastery of the house—if she takes exception to her husband, *he* has to go. "On a winter day a dripping roof drives a man from his house—so does an evil-tongued woman" (27.15)[7]— she makes the house flow with her continual abuse and daily chattering, and throws him out of his own house—that is, from the Church. * * *

4. Note that the text of the *Proverbs of Solomon* used by Jerome is often very different from that used by the King James version, and sometimes even from the Vulgate (see p. 336, n. 8).
5. Not in the King James (= *WBP*, 376–77).
6. Not in the King James (= *WBP*, 778–81).

7. Chaucer (*WBP*, 278–80, *Melibee*, VII, 1085 ff.) used a combined version of the "three-things" proverb: see Robinson's note to *Melibee*, VII, 1086, in Chaucer, *Works* (Boston: Houghton-Mifflin, 1957) 742. I have found this "new" proverb frequently in Medieval Latin texts.

We must not fail to mention the riddling saying, "The blood-sucking leech had three daughters, beloved in love, and they could not be satisfied; the fourth could never say 'Enough!': Hell, the love of a woman, the earth which cannot be sated by water, fire which never says, 'Enough!' "[8] (Prov. 30.15–16). The leech is the devil; those "beloved in love" are the devil's daughters who cannot be satisfied with the blood of those they have slain— Hell, a woman's love, dry earth, and burning fire. Here he is not talking about just a whore or an adulteress—the love of woman is accused in general: it is always insatiable; when quenched it burns; after a supply it is still hungry; it enfeebles a virile spirit and does not let it think of anything but the passion which it sustains. We read of something similar in the following proverb: "By three things is the earth moved, and the fourth cannot be tolerated: if a slave rules, if a foolish man is sated with bread, if a hateful wife has a good husband, and if a serving-wench throws out her own mistress" (Prov. 30.21–23).[9] In this heap of evils is numbered a wife; if you reply that it specifies "a *hateful* wife," I will say what I said above .* * * he who takes a wife is in doubt whether he is marrying a hateful wife or a loving one. If the former, she cannot be borne; if she is loving, her love is compared to Hell, to dry earth and to fire.

[Jerome continues with an argument based on Ecclesiastes 3.1 ("To everything there is a season . . .") and an interpretation of the role of sex in Paradise. In i, 30 (col. 251) he digresses in order to stress the point that the highly erotic Song of Songs is not to be interpreted literally, but is a symbol of the marriage of the Old and New Law through the visitation of Christ. He emphasizes the choice of a virgin to be mother of Christ, demonstrating the importance of virginity in the Christian religion. In i, 33 (col. 255) he reverts to the topic of widows and virgins:]

If, because baptism makes a man new, there is no difference between a virgin and a widow once they are baptized, by the same argument prostitutes and whores, once baptized, will be equated with virgins. For if past marriage does not harm a baptized widow, then the past pleasures of a prostitute, the exposure of her body to everyone's lust, will after baptism obtain the same reward as virginity! It is one thing to join to God a mind which is pure and is not polluted by any memories; it is quite another thing to remember the vile necessity of the embraces of a man, and to simulate in one's memory what one does not do physically.

[In i, 34 (col. 256-), he says that the early church was given lighter instructions by Paul because it was still weak, like a child that can drink only milk. To be perfect, however, is more difficult: he cites the story of the man who was told by Christ to give away all his goods.[1]

---

8. Jerome's Latin text of the Proverb makes little sense: it is the text neither of (his own) Vulgate Latin translation nor of the King James version. I have modified my translation according to the Vulgate version: the alteration does not affect Jerome's interpretation (= *WBP*, 371–75).
9. *WBP*, 362–67.
1. *WBP*, 107–11.

Married men are only chosen as priests *faute de mieux*: there may be no one else available, or those who are celibate may have other faults. He then turns to a difficult problem:]

[i, 36, cols. 259–61] But you will say, "If everyone becomes a virgin, how is the human race to survive?" I will reply with an analogy: if all women were widows, or chaste in marriage, how would mortal progeny be propagated? According to this argument, it would cease to exist altogether.[2] Now, if everyone was a philosopher, there would be no farmers; and not only farmers—there would be no orators, no lawyers, no teachers of any subjects. If everyone was a king, who would be a soldier? If everyone were head, what would we say they were head of, if all the limbs were removed? Are you really afraid that if more people pursued virginity, prostitution and adultery would cease to exist, and that there would be no children squalling in the towns and villages? Every day the blood of lechers is spilled, acts of adultery are condemned, and in the very law-courts and tribunals lust dominates. There is no need to fear that all will become virgins: virginity is hard, and therefore rare—"many are called, but few are chosen" (Matt. 20.16, etc.). Many people can begin, but few persevere, and therefore those who do persevere win a great reward. If everyone could be a virgin, God would never have said, "Let him receive who can receive" (Matt. 19.12), and the Apostle Paul would not have hesitated in his advice when he said, "But on virgins, I have no instructions from God" (1 Cor. 7.25).

And you will say, "Why were genitals created? Why were we made in such a way by the most wise Creator, as to share passions for each other and to long for natural copulation?"[3] My modesty in replying involves me in a risk, and I am caught between two rocks, the Symplegades of necessity and modesty, pulled this way and that, fearing the loss of my case or of my honor. I flush with shame to reply to the question, but if my modesty causes me to remain silent, I shall be thought to have given up my position, and will give my opponent the chance of beating me. Better to fight with one's eyes shut, like the gladiators who are blindfolded, than not to ward off his arrows with the shield of truth. Now I *could* say, "In the same way that the posterior section of the body and bowels, through which the excrement of the belly is removed, is hidden from the eyes, and is placed as it were behind one's back, similarly God has hidden away that which is beneath the stomach for bringing out the moistures and liquids which irrigate the veins of the body."

Since, however, the organs themselves and the construction of the genitals, the distinction between men and women, and the receptacles of the womb made to receive and nourish the foetus—since all these indicate the difference between the sexes, I will make this brief reply: Are we, then, never to cease from lust, so that we shouldn't have these limbs to no purpose? Why should a man abstain from his wife? Why should a widow keep

2. Exact translation uncertain. The Latin is *Hac ratione nihil omnino erit, ne aliud esse desistat.*

3. *WBP*, 115 ff. The Wife seems to accept Jerome's argument, but with a slightly different emphasis.

herself chaste, if we were born only in order to live like animals? or, What harm will it do me, if my wife sleeps with someone else? For in the same way that the job of teeth is to chew, and to transmit what is chewed into the stomach, and there is no harm in anyone giving my wife bread, similarly, if it is the job of genitals always to follow their nature, then let someone else's virility surpass my lassitude, and let any chance lust quench my wife's eager appetite. What does the Apostle mean by exhorting continence, if it is against nature? Or God himself, by prescribing kinds of eunuchs (cf. Matt. 19.12)? The Apostle, who recommended his chastity to us, should constantly be assailed by this question, "Why do *you* have a tool, Paul? Why are you distinguished from the female sex by beard, hair, and other physical characteristics? Why don't your breasts swell, your hips spread out, your chest narrow? Your voice is older, your tone more fierce, and your brow shaggier. There is no point in your having all these male characteristics, if you do not have sexual intercourse." I have had to descend to a ridiculous kind of argument, but it was you who forced me to make this bold reply.

Our Lord and Savior, although in the form of God, deigned to take on the form of a servant, obedient to his Father, obedient till his death on the Cross. Why, then, was it necessary for him to be born with these limbs which he was not going to use?[4] For he was circumcised in order to indicate his sex. Why in his love did he castrate John the Apostle and John the Baptist, whom he had created as men? Therefore, let us, who believe in Christ, follow the example of Christ. * * * Certainly, at the Resurrection of the flesh our bodies will be of the same substance as now, though increased in glory. For the Savior had the same body after death as he had when he was crucified, to the extent that he showed his hands perforated by nails and the wound in his side. * * * "In the resurrection of the dead, they neither marry nor are given in marriage, but will be like angels" (Matt. 22.30). What others are going to be in heaven, virgins have already begun to be on this earth. If we are promised the likeness of angels (who are not distinguished into sexes), either we shall lack sex, like the angels, or, what is clearly proved to be the case, we shall arise in our own sex, but not perform the offices of sex.

> [He continues with an exposition of various statements of the Apostles, directed mainly to show that "living by the spirit" precludes marriage, and that the opposite is the way of death. In i, 39 (col. 265-), he lists various precepts to chastity in the writings of other Apostles (notably 2 Pet. 2.9–22). In i, 40 (col. 267), he gives a description of the vicious life and habits of Jovinian himself, "a dog returning to his vomit" (2 Pet. 2.22). He summarizes the teachings of the early church:]

[i, 40, col. 270] The church does not condemn marriage, it relegates it; it does not reject it, but weighs it, knowing that in a great house there are

---

4. WBP, 139.

not only gold and silver containers, but ones of wood and clay;[5] some are to our honor, some to our shame; whoever purifies himself will be an honorable container, prepared as is necessary for every good work.

[(i, 41, col. 270) Jerome realizes that his opponents may argue that this "new religion" (Christianity) is recommending a dogma which runs counter to nature; he therefore turns to pagan history and literature to produce examples of the honor in which virginity is held even by non-Christians. His examples include Atalanta, Harpalice, Camilla, Leo, Iphigeneia, the Sibyl, pagan priestesses and Vestal Virgins, the sign of the Zodiac, etc. He lists examples of women who have committed suicide rather than lose their virginity. (i, 42, col. 273-) He gives examples of pagan stories of virgin birth, including the Buddha, Athene, Bacchus, Plato (born of Apollo by Perictione), etc.

(i, 43, col. 273) He continues with examples of famous widows from pagan literature who would not take a second husband, including Dido (!), etc. (i, 46, col. 275) He lists famous Roman women, beginning with Lucretia. After this he quotes at length from Theophrastus in i, 47, cols. 276–78 (see above, pp. 326–28).]

[i, 48, cols. 278–80] Does the co-heir of Christ really want a human heir?[6] Does he long to have children, and to delight in a succession of descendants who may be seized by Antichrist? We read that Moses and Samuel set others before their own sons, and did not regard as their own children those whom they saw offending God.

After his divorce from Terentia Cicero was asked by Hirtius to marry the latter's sister; Cicero refused, and said that it was not possible to give attention both to philosophy and a wife. This fine wife, who had drunk wisdom from the Ciceronian spring, then married Sallust, his enemy, and her third husband was Messala Corvinus—she devolved down the ladder of eloquence, so to speak.

Socrates had two wives, Xantippe and Myron, niece of Aristeides. They used to quarrel frequently, and Socrates used to laugh at them because they quarreled over such a terrible picture of a man, snub-nosed, bald-headed, shaggy-armed, and bow-legged; finally they turned their rage on him, and made him pay heavily—from then on he was put to flight and persecuted by them. On one occasion Xantippe was standing above him and wouldn't stop shouting at him; suddenly he found himself deluged by dirty water; he merely wiped his head and said, "I knew this thunder was sure to be followed by rain."[7]

Lucius Sylla the Lucky (if he hadn't been married) had a wife Metella who was openly unfaithful, and, because we are always the last to hear of our own misfortunes, Sylla didn't know about it even when it was common gossip in Athens; he finally learnt the secrets of his own home through the abuse of an enemy.

5. *WBP*, 99–101.
6. This picks up the final remarks of Theophrastus
(see above, p. 328).
7. *WBP*, 727–32.

Pompey also had an unfaithful wife, Mutia, who was always surrounded by Easterners and crowds of eunuchs from the Pontus; everyone thought he knew about her and was suffering in silence, but a fellow-soldier mentioned it to him on an expedition, and by this sad message shook the conqueror of the world.

Cato the Censor had a lowly born wife, Actoria Paula, who was a drunkard, violent, and, what is hard to credit, arrogant towards Cato: I mention this in case anyone thinks that by marrying a poor woman he ensures married bliss for himself.

Philip, King of Macedon (the object of Demosthenes' tirades, the *Philippics*) was once shut out of his bedroom by his angry wife: he suffered in silence, and consoled himself for his misfortune with tragic verses. At Olympia the orator Gorgias once recited a book "On Concord" to the Greeks who were quarreling amongst themselves. His opponent Melanthius retorted: "Here is a man preaching to us about concord, who can't get concord in one house between his wife, his serving-wench and himself!"—his wife was jealous of the serving-girl's good looks, and was continually abusing her husband (in fact the most pure of men).

All Euripides' tragedies are indictments of women: Hermione, for instance, says "the counsels of evil women deceived me." * * *[8] We read of a noble at Rome who was defending himself among his friends for divorcing a rich, chaste, and beautiful wife; he stretched out his foot, and said, "This shoe that you see here looks fine and new to you: I alone know where my own shoe pinches." Herodotus writes that a woman takes off her chastity with her clothes.[9] Our Comic says that no one is fortunate who has married. Need I mention Pasiphae, Clytemnestra, Eriphyle?[1] The first was deep in luxury, being a king's wife, but is said to have sought the embrace of a bull; the second killed her husband for the love of her paramour; the third betrayed Amphiareus, by putting a golden necklace above her husband's safety. The tragedies are full of it, cities, kingdoms, homes are overthrown by it—the quarrel between wives and sweethearts. Parents take up weapons against their children; poisonous feasts are set out; for the rape of one woman Europe and Asia endured a ten-year war. We hear of some women married one day, divorced on the second day, and married again on the third: both husbands deserve censure, the one for being too quickly displeased, the other for being too quickly pleased. Epicurus, the prophet of pleasure, (although his pupil Metrodorus married Leontia) said that few wise men should undertake marriage, because there were many disadvantages in it. In the same way that riches, honors, bodily health, and the other things which we call "morally indifferent" are in themselves neither good nor bad, and become good or bad only according to the way they are used and their result, so women are in this category of "both good and bad." Now it is a serious thing for a wise man to be in doubt whether he is going to marry a good wife or a bad one! Jokingly Chrysippus told the Romans to marry in

---

8. The omitted passage explains the point of a somewhat obscure mother-in-law joke by Terence.

9. *WBP*, 782–83.

1. *WBP*, 733–46.

order not to offend the "Jupiter of Marriage and Birth," for by this they would not marry at all, because they do not have a "Jupiter of Marriage"! * * *[2]

[i, 49, col. 280] Some of the above remarks are taken from writings on marriage by Aristotle, Plutarch, and Seneca. I here add some more: Love of beauty is loss of reason, and is the neighbor to insanity, a foul and inappropriate blemish on a blessed spirit. It destroys wise counsel, breaks high and noble spirits, drags them down from the loftiest to the meanest thoughts; it makes men quarrelsome, angry, rash, roughly imperious, servilely fawning, useless to everyone, and finally useless to love itself; for when it rages insatiably in the lust for enjoyment, it wastes many hours in suspicions, tears, and complaints. It makes one hate oneself, and finally hate love itself. The whole condemnation of love is set out by Plato [in the *Phaedro*], and Lysias expounds all its disadvantages—one takes a wife in madness, not in judgment; above all, the beauty of women needs the most strict guard. Further, Seneca tells us that he knew a fine man, who, when he was going out used to wrap his wife's girdle round his breast; not for a moment could he do without her presence; husband and wife would not drink anything unless both their lips had touched it; they did many equally foolish things, into which the sudden passion of burning love forced them. The origin of their love was honorable, but its size became monstrous. But in any case it makes no difference from what fine cause a man goes insane. Xystus says in his *Sentences* "the too eager lover of his own wife is an adulterer."[3] All love for another man's wife is disgraceful, but so is too great love for one's own wife[?].[4] A wise man should take a wife out of careful consideration, not out of love. He should keep a check on the urge of pleasure, not be rushed headlong into intercourse. Nothing is worse than to love a wife as one would a mistress. There are some who say that they couple with their wives and produce children for the sake of the state and the human race; they should at any rate imitate the animals, and not destroy their sons once their wife's womb has begun to swell. Let them behave to their wives as husbands, not as lovers. * * *[5] Thus satiety dissolves marriage of that sort swiftly. As soon as the pander of lust has gone, what once pleased is now cheapened. "What," says Seneca, "should I say of the poor men who for the most part marry to acquire the name of 'husband' in order to avoid the laws against celibacy?"

How can a married man control morals, order chastity, and keep the authority of a husband? The wisest of men says that chastity should be kept above all: once it is lost, all virtue tumbles. In this consists the chief of women's virtues. Chastity honors the poor woman, extolls the rich, redeems the ugly, adorns the beautiful: she deserves well of her ancestors because she has not soiled their line with a furtive conception; she deserves well of her children, who need have no shame of their mother nor doubt about

---

2. Jerome's comment on this joke is obscure.
3. See C. S. Lewis, *The Allegory of Love* (London: Oxford UP, 1936) 15 and n.5.

4. Translation uncertain.
5. The omitted passage is difficult and obscure.

who their father is, and most of all from herself, since she protects herself from insults on her outer body [?].[6] Captivity brings no greater misfortune than to be the object of another's lust. Men are honored by the consulship, eloquence extols their name forever, military glory and the triumph over a new people ennobles them. There are many things which bring glory to fine minds: a woman's virtue is properly her chastity. This made Lucretia the equal of Brutus—or even his superior, for he learnt from this woman that it is not possible to be a slave. It made Cornelia equal of Gracchus, Portia of the second Brutus. Tanaquilla is more famous than her husband—age has buried him among the names of kings, but her virtue (rare among all women) has fixed her name too firmly in the memory of all ages ever to be erased. Therefore let married women imitate Theano, Celobulina, Gorguntes, Timoclia, the Claudias and the Cornelias, and although they may see Paul pardoning evil women for their bigamy, let them read that even before the Christian religion shone forth in the world, faithful wives had glory among their sex: through virgins it was the custom to honor the goddess Fortune; no priest married twice or committed bigamy. Even today the High Priests at Athens are still castrated by a draught of hemlock; after they have been selected for the priesthood, they cease to be men.

End of Book One

WALTER MAP

From *The Letter of Valerius to Ruffinus, against Marriage*†

[This letter was written by the celebrated Walter Map, archdeacon of Oxford, probably before 1180; it was an early work and was not at first credited to him (because of the pseudonyms). Map therefore inserted it in his much longer work *De Nugis Curialium* (1181–93) ed. M. R. James (Anecdota Oxoniensia 14, 1914)—the letter is on pp. 142–58. Here he firmly asserted his authorship. The tone of the antifeminism is more akin to that of Theophrastus than of Jerome: it is philosophical rather than religious. It is referred to by the Wife of Bath as *Valerie*. I have made a few omissions.]

* * *

I had a friend who lived the life of a philosopher; after many visits over a long time I once noticed that he had changed in his dress, his bearing and his expression: he sighed a lot, his face was pale and his dress vulgarly ostentatious; he said little and was sombre, but was arrogant in a strange

---

6. Translation uncertain.
†Prepared for this volume by A. G. Rigg; see headnote, p. 326. The present translation is based on the 1914 edition by M. R. James. Since then the James edition has been revised by C. M. L. Brooke and R.

A. B. Mynors, as Walter Map, *De nugis curialium; Courtiers' Trifles* (Oxford: Clarendon Press, 1983). The new edition includes a revised translation and will be useful to anyone desiring access to the full text.

way; he had lost his old wit and jollity. He said he was not well, and indeed he wasn't. I saw him wandering about alone, and in so far as respect for me allowed he refused to speak to me. I saw a man in the grip of Venus's paralysis: he seemed all suitor, not at all a philosopher. However, I hoped that he would recover after his lapse: I pardoned what I didn't know; I thought it was a joke, not something brutally serious: he planned not to be loved but to be wived—he wanted to be not Mars but Vulcan. My mind failed me; because he was bent on death, I began to die with him. I spoke to him, but was repulsed. I sent people to talk to him, and when he wouldn't listen to them I said "An evil beast hath devoured him" (Gen. 37.33). To fulfill all the good turns of friendship I sent him a letter in which I altered the names, and called myself (Walter) Valerius and him (John, a red-head [Lat. *rufus*]) Ruffinus, and called the letter "the letter of Valerius to Ruffinus the philosopher, against marrying."

I am forbidden to speak, and I cannot keep silent. I hate the cranes, the voice of the night-owl, the screech-owl and the other birds which gloomily predict with their wails the sadness of foul winter, and you mock the prophesies of disaster which will surely come true if you continue as you are. Therefore I am forbidden to speak, for I am a prophet not of pleasure but of truth.

I love the nightingale and the blackbird, for with their soft harmony they herald the joy of the gentle breeze, and above all the swallow,[1] which fills the season of longed-for joy with its fulness of delights, and I am not deceived. You love parasites and hangers-on with their sweet flatteries, and above all Circe who pours on you joys full of sweet-scented delight, to deceive you: I cannot keep silent, lest you are turned into a pig or an ass.[2]

The servant of Babel pours out for you honeyed poison, which "moveth itself aright" (Prov. 23.31) and delights and leads astray your spirit: therefore I am forbidden to speak. I know that "at the last it biteth like a serpent" (ibid.) and will give a wound which will suffer no antidote: therefore I cannot keep silent.

You have many to persuade you to pleasure, and they are pleasant to hear; I am a stumbling speaker of bitter truth which makes you vomit: therefore I am forbidden to speak. The voice of the goose among swans is held to be a poor delight for men to hear, but it taught the senators to save the city from fire, the treasure-houses from plunder, and themselves from the arrows of their foes. Perhaps you too will realize with the senators, for you are no fool, that the swans sing death, and the goose screeches safety: therefore I cannot keep silent.

You are all afire with longing, and, seduced by the nobility of its fine head do not realize that you are seeking the chimaera;[3] you refuse to rec-

---

1. This word also usually means "nightingale," but clearly Map had a different bird in mind from the first.
2. I.e., by Circe.
3. The image of the Chimaera (ultimately from Lucretius V, 903) was developed as an example

against prostitutes by Marbod of Rennes (fl. A.D. 1100) in his *Liber Decem Capitulorum*, ed. W. Bulst (Heidelberg, 1947) 3. 45–49, and came to be almost a proverb. The passage from Map was used by Lydgate, *Reson & Sensualyte*, ll. 3370–78, and is quoted in the margin of one MS at this point.

ognize that that three-formed monster is graced with the face of a noble lion, is sullied by the belly of a stinking goat, and is armed in its tail with a poisonous serpent: therefore I am forbidden to speak.

Ulysses was enticed by the harmony of the Sirens, but, because he knew the voices of the sirens and the drinks of Circe, he restrained himself with the chains of virtue, so that he avoided the whirlpool. I trust in the Lord and hope that you will imitate Ulysses, not Empedocles who was overcome by his philosophy (or rather, melancholy), and chose Etna as his tomb. In order that you may take notice of the parable you hear, I cannot keep silent.

But your present flame, by which the worse choice pleases you, is stronger than the flame which draws you to me; therefore, lest the greater flame draws the lesser to it, and I myself perish, I am forbidden to speak. That I may speak with the spirit by which I am yours, let the two flames be weighed in any scale, equal or not, and let your decision, whatever it is, be at my risk: you must pardon me, for the impatience of the love I have for you will not let me keep silent.

After the first creation of man the first wife of the first Adam sated the first hunger by the first sin, against God's command. The sin was the child of Disobedience, which will never cease before the end of the world to drive women tirelessly to pass on to the future what they learned from their mother. Friend, a disobedient wife is dishonor to a man: beware.

The Truth which cannot be deceived said of the blessed David, "I have found a man according to my heart" (1 Sam. 13.14). But by love of a woman he fell conspicuously from adultery to homicide, to fulfil the saying "scandals never come singly" (Matt. 18.7). For every iniquity is rich in followers, and whatever house it enters, it hands over to be soiled by abuse. Friend, Bathsheba was silent, and has never been criticized for anything; yet she became the spur which caused the fall of her perfect husband, the arrow of death for her innocent spouse. Is she innocent who strives with both eloquence, like Sampson's Delilah, and beauty, like Bathsheba, when the latter's beauty triumphed alone, even without intending to? If you are no closer than David to the heart of God, do not doubt that you too can fall.

Solomon, Sun of men, treasure of God's delights, singular home of wisdom, was clouded over by the cloud of darkness and lost the light of his soul, the smell of his glory, and the glory of his house by the witchery of women: finally, he bowed down before Baal, and from a priest of the Lord was turned into a servant of the Devil, so that he can be seen to have fallen from a higher precipice than Phoebus in the fall of Phaeton, when he became Admetus's shepherd instead of Jupiter's Apollo. Friend, if you are not wiser than Solomon—and no man is—you are not too great to be bewitched by a woman. Open your eyes and see.[4]

---

4. Cf. Chaucer, *Parson's Tale*, X, 955: "Ful ofte tyme I rede that no man truste in his owene perfeccioun, but he be stronger than Sampson, and hoolier than David, and wiser than Salomon." See also *Sir Gawain & the Green Knight*, 2416–19. The list was used often: Map may be the direct source of many of the occurrences.

[Map continues his argument with a pun on *amare* "love" and *amarus* "bitter"; he says that chastity perished with Lucretia, Penelope, and the Sabine women. As examples of women's viciousness, he cites Scilla and Mirra. He quotes the stories of Jupiter, who became a bull in order to love Europa ("a woman will make you roar too"); Phoebus Apollo, whose light was eclipsed because of Leucithoe; Mars, who was put in chains by Vulcan when he was found sleeping with Venus, Vulcan's wife ("consider the chains which you cannot see but are beginning to feel, and tear yourself free while they can still be broken"). He notes that Paris passed an unfavorable judgment on Pallas Athene (when he preferred Helen), because she promised profit not pleasure ("would you make the same decision?"). He reminds his friend of the fate of Julius Caesar, who did not heed the advice of the soothsayer on the day of his assassination. He then gives a series of anecdotes:]

King Phoroneus [famous for his legal innovations] on the day on which he went the way of all flesh said to his brother Leontius, "I would not have fallen short of the highest summit of good fortune, if only I had never had a wife." Leontius said, "How has a wife impeded you?" He replied, "All married men know!" Friend, would that you had experienced marriage, but were not married, so that you would know what an impediment it is to felicity!

The Emperor Valentius, eighty years old and still a virgin, when on the day of his death he heard the praises of his triumphs recounted—and he had had many—said that he was only proud of one victory. Asked "Which?" he said, "When I conquered my worst enemy, my own flesh." Friend, this emperor would have left the world without glory, if he had not boldly resisted that with which you have now made a pact.

After his divorce from Terentia, Cicero would not marry again; he said it was not possible to give one's attention both to a wife and to philosophy.
* * *
Canius of Cadiz, a poet of a light and pleasant wit, was reproved by the sombre hen-pecked historian Livy of Phoenicia, because he enjoyed the loves of many women: "You cannot share in our philosophy when you yourself are shared by so many: Tityus does not love Juno with a liver torn into so many pieces by vultures!" Canius replied: "Whenever I slip, I get up more cautiously; when I am pushed down a little, I come up for air more quickly. The alternations of my nights make my days happier: a perpetuity of darkness is like hell. The first lilies of the springtime sun spread with a more effusive joy if they enjoy winds both from the South-east and the South-west—more than those which are blown over by the single blast of the fiery South wind. Mars broke his chains and sits at the heavenly banquet, from which hen-pecked Vulcan is excluded, held back by a long rope. Many threads bind less firmly than one chain: from philosophy I obtain pleasure—you go to it for relief!" Friend, I approve the words of both, but the lives of neither, but it is true that many diseases, which con-

tinually interrupt health, do less harm than a single disease which continually afflicts one with incurable illnesses.

Weeping, Pacuvius said to his neighbor Arrius, "Friend, I have in my garden an unlucky tree: my first wife hanged herself on it, then my second wife, and now the third." Arrius replied, "I'm surprised you find yourself able to weep in all these successes"; then he said, "Good Lord, think how many sorrows that tree has saved you!" Thirdly he said, "Friend, let me have some shoots of that tree to plant for myself." Friend, I'm afraid you may have to beg shoots of that tree when you won't be able to find any.[5]

Sulpicius, who had divorced a noble and chaste wife, knew where his own shoe pinched him. Friend, be careful that you don't have a pinching shoe which you can't take off.

Cato of Utica said, "If the world could exist without women, our company would not differ from that of the gods." Friend, Cato said nothing that he hadn't experienced and known; none of these men who attacked the deceits of women did so without having themselves been deceived—they were fully experienced and aware. You should believe them, for they tell the truth: they know that love pleases and then the loved one stabs [or: and stabs the loved one]; they know that the flower of Venus is a rose, but under its bright colour lie hidden many thorns.

Metellus would not marry the daughter of Marius, although she was rich in dowry, beautiful to look at, famous in birth, and of good reputation; he said, "I prefer to be mine than hers"; Marius said, "But she will be yours"; Metellus retorted, "A man has to be a woman's, because it is a point of logic that the predicates are only what the subject allow."[6] Thus by a joke Metellus turned away a load from his back. Friend, even if it is fitting to take a wife, it is not expedient. May it be love (and not blind love) that is in question, not income; may you choose beauty, not clothes; her mind, not her gold; may your bride be a wife, not a dowry. If it can possibly happen in this way, you may be able to be a predicate in such a way that you do not derive anger from the subject!

Lais of Corinth, a renowned beauty, only deigned to accept the embraces of kings and princes, but she tried to share the bed of the philosopher Demosthenes, so that she would seem, by breaking his notorious chastity, to have made rocks move by her beauty (as Amphion did with his lyre), and having attracted him by her blandishments treat him at her pleasure. When Demosthenes was enticed to her bedroom, Lais asked him for a hundred talents for the privilege; he looked up to heaven and said "I don't pay so much to feel penitent!" Friend, would that you might lift your attention to heaven, and avoid that which can only be redeemed by penitence.

Livia killed her husband whom she hated greatly; Lucilia killed hers, whom she loved to excess.[7] The former intentionally mixed poison, the

---

5. WBP, 757–64 (with Latumyus inexplicably for Pacuvius).
6. Puns on predicate and subject (that which is literally "placed underneath," but logically governs the predicate) abound in Medieval Latin antifeminist writers, both serious and frivolous.
7. WBP, 747–56 (with Lucye for Lucilia).

latter was deceived and poured out madness as a cup of love. Friend, these women strove with opposite intentions, but neither was cheated of the end of female treachery, that is, their natural evil. Women walk by varying and diverse paths, but whatever the paths they wander, whatever the by-ways they take, there is one result, one finishing-post for all their routes, one head and point of agreement of all their ways—mischief. Take the example of these two women as evidence that woman, whether she loves or hates, is bold in everything—crafty, when she wants to do harm (which is always), and when she tries to help frequently gets in the way, and so turns out to do harm even unintentionally. You are placed in the furnace: if you are gold, you will come out gold.

Deianeira clothed Hercules in a shirt, and brought vengeance on the "hammer of monsters" with the blood of a monster: what she had contrived to bring her happiness resulted in her tears * * * [women always look to their own pleasure, and never think of its effect on other people]. Hercules fulfilled twelve inhuman labors, but by the thirteenth, which surpassed all inhumanity, he was consumed. Thus the bravest of men lay dead, to be lamented like the most pitiful man,—he who had held up on his shoulders the span of the world without a groan.

Finally, what woman, among so many thousand thousands, ever saddened the eager and consistent suitor by a permanent refusal? Which one ever invariably cut off the words of a wooer? Her reply always savors of her favor, and however hard she may be she will always have hidden in her words some hint of encouragement for your plea. Any woman may say "No," but none say "No" for ever.

> [His examples of unchastity[8] are inappropriately Jupiter's visit to Danae in a shower of gold, and Perictione's virgin-birth of Plato out of Apollo: they are taken from Jerome (see above, p. 339) where they are used more appropriately. Map concludes his letter with a justification of his use of pagan examples, which may offer even a Christian a good example—in any case one should note that the pagans applied themselves to learning even without the promise of eternal felicity, simply to avoid ignorance—how much more should we pay attention to Scripture! He wants Ruffinus to marry not Venus but Pallas. The hand of the surgeon is hard, but it cures; the way to life is narrow and difficult, as was Jason's to the Golden Fleece. . . . Hard beginnings are rewarded by a sweet result. If you need any more evidence, read Theophrastus, or Seneca's *Medea*.]

8. Cf. *WBP*, 765 ff.

From the Gospel According to St. John†

Chapter 4

* * *

5. He cometh therefore to a city of Samaria, which is called Sichar, near the land which Jacob gave to his son Joseph.

6 Now Jacob's well was there. Jesus therefore being wearied with his journey, sat thus on the well. It was about the sixth hour.

7 There cometh a woman of Samaria, to draw water. Jesus saith to her: Give me to drink.

8 For his disciples were gone into the city to buy meats.

9 Then that Samaritan woman saith to him: How dost thou, being a Jew, ask of me to drink, who am a Samaritan woman? For the Jews do not communicate with the Samaritans.

10 Jesus answered, and said to her: If thou didst know the gift of God, and who he is that saith to thee, Give me to drink; thou perhaps wouldst have asked of him, and he would have given thee living water.

11 The woman saith to him: Sir, thou hast nothing wherein to draw, and the well is deep; from whence then hast thou living water?

12 Art thou greater than our father Jacob, who gave us the well, and drank thereof himself, and his children, and his cattle?

13 Jesus answered, and said to her: Whosoever drinketh of this water, shall thirst again; but he that shall drink of the water that I will give him, shall not thirst for ever:

14 But the water that I will give him, shall become in him a fountain of water, springing up into life everlasting.

15 The woman saith to him: Sir, give me this water, that I may not thirst, nor come hither to draw.

16 Jesus saith to her: Go, call thy husband, and come hither.

17 The woman answered, and said: I have no husband. Jesus said to her: Thou hast said well, I have no husband:

18 For thou hast had five husbands: and he whom thou now hast, is not thy husband. This thou hast said truly.

19 The woman saith to him: Sir, I perceive that thou art a prophet.

20 Our fathers adored on this mountain, and you say, that at Jerusalem is the place where men must adore.

21 Jesus saith to her: Woman, believe me, that the hour cometh, when you shall neither on this mountain, nor in Jerusalem, adore the Father.

22 You adore that which you know not: we adore that which we know; for salvation is of the Jews.

23 But the hour cometh, and now is, when the true adorers shall adore

---

† For this and the following Bible selections, we print the Douay/Rheims translation of the Latin Vulgate Bible, first published in 1582 and 1609, from the edition published by P. J. Kenedy and Sons (New York, 1914).

the Father in spirit and in truth. For the Father also seeketh such to adore him.

24 God is a spirit; and they that adore him, must adore him in spirit and in truth.

25 The woman saith to him: I know that the Messias cometh (who is called Christ); therefore, when he is come, he will tell us all things.

26 Jesus saith to her: I am he, who am speaking with thee.

27 And immediately his disciples came; and they wondered that he talked with the woman. Yet no man said: What seekest thou? or, why talkest thou with her?

28 The woman therefore left her water-pot, and went her way into the city, and saith to the men there:

29 Come, and see a man who has told me all things whatsoever I have done. Is not he the Christ?

30 They went therefore out of the city, and came unto him.

31 In the mean time the disciples prayed him, saying: Rabbi, eat.

32 But he said to them: I have meat to eat, which you know not.

33 The disciples therefore said one to another: Hath any man brought him to eat?

34 Jesus saith to them: My meat is to do the will of him that sent me, that I may perfect his work.

35 Do not you say, There are yet four months, and then the harvest cometh? Behold, I say to you, lift up your eyes, and see the countries; for they are white already to harvest.

36 And he that reapeth receiveth wages, and gathereth fruit unto life everlasting: that both he that soweth, and he that reapeth, may rejoice together.

37 For in this is the saying true: That it is one man that soweth, and it is another that reapeth.

38 I have sent you to reap that in which you did not labour: others have laboured, and you have entered into their labours.

39 Now of that city many of the Samaritans believed in him, for the word of the woman giving testimony: He told me all things whatsoever I have done.

40 So when the Samaritans were come to him, they desired that he would tarry there. And he abode there two days.

41 And many more believed in him because of his own word.

42 And they said to the woman: We now believe, not for thy saying: for we ourselves have heard him, and know that this is indeed the Saviour of the world.

* * *

From St. Paul to the Corinthians 1

Chapter 7

Now concerning the things whereof you wrote to me: It is good for a man not to touch a woman.

2 But for fear of fornication, let every man have his own wife, and let every woman have her own husband.

3 Let the husband render the debt to his wife, and the wife also in like manner to the husband.

4 The wife hath not power of her own body, but the husband. And in like manner the husband also hath not power of his own body, but the wife.

5 Defraud not one another, except, perhaps, by consent, for a time, that you may give yourselves to prayer; and return together again, lest Satan tempt you for your incontinency.

6 But I speak this by indulgence, not by commandment.

7 For I would that all men were even as myself: but every one hath his proper gift from God; one after this manner, and another after that.

8 But I say to the unmarried, and to the widows: It is good for them if they so continue, even as I.

9 But if they do not contain themselves, let them marry. For it is better to marry than to be burnt.

10 But to them that are married, not I but the Lord commandeth, that the wife depart not from her husband.

11 And if she depart, that she remain unmarried, or be reconciled to her husband. And let not the husband put away his wife.

12 For to the rest I speak, not the Lord. If any brother hath a wife that believeth not, and she consent to dwell with him, let him not put her away.

13 And if any woman hath a husband that believeth not, and he consent to dwell with her, let her not put away her husband.

14 For the unbelieving husband is sanctified by the believing wife; and the unbelieving wife is sanctified by the believing husband: otherwise your children should be unclean; but now they are holy.

15 But if the unbeliever depart, let him depart. For a brother or sister is not under servitude in such *cases*. But God hath called us in peace.

16 For how knowest thou, O wife, whether thou shalt save thy husband? Or how knowest thou, O man, whether thou shalt save thy wife?

17 But as the Lord hath distributed to every one, as God hath called every one, so let him walk: and so in all churches I teach.

18 Is any man called, being circumcised? let him not procure uncircumcision. Is any man called in uncircumcision? let him not be circumcised.

19 Circumcision is nothing, and uncircumcision is nothing: but the observance of the commandments of God.

20 Let every man abide in the same calling in which he was called.

21 Wast thou called, being a bondman? care not for it; but if thou mayest be made free, use it rather.

22 For he that is called in the Lord, being a bondman, is the freeman of the Lord. Likewise he that is called, being free, is the bondman of Christ.

23 You are bought with a price; be not made the bondslaves of men.

24 Brethren, let every man, wherein he was called, therein abide with God.

25 Now concerning virgins, I have no commandment of the Lord; but I give counsel, as having obtained mercy of the Lord, to be faithful.

26 I think therefore that this is good for the present necessity, that it is good for a man so to be.

27 Art thou bound to a wife? seek not to be loosed. Art thou loosed from a wife? seek not a wife.

28 But if thou take a wife, thou hast not sinned. And if a virgin marry, she hath not sinned: nevertheless, such shall have tribulation of the flesh. But I spare you.

29 This therefore I say, brethren; the time is short; it remaineth, that they also who have wives, be as if they had none;

30 And they that weep, as though they wept not; and they that rejoice, as if they rejoiced not; and they that buy, as though they possessed not;

31 And they that use this world, as if they used it not: for the fashion of this world passeth away.

32 But I would have you to be without solicitude. He that is without a wife, is solicitous for the things that belong to the Lord, how he may please God.

33 But he that is with a wife, is solicitous for the things of the world, how he may please his wife: and he is divided.

34 And the unmarried woman and the virgin thinketh on the things of the Lord, that she may be holy both in body and in spirit. But she that is married thinketh on the things of the world, how she may please her husband.

35 And this I speak for your profit: not to cast a snare upon you; but for that which is decent, and which may give you power to attend upon the Lord, without impediment.

36 But if any man think that he seemeth dishonoured, with regard to his virgin, for that she is above the age, and it must so be: let him do what he will; he sinneth not, if she marry.

37 For he that hath determined being steadfast in his heart, having no necessity, but having power of his own will; and hath judged this in his heart, to keep his virgin, doth well.

38 Therefore, both he that giveth his virgin in marriage, doth well; and he that giveth her not, doth better.

39 A woman is bound by the law as long as her husband liveth; but if her husband die, she is at liberty: let her marry to whom she will; only in the Lord.

40 But more blessed shall she be, if she so remain, according to my counsel; and I think that I also have the spirit of God.

From St. Paul to the Ephesians

Chapter 5

Be ye therefore followers of God, as most dear children;

2 And walk in love, as Christ also hath loved us, and hath delivered himself for us, an oblation and a sacrifice to God for an odour of sweetness.

3 But fornication, and all uncleanness, or covetousness, let it not so much as be named among you, as becometh saints:

4 Or obscenity, or foolish talking, or scurrility, which is to no purpose; but rather giving of thanks.

5 For know you this and understand, that no fornicator, or unclean, or covetous person (which is a serving of idols), hath inheritance in the kingdom of Christ and of God.

6 Let no man deceive you with vain words. For because of these things cometh the anger of God upon the children of unbelief.

7 Be ye not therefore partakers with them.

8 For you were heretofore darkness, but now light in the Lord. Walk then as children of the light.

9 For the fruit of the light is in all goodness, and justice, and truth;

10 Proving what is well pleasing to God.

11 And have no fellowship with the unfruitful works of darkness, but rather reprove them.

12 For the things that are done by them in secret, it is a shame even to speak of.

13 But all things that are reproved, are made manifest by the light; for all that is made manifest is light.

14 Wherefore he saith: *Rise thou that sleepest, and arise from the dead: and Christ shall enlighten thee.*

15 See therefore, brethren, how you walk circumspectly: not as unwise,

16 But as wise: redeeming the time, because the days are evil.

17 Wherefore become not unwise, but understanding what is the will of God.

18 And be not drunk with wine, wherein is luxury; but be ye filled with the holy Spirit,

19 Speaking to yourselves in psalms, and hymns, and spiritual canticles, singing and making melody in your hearts to the Lord;

20 Giving thanks always for all things, in the name of our Lord Jesus Christ, to God and the Father:

21 Being subject one to another, in the fear of Christ.

22 Let women be subject to their husbands, as to the Lord:

23 Because the husband is the head of the wife, as Christ is the head of the church. He *is* the saviour of his body.

24 Therefore as the church is subject to Christ, so also let the wives be to their husbands in all things.

25 Husbands, love your wives, as Christ also loved the church, and delivered himself up for it:

26 That he might sanctify it, cleansing it by the laver of water in the word of life:

27 That he might present it to himself a glorious church, not having spot or wrinkle, or any such thing; but that it should be holy, and without blemish.

28 So also ought men to love their wives as their own bodies. He that loveth his wife, loveth himself.

29 For no man ever hated his own flesh; but nourisheth and cherisheth it, as also Christ doth the church:

30 Because we are members of his body, of his flesh, and of his bones.

31 *For this cause shall a man leave his father and mother, and shall cleave to his wife, and they shall be two in one flesh.*

32 This is a great sacrament; but I speak in Christ and in the church.

33 Nevertheless let every one of you in particular love his wife as himself: and let the wife fear her husband.

From St. Paul to Timothy 1

Chapter 2

*   *   *

9 In like manner women also in decent apparel. adorning themselves with modesty and sobriety, not with plaited hair, or gold, or pearls, or costly attire,

10 But as it becometh women professing godliness, with good works.

11 Let the woman learn in silence, with all subjection.

12 But I suffer not a woman to teach, nor to use authority over the man: but to be in silence.

13 For Adam was first formed; then Eve.

14 And Adam was not seduced; but the woman being seduced, was in the transgression.

15 Yet she shall be saved through child-bearing; if she continue in faith, and love, and sanctification, with sobriety.

Chapter 5

*   *   *

3 Honour widows, that are widows indeed.

4 But if any widow have children, or grandchildren, let her learn first to govern her own house, and to make a return of duty to her parents: for this is acceptable before God.

5 But she that is a widow indeed, and desolate, let her trust in God, and continue in supplications and prayers night and day.

6 For she that liveth in pleasures, is dead while she is living.

7 And this give in charge, that they may be blameless.

8 But if any man have not care of his own, and especially of those of his house, he hath denied the faith, and is worse than an infidel.

9 Let a widow be chosen of no less than threescore years of age, who hath been the wife of one husband.

10 Having testimony for her good works, if she have brought up children, if she have received to harbour, if she have washed the saints' feet, if she have ministered to them that suffer tribulation, if she have diligently followed every good work.

11 But the younger widows avoid. For when they have grown wanton in Christ, they will marry:

12 Having damnation, because they have made void their first faith.

13 And withal being idle they learn to go about from house to house: and are not only idle, but tattlers also, and busy-bodies, speaking things which they ought not.

14 I will therefore that the younger should marry, bear children, be mistresses of families, give no occasion to the adversary to speak evil.

15 For some are already turned aside after Satan.

16 If any of the faithful have widows, let him minister to them, and let not the church be charged: that there may be sufficient for them that are widows indeed.

* * *

From St. Paul to Timothy 2

Chapter 2

* * *

14 Of these things put them in mind, charging them before the Lord. Contend not in words, for it is to no profit, but to the subverting of the hearers.

15 Carefully study to present thyself approved unto God, a workman that needeth not to be ashamed, rightly handling the word of truth.

16 But shun profane and vain babblings: for they grow much towards ungodliness.

17 And their speech spreadeth like a canker: of whom are Hymeneus and Philetus:

18 Who have erred from the truth, saying, that the resurrection is past already, and have subverted the faith of some.

19 But the sure foundation of God standeth firm, having this seal: the Lord knoweth who are his; and let every one depart from iniquity who nameth the name of the Lord.

20 But in a great house there are not only vessels of gold and of silver, but also of wood and of earth : and some indeed unto honour, but some unto dishonour.

21 If any man therefore shall cleanse himself from these, he shall be a vessel unto honour, sanctified and profitable to the Lord, prepared unto every good work.

22 But flee thou youthful desires, and pursue justice, faith, charity, and peace, with them that call on the Lord out of a pure heart.

23 And avoid foolish and unlearned questions, knowing that they beget strifes.

24 But the servant of the Lord must not wrangle: but be mild towards all men, apt to teach, patient,

25 With modesty admonishing them that resist the truth: if peradventure God may give them repentance to know the truth,

26 And they may recover themselves from the snares of the devil, by whom they are held captive at his will.

GEOFFREY CHAUCER

The Remedy against Lechery †

Remedium contra peccatum Luxurie.°   *The remedy against the sin of lechery.*

Now comth the remedie agayns Lecherie, and that is, generally, Chastitee and Continence, that restreyneth alle the desordeynce moev-

915 inges° that comen of fleshly talentes.° / And evere   *disorderly stirrings / desires*
the gretter merite shal he han, that most res-
treyneth the wikkede eschaufinges° of the ordure°   *burnings / filth*
of this sinne. And this is in two maneres,° that   *kinds*
is to seyn, chastitee in mariage, and chastitee
of widwehode.° / Now shaltow° understonde,   *widowhood / shalt thou*
that matrimoine is leefful° assemblinge of man   *allowable*
and of womman, that receyven by vertu of the
sacrement the bond thurgh which they may
nat be departed° in al hir lyf, that is to seyn,   *separated*
whyl that they liven bothe. / This, as seith the
book, is a ful greet sacrement. God maked it,
as I have seyd, in paradys, and wolde himself
be born in mariage. / And for to halwen° mar-   *hallow*
iage, he was at a weddinge, whereas he turned
water into wyn;° which was the firste miracle   *wine*
that he wroghte° in erthe° biforn hise disciples.   *performed / on earth*
/ Trewe° effect of mariage clenseth° fornica-   *True / purifies*

† From the *Parson's Tale.*

cioun and replenisseth° holy chirche of good — *replenishes*
linage; for that is the ende of mariage; and it
chaungeth deedly sinne into venial sinne bitwixe
hem that been y-wedded, and maketh the hertes° — *hearts*
al oon° of hem that been y-wedded, as wel as — *all one*
920 the bodies. / This is verray° mariage, that was — *true*
establissed by God er° that sinne bigan, whan — *before*
naturel lawe was in his right point° in paradys; — *rightful position*
and it was ordeyned that o° man sholde have — *one*
but o womman, and o womman but o man, as
seith Seint Augustin, by manye resouns. /

First, for mariage is figured° bitwixe Crist and — *symbolized*
holy chirche. And that other is, for a man is
heved° of a womman; algate,° by ordinaunce it — *the head / in every way*
sholde be so. / For if a womman had mo° men — *more*
than oon,° thanne sholde she have mo hevedes° — *one / more heads*
than oon, and that were an horrible thing biforn
God; and eek° a womman ne mighte nat plese° — *also / please*
to many folk at ones.° And also ther ne sholde — *once*
nevere be pees° ne reste amonges hem; for ever- — *peace*
ich° wolde axen° his owene thing. / And forther- — *each one / ask for*
over,° no man ne sholde knowe his owene — *moreover*
engendrure,° ne who sholde have his heritage; — *offspring*
and the womman sholde been the lasse° biloved, — *less*
fro the time that she were conioynt° to many — *conjoined*
men. /

Now comth, how that a man sholde bere him° — *conduct himself*
with his wyf; and namely in two thinges, that
is to seyn in suffraunce° and reverence, as shewed — *patience*
925 Crist whan he made first womman. / For he ne
made hir nat of the heved° of Adam, for she — *head*
sholde nat clayme to greet lordshipe. / For theras
the womman hath the maistrie, she maketh to
muche desray;° ther neden none ensamples° of — *disorder / examples*
this. The experience of day by day oghte suf-
fyse.° / Also certes, God ne made nat womman — *ought to suffice*
of the foot of Adam, for she ne sholde nat been
holden to lowe; for she can nat paciently suffre:° — *endure*
but God made womman of the rib of Adam,
for womman sholde be felawe° unto man. / Man — *a companion*
sholde bere him to° his wyf in feith, in trouthe,° — *conduct himself toward / loyalty*
and in love, as seith seint Paul: that "a man
sholde loven his wyf as Crist loved holy chirche,
that loved it so wel that he deyde° for it." So — *died*
sholde a man for his wyf, if it were nede.° / — *necessary*

Now how that a womman sholde be subget° — *subject*

to hir housbonde, that telleth seint Peter. First,
930 in obedience. / And eek, as seith the decree, a
womman that is a wyf, as longe as she is a wyf,
she hath noon auctoritee to swere° ne bere wit-   swear (legal) oaths
nesse withoute leve° of hir housbonde, that is   permission
hir lord; algate,° he sholde be so by resoun. /   at least
She sholde eek serven him in alle honestee,°   modesty, chastity
and been attempree° of hir array.° I wot° wel   modest / clothing / know
that they sholde setten hir entente[1] to plesen
hir housbondes, but nat by hir queyntise° of   refinement
array. / Seint Jerome seith that wyves that been
apparailled in silk and in precious purpre° ne   purple
mowe nat clothen hem in Jesu Crist. What seith
Seint John eek in this matere? / Seint Gregorie
eek seith, that no wight° seketh precious array   person
but only for veyne glorie,[2] to been honoured
the more biforn the peple. / It is a greet folye, a
womman to have a fair array outward and in
935 hirself be foul inward.° / A wyf sholde eek° be   within / also
mesurable in lokinge and in beringe° and in   bearing
laughinge, and discreet in alle hir wordes and
hir dedes.° / And aboven alle worldly thing she   deeds
sholde loven hir housbonde with al hir herte,
and to him be trewe of hir body; / so sholde an
housbonde eek be to his wyf. For sith° that al   since
the body is the housbondes, so sholde hir herte
been, or elles ther is bitwixe hem two, as in
that,° no parfit mariage. / Thanne shal men   as far as that is concerned
understonde that for three thinges a man and
his wyf fleshly mowen assemble.° The firste is   may have intercourse
in entente of engendrure of° children to° the   engendering / in
service of God, for certes that is the cause fynal°   ultimate purpose
of matrimoine. / Another cause is to yelden°   pay
everich of hem to other the dette of hir bodies,
for neither of hem hath power over his owene
body. The thridde is for to eschewe lecherye
and vileinye. The ferthe is, for sothe,° deedly   in truth
940 sinne. / As to the firste, it is meritorie;° the sec-   meritorious
onde also, for, as seith the decree, that she hath
merite of chastitee that yeldeth to hir housbonde the dette of hir body, ye, though it be
agayn hir lykinge and the lust° of hir herte. /   desire
The thridde manere is venial sinne, and, trewely,
scarsly may ther any of thise be withoute venial

1. I.e., seek, intend.   2. I.e., pride.

sinne, for the corrupcion and for the delyt.° /   *pleasure (of it)*
The fourthe manere is, for to understonde, if
they assemble only for amorous love and for
noon of the forseyde causes, but for to accom-
plice° thilke brenninge° delyt, they rekke° nev-   *accomplish, satisfy / burning / care*
ere how ofte. Sothly it is deedly sinne; and yet,
with° sorwe, somme folk wol peynen hem° more   *to their / exert themselves*
to doon than to hir appetyt suffyseth.° /   *suffices for their sexual needs*

The seconde manere of chastitee is for to been
a clene° widewe, and eschue the embracinges   *chaste*
of man, and desyren the embracinge of Jesu
Crist. / Thise been tho that han been wyves and
han forgoon° hir housbondes, and eek wom-   *lost*
men that han doon° lecherie and been releeved°   *practiced / relieved (of guilt)*
945   by Penitence. / And certes, if that a wyf coude
kepen hir al chaast by licence° of hir hous-   *permission*
bonde, so that she yeve° nevere noon occasion   *give*
that he agilte,° it were to hire a greet merite. /   *sin (with her)*
Thise manere wommen that observen° chasti-   *practice*
tee moste° be clene in herte as well as in body   *must*
and in thoght, and mesurable° in clothinge and   *moderate, modest*
in contenaunce; and been abstinent in etinge
and drinkinge, in spekinge, and in dede.° They   *deed*
been the vessel or the boyste° of the blissed   *box (of ointments)*
Magdelene, that fulfilleth° holy chirche of° good   *fills / with*
odour. / The thridde manere of chastitee is vir-
ginitee, and it bihoveth° that she be holy in herte   *is necessary*
and clene of body. Thanne is she spouse to Jesu
Crist, and she is the lyf° of angeles. / She is the   *beloved*
preisinge of³ this world, and she is as thise mar-
tirs in egalitee;° she hath in hir that° tonge may   *equal to the martyrs / that which*
nat telle ne herte thinke. / Virginitee baar° oure   *gave birth to*
950   lord Jesu Crist, and virgine was himselve. /

Another remedie agayns Lecherie is specially
to withdrawen° swiche thinges as yeve occasion   *take away, avoid*
to thilke vileinye, as ese,° etinge and drinkinge;   *such as ease*
for certes, whan the pot boyleth strongly, the
best remedie is to withdrawe the fyr. / Slepinge
longe in greet quiete is eek a greet norice° to   *nurse*
Lecherie. /

Another remedie agayns Lecherie is that a
man or a womman eschue the companye of hem
by whiche he douteth° to be tempted; for al be   *fears*
it so that the dede is withstonden,° yet is ther   *resisted*

---

3. I.e., most praiseworthy in.

greet temptacioun. / Soothly a whyt wal,
although it ne brenne° noght fully by stikinge   *burn*
of° a candele, yet is the wal blak° of the   *holding against it / blackened*
leyt.° / Ful ofte tyme I rede that no man truste°   *by the flame / should trust*
in his owene perfeccioun, but° he be stronger   *unless*
than Sampson, and holier than Daniel, and
955 wyser than Salomon. /

JOHN GOWER

The Tale of Florent †

*   *   *

Mi Sone, and I thee rede° this,   *advise*
What so befalle of other weie,°   *otherwise*
That thou to loves heste° obeie   *command*
Als ferr as thou it myht suffise;°   *be able*
1400 For ofte sithe° in such a wise°   *oftentimes / way*
Obedience in love availeth,
Wher al a mannes strengthe faileth.
Wherof, if that the list to wite°   *it pleases thee to know*
In a cronique° as it is write,   *chronicle*
1405 A gret ensample° thou myht fynde,   *example*
Which now is come to my mynde.

Ther was whilom° be° daies olde   *once upon a time / in*
A worthi knyht, and as men tolde
He was nevoeu° to th'emperour   *nephew*
1410 And of his court a courteour.°   *courtier*
Wifles° he was, Florent he hihte,°   *Wifeless / was called*
He was a man that mochel myhte.°   *could (do) a great deal*
Of armes he was desirous,
Chivalerous and amorous,
1415 And for the fame of worldes speche,°   *worldly reputation*
Strange aventures forto seche,°   *seek*
He rod the Marches al aboute.
And fell° a time, as he was oute,   *there befell*
Fortune, which may every thred
1420 Tobreke° and knette° of mannes sped,°   *Break apart / knit up / success*

† *Confessio Amantis* 1.1396–1871. Text based on *The Works of John Gower*, ed. G. C. Macaulay (Oxford: Clarendon Press, 1899–1902) 2.74–86. Notes are by the editors of this volume. The framing device in the *Confessio* is the lover-narrator's confession to Genius, who instructs him with many *exempla* organized according to the seven deadly sins.

The *Tale of Florent* is told to counteract disobedience, one of the subdivisions of Pride. Gower completed the first version of the *Confessio* in 1390, having begun it some four years earlier. A revised version was completed in 1392–93. On Gower's relationship to Chaucer, see the headnote, p. 267.

Schop,° as this knyht rod in a pas,°   *Arranged / at a walk*
That he be strengthe° take was,   *by force*
And to a castell thei him ladde,°   *led*
Wher that he fewe frendes hadde;
1425 For so it fell that ilke stounde°   *at that same time*
That he hath with a dedly wounde,
Feihtende, his oghne hondes slain°   *Fighting, (with) his own hands slew*
Branchus, which to the Capitain
Was sone and heir, wherof ben wrothe°   *angry*
1430 The fader and the moder bothe.
That knyht Branchus was of his hond
The worthieste of al his lond,
And fain° thei wolden do vengance°   *willingly / take revenge*
Upon Florent, bot° remembrance   *except for*
1435 That thei toke of his worthinesse
Of knyhthod and of gentilesse,
And how he stod of cousinage°   *was related*
To th'emperour, made hem° assuage,°   *them / abate (their anger)*
And dorsten° noght slen° him for fere.°   *(they) dared / slay / out of fear*
1440 In gret desputeisoun° thei were   *argumentation*
Among hemself, what was the beste.
    Ther was a lady, the slyheste°   *most clever*
Of alle that men knewe tho,°   *then*
So old sche myhte unethes go,°   *could scarcely walk*
1445 And was grantdame° unto the dede;°   *grandmother / dead (man)*
And sche with that began to rede,°   *counsel*
And seide how sche wol bringe him inne,
That° sche schal him to dethe winne°   *So that / bring to*
Al only of his oghne grant,°   *by his own consent*
1450 Thurgh strengthe of verray° covenant   *a true*
Withoute blame of eny wiht.°   *person*
Anon° sche sende for this kniht,   *Immediately*
And of hire sone sche alleide°   *alleged, cited*
The deth, and thus to him sche seide:
1455 "Florent, how so thou be to wyte°   *blame*
Of Branchus deth, men schal respite°   *delay*
As now° to take vengement,°   *Just now / revenge*
Be so° thou stonde in juggement   *If*
Upon certein condicioun—
1460 That thou unto a questioun
Which I schal axe° schalt ansuere;   *ask*
And over this thou schalt ek° swere,   *also*
That if thou of the sothe° faile,   *truth*
Ther schal non other thing availe,
1465 That thou ne schalt thi deth receive.
And for men schal thee noght deceive,

That thou therof myht ben avised,°   *take counsel*
Thou schalt have day and tyme assised°   *fixed, appointed*
And leve° saufly° forto wende,°   *permission / safely / depart*
1470 Be so that° at thi daies ende   *If*
Thou come ayein° with thin avys.'"°   *again / conclusion*
    This knyht, which worthi was and wys,
This lady preith° that he may wite,°   *beseeches / know*
And have it under seales write,
1475 What questioun it scholde be,
For which he schal in that degree
Stonde of his lif in jeupartie.°   *jeopardy*
With that sche feigneth compaignie,°   *friendliness*
And seith: "Florent, on love it hongeth° *depends, concerns*
1480 Al that to myn axinge° longeth:°   *asking, question / belongs*
What alle wommen most desire,
This wole I axe, and in th'empire
Wher as° thou hast most knowlechinge° *Where / largest acquaintance*
Tak conseil upon this axinge."
1485   Florent this thing hath undertake,
The day was set, the time take;
Under his seal he wrot his oth°   *oath*
In such a wise,° and forth he goth   *way*
Hom to his emes° court ayein;°   *uncle's / again*
1490 To whom his aventure plein
He tolde, of that him is befalle.
And upon that thei weren alle
The wiseste of the lond asent,°   *sent for*
Bot natheles° of on° assent   *nevertheless / one*
1495 Thei myhte noght acorde plat.°   *plainly*
On° seide this, an othre that.   *One*
After° the disposicioun   *According to*
Of naturel complexioun,°   *temperament*
To som womman it is plesance°   *a pleasure*
1500 That to an other is grevance;°   *a vexation*
Bot such a thing in special,°   *particular*
Which to hem alle in general
Is most plesant, and most desired
Above alle othre and most conspired,° *sighed after*
1505 Such o thing conne° thei noght finde *could*
Be constellacion ne kinde.[1]
And thus Florent withoute cure°   *remedy*
Mot stonde upon his aventure,°   *Must endure his fortune*
And is al schape° unto the lere,°   *prepared / loss*
1510 As in defalte of his answere.

---

1. Through astrological or natural investigation.

This knyht hath levere° forto dye — *rather*
Than breke his trowthe° and forto lye — *vow*
In place ther as he was swore,
And schapth him gon ayein° therfore. — *prepares himself to return again*
1515 Whan time cam he tok his leve,
That lengere° wolde he noght beleve,° — *longer / remain*
And preith° his em he be noght wroth, — *begs*
For that is a point of his oth,
He seith, that noman schal him wreke,° — *avenge*
1520 Thogh afterward men hiere speke° — *hear (it) said*
That he par aventure° deie.° — *by chance / die*
And thus he wente forth his weie° — *way*
Alone as knyht aventurous,
And in his thoght was curious
1525 To wite° what was best to do; — *know*
And as he rod al one° so, — *all alone*
And cam nyh° ther° he wolde be, — *nigh (near) / where*
In a forest under a tre
He syh° wher sat a creature, — *saw*
1530 A lothly° wommannysch figure, — *loathly*
That forto speke of fleisch and bon° — *flesh and bone*
So foul yit° syh° he nevere non. — *yet, until then / saw*
This knyht behield hir redely,° — *intently*
And as he wolde have passed by,
1535 Sche cleped° him and bad abide; — *called*
And he his horse heved° aside — *pulled*
Tho° torneth, and to hire he rod, — *Then*
And there he hoveth° and abod, — *remained*
To wite° what sche wolde mene.° — *know / say*
1540 And sche began him to bemene,° — *speak*
And seide: "Florent, be° thi name, — *by*
Thou hast on honde such a game,
That bot° thou be the betre avised, — *unless*
Thi deth is schapen° and devised, — *arranged*
1545 That al the world ne mai the save,
Bot if that° thou my conseil have." — *Unless*
Florent, whan he this tale herde,
Unto this olde wyht° answerde — *person*
And of hir conseil° he hir preide.° — *advice / begged*
1550 And sche ayein° to him thus seide: — *again, in turn*
"Florent, if I for the so schape,
That thou thurgh me thi deth ascape° — *escape*
And take worschipe of° thi dede, — *receive honor for*
What schal I have to my mede?"° — *for my reward*
1555 "What° thing," quod he, "that thou wolt axe."° — *Whatever / ask*
"I bidde° nevere a betre taxe,"° — *ask / no better fee*

Quod sche, "bot ferst, er° thou be sped,° — *before / have hastened off*
Thou schalt me leve° such a wedd,° — *leave / pledge*
That I wol have thi trowthe° in honde — *troth, promise*
1560 That thou schalt be myn housebonde."
"Nay," seith Florent, "that may noght be."
"Ryd thanne forth thi wey," quod sche,
"And if thou go withoute red,° — *advice*
Thou schalt be sekerliche° ded." — *surely*
1565 Florent behihte° hire good ynowh—° — *promised / goods enough*
Of lond, of rente,° of park,° of plowh—° — *income / forest / ploughland*
Bot al that compteth sche at noght.° — *she considers worth nothing*
Tho° fell this knyht in mochel° thoght; — *Then / much*
Now goth he forth, now comth ayein,
1570 He wot° noght what is best to sein,° — *knows / say*
And thoghte, as he rod to and fro,
That chese° he mot° on° of the tuo,° — *choose / must / one / two*
Or° forto take hire to his wif — *Either*
Or elles° forto lese° his lif. — *else / lose*
1575 And thanne he caste° his avantage, — *considered*
That sche was of so gret an age,
That sche mai live bot a while,
And thoghte° put hire in an ile,° — *thought to / on an island*
Wher that noman hire scholde knowe,
1580 Til sche with deth were overthrowe.
And thus this yonge lusti° knyht — *vigorous*
Unto this olde lothly° wiht° — *loathly / person*
Tho seide: "If that non other chance
Mai make° my deliverance, — *bring about*
1585 Bot only thilke same° speche — *that same*
Which, as thou seist, thou schalt me teche,
Have hier myn hond, I schal thee wedde."
And thus his trowthe° he leith to wedde.° — *troth, pledge / sets forth*
With that sche frounceth° up the browe: — *wrinkles*
1590 "This covenant I wol allowe,"° — *accept*
Sche seith: "if eny other thing
Bot° that° thou hast of my techyng — *Except / what*
Fro deth thi body mai respite,° — *delay, put off*
I woll thee of thi trowthe acquite,° — *release*
1595 And elles° be non other weie. — *otherwise*
Now herkne me what I schal seie: — *say*
Whan thou art come into the place,
Wher now thei maken gret manace° — *show great hostility*
And upon thi comynge abyde,
1600 Thei wole anon° the same tide° — *at once / time*
Oppose thee of° thin answere. — *Demand from thee*
I wot° thou wolt nothing° forbere° — *know / not at all / hold back*

Of that° thou wenest° be thi beste,° — *With what / thinkest / best (answer)*
And if thou myht so finde reste,° — *peace*
1605 Wel is,° for thanne is ther nomore. — *it is*
And elles this schal be my lore,° — *teaching*
That thou schalt seie, upon this molde° — *earth*
That alle wommen lievest° wolde — *most dearly*
Be soverein of° mannes love; — *sovereign over, master of*
1610 For what° womman is so above, — *whatever*
Sche hath, as who seith,° al hire wille; — *as it is said*
And elles may sche noght fulfille
What thing hir were lievest have.
With this answere thou schalt save
1615 Thiself, and other wise noght.
And whan thou hast thin ende wroght,
Com hier ayein, thou schalt me finde,
And let nothing out of thi minde."° — *escape thy memory*
He goth him forth with hevy chiere,° — *sad countenance, mood*
1620 As he that not° in what manere — *knows not*
He mai this worldes joie atteigne;° — *attain*
For if he deie,° he hath a peine, — *die*
And if he live, he mot him binde
To such on° which of alle kinde° — *a one / the species*
1625 Of wommen is th'unsemlieste.° — *the unseemliest, ugliest*
Thus wot° he noght what is the beste, — *knows*
Bot be him lief° or be him loth,° — *dear, desirable / loath, distasteful*
Unto the castell forth he goth,
His full answere forto yive,° — *give*
1630 Or° forto deie° or forto live. — *Either / die*
Forth with his conseil° cam the lord, — *council*
The thinges° stoden of record;° — *Everything / as previously arranged*
He sende up for the lady sone,° — *immediately*
And forth sche cam, that olde mone.° — *crone*
1635 In presence of the remenant° — *rest*
The strengthe of al the covenant
Tho° was reherced openly, — *Then*
And to Florent sche bad forthi° — *therefore*
That he schal tellen his avis,° — *conclusion*
1640 As he that woot° what is the pris. — *knows*
Florent seith al that evere he couthe,° — *knew*
Bot such word cam ther non to mowthe,° — *mouth*
That he for yifte° or for beheste° — *by any gift / promise*
Mihte eny wise° his deth areste.° — *in any way / prevent*
1645 And thus he tarieth longe and late,
Til that this lady bad° algate° — *commanded / finally, at last*
That he schal for the dom° final — *judgment*
Yive° his answere in special° — *Give / particular*

Of that sche hadde him ferst opposed:°   *first put to him*
650 And thanne he hath trewly supposed
That he him may of nothing yelpe,°   *boast*
Bot if° so be tho° wordes helpe   *Unless / those*
Whiche as the womman hath him tawht;°   *taught*
Whereof he hath an hope cawht°   *caught, conceived*
655 That he schal ben excused so,
And tolde out plein° his wille tho.°   *plainly / then*
And whan that this matrone herde
The manere how this knyht ansuerde,
Sche seide: "Ha, treson!° Wo thee be,°   *treason / Woe be to thee*
660 That hast thus told the privite,°   *the secret knowledge*
Which° alle wommen most desire!   *What*
I wolde that thou were afire!"
Bot natheles° in such a plit°   *nevertheless / plight*
Florent of° his answere is quit,°   *for / released*
665 And tho° began his sorwe newe,   *then*
For he mot gon, or ben untrewe,
To hire which his trowthe hadde.
Bot he, which alle schame dradde,°   *feared*
Goth forth in stede of° his penance,   *to the place of*
670 And takth the fortune of his chance,
As he that was with trowthe affaited.°   *governed by truth*
This olde wyht° him hath awaited   *person*
In place wher as° he hire lefte.   *where*
Florent his wofull heved° uplefte°   *head / uplifted*
675 And syh° this vecke° wher sche sat,   *saw / hag, old woman*
Which was the lothlieste what°   *thing*
That evere man caste on his yhe:°   *eye*
Hire nase° bass,° hire browes hyhe,°   *nose / low, long / high*
Hire yhen° smale and depe set,   *eyes*
680 Hire chekes ben with teres wet
And rivelen° as an emty skyn°   *shriveled / skin*
Hangende doun unto the chin;
Hire lippes schrunken ben for age,
Ther was no grace in the visage;
1685 Hir front° was nargh,° hir lockes° hore,°   *forehead / narrow / locks (of hair) / hoary*
Sche loketh forth° as doth a More;°   *looks / Moor*
Hire necke is schort, hir schuldres courbe,°   *stooped*
That myhte a mannes lust destourbe;°   *trouble, destroy*
Hire body gret° and nothing° smal,   *large / not at all*
1690 And shortly to descrive° hire al,   *describe*
Sche hath no lith° withoute a lak;°   *limb / defect, fault*
Bot lich° unto the wollesak°   *like / woolsack*
Sche proferth hire° unto this knyht,   *proffers herself*
And bad him, as he hath behyht,°   *promised*

1695 So as° sche hath ben his warant,° — *Since / protection*
That he hire holde covenant,° — *keep the covenant with her*
And be° the bridel sche him seseth.° — *by / seizes*
Bot Godd wot how that sche him pleseth
Of° suche wordes as sche spekth. — *By*
1700 Him thenkth° welnyh° his herte brekth — *It seems to him / almost*
For° sorwe that he may noght fle, — *Out of*
Bot if° he wolde untrewe be. — *Unless*
   Loke how° a sek° man for his hele° — *Just as / sick / health*
Takth baldemoine° with canele,° — *gentian (a medicinal root) / cinnamon*
1705 And with the mirre° takth the sucre,° — *myrrh / sugar*
Ryht upon such a maner lucre° — *kind of profit, reward*
Stant° Florent, as in this diete: — *Stands*
He drinkth the bitre° with the swete, — *bitter*
He medleth° sorwe with likynge,° — *mixes / pleasure (at being alive)*
1710 And liveth, as who seith, deyinge;
His youthe schal be cast aweie° — *away*
Upon such on,° which as the weie° — *a one / like the road*
Is old and lothly° overal. — *loathly*
Bot nede he mot that nede schal:[2]
1715 He wolde algate his trowthe holde,° — *keep his troth, promise*
As every knyht therto is holde,° — *beholden, bound*
What happ° so evere him is befalle. — *fortune, chance*
Thogh sche be the fouleste of alle,
Yet to th'onour of wommanhiede° — *womanhood*
1720 Him thoghte he scholde taken hiede;° — *heed*
So that for pure gentilesse,° — *nobility, courtesy*
As he hire couthe best adresce,° — *knew best how to position her*
In ragges, as sche was, totore° — *all torn*
He set hire on his hors tofore° — *before (him)*
1725 And forth he takth his weie° softe;° — *way / gently*
No wonder thogh he siketh° ofte. — *sighs*
Bot as an oule° fleth° by nyhte — *owl / flies*
Out of alle othre briddes syhte,° — *sight*
Riht so° this knyht on daies brode° — *Just so / in broad daylight*
1730 In clos° him hield, and schop° his rode° — *hiding / arranged / ride*
On nyhtes time, til the tyde° — *time*
That he cam there° he wolde abide. — *there where*
And prively° withoute noise — *secretly*
He bringth this foule grete coise° — *hag (lit. rump, thigh)*
1735 To his castell in such a wise° — *way*
That noman myhte hire schappe° avise,° — *form / discern*
Til sche into the chambre cam:
Wher he his prive conseil° nam° — *private counsel / took*

2. I.e., there's no denying necessity.

Of suche men as he most troste,° — trusted
1740 And tolde hem that he nedes moste° — needs must
This beste° wedde to his wif, — beast
For elles hadde he lost his lif.
The prive° wommen were asent,° — confidential / sent for
That scholden ben of his assent.
1745 Hire ragges thei anon of drawe,° — take off
And, as it was that time lawe,
She hadde bath, sche hadde reste,
And was arraied to the beste;
Bot with no craft of combes brode° — wide combs
1750 Thei myhte hire hore lockes schode,° — part
And sche ne wolde noght be schore° — shorn
For no conseil;° and thei therfore, — On anyone's advice
With such atyr° as tho° was used, — attire / then
Ordeinen° that it was excused, — Ordained
1755 And hid so crafteliche° aboute, — skillfully
That noman myhte sen hem oute.° — discern them (the locks of her hair)
Bot when sche was fulliche arraied
And hire atyr was al assaied,° — examined, inspected
Tho was sche foulere on to se;° — fouler to look on
1760 Bot yit° it may non other° be, — yet / not otherwise
Thei were wedded in the nyht.
So wo begon° was nevere knyht — woebegone
As he was thanne of mariage.
And sche began to pleie° and rage,° — play / carry on wantonly, foolishly
1765 As who° seith, I am wel ynowh;° — Like one who / happy enough
Bot he thereof nothing ne° lowh,° — not at all / laughed
For° sche tok thanne chiere on honde° — So / became more cheerful
And clepeth° him hire housebonde, — calls
And seith, "My lord, go we to bedde,
1770 For I to that entente° wedde, — for that reason
That thou schalt be my worldes blisse;"
And profreth° him with that to kisse, — proffers
As° sche a lusti° lady were. — As if / jolly
His body myhte wel be there,
1775 Bot as of° thoght and of memoire° — for / memory
His herte was in purgatoire.° — purgatory
Bot yit for strengthe of matrimoine
He myhte make non essoine,° — excuse
That he ne mot algates plie° — could not in any way comply
1780 To gon to bedde of° compaignie. — in
And whan thei were abedde naked,
Withoute slep he was awaked;° — Sleepless, he lay awake
He torneth on that other side,
For that he wolde hise yhen° hyde — eyes

1785 Fro lokynge on that foule wyht.°   *creature*
    The chambre was al full of lyht,
    The courtins were of cendal³ thinne;
    This newe bryd° which lay withinne,   *bride*
    Thogh it be noght with his acord,
1790 In armes sche beclipte° hire lord,   *embraced*
    And preide,° as° he was torned fro,°   *begged / since / away*
    He wolde him torne ayeinward° tho;   *around*
    "For now," sche seith, "we ben bothe on."°   *one*
    And he lay stille as eny ston,
1795 Bot evere in on° sche spak and preide,   *continually*
    And bad him thenke on that° he seide,   *what*
    Whan that he tok hire be the hond.
      He herde and understod the bond,
    How he was set to his penance,
1800 And as it were a man in trance
    He torneth him al sodeinly,°   *suddenly*
    And syh° a lady lay him by   *saw*
    Of eyhtetiene wynter age,⁴
    Which was the faireste of visage°   *appearance*
1805 That evere in al this world he syh.
    And as he wolde have take hire nyh,°   *nigh, close*
    Sche put hire hand and be his leve°   *by his leave, with his permission*
    Besoghte him that he wolde leve,°   *leave off*
    And seith that forto wynne or lese°   *lose*
1810 He mot on of tuo thinges chese:°   *choose*
    Wher° he wol have hire such on nyht,°   *Whether / at night*
    Or elles upon daies lyht,°   *by day's light*
    For he schal noght have bothe tuo.
    And he began to sorwe tho
1815 In many a wise, and caste his thoght,°   *pondered*
    Bot for al that yit cowthe he noght°   *he didn't know how to*
    Devise himself° which was the beste.   *Decide (for) himself*
    And sche, that wolde his hertes reste,
    Preith° that he scholde chese algate,°   *Begs / nevertheless*
1820 Til ate laste longe and late
    He seide: "O ye, my lyves hele,°   *health, prosperity*
    Sey what you list° in my querele,°   *pleases you / on my behalf*
    I not° what ansuere I schal yive;°   *know not / give*
    Bot evere whil that I may live,
1825 I wol that ye be my maistresse,
    For I can noght miselve gesse°   *guess, determine*
    Which is the beste unto my chois.
    Thus grante I yow myn hole vois:°   *my whole voice, my full assent*

3. A kind of silk.   4. I.e., eighteen years old.

Ches for ous bothen,° I you preie,   *both*
1830 And what as evere that ye seie,
Riht as ye wole,° so wol I."   *Just as you wish*
    "Mi lord," sche seide, "grant merci,°   *many thanks*
For of this word that ye now sein,°   *say*
That ye have made me soverein,
1835 Mi destine° is overpassed,   *destiny / fate / overcome*
That° nevere hierafter schal be lassed°   *So that / lessened*
Mi beaute, which that I now have,
Til I be take into my grave;
Bot nyht and day as I am now
1840 I schal alwey be such to yow.
The kinges dowhter of Cizile°   *Sicily*
I am, and fell bot siththe awhile,°   *it happened but a while ago*
As I was with my fader late,°   *recently*
That my stepmoder for an hate,°   *hatred*
1845 Which toward me sche hath begonne,°   *established, nurtured*
Forschop me,° til I hadde wonne   *Changed my shape*
The love and sovereinete
Of what knyht that in his degre
Alle othre passeth of good name.
1850 And, as men sein,° ye ben the same;   *say*
The dede proeveth it is so—
Thus am I youres evermo."
Tho was plesance° and joye ynowh,°   *delight / enough*
Echon° with other pleide° and lowh;°   *Each one / played / laughed*
1855 Thei live longe and wel thei ferde,°   *fared*
And clerkes that this chance° herde   *happening, story*
Thei writen it in evidence,
To teche how that obedience
Mai wel fortune° a man to love   *bring about*
1860 And sette him in his lust above,°   *give him happiness, delight*
As it befell unto this knyht.
    Forthi,° my Sone, if thou do ryht,   *Therefore*
Thou schalt unto thi love obeie,
And folwe hir will be alle weie.°   *in all ways*
1865 Min holy fader, so I wile:
For ye have told me such a skile°   *reason*
Of° this ensample° now tofore,°   *By / example / foregoing*
That I schal evermo therfore
Hierafterward myn observance
1870 To love and to his obeissance°   *obedience*
The betre kepe.

                    *   *   *

The Clerk's Prologue and Tale

The *Clerk's Tale* is a close translation of Petrarch's Latin version of the story of Griselda, although Chaucer also relied on a French translation of Petrarch as well. Petrarch had expanded the story from the final tale of Boccaccio's *Decameron*, and his narrative became highly popular in the late fourteenth century. Petrarch wrote to Boccaccio about his interest in the story and also recorded the responses of some friends. Further evidence of medieval reaction to it can be found in the comments of an anonymous Parisian citizen (probably like the Franklin in social status) who included a French translation of the tale in a book that he wrote for his fifteen-year-old bride to instruct her in the duties of a good wife.

GIOVANNI BOCCACCIO

From the *Decameron*, Tenth Day, Tenth Tale†

The marquis of Saluzzo, by the requests of his vassals, is urged to take a wife, and in order to have his own way in the matter, he picks the daughter of a peasant from whom he has two children; he pretends to her that he has had them killed; then, under the pretense that she has displeased him, he pretends to have taken another wife, and has their own daughter brought into the house as if she were his new wife once he has his real wife driven out in nothing more than her shift; after he discovers that she has patiently endured it all, he brings her back home, more beloved than ever, shows their grown children to her, and honors her, and has others honor her, as the marchioness.

* * *

A long time ago, among the various marquises of Saluzzo, there was the first-born son of the family, a young man named Gualtieri who, having no wife or children, spent his time doing nothing but hawking and hunting, and never thought of taking a wife or of having children—and this was very wise on his part. This did not please his vassals, and they begged him on many an occasion to take a wife so that he would not be without an heir

† From *The Decameron*, ed. and trans. Mark Musa and Peter E. Bondanella (New York: W. W. Norton, 1977) 133–42. With this story—the one hun- dredth—the tale-telling ends, and the young people return to Florence. See the tenth-day conclusion, pp. 249–51.

and they left without a master; they offered to find him a wife born of the kind of mother and father that might give him good expectations of her and who would make him happy. To this Gualtieri answered:

"My friends, you are urging me to do something that I was determined never to do, for you know how difficult it is to find a woman with a suitable character, and how plentiful is the opposite kind of woman, and what a wretched life a man would lead married to a wife that is not suitable to him. And to say that you can judge the character of a daughter by examining those of her father and mother is ridiculous (which is the basis of your argument that you can find a wife to please me), for I do not believe that you can come to know all the secrets of the father or mother; and even if you did, a daughter is often unlike her father and mother. But since you wish to tie me up with these chains, I will do as you request; and so that I shall have only myself to blame if things turn out badly, I want to be the one who chooses her; and I tell you now that if she is not honored by you as your lady—no matter whom I choose—you will learn to your great displeasure how serious a matter it was to compel me with your requests to take a wife against my will!"

His worthy men replied that they would be happy if he would only choose a wife. For some time Gualtieri had been pleased by the manners of a poor young girl who lived in a village near his home, and since she seemed very beautiful to him, he thought that life with her could be quite pleasant; so, without looking any further, he decided to marry her, and he sent for her father, who was extremely poor, and made arrangements with him to take her as his wife. After this was done, Gualtieri called all his friends in the area together and said to them:

"My friends, you wished and continue to wish that I take a wife, and I am ready to do this, but I do so more to please you than to satisfy any desire of mine to have a wife. You know what you promised me: to honor happily anyone I chose for your lady; therefore, the time has come for me to keep my promise to you, and for you to do the same for me. I have found a young girl after my own heart, very near here, whom I intend to take as my wife and bring home in a few days; so, make sure that the wedding celebrations are splendid and that you receive her honorably, so that I may consider myself as content with your promise as you are with mine."

The good men all happily replied that this pleased them very much and that, whoever she was, they would treat her as their lady and honor her in every way they could; and soon after this, they all set about preparing for a big, beautiful, and happy celebration, and Gualtieri did the same. He had a great and sumptuous wedding feast prepared, and he invited his friends and relatives and the great lords and many others from the surrounding countryside; and besides this, he had beautiful and expensive dresses cut out and tailored to fit a young girl who he felt was about the same size as the young girl he had decided to marry; he also saw to it that girdles and rings were purchased and a rich, handsome crown, and everything else a new bride might require. When the day set for the wedding arrived, Gual-

tieri mounted his horse at about the middle of tierce, and all those who had
come to honor him did the same; when all was arranged, he said:

"My lords, it is time to fetch the new bride."

Setting out on the road with the entire company, they arrived at the little
village; they came to the house of the girl's father and found her returning
from the well in great haste in order to be able to see the arrival of Gualtieri's bride in time with the other women; when Gualtieri saw her, he
called her by name—that is, Griselda—and asked her where her father was;
to this she replied bashfully:

"My lord, he is in the house."

Then Gualtieri dismounted and ordered all his men to wait for him;
alone, he entered that wretched house, and there he found Griselda's father,
who was called Giannucolo, and he said to him:

"I have come to marry Griselda, but before I do, I should like to ask her
some things in your presence."

And he asked her, if he were to marry her, would she always try to please
him, and would she never become angry over anything he said or did, and
if she would always be obedient, and many other similar questions—to all
of these she replied that she would. Then Gualtieri took her by the hand,
led her outside, and in the presence of his entire company and all others
present, he had her stripped naked and the garments he had had prepared
for her brought forward; then he immediately had her dress and put on her
shoes, and upon her hair—as disheveled as it was—he had a crown placed;
then, while everyone was marveling at the sight, he announced:

"My lords, this is the lady I intend to be my wife, if she will have me as
her husband."

And then, turning to Griselda who was standing there blushing and per-
plexed, he asked her:

"Griselda, do you take me for your husband?"

To this she answered: "Yes, my lord."

And he replied: "And I take you for my wife."

In the presence of them all he married her; then he had her set upon a
palfrey and he led her with an honorable company to his home. The wedding feast was great and sumptuous, and the celebration was no different
from what it might have been if he had married the daughter of the king of
France. The young bride seemed to have changed her soul and ways along
with her garments: she was, as we have already said, beautiful in body and
face, and as she was beautiful before, she became even more pleasing,
attractive, and well-mannered, so that she seemed to be not the shepherdess
daughter of Giannucolo but rather the daughter of some noble lord, a fact
that amazed everyone who had known her before; moreover, she was so
obedient and indulgent to her husband that he considered himself the happiest and the most satisfied man on earth, and she was also so gracious and
kind towards her husband's subjects that there was no one who was more
beloved or willingly honored than she was; in fact, everyone prayed for her
welfare, her prosperity, and her further success. Whereas everyone used to

say that Gualtieri had acted unwisely in taking her as his wife, they now declared that he was the wisest and the cleverest man in the world, for none other than he could have ever recognized her noble character hidden under her rude garments and her peasant dress.

In short, she knew how to comport herself in such a manner that before long, not only in her husband's marquisate but everywhere, her virtue and her good deeds became the topic of discussion, and for anything that had been said against her husband when he married her, she now caused the opposite to be said. Not long after she had come to live with Gualtieri, she became pregnant, and in the course of time she gave birth to a daughter, which gave Gualtieri much cause for rejoicing. But shortly afterwards, a new thought entered his mind: he wished to test her patience with a long trial and intolerable proofs. First, he offended her with harsh words, pretending to be angry and saying that his vassals were very unhappy over her because of her low birth and especially now that they saw her bear children; they were most unhappy over the daughter that had been born and did nothing but mutter about it. When the lady heard these words, without changing her expression or her good intentions in any way, she answered:

"My lord, do with me what you believe is best for your honor and your happiness, and I shall be completely happy, for I realize that I am of lower birth than they and am not worthy of this honor which your courtliness has bestowed upon me."

This reply was very gratifying to Gualtieri, for he realized that she had not become in any way haughty because of the respect which he or others had paid her. A short time later, after he had told his wife in vague terms that his subjects could not tolerate the daughter to whom she had given birth, he spoke to one of her servants and sent him to her, and with a very sad expression, he said to her:

"My lady, since I do not wish to die, I must do what my lord commands. He has commanded me to take this daughter of yours and to . . ." And he could say no more.

When the lady heard these words and saw her servant's face, she remembered what her husband had said to her and understood that her servant had been ordered to murder the child; therefore, she quickly took the girl from the cradle, kissed her and blessed her, and although she felt a great pain in her heart, without changing her expression she placed her in her servant's arms and said to him:

"There, do exactly what your lord and mine has ordered you to do; but do not abandon her body to be devoured by the beasts and birds unless he has ordered you to do so."

The servant took the child and told Gualtieri what the lady had said, and he was amazed at her perseverance; then he sent the servant with his daughter to one of his relatives in Bologna, begging her to raise and educate the girl carefully but without ever telling whose daughter she was. Shortly after this, the lady became pregnant again, and in time she gave birth to a male child, which pleased Gualtieri very much; but what he had already done did not satisfy him, and he wounded the lady with even a greater hurt, telling her one day in a fit of feigned anger:

"Lady, since you bore me this male child, I have not been able to live with my vassals, for they bitterly complain about a grandson of Giannuco-lo's having to be their lord after I am gone; because of this, I am very much afraid that unless I want to be driven out, I must do what I did the other time, and must eventually abandon you and take another wife."

The lady listened to him patiently and made no other reply than this:

"My lord, think only of making yourself happy and of satisfying your desires and do not worry about me at all, for nothing pleases me more than to see you contented."

After a few days, Gualtieri sent for his son in the same way he had sent for his daughter, and he again pretended to have the child killed, actually sending him to be raised in Bologna as he had his daughter; and the lady's face and words were no different from what they were when her daughter had been taken, and Gualtieri was greatly amazed at this and remarked to himself that no other woman could do what she had done: if he had not seen for himself how extremely fond she was of her children as long as they found favor in his sight, he might have believed that she acted as she did in order to be free of them, but he realized that she was doing it out of obedience.

His subjects, believing he had killed his children, criticized him bitterly and regarded him as a cruel man, and they had the greatest of compassion for the lady; but she never said anything to the women with whom she mourned the deaths of her children. Then, not many years after the birth of their daughter, Gualtieri felt it was time to put his wife's patience to the ultimate test: he told many of his vassals that he could no longer bear having Griselda as a wife and that he realized he had acted badly and impetuously when he had taken her for his wife, and that he was going to do everything possible to procure a dispensation from the pope so that he could marry another woman and abandon Griselda; he was reprimanded for this by many of his good men, but to them he answered that it was fitting that this be done.

When the lady heard about these matters and it appeared to her that she would be returning to her father's house (perhaps even to guard the sheep as she had previously done) and that she would have to bear witness to another woman possessing the man she loved, she grieved most bitterly; but yet, as with the other injuries of Fortune which she had suffered, she determined to bear this one too with a stern countenance. Not long afterwards, Gualtieri had forged letters sent from Rome, and he showed them to his subjects, pretending that in these letters the pope had granted him the dispensation to take another wife and to abandon Griselda; and so, having his wife brought before him, in the presence of many people he said to her:

"Lady, because of a dispensation which I have received from the pope, I am able to take another wife and to abandon you; and since my ancestors were great noblemen and lords of these regions while yours have always been peasants, I wish you to be my wife no longer and to return to Gian-nucolo's home with the dowry that you brought me, and I shall then bring home another more suitable wife, whom I have already found."

When the lady heard these words, she managed to hold back her tears only with the greatest of effort (something quite unnatural for a woman), and she replied:

"My lord, I have always realized that my lowly origins were not suitable to your nobility in any respect, and the position I have held with you, I always recognized as having come from God and yourself; I never made it mine or considered it given to me—I always kept it as if it were a loan; if you wish to have it back again, it must please me (as it does) to return it to you: here is your ring with which you married me—take it. You order me to take back with me the dowry I brought you, and to do this no accounting on your part, nor any purse or beast of burden, will be necessary, for I have not forgotten that you received me naked; and if you judge it proper that this body which bore your children should be seen by everyone, I shall leave naked; but I beg you, in the name of my virginity which I brought here and which I cannot take with me, that you at least allow me to carry away with me a single shift in addition to my dowry."

Gualtieri, who felt closer to tears than anyone else there, stood neverthe-less with a stern face and said:

"You may take a shift."

Many of those present begged him to give her a dress, so that this woman who had been his wife for more than thirteen years would not be seen leaving his home so impoverished and in such disgrace as to leave clad only in a shift; but their entreaties were in vain, and in her shift, without shoes or anything on her head, the lady commended him to God, left his house, and returned to her father, accompanied by the tears and the weeping of all those who witnessed her departure.

Giannucolo, who had never believed that Gualtieri would keep his daughter as his wife, and who had been expecting this to happen any day, had kept the clothes that she had taken off that morning when Gualtieri married her; he gave them back to her, and she put them on, and began doing the menial tasks in her father's house as she had once been accus-tomed to doing, suffering the savage assaults of a hostile fortune with a brave spirit.

After Gualtieri had done this, he led his vassals to believe that he had chosen a daughter of one of the counts of Panago for his new wife; and as he was making great preparations for the wedding, he sent for Griselda to come to him, and when she arrived he said to her:

"I am bringing home the lady I have recently chosen as my wife, and I intend to honor her at her first arrival; you know that I have no women in my home who know how to prepare the bedchambers or to do the many chores that are required by such a grand celebration; you understand these matters better than anyone in the house; therefore, I want you to arrange everything: invite those ladies whom you think should be invited, and receive them as if you were the lady of the house; then when the wedding is over, you can return to your home." 3 of swords

These words were like a dagger in Griselda's heart, for she had not yet been able to extinguish the love that she bore for him (as she had learned to do without her good fortune), and she answered:

"My lord, I am ready and prepared."

And so in a coarse, peasant dress she entered that house which a short time before she had left dressed only in a shift, and she began to clean and arrange the bedchambers, to put out hangings and ornamental tapestries on the walls, to make ready the kitchen, and to put her hands to everything, just as if she were a little servant girl in the house; and she never rested until she had organized and arranged everything as it should be. After this, she had invitations sent in Gualtieri's name to all the ladies of the region and then waited for the celebration; when the day of the wedding came, in the poor clothes she had on and with a pleasant expression on her face and a noble manner, she courageously received all the ladies who arrived for the celebration.

Gualtieri had had her children carefully raised in Bologna by one of his relatives who had married into the family of the counts of Panago; the daughter was already twelve years of age and the most beautiful thing anyone had ever seen, and the boy was already six; he sent a message to his relative in Bologna, requesting him to be so kind as to come to Saluzzo with his daughter and his son, and to organize a handsome and honorable retinue to accompany them, and not to reveal her identity to anyone but to tell them only that he was bringing the girl as Gualtieri's bride.

The nobleman did what the marquis had asked him: he set out, and after several days he arrived at Saluzzo at about suppertime with the young girl, her brother, and a noble company, and there he found all the peasants and many other people from the surrounding area waiting to see Gualtieri's new bride. She was received by the ladies and then taken to the hall where the tables were set, where Griselda, dressed as she was, met her cheerfully and said to her:

"Welcome, my lady!"

Many of the women had begged Gualtieri (but in vain) either to allow Griselda to stay in another room or that she be permitted to wear some of the clothing that had once been hers so that she would not have to meet his guests in such clothing. Everyone sat down at the table and was served, and they all stared at the young girl and agreed that Gualtieri had made a good exchange; but it was Griselda who praised her and her little brother more than any of the others did.

Gualtieri finally felt that he had seen as much evidence as he needed to of his wife's patience; he observed that the new arrangement had not changed Griselda one bit, and since he was certain that her attitude was not due to stupidity, for he knew her to be very wise, he felt that it was time to remove her from the bitterness which he felt she must be concealing under her impassive face; so, he had her brought to him, and in the presence of everyone, he said to her with a smile:

"What do you think of my new bride?"

"My lord," replied Griselda, "she seems very beautiful to me; and if she is as wise as she is beautiful (which I believe to be the case), I have no doubt that you will live with her as the happiest lord in the world; but I beg you as strongly as I can not to inflict those wounds upon her which you inflicted upon the other woman who was once your wife, for I believe that she could scarcely endure them, both because she is younger and because she has been brought up in a more delicate fashion, while the other woman was used to continuous hardships from the time she was a little girl."

When Gualtieri saw that she firmly believed the girl was to be his wife, yet in spite of this said nothing but good about her, he made her sit beside him, and he said:

"Griselda, it is time now for you to reap the fruit of your long patience, and it is time for those who have considered me cruel, unjust, and bestial to realize that what I have done was directed toward a pre-established goal, for I wanted to teach you how to be a wife, to show these people how to know such a wife and how to choose and keep one, and to acquire for myself lasting tranquility for as long as I was to live with you; when I went to take you for my wife, I greatly feared that this tranquility I cherished would be lost, and so, to test you, I submitted you to the pains and trials you have known. But since I have never known you to depart from my wishes in either word or deed, and since I now believe I shall receive from you that happiness which I always desired, I intend to return to you now what I took from you for a long time and to soothe with the greatest of delight the wounds that I inflicted upon you; therefore, with a happy heart receive this girl, whom you suppose to be my bride, and her brother as your very own children and mine; they are the ones you and many others have long thought I had brutally murdered; and I am your husband, who loves you more than all else, for I believe I can boast that no other man exists who could be so happy with his wife as I am."

After he said this, he embraced and kissed her, and she was weeping for joy; they arose and together went over to their daughter who was listening in amazement to these new developments; both of them tenderly embraced first the girl and then her brother, thus dispelling their confusion as well as that of many others who were present. The ladies arose from the tables most happily, and they went with Griselda to her bedchamber, and with a more auspicious view of her future, they took off her old clothes and dressed her in one of her noble garments, and then they led her back into the hall as the lady of the house, which she had, nonetheless, appeared to be even in her tattered rags.

Everyone was most delighted about how everything had turned out, and Griselda with her husband and children celebrated in great style, with the joy and feasting increasing over a period of several days; and Gualtieri was judged to be the wisest of men (although the tests to which he had subjected his wife were regarded as harsh and intolerable) and Griselda the wisest of them all.

The count of Panago returned to Bologna several days later, and Gualtieri took Giannucolo away from his work, setting him up as his father-in-law in such a way that he lived the rest of his life honorably and most happily. After giving their daughter in marriage to a nobleman, Gualtieri lived a long and happy life with Griselda, always honoring her as much as he could.

What more can be said here, except that godlike spirits do sometimes rain down from heaven into poor homes, just as those more suited to governing pigs than to ruling over men make their appearances in royal palaces. Who besides Griselda could have endured the severe and unheard-of trials that Gualtieri imposed upon her and remained with a not only tearless but happy face? It might have served Gualtieri right if he had run into the kind of woman who, once driven out of her home in nothing but a shift, would have allowed another man to shake her up to the point of getting herself a nice-looking dress out of the affair!

* * *

FRANCIS PETRARCH

A Fable of Wifely Obedience and Devotion †

In the chain of the Apennines, in the west of Italy, stands Mount Viso, a very lofty mountain, whose summit towers above the clouds and rises into the bright upper air. It is a mountain notable in its own nature, but most notable as the source of the Po, which rises from a small spring upon the mountain's side, bends slightly toward the east, and presently, swollen with abundant tributaries, becomes, though its downward course has been but brief, not only one of the greatest of streams but, as Vergil called it, the king of rivers. Through Liguria its raging waters cut their way, and then, bounding Aemilia and Flaminia and Venetia, it empties at last into the Adriatic sea, through many mighty mouths. Now that part of these lands, of which I spoke first, is sunny and delightful, as much for the hills which run through it and the mountains which hem it in, as for its grateful plain. From the foot of the mountains beneath which it lies, it derives its name; and it has many famous cities and towns. Among others, at the very foot of Mount Viso, is the land of Saluzzo, thick with villages and castles. It is ruled over by noble marquises, the first and greatest of whom, according to tradition, was a certain Walter, to whom the direction of his own estates and of all the land pertained. He was a man blooming with youth and

† From Robert Dudley French, *A Chaucer Handbook*, 2/e, © 1947, pp. 291–311. Reprinted by permission of Prentice-Hall, Inc., Englewood Cliffs, New Jersey. French's translation, originally made from a much earlier text of Petrarch's story, was changed in his second edition to reflect the more accurate version edited by J. Burke Severs, which appears both in Bryan and Dempster's *Sources and Analogues* and in Severs's own *The Literary Relationships of Chaucer's* Clerkes Tale (New Haven: Yale UP, 1942). As the letters on pp. 388–91 make clear, Petrarch translated and adapted Boccaccio's story in 1373.

beauty, as noble in his ways as in his birth; marked out, in short, for leadership in all things,—save that he was so contented with his present lot that he took very little care for the future. Devoted to hunting and fowling, he so applied himself to these arts that he neglected almost all else; and—what his subjects bore most ill—he shrank even from a hint of marriage. When they had borne this for some time in silence, at length they came to him in a company; and one of their number, who had authority and eloquence above the rest and was on more familiar terms with his overlord, said to him, "Noble Marquis, your kindness gives us such boldness that we come separately to talk with you, with devoted trust, as often as occasion demands, and that now my voice conveys to your ears the silent wishes of us all; not because I have any especial privilege, unless it be that you have shown by many signs that you hold me dear among the others. Although all your ways, then, justly give us pleasure and always have, so that we count ourselves happy in such an overlord, there is one thing in which we should assuredly be the happiest of all men round about, if you would consent to it and show yourself susceptible to our entreaties; and that is, that you should take thought of marriage and bow your neck, free and imperious though it be, to the lawful yoke; and that you should do this as soon as possible. For the swift days fly by, and although you are in the flower of your youth, nevertheless silent old age follows hard upon that flower, and death itself is very near to any age. To none is immunity against this tribute given, and all alike must die; and just as that is certain, so is it uncertain when it will come to pass. Give ear, therefore, we pray you, to the entreaties of those who have never refused to do your bidding. You may leave the selection of a wife to our care, for we shall procure you such an one as shall be truly worthy of you, and sprung of so high a lineage that you may have the best hope of her. Free all your subjects, we beseech you, of the grievous apprehension that if anything incident to our mortal lot should happen to you, you would go leaving no successor to yourself, and they would remain deprived of a leader such as their hearts crave."

Their loyal entreaties touched the man's heart, and he made answer: "My friends, you constrain me to that which never entered my thoughts. I have had pleasure in complete liberty, a thing which is rare in marriage. Nevertheless, I willingly submit to the wishes of my subjects, trusting in your prudence and your devotion. But I release you from the task, which you have offered to assume, of finding me a wife. That task I lay on my own shoulders. For what benefit can the distinction of one confer upon another? Right often, children are all unlike their parents. Whatever is good in a man comes not from another, but from God. As I entrust to Him all my welfare, so would I entrust to Him the outcome of my marriage, hoping for His accustomed mercy. He will find for me that which shall be expedient for my peace and safety. And so, since you are resolved that I should take a wife, so much, in all good faith, I promise you; and for my part, I will neither frustrate nor delay your wishes. One promise, in your turn, you must make and keep: that whosoever the wife may be whom I shall choose, you will yield her the highest honor and veneration; and let there be none among you who ever shall dispute or complain of my decision. Yours it was that I, the freest of all the men you have known, have submitted to the yoke of marriage; let it be mine to choose that yoke; and whoever my wife may be, let her be your mistress, as if she were the daughter of a prince of Rome."

Like men who thought it hardly possible that they should see the wished-for day of the nuptials, they promised with one accord and gladly that they should be found in nothing wanting; and with eager alacrity they received the edict from their master, directing that the most magnificent preparations be made for a certain day. So they withdrew from conference; and the marquis, on his part, laid care upon his servants for the nuptials and gave public notice of the day.

Not far from the palace, there was a village, of few and needy inhabitants, one of whom, the poorest of all, was named Janicola. But as the grace of Heaven sometimes visits the hovels of the poor, it chanced that he had an only daughter, by name Griseldis, remarkable for the beauty of her body, but of so beautiful a character and spirit that no one excelled her. Reared in a frugal way of living and always in the direst poverty, unconscious of any want, she had learned to cherish no soft, no childish thoughts; but the vigor of manhood and the wisdom of age lay hidden in her maiden bosom. Cherishing her father's age with ineffable love, she tended his few sheep, and as she did it, wore her fingers away on the distaff. Then, returning home, she would prepare the little herbs and victuals suited to their fortune and make ready the rude bedchamber. In her narrow station, in fine, she discharged all the offices of filial obedience and affection. Walter, passing often by that way, had sometimes cast his eyes upon this little maid, not with the lust of youth, but with the sober thoughts of an older man; and his swift intuition had perceived in her a virtue, beyond her sex and age, which the obscurity of her condition concealed from the eyes of the common throng. Hence it came about that he decided, at one and the same time, to take a wife—which he had never before wished to do—and to have this woman and no other.

The day of the nuptials drew on, but no one knew whence the bride should come, and there was no one who did not wonder. Walter himself, in the meanwhile, was buying golden rings and coronets and girdles, and was having rich garments and shoes and all necessities of this kind made to the measure of another girl, who was very like Griseldis in stature. The longed-for day had come, and since not a word about the bride was to be heard, the universal bewilderment had risen very high. The hour of the feast arrived; and already, the whole house was in a great ferment of preparation. Then Walter came out of the castle, as if he were setting out to meet his approaching bride, and a throng of noble men and matrons followed in his train.

Griseldis, ignorant of all the preparations which were being made on her account, had performed what was to be done about her home; and now, with water from the distant well, she was crossing the threshold of her father's house, in order that, free from other duties, she might hasten, with the girls who were her comrades, to see her master's bride. Then Walter, absorbed in his own thoughts, drew near and, calling her by name, asked her where her father was; and when she had replied, reverently and humbly, that he was within, "Bid him," he said, "come hither."

When the old man was come, Walter took him by the hand and drew him a little aside; and lowering his voice, he said, "Janicola, I know that I am dear to you. I have known you for my faithful liegeman, and I believe you wish whatever suits my pleasure. One thing in particular, however, I should like to know: whether you would take me, whom you have as your master, for a son-in-law, giving me your daughter as a wife?"

Stupefied at this unlooked-for matter, the old man went rigid. At length, hardly able to stammer out a few words, he replied, "It is my duty to wish or to deny nothing, save as it pleases you, who are my master." "Let us, then, go in alone," said the marquis, "that I may put certain questions to the girl herself in your presence." They entered the house, therefore, while the populace stood expectant and wondering, and found the maiden busying herself about her father's service and abashed by the unexpected advent of so great a throng of strangers. Walter, approaching her, addressed her in these words: "It is your father's pleasure and mine that you shall be my wife. I believe that this will please you, too. But I have one thing to ask you: when that is done which shortly shall take place, will you be prepared, with consenting mind, to agree with me in all things; so that you dispute my wish in nothing, and permit me, with mind consenting, and without remonstrance of word or look, to do whatever I will with you?"

Trembling at this marvelous thing, the girl made answer: "I know myself unworthy, my lord, of so great an honor; but if it be your will, and if it be my destiny, I will never consciously cherish a thought, much less do anything, which might be contrary to your desires; nor will you do anything, even though you bid me die, which I shall bear ill."

"It is enough," said he; and so, leading her out before the throng, he showed her to the people, and said, "This is my wife, this is your lady; cherish her and love her; and if you hold me dear, hold her most dear of all." Then, lest she carry into her new home any relic of her former fortune, he commanded her to be stripped, and clad from head to heel with new garments; and this was done, reverently and swiftly, by matrons who stood around her and who embraced her each in turn. So this simple peasant girl, new clad, with her dishevelled tresses collected and made smooth, adorned with gems and coronet, was as it were suddenly transformed, so that the people hardly knew her. And Walter solemnly plighted her his troth with a precious ring, which he had brought with him for that purpose; and having placed her on a snow-white horse, he had her conducted to the palace, the populace accompanying her and rejoicing. In this way, the nuptials were celebrated, and that most happy day was passed.

Shortly thereafter, so much did God's favor shine upon the lowly bride, it seemed she was reared and bred, not in a shepherd's cottage, but in the imperial court; and to all she became dear and venerable beyond belief. Even those who had known her from her birth could hardly be persuaded she was Janicola's daughter; such was the graciousness of her life and of her ways, the gravity and sweetness of her speech, by which she had bound the hearts of all the people to her with the bond of a great love. And already her name, heralded by frequent rumor, had spread abroad, not only within the confines of her fatherland, but through every neighboring province; so that many men and matrons, with eager desire, came flocking to see her. So, graced by a marriage, which, however humble, was distinguished and prosperous, Walter lived in the highest peace and honor at home; and abroad he was held in the highest esteem; and because he had so shrewdly discovered the remarkable virtue hidden under so much poverty, he was commonly held to be a very prudent man. Not only did his wife attend adroitly to those domestic matters which pertain to women; but when occasion demanded, in her husband's absence, she undertook state affairs, settling and composing the country's law-suits and disputes among the nobles, with such weighty opinions and so great a maturity and fairness of judgment, that all declared this woman had been sent down from heaven for the public weal.

Not long time had passed ere she became pregnant; and after she had held her subjects for a time in anxious expectation, at length she bore the fairest of daughters. Though they had preferred a son, nevertheless she made both her husband and her country happy by this proof of the fertility they longed for. In the meanwhile, it so happened, when his little daughter had been weaned, that Walter was seized with a desire more strange than laudable—so the more experienced may decide—to try more deeply the fidelity of his dear wife, which had been sufficiently made known by experience, and to test it again and again. Therefore, he called her alone into his chamber and addressed her thus, with troubled brow:

"You know, Griseldis—for I do not think that amid your present good fortune you have forgotten your former state—you know, I say, in what manner you came into this house. To me, indeed, you are dear enough and well beloved; but to my nobles, not so; especially since you have begun to bear children. For they take it most ill that they should submit to a lowborn mistress. Since, therefore, I desire peace with them, I must follow another's judgment, not my own, in the case of your daughter, and do that which is most grievous to me. But I would never do it without letting you know, and I wish you to accommodate your will to mine and to show that obedience which you promised at the outset of our married life."

She listened without a protesting word or glance. "You are our master," she said, "and both this little girl and I are yours. Do, therefore, as you will with your own; for nothing can please you which would displease me. There is absolutely nothing which I wish to have or fear to lose, save you. This is fixed in the very center of my heart, and never, either by lapse of years or by death, will it be torn away. Anything can happen ere I shall change my mind."

Happy in her reply, but feigning sadness in his looks, he left her; and a little later, he sent to her one of his underlings, a most faithful man, whose services he was wont to use in his most weighty affairs, and whom he instructed in the task before him. The fellow, coming to Griseldis by night, said to her, "Spare me, my lady, and do not lay to my blame what I am forced to do. You are right knowing, and you understand what it is to be subject to a master; nor is the harsh necessity of obedience unknown to one endowed with so much sense, though inexperienced. I am bidden to take this little baby girl, and—" Here, breaking off his speech, he ceased, as if he would indicate his cruel business by his silence. Suspect was the reputation of the man, suspect his face, suspect the hour, suspect his words. By these tokens, she clearly knew her sweet daughter was to be killed; yet she shed no tear, she breathed no sigh,—a thing most hard, even for a nurse, much more so for a mother. But taking up the little girl, with tranquil brow, she looked at her a little, and kissing her, blessed her and made the sign of the Holy Cross upon her. Then she gave the child to the fellow, and said, "Go; and whatever our lord hath laid upon you, see that you perform it. One thing I beg of you: take care lest beasts or birds tear her little body; and this, only if no contrary orders have been laid upon you."

The fellow returned to his master and told him what he had said and how Griseldis had replied; and when he had given him his daughter, paternal pity touched the marquis to the heart. Nevertheless, he did not relax the rigor of his purpose. He ordered his slave to wrap the child in cloths, to place it in a wickerwork basket upon a beast of burden, and carry it, secretly and with all the diligence he could command, to Bologna, to Walter's sister, who had married the Count of Panago. He should hand the child over to her, to be cherished with maternal care, to be reared in gentle ways, and to be concealed, moreover, with so much care that no one could know whose daughter she was. The slave journeyed thither and fulfilled with care what had been laid upon him.

Walter, in the meanwhile, though he often studied his wife's face and words, never detected any sign of a change of feeling: equal alacrity and diligence, her accustomed complaisance, the same love, no sadness, no mention of her daughter! Never did the girl's name fall from her mother's lips, either by design or by chance. In this way, four years went by; and being again with child, behold she brought forth a most excellent son, a great delight to his father and all their friends. But when, after two years, this child had been weaned, the father fell back into his former caprice. And again he said to his wife, "Once before you have heard that my people bear our marriage ill, especially since they knew you capable of bearing children; but it has never been so bad as since you gave birth to a son. For they say—and the murmur of it comes often to my ears, 'So, when Walter dies, Janicola's grandson shall rule over us, and so noble a land will be subject to such a master.' Each day many things of this tenor are current among my people; and I, eager for peace and—to say sooth—fearing for myself, am therefore moved to dispose of this infant as I disposed of his sister. I tell you this beforehand, lest the unexpected and sudden grief disturb you."

To which she made answer: "I have said, and I say again, that I can have no wishes save yours. In these children, indeed, I have no share, beyond the pangs of labor. You are my master and theirs: use your power over your own. Nor seek my consent; for when I entered your house, as I put off my clothes, so I put off my wishes and desires, and put on yours. Whatever you wish to do, therefore, about anything whatsoever, that is what I wish, too. Nay, if I could foresee your future wishes, I should begin beforehand, whatever it might be, to wish and desire what you wish. Now I gladly follow your desire, which I cannot anticipate. Suppose it pleased you that I should die, I would die gladly; nor is there any other thing—not death itself—to equal our love."

Marvelling at the steadfastness of the woman, he took his departure, his face agitated with emotion; and straightway he sent to her the servant whom he had sent before. The latter, with many a plea of the necessity of obedience, and with many an entreaty for forgiveness, if he had done or was doing her a wrong, demanded her child, as one who is about to commit a monstrous crime. But she, with unchanged mien, whatever might be passing in her mind, took up in her arms the son who was so well beloved, not only by his mother but by everyone, for the beauty of his body and his disposition; and she made upon him the sign of the Cross, blessing him, as she had blessed her daughter, clinging to him just a little while with her eyes, and bending down to kiss him; but she gave absolutely no other sign of her grief. Then she gave him to the fellow who had come to seek him, and she said, "Take him, too, and do what you are bidden. But one thing I beg of you: that if it can be done, you will protect the tender limbs of my beautiful baby against the ravages of birds and beasts."

The man, returning to his master with these words of hers, drove him to yet greater wonder, so that if he had not known her for the most loving of mothers, he might have had some faint suspicion that the strength of the woman came from a certain hardness of heart; but while she was strongly attached to all that were hers, she loved no one better than her husband. The servant was then bidden to set out for Bologna and to take the boy where he had taken his sister.

These trials of conjugal affection and fidelity would have been sufficient for the most rigorous of husbands; but there are those who, when once they have begun anything, do not cease; nay, rather, they press on and cling to their purpose. Keeping his eyes upon his wife, therefore, Walter watched continually for any change in her behavior toward him, and he was not able to find any at all, save that she became each day more devoted and more obedient to his wishes; so that it seemed there was but one mind between them, and that not common to them both, but, to say truth, the husband's alone; for the wife had declared, as has been said, that she had no wishes of her own.

Little by little, an ugly rumor about Walter had begun to spread abroad; namely, that with savage and inhuman cruelty, out of regret and shame for his humble marriage, he had ordered his children slain; for neither did his children appear, nor had anyone heard where in the world they were. Wherefore, he who had once been a man of spotless reputation, dear to his people, had become in the eyes of many men infamous and hateful. Not on that account, however, was his stern purpose altered, but he persevered in the severity which he had assumed and in his harsh caprice of testing his wife. And so, when twelve years had passed since the birth of his daughter, he sent envoys to Rome to bring back thence documents bearing the appearance of a papal bull, which should cause the rumor to circulate among the people that license had been granted him by the Roman pontiff, with a view to his own peace and that of his people, to annul his first marriage and to take another wife; nor was it difficult, in fact, to convince those untutored Alpine folk of anything you pleased. When this rumor reached Griseldis, she was sad, I think; but as one who had made her decision, once and for all, about herself and her destiny, she stood unshaken, awaiting what should be decreed for her by him to whom she had submitted herself and all that was hers.

Walter had already sent to Bologna and had asked his kinsman to send him his children, spreading the story in every quarter that this maiden was to be Walter's bride. His kinsman faithfully performed these orders and set out upon his journey on the appointed day, bringing with him, amid a brilliant throng of noblemen, the young maiden, who was now of marriageable age, of excellent beauty, and adorned with magnificent attire; and with her he brought her brother, who was now in his seventh year.

Walter, in the meanwhile, with his accustomed inclination to try his wife, even to the heights of grief and shame, led her forth before the multitude and said, "I have been wont to take ample delight in our marriage, having regard for your character, not your lineage; but now, since I perceive that great place is always great servitude, it is not permitted me to do what any peasant may. My people compel me—and the Pope consents—to take another wife. Already my wife is on her way, and presently she will be here. Therefore, be of stout heart, and yielding your place to another, take back your dowry and return to your former home with equal mind. No good fortune lasts forever."

She made answer: "My lord, I have always known that there was no proportion between your greatness and my lowly station. I have never considered myself worthy to be—I will not say, your wife, but your servant; and in this house, in which you have made me mistress, I call God to witness that I have remained in spirit as a handmaid. For these years, therefore, that I have dwelt with you in honor far beyond my deserts, I give thanks to God and you. For the rest, I am ready, with good heart and peaceful mind, to return to my father's house, to pass my age and to die where I have passed my youth, always happy in the honorable estate of widowhood, since I have been the wife of such a man. I readily yield place to your new bride—and may her coming bring you joy!—and I will not take away any ill feeling from this place, where I was wont to live most happily, while it so pleased you. But as for my dowry, which you bid me take back with me, I see of what sort it is, and it has not been lost; for as I came to you long since, stripped at my father's threshold of all my clothes and clad in yours, I had no other dowry but nakedness and devotion. Lo, therefore, I strip off this dress and restore this ring, with which you wed me. And the other rings and finery, with which your gifts have enriched me to the point of envy, are in your chamber. Naked I came from my father's house, and naked shall I return again—save that I think it unseemly that this belly, in which the children you begot were shaped, should appear naked before the people. Wherefore, if it please you—but not otherwise— I pray and beseech you, as the price of the maidenhood which I brought hither and do not take hence, bid me keep one shift, out of those I have been wont to wear, that I may cover therewith the belly of her who was once your wife."

The tears welled into her husband's eyes, so that they could no longer be restrained; and so, turning his face aside, "Take your one shift," he said, and his voice trembled so that he could scarcely say it. So, weeping, he took his departure. Before them all, she stripped off her clothes, keeping upon her only her shift; and covered with that alone, she went forth before them with feet and head quite bare. Followed by many, who wept and railed at fortune, she alone dry-eyed and to be honored for her noble silence, returned to her father's house. The good man, who had always held his daughter's marriage in suspicion and had never allowed himself high hopes, ever expecting it to turn out that so high-born a husband, proud after the fashion of noblemen, would one day be sated with so lowly a bride and send her home, had kept her coarse and well-worn gown hidden away in some corner of his narrow dwelling. Hearing the uproar, not of his daughter, who returned in silence, but of the accompanying throng, he ran to meet her at the threshold and covered her, half naked as she was, with the old gown. She remained with her father a few days, showing marvelous equanimity and kindness; for she gave no sign of the sadness of her heart and showed no trace of her more favorable lot, since, forsooth, she had always dwelt amid riches with lowly and humble spirit.

Now the Count of Panago was drawing near; and, on every hand, rumors of the new nuptials were rife. Sending forward one of his train, he announced the day on which he would arrive at Saluzzo. The day before, therefore, Walter sent for Griseldis, and when she had come with all fidelity, he said to her, "It is my desire that the maiden who is coming on the morrow to dine with us should be received sumptuously, as well as the men and matrons who come with her and such of our own people as are present at the feast, so that honor of place and welcome may be preserved unspotted, according to the dignity of each and all. But I have no women in the house who are suited to cope with this task; therefore, though your garments are but poor, you may best assume the duty of receiving and placing my guests, for you know my ways."

"I will do this," said she, "and whatever else I see will please you, not only willingly, but eagerly. Nor shall I grow weary or sluggish in this labor, so long as the least remnant of my spirit shall last." And when she had said this, straightway she caught up the implements of servant's toil and set to work, sweeping the house, setting the tables, making the beds, and urging on the others, like the best of handmaids.

At the third hour of the next day, the count arrived; and all the people vied in commending the manners and the beauty of the maiden and her youthful brother. There were those who said that Walter had been fortunate and prudent in the change he made, since this bride was more delicate and of nobler breeding, and had so fine a kinsman into the bargain. So, while the preparations for the feast went feverishly on, Griseldis, who had been present everywhere and solicitous of all—not cast down by so grievous a lot nor confused with shame for her old-fashioned clothing, but serene of countenance—came to meet the maiden as she entered. Bending the knee before her, after the manner of servants, with eyes cast reverently and humbly down, she said, "Welcome, my lady." Then she greeted others of the guests with cheerful face and marvelous sweetness in her words, and she managed the vast household with great skill; so that everyone greatly wondered—especially the newcomers—whence came that dignity of manner and that discretion beneath such a dress. She, in her turn, could not grow weary of praising the maiden and the boy: now she extolled the maiden's beauty, now the boy's.

Just as they were to sit down at the tables, Walter turned toward her and said before them all, as if he were making game of her, "What think you, Griseldis, of this bride of mine? Is she pretty and worthy enough?"

"Surely," said she, "no prettier or worthier could be found. Either with her or with no one, can you lead a life of tranquillity and happiness; and that you may find happiness is my desire and my hope. One thing, in all good faith, I beg of you, one warning I give you: not to drive her with those goads with which you have driven another woman. For since she is younger and more delicately nurtured, I predict she would not be strong enough to bear so much."

Walter, seeing the cheerfulness with which she spoke, and turning over in his mind the steadfastness of the woman, who had been so often and so bitterly injured, took pity on the unworthy fate that had befallen her so unjustly. Able to bear it no longer, he cried out, "It is enough, my Griseldis! Your fidelity to me is made known and proved; nor do I think that under heaven there is another woman who has undergone such trials of her conjugal love." And saying this, with eager arms he embraced his dear wife, who stood all overcome with stupor and as if waking from a troubled sleep. "And you," he said, "are my only wife. I have no other, nor ever shall have. This maiden, whom you think to be my bride, is your daughter; and he, who is thought to be my kinsman, is your son. They whom you believed you had lost, each in turn, you get back both together. Let all know, who thought the contrary, that I am curious and given to experiments, but am not impious: I have tested my wife, not condemned her; I have hidden my children, not destroyed them."

Almost out of her wits for joy and beside herself with maternal love, on hearing these words, Griseldis rushed into her children's arms, shedding the most joyous tears. She wearied them with kisses and bedewed them with her loving tears. And straightway the ladies gathered about her with alacrity and affection; and when her vile apparel had been stripped off her, they clothed her in her accustomed garments and adorned her. The most joyous plaudits and auspicious words from all the throng resounded all about; and the day was the most renowned that ever was for its great joy and sorrow,—more renowned, even, than the day of her nuptials had been.

Many years thereafter they lived in great peace and concord; and Walter, who had appeared to neglect his father-in-law, lest he should stand in the way of the experiment he had conceived, had the old man moved into his palace and held him in honor. His own daughter he gave in noble and honorable marriage, and his son he left behind him as his heir, happy in his wife and in his offspring.

This story it has seemed good to me to weave anew, in another tongue, not so much that it might stir the matrons of our times to imitate the patience of this wife—who seems to me scarcely imitable—as that it might stir all those who read it to imitate the woman's steadfastness, at least; so that they may have the resolution to perform for God what this woman performed for her husband. For He cannot be tempted by evil, as saith James the Apostle, and He himself tempts no man. Nevertheless, He often proves us and suffers us to be vexed with many a grievous scourge; not that He may know our spirit, for that He knew ere we were made, but that our own frailty may be made known to us through notable private signs. Therefore I would assuredly enter on the list of steadfast men the name of anyone who endured for his God, without a murmur, what this obscure peasant woman endured for her mortal husband.

FRANCIS PETRARCH

[Two Letters to Boccaccio] †

I

Your book, written in our mother tongue and published, I presume, during your early years, has fallen into my hands, I know not whence or how. If I told you that I had read it, I should deceive you. It is a very big volume, written in prose and for the multitude. I have been, moreover,

† From *Petrarch: The First Modern Scholar and Man of Letters*, trans. James Harvey Robinson and Henry Winchester Rolfe (New York: G. P. Putnam's Sons, 1914) 191–96. Although Robinson and Rolfe print these two selections as parts of one letter, the first was written in 1373 as the preface to Petrarch's translation, the second in 1374, when Petrarch found that his original letter had not reached Boccaccio and sent him another copy of his translation.

occupied with more serious business, and much pressed for time. You can easily imagine the unrest caused by the warlike stir about me, for, far as I have been from actual participation in the disturbances, I could not but be affected by the critical condition of the state. What I did was to run through your book, like a traveller who, while hastening forward, looks about him here and there, without pausing. I have heard somewhere that your volume was attacked by the teeth of certain hounds, but that you defended it valiantly with staff and voice. This did not surprise me, for not only do I well know your ability, but I have learned from experience of the existence of an insolent and cowardly class who attack in the work of others everything which they do not happen to fancy or be familiar with, or which they cannot themselves accomplish. Their insight and capabilities extend no farther; on all other themes they are silent.

My hasty perusal afforded me much pleasure. If the humour is a little too free at times, this may be excused in view of the age at which you wrote, the style and language which you employ, and the frivolity of the subjects, and of the persons who are likely to read such tales. It is important to know for whom we are writing, and a difference in the character of one's listeners justifies a difference in style. Along with much that was light and amusing, I discovered some serious and edifying things as well, but I can pass no definite judgment upon them, since I have not examined the work thoroughly.

As usual, when one looks hastily through a book, I read somewhat more carefully at the beginning and at the end. At the beginning you have, it seems to me, accurately described and eloquently lamented the condition of our country during that siege of pestilence which forms so dark and melancholy a period in our century. At the close you have placed a story which differs entirely from most that precede it, and which so delighted and fascinated me that, in spite of cares which made me almost oblivious of myself, I was seized with a desire to learn it by heart, so that I might have the pleasure of recalling it for my own benefit, and of relating it to my friends in conversation. When an opportunity for telling it offered itself shortly after, I found that my auditors were delighted. Later it suddenly occurred to me that others, perhaps, who were unacquainted with our tongue, might be pleased with so charming a story, as it had delighted me ever since I first heard it some years ago, and as you had not considered it unworthy of presentation in the mother tongue, and had placed it, moreover, at the end of your book, where, according to the principles of rhetoric, the most effective part of the composition belongs. So one fine day, when, as usual, my mind was distracted by a variety of occupations, discontented with myself and my surroundings, I suddenly sent everything flying, and, snatching up my pen, I attacked this story of yours. I sincerely trust that it will gratify you that I have of my own free-will undertaken to translate your work, something I should certainly never think of doing for anyone else, but which I was induced to do in this instance by my partiality for you and for the story. Not neglecting the precept of Horace in his *Art of Poetry*, that the careful translator should not attempt to render word for word, I have told your tale in my own language, in some places changing or even adding a few words, for I felt that you would not only permit, but would approve, such alterations.

Although many have admired and wished for my version, it seemed to me fitting that your work should be dedicated to you rather than to anyone else; and it is for you to judge whether I have, by this change of dress, injured or embellished the original. The story returns whence it came; it knows its judge, its home, and the way thither. As you and everyone who reads this knows, it is you and not I who must render account for what is essentially yours. If anyone asks me whether this is all true, whether it is a history [*historia*] or a story [*fabula*], I reply in the words of Sallust, "I refer you to the author"—to wit, my friend Giovanni. With so much of introduction, I begin.

*   *   *

II

My affection for you has induced me to write at an advanced age what I should hardly have undertaken even as a young man. Whether what I have narrated be true or false I do not know, but the fact that you wrote it would seem sufficient to justify the inference that it is but a tale. Foreseeing this question, I have prefaced my translation with the statement that the responsibility for the story rests with the author; that is, with you. And now let me tell you my experiences with this narrative [*historia*], or tale [*fabula*], as I prefer to call it.

In the first place, I gave it to one of our mutual friends in Padua to read, a man of excellent parts and wide attainments. When scarcely half-way through the composition, he was suddenly arrested by a burst of tears. When again, after a short pause, he made a manful attempt to continue, he was again interrupted by a sob. He then realized that he could go no farther himself, and handed the story to one of his companions, a man of education, to finish. How others may view this occurrence I cannot, of course, say; for myself, I put a most favourable construction upon it, believing that I recognise the indications of a most compassionate disposition; a more kindly nature, indeed, I never remember to have met. As I saw him weep as he read, the words of the Satirist came back to me:

> Nature, who gave us tears, by that alone
> Proclaims she made the feeling heart our own;
> And 't is our noblest sense. [1]

Some time after, another friend of ours, from Verona (for all is common between us, even our friends), having heard of the effect produced by the story in the first instance, wished to read it for himself. I readily complied,

---

1. Juvenal, xv., 131–33, as translated by William Gifford [*Translators*].

as he was not only a good friend, but a man of ability. He read the narrative from beginning to end without stopping once. Neither his face nor his voice betrayed the least emotion, nor a tear or a sob escaped him. "I too," he said at the end, "would have wept, for the subject certainly excites pity, and the style is well adapted to call forth tears, and I am not hard-hearted; but I believed, and still believe, that this is all an invention. If it were true, what woman, whether of Rome or any other nation, could be compared with this Griselda? Where do we find the equal of this conjugal devotion, where such faith, such extraordinary patience and constancy?" I made no reply to this reasoning, for I did not wish to run the risk of a bitter debate in the midst of our good-humoured and friendly discussion. But I had a reply ready. There are some who think that whatever is difficult for them must be impossible for others; they must measure others by themselves, in order to maintain their superiority. Yet there have been many, and there may still be many, to whom acts are easy which are commonly held to be impossible. Who is there who would not, for example, regard a Curtius, a Mucius, or the Decii, among our own people, as pure fictions; or, among foreign nations, Codrus and the Philæni; or, since we are speaking of woman, Portia, or Hypsicratia, or Alcestis, and others like them?[2] But these are actual historical persons. And indeed I do not see why one who can face death for another, should not be capable of encountering any trial or form of suffering.

* * *

From Le Ménagier de Paris †

* * *

Dear sister [dear wife], this story was translated by master Francis Petrarch, the poet crowned at Rome,[1] not in order to move good women to have patience amid the tribulations which their husbands cause them solely because of their love for those husbands. It was translated to show that since God, the Church, and Reason would have them be obedient; and since their husbands would have them endure a great deal; and since, to avoid worse,

2. All these examples from classical history and legend involve stories of acts of extraordinary courage or self-sacrifice. The first three are Roman: Marcus Curtius leapt into a chasm in order to close it; Caius Mucius Scaevola, captured by enemies, put his hand into a fire to show that he did not fear their threats; the Decii—father, son, and grandson—all died in battle for Rome. Codrus was the last king of Athens and sacrificed himself because of a prophecy that success in battle would come to the side whose king died. The Philæni were two brothers who consented to being buried alive in order to secure extended territory for Carthage. The three women Petrarch cites are more directly related to his story of wifely devotion: Portia killed herself when she learned of the death of Brutus; Hypsicratia so loved Mithridates

that she accompanied him everywhere, even in battle; Alcestis gave up her life so that Admetus could live.
† Translated for this volume by Glending Olson and V. A. Kolve: *Le Ménagier de Paris,* ed. Jérôme Pichon, 2 vols. (Paris: Crapelet, 1846) I. 124–26. The book was written by a wealthy householder of Paris—a member of the upper bourgeoisie—for the instruction of his young wife, sometime between 1392 and 1394. His paraphrase of Petrarch's version of the Griselda story is one of several tales through which he discusses the obedience and humility a wife should show her husband.
1. In 1341, Petrarch was given the laurel crown for poetry, in imitation of ancient custom. Cf. *Clerk's Prologue,* ll. 31–33.

it is necessary that they submit themselves completely to their husbands' wills, enduring patiently whatever their husbands desire; and what is more, since these good women must conceal such troubles, keep silent about them, and indeed come to terms with them while seeking always, with a happy spirit, to draw closer to the favor and love of those mortal husbands: how much greater then the reason for which men and women ought to suffer in patience the tribulations which God, who is immortal and eternal, sends to them. Whether it be the death of friends; the loss of goods, children, or kinfolk; the distress brought about by enemies, captures, slaughters, destruction, fire, tempest, thunderstorms, floods or other unexpected disasters: one ought always to endure it patiently and turn oneself again, with love and solicitude, to the love of the immortal Sovereign, eternal and everlasting God. This we may learn by the example of this pitiable woman, born into poverty among simple people without rank or learning, who suffered so much for her mortal husband [ami].

I have set down this story here only in order to instruct you, not to apply it directly to you, and not because I wish such obedience from you. I am in no way worthy of it. I am not a marquis, nor have I taken in you a shepherdess as my wife. Nor am I so foolish, arrogant, or immature in judgment as not to know that I may not properly assault or assay you thus, nor in any such fashion. God keep me from testing you in this way or any other, under the color of lies and dissimulations. Nor do I wish to test you in yet some other manner, for I am fully satisfied by the proof already established through the good name of your ancestors and of yourself, along with what I feel and see and know from direct experience.

I apologize if this story deals with too great cruelty—cruelty, in my view, beyond reason. Do not credit it as having really happened; but the story has it so, and I ought not to change it nor invent another, since someone wiser than I composed it and set it down. Because other people have seen it, I want you to see it too, so that you may be able to talk about everything just as they do.

* * *

The Franklin's Prologue and Tale

The story told in the *Franklin's Tale* appears twice in Boccaccio: first in book 4 of the *Filocolo* as one of the questions of love debated by a group of young men and women at their leisure; second in the *Decameron*, in a shorter version told on the final day as one of the tales illustrating the theme of generosity. Although there is not complete agreement on the nature of Chaucer's indebtedness to either of these stories, scholars tend to favor the *Filocolo* version, written ca. 1336–38 and here printed in a new English translation, as the most likely source. We also include as background to some of the Franklin's ideas a passage discussing love and marriage from a fourteenth-century English translation of Bartholomaeus Anglicus's popular thirteenth-century encyclopedia, *De proprietatibus rerum*. Certain of the biblical texts and the passage from the *Parson's Tale*, printed above as background to the *Wife of Bath's Prologue and Tale*, will be of interest to readers of the present tale as well.

GIOVANNI BOCCACCIO

From *Il Filocolo*, Book 4 †

[Fourth Question of Love]

[Menedon begins his story:]

In the land where I was born I remember that there was a very rich and noble knight, who loved with a perfect love a noble lady of that land, and took her for his wife. Another knight named Tarolfo became enamored of this lady, who was most beautiful, and loved her with so much love that he had eyes for nothing but her, and desired no other thing. He strove to win her love in many ways, by passing frequently before her house, by jousting, by doing battle, and by other deeds—often sending messengers to her, possibly promising great gifts, in order to make clear his intent. All of these things the lady suffered in silence, without giving any sign or answer to the knight, saying to herself, "When he notices that he cannot obtain any favor-

† Translated for this volume by Luigi Chinatti. For the text, see Giovanni Boccaccio, *Decameron, Filocolo, Ameto, Fiammetta*, ed. E. Bianchi, C. Salinari, N. Sapegno (Milan: Ricciardi, 1952). *Sources and Analogues*, pp. 378–83, prints the text of the narrative, but not the discussion of the "question."

able sign or response from me, perhaps he will cease loving and wooing me." But despite all this, Tarolfo did not cease, following the good teaching of Ovid, who says "A man should not stop persevering because of a woman's hardness, for the soft water by its continuous motion wears away the hard rock." The lady, fearful that these things should reach her husband's ear, and that he should think they had happened with her consent, decided to tell him everything. But reconsidering, she said, "If I were to tell him, I might cause something to happen between them which would make me forever unhappy. I must be rid of him in another way." And she thought of an ingenious trick. She sent word to Tarolfo that if he loved her as much as he claimed, she wished to have from him a gift. She swore by her gods and by the loyalty of a well-born lady that when she received it she would do his every wish; and that if he did not choose to grant what she asked, he should resolve in his heart to woo her no longer, unless he wished her to reveal all this to her husband. And the gift that she asked for was this: she said that she wished to have in the month of January, in that city, a large and beautiful garden filled with herbs and flowers and trees and fruits, as though it were the month of May. To herself she said, "This is an impossible thing, and I shall rid myself of him in this way." On hearing this, Tarolfo—though it seemed impossible, and though he understood why the lady asked it of him—replied that he would never rest nor return again into her presence until he could give her the gift that she had asked.

Then he departed from that city with such company as he wished, searching throughout the lands to the west for advice that might help him accomplish his desire. Not finding it there, he searched in the very hottest regions, arriving finally in Thessaly, to which he had been sent by a knowledgeable man. After staying there for several days without having found what he was looking for, almost despairing of his intent, he rose one morning before sunrise and went alone across the wretched plain that had once been all bathed in Roman blood. Having gone a long way, he saw at the foot of a mountain a bearded man, neither young nor very old, whose clothing indicated that he was poor. Small in stature and very lean, he was gathering herbs and digging with a small knife for various roots, with which he had already filled one large pocket of his robe. When Tarolfo saw this, he marveled and wasn't sure what it might be; but when he knew for certain that it was a man, he approached and greeted him, asking who he was, and from whence he came, and what he was doing in such a place and at such an hour. To which the little old man responded, "I am from Thebes, and Theban is my name. I go about this plain gathering herbs to earn a living, making from their juices medicines useful for various infirmities. It is necessity, not pleasure, that makes me come here at this hour. But who are you, whose appearance seems to me noble, and who walk here so alone?"

To which Tarolfo replied, "I come from the farthest west, and am a wealthy knight, driven and obsessed by thoughts of an undertaking I have not been able to accomplish, and so I walk alone in this fashion in order to lament the more freely." To which Theban said, "Do you not know what

kind of place this is? And why did you not take another way? You might
easily be set upon here by angry spirits." Tarolfo responded, "God may do
what he wishes, here as elsewhere. He has my life and my honor in his
hands; let him do with me what he wills. Truly, death would be a very rich
treasure to me." Then Theban said, "What is the undertaking you cannot
achieve, and for which you live in such sorrow?" Tarolfo replied, "It is
something I now think cannot be accomplished, since I have found no
useful counsel here." Theban asked, "Do you dare to name it?" and Tarolfo
answered, "Yes, but to what use? Probably none!" "But to what harm?"
Theban replied; and then Tarolfo said, "I seek advice as to how one might
have in the coldest month a garden full of flowers and fruits and herbs, as
beautiful as if it were the month of May; but I do not find anyone who can
offer me true assistance or good counsel."

Theban stood silent for a moment, thinking to himself, and then said,
"You and many others judge the knowledge and power of men according
to their clothing. If my robe had been like yours, or if you had found me
in the company of rich princes instead of gathering herbs, you would not
have found it so difficult to tell me your need. But often under the shabbiest
garments there is hidden the greatest treasury of knowledge. Let no one,
therefore, hide his need from someone who offers advice or help, as long
as he does not compromise himself by revealing it. What would you give
to him who helped bring about what you are looking for?"

Tarolfo looked into his face as he spoke these words, wondering if he
might be making fun of him, for it seemed incredible to him that Theban
could have this power unless he were God. Nevertheless, Tarolfo answered
thus, "In my country I am lord of many castles and many treasures, all of
which I would divide in half with him who grants me this wish." "Truly,"
said Theban, "if I were to do this I would no longer need to go about
gathering herbs." "I promise you," said Tarolfo, "if you can really bring
these things about, and give them to me, you will never again need to
struggle to become rich; but how and when can you furnish me this?" Said
Theban, "The time is up to you; do not trouble yourself about the manner.
I will come with you, trusting your promise, and when we arrive there
where you wish to be, you will give the command, and I will furnish everything without fail." Tarolfo was so happy over this event he could hardly
have felt more happiness had he then held his lady in his arms, and he
said, "I am very eager that what you promise be accomplished. Let us leave
without delay, and go there where it must be done." Theban threw away
his herbs, and took his books and other things necessary to the work, and
set out with Tarolfo. In a brief time they arrived at the desired city, very
near to the month for which the garden had been requested. Here they
rested silently and secretly until the proper time. When the month began,
Tarolfo commanded that the garden be prepared so that he might give it to
his lady.

When Theban had received this command, he waited for the night and,
when it had come, saw that the horns of the moon had returned to a full

circle, all resplendent above the familiar lands. Then he left the city, leaving behind his clothes and shoes, with his hair spread out upon his naked shoulders, all alone. The night passed by slow degrees; birds, beasts and men rested without any murmuring; on the trees the unfallen leaves stood without any movement, and the moist air rested at peace. Only the stars were shining when, after circling the city many times, he came to the place beside a river that it pleased him to choose for his garden. Here three times he extended his arms toward the stars, turning himself toward them; and bathing his white hair in the running water an equal number of times, he asked in a loud voice for their aid. Kneeling on the bare ground, he began to speak thus: "Aid me, oh night, most faithful concealer of lofty affairs; and you stars, who together with the moon follow the shining day; and you, highest Hecate, who come as helper to the enterprises begun by men; and you, holy Ceres, renewer of the ample face of the earth; and all you verses and arts and herbs; and you, earth that produced potent plants. Aid me, air, winds, mountains, rivers and lakes, and every god of the woods and of the secret night, with whose help I once turned back the flowing waters to their sources, and once made moving things to stand still and still things to move; you who once gave to my verses the power to dry up the seas and search freely their depths; with whose help I have made clear the cloudy weather, and filled the clear skies with dark clouds, causing the winds to cease or to blow at my pleasure, and with them breaking the harsh jaws of frightening dragons; with whose help I made also the still forests move, and the lofty mountains tremble, and spirits of the dead return to their bodies from the Stygian swamps and come forth alive from their sepulchers; with whose help I drew you, oh moon, to your full roundness, which formerly the sounding of horns used to help accomplish; with whose help I made pale also at times the clear face of the sun. Be present, all of you, and give me your aid. I have need now for the juices of herbs by which some part of the arid earth, despoiled of its bloom and fruit and herbs first by autumn and then by the fierce cold of winter, may be returned to flower, thereby making spring appear before its proper time."

When he had said this, he added many other things quietly to his prayers, and when he had finished, the stars did not shed their light in vain, for, more swiftly than the flight of any bird, a chariot drawn by two dragons appeared before him, which he mounted. Taking in his hands the reins of the dragons' bridles, he was carried up into the air. Making his journey through the high regions, he left behind Spain and all of Africa, and sought out the island of Crete, and then Pelion, Othrys and Ossa, Mount Nerius, Pachinus, Pelorus, and Appenine. In brief course he searched all of these, from each uprooting and cutting with a sharp sickle those roots and herbs that he wanted; nor did he forget those which he had picked when he was found by Tarolfo in Thessaly. He took stones from Mount Caucasus and from the sands of the Ganges, and from Libya he brought the tongues of venemous serpents. He visited the watery banks of the Rhone, the Seine in Paris, the great Po, the Arno, the imperial Tiber, the Don, and the Danube, taking from them also those herbs that he thought necessary; and these he added to others gathered on the summits of the wild mountains. He sought out the islands of Lesbos, and Colchis, and Patmos, and every other where he had heard of things useful to his purpose.

He returned with these things before the third day had passed, to the place from which he had departed; and the dragons, from the mere odor of the collected herbs, cast off their ancient scales and were renewed and returned to youth. Dismounting there, he built two altars from the grassy earth: on the right that of Hecate, and on the left that of [Ceres] the goddess of renewal. When these were finished, and devout fires had been lighted upon them, he began to circle them, quietly murmuring, with his hair loose upon his aged shoulders; and he repeatedly dipped the burning wood in the blood he had collected. Then placing the wood again upon the altars, and wetting with it at times the soil which he had prepared for the garden, he sprinkled the land three times with fire, water and sulphur. Then he placed an immense vase full of blood, milk and water on the burning flames, and made it boil for a long time, adding herbs and roots collected in strange places, putting in with them various seeds and flowers of unknown herbs, and adding stones found in the farthest East, along with frost gathered the previous nights, and the flesh and wings of infamous witches, the essential part of a wolf's testicles, the scaly skin of a Libyan snake, and finally the liver and lungs of an ancient stag; and with these things a thousand more besides, either nameless or so strange that my memory does not recall them. Then he took a branch from an old olive tree, and with it began to mix together all these things. And as he did this, the dry branch began to turn green, and shortly to sprout leaves; thus apparelled, it became laden with black olives not long after. When Theban saw this, he took the boiling liquors and began to spread and sprinkle them everywhere about the chosen spot, in which he had planted as many twigs as the number and kinds of trees he wanted there; and as soon as the earth felt this, it began to bloom everywhere, producing new and beautiful grasses, and the dry twigs all turned into green and fruitful plants.

When this was done, Theban entered the city and returned to Tarolfo, whom he found lost in thought, almost afraid of having been tricked because of the long delay. He said to him, "Tarolfo, that which you have required is done, and is at your disposal." This pleased Tarolfo greatly, and, there being the next day in the city a solemn festival, he went to his lady, whom he had not seen for a long time, and spoke to her thus: "My lady, after long labor I have provided what you commanded. When it will please you to see it or to take it, it is at your disposal."

The lady marveled greatly at seeing him, and even more upon hearing what he had to say. Not believing him, she answered, "I am very pleased; you shall show it to me tomorrow." The following day, Tarolfo went to his lady and said, "My lady, may it please you to come to the garden which you requested of me, in this cold month." The lady then set out with many companions, and, arriving at the garden, entered it through a beautiful portal; therein they felt no coldness like that outside, but temperate and sweet air. The lady went everywhere about the garden, admiring and gathering herbs and flowers, which she saw there in great abundance; and the power of the sprinkled liquors had wrought even more, for the fruits that August usually produces adorned all the trees here in this harsh time, and many of the people who had come with her ate of them. This seemed to the lady a most beautiful and wonderful thing; she did not remember ever having seen anything so beautiful. When by various means she knew this to be a real garden, and that the knight had fulfilled what she had asked, she turned to Tarolfo and said, "Without a doubt, sir knight, you have earned my love, and I am ready to grant what I promised you. But I would ask one favor of you: that you wait until my husband goes hunting, or somewhere out of the city, before asking me to fulfill your desire, so that you may take your pleasure more discreetly and without any fear." This pleased Tarolfo, who took his leave and departed from the garden, almost content.

This garden became known to all the people of the country, although no one knew for a long time how it had come into being. But the gentle lady to whom it had been given departed from it sorrowing, returning to her bedchamber full of melancholy. Wondering in what way she might avoid what she had promised, and finding no legitimate excuse, she grieved all the more. Her husband upon seeing this began to marvel greatly, and to ask her what was wrong. She said there was nothing wrong—being ashamed to reveal to him the promise she had made in requesting the gift, and fearing that he might think her evil. Finally, unable to resist the continual proddings of her husband, who still desired to know the reason for her melancholy, she told him from beginning to end why she lived in such grief. When he heard this, the knight fell into long thought, and then, knowing in his mind the purity of this woman, said to her thus: "Go, and fulfill your vow in secret, freely granting to Tarolfo what you have promised. He has earned it justly and with great effort." The lady began to weep, saying "May the gods keep me far from such an error; by no means will I do this. I would kill myself before doing anything that would cause you dishonor or displeasure." To which the knight said, "My lady, I do not want you to kill yourself because of this, nor do I wish that you make yourself sad because of it. It is no displeasure to me. Go and do what you have promised, for I will hold you no less dear; but when this is done, refrain from ever again making such a promise, however impossible the gift you request may seem to you."

In accord with her husband's will, she went, adorned and beautiful, with attendants, to the house of Tarolfo. There, blushing with shame, she presented herself before him. When Tarolfo saw her, he got up from the side of Theban, with whom he had been sitting, and approached her full of wonder and joy, receiving her honorably and asking the reason for her coming. To which the lady answered, "I have come to do your every pleasure; do with me what you will." Then Tarolfo said, "You surprise me greatly, considering the hour and the company with which you have come. This cannot be, unless something has happened between you and your husband. Tell me, I pray you." The lady then told Tarolfo in detail everything that had happened. Hearing this, Tarolfo more than ever began to marvel and to ponder it deeply, thinking about the great generosity of her husband, who had sent her to him, and saying to himself that anyone who would consider doing villainy to so generous a man would be worthy of the greatest blame. And so he said to her, "Gentle lady, you have done your duty loyally, as a noble woman should, and therefore I think of myself as having received from you that which I desired. And so, when it pleases you, you may return to your husband. Thank him on my behalf for this great generosity, and ask that he forgive me for the folly that I have committed in the past, assuring him that in the future such things will never again be done by me." Thanking Tarolfo for such a courtesy, the lady left happily to return to her husband, to whom she related in detail everything that had happened.

When Theban returned to Tarolfo, he asked what had happened, and Tarolfo told it all to him in turn; to which Theban said, "Have I therefore lost, because of this, that which you promised me?" Tarolfo responded, "No, on the contrary, when it pleases you, go and take half of my castles and my treasure, as I promised you, for I consider myself entirely satisfied with your service." To which Theban answered, "Since the knight was generous to you with his wife, and you were not villainous toward him, may it never please the gods that I should be less courteous. Beyond anything in the world I am pleased to have served you, and I wish those things that I was to have claimed in payment to remain your own, as if it had never happened." He did not wish to take a single thing that belonged to Tarolfo.

The question then is this: Which of these was the most generous? Was it the knight, who permitted his wife to go to Tarolfo? Or Tarolfo, who, when the lady came to him, sent her back to her husband—the lady he had always desired, and for whom he had done so much in order to bring things to that point? Or was it Theban, who leaving behind his country, and already an old man, came here to earn the promised gifts, struggled to accomplish what he had promised, and having earned them, renounced them all, remaining as poor as before?

"The story is most beautiful and so is the question," said the queen, "and in truth each of the men was very generous, considering how the first was courteous in respect to his honor, the second in respect to his lustful desire, and the third in respect to the wealth he had acquired. And therefore, if we wish to know who performed the greatest generosity or courtesy, it is necessary to consider which of these three things is the most valuable. When we have understood that, we will know clearly who that person is, because he who gives most is considered most generous. Of these three things, one is dear, that is, honor, which Paulus Aemilius, having defeated Perseus, desired more than the treasures he had earned. The second is to be avoided, that is, lustful relationships, according to the teaching of Sophocles and Xenocrates, who said that lust is to be avoided as one avoids a raging tyrant. The third is not to be desired, that is, riches, because more often than not they are troublesome to a virtuous life, and one can live virtuously in moderate poverty, as Marcus Curtius, Attilius Regulus and Valerius Publicola show in their deeds. Therefore, if among these three things only honor is dear, and the others not, then he was most generous who gave his lady, although he acted less than wisely. He was also the first to be generous, whereupon the others followed. Therefore, in our opinion, he who gave the woman, upon whom his honor depended, was more generous than the others."

Said Menedon, "I agree that all this may be as you say—since it is you who have said it—but it seems to me that each of the others was more generous, and you shall hear how. It is true that the first man granted his wife, but in doing this he was not so generous as you claim. Even if he had wanted to deny her to Tarolfo, he could not justly have done so because of the vow made by the woman, which had to be observed. He who grants what he cannot deny does well, inasmuch as he is generous with it, but he gives little. And therefore, as I said, each of the others was more courteous.

"Furthermore Tarolfo had for a long time already loved and desired the lady above all other things, and had struggled long to have her, undertaking to search for things almost impossible to have, in order to satisfy her request. Once he had obtained them, he deserved to have her because of her pledge. And when this pledge was kept, as we said, there is no doubt that the honor of the husband was in his hands, and also the release to her of what she had promised him. He did this, and was therefore generous in respect to the honor of the husband, her oath, and his own long-lived desire. It is a great thing to have suffered thirst for a long time, and then to come upon a fountain and not drink in order to let someone else drink.

"The third man also was very generous, if we consider that poverty is one of the hardest things in the world to bear, for it drives away both joy and rest, puts honor to flight, conceals virtue, and brings bitter cares so that everyone naturally attempts to flee from it, with ardent desire. In many men this desire to live splendidly and at leisure is kindled so fiercely that they give themselves to dishonest gains and base adventures, perhaps because they do not know the means, or are not able, to satisfy their desire in any other way; and for these things sometimes they deserve to die, or to be forever exiled from their lands. How pleasing and dear therefore must these riches be to one who has earned and possessed them fairly? And who can doubt the extreme poverty of Theban, if you remember that he forsook his evening rest to go about in dangerous places, gathering herbs and digging roots, in order to sustain his life? That this poverty concealed his virtue one can also believe, since Tarolfo thought he was being mocked by Theban when he first saw him dressed in such vile clothing. And so too one can well believe that Theban desired to leave such misery and become rich, since he came all the way from Thessaly to Spain, exposing himself to dangerous things through perilous and uncertain paths of the air, in order to fulfill his promise, and to receive what had been promised by another. One must believe that whoever undergoes so many things of this kind in order to flee poverty, knows it to be full of every suffering and every grief. And the greater the poverty he left in entering a life of riches, the more is that new life precious to him. Therefore, if a man has come from poverty to riches, and takes delight in that life, how great and how generous is he when he gives it up, and consents to return to that state that he sought to flee with such difficulty? Men do many great and generous things, but this seems to me the greatest, especially considering the old age of the donor, because avarice is usually much more powerful in old men than in young. Therefore, I maintain that each of the two others was more generous than the first one commended by you, and that the third was most generous of all."

"You defend your opinion as well as anyone could," said the queen, "but we intend to demonstrate briefly why you should hold our opinion rather than your own. You wish to say that the husband was not generous in yielding his wife because he was justly obliged to do so by the oath she made—and that would indeed be so if the oath were binding. But the lady, insofar as she is a part of her husband, or rather, of one body with him, could not take that oath without his will; and if she did so, it was null, because a first sacrament lawfully made cannot justly be replaced by any subsequent one, and especially not by those that are not made properly and for a rightful reason. In matrimonial relationships it is the custom to swear that the man will be always content with his wife, and the woman with the husband, and that the one will never exchange the other for any other person. Therefore, the woman could not swear such an oath, and if she did so, as we have already said, she swore an unlawful thing, contrary to her first oath, and it could not be valid. Since it was not valid, the husband should not have sent his wife to Tarolfo unless it pleased him to do so. When he did send her, then it was he who was generous with his honor— more generous than Tarolfo, as you have maintained. Since the wife's oath was invalid, its renunciation cannot be an act of generosity.

"Therefore, Tarolfo was generous only in renouncing his lustful desire, which everyone should do as his proper duty, because we are all bound by reason to abandon vice and to follow virtue. Whoever does what he is bound by reason to do (you have admitted this is the case) is generous in nothing— though whatever one does of good beyond this, that ought truly to be called generosity. But because you are perhaps still thinking how dear to the husband must be the honor of a chaste wife, we will go further in our reasoning, and demonstrate, so that you may see it more clearly, that Tarolfo and Theban showed no generosity in respect to the husband. You must know that chastity and other virtues give to their possessors no other reward than honor, and that this honor, among virtuous men, can make the least among them the most excellent. This honor, if men sustain it humbly, makes them friends of God, and consequently makes them live and die happily, thereafter to possess their eternal reward. If the woman preserves this honor for her husband, he lives happily and is certain of his offspring, going about with an untroubled face among the people, content to see her honored above all other women for this virtue. In his mind this is a clear sign that she is good, and fears God, and loves him, for it should please him not a little to feel that she is his in eternal union, indivisible except by death. Through this blessing, he is seen to multiply continually in earthly and spiritual wealth. In contrast, he whose wife lacks this virtue can pass no hour in real tranquility, and nothing is to his liking; the one desires the death of the other. He senses himself an object of gossip among even the most wretched people because of this low vice; it seems to him that such a thing must be believed by whoever hears it. And even if he possessed all other virtues, this vice would seem to have the force to contaminate and ruin them all. Therefore, the chastity of a good woman is the greatest honor that she can give to a husband, and it is greatly to be cherished. He to whom such a gift is granted may consider himself blessed through grace, although we believe that there are few men who qualify to be envied for this blessing.

"But returning to our argument, consider how much the husband gave. We have not forgotten that you said Theban was more generous than the others because, having become rich through his labors, he did not hesitate to return to the misery of poverty by giving up all that he had acquired. It is clear that you do not understand what poverty is, for it surpasses any wealth as long as we receive it happily. Perhaps Theban already because of his newly earned riches felt full of bitter and sundry cares. Perhaps he already imagined that Tarolfo might conclude he had done a foolish thing, and try to kill him in order to regain his castles. Perhaps he already lived in fear that his subjects might betray him. He had entered into the cares of governing his lands. He now knew all the deceits practiced by his tenants. He imagined himself envied by many because of his riches, and feared that thieves might secretly take them away. He was full of so many various and sundry thoughts and cares that all tranquility fled from him. Whereupon, remembering how in his earlier life he had lived happily without such cares, he said to himself: "I desired to become wealthy so that I might have peace, but I see that wealth increases difficulties and worries, and puts all rest to flight." And desiring to return to his former life, he returned those riches to him who had given them. Poverty consists in riches refused; it is an unknown good, that puts cares to flight, as Diogenes understood full well. Poverty needs only that which nature requires. He who confronts it in patience lives secure from every treachery, and the power to achieve great honor is by no means taken from him, so long as he lives virtuously, in the manner we have described. And therefore, when Theban cast off this burden, he was not generous, but wise. He was gracious to Tarolfo in that it pleased him to give his riches to him rather than to another—for he might have given them to many others.

"But the husband was more generous than the rest because he was willing to give up his honor. Think on this point in conclusion: the honor that he renounced was irrecoverable—which is not the case with many other things, such as the honor that is risked in battles, or contests, or the like, which if it is lost at one time may be recovered at another. Let this suffice in answer to your question."

GIOVANNI BOCCACCIO

From the *Decameron*, Tenth Day, Fifth Tale†

Madonna Dianora asks Messer Ansaldo to give her a garden that would be as beautiful in January as in May; by hiring a magician, Messer Ansaldo manages to grant her wish; her husband agrees that she must fulfill Messer Ansaldo's desires, but when Messer Ansaldo hears of her husband's generosity, he frees her from her promise, and the magician, refusing to accept anything from him, also frees Messer Ansaldo from his.

Every member of the merry company had already praised Messer Gentile to the skies, when the King ordered Emilia to continue, and she, longing to speak, self-confidently began as follows:

Tender ladies, no one can reasonably say that Messer Gentile did not act generously, but if anyone were to claim that it would be impossible to act more generously, it would not be hard to show the contrary, as I mean to show you in this little tale of mine.

In Friuli, a rather cold province but one which boasts of beautiful mountains, many rivers, and clear springs, there is a town called Udine, in which there once lived a beautiful and noble lady named Madonna Dianora, the wife of a very wealthy man named Gilberto, a very pleasant and amiable person. Such was this lady's worth that she was greatly loved by a famous and noble baron of high rank, whose name was Messer Ansaldo Gradense and who was known everywhere for his feats of arms and chivalry. And while Messer Ansaldo loved Madonna Dianora passionately and did everything he could to be loved in return by her, often sending her numerous messages with this end in mind, he labored in vain. And when the lady, having become weary of the knight's entreaties, realized that no matter how much she denied him everything he requested, he nevertheless continued to love her and to implore her, she decided to rid herself of him by making a strange and, in her judgment, impossible request.

And so she said the following to a woman who often came to her on his behalf:

† From THE DECAMERON by Giovanni Boccaccio, translated by Mark Musa and Peter Bondanella. Pp. 623–27. Copyright © 1982 by Mark Musa and Peter Bondanella. Reprinted by arrangement with NAL Penguin Inc., New York, NY.

"Good woman, you have assured me many times that Messer Ansaldo loves me above all other things, and you have, on his behalf, offered me marvelous gifts; he may keep these gifts, for they could never bring me to love him or to fulfill his pleasure. But if I could be certain he loved me as much as you say he does, I would be moved without a doubt to love him and to do whatever he wished. And so, whenever he is willing to provide me with proof by doing what I request, I shall be ready to do whatever he wants."

The good woman said: "What is it, my lady, that you wish him to do?"

The lady replied:

"What I desire is this: in the month of January which is soon to come, I want there to be on the outskirts of town a garden full of green grass, flowers, and leafy trees no different from one in the month of May; if he is unable to do this, he should never again send you or anyone else to me, for if he continues to bother me, just as until now I have completely concealed everything from my husband and my relatives, I shall, by complaining to them about him, seek to get rid of him."

When the knight heard his lady's request and offer, no matter how difficult or rather impossible a task he felt it was to fulfill, and in spite of the fact that he realized the lady had made this request for no other reason than to destroy his hope, nevertheless, he made up his mind to try to do what he could. He sent word to all parts of the world to find out if there was someone who might provide him with assistance or advice, and a certain man came to him who offered to do it by means of magic, provided he was well paid. Messer Ansaldo came to an agreement with him for an enormous sum of money and then happily awaited the time the lady had set for him. When it arrived and the weather was bitter cold and everything was covered with snow and ice, in a most beautiful meadow near the town, the worthy man, on the night before the first day of January, employed his magic to such effect that on the following morning there appeared, according to the testimony of those who saw it for themselves, one of the most beautiful gardens that had ever been seen, with grass, trees, and fruit of every kind. As soon as Messer Ansaldo saw the garden, with great joy he had gathered some of the most beautiful fruits and flowers growing there and then secretly had them presented to the lady, inviting her to come and see the garden she had requested so that she would not only realize how much he loved her but would also recall the promise she had made to him, sealed with her oath, and in so doing would seek, as a woman of good faith, to keep her promise.

The lady had heard much talk about the marvelous garden, and when she saw the flowers and fruit, she began to regret her promise. In spite of her regret, curious as she was to see so unusual a thing, she went with many other ladies of the town to have a look at the garden; after praising it very highly, and not without amazement, she returned home the most sorrowful of women, thinking about what she was obliged to do because of it. So intense was her grief that she was unable to conceal it, and her husband, who could not help noticing it, insisted on knowing the cause of it. Out of shame, the lady kept silent for a long time; then, finally compelled to speak, she revealed everything to him.

When Gilberto heard all this, at first he was very much disturbed; but then, when he considered his wife's pure intentions, he put aside his anger and said:

"Dianora, it is not proper for a wise or virtuous woman to pay attention to messages of that sort or to fix a price on her chastity with anyone, under any circumstances. Words received by the heart through the ears have more power than many would believe, and almost everything becomes possible for lovers. Hence, you did wrong first by listening and then by bargaining, but since I know the purity of your heart, I shall allow you, in order to absolve you of the obligation of your promise, to do something which perhaps no other man would allow, being also moved by my fear of the magician, whom Messer Ansaldo, if we were to disappoint him, would perhaps have do us harm. I want you to go to him, and by any means possible, short of your chastity, seek to be released from this promise, and if that is impossible, then this one time you must give him your body, but not your heart."

When the lady heard her husband, she wept and refused to accept such a favor from him. But no matter how much the lady objected, Gilberto insisted that she do it, and so, the following morning, around daybreak, without dressing up too much, the lady, preceded by two of her retainers and followed by one of her maidservants, went to Messer Ansaldo's home.

When he heard that the lady had come to him, he was quite amazed, and so, rising, he sent for the magician, and said to him: "I want you to see how much good your art has procured me." And then he went to greet her, and with no display of unbridled passion, with reverence he received her courteously, after which he had everyone go into a beautiful room where a big fire was burning, and after arranging for her to be seated, he said:

"My lady, I beg you, if the long love which I have borne you deserves any reward, be good enough to tell me the real reason why you have come here at such an hour and with such an escort."

Ashamed and with tears welling in her eyes, the lady replied:

"Sir, neither because I love you, nor because of my promise do I come here, but, rather, because of my husband's orders. Having more consideration for the labors of your unbridled passion than for his or my honor, he has made me come here; and it is at his command that I am disposed, this one time, to fulfill your every desire."

If Messer Ansaldo was astonished when she began speaking, he was even more so after she finished. Moved by Gilberto's generosity, his passion began to change into compassion, and he said:

"My lady, since things are as you say, God forbid that I should soil the honor of a man who has taken pity on my love, and so, as long as you wish to stay here, you will be treated just as if you were my sister, and whenever you like, you are free to leave, provided that you give your husband such

:hanks as you deem befitting such courtesy as his, and that henceforth you always consider me as a brother and your servant."

When the lady heard these words, happier than ever before, she said:

"Nothing could ever make me believe, considering your manners, that anything else could have resulted from my coming here than what I see you have made of it, and I shall always be obliged to you for this."

And having taken her leave, honorably escorted, she returned to Gilberto and reported to him what had happened; and as a result, a very close and loyal friendship grew up between Gilberto and Messer Ansaldo.

When Messer Ansaldo was ready to give the magician his promised fee, the magician, having witnessed the generosity of Gilberto toward Messer Ansaldo and that of Messer Ansaldo toward the lady, said:

"God forbid that having seen Gilberto so generous with his honor and you with your love, I should not be just as generous with my reward; and so, recognizing the justice of leaving the reward with you, it is my intention that you keep it."

The knight was embarrassed and tried to make him take if not all of the money, at least a part of it; but he labored in vain, and after the third day, when the magician had removed his garden and wanted to depart, Messer Ansaldo bid him Godspeed. And with his sensual passion for the lady extinguished in his heart, there remained the honest flame of affection.

What shall we say of this, loving ladies? Shall we place the lady who was almost dead and the love already grown lukewarm through lost hope above the generosity of Messer Ansaldo, who was more warmed with love than ever and kindled with even more hope, who held in his very hands the catch he had pursued for so long a time? It seems foolish to me to believe that his kind of generosity could ever be compared to the other.

BARTHOLOMAEUS ANGLICUS

[On Love and Marriage] †

De viro.

A man hatte° *vir* in latyn, and hath that   *is called*
name of° myght and vertu° and strengthe. So   *because of / power*
seith Isidre.[1] For in myght and strengthe a man
passith° a womman, and a man is the hed of   *surpasses*
a womman, as the apostil seith.[2] Therfore a
man is holde° to rule his wif, as the heed hath   *bound*

---

†Text based on *On the Properties of Things: John Trevisa's Translation of Bartholomaeus Anglicus de Proprietatibus Rerum*, ed. M. C. Seymour et al. Reprinted by permission of Oxford University Press. 2 vols. (Oxford: Oxford UP, 1975) I. 307–9.
1. Isidore of Seville (d. 636), author of a popular medieval encyclopedia, the *Etymologies*. The explanations of the meanings of the Latin words *vir* (man), *maritus* (husband), and *sponsus* (bridegroom) in this paragraph are based on Latin etymologies that the English translation cannot reproduce.
2. St. Paul, in Ephesians 5.23; see p. 352.

the cure° and reule of al the body. And a man
hatte *maritus*, as it were wardinge° and
defendinge the modir, for he taketh so the
charge, the warde,° and the kepinge of his wif
that is modir of children, and hatte *sponsus*
also, and hath that name of *spondere*,° for a
behotith' and obligith himsilf. For in the
contract of weddinge he plightith his treuthe,°
and oblegith himsilf to lede his lif with his wif
withoute departinge,° and to paye dettis° to
here° and to kepe to here feith and companie,
and that he schal leve hire for none othir. A
man hath so gret love to his wif that because
of here he aventurith him° to al perilus,° ande
settith [here] love tofore his modir love,° and
for to dwelle with his wif he forsaketh his fadir
and modir and his contray, as oure lord seith:
Herefore a man schal forsake fadir and modir
and abide with his wif.[3]

Tofore° the weddinge the spouse fondith°
to winne the love of hise spouse that° he wow-
ith° with giftis, and certifieth of his wille° with
lettres and messingeres and with divers sondes,°
and geveth many giftis and meche good and
catelle,° and behotith° wel more. And to plese
hire he puttith hym° to divers pleyes and games
among gederinge° of puple, and usith° ofte
dedis of myght and of maistrie,° and maketh
hym gay° and semeliche° in divers clothinge
and aray. And alle that he is i-prayed° to geve
othir° to doo for here love he geveth and doth
anon with alle his myght, and werneth none
bone° that is i-prayed in here name and for
here love. He spekith to here plesingeliche,°
and beholdith hire in the face with plesinge
and glad chere° and with a scharp eye, and
assentith° to hire at the laste, and tellith open-
liche his wille and his assent° in presence of
hire frendes, and spousith° hire with a ring
and taketh hire to wif, and geveth hire grete
giftis in tokene of the contract of weddinge,
and maketh to hire chartres and dedes° of
graunt° and of giftis, and maketh revels and
festis of spousailes,° and geveth many goode

care	
keeping	
guardianship	
from "to betroth"	
he promises	
troth	
parting from her / debts	
her	
himself / perils	
love for his mother	
Before / strives	
whom	
woos / makes known his intentions	
messages	
many goods and possessions / promises	
himself	
gathering / practices	
prowess	
well-dressed / comely	
asked	
or	
refuses no boon, request	
pleasantly	
countenance	
submits	
intent	
espouses, marries	
deeds	
allowance	
wedding feasts	

3. Ephesians 5.31; see p. 353.

giftis to frendis and gestis, and comfortith and gladith his gestis with songis and pipis and with instrumentis of musik. And hereaftir he bryngith his spouse into the privetees° of his chambre, and fongith hire to felawe° and maketh hire felawe in bedde and at bourde.[4] And thanne he maketh hire lady of his money and of his meyne.° Thanne he hath hire cause as moche to herte as his owne, and taketh the charge and keping of here. And for special love he amendith° hire yif sche doth amys,° and taketh hede° of here beringe and goynge,° of spekinge and lokynge, and of here passinge° and agencomynge° and entringe.

privacy
takes her as a companion

household

corrects / wrong
heed / behavior
departing
returning

No man hath more welthe than he that hath a good womman to wif. Ne no man is more wrecche nothir° hath woo and sorwe than he that hath an yvel wif, crienge, jangelinge,° chidinge and skoldinge, drunkelew° and unstedefast and contrarye° to hym, costlew,° stoute and gay,[5] envyous, noyful,° and lepinge ouer londes and contrayes, and mychinge,° suspicious, and wrethful. Fulgencius touchith al this matere in a certeyn sermon *de nupciis in Chana Galile.*[6] And so he likneth° Crist to the goode man, and holy chirche to a goode wif, and the synagoge to an evel wif that breketh spousehode.° In a goode spouse and wif nedith thes condicions: that sche be busy and devoute in goddes servyse; meke° and servisable to here housbonde, and faire spekinge and goodlich° to here meyne;° merciable and good to wrecchis that beth nedy; esi° and pesible° to here neighbores; redy, ware,° and wys in thinges that schal be i-voided; rightful and pacient in soffringe;° besi [and] diligent in here doinge and dedis; manerliche in clothinge; sobre in movinge; ware in spekinge; chast° in lokinge; honest in beringe; sad° in goynge,° schamfast° among the puple; meri and glad with here housbonde; and chast in privete. Such a wif is worthi to be i-preised,° that fon-

nor
chattering
prone to drunkenness
hostile / extravagant
troublesome

thieving

likens, compares

commits adultery

meek

kind / household
agreeable
peaceful / wary, careful

suffering

chaste, modest
steady / behavior
modest

praised

4. Literally "at table," but the phrase "bed and board" refers to the full range of a wife's sexual and domestic responsibilities and privileges.
5. Haughty and ostentatiously dressed.

6. We have not been able to find a sermon on the marriage at Cana (John 2.1–11) in the extant works of either Fulgentius, bishop of Ruspe, or Fulgentius the mythographer.

dith° more to plese here housbonde with heer°   *strives / hair*
homliche i-wounde° than with heer gailiche   *simply braided*
i-pinchid,° and i-wrolled° more with vertues   *gaily curled / wrapped*
than with faire and gay clothinge. Sche usith
the goodnes of matrimoni more bicause of
children than of fleischliche likynge,° and hath   *physical pleasure*
more likinge in spousehod in children of grass
than of kynde.[7] Of a goode wif be this inowgh°   *enough*
at this tyme.

---

7. For spiritual than for earthly reasons.

The Pardoner's
Prologue and Tale

As in the case of the Wife of Bath, the relationship between the Pardoner's prologue and his tale is exceptionally provocative. The Pardoner's open revelation of his own hypocrisy and avarice, which frames the narrative, has precedent in the speech of False Seeming *(Faus Semblant)* from the *Romance of the Rose*. The basis of the story of the rioters and the treasure is an exemplum found in various forms in the Middle Ages and Renaissance, known in its fullest version as *The Hermit, Death, and the Robbers*. The Pardoner's discussion of the tavern sins owes much to traditional lore, such as Thomas of Cantimpré's exemplum about swearing. The grim atmosphere of death in the tale reflects in part the impact of the plague on late medieval consciousness, which is treated in the prologues of Boccaccio and Sercambi on pp. 236–49 and 251–55.

JEAN DE MEUN

From the *Romance of the Rose*†

[False Seeming's Speech]

* * *

* * * False Seeming began his lecture and said to all in hearing:
"Barons, hear my theme: he who wants to become acquainted with False Seeming must seek him in the world or in the cloister. I dwell in no place except these two, but more in one and less in the other. Briefly, I am lodged where I think that I am better hidden. The safest hiding place is under the most humble garment. The religious are very covert, the worldly more open. I do not want to blame or defame the religious calling, in whatever habit one may find it. I shall not, as I may, blame the humble and loyal religious life, although I do not love it.

† From Guillaume de Lorris and Jean de Meun, *The Romance of the Rose*, trans. Charles Dahlberg (Princeton: Princeton UP, 1971) 194–98, 202–5, 208–9. Copyright © 1971 by Princeton University Press. Excerpts reprinted by permission of Princeton University Press. Jean de Meun wrote his vast conclusion to Guillaume's poem ca. 1275–77. In this passage, False Seeming *(Faus Semblant)* offers his service to the God of Love in an assault upon the Castle wherein Jealousy has imprisoned the Rose and Fair Welcoming *(Bel Accueil)*, the object of the Lover's quest. False Seeming (who personifies an aspect of the Lover's mind and a part of his erotic strategy) here presents his credentials—an extended self-portrait of hypocrisy exultant—to the God of Love and his assembled barons. On Chaucer's knowledge of this poem, see p. 311 of this volume.

"I have in mind the false religious, the malicious criminals who want to wear the habit but do not want to subdue their hearts. The religious are all compassionate; you will never see a spiteful one. They do not care to follow pride, and they all want to live humbly. I never dwell with such people, and if I do, I pretend. I can indeed assume their habit, but I would rather let myself be hanged than desert my main business, whatever face I put on it.

"I dwell with the proud, the crafty, the guileful, who covet worldly honors and who carry out large dealings, who go around tracking down large handouts and cultivating the acquaintance of powerful men and becoming their followers. They pretend to be poor, and they live on good, delicious morsels of food and drink costly wines. They preach poverty to you while they fish for riches with seines and trammel nets. By my head, evil will come of them. They are neither religious nor worldly. To the world they present an argument in which there is a shameful conclusion: this man has the robe of religion; therefore he is a religious. This argument is specious, not worth a knife of privet; the habit does not make the monk. Nevertheless no one knows how to reply to the argument, no matter how high he tonsures his head, even if he shaves with the razor of the *Elenchis*, that cuts up fraud into thirteen branches.[1] No man knows so well how to set up distinctions that he dare utter a single word about it. But whatever place I come to, no matter how I conduct myself, I pursue nothing except fraud. No more than Tibert the cat has his mind on anything but mice and rats do I think of anything except fraud. Certainly by my habit you would never know with what people I dwell, any more than you would from my words, no matter how simple and gentle they were. You should look at actions if your eyes have not been put out; for if people do something other than what they say, they are certainly tricking you, whatever robes they have or whatever estate they occupy, clerical or lay, man or woman, lord, sergeant, servant, or lady.

* * *

"But indeed I want to promise you to further the causes of all your friends, provided that they want my companionship. They are dead if they don't receive me, and they will serve my friend, or, by God, they will never succeed! Without fail, I am a traitor, and God has judged me a thief. I am perjured, but one hardly knows before the end what I am bringing to an end, for several who never recognized my fraud have received their deaths through me, and many are receiving them and will receive them without ever recognizing it. The man who does so, if he is wise, protects himself from it, or it will be his great misfortune. But the deception is so strong that it is very difficult to recognize it. For Proteus, who was accustomed to change into whatever form he wished, never knew as much fraud or guile as I practice; I never entered a town where I was recognized, no matter how much I was heard or seen. I know very well how to change my garment, to

---

1. The allusion is to scholastic subtlety in argumentation; an *elenchus* is a procedure of refutation.

take one and then another foreign to it. Now I am a knight, now a monk; at one time I am a prelate, at another a canon; at one hour a clerk, at another a priest; now disciple, now master, now lord of the manor, now forester. Briefly I am in all occupations. Again I may be prince or page, and I know all languages by heart. At one hour I am old and white, and then I have become young again. Now I am Robert, now Robin, now Cordelier, now Jacobin. And in order to follow my companion, Lady Constrained Abstinence, who comforts me and goes along with me, I take on many another disguise, just as it strikes her pleasure, to fulfill her desire. At one time I wear a woman's robe; now I am a girl, now a lady. At another time I become a religious: now I am a devotee, now a prioress, nun, or abbess; now a novice, now a professed nun. I go through every locality seeking all religions. But, without fail, I leave the kernel of religion and take the husk. I dwell in religion in order to trick people; I seek only its habit, no more. What should I tell you? I disguise myself in the way that pleases me. The time is very much changed in me; my deeds are very different from my words."

At this point False Seeming wanted to stay silent, but Love did not pretend that he was annoyed at what he heard; instead, to delight the company, he said to him:

"Tell us more especially in what way you serve disloyally. Don't be ashamed to speak of it, for, as you tell us of your habits, you seem to be a holy hermit."

"It is true, but I am a hypocrite."

"You go around preaching abstinence."

"True, indeed, but I fill my paunch with very good morsels and with wines such as are suitable for theologians."

"You go around preaching poverty."

"True, abundantly richly. But however much I pretend to be poor, I pay no attention to any poor person. I would a hundred thousand times prefer the acquaintance of the King of France to that of a poor man, by our lady, even though he had as good a soul. When I see those poor devils all naked, shivering with cold on those stinking dunghills, crying and howling with hunger, I don't meddle in their business. If they were carried to the Hôtel-Dieu, they wouldn't get any comfort from me, for they wouldn't feed my maw with a single gift, since they have nothing worth a cuttlefish. What will a man give who licks his knife? But a visit to a rich usurer who is sick is a good and pleasant thing. I go to comfort him, for I expect to bring away money from him. And if wicked death stifles him, I will carry him right up to his grave. And if anyone comes to reprove me for avoiding the poor, do you know how I escape from him? I give out behind my cloak that the rich man is more stained with sin than the poor, and has greater need of counsel, and that that is the reason that I see him and advise him.

* * *

"Working can give me no pleasure: I have nothing to do with it, for there is too great difficulty in working. I prefer to pray in front of people and cover my foxlike nature under a cloak of pope-holiness."

"What's this?" said Love. "The devil! What are your words? What have you said here?"

"What?"

"Great and open disloyalty. Don't you fear God then?"

"Certainly not. The man who wants to fear God can hardly attain anything great in this world, for the good, who avoid evil, live legitimately on what they have, and keep themselves according to God, scarcely get from one loaf to the next. Such people drink too much discomfort; there is no life that displeases me so much.

"But consider how usurers, counterfeiters, and loan sharks have money in their storehouses. Bailiffs, beadles, provosts, mayors, all live practically by rapine. The common people bow to them, while they, like wolves, devour the commoners. Everybody runs over the poor; there isn't anyone who does not want to despoil them, and all cover themselves with their spoil. They all snuff up their substance and pluck them alive without scalding. The strongest robs the weakest. But I, wearing my simple robe and duping both dupers and duped, rob both the robbed and the robbers.

"By my trickery I pile up and amass great treasure in heaps and mounds, treasure that cannot be destroyed by anything. For if I build a palace with it and achieve all my pleasures with company, the bed, with tables full of sweets—for I want no other life—my money and my gold increases. Before my treasure can be emptied, money comes to me again in abundance. Don't I make my bears tumble? My whole attention is on getting. My acquisitions are worth more than my revenues. Even if I were to be beaten or killed, I still want to penetrate everywhere. I would never try to stop confessing emperors, kings, dukes, barons, or counts. But with poor men it is shameful; I don't like such confession. If not for some other purpose, I have no interest in poor people; their estate is neither fair nor noble.

"These empresses, duchesses, queens, and countesses; their high-ranking palace ladies; these abbesses, beguines, and wives of bailiffs and knights; these coy, proud bourgeois wives, these nuns and young girls; provided that they are rich or beautiful, whether they are bare or well turned out, they do not go away without good advice.

"For the salvation of souls, I inquire of lords and ladies and their entire households about their characteristics and their way of life; and I put into their heads the belief that their parish priests are animals in comparison with me and my companions. I have many wicked dogs among them, to whom I am accustomed to reveal people's secrets, without hiding anything; and in the same way they reveal everything to me, so that they hide nothing in the world from me.

"In order that you may recognize the criminals who do not stop deceiving people, I will now tell you here the words that we read of Saint Matthew, that is to say, the evangelist, in the twenty-third chapter: 'Upon the chair of Moses' (the gloss explains that this is the Old Testament), 'the scribes and pharisees have sat.' These are the accursed false people that the letter calls hypocrites. 'Do what they say, but not what they do. They are not slow to speak well, but they have no desire to do so. To gullible people they attach heavy loads that cannot be carried; they place them on their shoulders, but they dare not move them with their finger.' "

"Why not?" asked Love.

"In faith," replied False Seeming, "they don't want to, for porters' shoulders are often accustomed to suffer from their burdens, and these hypocrites flee from wanting to do such a thing. If they do jobs that may be good, it is because people see them. They enlarge their phylacteries and increase their fringes; since they are haughty, proud, and overbearing, they like the highest and most honorable seats at tables and the first in the synagogues. They like people to greet them when they pass along the street, and they want to be called 'master,' when they shouldn't be called, for the gospel goes against this practice and shows its unlawfulness.

"We have another custom toward those that we know are against us. We want to hate them very strongly and attack them all by agreement among ourselves. He whom one hates, the others hate, and all are bent on ruining him. If we see that he may, through certain people, win honor in the land, income, or possessions, we study to find out by what ladder he may mount up, and the better to capture and subdue him, we treacherously defame him to those people, for we do not love him. We cut the rungs from his ladder, and we strip him of his friends in such a way that he will never know by a word that he has lost them. If we troubled him openly, we would perhaps be blamed for it and thus miss out in our calculation; if he knew our worst intention, he would protect himself against it so that we would be reprimanded for it.

"If one of us has done something very good, we consider that we have all done it. Indeed, by God, if he was pretending it, or if he no more than condescends to brag that he has advanced certain men, we make ourselves partners in the deed and, as you should well know, we say that these people have been helped on by us. In order to win people's praise we tell lies to rich men and get them to give us letters bearing witness to our goodness, so that throughout the world people will think that every virtue abounds in us. We always pretend to be poor, but no matter how we complain, we are the ones, let me tell you, who have everything without having anything.

"I also undertake brokerage commissions, I draw up agreements, I arrange marriages, I take on executor's duties, and I go around doing procurations. I am a messenger and I make investigations, dishonest ones, moreover. To occupy myself with someone else's business is to me a very pleasant occupation. And if you have any business to do with those whom I frequent, tell me, and the thing is done as soon as you have told me. Provided that you have served me well, you have deserved my service. But anyone who wanted to punish me would rob himself of my favor. I neither love nor value the man by whom I am reproved for anything. I want to reprove all the others, but I don't want to hear their reproof, for I, who correct others, have no need of another's correction.

* * *

"But to you I dare not lie. However, if I could feel that you would not recognize it, you would have a lie in hand. Certainly I would have tricked you, and I would never have held back on account of any sin. And I would indeed desert you if you were to treat me poorly."

The god smiled at this wonder, and everyone laughed with amazement and said, "Here is a fine sergeant, of whom people should indeed be proud!"

"False Seeming," said Love, "tell me: since I have brought you so near to me that your power in my court is so great that you will be king of camp followers here, will you keep your agreement with me?"

"Yes, I swear it and promise you; neither your father nor your forefathers ever had sergeants more loyal."

"How! It is against your nature."

"Take your chances on it, for if you demand pledges, you will never be more sure, in fact, not even if I gave hostages, letters, witnesses, or security. I call on you as witness of the fact that one can't take the wolf out of his hide until he is skinned, no matter how much he is beaten or curried. Do you think that I do not deceive and play tricks because I wear a simple robe, under which I have worked many a great evil? By God! I shall never turn my heart from this kind of life. And if I have a simple, demure face, do you think that I may cease doing evil? My sweetheart Constrained Abstinence has need of my providence. She would long ago have been dead and in a bad plight if she hadn't had me in her power. Grant that we two, she and I, may carry out the task."

"So be it," said Love, "I believe you without guarantee."

And the thief with the face of treachery, white without and black within, knelt down on the spot and thanked him.

*   *   *

The Hermit, Death, and the Robbers †

Here is the story of a hermit who, walking through a forest, found a very great treasure.

One day a hermit, walking through a forest, found a cave that was very large and well hidden, and went toward it to rest for he was very tired. Just as he reached the cave, he saw at a certain place within it a great brightness, because there was much gold there. As soon as he recognized what it was, he swiftly took his leave, and began running through the desert as fast as he could go. While running thus, this hermit happened upon three bold thieves who haunted that forest to rob anyone who passed through it, and who had not yet realized that this gold was there. As they stood in hiding, they saw this man running away with no one in pursuit, and were a little frightened. But they came out of hiding nevertheless, in order to learn why he was fleeing, for they marveled greatly at it. And he answered, "My brothers, I

---

† Translated for this volume by V. A. Kolve. The tale survives in a Renaissance collection of stories— Borghini's 1572 *Libro di novelle e di bel parlar gentile*—but materials in that collection have been traced back to the thirteenth century. For the Italian text, and reference to the antecedents, see *Sources and Analogues*, pp. 416–19.

flee death, who comes after me, pursuing me." Seeing neither man nor beast chasing him, they said, "Show us who is pursuing you, and lead us to the place where he is." Then the hermit said to them, "Come with me, and I will show him to you," while begging them every step of the way not to go seeking death, whom he himself was fleeing. But they, wishing to find death, and to see how he was made, would not settle for anything else. The hermit, seeing he could not do otherwise, and being frightened of them, led them to the cave from which he had fled, and said to them, "Here is death, which pursued me," and showed them the gold that was there.

They immediately knew what it was, and began to rejoice greatly and to make merry together. They dismissed the good man, who went away about his own affairs, and remarked to each other on what a great simpleton he was. The three robbers stayed together, guarding the treasure and discussing what they wished to do with it. One said, "It seems to me, since God has given us this great good fortune, that we should not leave here until we carry away all this treasure." Another said, "Let us do otherwise. Let one of us take a part of it and go to town and sell it, and get some bread and some wine and whatever else is necessary; and let him be as clever about this as he can, until he has obtained what we need." All three agreed to this together.

Now the Devil, who is crafty and inclined always to do as much evil as he can, put this thought into the heart of him who was going into town for provisions: "As soon as I am in town," he said to himself, "I want to eat and drink my fill, provide myself with certain things that have become necessary to me, and then poison the food which I carry back to my fellows. Once they are both dead, I shall be Lord of all that treasure. It seems so great, I think I shall be the richest man in this whole region." He did all those things, just as they had come into his mind. He took as much food for himself as he needed, poisoned all the rest, and brought it thus to his friends.

But while he went to town in the fashion I have told you, thinking evil and plotting to kill his friends so that everything would remain to himself, they were thinking no better of him. They said to each other, "As soon as this friend of ours returns with the bread and the wine and the other things we need, we will murder him, and then eat as much as we want, and afterward we'll have this great treasure just between the two of us. Since there will be fewer of us, each one will have a larger part of the treasure." When the one who had gone to town to buy the things they needed came back, his friends attacked him, as soon as they saw him, with lances and knives, and murdered him. When he was dead, they ate what he had brought, and as soon as they were full, both fell dead. And thus they died all three, for each killed the other, as you have heard, and did not possess the treasure.

Thus does our Lord God repay traitors: they went seeking death, and found it in such manner as they deserved. The wise man fled from it wisely. The gold remained free as before.

THOMAS OF CANTIMPRÉ

From *Liber de Apibus*†

Exemplum 103

In the city of Louvain, within the boundaries of Brabant we saw a noble and worthy citizen who, rising to go to matins on the holy night of Good Friday, passed in front of a tavern in which dissolute young men were sitting, playing at dice and vying with one another in blasphemies and oaths. Continuing on his way, this citizen found men in the street near the tavern who were making loud lamentation over a certain stranger who was badly wounded and bleeding. When he asked the men who had inflicted these wounds they answered: "Those young men who are playing dice." Entering the tavern, the citizen upbraided the young men for playing on that night and asked them sternly why they had so cruelly beaten the stranger who had been with them. Much astonished, the young men denied that anyone had come in since they had sat down, and protested that they had wounded no one either by word or blow. Going forth quickly with the citizen, they sought for the bleeding stranger but could not find him. Having now recovered their senses, each of them realized that by their terrible oaths they had again insulted the Lord Christ and by their taunts had crucified him afresh.

---

†Trans. Carleton Brown, *The Pardoner's Tale*, by Geoffrey Chaucer (Oxford: Oxford UP, 1935) xvii–xviii. Reprinted by permission of Oxford University Press. Thomas Cantimpré (or Chantimpré) was born in Brabant ca. 1200 and died ca. 1270; the story here translated was written sometime before 1263. As an exemplum, it is less a tale in its own right than a narrative abstract, which a preacher could use to illustrate and make vivid his theme, and which he would characteristically expand in the telling, through further dialogue and detail, to the level of his ability and the needs of his sermon audience.

The Prioress's Prologue and Tale

Stories of the miracles performed by the Virgin Mary constitute one of the most familiar genres in medieval literature, and there are many analogues, in a variety of languages, to the *Prioress's Tale*. The richest, and in many ways the closest to Chaucer, is a fifteenth-century Latin version, here translated into English for the first time by A. G. Rigg. We also include a verse analogue from the Vernon manuscript, an important fourteenth-century collection of English religious and didactic literature. The song sung by Chaucer's "litel clergeoun," the *Alma Redemptoris Mater*, is printed both in Latin and in Cardinal Newman's English translation.

anti-Semitic

The Story of the *Alma Redemptoris Mater*†

The Mother of Grace never forgets those who remember her, and so the memory of her should be continually brought to mind; praise should be lavished upon her, and we should preach her mighty works as often as possible. Although the treasure-chest of all goodness has no need of our good offices, nevertheless it is beneficial and salutary for us to heap praises on her goodness. I have, therefore, decided to take care to entrust the following chapter to writing, so that the story may come to the notice of future generations, and so that those who hear it may be inspired all the more deeply and firmly to remember the Virgin.

There was once a certain boy born and bred in the city of Toledo; by the diligence of his mother he was sent to be instructed at school; he learned to dot his "i"s and to make the forms of letters; he learned the alphabet, and how to marry letter to letters and figure to figures properly. When he had learned how to join letters, he gladly passed on to music, in order that the understanding of the voice might be open to him as well as knowledge acquired by words.

†Translated and annotated for this volume by A. G. Rigg. The original Latin is printed in *Sources and Analogues*, pp. 480–85, from the unique MS Trinity College, Cambridge 0.9.38. The MS was compiled ca. 1450, mainly from material written much earlier; on the other hand, several stylistic features of this story resemble those of another Latin narrative in the MS, and both of them may have been "retouched" by the scribe with his own rhetorical embellishments (such as frequent biblical quotation, for purely literary effect, not always aptly). There is, however, no a priori reason for saying that Chaucer could not have known the story in a version very close to this. The punctuation in SA is frequently deficient, and the following corrections should be made: 480 / 28 for *precanere* read *precauere*; 481 / n. 3 MS reads *diffitetur*; 481 / 22 delete *animis*; 482 / 41 *cunque* read *scilicet*; 483 / 22 *quanto* read *quanta*; 483 / 32 *suo* read *sue*; 484 / 20 *monumentum* read *monimentum*. Several unnecessary emendations of typical MS spellings are made in SA. The following emendations are necessary: 480 / 11 for *figura* read *figuram*; 481 / 6–7 *doctam* read *docta*; 483 / 22 *que* read *qui*; 484 / 9 *excitato* read *excitatus*.

Every day he dutifully made his reading, according to what the authority of his teacher required of him. Each day, when he had fulfilled his educational duty, the hour of mealtime followed, and this little boy then used to go to the house of a canon of Mother Church; by the help of this canon the boy relieved his hunger and cheated the demands of that most importunate of debt-collectors, his stomach. He went there in hope of satisfying his hunger with the rich man's crumbs; every day he was given a measure of the crumbs which fell from the table of his masters and of the fragments left over by those who had eaten. He carefully collected everything that was given him, not in a shepherd's bag but in a little pocket at his breast; for his own use he kept the smallest and most worthless scraps, setting aside the bigger and better portions for his mother. O Lord, you who look into and know our hearts—you know what lies within man!

One day the boy was assigned as his daily schoolwork that sweet and delightful antiphon in praise of the Virgin Mother, whose opening line is "Alma Redemptoris Mater."[1] The boy was anxious not to suffer the terrifying taunts of his schoolmaster, and so he carefully learned the antiphon by heart, and meditated on it, both because it was difficult to learn and because it is a delightful song to sing. In my opinion, however, he learned and sang the antiphon so often not so much because of the sweetness of the song as because of the memory and love of the Virgin Mother. For more worthy than the string of the harp is the heart of the player who prays out of love.[2] The judge who judges the hearts of men is more affected by the love from the heart than by the loudness of the harp, more by the prayer than by the voice which makes the prayer: when one learns to pray in faith one also learns to speak with beauty. Why is this? Because the voice never sounds pleasant unless the spirit leads the voice and prayer in the singing.

One day, when the hour of breakfast had arrived, the boy, who had earned rest by his hard work, was released from school; he practiced with effect what he had learned from usage, like the calf of Ephraim who was taught to love treading.[3] He proceeded in the direction of the house of the canon by whose mercy he used to relieve his own misfortune. By chance he happened to go into the courtyards of Jewry where that stiffnecked race lives, that detestable family—the race which objects to the fruitfulness of the Virgin Mary and denies that the Son of God was made incarnate in her womb. A great number of the sons of the synagogue had gathered together in a house there, strengthening by their number that brotherhood of iniquity, that oppressive branch of sin. The boy arrived close by the house, singing the antiphon we have mentioned above, the *Alma Redemptoris Mater*. His intention was to pass through the area, but he did not get through unharmed. Among the Jews was a certain young Hebrew boy who had been taught a little Latin and understood the Latin idiom. They heard the song,

1. The hymn was probably composed in the eleventh century; for text and translation, see p. 427.
2. *Sources and Analogues* notes the presence of a rhyme on which this conceit is based in another MS, but in fact a later hand has added it in this text also; the rhyme puns on *amor, clamor, vox, votum,* etc.
3. Hosea 10.11 (all quotations are from the Vulgate): the line is not clarified by the biblical passage.

and wondered what it was; Satan came among them, and one of them asked the Hebrew who knew Latin what the Christian boy was singing. The Hebrew replied that the boy was singing an antiphon composed in praise of the Virgin Mary; its delightful sweetness was intended to inspire the minds of the listeners to the memory of Mary. At the mention of the name of the Virgin, the Jew cried out; Satan put it into his heart to betray and kill the innocent boy.

He therefore treacherously asked his colleague to bring the boy in: if he couldn't do what was required simply by asking, he was to offer the boy a bribe. So the innocent boy was summoned and brought in, introduced— or, rather, traduced. They took firm hold of him; "their rejoicing was as that of him who eats the poor in secret."[4] Without delay they made themselves ready for the murder, and prepared to condemn the innocent boy to death. The lamb was seized by the wolves; one of them set a knife to his throat, and his tongue was cruelly cut out; his stomach was opened and his heart and liver taken out. They imagined that they were offering a double sacrifice, firstly by cutting the throat from which emerged the voice of praise, and secondly by tearing out the heart which incessantly meditated on the memory of the Virgin. They thought they were obeying God, but in fact they were making a sacrifice not to God but to the devils of hell. It is usual for malice to cease after death, but although they had killed the boy, their malice did not come to an end: they threw his corpse into a place of the coarsest filth, where nature purges itself in secret.

Immediately the blessed mother of the Redeemer arrived by his side; her gracious mercy was present; she appeared to place a pebble (which looked very like a stone) on and within the mouth of the dead boy. When the pebble had been put in place, the boy's heart and throat opened up; his voice and power of speech returned, and he began to sing the *Alma Redemptoris Mater*.

In the meantime the boy's mother was anxious at his delay: he was her only son. She was alarmed at his unusually long delay, and suddenly began to be afraid and frightened at his daylong absence. For a mother does not easily forget the child of her womb and the joy that a man is born into the world. Thus, scarcely in control of herself, she set aside her domestic task, and went out into the courtyards and walked through the streets of the town; everywhere she looked at the passersby, and carefully scrutinized everyone she met. But nowhere did she see the face of her son. She walked on and on, into the Jewish quarter, scarcely able to support herself for her grief: her soul slept for weariness when she pictured as dead the child whom she had loved in life. She was now close to the house where the progeny of vipers had committed the crime. Suddenly she heard her son singing the *Alma Redemptoris Mater*: that is, she heard his voice, but she saw no one. She stopped in amazement, but just as a sheep recognizes its lamb by its bleat alone, so this mother recognized her own son by the uniqueness of his singing voice: she was in labour close to death when she bore him, and

4. Habakkuk 3.14.

so now she was in labour again, shouting and not sparing her voice. She could not put a guard on her mouth; however hoarse her throat became through her shouting, she incessantly cried out at the doors of her bloody enemies, "Give me back my son! Give me back my son!" As she repeated the words again and again, her grief was opened up. Time and again, as she stood outside the house she begged the Jews for her son, but the cruel and treacherous Jews would not give her any satisfaction; on stumbling feet she went to the house of the canon, and told him the whole sequence of events. In great grief and sorrow for the boy, the canon came to the house and demanded back the body from the murderers, but the perfidious Jews still refused to satisfy his demand in any way. Nevertheless he also heard and recognized the voice of the innocent child sweetly singing the *Alma Redemptoris Mater.*

Together they ran to the Archbishop of the city of Toledo and told him the sequence of events. He gathered a huge company of men and quickly went to investigate. He entered the guilty and treacherous house, breaking down the doors in his way, and roughly ordered the killer to produce the remains of the murdered innocent as quickly as possible—for he was sure that the boy was dead, in view of the great secrecy with which the malicious Jews had hidden him. All of them had conspired in the murder, but the main culprit in the murder, fearing the majesty of the Archbishop, confessed the truth of all his wickedness—how, out of envy at the mother of the Redeemer, he had extinguished the life of an innocent child, just because he had sung such a sweet song in honour of the Virgin Mother. After his confession of the crime—or rather his conviction—he put himself under the judgment of the Archbishop, and asked him for his mercy rather than his condemnation. He led the Archbishop by the hand, for all was darkness and gloom where the boy lay dead in the depths. The singing voice was their leader and guide, and at last they arrived where the dead boy miraculously continued to sing the *Alma Redemptoris Mater* without ceasing—for when the dead boy's voice had finished the end of the antiphon, it would begin the same song over again throughout the whole day.

The boy was lifted out, like a second Joseph out of the pit;[5] with speed and rejoicing he was taken to the church. The song to the Virgin did not leave his lips; continually he sang the *Alma Redemptoris Mater.* The people were summoned, and the clergy sat down in complete devotion. The Archbishop began to celebrate the divine office in honour of the blessed Virgin. The moment came when the congregation was ordered to be silent; the preacher began to speak, bringing a message of salvation through the gospel. At this moment the boy also became quiet, and placed "a door of circumstance"[6] on his lips, so that the words of the gospel would not be misheard or misunderstood because of the sound of his voice.

The congregation listened with faith and devotion to the reading, and when the message of salvation was over, once again the boy miraculously began to sing the antiphon. How great then was the pious devotion of the clergy's prayers! How great was the effusion of tears among the congregation in its place, when the dead boy began again what he had just stopped, going through in his song what he had just passed over in silence! The health-giving Host was offered devoutly on the altar and the memory of the Lord's Passion worshipped, and all this time the boy's voice continued to sing of the purity of Mary. When the mysteries of our Redemption had been per-formed, the Archbishop turned to the congregation and delivered a sermon in praise of the innocence of the Virgin—though while he reverently called to memory the mother, of course he did not neglect to honour Christ as well. At the end of the sermon he wept and encouraged the clergy and people altogether to beseech the Virgin's son with the aroma of devotion and the sweet scent of pious prayer, and to pray by the merits of his mother and the prayers of the precious Virgin that Christ should deign to restore the boy to life, and breathe the breath of life into the dead corpse.

The clergy and the people poured out their souls within themselves, giv-ing out their hearts like water in the sight of the Lord, letting their tears flow in a willing shower in the evening, a shower of tears, for their tears "were on their cheeks."[7] They prayed in supplication; in faith they beseeched; they were not beset by a cloud of mistrust about the efficacy of their prayer, for it went straight up to the Trinity: their faith swiftly penetrated to heaven, and their blessed trust was faithfully and joyfully repaid. In reply to their public and private prayers, the Virgin Mother (as I imagine) looked into the face of Christ and beseeched him in what I picture as a familiar fashion; and immediately the boy's cut throat was allowed to breathe again, his previously torn flesh was restored fully, and his tongue, which sang divine praise, was given back to him; his heart and liver which had been removed were put back again, or were created anew by divine aid. His soul was summoned back again into its vessel and vehicle, and the boy became whole again; the immortal spirit was again married to the dead flesh. He who was dead came to life again and returned; the boy awoke, aroused, as it were, from a deep sleep. Even now he did not cease his praise of Mary, and his sweet voice continued to sing the *Alma Redemptoris Mater*. Truly blessed are you, Mother of the Redeemer, for coming to the help of the dead boy who lacked the power to rise again: she who, to the amazement of Nature,[8] gave birth to her own creator, again astonished Nature by pouring back the vital spirit into the dead child through the intercession of her prayer.

At the sight of this amazing miracle, the congregation of the faithful rejoiced, and at the sight they dissolved into tears: they still wondered if it was an illusion. When they looked at the revived boy's face, they discovered the pebble which Mary had placed in his mouth; they removed it, and immediately he stopped his singing of the antiphon. He lost the impelling power of speech which before had not allowed him to be silent. The pebble was placed as a sign in the cathedral church, to act as a monument of the event and as evidence of the miracle, to be kept there for ever.

---

7. Lamentations 1.2; cf. Joel 2.23.
8. The phrase *Natura mirante*, "to Nature's amaze-   ment," is taken from the antiphon *Alma Redempto-ris Mater*.

The Archbishop now asked the boy to tell him the whole sequence and order of the affair, and he answered the pontiff to his satisfaction, giving him a full and true account of the whole series of events—the crime of the Jews, his own martyrdom and the assistance of the Virgin Mary. He attributed everything to the Mother of God: whatever had happened to him was done by the Mother of Grace, who had thus aided his wretchedness from the abundance of her mercy. As he told his story, he pointed with his finger at the murderer, but this boy, who had been raised from death, prayed humbly but insistently that his murderer should not be condemned to die for the crime. At last the boy rose, and gave thanks fully to his saviour, the Virgin, and, now made whole in every particular, lived long after in the city of Toledo.

The Jew was more sure of his punishment than hopeful for mercy, but after seeing the miracle he confessed himself guilty and worthy of execution; nevertheless, he asked first to be bathed by the saving water of baptism. The Archbishop was more eager for the saving of a soul than for the punishment of the crime; he baptized the Jew and entrusted him to the church; having marked him with the sign of our faith, he remitted the penalty and pardoned the crime. Afterward the Jew, who had before been the most impious persecutor of the name of the Virgin, became her most pious devotee. There was also an infidel who witnessed the miracle and who became a member of the Christian faith. Thus, in the faith of Christ, the two walls of the cornerstone, from both circumcised and uncircumcised,[9] were joined together. The second man, now a believer instead of an infidel, was prosperous and very rich: he built a church in honour of the Virgin Mother, where her memory is memorably celebrated. Thus the kindly Mother of the Redeemer helps everyone with success; by her deserts may she commend to God those of us who are mindful of her, and help them by her good actions. AMEN.

A Miracle of Our Lady†

"Hou the Jewes, in despit° of Ure Lady, threwe   scorn
a chyld in a gonge"°   privy

Wose° loveth wel Ure Ladi,   *Whoever*
Heo° wol quiten his wille wel whi,[1]   *She*

---

9. The image of the two walls meeting at the cornerstone comes from Ephesians 2.11–22 and Psalms 117.22, the antiphon for the Magnificat on December 22. The passage was interpreted in this way, as the union of circumcised and uncircumcised, by Gregory: see *The Christ of Cynewulf*, ed. A. S. Cook (1900; Hamden: Archon Books, 1964) 75.

†Text based on *The Minor Poems of the Vernon MS*, ed. Carl Horstmann and F. J. Furnivall, EETS o.s. 98, 117 (London, 1892, 1901) I. 141–45. The MS

was made in the late fourteenth century, sometime after 1382, and is a vast miscellany of religious or didactic pieces, written in Middle English and Anglo-Norman. It once included a comprehensive collection of Miracles of the Virgin—the index lists forty-two—but most of that part of the MS was destroyed long ago. Only eight Miracles, of which this is the second, survive in full; a ninth is fragmentary.

1. She will for that (reason) repay well his determination.

Othur° in his lyf or at his ende,   *Either*
The ladi is so freo° and hende.°   *generous / gracious*
5 Hit fel sumtyme° in Parys,°   *It happened once / Paris*
As witnesseth in Holy Writ storys,
In the cite bifel this cas:°   *case, adventure*
A pore child was° of porchas,°   *there was / income*
That with the beggeri that he con wynne[2]
10 He fond° sumdel what of° his kinne—   *supported / certain of*
His fader, his moder, and eke himself.
He begged in cite bi everi half.°   *in every section*
    The child non othur craftus° couthe°   *skills / knew*
But winne hys lyflode° with his mouthe.   *livelihood*
15 The childes vois was swete and cler;
Men lusted° his song with riht good cher.   *listened to*
With his song that was ful swete
He gat mete° from strete to strete.   *obtained food*
Men herked° his song ful likyngly:°   *listened to / pleasurably*
20 Hit was an antimne° of Ure Lady;   *anthem*
He song that antimne everiwher,
I-called Alma Redemptoris Mater,
That is forthrightly° to mene°   *plainly, simply / mean*
"Godus° moder, mylde and clene,°   *God's / chaste*
25 Hevene gate and sterre of se,°   *star of the sea*
Save thi peple from synne and we."°   *woe*
That song was holden deynteous;°   *considered precious*
The child song hit from hous to hous.
For° he song hit so lykynglye,°   *Because / pleasingly*
30 The Jewes hedde° alle to hym envye.   *had*
Til hit fel on a Setersday°   *Saturday*
The childes wey thorw the Jewerie° lay;   *the Jewish quarter*
The Jewes hedden that song in hayn,°   *hate*
Therfore thei schope° the child be slayn.   *made plans that*
35 So lykingly the child song ther,
So lustily song he never er.°   *before*
    On° of the Jewes malicious   *One*
Tilled° the child in to his hous.   *Enticed*
His malice there he gan to kuythe:°   *show*
40 He cutte the childes throte alswithe.°   *quickly*
The child ne spared nout° for that wrong   *did not cease*
But never-the-latere° song forth his song.   *nevertheless*
Whon he hedde endet, he eft° bigon;   *again*
His syngyng couthe stoppe no mon.°   *no man knew how to stop*
45 Therof the Jeuh was sore anuyet,°   *annoyed, troubled*
Leste his malice mihte ben aspyet.°   *spied out, discovered*

---

2. Who with the money that he earned by begging.

The Jeuh bithouhte him of a gynne:°   *stratagem*
Into a gonge-put° fer withinne   *privy-pit*
The child adoun therinne he throng;°   *thrust*
50 The child song evere the same song.
So lustily the child con crie,
That song he never er so hyghe.°   *loudly*
Men mihte him here fer and neer,
The childes vois was so heigh and cleer.
55   The childes moder was wont to abyde°   *wait (for him)*
Every day til the non-tyde;°   *noontime*
Then was he wont to bring heom° mete   *them*
Such as he mihte with his song gete.
Bote that day was the tyme apast;
60 Therfore his moder was sore agast.°   *afraid*
With syk° and serwe° in everi strete   *sighing / sorrow*
Heo souhte wher° heo mihte with him mete.   *She sought (the place) where*
Bote whon heo com in to the Jewery,
Heo herde his vois so cler of cry.
65 Aftur that vois his modur dreuh;°   *drew, followed*
Wher he was inne, therbi heo kneuh.°   *knew*
  Then of hire child heo asked a siht.°   *sight*
The Jew withnayted° him anon-riht°   *denied / promptly*
And seide ther nas non such child thrinne.°   *therein*
70 The childes moder yit nolde not blinne,°   *cease*
But ever the moder criede in on.°   *continually*
The Jeuh seide evere ther nas such non.
Then seide the wommon, "Thou seist wrong.
He is herinne, I knowe his song."
75 The Jeuh bigon to stare° and swere   *glare*
And seide ther com non such child there.
But never-the-latere men mihte here
The child song evere so loude and clere,
And ever the lengor, herre° and herre,   *higher, louder*
80 Men mihte him here bothe fer and nerre.
  The modur coude° non othur won:°   *knew / hope*
To meir° and baylyfs° heo is gon.   *mayor / bailiffs*
Heo pleyneth° the Jeuh hath don hire wrong   *complains*
To stelen hire sone so for his song.
85 Heo preyeth to don hire lawe and riht,°   *justice*
Hire sone don° come bifore heore siht.   *To cause her son to*
Heo preyeth the meir par charite°   *in the name of charity*
Of him to have freo lyvere.°   *to take legal custody*
Thenne heo telleth the meir among°   *at this time*
90 Hou heo lyveth bi hire sone song.
The meir then hath of hire pite,
And sumneth° the folk of that cite.   *summons*

He telleth hem of that wommons sawe°   *story*
And seith he mot don° hire the lawe,   *enforce (for)*
95 And hoteth° hem with hym to wende,°   *orders / go*
To bringe this wommons cause to ende.
    Whon thei cum thider, for al heore noyse
Anon thei herde the childes voyse.
Riht as an angeles vois hit were,
100 Thei herde him never synge so clere.
Ther the meir maketh entre,
And of the child he asketh lyvere.°   *delivery (into his possession)*
The Jeuh may nought the meir refuse,
Ne of the child hym wel excuse;
105 But nede he moste knouleche° his wrong,   *acknowledge*
Ateynt° bi the childes song.   *Convicted*
    The meir let serchen hym° so longe   *had him searched for*
Til he was founden in the gonge,
Ful depe i-drouned in fulthe° of fen.°   *filth / muck, dung*
110 The meir het drawe the child° up then,   *ordered the child raised*
With fen and fulthe riht foule biwhorven,°   *bespattered*
And eke the childes throte i-corven.°   *carved, cut*
Anon-riht, er thei passede forthere,
The Jeuh was jugget° for that morthere.°   *judged / murder*
115 And er the peple passede in sonder,°   *apart*
The bisschop was comen to seo that wonder.
    In presence of bisschop and alle ifere,°   *together*
The child song evere iliche° clere.   *continually*
The bisschop serchede with his hond;
120 Withinne the childes throte he fond
A lilie flour, so briht and cler,
So feir a lylie nas nevere seyen er,
With guldene° lettres everiwher: *golden*
"Alma Redemptoris Mater."
125 Anon° that lilie out was taken,   *As soon as*
The childes song bigon to slaken.
That swete song was herd no more,
But as a ded cors° the child lay thore.°   *corpse / there*
    The bisschop with gret solempnete°   *ceremony*
130 Bad bere the cors° thorw al the cite;   *Ordered the body carried*
And hymself with processioun
Com with the cors thorw al the toun,
With prestes and clerkes that couthen° syngen.   *knew how to*
And alle the belles he het hem ryngen,
135 With torches brennynge and clothus riche;
With worschipe thei ladden that holi liche.°   *body*
In to the munstre° whon thei kem,°   *minster, church / came*
Bigonne the masse of requiem,°   *Requiem Mass*

As for the dede men is wont.°   *customary*
140 But thus sone thei weren i-stunt:°   *astounded*
The cors aros in heore° presens,   *their*
Bigon then "Salve sancta parens."°   *"Hail, holy parent" (antiphon)*
Men mihte wel witen° the sothe° therbi: *know / truth*
The child hedde i-servet Ur Swete Ladi,
145 That worschipede° him so on erthe her°   *honored / here*
And brouhte his soule to blisse al cler.
    Therfore I rede° that everi mon   *advise*
Serve that ladi wel as he con,
And love hire in his beste wyse.°   *way*
150 Heo wol wel quite° him his servise.   *repay*
Now, Marie, for thi muchele° miht,   *great*
Help us to hevene that is so briht!

Alma Redemptoris Mater†

Alma Redemptoris Mater quae pervia coeli
Porta manes, et stella maris, succurre cadenti,
Surgere qui curat, populo; tu quae genuisti,
Natura mirante, tuum sanctum Genitorem,
Virgo prius ac posterius, Gabrielis ab ore,
Sumens illud Ave, peccatorum miserere.

Kindly Mother of the Redeemer, who art ever of heaven
The open gate, and the star of the sea, aid a fallen people,
Which is trying to rise again; thou who didst give birth,
While Nature marveled how, to thy Holy Creator,
Virgin both before and after, from Gabriel's mouth
Accepting the All hail, be merciful toward sinners.

           (trans. John Henry Newman)

---

† This is one of four antiphons of the Blessed Virgin Mary used to conclude Compline, the final hour of the canonical day. Each is assigned to a different portion of the church year, the present antiphon being sung from Saturday before the first Sunday of Advent through February 1. Cardinal Newman's translation is printed from *Tracts for the Times* 75 (3.23 in the bound editions of 1840–42, rpt. New York: AMS Press, 1969).

The Nun's Priest's
Prologue and Tale

On one level the *Nun's Priest's Tale* is a beast fable; the genre and its goals may be illustrated by brief selections from William Caxton's translation of Aesopic stories. For the expansion of fable into beast-epic, Chaucer knew of the tales of Reynard the Fox, which circulated widely in France and elsewhere. Robert A. Pratt has argued that the confrontation of Reynard and Chanteclere in branch 2 of the *Roman de Renart* is one of Chaucer's direct sources. The learned and mock-heroic inflations of the *Nun's Priest's Tale* derive from many places; we include Macrobius's authoritative chapter on dreams and Geoffrey of Vinsauf's rhetorical lament on the death of King Richard I. The courtly elements of Chaucer's story could even have been suggested by the encyclopedic tradition, as may be seen in a portion of Bartholomaeus Anglicus's description of the cock, here printed in John of Trevisa's fourteenth-century English translation.

WILLIAM CAXTON

From Aesop's Fables†

[Book I]

Here begyneth the preface or prologue of the fyrst book of Esope.

I, Romulus, son of Thybere[1] of the cyte of Atyque,° gretyng.   *Attica*
Esope, man of Grece, subtyll and ingenyous, techeth in his fables
how men ought to kepe and rewle them° well. And to th'ende   *themselves*
that he shold shewe the lyf and customes of al maner of men,
he induceth° the byrdes, the trees and the beestes spekynge, to   *introduces*
th'ende that the men may knowe wherfore the fables were found.°   *invented*
In the whiche he hath wreton the malyce of the evylle people
and the argument of the improbes.° He techeth also to be hum-   *wicked*
ble and for to use wordes, and many other fayr ensamples reherced
and declared here after, the whiche I, Romulus, have translated
oute of Grekes tongue in to Latyn tongue, the which yf thou

---

†Text based on Caxton's 1484 edition as printed in *The Fables of Aesop*, ed. Joseph Jacobs, 2 vols. (London: David Nutt, 1889) 2.3, 21.
1. Tiberius. The "Romulus" version of Aesop's fables

circulated widely in the Middle Ages; the author is unknown, but it was certainly not the Roman emperor's son.

rede them, they shalle aguyse° and sharp thy wytte and shal gyve   *adorn*
to the cause of ioye.

* * *

The xv fable is of the raven and of the foxe.

They that be glad and ioyefull of the praysynge of flaterers
oftyme repente them therof, wherof Esope reherceth to us suche
a fable. A raven whiche was upon a tree, and held with his bylle
a chese, the whiche chese the fox desyred moche to have; wherfore the foxe wente and preysed hym by suche wordes as folowen:
"O gentyll raven, thow art the fayrest byrd of alle other byrdes.
For thy fethers ben so fayr, so bright, and so resplendysshynge,°   *resplendent*
and can also so wel synge, yf thow haddest the voys clere and
small thow sholdest be the moost happy of al other byrdes." And
the foole whiche herd the flateryringe wordes of the foxe beganne
to open his bylle for to synge. And then the chese fylle to the
grounde, and the fox toke and ete hit. And whan the raven
sawe that for his vayn glorye he was deceyved, wexed° hevy   *he became*
and sorowfull and repented hym of that° he had byleved the   *the fact that*
foxe. And this fable techeth us, how men ought not to be glad,
ne take reioysshynge in the wordes of caytyf° folke, ne also to   *cunning*
leve° flatery ne vayn glory.   *believe*

* * *

From *Le Roman de Renart*, Branch 2†

How Chanteclere Makes a Fool of Reynard

It happened on a day that Reynard the Fox, well-versed in evil arts and
guile, came trotting up to a farm set in the woods. The farm possessed many
chickens, ducks, and geese. The lord of that land was Constantine of Noyes,
a farmer of great wealth. His house was full to the bursting with fowl and
bacon and salted meat. He also had plenty of grain set by, and the orchards
bore their many and various fruits in season. It was here that Reynard came
for his own amusement.

The courtyard was enclosed by a palisade of sharp oak stakes and spiny
hawthorn, and there Sir Constantine had placed his hens, as in a kind of
fortress. Reynard addressed himself to the palisade, but though his resource-
fulness was great, the spines were sharper still. At last he squatted in the
road, angry and upset, yet not wanting to abandon the hens. If he tried to
leap the stockade wall, he would be seen, and the hens that pecked the dirt
not two feet beyond would disappear. The fox paced angrily up and down,

†Translated for this volume by Elizabeth Hanson-
Smith from *Le Roman de Renart*, ed. Ernest Martin
(Strasbourg: Trübner, 1882) 1. 91–104. The French
text is reprinted in *Sources and Analogues*, pp. 646–
58.

until he spied a broken stake. At once he plunged through the wall. Where the stockade was broken, the farmer had planted cabbages, and Reynard dropped down among them, hoping he had not been seen. But the chickens had heard the noise of his fall, and every one of them took flight.

Master Chanteclere the Cock, who had been scratching in a dusty path, came toward the band of chickens. Plumes spread and neck outstretched, he demanded haughtily why they had fled. Pinte of the Large Eggs, who roosted at the cock's right hand, was the wisest, and she told him what had happened: "We were all terrified," she said.

"But why?" the rooster demanded. "What have you seen?"

"Some kind of wild beast, who would have done great harm, if we hadn't fled the garden."

"I beg your pardon," Chanteclere replied, "but this is just a trifle. Don't worry yourself about it further."

"By my faith," said Pinte, "I loyally swear to you I saw him clearly."

"And how did you catch sight of whatever it was?"

"How? I saw the enclosure shake and the cabbage leaf tremble where he lies in wait."

"Pinte," exclaimed the cock, "you're a fool! I don't know of any fox or polecat strong enough to breach our walls. I promise you by the loyalty I owe you, there is nothing there. Go on back!" And the rooster returned to his dust.

He who fears nothing, except a dog or fox, will always be quite confident—as long as he thinks himself safe. And thus Chanteclere acted quite disdainfully, for he feared nothing but the fox.

As one bored with both singing and scratching, one eye open, the other shut, the cock at last flew up under the eaves and took his rest. Roosting there in delicious sleep, Chanteclere began to dream. (Now don't think I'm making this up—it's the whole truth, and you can find it written down.) He dreamed that something entered the courtyard, although it was securely locked, and came up to him, face to face. Chanteclere shuddered at this. The creature had a fur mantle of red and white, its collar trimmed in bone. Here Chanteclere tossed and turned in his sleep. Suddenly the cloak was wrapped about him, by force. And most strange, he was forced into it through the narrow collar, so that his head was at the creature's tail. Great was the pain that Chanteclere suffered for that dream, and he thought himself cursed in that vision. At last he struggled into wakefulness and heaved a sigh, saying "Holy Spirit, save my body from that prison, and keep me safe!" Off he rushed, no longer quite so secure, and came upon the hens, who pecked beside the hawthorn. He did not cry out to them at once, but called Pinte aside to take counsel with her first.

"Pinte," he said, for he trusted her, "I can't hide my sorrow and despair. And fear. I think some bird of prey or wild beast is going to harm us."

"Dear sweet lord," cried Pinte, "never say that aloud! For shame! You'll frighten us all. You betray yourself in saying you are afraid. By all the saints to whom we pray, you're like the dog who whines before the stone is cast. Why are you frightened? What's the matter with you?"

"You don't know," he answered, "what a strange dream I've had. It seemed to me there was an evil apparition within the enclosure of this very farm. That is why you see me pale and trembling. It seemed to me some animal came in, wearing a mantle of red fur, sown together without scissors or seam, trimmed in bone, all white and hard. He forced me to dress in his mantle, and I had to put it on over my head, collar first. When I awoke I was no longer wrapped up in fur, but I marvel still at the tightness of that collar, and at the tail that seemed to be in front of my face. That is why I despair. Pinte, I am tormented by this dream. By the loyalty you owe me, tell me, do you know what this signifies?"

Pinte, his trusted one, answered then, "You have told me your dream, but please God, it won't come true. If you wish an explanation of it, I know well what it is, for what you have seen while dreaming, that thing dressed in a red cloak—that is the fox. He's easily known by his red fur coat. The trim of bone, that was his teeth, by which he forced you inside him. The collar that did not fit, that was so horribly tight for you—that is the gullet of the beast, that's how you entered his belly. The tail means, no doubt— by all the saints in all the world!—that when the fox has swallowed you, his tail will be before your nose! Now you know the meaning of your dream, God help me. Gold and silver can't save you. And it will all come to pass before high noon. But if you still don't believe me, take a look over there, for he lies in wait, quietly, in the cabbage patch, ready to betray and deceive you."

When Chanteclere had heard this interpretation of his dream, he said, "Pinte, these are traitorous words! You say I'll be conquered by a beast who is even now inside our stockade. Cursed is the man who believes that! You've told me nothing I care to hear. No matter what, I won't believe I'll suffer for this dream."

"Sire," she answered, "God forbid it should be so, but I swear to you, if things don't turn out as I've predicted, I am no longer your true love."

"Oh, Pinte," said Chanteclere, "never mind!"

Chanteclere considered that interpretation a wild tale, and walked back to take his pleasure in his patch of dust, where he soon began to slumber again.

Meanwhile, Reynard had waited patiently and looked on, much amused. Once certain the cock had fallen asleep, Reynard crept up, one paw after another, soundlessly. If once the fox had Chanteclere in his teeth, he would make a meal of him. He longed for chicken dinner, but when he sprang, heavy-handed, he missed. While Chanteclere flew to the top of a dung-heap, well out of reach, Reynard cursed himself for failing. But at once the fox began again to plot a way to trick poor Chanteclere. If he did not eat that rooster, his time was wasted.

"Dear Chanteclere," he called, "don't fly away for this trifle. After all, you and I are first cousins, quite closely related."

Chanteclere gained confidence at this, and sang a little song for joy.

Reynard said to his cousin, "Do you remember Chanteclin, your dear father, who begot you? No other cock could sing the way he did. The country folk miles away could hear him. When he sang, he took a good deep breath and closed his eyes tight. Ah, but his voice was grand. He wasn't always peering about him, when he let go in the pleasures of song."

"Reynard, cousin," said Chanteclere, "are you trying to pull a trick?"

"Of course . . ." answered Reynard, "I am not. But now, please sing! Shut those eyes and go to it! You know we are of one flesh, one blood— and I would rather lose a leg than see you come to grief."

Said Chanteclere, "I don't believe you. Remove yourself a little way before I sing a song. There won't be a neighbor far or near who cannot hear my falsetto!"

Reynard smiled broadly: "Well, do it loudly, then! Sing, cousin! Let it be known you were born of my uncle Chanteclin."

The cock began quite loudly, letting out a terrific din, but with only one eye closed, and the other open, watching Reynard, whom he strongly suspected of mischief.

Reynard said, "This is nothing. Chanteclin sang far differently. He'd close his eyes tight and his great crowing could be heard for miles beyond the palisade."

Chanteclere at last believed him, and screwing his eyes up tight in the effort, he sent forth his melody. Reynard did not hesitate a moment, but seized the cock by the neck, and off he raced in high spirits, for he'd won his prey.

Pinte saw that Reynard had her love, and she fell into a frenzied despair when she saw the cock being carried off. She wailed after them, "Sire, I told you so! But you scorned my words and called me a fool. Now those words are proven true and it is your own reasoning that brought you to ruin. I was a fool to cry 'fox' before you had actually seen him. Now Reynard has you and bears you off. Alas! Misery! I shall die! For if I lose my lord and master, my honor too is lost forever!"

The good old woman of the manor opened the door to her yard, for it was evening, and she wished to put her hens back in the coop. "Come, Pinte, Bise, Rosette!" she called, but none of them answered. She wondered what was wrong, until she heard her cock yelling, as best he could, and saw the fox running off with him. She knew she couldn't catch them and raised a cry for help. All the peasants on the farm came running when they heard her bawling so. They asked her what was wrong.

"Alas," she sighed heavily, "what a wicked thing has happened!"

"But what is it?" they demanded.

"I have lost my rooster—the fox has him!"

"You foul old hag!" shouted Constantine. "Didn't you stop him?"

"Sire," she replied, "You do me wrong. By holy God, I couldn't catch him. He wouldn't wait for me."

"Why didn't you hit him?"

"I couldn't find a stick. But anyway, he ran so fast, a Breton hound couldn't have caught up with him."

"Where did he go?"

"That way."

And off the peasants ran in great haste, shouting, "Over there, he's over there!"

Reynard leaped through the hole in the palisade and bore the cock to earth with him, but the noise he made was heard by all. "After him!" Constantine shouted and called his mastiffs: "Mauvoisin! Bardol! Travers! Humbaut! Rebors! After him! After Renard the Red!"

Now Chanteclere was in great peril if he didn't think of some trick. And so he said, "Lord Reynard, don't you hear the shameful things those peasants say? Constantine recognized you and called you all sorts of names. When he shouts, 'Reynard is stealing my rooster!' you should say, 'In spite of all your efforts!' There's nothing that would annoy him more."

No one is so wise that he can't be fooled sometime: Reynard had tricked all the world, but this time he himself was deceived. The peasants raised the cry again, and Reynard turned to shout back, "In spite of all your efforts! I'll steal him any time I please!"

But with these words, Chanteclere felt those terrible jaws go slack, and beating his wings with all his might, he flew into an apple-tree. Reynard sat down on a dung-heap below him, chagrined, enraged, tormented by the cock who had escaped. Chanteclere just laughed: "Reynard," he said, "how's the world treating you these days?"

The traitor shook with rage and in sheer bad humor said, "Cursed be the mouth that speaks when it should be silent."

"Amen, amen," said the rooster. "Yes, and I wish him every evil who shuts his eyes and goes to sleep when he should stay awake. Cousin Reynard," he continued, "no one should ever trust you. Cursed be your cousinage! It almost ruined me. Reynard, you liar, get out of here! If you wait around, you'll lose your hide!"

Reynard was always very careful of his fur coat. He spoke not a word more, but turned at once and ran. Through the hedge beside the plain, straight down the road he fled. But his heart was heavy because of the rooster, who had escaped when he'd had him in his hands.

MACROBIUS

[On Dreams]†

* * *

After these prefatory remarks, there remains another matter to be considered before taking up the text of *Scipio's Dream*. We must first describe the many varieties of dreams recorded by the ancients, who have classified

†From *Commentary on the Dream of Scipio*, trans. William Harris Stahl (New York: Columbia UP, 1952) 87–90. Copywright © 1952 Columbia University Press. By permission. Stahl's notes have been omitted.

and defined the various types that have appeared to men in their sleep, wherever they might be. Then we shall be able to decide to which type the dream we are discussing belongs.

All dreams may be classified under five main types: there is the enigmatic dream, in Greek *oneiros*, in Latin *somnium;* second, there is the prophetic vision, in Greek *horama*, in Latin *visio;* third, there is the oracular dream, in Greek *chrematismos*, in Latin *oraculum;* fourth, there is the nightmare, in Greek *enypnion*, in Latin *insomnium;* and last, the apparition, in Greek *phantasma*, which Cicero, when he has occasion to use the word, calls *visum.*

The last two, the nightmare and the apparition, are not worth interpreting since they have no prophetic significance. Nightmares may be caused by mental or physical distress, or anxiety about the future: the patient experiences in dreams vexations similar to those that disturb him during the day. As examples of the mental variety, we might mention the lover who dreams of possessing his sweetheart or of losing her, or the man who fears the plots or might of an enemy and is confronted with him in his dream or seems to be fleeing him. The physical variety might be illustrated by one who has overindulged in eating or drinking and dreams that he is either choking with food or unburdening himself, or by one who has been suffering from hunger or thirst and dreams that he is craving and searching for food or drink or has found it. Anxiety about the future would cause a man to dream that he is gaining a prominent position or office as he hoped or that he is being deprived of it as he feared.

Since these dreams and others like them arise from some condition or circumstance that irritates a man during the day and consequently disturbs him when he falls asleep, they flee when he awakes and vanish into thin air. Thus the name *insomnium* was given, not because such dreams occur "in sleep"—in this respect nightmares are like other types—but because they are noteworthy only during their course and afterwards have no importance or meaning.

Virgil, too, considers nightmares deceitful: "False are the dreams *(insomnia)* sent by departed spirits to their sky." He used the word "sky" with reference to our mortal realm because the earth bears the same relation to the regions of the dead as the heavens bear to the earth. Again, in describing the passion of love, whose concerns are always accompanied by nightmares, he says: "Oft to her heart rushes back the chief's valour, oft his glorious stock; his looks and words cling fast within her bosom, and the pang withholds calm rest from her limbs." And a moment later: "Anna, my sister, what dreams *(insomnia)* thrill me with fears?"

The apparition *(phantasma* or *visum)* comes upon one in the moment between wakefulness and slumber, in the so-called "first cloud of sleep." In this drowsy condition he thinks he is still fully awake and imagines he sees specters rushing at him or wandering vaguely about, differing from natural creatures in size and shape, and hosts of diverse things, either delightful or disturbing. To this class belongs the incubus, which, according to popular belief, rushes upon people in sleep and presses them with a weight which they can feel. The two types just described are of no assistance in foretelling the future; but by means of the other three we are gifted with the powers of divination.

We call a dream oracular in which a parent, or a pious or revered man, or a priest, or even a god clearly reveals what will or will not transpire, and what action to take or to avoid. We call a dream a prophetic vision if it actually comes true. For example, a man dreams of the return of a friend who has been staying in a foreign land, thoughts of whom never enter his mind. He goes out and presently meets his friend and embraces him. Or in his dream he agrees to accept a deposit, and early the next day a man runs anxiously to him, charging him with the safekeeping of his money and committing secrets to his trust. By an enigmatic dream we mean one that conceals with strange shapes and veils with ambiguity the true meaning of the information being offered, and requires an interpretation for its understanding. We need not explain further the nature of this dream since everyone knows from experience what it is. There are five varieties of it: personal, alien, social, public, and universal. It is called personal when one dreams that he himself is doing or experiencing something; alien, when he dreams this about someone else; social, when his dream involves others and himself; public, when he dreams that some misfortune or benefit has befallen the city, forum, theater, public walls, or other public enterprise; universal, when he dreams that some change has taken place in the sun, moon, planets, sky, or regions of the earth.

*   *   *

GEOFFREY OF VINSAUF

[Lament on the Death of Richard I]†

Once defended by King Richard's shield, now undefended, O England, bear witness to your woe in the gestures of sorrow. Let your eyes flood with tears, and pale grief waste your features. Let writhing anguish twist your fingers, and woe make your heart within bleed. Let your cry strike the heavens. Your whole being dies in his death; the death was not his but yours. Death's rise was not in one place only but general. O tearful day of Venus! O bitter star! That day was your night; and that Venus your venom. That day inflicted the wound; but the worst of all days was that other—the day after the eleventh—which, cruel stepfather to life, destroyed life. Either day, with strange tyanny, was a murderer. The besieged one pierced the besieger; the sheltered one, him without cover; the cautious one pierced the incautious;

† Reprinted from the *Poetria Nova of Geoffrey of Vinsauf*, translated by Margaret F. Nims, by permission of the publisher; © 1967 by Pontifical Institute of Mediaeval Studies, Toronto. pp. 29–31. This passage is one of several examples given by Geoffrey to illustrate the use of apostrophe as a device of amplification.

the well-equipped soldier pierced an unarmed man—his own king! O soldier, why, treacherous soldier, soldier of treachery, shame of the world and sole dishonour of warfare; O soldier, his own army's creature, why did you dare this against him? Why did you dare this crime, this hideous crime? O sorrow! O greater than sorrow! O death! O truculent death! Would you were dead, O death! Bold agent of a deed so vile, how dare you recall it? You were pleased to remove our sun, and condemn day to darkness. Do you realize whom you snatched from us? To our eyes he was light; to our ears, melody; to our minds an amazement. Do you realize, impious death, whom you snatched from us? He was the lord of warriors, the glory of kings, the delight of the world. Nature knew not how to add any further perfection; he was the utmost she could achieve. But that was the reason you snatched him away: you seize precious things, and vile things you leave as if in disdain. And Nature, of you I complain: for were you not, when the world was still young, when you lay new-born in your cradle, giving zealous attention to him? And that zeal did not flag before your old age. Why did such strenuous effort bring this wonder into the world, if so short an hour stole the pride of that effort away? You were pleased to extend your hand to the world and then to withdraw it; to give thus, and then to recall your gift. Why have you vexed the world? Either give back to us him who is buried, or give us one like him in excellence. But you have not resources for that; whatever you had that was wondrous or precious was expended on him. On him were exhausted your stores of delight. You were made most wealthy by this creature you made; you see yourself, in his fall, most impoverished. If you were happy before, in proportion to happiness then is your misery now. If heaven allow it, I chide even God. O God, most excellent of beings, why do you fail in your nature here? Why, as an enemy would, do you strike down a friend? If you recall, your own Joppa gives evidence for the king—alone he defended it, opposed by so many thousands. Acre, too, gives evidence—his power restored it to you. The enemies of the cross add their witness—all of them Richard, in life, inspired with such terror that he is still feared now he is dead. He was a man under whom your interests were safe. If, O God, you are, as befits your nature to be, faithful and free of malice, just and true, why then did you shorten his days? You could have shown mercy to the world; the world was in need of him. But you choose to have him with you, and not with the world; you would rather favour heaven than the world. O Lord, if it is permissible to say it, let me say—with your leave—you could have done this more graciously, and with less haste, if he had bridled the foe at least (and there would have been no delay to that end; he was on the verge of success). He could have departed more worthily then to remain with you. But by this lesson you have made us know how brief is the laughter of earth, how long are its tears.

BARTHOLOMAEUS ANGLICUS

[On the Cock]†

* * * Also the kok is hoot and drie of complexioun, and therfore he is ful bolde and hardy, and so
fightith boldeliche for his wyfes agenst his adversaries
and assaileth and resith on° hem and tereth and   *attacks*
woundeth ham with bile and with spores.° And whan   *back-claws*
he hath the maistrie he singeth anon, and or° he sin-   *before*
geth he betith himself with his wynges to make him
the more able to singe. And he usith° fer in the nyght   *is accustomed*
to singe moost cleereliche and strongliche, and aboute
the morwetyde° he schapith° lyght voys and song, as   *morning / produces*
Ambrose saith. The cok bereth a comb on his hede
in stede of a crowne, and yif he lesith° his comb he   *loses*
lesith his hardinesse and is the more slow and coward
to assaile his adversarie. And he loveth cherliche° his *tenderly*
wyves. And whenne he fyndeth mete° he clepith his   *food*
wifes togedres with a certeyn voys and spareth his owne
mete to fede therwith his wifes. And settith next to
him on rooste the henne that is most fatte and tendre
and loveth hire best and desireth most to have hire
presence. In the morwetide whanne he fleeth to gete
his mete, furst he leith his side to hire side and bi
certeyne tokenes and beckes,° as it were love tacchis,° *gestures / indications*
a woweth° and prayeth hire to tredinge;° and fightith   *he woos / copulation*
for hire specialliche as though he were jelous, and
with byle and spores he chacith and dryveth awey from
him cokkes that cometh nyghe° his wifes. And in   *near*
fightinge he smytith the grounde with his bile and
rereth up the weyes aboute his necke to maken him
the more bolde and hardy, and meveth the fetheres
of his taile upwarde and donwarde that he mowe so
the more abilliche° come to the bataile.   *ably*

* * *

†Text based on *On the Properties of Things: John Trevisa's Translation of Bartholomaeus Anglicus* De Proprietatibus Rerum, ed. M. C. Seymour et al., 2 vols. (Oxford: Oxford UP, 1975) 1. 627. Reprinted by permission of Oxford University Press.

CRITICISM†

† In this Norton Critical Edition, we have numbered the lines of each prologue and tale separately. The standard editions of the complete *Canterbury Tales* number lines according to fragments (sequences of tales and framing passages that are clearly linked to each other), using either letters or Roman numerals to specify the fragment. In the following essays, whenever a critic cites passages from Chaucer included in this edition for which the standard line numbering differs from ours, we have added the NCE line numbers in brackets. We have made no changes whenever the essays quote either passages not included in our selections or passages where our numbering corresponds to that of the standard editions.

F. R. H. DU BOULAY

The Historical Chaucer†

The world in which Chaucer lived was small in terms of people but large in terms of geography. A magical journey backwards in time would place us in an England where the most terrifying noise would not be made by bomb or jet but the yelling of a murderous crowd, and where for every twenty people on today's streets there would be only one. The south-east was already more heavily populated than the rest of the country, but the London throngs would have seemed comparatively thin. Perhaps the age-structure of the population would also have appeared different. Many children died, and to be fifty was to be quite old. When Chaucer began his literary career the bubonic plague had recently taken a specially heavy toll of the very young, so that by modern standards English life was carried on by a large majority of people who were between twenty and forty years old. The children, as was customary, fitted into the work of the adult world without the doting attention of today. Above all, the effective leadership of society was in the hands of relatively few men. The historian who reads the records of government, law and commerce between 1340 and 1400 is constantly surprised by meeting the same people and noticing how often they knew each other and were connected with the same affairs. In his brilliant *Some New Light on Chaucer*, Professor J. M. Manly tried to identify some of the characters in *The Canterbury Tales* with real people, and even if he does not always carry conviction it is a remarkable sign of society's smallness that such attempts at identification could be made. Another illustration of this close community is furnished by the account-book of Gilbert Maghfeld, a London merchant and money-lender. His customers between 1390 and 1395 included nobles, knights, clerks and merchants from England and abroad, and of these no less than thirty to forty are known to have been associated in some way with Chaucer.[1]

Though lightly peopled, the world of Chaucer was mobile. War, diplomacy, trade, administration and the impulses of religion shifted men and women of even humble station about the country and far beyond its shores. The framework of a pilgrimage from Southwark to Canterbury which Chaucer chose for his best-known collection of tales is not out of keeping with historical truth, but the theme of the journey appears even more clearly after a closer look at the pilgrims. There were thirty-two of them, and out of these at least thirteen not counting Chaucer himself were regular travellers by profession or taste. The knight as a chivalric crusader had seen Granada,

†Reprinted from *Writers and Their Background: Geoffrey Chaucer*, edited by Derek Brewer. Athens, Ohio: Ohio University Press, 1974. pp. 33–57. Reprinted by permission of Ohio University Press and Unwin Hyman Limited.

1. J. M. Manly, *Some New Light on Chaucer*, New York 1926; for remarks on Maghfeld's account-book and excerpts from it see *Chaucer's World*, compiled by Edith Rickert, ed Clair C. Olson and Martin M. Crow, New York 1948, pp. 185–93.

North Africa, Armenia, Russia, Lithuania and Prussia.[2] The squire like his literary creator had fought in Flanders, Artois and Picardy. The monk coursed over the countryside with a string of hunters. Unlike the monk the friar belonged to a religious order in which travel was part of the vocation itself, necessary for study, preaching and organized begging. The merchant's business trips to the Low Countries were a commonplace activity upon which depended the export-import trade and credit transactions of Merchant Venturers and other groups from English towns. The Serjeant-at-Law made his assize-circuits just as his modern counter-part does and incidentally helped by so doing to bring to remoter shires the English of the king 'that is lord of this langage'.[3] As a well-to-do landowner the franklin had been commissioned as sheriff and justice of the peace and elected as a parliamentary 'knight' for his shire, so that he was familiar with constant journeying, at least within the realm. The shipman like the friar was so much a medieval byword for rootlessness that he was regarded as a good spy in war and a bad surety in the courts.[4] Chaucer's example was evidently experienced on both the Bordeaux and Baltic routes. The reeve was an agricultural overseer from Norfolk and accustomed to presenting biannual accounts to his lord's auditors. The summoner was a specialized postman whose round covered an entire diocese and made him an embarrassingly familiar figure. The pardoner was one of a whole crowd of 'Rome-runners', and the manciple, if he were like many other estate-officials, was probably the servant of more than one lord and liable to serve in several parts of England in any one year.

The rustic members of this company have been called the manorial aristocracy, and it is true that we do not meet the poorest villagers among them, nor did Chaucer write about the mass of small-holders as did Langland about the cottage-dwellers he felt to be his neighbours. But even Langland envisaged pilgrimage, and the estate-documents of the time leave no doubt that the manorial poor travelled too, bound on errands or carrying-services for their masters, service in wars, or in search of wage labour.

Of course this pilgrimage to Canterbury was a literary construct, yet behind it lay a constant historical reality which can to some extent be measured. Offerings at the shrine of Becket in Canterbury Cathedral amounted during the fourteenth century to some £300 or £400 a year, more during the second half of the century, and they only declined permanently after 1420.[5] If aristocratic pilgrims were more noticed in the monks' records they sometimes cost the cathedral more than they gave: most of the donors were the anonymous, humble people who were doubtless often able to make the journey because their fortunes were improving through the forces of economic change.

2. For maps of the crusading journeys to Prussia and Lithuania undertaken in the 1390s by Henry of Derby and his knightly companions, see *Richard II*, ed. F. R. H. Du Boulay and Caroline M. Barron, 1971, pp. 163, 166.
3. *The Works of Geoffrey Chaucer*, ed. F. N. Robin-son, 2nd edn, 1957, p. 546.
4. *The Paston Letters, 1422–1509*, ed James Gairdner, 1900–08, I, Nos. 146, 195.
5. C. Eveleigh Woodruff, 'The financial aspect of the cult of St. Thomas of Canterbury', *Archaeologia Cantiana* XLIV, 1932, esp. pp. 18–25.

For Chaucer's lifetime spanned a period of economic transition so important that neither his career nor his writing can be properly understood without some brief reference to it. It is basically a question of demography. The first and most lethal epidemic of plague occurred in 1348–9, when Chaucer was a small boy. During his middle years there were further epidemics, so that within a generation the population of Britain like that of Europe as a whole had been severely reduced. Historians often argue that the horrors of pestilence made late medieval men and women preoccupied with death and filled their art and literature with fantasies of mortality, but the most striking historical consequence seems to have been a sharper appetite for a better life. As people died the pressure of population on land was relieved. The survivors inherited property more quickly. Poorer fields could go out of cultivation, leaving men in possession of the most productive arable. In general the price of basic foodstuffs remained low while the wages of labourers rose. The unskilled man who got 1d a day in 1300 got 4d or 5d by 1400. In short, labouring men benefited from the very fewness of their numbers and could expect to have more to spend after rents had been paid and food bought or grown. It is not surprising that lords and knights thought their inferiors were becoming uppish and attempted, though without success, to control wages and prevent the flaunting of fine clothes and personal possessions by folk whose fathers had known better how to keep to their station.

Chaucer's age was consequently one of unusual tension, born of betterment rather than oppression. The Great Revolt of 1381 was only the biggest explosion in a fire of change. Up the ladder of society inferior answered back to superior with sharp criticism and occasional blows, whether it was bondmen against lords and lawyers, commons against the tax-men, middling townsmen against the big financiers, laymen against rich, endowed clergy, or warlike nobles against a young king who wanted peace with France and respectful acquiescence for his tactless spending on personal friends. These conflicts sometimes merged into each other and are in any case too complex for full discussion here, but a word must be given to the problem of social class which clearly coloured Chaucer's own assumptions.

The fundamental distinction in English society was between those who were *gentils* and those who were not, in very much the same way as this was true at least up until the early twentieth century. A squire in a noble household was usually *gentilhomme* no less than the king himself. By about 1425 this simple class distinction was being frequently expressed in the English language by the word 'gentleman' which was taking the place of the older Latin *generosus* and French *gentil*. This is not to say that more numerous gradations in rank were of no account. It was an aristocratic society in which king, nobles, prelates and knights all received particular expressions of deference. It was also a world of social mobility which in fact sharpened the sense of status. Merchants who had just climbed into *gentilesse* could be despised by those who had forgotten any remoter taint of trade. Even the de la Poles, dukes of Suffolk and most splendid of medieval *arrivistes*, could now and then be reminded without much delicacy how they were 'worship-ful men grown to fortune of the world.'[6] But the bisection of society into gentle and simple was understood clearly enough and is the basic historical reality of late medieval class structure. It makes no difference that Chaucer wrote moralizing lines to the effect that a real gentleman is a man who behaves decently. 'Handsome is as handsome does' is an acceptable motto to the most snobbish societies, just as in our own somewhat more relaxed days 'nature's gentleman' remains a wholly intelligible alternative for a rough diamond. To this extent the social historian must differ from the literary scholar who sees equal reality in literary statements of fourteenth-century class distinction.[7] The idea of 'degree', according to which men were ranked by their function in society, was certainly attractive to the theological cast of mind that understood society's God-given architecture in terms of men's vocations and mutual dependence. But it was of no more social significance than are ranks and regiments in the armed services of today. As to the theoretical division of men into those who fight, those who pray and those who work (such as the knight, the clerk and the ploughman), this was only a more primitive version of 'degree': if it is 'the only class system known to medieval theory', then it must be answered that the class distinctions which possess the greatest everyday importance are those least subject to theory.

Hence, when we enquire about Chaucer's place in Society (which must have been of more account to him than society), we may accept that he was a gentleman because he had a courtly upbringing and worked, behaved and wrote like one. True, his origins were mercantile, his position modest, his ambitions even a trifle eccentric in their artistic solitariness. But he was not a hired craftsman who came in at the back door and downed his ale with the life-long servants. He 'communed with gentle wights'.

The sort of people who gathered for their entertainment round a public reader would have been aware of changes that were taking place in lan-guage. Three of these changes were leaving their mark upon the fourteenth century. English was moving towards a standardized form. French was being forgotten, and the ability to read and write in English was becoming more widespread amongst lay people. In a well-known passage of *Troilus* Chaucer alludes to the variations which still existed in English and hopes that what he is writing will be understood.

> And for ther is so gret diversite
> In Englissh and in writyng of oure tonge,
> So prey I God that non myswrite the,
> Ne the mysmetre for defaute of tonge . . .

Yet the very apostrophe suggests the marvellous possibility of a wider com-prehension:

6. For all this, see the present writer's *An Age of Ambition*, 1970, chap. 4.
7. A skilful literary analysis is by D. S. Brewer, 'Class distinctions in Chaucer', *Speculum* XLIII, 1968, pp. 290–308.

And red wherso thow be, or elles songe,
That thou be understonde, God I biseche!
(V, 1793–98).

And no one who has glanced at the provincial literature of the same age can doubt that the future lay on the sophisticated London tongues of Chaucer and his friends, not with the up-country authors of *Pearl*, *Gawayne* or *Sir Orfoo*. There is a historical point here too. In the mid-fourteenth century the richer classes of London society were being reinforced by immigrants from the east midlands who brought their speech with them and fused it with existing London language as the vehicle of communication between Englishmen of position. These people were merchants who dealt in major commodities like wool and wine, so that the economic drift to the south-east accomplished changes in society and speech as well as in production and government. Once more, the de la Poles of Hull provide a leading instance, but so too does the Chaucer family of Ipswich whose migration to the capital helped the victory of the very language used by its most famous member. The fact that French was concurrently becoming a foreign tongue is probably a parallel development rather than a consequence of this slowly forming linguistic identity. Enmity with France never stopped the interchange of ideas and people across the Channel, but the standardization of speech into its modern shapes was occurring none the less, and indeed in France and Germany as well as England. It was encouraged the more vigorously in England because London stood as a capital city in a relatively small country, whereas France was larger and even more regionalized, and Germany had no capital at all. So to London wealth and substantial people were drawn, and thence flowed the torrent of administration and law, expressed in the dialect of Europe's most centralized government. All the standard history books tell how English began to be used in London courts and parliaments in the 1360s. French was becoming an accomplishment rather than a habit, and a sidelight on this comes from the will of James de Peckham, a Kentish gentleman who died in the same year as Chaucer. His codicil of 30 September 1400 ordering the bequest of 10 oxen and 200 sheep added that 'my executors shall distribute all my books in French to those who know how to use them'.[8]

With language went literacy in the sense of an ability to read and even write in the mother tongue. The great collections of private correspondence like the Paston Letters begin to survive from about this time. If Chaucer himself had been an exception as a literate layman it would hardly have made sense for him to describe so naturally the exchange of love-letters between Troilus and Criseyde:

---

8. Lambeth Palace Library, Register of Archbishop Arundel, I, fos. 176b–177a: . . . *volo ut executores mei distribuant omnes libros meos gallicos scientibus illos occupare* . . .'

The lettres ek that she of olde tyme
Hadde hym ysent he wolde allone rede,
An hondred sithe atwixen noon and prime . . .
                                          (V, 470–2).

So too does his midnight remedy invite a flash of sympathy from fellow
insomniacs: 'to rede, and drive the night away'. (*The Booke of the Duchess*
49).

Evidence does not exist to make possible any geography of literacy, though
we may guess that more people who could read and write lived in the south-
east and east of England than elsewhere. But certainly the most advanced
institutions of government had their home in and about London. The king
himself was often on the move, accompanied by friends and counsellors.
But the established departments of state were organized in permanent buildings spread out over the metropolis, like the Exchequer and Chancery at
Westminster, and the Wardrobe's permanent offshoots, the Great and Privy
Wardrobe which housed bulk supplies and armaments in Baynard's Castle
and the Tower within the City walls. Household departments both station-
ary and itinerant possessed seals as the essential instruments to authenticate
orders, commissions and grants of property and privilege. To remove the
seals from the effective control of the king was an organized baronage's chief
answer to his supposed misrule, yet at the same time the action most likely
to arouse the king's vengeful anger. During the reigns of Edward III (1327–
77) and Richard II (1377–99), the internal politics of England turned prin-
cipally round the problem of controlling such commissions and grants, in
peace and in war, and of how the groups of politically influential men
combined with and against each other in ever-changing factions: nobles,
parliamentary knights, bishops and merchants; king's friends and king's critics, allies or enemies of each other according to a thousand personal interests, but never parties in a modern sense. There is no place here for a
detailed chronicle, but it may be helpful to explain two basic characteristics
of political life. Medieval government at every level was organized through
households; and the disposition of property was the stuff of politics.

Public affairs in modern times are carried on in offices and committees
which operate for the most part in office hours and rely heavily upon
administrative standing orders and the services of secretaries. In the fourteenth century the household of an important man was also to a great extent
the place where political decisions were taken. Private and public life were
not yet clearly distinguished. This is true of insignificant country lords with
small estate councils and a handful of armed retainers, of merchants who
slept near their bales and accounts, and of the king himself whose advisers
might talk gravely with their master in a private room whilst his immense
entourage prepared the meals, mended the waggons, or rollicked in halls
and yards. Our imaginative picture of minstrels and large-scale catering is
sound enough if we remember also that the household was a moving centre
of government where messengers to and from the outside world sped like

bees. Charters, letters and writs drawn up with professional care in Chancery or Exchequer often awaited their ultimate authority from this pell-mell dwelling.

The subject-matter of public business was in a curious way equally private. At tense moments educated men might speak of the crown in distinction from the king, or of 'the law and course of parliament', but the underlying realities were cornfields, flocks of sheep, rents, pensions from the Exchequer, rake-offs from customs houses or judicial courts, and, perhaps above all, the capital gains that accrued from rich marriages. The king's task was to walk on the knife-edge between all-round generosity and the insolvency which left him desperate.

One of the medieval historian's greatest difficulties is to discover in detail the jealousies and ambitions which set men at daggers drawn or brought them for a time into sworn friendship, but the generalized picture is quite a simple one. The royal household and noble households were the same in kind but different in degree. Their outward form was a family structure of men and women living according to rank yet with a good deal of informality, and in a milieu where kindness to a young knight or an unexpected flirtation might have the most serious political undertones. Everybody wanted security and income, and these things were in the gift of the dynasts: offices, pensions, manors or the hand of a girl with an inheritance whence might spring another young family to struggle and jockey in its turn for livelihood and power. All this is quite different from modern family life of which the function at its best is fulfilled by twenty years of intimate parental care. The medieval *familia* embraced other people's children as well who from early adolescence shared in the work of the adult world, whether they were apprentices, religious postulants or pages.

To call Chaucer's age violent is not very illuminating as this is true of almost all epochs, but the particular forms violence took are of interest. In the first place there was endemic warfare. When Chaucer was born the young Edward III had just reopened the war with France which was fundamentally about the king of England's lands and status across the Channel. The 'Hundred Years War' (1337–1453) sounds like a distinct episode but was in fact a fresh series of phases in a conflict so old that it was part of the folk-memory. In the middle years of the fourteenth century war took the form of sea fights, raids across the Scottish border and, more centrally, long-range expeditions or *chévauchées* into France under a king with unusual gifts of affability and comradeship with his own nobility. Thousands of people were involved besides the knights, men-at-arms and archers, from the clothiers who made uniforms for the retinues to the craftsmen who supplied bowstrings and the shipmen who ferried grain for the armies overseas.[9] But war is never a unifying activity for long, and cracks soon widened in the fabric of English society. These were of two kinds: the little fissures of outrage committed by men habituated to the violent seizure of what they wanted;

9. H. J. Hewitt, *The Organization of War under Edward III*, 1966.

and the crevasses which opened when the dramatic victories of Crécy and Poitiers were over and the slog had to be paid for by taxation, when financiers were caught profiteering, and (worst of all) when a new young king, wilful, cliquish and extravagant, actually wanted to make peace with his ancient adversary and use his soldiers nearer home. Two examples of political shock may be chosen for their bearing on Chaucer's life.

In 1376 a group of highly-placed courtiers and London financiers was impeached in parliament for peculation, at the instigation of Peter de la Mare, knight of the shire for Herefordshire and the earliest known Speaker of the Commons. The incident is complex because it was part of an aristocratic wrangle, and is also especially famous for the earliest eyewitness account of a debate amongst the parliamentary Commons. But to the point here is the person of Richard Lyons, the chief merchant culprit, for he was a man of similar background to Chaucer's and a London neighbour, though he had made himself of much greater political importance. Little is known of Lyons's origins apart from the fact that he was illegitimate. But by 1359 he was buying houses and shops in London and in the 1360s was a prominent vintner with a group of taverns which sold sweet wine. He had a country property in Essex as well and was to represent Essex in the parliament of 1380. In the 1370s he was lessee of much of the petty custom and subsidy in English ports and able to lend the government money and buy the government's debts at a heavy discount. Professor Myers calls him 'not so much a thief as a rich individual who could help to rescue a virtually bankrupt government'.[1] After his impeachment his wealth was confiscated, but he soon got it back. The present interest lies in seeing how an obscure vintner could become so rich and how his heart lay where his treasure was. His confiscated possessions were worth nearly £2500 and he owned a fairly large ship. In 1380 he bought exemption for life from being made sheriff, escheator, coroner, J.P. or collector of taxes against his will. Probably these tasks would have interfered too much with business, and the exemption is suggestive of the fact that these important offices were not always either desired or voluntary. Lyons's end was neither happy nor dignified, for he was murdered in Cheapside by the rebels of 1381, his house at Overhall in Essex was wrecked and a woman called Isabella spent fruitless years of litigation in claiming to be his widow, though the executors argued that the marriage had been annulled in 1363. Stow saw his tomb in St. James Garlickhithe, with his effigy showing 'hair rounded by his ears and curled, and a little beard forked', like the king he served. Compared with Lyons, we may reflect that Chaucer had the better part in remaining a politically modest figure.

Ten years after the Good Parliament the court was again attacked, this time by the impeachment of Michael de la Pole, earl of Suffolk and Chancellor. The opposition of the autumn and winter of 1386 was led by Thomas of Woodstock (duke of Gloucester since 1385) and the earl of Arundel. The

1. A. R. Myers, 'The Wealth of Richard Lyons' in *Essays in Medieval History presented to Bertie Wilkinson,* ed T. H. Sandquist and M. R. Powicke, Toronto 1969.

most recent research has shown that it was indeed the king himself, not yet twenty, who was the real target of attack,[2] for his extravagance and political partisanship; and the crisis of the next two years during which many of the king's friends were executed or exiled was a most violent confrontation in which the king's possession of the throne and perhaps of his life itself hung in balance. It has proved all too tempting for scholars to argue that Chaucer's surrender of his post in the customs was a minor consequence of this massive political purge, but as we shall see this seems on balance unlikely. The events of 1386–8 are more useful as a prominent instance of political upheaval which help to explain the prudence of Chaucer's life but did not involve any punishment for his associations.[3]

The Church which might have stood as a city of peace in so unquiet a world shared in fact in all that world's frictions and political malice. This is not to deal out the almost total disapproval bestowed upon late medieval Catholicism by disdainful critics like G. M. Trevelyan. In parishes, monasteries and even in the lives of certain bishops there are examples of fidelity, study and the works of charity. But the deep connections between secular and ecclesiastical government involved the Church in precisely the same imperfections as the world itself of which it was part, and attracted criticisms which reasonably condemned many blemishes. It may at the same time be remembered that the criticisms themselves are a sign of grace, and that not every revolted conscience belonged to a heretic or cynic.

In 1305 the papacy had moved to Avignon, and fourteenth-century Englishmen had grown accustomed to thinking of a *curia* where the cardinals were mostly French as an institution hostile to English interests. Papal taxation had been loudly resented even in the early thirteenth century; the resentment did not abate even after kings in the fourteenth century had moderated its impact upon their subjects. The claims of popes to provide their direct nominees to church benefices and the unremitting hostility of English parliaments to such papal provisions are prominent in the records of the fourteenth century. If this was material enough for an English political anti-papalism, the Great Schism which began in 1378 was an enormous aggravation. It is arguable that before 1378 the popes had the will of peace-makers between England and France, but afterwards the divided papacy was yet another *casus belli*.

Perhaps a gaze too firmly fixed on Rome or Avignon causes optical illusions in students of Chaucer. Understanding of Englishmen's attitudes must in the best analysis be sought in England itself. Here was a society both religious and anti-clerical, and to miss the fact that both these attitudes co-existed is to misread the age. Indeed, it is doubtful whether anti-clericalism can occur in an irreligious society.

In the fourteenth century there were at least three different kinds of hos-

2. J. J. N. Palmer, 'The Impeachment of Michael de la Pole in 1386', *Bulletin of the Institute of Historical Research* XLII, 1969, pp. 96–101.
3. This is the place to applaud the general sound

historical sense displayed in a now quite old work: J. R. Hulbert, *Chaucer's Official Life* (Ph.D. dissertation), Chicago 1912.

tility to clergy. Occasionally there was anger against senior prelates who were also high government officials, like the bishops of Chichester and Lichfield, Chancellor and Treasurer respectively, who were dismissed for inefficiency by Edward III in 1340 and replaced by laymen on the grounds that their clerical order gave them undue protection against punishment. Similarly, William of Wykeham, bishop of Winchester, was thrown out of the Chancellorship in 1371, and Simon of Sudbury, archbishop of Canterbury and Treasurer of England, had his head cut off by the rebels in 1381. Secondly, bitter feelings were often shown towards the friars. The *Summoner's Tale* is a well-known joke in this vein, but the belief that the friars had betrayed their ministry to the poor is expressed with more solemn indignation in *The Vision of Piers the Plowman*. Yet hatred of the mendicants was more keenly felt by other kinds of clergyman than by laymen. The friars were competitors with the secular clergy for the alms and esteem of parishioners and for academic privileges in the universities. No amount of literary vilification can hide the fact that lay men and women continued to leave bequests of money to the orders of friars right up until the Reformation, so that friar-baiting was in a sense a clerical variety of anticlericalism. Third, and most important, was a disgust with the wealthy, established, sacerdotal Church which was felt with varying intensity by a wide range of people, from outright Lollard heretics to those who were entirely orthodox in fundamental belief and practice, yet devoted in their hearts to the simplicities of the New Testament and the application of moral principles to everyday life. It is difficult to avoid the conclusion that Chaucer himself moved in these circles, and equally difficult to show that in Richard II's reign there was any clear dividing line between Lollards and what, for lack of a better term, may be called orthodox evangelicals.

The careers of the so-called Lollard knights reflect these ambiguities. In the chronicles at least ten distinguished laymen are named and portrayed as supporters of heresy and heretics themselves. The interpretation of their activities is still controversial but any account of Chaucerian society must at least face the same problem.[4] Seven of these men formed a closely-knit group of friends, namely, the knights Richard Stury, Lewis Clifford, Thomas Latimer, William Nevill, John Clanvowe, John Montagu (earl of Salisbury from 1397) and John Cheyne. All were courtiers and members of the king's household. Stury, Clifford, Nevill and Clanvowe were knights of the king's Chamber and thus members of an intimate circle of which Chaucer, as an esquire of the Chamber, was also part. In 1372 when Chaucer was certainly occupying this position he was about 30 years old; Stury would then have been about 45, Clifford about 40, Nevill and Clanvowe roughly Chaucer's age. They were therefore more or less contemporaries, and they lived the same kind of life. By 1378 they were mostly veteran campaigners who knew

4. W. T. Waugh, 'The Lollard Knights' in *Scottish Historical Review* XI, 1914, pp. 55–92 held that most of them were never serious Lollards and all made orthodox ends. Conversely, the genuine and lasting Lollardy of these knights was argued by the late K. B. McFarlane in a paper read to the *Canterbury and York Society* on 13 December 1962 and now published in fuller form in *Lancastrian Kings and Lollard Knights*, Oxford 1972.

other lands and had also, except for Latimer, travelled on diplomatic missions. In September 1385 the same Wardrobe account records the issue of black cloth for mourning the king's mother to Clanvowe, Clifford, Clifford's son-in-law, La Vache, and Chaucer. Several of this circle had literary tastes. Clifford had brought Chaucer a copy of a poem written in his honour by Eustache Deschamps, praising him for his wisdom and his ability as translator of the *Roman de la Rose*, which is, incidentally, more a satire in its English form against false love and corrupt morals than a work of courtly love.[5] Stury also owned a copy. Montagu was a versifier praised by Christine de Pisan. Clanvowe was himself a sincerely moralizing author who will be referred to again. The group were also knights, and individually much more well-to-do than Chaucer. Although Clifford began as an almost landless man in a Devonshire village, by 1389 he had nearly £400 a year in annuities and was exchanging them quickly for land, an intelligent business move which Chaucer too may have been making when in 1388 he granted his Exchequer annuities to John Scalby. Several of the knights married heiresses and some invested in the English lands of Norman abbeys confiscated by the king, and thus had an interest in the disendowment of the Church at a time when Lollards were demanding the same thing. But financial success formed no barrier between these men and Chaucer. Nevill and Clanvowe acted as witnesses to a deed in Chaucer's interest.[6] Clifford was his close friend and the father-in-law of Sir Philip La Vache whom Chaucer in his popular poem *Truth* advised to shun the servitude of this world. Whether the knights were Lollards in any exact sense must remain an open question. They were called such in the chronicles, but chroniclers were emotionally hostile even to implicit criticisms of the Church. True, Latimer was accused of heresy before the king's council, and when Wycliff's disciple, master Nicholas Hereford, was arrested Nevill asked to have his custody 'because of the honesty of his person'. Clifford, Latimer and Cheyne drew up wills which used phrases dear to Lollards, like referring to their bodies as 'stinking carrion', and requesting burial in cheap cloth and without funeral pomp, and to supervise the execution of these wills they chose Lollard overseers. Yet it remains possible that as a group they showed in exaggerated form the sentiments felt by many orthodox contemporaries. What betrays this attitude to the historian is less the ambiguous record of action than the common feeling behind Chaucer's own poem *Truth* (before 1390?) and the English tract by Clanvowe later entitled *The Two Ways* (1391?).[7] The message of Chaucer is that the world is a wilderness, not a home, through which the wise man goes as a pilgrim in dread of avarice and self-advancement:

> Hold the heye wey, and lat thy gost thee lede:
> And trouthe thee shal delivere, it is no drede.

5. D. W. Robertson, *Chaucer's London*, New York 1968, p. 209.
6. *Chaucer Life-Records*, ed M. M. Crow and C. C. Olson, Oxford 1966, p. 343.

7. V. J. Scattergood, 'The two ways: an unpublished religious treatise by Sir John Clanvowe', in *English Philological Studies* X, 1967, pp. 33–56.

In Clanvowe's pamphlet the meaning is the same and even the imagery similar. No more than Chaucer does he attack or defend the Church's institutions, but begs Christians to avoid the 'broad way' that leads to hell and enter the 'narrow way' to heaven. Insistent that salvation lies through a life in which scriptural teaching is observed he speaks with the same voice as Chaucer in his moments of direct simplicity or, for the matter of that, of Langland when he uses the metaphor of pilgrimage and prefers Do-Wel to triennials. It is an authentic English voice of late fourteenth-century spirituality.

> For that that is cleped richesse it is greet trauail to geten it and it is greet drede to keepen it and to departe therfro it is greet heuynesse, so that fro the first getynge to the laste forgoying it is alle sorewe . . .

Nothing in the rhythmic phrases of Clanvowe is wholly out of accord with what little of his private mind Chaucer himself permits us to hear. So we come from the world of Chaucer to the man himself.

There can be no intention here to rehearse in detail the well-known fragments of Chaucer's biography, but rather to offer the view of a single historian about what in that life is important to understanding the poet. His life indeed begins and ends in historical obscurity, and even the extraordinary labours which have culminated in the *Life-Records* leave us in a twilight unimaginable to students of post-Plantagenet England. The first frustration is of a natural wish to know about the domestic life of a poet who wrote so much of marriage and children. The most that can be said is that Chaucer was probably married to Philippa de Roet from about 1366 to 1387, by which time she was dead, and that he had a son called Thomas who rose higher in the world than his father, probably also a son called Lewis, and just possibly a surviving daughter called Elizabeth. To attempt deductions from the poetry about Chaucer's happiness or otherwise in the married state seems a waste of time like so much other effort which, unsupported by real evidence, has been put into the Chaucer industry. Yet enough is known of the fourteenth-century milieu to allow a reflection that Chaucer was lucky in having legitimate parents, a settled home, a father who did not die till his son was about 22, and a marriage which lasted some 21 years. Despite the Christian teaching about monogamy and fidelity it was an age when family life was often brief and fragile. Parents frequently died young, leaving the survivor to re-marry quickly. Bastardy was exceedingly common. Children were likely to be shunted off to fend for themselves at quite an early age. Chaucer's own maternal grandmother Mary was married three times. His father John was abducted by an aunt who tried to marry him off at the age of about 11. In fact, many of Chaucer's contemporaries had a rough youth, such as Langland who was illegitimate and resented it, or Boccaccio legitimized after his birth and estranged from a father 'old, coarse and mean'.[8] Richard Lyons was also illegitimate; Dante and Petrarch exiles; Boccaccio, Dante and Petrarch had step-mothers; Boccaccio and

---

8. John Larner, *Culture and Society in Italy, 1290–1420*, 1971, p. 216.

Petrarch had many illegitimate children. Even Chaucer's sister-in-law was a mistress for many years before she became John of Gaunt's third wife, and her very marriage attracted sneers rather than rejoicing.

Like the great Italians, Chaucer started from a mercantile background and was educated in letters—we do not know where—at an early age. Literary originality was rare among the old landed families. But he did not have the advantages or disadvantages of being a tonsured cleric and in this he was unlike Langland, Froissart, Boccaccio, Petrarch, Hoccleve and Lydgate. Although the literate layman was becoming quite a common figure as a reader it was still exceptional for a layman to be a professional poet, let alone a great one. In this he is perhaps to be compared only with Dante.

Undoubtedly the career of Chaucer was made possible by his acceptance into courtly households. It is not necessary to suppose either that he was a faintly bourgeois usher or the partisan of any longlasting political faction. He had a foot in several worlds: the courtly, the mercantile and the literary, but as already explained he lived naturally as a gentleman, like many other Englishmen of the governing class, with jobs to do and the usual rewards in return. Further, it was easy to pass from one household to another. Chaucer began as an adolescent in the household of Elizabeth, countess of Ulster, wife of Lionel, duke of Clarence, who was the second son of Edward III and one of Richard II's uncles. By 1367 he was in Edward III's household and from then on until his death he was connected with the royal court in one way or another even though he did not always travel about with the king as one of his personal entourage. Another point is worth making. There were times when political and personal hostility (much the same thing) existed between some of the magnates and the king, and even between Richard II and his uncle John of Gaunt, and as everyone knows Gaunt's son Henry ultimately deposed his cousin. But factions however savage were transient, and although royal or noble servants connected with unpopular policies might on occasion be dismissed or even destroyed, there were whole substrata of courtiers, officials and servants who did not suffer if they did not seem to pose any political threat or to have committed any political crime. Guilt by association was not taken very far. It is hard to believe that Chaucer was not liked and valued, and not because he was a wary trimmer but for his genial skill in bringing 'mirth and solas' to his neighbours and a personal inability to get seriously diverted from practising his gift. This seems the explanation of his professional and financial survival. Doubtless he was welcome in the great Lancastrian family. In 1386 his wife was admitted to the fraternity of Lincoln Cathedral in the presence of Gaunt and along with Henry of Derby and a galaxy of Lancastrian luminaries. It was both a distinguished occasion and a family affair. This sort of thing did not prevent Chaucer continuing in the service of Richard II, and even riding through England on his urgent business within a year of Derby's landing. On the day of Henry IV's coronation Chaucer, still king's esquire, received a handsome rise in his pension.[9] There is no contradiction in all

9. *Life-Records*, pp. 91, 62, 525.

this, for it is a sequence of rewards for uncomplicated service and friendship, the bright lining of political storm-clouds.

Much of Chaucer's employment was too fleeting, too ordinary or of too little significance in his life to merit discussion in a short essay, but his work at the London Customs House is worth a moment's attention. He was appointed Controller of the wool custom, the wool subsidy and the petty custom in London in 1374, increasingly allowed deputies to do the work at the wool quay, and replaced in these posts in December 1386. It is sometimes said that these were important posts from which he was dismissed when the Wonderful Parliament placed the king's government in commission under the power of Gloucester, Arundel and Warwick. Neither of these suppositions is likely. It is true that the wool custom was one of the chief props of the crown's finances despite the decline in exports of raw wool, by reason of the high tariff and the relative efficiency of its collection by the best civil service in Christendom. But the really important officials were the Collectors and not the Controllers. The Collector was usually a London merchant-financier who lent the crown money and spent his time in the customs service in repaying himself out of the £18,000 or so annual revenue which flowed through his hands. His work was in the technicalities of the credit system while the actual collecting was done by deputies. The Controller *(contrarotulator)* was intended to act as a check on the Collector, returning to the Exchequer his own counter-roll which detailed the exports and imports. In fact, of course, he was so inferior in wealth and status that he was no effective check. The idea was that the Collector had one half of the customs seal (the cocket) and the Controller the other half, and that the application of this seal to documents of consignment would show that the customs had been paid. But the Controller's half had to be surrendered to the king's creditors, and when this happened the Controller was virtually deprived of office and the creditor was made Controller in all but name. In 1379, for instance, the City of London held half the cocket seal, which meant that the great financier John Philipot held one half of the seal as Collector and the other as Mayor.[1] No doubt the job of Controller needed expertise, especially in accounting at the Exchequer, and it yielded a salary equivalent to the income of a simple country knight. But it was 'a modest office for a modest man'. Nor, despite parliamentary petitions that life-holders of Controllerships should have their appointments annulled, is there evidence that any of them was discharged after investigations or purges. Chaucer's service for 12½ years had in 1386 already run beyond the usual term. Once more the attempt to dramatize the events of his external life must fail.

The years 1385–6 saw the beginning of serious political disturbance in England, and at the same time a number of changes occurred in Chaucer's life, so that scholars have naturally assumed some connection between the two. The changes are interesting, but the assumption does not carry strong

1. An expert study is Olive Coleman's 'The Collectors of Customs in London under Richard II' in *Studies in London History presented to P. E. Jones*, 1969, pp. 181–96.

conviction. In 1385 Chaucer got a permanent deputy at the wool quay and also became one of the J.P.'s for Kent. In the late summer of 1386 he was elected knight of the shire for Kent in the parliament that was to meet at Westminster on 1 October, he gave up his house at Aldgate, and by December had ended his employment at the Customs House altogether. No direct evidence survives to tell us what property he acquired in Kent, but what most likely happened is that now, past his fortieth year and perhaps with a sick wife, he went to live in north Kent and hoped to give more time to his writing in agreeable surroundings. Of course the idealization of May and the cult of the daisy were stock literary forms. But it is hard to reject as mere devices the expressed delight at the tranquillity of gardens in the Prologue to the *Legend of Good Women*, whether that poem was written before or after Chaucer's exit from the city. At this point it will be timely to say something of Chaucer's connection with Kent. The county was as much the scene of his life as London. On occasion he uses Kentish dialect forms, the road to Canterbury he knew in actuality as well as imagination, and close investigation shows that many of the people he knew lived near Greenwich, the Cray valley or within sight of the North Downs, then a prosperous residential area and even now offering a certain freshness to the London worker.

As early as 1375 Chaucer had a considerable financial profit out of Kent through the custody of a Canterbury heir called Edmund Staplegate,[2] but by the time he was appointed J.P. for the county in 1385 he probably possessed property in the part of Kent nearest to London.[3] When in 1387 he was placed on a commission to enquire into the abduction of a young heiress, the session was held at Dartford and the other three commissioners possessed land and interests in the same area. The centre of the enquiry was indeed Bexley, North Cray, Sidcup and Chislehurst, whence came plaintiff, defendant and jurors as well as commissioners, and the wills of some of their descendants are extant and derive from the same region.[4] Again in 1388 the transfer of a small action for debt against Chaucer suggests that the Exchequer considered Kent to be his home. Frequently during the 1390s official records hint at Chaucer's association with the Woolwich and Greenwich areas, and a manuscript of 'Lenvoy a Scogan' dating from *c.* 1393 has a marginal note which says that Chaucer was then living in Greenwich. This is made virtually certain by the series of deeds dated 1395–

2. *Life-Records*, Ch. 12.
3. The only other esquires in this list of Kentish J.P.'s were Hugh Fastolf who was Deputy Constable of Dover Castle and William Topcliffe who was a lifelong servant of the archbishop and probably lived in Maidstone, F. R. H. Du Boulay, *The Lordship of Canterbury*, 1966, pp. 394, 396, 398.
4. William Hall (1512) and Thomas Hall (1526), yeomen of Bexley (Public Record Office, filed will and Prerogative Court of Canterbury (PCC) Will Register 20 Porch); William Swetesyre (1527), yeoman of North Cray (ibid., 23 Porch). For these, see my pamphlet *Medieval Bexley*, Bexley Corporation

Public Libraries 1961. The case clearly concerned the Bexley Halls, so *Life-Records* p. 379 note 3 is wrong, but p. 381 is on the right lines. Rickhill, the chief commissioner and a man connected with the death of the duke of Gloucester in 1397, was from Rochester, where his second wife, Rose, died in 1418 or 1419 (*Register of Henry Chichele, archbishop of Canterbury, 1414–43*, ed E. F. Jacob, II, Oxford 1938, pp. 161–2). Thomas Carshill (Cressell), one of the defendants, had a descendant, Richard Cressell, gent., still living in Chislehurst in 1508 (PCC Will Register 12 Bennett).

6 transferring Spittlecombe in East Greenwich from Archbishop Arundel to Gregory Ballard. The technical details do not matter here, but the witness-list fairly clearly numbers Chaucer among the Greenwich residents. Chaucer was also one of the attorneys appointed by Ballard to take possession in his behalf which would have been most conveniently done by a local inhabitant. There is an additional point. Gregory Ballard was a busy official who during his life served both the king and Archbishop Arundel, the king's enemy. He was butler to Richard II in the 1390s (a post later held by Thomas Chaucer) and both Treasurer (1398–1401) and Steward of the estates (1400–12) to the archbishop. His will made in October 1415 shows him a well-to-do inhabitant of Greenwich, accustomed to travel, and leaving a widow, one son and at least four menservants.[5] When Arundel suffered forfeiture in 1397 Ballard received this property from the king, yet again became the archbishop's counsellor when Arundel was restored to favour. His career illustrates the kind of friend Chaucer had in prosperous north Kent: a modest landholder with professional skills, accustomed to riding over southern England and giving official orders, and surviving the cross-winds of political fortune.

The years 1385–6 formed a dividing-point in Chaucer's life. Hitherto his work had been carried on in contact with communities, whether in great households or in the bustle of city life. Thereafter his appointments required him to travel about but to live less closely surrounded by his fellow men. From 1389 to 1391 he was Clerk of the King's Works with responsibilities for buildings and repairs at various royal residences; from at latest 1391 till the end of his life he was one of the deputy foresters of North Petherton, Somerset. There is no evidence that as Clerk of the Works he was unsatisfactory, and his duties in Somerset, if any, are quite obscure. The impression is that as he grew older he continued to be favoured on all sides, received posts which made decreasing demands on him, and was granted emoluments to maintain him at a decent standard of living. The debts which have attracted such attention were nothing unusual, but rather indicate a certain affluence, for his income tended to rise and was paid with remarkable regularity for the times, and the ability to borrow money was then as now a sign of creditworthiness. His service as Justice of the Peace for Kent in 1385–9 has left no trace of any personal activities, nor does the commission mark him out from scores of country gentry who were thus associated with magnates in the shires, but his election to parliament in 1386 merits comment. It was the last time that Chaucer found himself at the centre of public affairs. Any personal part played by him is quite unknown (again, the same is true of many others) but the occasion can be made to illustrate with some satisfying detail the society in which he found himself.

During the thirteenth and fourteenth centuries the king's government was always trying to persuade men of suitable substance to take up knighthood and thus formally qualify themselves for various kinds of public duty

---

5. *The Lordship of Canterbury*, pp. 394, 398; *Register Chichele* II, pp. 114–15. These works add to the information in *Life-Records*, p. 509 note 2.

in their localities. This is true of Londoners as well as of rural landholders, but resistance to so expensive a distinction was stubborn. Consequently, many of the parliamentary 'knights of the shire' were not true knights at all, cermonially girt with the sword and styled *chivaler*, but squires and gentlemen more interested in their estates than in the warrior pursuits so admired by monastic chroniclers and other desk-romantics who liked to deplore the softness of the times. Likewise, election to parliament was not always the prized honour it later became. Absence from one's domestic concerns might be awkward; travel had its risks, and so too did business among the powerful and demanding men who surrounded the king; and four shillings a day would not seem much when faced with the need to furbish accommodation, as were the four citizens of London who travelled to the Cambridge parliament of 1389 and had to spend £112 7s 0d restoring and equipping a ruined house for their stay.[6]

In any parliament there were men who had never been there before and some who would serve once only. For all that, the parliamentary knights were becoming an influential body in petitioning the king, arguing about taxation and at critical moments supporting the king's aristocratic opponents. Politics were still 'lords' matters', and the political leaders were the higher nobility. Between the ordinary run of barons and knights there was no very sharp social division. It was a strongly held opinion that the knights in parliament ought to have some property in the shires they represented. The rule of primogeniture in aristocratic inheritance meant that a knight could well be a lord's close kinsman and even if he were not many knights were followers and retainers of the lords. Likewise, a knight could have ties of business or relationship with a burgess, although the townsmen enjoyed less prestige than the knights when they met in parliamentary sitting. In brief, the Commons in parliament were by Chaucer's day becoming a homogeneous group, yet one in which wide differences of career and importance could be found.[7]

In the parliament which met on 1 October 1386 only 38 out of the 71 shire representatives present were real knights.[8] No pattern can be discerned. Both representatives for Sussex and Buckinghamshire happened to be knights, but neither for Kent or Bedfordshire. If anything, the north, the east midlands and the west country produced on this occasion more knights than the south-east. But there was a tendency for men of greater wealth to be knights, whether they had inherited it, married it or been granted it for good service. A constant feature in the lives of shire knights is that they also at some time acted as sheriff, Justice of the Peace and commissioner for the various tasks of local government. A few instances must suffice to show how diverse were the men whose characteristics might seem at first glance so similar. Ralph Carminew of Cornwall was elected but never sat in the par-

6. *English Historical Documents, 1327–1485*, ed A. R. Myers, 1969, pp. 451–2.
7. The following biographical details have been made available before their official publication by courtesy of the *History of Parliament Trust*, London, and special thanks are due to its Secretary, Mr. E. L. C. Mullins.
8. *Calendar of Close Rolls, 1385–89*, H.M.S.O., pp. 298–9.

liament at all because he was pulled over a cliff on 9 October by a pair of greyhounds he was leading. He had been to parliament twice before, but his fellow Cornishman, John Bevyle, sat only the once even though he was unusually young at this time; as sheriff of Cornwall he complained of his 'great losses and costs in office', but he married an heiress and became richer than his father. Walter atte Lee of Hertfordshire sat for parliament eleven times and was a king's knight and vigorous soldier, but Thomas atte Lee, esquire, his colleague and probable kinsman, never came to parliament again although he was a favoured retainer of the king. Sir Thomas Broke of Somerset, who sat twelve times, owed his position largely to marriage with the rich widow of a Bristol merchant who had sixteen manors in the west country. They lived in a stone mansion at Holditch (now in Dorset) where they had a deer-park. The family became connected with the Cobhams, notorious for Lollardy, and Broke himself requested in his will (1415) a simple grave that might be trampled by people going to church, and left no bequests to religious institutions. The knights for Northumberland were quite different again: Sir Bertram de Montboucher and Sir Robert de Claveryng were both campaigners much occupied with the unremitting border struggle against the Scots. Chaucer's Kentish colleagues were less distinguished. Hardly anything is known of the Rochester burgesses, Piers Pope and John Fleming, not even their connection with Rochester. One of the Canterbury burgesses, called L. H. Holt, was in 1387 a trustee for the property of Edmund Staplegate, former ward of Chaucer.[9] The other shire representative was William Bettenham of Hawkhurst who owed large sums of money, including £66 13s 4d to Sir Richard Stury. He must have been related to Stephen Bettenham, esquire of Cranbrook, and it is interesting that whereas William obtained a papal licence to have a private altar, Stephen showed signs of the evangelical views that were common in Kent, for he asked in his will that money should be given to the poor rather than spent on a funeral feast 'which is rather called the solace of the living and dissipation of goods than refreshment and salvation of souls'. He cannot have been a wholehearted Lollard as he did not forbid obsequies but merely wished to avoid a multiplicity of masses for his soul.[1] Chaucer could almost have made a variegated pilgrimage out of his fellow-parliamentarians.

Nothing is more natural than the wish to give genius a human face. Yet five hundred documents excavated with monumental labour and printed in the *Life Records* still leave the figure veiled. There can be little surprise at the exasperation of scholars with Chaucer's habit of slipping into the background of historical events. Some have preferred the most fearful precision of conjecture rather than a blurring of the biographical edges and have argued for almost anything but the commonplace: domestic misery, political cowardice, insolvency, incompetence, rape, or even a *diseur's* subjection to the patronizing tolerance of courtiers. Criticism is disfigured by such

9. See p. 455 above. Edmund Staplegate was also a landlord of James de Peckham who arranged masses to be said for him. See the will referred to on p. 445,

n. 8.
1. *Register Chichele*, II, pp. 33–6.

rash dramatizations; nor does Chaucer's fame need the aid of worldly distinction. There is indeed a biographical singularity about him if we will see it. It is, I dare to say, in a personal modesty which was real and not simply a device of rhetoric designed to charm an audience. Geoffrey Chaucer did not struggle for the kind of advancement which his son Thomas achieved. There is no question of an actual poverty or public neglect (though the absence of his last will is one of the worst gaps in the evidence), for his financial means never failed and his son cannot have begun a well-heeled life on nothing. But the poet's own life-work was truly in poetry which he generated in quiet reading and expressed as professional entertainment. To a society not surfeited with mental recreation he brought mirth and solace. Implicit in the solace was an assumption that even a story has a 'signification', a morality that assured his hearers of values beyond mere storytelling. In the fourteenth century it was impossible that it should be otherwise, and Chaucer did not speak a language wholly different from that of Langland or the preachers, mystics, or religious lyricists. In a sense his outlook was a spiritual one, while entirely compatible with the conventions of courtly love, mild pessimism, irony, a sense of destiny and pleasurable indecency. For the historian the literature's integrity is matched by that of the man when he is compared with the great Italians he admired and used. Despite similarities in mercantile origins, life at courts, public position and dedication to letters, we miss in Chaucer the spiritual violence of Dante, the bitterness of Boccaccio, the vanity of Petrarch. It is a dubious excuse to argue that he did not suffer as they did; that he was able to stand outside the pain of his own utterances, unlike Boccaccio for whom *Il Filostrato* was a shield 'for his secret and amorous grief'. If Troy was London, the *Troilus* is incredible as a mere entertainment, indited without sentiment as the author claimed.[2] The fifth book of *Troilus and Criseyde* is the Everest of Chaucer's Himalayas and cannot have been climbed without cost. When at nightfall the warden of the gates began to call in the townsmen and their beasts, and Troilus at last gave up his gazing for the woman who did not come, the poet was communicating an experience satisfying to the historian, who is fiction's enemy, and the historian must be silent and content.

ARTHUR W. HOFFMAN

Chaucer's Prologue to Pilgrimage: The Two Voices†

Criticism of the portraits in Chaucer's General Prologue to *The Canterbury Tales* has taken various directions: some critics have praised the portraits especially for their realism, sharp individuality, adroit psychology, and vividness of felt life; others, working in the genetic direction, have pointed

2. *Troilus*, II, 13, and, for the closing of the gate, V, 1177–80.

† From *ELH: A Journal of English Literary History* 21 (1954): 1–16. Reprinted by permission of The Johns Hopkins University Press.

out actual historical persons who might have sat for the portraits; others, appealing to the light of the medieval sciences, have shown the portraits to be filled, though not burdened, with the lore of Chaucer's day, and to have sometimes typical identities like case histories. Miss Bowden,[1] in her recent study of the Prologue, assembles the fruits of many earlier studies and gives the text an impressive resonance by sketching historical and social norms and ideals, the facts and the standards of craft, trade, and profession, so that the form of the portraits can be tested in the light of possible conformities, mean or noble, to things as they were or to things as they ought to have been.

It is not unlikely that the critics who have explored in these various directions would be found in agreement on one commonplace, a metaphor which some of them indeed have used, the designation of the portraits in the General Prologue as figures in a tapestry. It is less likely that all of the critics would agree as to the implications of this metaphor, but it seems to me that the commonplace deserves to be explored and some of its implications tested. The commonplace implies that the portraits which appear in the General Prologue have a designed togetherness, that the portraits exist as parts of a unity.

Such a unity, it may be argued, is partly a function of the exterior framework of a pilgrimage to Canterbury; all the portraits are portraits of pilgrims:

> At nyght was come into that hostelrye
> Wel nyne and twenty in a compaignye,
> Of sondry folk, by aventure yfalle
> In felaweshipe, and pilgrimes were they alle,   (23–26)[2]

But the unity of the Prologue may be also partly a matter of internal relationships among the portraits, relationships which are many and various among "sondry folk." One cannot hope to survey all of these, but the modest objective of studying some of the aesthetically important internal relationships is feasible.

If one begins with the unity that is exterior to the portraits, the unity that contains them, one faces directly the question of the nature of pilgrimage as it is defined in this dramatic poem. What sort of framework does the Prologue in fact define? Part of the answer is in the opening lines, and it is not a simple answer because the definition there ranges from the upthrust and burgeoning of life as a seasonal and universal event to a particular outpouring of people, pilgrims, gathered briefly at the Tabard Inn in Southwark, drifting, impelled, bound, called to the shrine of Thomas a Becket at Canterbury. The pilgrimage is set down in the calendar of seasons as well as in the calendar of piety; nature impels and supernature draws. "Go, go, go," says the bird; "Come," says the saint.

In the opening lines of the Prologue springtime is characterized in terms

1. Muriel Bowden, A Commentary on the General Prologue to the Canterbury Tales (New York, 1948).
2. All references to the text of The Canterbury Tales are to The Poetical Works of Chaucer, ed. F. N. Robinson (Cambridge, Mass., 1933).

of procreation, and a pilgrimage of people to Canterbury is just one of the many manifestations of the life thereby produced. The phallicism of the opening lines presents the impregnating of a female March by a male April, and a marriage of water and earth. The marriage is repeated and varied immediately as a fructifying of "holt and heeth" by Zephirus, a marriage of air and earth. This mode of symbolism and these symbols as parts of a rite of spring have a long background of tradition; as Professor Cook[3] once pointed out, there are eminent passages of this sort in Aeschylus and Euripides, in Lucretius, in Virgil's *Georgics*, in Columella, and in the *Pervigilium Veneris*, and Professor Robinson cites Guido delle Colonne, Boccaccio, Petrarch, and Boethius. Zephirus is the only overt mythological figure in Chaucer's passage, but, in view of the instigative role generally assigned to Aphrodite in the rite of spring, she is perhaps to be recognized here, as Professor Cook suggested, in the name of April, which was her month both by traditional association and by one of the two ancient etymologies.[4] Out of this context of the quickening of the earth presented naturally and symbolically in the broadest terms, the Prologue comes to pilgrimage and treats pilgrimage first as an event in the calendar of nature, one aspect of the general springtime surge of human energy and longing. There are the attendant suggestions of the renewal of human mobility after the rigor and confinement of winter, the revival of wayfaring now that the ways are open. The horizon extends to distant shrines and foreign lands, and the attraction of the strange and faraway is included before the vision narrows and focusses upon its English specifications and the pilgrimage to the shrine at Canterbury with the vows and gratitude that send pilgrims there. One way of regarding the structure of this opening passage would emphasize the magnificent progression from the broadest inclusive generality to the firmest English specification, from the whole western tradition of the celebration of spring (including, as Cook pointed out, such a non-English or very doubtfully English detail as "the droghte of March") to a local event of English society and English Christendom, from natural forces in their most general operation to a very specific and Christian manifestation of those forces. And yet one may regard the structure in another way, too; if, in the calendar of nature, the passage moves from general to particular, does it not, in the calendar of piety, move from nature to something that includes and oversees nature? Does not the passage move from an activity naturally generated and impelled to a governed activity, from force to *telos*? Does not the passage move from Aphrodite and *amor* in their secular operation to the sacred embrace of "the hooly blisful martir" and of *amor dei*?

The transition from nature to supernature is emphasized by the contrast between the healthful physical vigor of the opening lines and the reference to sickness that appears in line 18. On the one hand, it is physical vitality which conditions the pilgrimage; on the other hand, sickness occasions pil-

3. Albert S. Cook, "Chaucerian Papers—I: I. Prologue 1–11," *Transactions of the Connecticut Academy of Arts and Sciences*, XXIII (New Haven, 1919), 5–21.
4. Cook, 5–10.

grimage. It is, in fact, rather startling to come upon the word "seeke" at the end of this opening passage, because it is like a breath of winter across the landscape of spring. "Whan that they were seeke" may, of course, refer literally to illnesses of the winter just past, but, in any event, illness belongs symbolically to the inclement season. There is also, however, a strong parallelism between the beginning and end of this passage, a parallelism that has to do with restorative power. The physical vitality of the opening is presented as restorative of the dry earth; the power of the saint is presented as restorative of the sick. The seasonal restoration of nature parallels a supernatural kind of restoration that knows no season; the supernatural kind of restoration involves a wielding and directing of the forces of nature. The Prologue begins, then, by presenting a double view of the Canterbury pilgrimage: the pilgrimage is one tiny manifestation of a huge tide of life, but then, too, the tide of life ebbs and flows in response to the power which the pilgrimage acknowledges, the power symbolized by "the hooly blisful martir."

After line 18 the process of particularizing is continued, moving from "that seson" just defined to a day and to a place and to a person in Southwark at the Tabard, and thence to the portraits of the pilgrims. The double view of pilgrimage is enhanced and extended by the portraits where it appears, in one aspect, as a range of motivation. This range of motivation is from the sacred to the secular and on to the profane—"profane" in the sense of motivations actually subversive of the sacred. All the pilgrims are, in fact, granted an ostensible sacred motive; all of them are seeking the shrine. The distances that we are made aware of are both *within* some of the portraits, where a gulf yawns between ostensible and actual motivation, and *between* the portraits, where the motivation of the Knight and the Parson is near one end of the spectrum, and the motivation of the Summoner and the Pardoner near the other end. There is such an impure but blameless mixture as the motivation of the Prioress; there is the secular pilgrimage of the Wife of Bath, impelled so powerfully and frankly by Saint Venus rather than drawn by Saint Thomas, and goaded by a Martian desire to acquire and dominate another husband; in the case of the Prioress, an inescapable doubt as to the quality of *amor* hesitates between the sacred and secular, and in the case of the thoroughly secular Wife of Bath, doubt hesitates between the secular and the profane while the portrait shows the ostensible motive that belongs to all the pilgrims shaken without ever being subverted, contradicted perhaps, brazenly opposed, but still acknowledged and offered, not, at any rate, hypocritically betrayed. In the area of motivation, the portraits seem to propose, ultimately, a fundamental, inescapable ambiguity as part of the human condition; prayer for the purification of motive is valid for all the pilgrims. And the pilgrims who move, pushed by impulse and drawn by vows, none merely impelled and none perfectly committed, reflect, in their human ambiguity, the broad problem of origins and ends, the stubbornness of matter and the power of spirit, together with ideas of cosmic resolution and harmony in which source and end are reconciled and seem to be the same, the purposes of nature and supernature found to be at one, the two restorative powers akin, the kinds of love not discontinuous, Saint Venus and Saint Thomas different and at odds yet not at war, within the divine purpose which contains both.

The portraits of the Knight and the Squire have a particular interest. The relationships between these two portraits are governed by and arise out of the natural relationship of father and son. Consanguinity provides the base for a dramatic relationship, and at the same time is the groundwork for a modestly generalized metaphor of age and youth. Each portrait is enhanced and defined by the presence of the other: the long roll of the Knight's campaigns, and the Squire's little opportunity ("so litel space"), a few raids enumerated in one line; a series of past tenses, a history, for the Knight, and for the Squire a present breaking forth in active participles; the Knight not "gay," wearing fustian soiled by his coat of mail, "bismotered," the Squire bright and fresh and colorful; the Knight meek and quiet,—or so the portrait leaves him—beside the Squire, who sings and whistles all the day. The Knight's love is an achieved devotion, a matter of pledges fulfilled and of values, if not completely realized, yet woven into the fabric of experience (ideals—"trouthe," "honour," "fredom," "curteisie"). The Squire is a lover, a warm and eager lover, paying court to his lady and sleeping no more than the nightingale. In the one, the acquired, tutored, disciplined, elevated, enlarged love, the piety; and in the other, the love channelled into an elaborate social ritual, a parody piety, but still emphatically fresh and full of natural impulse. One cannot miss the creation of the Squire in conventional images of nature, the meadow, the flowers, the freshness like May, the lover like the nightingale,—comparisons that are a kind of re-emergence of the opening lines of the Prologue, the springtime surge of youthful, natural energy that animates the beginning. "Go, go, go," the bird's voice, is a major impulse in the portrait of the Squire and in the Squire's pilgrimage; the Knight's pilgrimage is more nearly a response to the voice of the saint. Yet the Squire is within the belt of rule, and learning the calendar of piety. The concluding couplet of the portrait

> Curteis he was, lowely and servysable,
> And carf biforn his fader at the table.   (99–100)

has the effect of bending all the youth, energy, color, audibleness, and high spirit of the Squire to the service of his father, the Knight, and to attendance on his pilgrimage, with perhaps a suggestion of the present submitting to the serious and respected values served and communicated by the past, the natural and the imposed submitting of the son to his natural father, and beyond him to the supernatural goal, the shrine to which the father directs his pilgrimage.

The portraits of the Knight and the Squire represent one of the ways in which portraiture takes into account and develops the double definition of pilgrimage which is established at the beginning. The double definition of pilgrimage is involved in a different way in the portrait of the Prioress; there it appears as a delicately poised ambiguity. Two definitions appear as two faces of one coin. Subsequently, when the portrait of the Prioress is seen together with the portraits of the Monk and the Friar, a sequence is realized, running from ambiguity to emphatic discrepancy, and the satire that circles the impenetrable duality of sacred and secular impulse in the case of the Prioress, knifes in as these impulses are drawn apart in the case of the Monk and strikes vigorously in the still wider breach that appears in the case of the Friar. What is illustrated within the portraits is amplified by a designed sequence.

The delicate balance in the picture of the Prioress has been generally recognized and has perhaps been only the more clearly exhibited by occasional seesawing in the critical interpretation of the portrait in which the satiric elements are sometimes represented as heavy, sometimes as slight, sometimes sinking the board, and sometimes riding light and high. There is, perhaps, no better illustration of the delicacy of the balance than the fact that the Prioress's very presence on a pilgrimage, as several commentators have pointed out, may be regarded as the first satiric touch. The very act of piety is not free from the implication of imperfection; the Prioress is obligated to a cloistered piety that serves and worships God without going on a journey to seek a shrine, and prioresses were specifically and repeatedly enjoined from going on pilgrimages. Prioresses did, nevertheless, go as pilgrims, so that Chaucer's Prioress is not departing from the norm of behavior of persons in her office so much as she is departing from the sanctioned ideal of behavior.[5] In the case of the Prioress, the blemish is sufficiently technical to have only faint satiric coloring; it is not the notable kind of blemish recognized in all times and all places. Nevertheless, it is precisely this kind of hint of a spot that places the Prioress at one end of a sequence in which the more obviously blemished Monk and Friar appear. If we pose a double question—What kind of woman is the Prioress, and what kind of prioress is the woman?—the portrait responds more immediately to the first part of the question, and leaves the answer to the second part largely in the area of implication. The portrait occupies forty-five lines, and more than three-fourths of the lines have to do with such matters as the Prioress's blue eyes, her red mouth, the shape of her nose and width of her forehead, her ornaments and dress, her table manners, her particular brand of French, her pets and what she fed them, and her tenderness about mice. It is, of course, one of the skilful arts of these portraits to work with surfaces and make the surfaces convey and reveal what lies beneath, but it should be observed that in the case of the Parson—or even in the case of the Knight— a character is arrived at almost entirely without physical and superficial detail. One need not take the emphatic surface in the portrait of the Prioress as necessarily pejorative in its implication; it need not follow that the Prioress is a shallow and superficial person, and, in consequence, sharply satirized. But the portrait does seem, by means of its emphasis on surfaces, to

5. The relevance of the ideal sanctioned character of an office to the portrait of a person will appear again strikingly in the case of the Summoner and the Pardoner.

define the Prioress as woman, and strongly enough so that tension between the person and her office, between the given human nature and the assumed sacred obligation is put vividly before us, and rather as the observation of a fact than as the instigation of a judgment. In the cases of the Monk and the Friar, the tension is so exacerbated that judgment is, in the case of the Monk, incited, and in the case of the Friar, both incited and inflamed to severity.

In the portrait of the Prioress the double view of pilgrimage appears both in an ambiguity of surfaces, and in an implied inner range of motivation. In the surfaces there is a sustained hovering effect: the name, Eglentyne, is romance, and "simple and coy" is a romance formula, but she *is* a nun, by whatever name, and "simple" and "coy," aside from their romance connotations have meanings ("simple" and "modest") appropriate enough to a nun; there are the coral beads and the green gauds, but they *are* a rosary; there are the fluted wimple and the exposed forehead, but the costume *is* a nun's habit; there is the golden brooch shining brightly, but it *is* a religious emblem. Which shall be taken as principal, which as modifying and subordinate? Are the departures or the conformities more significant of her nature? Are her Stratford French and her imitation of court manners more important than the fact that she sings well and properly the divine service? Do we detect vanity in her singing well, or do we rely on what she sings and accept her worship as well performed—to the glory of God? The ambiguity of these surface indications leads into the implied range of motivation; this implied range has been generally recognized in the motto—"*Amor vincit omnia*"— on the Prioress's golden brooch, and the implications set up in the portrait as a whole seem to be clustered and tightly fastened in this ornament and symbol.

The motto itself has, in the course of history, gone its own double pilgrimage to the shrine of Saint Venus and to sacred shrines; the original province of the motto was profane, but it was drawn over to a sacred meaning and soon became complexly involved with and compactly significant of both. Professor Lowes comments on the motto as it pertains to the Prioress:

> Now is it earthly love that conquers all, now heavenly; the phrase plays back and forth between the two. And it is precisely that happy ambiguity of the convention—itself the result of an earlier transfer— that makes Chaucer's use of it here . . . a master stroke. *Which of the two loves does "amor" mean to the Prioress?* I do not know; but I think she thought she meant love celestial.[6]

Professor Lowes, presumably, does not really expect to see the matter concluded one way or the other and finds this very inconclusiveness, hovering between two answers, one of the excellences of the portrait. There is, however, a certain amount of illumination to be gained, though not an answer to the question as formulated by Professor Lowes, by asking the question

6. John Livingston Lowes, *Convention and Revolt* (Boston and New York, 1919), p. 66.

another way and considering an answer in terms that lie outside of the
Prioress's motivation. Put the question in this form: Which of the two loves
does the *portrait* in the context of the Prologue mean by *amor?* The answer
to this question, of course, is *both.* On the one hand, profane love or the
love of earthly things does overcome all; the little vanities and pretensions,
the love of color and decoration and dress, the affection squandered in little
extravagances toward pets, the pity and tender emotion wasted upon a trapped
mouse—the multiplicity of secular, impulsive loves threatens to and could
ultimately stifle the dedication to the celestial love. This answer is, in fact,
a version of the Prioress's character and motivation sometimes offered. It
actually implies one half of the view of pilgrimage—the natural powers that
move people and that may usurp the whole character. But the other answer—
celestial love conquers all things—also applies to the portrait, though it is
not very easily arrived at in terms of the Prioress's motivation. Here we are
dealing with the ostensible meaning of the motto, the ideal meaning of the
motto as worn by a prioress—what it ought to mean in terms of her office.
And, no matter what the impurity of the Prioress's motives, no matter what
she means or thinks she means by the motto, the motto does, in the calendar of piety, mean that God's love is powerful over all things, powerful
in this case over the vanity that may be involved in the wearing of the
brooch, powerful over all the shallowness and limitation and reduction and
misdirection of love that the Prioress may be guilty of, powerful over all her
departures from or misunderstandings of discipline and obligation and vow,
powerful over all inadequacy, able to overcome the faults of God's human
instruments and make this woman's divine office valid. The motto, and the
portrait of which it is the conclusion, appreciate both the secular impulses
and the sacred redemptive will, but there is no doubt which love it is that
is crowned with ultimate power.

Chaucer has found ways, as in the case of the Prioress, of making an
ideal or standard emerge within a portrait. The standard may be ambigu-
ously stated or heavily involved in irony, but it is almost always present,
and nowhere with greater effectiveness than in the most sharply satiric portraits. This, I take it, is the effect of the formula of worthiness which is
applied to so many of the pilgrims. A character is declared to be "worthy"
or "the best that ever was" of his craft or profession or office, and frequently
under circumstances that make the statement jarring and the discrepancy
obvious. There is a definite shock, for example, when Friar Huberd is declared
to be a "worthy lymytour," or the Pardoner "a noble ecclesiaste." Even
when the satiric thrust has two directions, striking both at the individual
and at the group to which he belongs, the implication has nevertheless been
lodged in the portrait that there could be, for example, a worthy friar, or a
pardoner who was indeed a noble ecclesiastic. The reader is, as it were,
tripped in the act of judging and reminded that if he condemns these figures, if they appear culpable, there must be some sort of standard by which
they are so judged, by which they appear so.

Chaucer has also adopted the method of including ideal or nearly ideal portraits among the pilgrims. There are, for example, the Knight and the Plowman, figures at either end of the secular range, and among the clerical figures there is the Parson. A host of relative judgments, of course, are set up by devices of sequence and obvious pairing and contrasting of portraits. It is the ideal portraits, however, that somehow preside over all these judgments and comparisons, and it is to them that the relative distinctions are presented for a kind of penultimate judgment. Prioress, Monk, and Friar, and all the other clerical figures are reckoned with the Parson who is, in fact, made to speak in an accent of judgment upon the clerical figures who go astray—". . . if gold ruste, what shal iren do?" (We may remember the Prioress's shining gold brooch, the Monk's gold pin, and, among the secular figures, the Physician who so doubly regarded gold as a sovereign remedy.)

Chaucer has used an interesting device for undergirding the ideal portrait of the Parson. He employs consanguinity with metaphorical effect. After the assertions which declare that the Parson "first . . . wroghte, and afterward . . . taughte," the actualizing of Christian ideals is supported by the representation of the Parson as brother to the Plowman. It is the Parson's Christian obligation to treat men as brothers, and the portrait abundantly affirms that he does so. Making him actually the brother of the Plowman brilliantly insists that what supernature calls for is performed by the Parson and, more than that, comes by nature to him.[7] The achieved harmony both comes from above and rises out of the ground; sacred and secular are linked, the shepherd of souls and the tiller of the soil. This is a vantage point from which the conflicts of secular and sacred, of nature and supernature, are seen in a revealing light, a point at which one sees reflected in the clear mirror of ideal characters and an actual-ideal relationship the fundamental double view of pilgrimage established in the beginning.

The double definition of pilgrimage is differently but nonetheless revealingly illuminated by the portraits of another fraternizing pair, the Summoner and Pardoner, who conclude the sequence of pilgrims. The illumination here is not clarified by way of ideal characters but somehow refracted and intensified by the dark surfaces upon which it falls. The darkness is most visible in connection with the theme of love, which appears here in a sinister and terrible distortion. The hot and lecherous Summoner, the type of sexual unrestraint, is represented as harmonizing in song with the impotent Pardoner, the eunuch; the deep rumbling voice and the thin effeminate voice are singing, "Com hider, love, to me!" The song, in this context, becomes both a promiscuous and perverted invitation and an unconscious symbolic acknowledgment of the absence of and the need for love, love that comes neither to the grasping physical endeavor of the Summoner nor to the physical incapacity of the Pardoner—nor to their perverted spirits. Love has been treated in the Prologue from the beginning as dual in character, a matter both of the body and the spirit, the *amor* sym-

---

7. There is, of course, plenty of actual basis for representing a parson as a son of the soil; the connection is not merely an artistic and symbolic device.

bolized by Venus, sung by the Squire, equivocally illustrated by the Prioress, lustily celebrated by the Wife of Bath; and the *amor dei*, the love shadowily there beyond all the secular forms of love, a hovering presence among the pilgrims and sometimes close, as to the Knight and the Parson and the Plowman, and symbolized in the saint's shrine which is the goal of all of them. On this view, the song of the Summoner and the Pardoner is a superb dramatic irony acknowledging the full extent of their need and loss, the love of God which they ought to strive for, the love which they desperately need.

The office which each of these men is supposed to fulfill should be taken into account. The Summoner is, ostensibly, an instrument through whom divine justice, in a practical way, operates in the world. There are, in the portrait, a few touches that may be reminders of the ultimate source of his authority and function: his *"Questio quid iuris,"* though it is represented satirically as the sum and substance of his knowledge, and posed as a question, *is* legitimately the substance of his knowledge—his province is law, especially the divine law; *"Significavit"* is the opening word of a legal writ, a dreaded worldly pronouncement of divine judgment, excommunication; he is physically a fearful figure from whom children run (not the divine love which suffers them to come), and some of the physical details may be reminders of noble and awesome aspects of divine justice—his "fyr-reed cherubynnes face" and the voice described in a significant analogy as like a trumpet, "Was nevere trompe of half so greet a soun." The Pardoner, on the other hand, is the ostensible instrument of divine mercy and love. Many of the pardoners, as Miss Bowden points out, went so far as to pretend to absolve both *a poena* and *a culpa*, thereby usurping, in the pretended absolution *a culpa*, a function which theological doctrine reserved to God and His grace. In any case, their legitimate functions were an appeal for charity and an extension of God's mercy and love. The Pardoner, it should be observed, is, compared to the Summoner, an attractive figure. We may be reminded of the superior affinity of the Pardoner's office by the veil which he has sewed upon his cap, the copy of St. Veronica's veil which is supposed to have received the imprint of Christ's face.[8]

The justice and love[9] of which the Summoner and Pardoner are emissaries are properly complementary and harmoniously, though paradoxically and mysteriously, related, so that the advances that are being made both of persons and of values are, in a very serious sense, proper to this pair. The

---

8. Later, in telling his story, the Pardoner acknowledges that his pardons are inferior versions of the supreme pardon which is Christ's. See *The Pardoner's Tale*, 915–918 [602–05].

9. This statement of the symbolic values behind the Summoner and the Pardoner is not a disagreement with, but merely an addition to, the point made by Kellogg and Haselmayer (Alfred L. Kellogg and Louis A. Haselmayer, "Chaucer's Satire of the Pardoner," *PMLA, LXVI* [March, 1951], 215–277)

when they assert: "In this paradox, this ironic portrait of justice and crime singing in close harmony, we reach the center of Chaucer's satire." (p. 275) There is, indeed, the strongest satiric impact in this affiliation of the man who should apprehend the wrongdoer with the criminal. In addition, however, if we are to see beyond the Summoner's disabilities to his representation of justice, we see in parallel vision beyond the Pardoner's disabilities a representation of love.

radical physical distinctness of Summoner and Pardoner is at this level the
definition of two aspects of supernature; there is the same employment of
physical metaphor here that there is in the portraits of the Parson and the
Plowman, but with the difference that light comes out of darkness, and out
of the gravest corruption of nature the supernatural relationship emerges
clarified in symbol. The Summoner cannot finally pervert, and the Pardoner's impotence cannot finally prevent; the divine justice and love are powerful even over these debased instruments—*Amor vincit omnia*. Beyond
their knowing, beyond their power or impotence, impotently both Pardoner
and Summoner appeal for the natural love—melody of bird-song and
meadows of flowers—and both pray for the celestial love, the ultimate pardon which in their desperate and imprisoned darkness is their only hope:
"Com hider, love, to me!"

The exterior unity achieved by the realistic device and broadly symbolic
framework of pilgrimage is made stronger and tighter in the portraits, partly
by local sequences and pairings, but most impressively by the illustration,
the variation and enrichment by way of human instances, of a theme of
love, earthly and celestial, and a general complex intermingling of the consideration of nature with the consideration of supernature. The note of love
is sounded in different keys all through the portraits:

The Knight

> . . . he loved chivalrie,
> Trouthe and honour, fredom and curteisie (45–46)

The Squire

> A lovyere and a lusty bacheler . . . (80)
> So hoote he lovede that by nyghtertale
> He sleep namoore than dooth a nyghtyngale.
> (97–98)

The Prioress

> . . . *Amor vincit omnia*. (162)

The Monk

> A Monk . . . that lovede venerie, . . . (166)
> He hadde of gold ywroght a ful curious pyn;
> A love-knotte in the gretter ende ther was.
> (196–197)
> A fat swan loved he best of any roost. (206)

The Friar

> In love-dayes ther koude he muchel help . . . (258)
> Somewhat he lipsed, for his wantownesse, . . . (264)

The Clerk

> For hym was levere have at his beddes heed
> Twenty bookes, clad in blak or reed,
> Of Aristotle and his philosophie,
> Than robes riche, or fithele, or gay sautrie.
> (293–296)

The Frankelyn

> Wel loved he by the morwe a sop in wyn;
> To lyven in delit was evere his wone,
> For he was Epicurus owene sone . . . (334–336)

The Physician

> He kepte that he wan in pestilence.
> For gold in phisik is a cordial,
> Therefore he lovede gold in special. (442–444)

The Wife of
Bath

> Of remedies of love she knew per chaunce,
> For she koude of that art the olde daunce.
>   (475–476)

The Parson

> But rather wolde he yeven, out of doute,
> Unto his povre parisshens aboute
> Of his offryng and eek of his substaunce. (487–489)
> . . . Cristes loore and his apostles twelve
> He taughte, but first he folwed it hymselve.
>   (527–528)

The Plowman

> With hym ther was a Plowman, was his brother, . . .
>   (529)
>
> Lyvynge in pees and parfit charitee.
> God loved he best with al his hoole herte
> At alle tymes, thogh him gamed or smerte,
> And thanne his neighebor right as hymselve.
>   (532–535)

The Summoner
and　　　　　. . . "Com hider, love, to me!" (672)
The Pardoner

The theme of restorative power attends upon the theme of love. It is, of course, announced at the beginning and defined in terms both of nature and supernature. Both the Physician, concerned with natural healing, and the Pardoner, the agent of a supernatural healing, appear under the rubric of "Physician, heal thyself." The worldly Physician is disaffected from God; the Pardoner is naturally impotent. Serious inadequacy in either realm appears as counterpart of inadequacy in the other. It is the Parson who both visits the sick and tends properly to the cure of souls; he works harmoniously in both realms, and both realms are in harmony and fulfilled in him.

The pilgrims are represented as affected by a variety of destructive and restorative kinds of love. Their characters and movement can be fully described only as mixtures of the loves that drive and goad and of the love that calls and summons. The pilgrims have, while they stay and when they move, their worldly host. They have, too, their worldly Summoner and Pardoner who, in the very worst way, move and are moved with them.

Nevertheless, the Summoner and Pardoner, who conclude the roll of the company, despite and beyond their appalling personal deficiency, may suggest the summoning and pardoning, the judgment and grace which in Christian thought embrace and conclude man's pilgrimage and which therefore, with all the corrosions of satire and irony, are also the seriously appropriate conclusion to the tapestry of Chaucer's pilgrims.

JILL MANN

[Characterization and Moral Judgement in the General Prologue Portraits]†

One reason why Chaucer is at pains to give his characters 'life' as individuals is obviously that they are to act as individuals in the drama of the *Canterbury Tales*; they talk and react to each other as individual human beings would do. The 'individual' aspect is therefore vital to the frame of the tales. The 'typical' aspect is, however, equally vital to Chaucer's purpose in the whole work. The most obvious aspect of the *Canterbury Tales*, even in its incomplete state, is its comprehensiveness. It clearly aims at universality, at taking up all the themes and styles of contemporary literature and making one glorious compendium of them. The *Prologue* in a sense constitutes a kind of sample of what is to follow by its wide range of tone and mood. The serious ideals—chivalric, religious, labouring—which operate in the portraits of Knight, Parson and Ploughman, furnish a serious tone in addition to the comic and savage ones on which Chaucer can draw in the main body of his work. But as well as this, the *Prologue* makes its own contribution to the genres included in the *Canterbury Tales*, by the clear reference to estates literature in its form and content. It is especially appropriate that estates literature should perform this introductory function, since it lays claim to a universality of its own, and since its subject-matter is the whole society, the 'raw material' from which the other genres select their own areas of interest.

The *Canterbury Tales*, however, is not a compendium of literary genres in any simple sense. The method of the work is not additive, but dialectic; the tales modify and even contradict each other, exploring subjects in a way that emphasises their different and opposed implications. Sometimes we can follow the development of one theme through various mutations; even where the unifying theme is absent, it is noteworthy that the stimulus for tale-telling is the quarrel. The overall effect of this process of exploring tensions and contradictions is to relativise our values until we reach the

†From the conclusion of *Chaucer and Medieval Estates Satire* (Cambridge: Cambridge UP, 1973), 189–202, 290–94. Reprinted with the permission of Cambridge University Press. We have renumbered the notes and expanded some of the references. A sampling of the estates literature against which Mann discusses Chaucer's portraits is printed above, pp. 264–70.

absolute values of the Parson, who is willing to admit of no compromise or modification—but in assigning these absolute values to a character *within* the *Tales* (and, moreover, not to the narrator) Chaucer in one sense makes these values relative too.

The same refusal to take up an absolute standpoint can be found in the *Prologue*. One important demonstration of this has emerged from a comparison with other estates material—the fact that the persons who suffer from behaviour attributed to some of the pilgrims are left out of account— what I have called 'omission of the victim'. I have already stressed the importance of not letting our awareness of these victims, an awareness for which other satiric works are responsible, lead us into supplying them in the *Prologue* for the purposes of making a moral judgement, whether on Prioress, Merchant, Lawyer or Doctor. Chaucer deliberately omits them in order to encourage us to see the behaviour of the pilgrims from their own viewpoints, and to ignore what they necessarily ignore in following their courses of action.[1] Of course, our blindness differs from theirs in being to some extent voluntary—for the pilgrims' viewpoint is not maintained everywhere in the *Prologue*—while their blindness is unconscious and a condition of their existence. The manipulation of viewpoint, and ignorance (wilful or unconscious), are traditionally taken as features of irony, and the omission of the victim is a functional part of the ironic tone of the *Prologue*. The tone, as we have noted, becomes more forthright and moves away from irony precisely at moments when we are made conscious of the victim, and in particular of the victim's attitude to the pilgrim.[2]

The omission of the victim is part of the *Prologue*'s peculiar social ethic, which extends even to the pilgrims that Chaucer presents as morally admirable. The Yeoman, for example, is certainly an honest and hard-working member of his profession. Yet fault has been found even with him, on the grounds that

> no practical application of his skill is indicated . . . The description stops short at the means, the end is never indicated. The result is the impression of a peculiarly truncated consciousness.[3]

As regards the particular portrait, this interpretation is surely mistaken; there is no criticism of the Yeoman as an individual. The comment may however usefully focus attention on the small part played by social ends in the *Prologue*. This has already been indicated in discussion of the individual por-

---

1. For observations on the way in which a growing sense of individual motives and points of view in the twelfth century is connected with the growing importance of the estates concept in the same period, see J. Le Goff, 'Métier et profession d'après les manuels de confesseurs au Moyen Âge', in *Beiträge zum Berufsbewusstsein des Mittelalterlichen Menschen*, ed. P. Wilpert, *Miscellanea Medievalia*, vol. 3 (Berlin, 1964), pp. 44–60. [Now available in translation in Le Goff's *Time, Work, and Culture in the Middle Ages* (Chicago, 1980).]
2. An exception might seem to be the presence of

the victim in the Friar's portrait, in the form of the 'sike lazars' he neglects; we come very close to abandoning the Friar's viewpoint here, but do not quite do so because the whole passage is clothed in the Friar's own terminology, not the narrator's, and we see the lepers from the Friar's point of view, not *vice versa*. In the Reeve's portrait, the situation is reversed; we do see the Reeve from the point of view of the 'hynes'.
3. M. F. Bovill, 'The Decameron and the Canterbury Tales: a comparative study' (unpublished, Oxford B. Litt. thesis, 1966), 60.

traits. The *effects* of the Knight's campaigning, of the Merchant's 'chevisaunce', of the Sergeant's legal activities, even of the Doctor's medicine, are not what Chaucer has in mind when he assures us of their professional excellence. It is by ignoring effects that he can present the expertise of his rogues on the same level as the superlative qualities of his admirable figures. His ultimate purpose in this is not to convey any naive enthusiasm for people, nor comic effect, although the Prologue is of course rich in comedy, nor is it even a 'connoisseur's appreciation of types', although this attitude characterises the narrator's ironic pose in presenting the individual estates. The overall effect of this method is rather to sharpen our perceptions of the basis of everyday attitudes to people, of the things we take into account and of the things we willingly ignore.

We may clarify this by pointing out that the distinction between Langland and Chaucer is not just, as is usually assumed, the distinction between a religious and secular writer, between didacticism and comedy.[4] It is true that Langland and most of the army of estates writers before him, have a continual sense of the rewards of Heaven and the punishments of Hell, which of itself provides a 'reason' for moral behaviour, and that this sense is lacking in Chaucer. But it is also true that Langland shows, in passages such as the ploughing of Piers's half-acre, the practical bases for, and effects of, specific moral injunctions, while Chaucer has no *systematic* platform for moral values, not even an implicit one, in the *Prologue*.

When we first compare Langland and Chaucer, there is a temptation to conclude as Manly did, that Chaucer's satire is convincing because

> He does not argue, and there is no temptation to refute him. He does not declaim, and there is no opportunity for reply. He merely lets us see his fools and rascals in their native foolishness and rascality, and we necessarily think of them as he would have us think. (*Some New Light on Chaucer* [London, 1926], p. 295)

Undoubtedly it is true that Chaucer not only persuades us that fools and rascals can be very charming people, but is at the same time taking care to make us suspect that they are fools and rascals. If, however, we examine more closely what considerations determine what 'he would have us think' of the pilgrims, we find that they are not always moral ones. For example, if we compare the portraits of the Friar and the Summoner, we find that many of the faults we attribute to them are identical: fondness for drink; parade of pretended knowledge; sexual licence and the corruption of young people; the encouragement of sinners to regard money-payments as adequate for release from sin. Yet what is our attitude to them? I think it is true to say that our judgement on the Friar is less harsh than our disgust for the

4. This is the distinction usually drawn; see, for example, P. F. Baum, *Chaucer, A Critical Appreciation* (Durham, 1958), p. 70, who says we are struck by the 'earnestness of the one and the detachment of the other . . . Langland is not amused. His sense of humour is as keen as Chaucer's, but unlike Chaucer's it is often bitter and barbed; it does not titillate. It exposes the comic and ridiculous without smile or laughter.' Cf. also R. Woolf, 'Chaucer as a Satirist in the *General Prologue* to the *Canterbury Tales*', *Critical Quarterly*, 1 (1959), 150–57.

Summoner.[5] The reasons for this, in a worldly sense, are perfectly adequate; the Friar's 'pleasantness' is continually stressed, he makes life easy for everyone, is a charming companion, has musical talent, he has a white neck and twinkling eyes and good clothes, while the Summoner revolts the senses with his red spotted face and the reek of garlic and onions.[6] But although adequate to account for our reactions, these considerations are not in any sense moral ones.

It is sometimes said that the physical appearance of the Summoner symbolises his inner corruption; there is certainly a link between physical ugliness and spiritual ugliness in other, moralising writers. But Chaucer is as it were turning their procedure round in order to point to its origins in our irrational, instinctive reactions. The explicit moralising attitude to beauty and ugliness—that they are irrelevant beside considerations of moral worth—coexists, paradoxically, with an implicit admission of their relevance in the use of aesthetic imagery to recommend moral values. In the *Ancrene Wisse*, for example, the author associates beautiful scents, jewels and so on, with heavenly values, and stinks and ugliness with the devil; he then finds himself in the difficult position of trying to encourage an ascetic indifference to *real* bad smells.[7] Chaucer makes this tension between moral judgement and instinctive emotional reaction into a central feature of the *Prologue* partly in order to create the ambiguity and complexity of response which persuades us that the characters are complex individuals, but at the same time to show us, in the *Prologue*, what *are* the grounds for our like or dislike of our neighbours. Moral factors have a part in our judgement, but on a level with other, less 'respectable' considerations. There is no hesitation in admiring the unquestioned moral worth of the Knight or Parson, but this will not prevent us from enjoying the company of rogues with charm, or despising those who have no mitigating graces.

I shall return in a moment to the significance of this lack of systematically expressed values, after noting some other means which produce it. The first of these again emerges in contrast to estates material, and consists of the simple but vivid similes which run through some of the portraits—head shining like glass, eyes twinkling like stars—and which plays a large part in convincing us of the attractiveness of such figures as the Monk and the Friar. The constant use of this sort of comparison creates a tone which is at

5. The lack of correlation between the moral status of the pilgrims and our response to them, seems to be implied in H. R. Patch's statement that Chaucer 'didn't necessarily like best' his ideal characters (*On Rereading Chaucer* [Cambridge, Mass., 1959] p. 155).

6. Other comparisons could be made. Are we prepared to accept, for example, that Chaucer thinks it morally worse for the Pardoner to be a homosexual than for the Shipman to be a murderer? Is it worse for the Reeve to terrify his underlings than for the Wife of Bath to be sexually promiscuous? The impossibility of answering these questions indicates

that there is no systematic moral scale determining our likes and dislikes in the *General Prologue*; attempts to find the *moral* grounds on which, for example, the Pardoner can be shown to be the worst of the pilgrims as well as the most disgusting, are strained and unconvincing (see G. Ethel, 'Chaucer's Worste Shrewe: the Pardoner', *Modern Language Quarterly* 20 (1959), 211–27).

7. This paradoxical situation characterises the whole work: see especially p. 45 fol. 21b, 26ff., and p. 55, fol. 27b, 11ff. (ed. J. R. R. Tolkien, EETS O.S. 249 [London, 1962].

once relaxed, colloquial and animated—the kind of style which, as Derek Brewer has pointed out, finds its best counterpart in the English romances, and which differs strikingly from the taut, pointed style of learned satire. Another type of simile is neutral or explanatory—'As brood as is a bokeler or a targe'—and occasional examples of this sort may be found in French or Anglo-Norman satire. But the first group, in which the stress on attractiveness runs counter to the critical effect of the satire, would destroy the intention of a moralising satirist. A writer like Langland deals in occasional vivid imagery, but its effect usually works together with the moral comment.

> And *as a leke* [leek] *hadde yleye· longe in the sonne*
> So loked he with lene chekes· lourynge foule [foully scowling].

> And *as a letheren purs·* lolled [drooped] his chekes.[8]

Occasionally the imagery works *with* the moral comment in the *General Prologue* also; we have noted that the animal imagery in the portraits of the Miller, Pardoner and Summoner persuades us that we are dealing with crude or unpleasant personalities. In both kinds of usage, the imagery does not reflect moral comment so much as create it; and the contradictory ways in which it is used means that it is also working to destroy the *systematic* application of moral judgements.

The role of the narrator and the use of irony in the *Prologue* have received abundant comments,[9] but they can in this connection take on a new light. It is the narrator who himself constantly identifies with the pilgrim's point of view—and that means the point of view of his estate—and encourages us to see the world from this angle. Even when the narrator distinguishes the pilgrim's view from his own, this also, paradoxically, makes us sharply aware of the series of insights into estates consciousness that we are given, and of the tension between their perspectives and our own which is implied in the 'his' of such phrases as 'his bargaynes'.

Moreover, the narrator acts as a representative for the rest of society in its relation to each estate. In this role, he shows us how often the rest of society is not allowed to go beyond the professional façade, to know what is the truth, or to apply any absolute values to professional behaviour. We are in a world of 'experts', where the moral views of the layman become irrelevant. The narrator assumes that each pilgrim is an expert, and presents him in his own terms, according to his own values, in his own language. All excellence becomes 'tricks of the trade'—and this applies to the Parson's virtues as well as to the Miller's thefts. In the *Prologue* we are in a world of

---

8. *Piers Plowman*, ed. W. W. Skeat, 2 vols. (London, 1886; rpt 1961), B-text, V 82–3 and 192. Even with Langland, this is not always true; the Doctor of Divinity who is as 'rody as a rose' is a case in point (XIII 99).

9. See especially E. T. Donaldson's article, 'Chaucer the Pilgrim', reprinted in *Speaking of Chaucer* (London, 1970), pp. 1–12. [See below, pp. 484–92.]

means rather than ends.[1] A large part of the narrator's criteria for judging people then becomes their success in social relationships at a *personal* level; they are judged on pleasantness of appearance, charm of manner, social accomplishments. Their social role is reduced to a question of sociability.

These criteria are of course ironically adopted, and we must therefore ask what is the significance of Chaucer's use of irony in the *Prologue*. We can take as starting-point the definition of irony offered by the thirteenth-century rhetorician Buoncompagno de Signa:

> Yronia enim est plana et demulcens verborum positio cum indignatione animi et subsannatione . . . Ceterum vix aliquis adeo fatuus reperitur qui non intelligat si de eo quod non est conlaudetur. Nam si commendares Ethyopem de albedine, latronem de custodia, luxuriosum de castitate, de facili gressu claudum, cecum de visu, pauperem de divitiis, et servum de libertate, stuperent inenarrabili dolore laudati, immo vituperati, quia nil aliud est vituperium quam alicuius malefacta per contrarium commendare vel iocose narrare.[2]

> Irony is the bland and sweet use of words to convey disdain and ridicule . . . Hardly anyone can be found who is so foolish that he does not understand if he is praised for what he is not. For if you should praise the Ethiopian for his whiteness, the thief for his guardianship, the lecher for his chastity, the lame for his agility, the blind for his sight, the pauper for his riches, and the slave for his liberty, they would

1. The concentration on means rather than ends has been held by sociologists to be characteristic of the social ethic of societies dominated by economic markets, and particularly of capitalism. See Max Weber, *Economy and Society* (trans. G. Roth and C. Wittich, 3 vols., New York, 1968), especially vol. 3, p. 1188: 'under capitalism . . . a person can practice *caritas* and brotherhood only outside his vocational life'. The ideology of capitalism has taken as its starting-point the division of labour, and implicitly assumed that the sum of each group's activities will be the social good. Therefore it has not considered it necessary to analyse the nature of this good or the way in which it was to be achieved. This raises the question of whether Chaucer felt the need to alter estates literature in order to express his consciousness that market relationships were assuming a new importance in his society, although the ironic tone which characterises the *Prologue* suggests that Chaucer is not *encouraging* the adoption of a capitalist ethic. Similar social characteristics have been especially associated with the city in a classic article by Louis Wirth (*American Journal of Sociology*, 34 (1938), 1–24):

> Our acquaintances [in the city] tend to stand in a relationship of utility to us in the sense that the role which each one plays in our life is overwhelmingly regarded as a means for the achievement of our own ends . . . The segmental character and utilitarian accent of interpersonal relations in the city find their institutional expression in the proliferation of specialized tasks which we see in

their most developed form in the professions. The operations of the pecuniary nexus lead to predatory relationships, which tend to obstruct the efficient functioning of the social order unless checked by professional codes and occupational etiquette.

Some further comments of Wirth's on the city also have striking resemblances with the world conjured up by the *General Prologue*:

> The city . . . tends to resemble a mosaic of social worlds in which the transition from one to the other is abrupt. The juxtaposition of divergent personalities and modes of life tends to produce a relativistic perspective and a sense of toleration of difference.

Chaucer may equally well, therefore, be recording a response to the kind of social relationships which were increasingly dominating the growing city of London. In some ways, the ethic of city life and the market ethic are indistinguishable—but the attempt to distinguish which of them is likely to have had most influence on Chaucer, and what contemporary events might most clearly have focussed for him a change in social consciousness, are questions I should like to pursue elsewhere.

2. Quoted by J. F. Benton, 'Clio and Venus: An Historical View of Medieval Love' in F. X. Newman (ed.), *The Meaning of Courtly Love* (New York, 1968), p. 37. The quotation is taken from Buoncompagno's *Rhetorica Antiqua* which was written about 1215.

be struck dumb with inexpressible grief to have been praised, but really vituperated, for it is nothing but vituperation to commend the evil deeds of someone through their opposite, or to relate them wittily. (trans. after Benton, pp. 28–9)

This definition is a useful starting-point, precisely because it does *not* fit Chaucer's habitual use of irony. For what he does so often is to commend the lecher, not for chastity, but for lechery—to enthuse, in fact, over his being the most lecherous lecher of all.

It is true that at certain moments Chaucer seems to be praising someone 'per contrarium'; we think of the 'gentil Pardoner'. But in making his definition, Buoncompagno assumes that the truth about the person ironically described is always clear to us; we know that an Ethiopian is really black. The baffling feature of the *Prologue*, as we have seen, is how often it weakens our grasp of the truth about a character, even while suggesting that it is somehow at odds with the narrator's enthusiastic praise. We begin to wonder whether the Ethiopian was not after all born of colonial parents, and white . . .

The same characteristics of Chaucerian irony are revealed if we analyse it in terms of a modern definition. Earle Birney suggests that the concept of irony always implies the creation of the illusion that a real incongruity or conflict does not exist, and that this illusion is so shaped that the bystander may, immediately or ultimately, see through it, and be thereby surprised into a move vivid awareness of the very conflict.[3] A large part in the creation and dispersal of the illusion in this ironic process in the *Prologue* is played by the narrator and the shifting attitudes he adopts. The shift can be sharp:

> Nowher so bisy a man as he ther nas,
> And yet he semed bisier than he was. (320–1)

or it can be more subtle, as in the case with Chaucer's constant exploitation of the different semantic values of words like 'worthy', 'gentil', 'fair'. To illustrate briefly: the adjective 'worthy' is used as the keyword of the Knight's portrait, where it has a profound and serious significance, indicating not only the Knight's social status, but also the ethical qualities appropriate to it. In the Friar's portrait, the word is ironically used to indicate the Friar's lack of these ethical qualities—but it can also be read non-ironically, as a reference to social status:

> For unto swich a worthy man as he
> Acorded nat, as by his facultee,
> To have with sike lazars aqueyntaunce.
> It is nat honest, it may nat avaunce,
> For to deelen with no swich poraille. (243–7)

3. 'English Irony Before Chaucer,' *University of Toronto Quarterly* 6 (1937), 538–57.

The reference to social status seems to be the only one in the portrait of the Merchant, who 'was a worthy man with alle' (283). By the time we reach the Franklin's portrait, the word is used with a vague heartiness which seems to indicate little beside the narrator's approval: 'Was nowher swich a worthy vavasour' (360).[4] This attempt to use words with something of the different emphases and connotations that they have in conversation rather than precise and consistent meaning, produces an impression of the complexity of the characters, for it too makes it difficult to pass absolute judgement on them. The shifting meaning given to the vocabulary parallels, and indeed, helps to produce, the shifting bases from which we approach the characters. And the ambivalence reflects not merely their moral ambiguity, but also our own; the shifting semantic values we give to words reveals in us relative, not absolute, standards for judging people. The characters whose own values are absolute are described in absolute terms; the others inhabit a linguistic realm which is more applicable to our everyday unthinking acceptance of different criteria.

The irony in this word-play has a more important role than to serve as a comic cloak for moral criticism. Chaucer uses it to raise some very serious questions. For example, in the Knight's portrait, the word 'curteisie' is associated with an absolute ideal to which one may devote one's whole life (46).[5] In the literary genre of the *chanson de geste*, from which the Knight seems to have stepped, this ideal provides the whole sphere of reference for action. The Squire's 'curteisie' (99), on the other hand, is linked with other characteristics, such as his devotion to love, and his courtly accomplishments, which make it seem not so much an exacting ideal, as part of a way of life for someone who occupies a particular social station.[6] The 'curteisie' in which the Prioress 'set ful muchel hir lest' (132) should be spiritual courtesy, as we have seen, but it has become in her case embarrassingly worldly; instead of striving to please a heavenly spouse by spiritual grace, she has become the female counterpart of the type represented by the Squire. At the same time as another idealistic and religious meaning of 'curteisie' is being evoked, the concrete manifestations of 'cheere of court' (139–40)— personal adornment and accomplished manners—are shown to be in sharp opposition to it. We are left with a sense of the contradictory values implied by the term. Is it a religious value or a secular one? Is it an absolute value, or merely appropriate to a certain social class or age-group? Is the refined behaviour involved in the conception to be defined as consideration of oth-

---

4. For these senses see *Oxford English Dictionary* 2: 'Of persons: Distinguished by good qualities, entitled to honour or respect on this account; estimable', and 3: 'Of persons: Holding a prominent place in the community; of rank or standing'.
5. *Middle English Dictionary* (2)—(perhaps too narrow a definition): 'Refinement of manners; gentlemanly or courteous conduct; courtesy, politeness, etiquette'. A. C. Cawley's gloss, 'gracious and considerate conduct' is better (see his edition of the

Canterbury Tales [rev. ed., London and New York, 1958], p. 2, n. to line 46).
6. 'Curteys' in this passage is glossed as 'Respectful, deferential, meek' by *MED* (3). It is important that the Squire 'proves' his 'curteisie' through his dexterous carving; this is an action which still has connotations of service to others, but to call this 'curteis' is half-way to applying the word to the refined table-manners of the Prioress.

ers, or as ritualised manners? The different uses of the word reflect not only our shifting attitude to the characters, but also to the idea itself.

This I take to be the essence of Chaucer's satire; it does not depend on wit and verbal pyrotechnic, but on an attitude which cannot be pinned down, which is always escaping to another view of things and producing comedy from the disparateness between the two. In some cases, the disparateness is indeed that between truth and illusion:

> And over al, *ther as profit sholde arise,*
> Curteis he was, and lowely of servyse. (249–50)

> For he hadde power of confessioun,
> As *seyde hymself,* moore than a curat. (228–9)

The necessity that the illusion should be seen through, should be dispersed, explains why we have the presentation of characters who are by any standards truly admirable, the use of words like 'worthy' to indicate moral as well as purely social values, and the use of unpleasant imagery to describe characters who are also morally unpleasant.

But in other instances we are not allowed to disperse the illusion, because we have only suspicions to set against it. What 'true' appellation are we to oppose to the description of the Franklin as a 'worthy vavasour'? Do we *know* that his feasts are selfish ones from which the poor are excluded? Do we feel his pleasant appearance to be *belied* by his character? And what about the Merchant—'Ther wiste no wight that he was in dette'—and yet we do not know either that his prosperity is a hollow pretence. Or the Reeve—'Ther koude no man brynge him in arrerage'—because he was honest, or because he was skilled at covering up his fraud?

I should say that all these ambiguities, together with the 'omission of the victim' and the confusion of moral and emotional reactions, add up to Chaucer's *consistent removal of the possibility of moral judgement.* In other words, our attention is being drawn to the *illusion*; its occasional dispersal is to demonstrate that it is an illusion, but the illusion itself is made into the focal point of interest. A comment of Auerbach on the irony of the *Libro de Buen Amor* of the Archpriest Juan Ruiz enables us to express this in other terms:

> What I have in mind is not so much a conscious irony of the poet, though that too is plentiful, as a kind of objective irony implicit in the candid, untroubled coexistence of the most incompatible things.[7]

The *General Prologue* leads us to discover in ourselves the coexistence of different methods of judging people, the coexistence of different semantic values, each perfectly valid in its own context, and uses this to suggest the way in which the coexistence of the people themselves is achieved. The

---

7. E. Auerbach, *Literary Language and its Public in Late Latin Antiquity and in the Middle Ages,* trans. R. Manheim (London, 1965), p. 322.

social cohesion revealed by the *Prologue* is not the moral or religious one of Langland's ideal, but the ironic one of the 'candid, untroubled coexistence of the most incompatible things'.

It is remarkable that many of the methods through which Chaucer achieves this significance for the *Prologue* are also those through which he persuades us of the individuality of the pilgrims. Thus, important for both irony and 'characterisation' in the *Prologue* is what may be called the lack of context. In estates satire, the estates are not described in order to inform us about their work, but in order to present moral criticism; the removal of this purpose in the *Prologue* results, as Rosemary Woolf has noted,[8] in the presentation of class failings as if they were personal idiosyncrasies, and thus gives us a sense of the individuality of the figures. Similarly the lack of narrative context, which would provide an apparent motive for mentioning many items of description by giving them storial significance,[9] creates the illusion of factual reporting in the *Prologue*, which has been convincingly related to Boccaccio's use of this technique in the *Decameron*.

> Gratuituous information . . . creates wonderfully the illusion of factual reporting. What other reason could there be for volunteering such a point if not that it actually happened?[1]

And the illusion of factual reporting in turn aids the creation of irony; there is no obligation to 'place' the pilgrims on a moral scale if one is simply reporting on their existence.

Yet the fascination of the actual is not quite the same for Chaucer and Boccaccio. The aim of the *Prologue* is not to describe human beings in the same spirit as that in which Browning's Fra Lippo Lippi painted people,

> Just as they are, careless of what comes of it
> . . . and count it crime
> To let a truth slip.

In order to show the distinction, the characterisation of the pilgrims may be briefly compared with Chaucer's great achievement in *Troilus and Criseyde*: the characterisation of Criseyde.

Coghill has made a useful distinction between Chaucerian characters who are presented through description, 'the selection and adding up of outward detail into the prime number that makes a human being', and those who grow out of speech and action, such as the Host.[2] This distinction can be taken further. Pandarus is a character who grows out of speech and action, but this is almost entirely observed from the outside. We do not see very far into the workings of his mind, and his inward attitude to such an

---

8. 'Chaucer as a Satirist', 152.
9. I owe this comment to Dr L. P. Johnson of Pembroke College, Cambridge. In *Troilus and Criseyde*, Chaucer skilfully incorporates descriptions of both hero and heroine at moments when they will have storial significance; Troilus is described as he rides past Criseyde's window (II 624ff.), and his appearance strongly affects Criseyde's deliberations on her feelings towards his love. Criseyde herself is described at the moment when the affair is consummated (III 1247ff.), as an indication of the 'heaven' in which Troilus is delighting.
1. Bovill, 'The Decameron and the Canterbury Tales', 48. See also 55ff. on Chaucer.
2. *The Poet Chaucer* (2nd edition, London, 1967), pp. 89–90.

apparently important matter as his own unrequited love-affair is left unde-
fined. With Criseyde, on the other hand, we are introduced to the minute-
by-minute workings of her mind, to a complex notion of her psychological
processes, and to a character subject to the influence of *time*. This development begins at the moment when she is first acquainted with Troilus's
love for her, and deliberates on what to do. Her plea to Pandarus to stay,
when he is marching out in anger with a threat of suicide because of her
first reaction of dismay, proceeds from a whole range of motives—fear, pity,
concern for her reputation, the consciousness that she has responded cruelly
to what is, on the surface, an innocent request.[3] The significance of the
two stanzas in which these turbulent reactions are described lies in their
mixed nature. Her responses are both calculating and instinctive, selfish
and charitable. No single motive can be isolated as the 'true' one.

This is equally true of Criseyde's deliberations, when left alone, on whether
to accept Troilus's love. Troilus's high social rank, his handsomeness, his
bravery, his intelligence and virtue, his suffering on her behalf, are all
admitted as influences, and conversely, fear of unpleasantness, of betrayal,
of what people will say (II 659–65, 701–28, 771–805). Criseyde is alter-
nately overwhelmed at the honour done to her and conscious that she well
deserves it (735–49). She tries to determine coolly and rationally what will
be the best course of action, and is then swayed by a song, a nightingale
and a dream (820ff., 918ff., 925ff.). This is a situation in which the workings of Criseyde's mind tell us more about her than the actual thoughts she
entertains. We have an extraordinarily realistic presentation of the complicated responses and decisions of human beings. One further touch is worth
noting, in Book IV, Criseyde earnestly assures Troilus that the reason for
her yielding to him was neither pleasure, his high rank, nor even his bravery, but 'moral vertu, grounded upon trouthe' (1667–73). The fact that we
have seen a very different situation in Book II does not mean that Criseyde
is insincere. It is a true statement with regard to the *present*—the time
dimension not only alters the character and our view of her, it retrospectively validates her selection of one single aspect of a complex past. There
is no single 'truth' in the sphere of human motives.

There is no ambiguity or depth of character comparable to this in the
Prologue. The state of the Merchant's finances is knowable, although we
do not know it, in a way that the state of Criseyde's mind is not knowable.
There is some ambiguity of mind indicated by external devices, such as the
motto on the Prioress's brooch. But comparison with the characterisation

---

3. Ed. F. N. Robinson, *The Works of Geoffrey
Chaucer*, 2d ed. (London, 1957), II 449–62:

Criseyde, which that wel neigh starf for feere,
So as she was the ferfulleste wight
That myghte be, and herde ek with hire ere
And saugh the sorwful ernest of the knyght,
And in his preier ek saugh noon unryght,
And for the harm that myghte ek fallen moore,
She gan to rewe, and dredde hire wonder soore,

And thoughte thus: 'Unhappes fallen thikke
Alday for love, and in swych manere cas
As men ben cruel in hemself and wikke;
And if this man sle here hymself, allas!
In my presence, it wol be no solas.
What men wolde of hit deme I kan nat seye:
It nedeth me ful sleighly for to pleye.'

of Criseyde reveals even more clearly that the complexity of the *Prologue* portraits consists much more in our attitude to them than in their own characteristics. Bronson seems to be saying something like this in claiming that we are much more deeply involved with the narrator than with any of the characters in the *General Prologue*, 'for he is almost the only figure in his "drama" who is fully realised psychologically and who truly matters to us'.[4] The centre of interest in the *Prologue* is not in any depiction of human character, in actuality for its own sake; it is in our relationship with the actual, the way in which we perceive it and the attitudes we adopt to it, and the narrator stands here for the ambiguities and complexities that characterise this relationship.

If we draw together the results of this discussion, we find that the ethic we have in the *Prologue* is an ethic of this world. The constant shifting of viewpoints means that it is relativist; in creating our sense of this ethic the estates aspect is of fundamental importance, for it means that in each portrait we have the sense of a specialised way of life. A world of specialised skills, experience, terminology and interests confronts us; we see the world through the eyes of a lazy Monk or a successful Merchant, and simultaneously realise the latent tension between his view and our own. But the tension is latent, because the superficial agreement and approval offered in the ironic comment has this amount of reality—it really reflects the way in which we get on with our neighbours, by tacit approval of the things we really consider wrong, by admiring techniques more than the ends they work towards, by regarding unethical behaviour as amusing as long as the results are not directly unpleasant for us, by adopting, for social reasons, the viewpoint of the person with whom we are associating, and at the same time feeling that his way of life is 'not our business'.

To say that the *General Prologue* is based on an ethic of this world is not to adopt the older critical position that Chaucer is unconcerned with morality. The adoption of this ethic at this particular point does not constitute a definitive attitude but a piece of observation—and the comic irony ensures that the reader does not identify with this ethic. Chaucer's inquiry is epistemological as well as moral. This is how the world operates, and as the world, it can operate no other way. The contrast with heavenly values is made at the end of the *Canterbury Tales*, as critics have noted,[5] but it is made in such a way that it cannot affect the validity of the initial statement—the world can only operate by the world's values. One's confidence in seeing this as the movement of the *Canterbury Tales* is increased by the observation that this parallels the movement in *Troilus and Criseyde*: consistent irony throughout the poem, the coexistence of incompatible things, the sharp demonstration of their incompatibility in the Epilogue and yet the tragic consciousness that their coexistence—indeed in the case of *Troilus* their unity—is as inevitable as their incompatibility. And yet the differ-

---

4. *In Search of Chaucer* (Toronto, 1960), p. 67.
5. See R. Baldwin, *The Unity of the Canterbury Tales* (Copenhagen, 1955), Chapters 5–7, and A.

W. Hoffman, 'Chaucer's Prologue to Pilgrimage: The Two Voices' [reprinted above, pp. 459–71].

ences between the two works are significant. The narrator in the *Troilus* is led by the conclusion of his story to reject his own—and our—experience of the beauty and nobility of what has gone before. Although we do not accept his Epilogue as the *only* valid response to the experience of the *Troilus*, this emotional rejection plays a large part in establishing the tragic finality of the work. The *Canterbury Tales* do not have the same sort of finality. The 'final statement' in the *Tales* comes not from the narrator, but from the Parson, who has not participated as we have in the worlds of the other pilgrims. In rejecting the world of the Miller, for example, he is not rejecting something for which he has felt personal enthusiasm—such as the narrator of the *Troilus* feels at the consummation of the love-affair. And *because* the final statement is given to the Parson, the narrator of the *Canterbury Tales* remains an observer who can sympathetically adapt to or report a whole range of experiences and attitudes to them. The relation between the *General Prologue* and the Parson's Tale is more subtle than a simple opposition between *cupiditas* and *caritas*.[6]

The *Prologue* presents the world in terms of worldly values, which are largely concerned with an assessment of façades, made in the light of half-knowledge, and on the basis of subjective criteria. Subjectivity characterises both the pilgrims' attitude to the world, and the world's (or the reader's) attitude to the pilgrims. But at least in their case, it must be repeated that their views on the world are not individual ones, but are attached to their callings—in medieval terms, their estates. The *Prologue* proves to be a poem about work. The society it evokes is not a collection of individuals or types with an eternal or universal significance, but particularly a society in which work as a social experience conditions personality and the standpoint from which an individual views the world. In the *Prologue*, as in history, it is specialised work which ushers in a world where relativised values and the individual consciousness are dominant.

---

6. These are Hoffman's terms. Hoffman's conception of the opposition between worldly and religious values is limited to the sphere of love. It seems to me that this is due to an interpretation of the spring-opening itself as particularly appropriate to love-poetry. It may therefore be worth noting that a spring-opening is found in all sorts of medieval poems: estates works, battle-poems and satires all begin this way. See, for example, 'Quant vei lo temps renovellar,' ed. T. Wright, *The Political Songs of England from the Reign of John to that of Edward II* (London, 1839, p. 3, and 'Serpserat Angligenam rabies quadrangula gentem,' *ibid.*, p. 19, a poem on the taking of Lincoln which begins with a lyrical spring description tending to the conclusion that in spring a Frenchman's fancy lightly turns to thoughts of war. Among satiric works, see the *Apocalipsis Goliae* (ed. K. Strecker [Rome, 1928]), the *Metamorphosis Goliae* (ed. Huygens, *Studi medievali*, Ser. 3, III (1962), 765), the debates 'Dum Saturno conjuge' (ed. T. Wright, *The Latin Poems Commonly Attributed to Walter Mapes* [London, 1841], pp. 237ff.) and 'Hora nona sabbati' (*Notices et Extraits des manuscrits de la Bibliothèque Nationale, et autres bibliothèques* 32, I pp. 289ff.), the *Vox Clamantis* and *Piers Plowman*. One might even ask whether the opening of the *Metamorphosis Goliae*—'Sole post Arietem Taurum subintrante'—is echoed in Chaucer's opening in the season when the sun 'Hath in the Ram his halve cours yronne.' The spring description is sometimes burlesqued in satire, but not necessarily for its associations with love: see Nigel de Longchamps, *Speculum Stultorum*, ed. J. H. Mozley and R. R. Raymo (Berkeley, 1960), 449ff., and 'Or vint la tens de May, que ce ros panirra,' ed. Wright, *Political Songs*, pp. 63ff. (R. Baldwin discusses the tradition of the spring-opening (*Unity of the Canterbury Tales*, pp. 21ff.), and comments that 'even the satirist' uses it, but does not follow up this remark.)

E. TALBOT DONALDSON

Chaucer the Pilgrim †

Verisimilitude in a work of fiction is not without its attendant dangers, the chief of which is that the responses it stimulates in the reader may be those appropriate not so much to an imaginative production as to an historical one or to a piece of reporting. History and reporting are, of course, honourable in themselves, but if we react to a poet as though he were an historian or a reporter, we do him somewhat less than justice. I am under the impression that many readers, too much influenced by Chaucer's brilliant verisimilitude, tend to regard his famous pilgrimage to Canterbury as significant not because it is a great fiction, but because it seems to be a remarkable record of a fourteenth-century pilgrimage. A remarkable record it may be, but if we treat it too narrowly as such there are going to be certain casualties among the elements that make up the fiction. Perhaps first among these elements is the fictional reporter, Chaucer the pilgrim, and the role he plays in the Prologue to the *Canterbury Tales* and in the links between them. I think it time that he was rescued from the comparatively dull record of history and put back into his poem. He is not really Chaucer the poet— nor, for that matter, is either the poet, or the poem's protagonist, that Geoffrey Chaucer frequently mentioned in contemporary historical records as a distinguished civil servant, but never as a poet. The fact that these are three separate entities does not, naturally, exclude the probability—or rather the certainty—that they bore a close resemblance to one another, and that, indeed, they frequently got together in the same body. But that does not excuse us from keeping them distinct from one another, difficult as their close resemblance makes our task.

The natural tendency to confuse one thing with its like is perhaps best represented by a school of Chaucerian criticism, now outmoded, that pictured a single Chaucer under the guise of a wide-eyed, jolly, rolypoly little man who, on fine Spring mornings, used to get up early, while the dew was still on the grass, and go look at daisies. A charming portrait, this, so charming, indeed, that it was sometimes able to maintain itself to the exclusion of any Chaucerian other side. It has every reason to be charming, since it was lifted almost *in toto* from the version Chaucer gives of himself in the Prologue to the *Legend of Good Women*, though I imagine it owes some of its popularity to a rough analogy with Wordsworth—a sort of *Legend of Good Poets*. It was this version of Chaucer that Kittredge, in a page of great importance to Chaucer criticism, demolished with his assertion that 'a naïf Collector of Customs would be a paradoxical monster'. He might well have added that a naïve creator of old January would be even more monstrous.

Kittredge's pronouncement cleared the air, and most of us now accept

† Reprinted by permission of the Modern Language Association from *Speaking of Chaucer* (New York: W. W. Norton, 1970) 1–12. Donaldson's essay originally appeared in *PMLA* 69 (1954): 928–36.

the proposition that Chaucer was sophisticated as readily as we do the proposition that the whale is a mammal. But unhappily, now that we've got rid of the naïve fiction, it is easy to fall into the opposite sort of mistake. This is to envision, in the *Canterbury Tales*, a highly urbane, literal-historical Chaucer setting out from Southwark on a specific day of a specific year (we even argue somewhat acrimoniously about dates and routes), in company with a group of persons who existed in real life and whom Chaucer, his reporter's eye peeled for every idiosyncrasy, determined to get down on paper—down, that is, to the last wart—so that books might be written identifying them. Whenever this accurate reporter says something especially fatuous—which is not infrequently—it is either ascribed to an opinion peculiar to the Middle Ages (sometimes very peculiar), or else Chaucer's tongue is said to be in his cheek.

Now a Chaucer with tongue-in-cheek is a vast improvement over a simple-minded Chaucer when one is trying to define the whole man, but it must lead to a loss of critical perception, and in particular to a confused notion of Chaucerian irony, to see in the Prologue a reporter who is acutely aware of the significance of what he sees but who sometimes, for ironic emphasis, interprets the evidence presented by his observation in a fashion directly contrary to what we expect. The proposition ought to be expressed in reverse: the reporter is, usually, acutely unaware of the significance of what he sees, no matter how sharply he sees it. He is, to be sure, permitted his lucid intervals, but in general he is the victim of the poet's pervasive—not merely sporadic—irony. And as such he is also the chief agent by which the poet achieves his wonderfully complex, ironic, comic, serious vision of a world which is but a devious and confused, infinitely various pilgrimage to a certain shrine. It is, as I hope to make clear, a good deal more than merely fitting that our guide on such a pilgrimage should be a man of such naïveté as the Chaucer who tells the tale of *Sir Thopas*. Let us accompany him a little distance.

It is often remarked that Chaucer really liked the Prioress very much, even though he satirized her gently—very gently. But this is an understatement: Chaucer the pilgrim may not be said merely to have liked the Prioress very much—he thought she was utterly charming. In the first twenty-odd lines of her portrait (A118 ff.) he employs, among other superlatives, the adverb *ful* seven times. Middle English uses *ful* where we use *very*, and if one translates the beginning of the portrait into a kind of basic English (which is what, in a way, it really is), one gets something like this: 'There was also a Nun, a Prioress, who was very sincere and modest in the way she smiled; her biggest oath was only "By saint Loy"; and she was called Madame Eglantine. She sang the divine service very well, intoning it in her nose very prettily, and she spoke French very nicely and elegantly'—and so on, down to the last gasp of sentimental appreciation. Indeed, the Prioress may be said to have transformed the rhetoric into something not unlike that of a very bright kindergarten child's descriptive theme. In his reaction to the

Prioress Chaucer the pilgrim resembles another—if less—simple-hearted enthusiast: the Host, whose summons to her to tell a tale must be one of the politest speeches in the language. Not 'My lady Prioresse, a tale now!' but, 'as curteisly as it hadde been a maide',

> My lady Prioresse, by youre leve,
> So that I wiste I sholde you nat greve,
> I wolde deemen that ye telle sholde
> A tale next, if so were that ye wolde.
> Now wol ye vouche sauf, my lady dere? (B² 1636–41)
> [Prioress's Tale 13–17]

Where the Prioress reduced Chaucer to superlatives, she reduces the Host to subjunctives.

There is no need here to go deeply into the Prioress. Eileen Power's illustrations from contemporary episcopal records show with what extraordinary economy the portrait has been packed with abuses typical of fourteenth-century nuns. The abuses, to be sure, are mostly petty, but it is clear enough that the Prioress, while a perfect lady, is anything but a perfect nun; and attempts to whitewash her, of which there have been many, can only proceed from an innocence of heart equal to Chaucer the pilgrim's and undoubtedly directly influenced by it. For he, of course, is quite swept away by her irrelevant *sensibilité*, and as a result misses much of the point of what he sees. No doubt he feels that he has come a long way, socially speaking, since his encounter with the Black Knight in the forest, and he knows, or thinks he knows, a little more of what it's all about: in this case it seems to be mostly about good manners, kindness to animals, and female charm. Thus it has been argued that Chaucer's appreciation for the Prioress as a sort of heroine of courtly romance *manquée* actually reflects the sophistication of the living Chaucer, an urbane man who cared little whether amiable nuns were good nuns. But it seems a curious form of sophistication that permits itself to babble superlatives; and indeed, if this is sophistication, it is the kind generally seen in the least experienced people—one that reflects a wide-eyed wonder at the glamour of the great world. It is just what one might expect of a bourgeois exposed to the splendours of high society, whose values, such as they are, he eagerly accepts. And that is precisely what Chaucer the pilgrim is, and what he does.

If the Prioress's appeal to him is through elegant femininity, the Monk's is through imposing virility. Of this formidable and important prelate the pilgrim does not say, with Placebo,

> I woot wel that my lord can more than I:
> What that he saith, I holde it ferm and stable, (E1498–9)

but he acts Placebo's part to perfection. He is as impressed with the Monk as the Monk is, and accepts him on his own terms and at face value, never sensing that those terms imply complete condemnation of Monk *qua* Monk. The Host is also impressed by the Monk's virility, but having no sense of

Placebonian propriety (he is himself a most virile man) he makes indecent jokes about it. This, naturally, offends the pilgrim's sense of decorum: there is a note of deferential commiseration in his comment, 'This worthy Monk took al in pacience' (B3155). Inevitably when the Monk establishes hunting as the highest activity of which religious man is capable, 'I saide his opinion was good' (A183). As one of the pilgrim's spiritual heirs was later to say, Very like a whale: but not of course, like a fish out of water.

Wholehearted approval for the values that important persons subscribe to is seen again in the portrait of the Friar. This amounts to a prolonged gratulation for the efficiency the deplorable Hubert shows in undermining the fabric of the Church by turning St Francis's ideal inside out:

> Ful swetely herde he confessioun
> And plesant was his absolucioun.
>
> For unto swich a worthy man as he
> Accorded nat, as by his facultee,
> To have with sike lazars aquaintaunce. (A221–2, 243–5)

It is sometimes said that Chaucer did not like the Friar. Whether Chaucer the man would have liked such a Friar is, for our present purposes, irrelevant. But if the pilgrim does not unequivocally express his liking for him, it is only because in his humility he does not feel that, with important people, his own likes and dislikes are material: such importance is its own reward, and can gain no lustre from Geoffrey, who, when the Friar is attacked by the Summoner, is ready to show him the same sympathy he shows the Monk (see D1265–67) [Friar's Prologue 1–3].

Once he has finished describing the really important people on the pilgrimage the pilgrim's tone changes, for he can now concern himself with the bourgeoisie, members of his own class for whom he does not have to show such profound respect. Indeed, he can even afford to be a little patronizing at times, and have his little joke at the expense of the too-busy lawyer. But such indirect assertions of his own superiority do not prevent him from giving substance to the old cynicism that the only motive recognized by the middle class is the profit motive, for his interest and admiration for the bourgeois pilgrims is centred mainly in their material prosperity and their ability to increase it. He starts, properly enough, with the out-and-out moneygrubber, the Merchant, and after turning aside for that *lusus naturae*, the non-profit-motivated Clerk, proceeds to the Lawyer, who, despite the pilgrim's little joke, is the best and best-paid ever; the Franklin, twenty-one admiring lines on appetite, so expensively catered to; the Gildsmen, cheered up the social ladder, 'For catel hadde they ynough and rente' (A373); and the Physician, again the best and richest. In this series the portrait of the Clerk is generally held to be an ideal one, containing no irony; but while it is ideal, it seems to reflect the pilgrim's sense of values in his joke about the Clerk's failure to make money: is not this still typical of the half-patronizing, half-admiring *un*understanding that practical men of business display towards academics? But in any case the portrait is a fine companion-piece for those in which material prosperity is the main interest both of the characters described and of the describer.

Of course, this is not the sole interest of so gregarious—if shy—a person as Chaucer the pilgrim. Many of the characters have the additional advantage of being good companions, a faculty that receives a high valuation in the Prologue. To be good company might, indeed, atone for certain serious defects of character. Thus the Shipman, whose callous cruelty is duly noted, seems fairly well redeemed in the assertion, 'And certainly he was a good felawe' (A395). At this point an uneasy sensation that even tongue-in-cheek irony will not compensate for the lengths to which Chaucer is going in his approbation of this sinister seafarer sometimes causes editors to note that *a good felawe* means 'a rascal'. But I can find no evidence that it ever meant a rascal. Of course, all tritely approbative expressions enter easily into ironic connotation, but the phrase *means* a good companion, which is just what Chaucer means. And if, as he says of the Shipman, 'Of nice conscience took he no keep' (A398), Chaucer the pilgrim was doing the same with respect to him.

Nothing that has been said has been meant to imply that the pilgrim was unable to recognise, and deplore, a rascal when he saw one. He could, provided the rascality was situated in a member of the lower classes and provided it was, in any case, somewhat wider than a barn door: Miller, Manciple, Reeve, Summoner, and Pardoner are all acknowledged to be rascals. But rascality generally has, after all, the laudable object of making money, which gives it a kind of validity, if not dignity. These portraits, while in them the pilgrim, prioress-like conscious of the finer aspects of life, does deplore such matters as the Miller's indelicacy of language, contain a note of ungrudging admiration for efficient thievery. It is perhaps fortunate for the pilgrim's reputation as a judge of men that he sees through the Pardoner, since it is the Pardoner's particular tragedy that, except in Church, every one can see through him at a glance; but in Church he remains to the pilgrim 'a noble ecclesiaste' (A708). The equally repellent Summoner, a practising bawd, is partially redeemed by his also being a good fellow, 'a gentil harlot and a kinde' (A647), and by the fact that for a moderate bribe he will neglect to summon: the pilgrim apparently subscribes to the popular definition of the best policeman as the one who acts the least policely.

Therefore Chaucer is tolerant, and has his little joke about the Summoner's small Latin—a very small joke, though one of the most amusing aspects of the pilgrim's character is the pleasure he takes in his own jokes, however small. But the Summoner goes too far when he cynically suggests that purse is the Archdeacon's hell, causing Chaucer to respond with a fine show of righteous respect for the instruments of spiritual punishment. The only trouble is that his enthusiastic defence of them carries *him* too far, so that after having warned us that excommunication will indeed damn our souls—

But wel I woot he lied right in deede:
Of cursing oughte eech gilty man him drede,
For curs wol slee right as assoiling savith— (A659–61)

he goes on to remind us that it will also cause considerable inconvenience
to our bodies: 'And also war him of a *Significavit*' (A662). Since a *Significavit* is the writ accomplishing the imprisonment of the excommunicate,
the line provides perhaps the neatest—and most misunderstood—Chaucer-
ian anticlimax in the Prologue.

I have avoided mentioning, hitherto, the pilgrim's reactions to the really
good people on the journey—the Knight, the Parson, the Plowman. One
might reasonably ask how his uncertain sense of values may be reconciled
with the enthusiasm he shows for their rigorous integrity. The question
could, of course, be shrugged off with a remark on the irrelevance to art of
exact consistency, even to art distinguished by its verisimilitude. But I am
not sure that there is any basic inconsistency. It is the nature of the pilgrim
to admire all kinds of superlatives, and the fact that he often admires superlatives devoid of—or opposed to—genuine virtue does not inhibit his equal
admiration for virtue incarnate. He is not, after all, a bad man; he is, to
place him in his literary tradition, merely an average man, or mankind:
homo, not very *sapiens* to be sure, but with the very best intentions, making
his pilgrimage through the world in search of what is good, and showing
himself, too frequently, able to recognize the good only when it is spectac-
ularly so. Spenser's Una glows with a kind of spontaneous incandescence,
so that the Red Cross Knight, mankind in search of holiness, knows her as
good; but he thinks that Duessa is good, too. Virtue concretely embodied
in Una or the Parson presents no problems to the well-intentioned observer,
but in a world consisting mostly of imperfections, accurate evaluations are
difficult for a pilgrim who, like mankind, is naïve. The pilgrim's ready
appreciation for the virtuous characters is perhaps the greatest tribute that
could be paid to their virtue, and their spiritual simplicity is, I think, enhanced
by the intellectual simplicity of the reporter.

The pilgrim belongs, of course, to a very old—and very new—tradition
of the fallible first person singular. His most exact modern counterpart is
perhaps Lemuel Gulliver who, in his search for the good, failed dismally
to perceive the difference between the pursuit of reason and the pursuits of
reasonable horses: one may be sure that the pilgrim would have whinnied
with the best of them. In his own century he is related to Long Will of *Piers
Plowman*, a more explicit seeker after the good, but just as unswerving in
his inability correctly to evaluate what he sees. Another kinsman is the
protagonist of the *Pearl*, mankind whose heart is set on a transitory good
that has been lost—who, for very natural reasons, confuses earthly with
spiritual values. Not entirely unrelated is the protagonist of Gower's *Confessio Amantis*, an old man seeking for an impossible earthly love that seems
to him the only good. And in more subtle fashion there is the teller of

Chaucer's story of *Troilus and Criseide*, who, while not a true protagonist, performs some of the same functions. For this unloved 'servant of the servants of love' falls in love with Criseide so persuasively that almost every male reader of the poem imitates him, so that we all share the heartbreak of Troilus and sometimes, in the intensity of our heartbreak, fail to learn what Troilus did. Finally, of course, there is Dante of the *Divine Comedy*, the most exalted member of the family and perhaps the immediate original of these other first-person pilgrims.

Artistically the device of the *persona* has many functions, so integrated with one another that to try to sort them out produces both over-simplification and distortion. The most obvious, with which this paper has been dealing—distortedly, is to present a vision of the social world imposed on one of the moral world. Despite their verisimilitude most, if not all, of the characters described in the Prologue are taken directly from stock and recur again and again in medieval literature. Langland in his own Prologue and elsewhere depicts many of them: the hunting monk, the avaricious friar, the thieving miller, the hypocritical pardoner, the unjust stewards, even, in little, the all-too-human nun. But while Langland uses the device of the *persona* with considerable skill in the conduct of his allegory, he uses it hardly at all in portraying the inhabitants of the social world: these are described directly, with the poet's own voice. It was left to Chaucer to turn the ancient stock satirical characters into real people assembled for a pilgrimage, and to have them described, with all their traditional faults upon them, by another pilgrim who records faithfully each fault without, for the most part, recognizing that it is a fault and frequently felicitating its possessor for possessing it. One result—though not the only result—is a moral realism much more significant than the literary realism which is a part of it and for which it is sometimes mistaken; this moral realism discloses a world in which humanity is prevented by its own myopia, the myopia of the describer, from seeing what the dazzlingly attractive externals of life really represent. In most of the analogues mentioned above the fallible first person receives, at the end of the book, the education he has needed: the pilgrim arrives somewhere. Chaucer never completed the *Canterbury Tales*, but in the Prologue to the Parson's Tale he seems to have been doing, rather hastily, what his contemporaries had done: when, with the sun nine-and-twenty degrees from the horizon, the twenty-nine pilgrims come to a certain—unnamed—*thropes ende* (I12), then the pilgrimage seems no longer to have Canterbury as its destination, but rather, I suspect, the Celestial City of which the Parson speaks.

If one insists that Chaucer was not a moralist but a comic writer (a distinction without a difference), then the device of the *persona* may be taken primarily as serving comedy. It has been said earlier that the several Chaucers must have inhabited one body, and in that sense the fictional first person is no fiction at all. In an oral tradition of literature the first person probably always shared the personality of his creator: thus Dante of the *Divine Comedy* was physically Dante the Florentine; the John Gower of the

Confessio was also Chaucer's friend John Gower; and Long Will was, I am sure, some one named William Langland, who was both long and wilful. And it is equally certain that Chaucer the pilgrim, 'a popet in an arm t'en-brace' (B1891), was in every physical respect Chaucer the man, whom one can imagine reading his work to a courtly audience, as in the portrait appearing in one of the MSS of *Troilus*. One can imagine also the delight of the audience which heard the Prologue read in this way, and which was aware of the similarities and dissimilarities between Chaucer, the man before them, and Chaucer the pilgrim, both of whom they could see with simul-taneous vision. The Chaucer they knew was physically, one gathers, a little ludicrous; a bourgeois, but one who was known as a practical and successful man of the court; possessed perhaps of a certain diffidence of manner, reserved, deferential to the socially imposing persons with whom he was associated; a bit absent-minded, but affable and, one supposes, very good company—a good fellow; sagacious and highly perceptive. This Chaucer was telling them of another who, lacking some of his chief qualities, never-theless possessed many of his characteristics, though in a different state of balance, and each one probably distorted just enough to become laughable without becoming unrecognizable: deference into a kind of snobbishness, affability into an over-readiness to please, practicality into Babbittry, per-ception into inspection, absence of mind into dimness of wit; a Chaucer acting in some respects just as Chaucer himself might have acted but unlike his creator the kind of man, withal, who could mistake a group of stock satirical types for living persons endowed with all sorts of superlative quali-ties. The constant interplay of these two Chaucers must have produced an exquisite and most ingratiating humour—as, to be sure, it still does. This comedy reaches its superb climax when Chaucer the pilgrim, resembling in so many ways Chaucer the poet, can answer the Host's demand for a story only with a rhyme he 'lerned longe agoon' (B1899)—*Sir Thopas*, which bears the same complex relation to the kind of romance it satirizes and to Chaucer's own poetry as Chaucer the pilgrim does to the pilgrims he describes and to Chaucer the poet.

Earlier in this paper I proved myself no gentleman (though I hope a scholar) by being rude to the Prioress, and hence to the many who like her and think that Chaucer liked her too. It is now necessary to retract. Undoubtedly Chaucer the man would, like his fictional representative, have found her charming and looked on her with affection. To have got on so well in so changeable a world Chaucer must have got on well with the people in it, and it is doubtful that one may get on with people merely by pretending to like them: one's heart has to be in it. But the third entity, Chaucer the poet, operates in a realm which is above and subsumes those in which Chaucer the man and Chaucer the pilgrim have their being. In this realm prioresses may be simultaneously evaluated as marvellously ami-able ladies and as prioresses. In his poem the poet arranges for the moralist to define austerely what ought to be and for his fictional representative—who, as the representative of all mankind, is no mere fiction—to go on affirming affectionately what is. The two points of view, in strict moral logic diametrically opposed, are somehow made harmonious in Chaucer's wonderfully comic attitude, that double vision that is his ironical essence. The mere critic performs his etymological function by taking the Prioress apart and clumsily separating her good parts from her bad; but the poet's function is to build her incongruous and inharmonious parts into an inseparable whole which is infinitely greater than its parts. In this complex structure both the latent moralist and the naïve reporter have important positions, but I am not persuaded that in every case it is possible to determine which of them has the last word.[1]

DONALD R. HOWARD

Chaucer the Man †

So much study has gone into the rhetorical workings of Chaucer's satire that almost anyone who reads Chaucer is now acutely aware of the persona or narrator in each poem. The fact of a disparity between the narrator and Chaucer himself has become a kind of premise or dogma of Chaucer criticism; we have become accustomed to phrases like "the fictional Chaucer," "the postures of the narrator," or "the finiteness of the narrator-role." And yet because his major poems confer upon him the status of a major figure, we continue to be interested in Chaucer the man despite the prevailing formalism of Chaucer criticism. We read minor works by him for which, were they anonymous, we should not take the trouble to turn a page. We talk about his education, thought, "development," "mind." And in his best poems we *feel* him as a "man speaking to men." As for the man himself, we have a few records, though none of these really proves that civil servant and poet were the same person. Mostly, we believe in him. Of course it is entirely possible that someone will come along and argue that the *Canterbury Tales* were an instance of group authorship, or were really written by John of Gaunt; but if someone did, we should all pooh-pooh him and ostracize him and direct plenty of irony at him.

My theme is that this man, whom we feel that we know, is a real and living presence in his works, and that his presence in them is what makes them interesting and good. I present this not as a corollary of any humanistic or existential principles, but as a fact. I say that we are interested in the fictive narrator, the rhetorical workings of the irony, the method of creating illusion and reality—all the "devices" of his high art—not because they are

1. Books referred to or cited in this paper are G. L. Kittredge, *Chaucer and His Poetry* (Cambridge, Mass., 1915), p. 45; Eileen Power, *Medieval People* (London, 1924), pp. 59–84. Robinson's note to A650 records the opinion that *a good felawe* means a 'rascal'. The medieval reader's expectation that the first person in a work of fiction would represent mankind generally and at the same time would physically resemble the author is commented on by Leo Spitzer in an interesting note in *Traditio*, iv. (1946), 414–22.

† Reprinted by permission of the Modern Language Association of America from *PMLA* 80 (1965): 337–43.

devices, but because everywhere *in* and *behind* them lies Chaucer the man. I will even go a step further: I say that this is the point which various analyses of "narrator" and "persona" have really proved.

It was, to begin with, the point of Professor Donaldson's famous article: he was attempting to show how Chaucer the poet masks himself behind the comic figure of Chaucer the pilgrim in order more effectively to say what he has to say [1] Professor Bronson's objection is that this is not a matter of the rhetoric of fiction, but a result of oral delivery—that it is a perfectly natural manner of ironic conversation. [2] The disagreement, it seems to me, is a kind of pseudo-problem. [3] Any such device, conversational or literary, is a matter of rhetoric and can be analyzed by distinguishing between the author and his projected persona. That the persona is wholly a fictive character—a "puppet"—with no element of the author's own character in it, is something which I think few would maintain. Is it not, after all, a matter of degree? Does not the writer project some element of himself into any character? Do we not all present ourselves in various roles to various people—even to ourselves? And can anyone know his "real" self well enough to present *or* conceal it? To borrow a phrase from Patrick Cruttwell, [4] the writer is by necessity an exhibitionist, and so presents something of himself in everything he writes. He may choose to do so by fragmenting himself behind various masks, but he does not, and cannot, make himself disappear. However we analyze his presence in his works, we are therefore all of us—myself, Professor Bronson, Professor Donaldson, and many another— "in search of Chaucer."

This search for an author on the part of his readers is a cultural phenomenon of some interest. We could say that the reader's curiosity is piqued by the self-projection of the author, and the more so if the author attempts a masked presentation of himself. But this is not quite the whole story, since authors would perhaps avoid more than a very elementary, or naive, self-presentation if they were not able to anticipate curiosity on the part of readers. Readers have, that is, a "sense of the author." Authors may encourage it, but they did not necessarily invent it. Simple and natural as it seems, it has not always been so important as it is in modern times. Indeed, our curiosity about the *private* life of the author—our desire to read his letters and know hidden facts about him—does not appear to have come into being until the eighteenth century; it begins, probably, with Boswell. [5] Before the eighteenth century, except perhaps in vituperative public controversies, the reader's curiosity was satisfied by what the writer *said* about himself. No one seems to have wondered, until quite recent times, whether or not (for

1. E. Talbot Donaldson, "Chaucer the Pilgrim," *PMLA*, LXIX (1954), 928–936. [See above, pp. 484–92.]
2. Bertrand H. Bronson, *In Search of Chaucer* (Toronto, 1960), pp. 25–32.
3. Cf. Robert M. Jordan, "Chaucer's Sense of Illusion: Roadside Drama Reconsidered," *ELH*, XXIX

(1962), 19–33.
4. "Makers and Persons," *Hudson Review*, XII (1959–60), 487–507. The idea is developed by Wayne C. Booth, *The Rhetoric of Fiction* (Chicago, 1961), esp. pp. 16–20, 67–77, 396–398.
5. Cruttwell, pp. 497–500.

example) Sir Philip Sidney really *did* look into his heart and write, just as no one tried to shed any light on the Dark Lady.

In the earlier Middle Ages, the sense of the author, the mention of his name, and the expression of his pride in his achievement were not entirely absent. But they were counterbalanced by frequent anonymity and by warnings against pride and worldly vanity. Moreover, the poet's name was sometimes mentioned only to ask forgiveness for shortcomings and request the prayers of readers;[6] Chaucer's "Retraction" would be an instance of the latter convention. It is only in the twelfth century that we begin to find open pride in authorship. Poets begin then to argue that true nobility springs from the individual intellect, and that letters are equal to arms as a means of conferring nobility.[7] By the time of the Italian Renaissance, the argument is carried further: poets begin to claim not merely a kind of nobility from what they write, but the power to confer fame upon others and the expectation of an earthly immortality through reputation.[8] In Chaucer we can find something like this Renaissance interest in fame, but it is very much more sparing than the extravagant claims of the humanists. *The House of Fame* shows Chaucer, quite early in his career, thinking about the problem of fame. Still, what does *The House of Fame* teach but the old medieval lesson that good or bad fame is often conferred unjustly in this transitory world? The envoy of the *Troilus* is a better place to look for Chaucer's hope of an earthly immortality:

> Go, litel bok, go, litel myn tragedye,
> Ther God thi makere yet, er that he dye,
> So sende myght to make in som comedye!
> But litel book, no makyng thow n'envie,
> But subgit be to alle poesye;
> And kis the steppes, where as thow seest pace
> Virgile, Ovide, Omer, Lucan, and Stace.
>
> (v. 1786–92)

Still, while the poet puts himself in very noble company, the passage is, in form at least, a conventional protestation of humility:[9] the poet's book is to be "subgit to alle poesye" and to kiss the steps where it sees these great poets

6. See Ernst Robert Curtius, *European Literature and the Latin Middle Ages*, trans. Willard R. Trask, Bollingen Series XXXVI (New York, 1953), pp. 515–518. Leo Spitzer, "Note on the Poetic and the Empirical 'I' in Medieval Authors," *Traditio*, IV (1946), 414–422, argues that medieval readers had little interest in the empirical person behind the "I," and tended to regard him as representative, though the autobiographical touch might add poignancy. R. W. Chambers, on the other hand, argues against the idea of "personas" in medieval poetry, showing with many examples that the dreamer or narrator in a medieval poem *is* the author; see "Robert or William Longland?" *London Mediaeval Studies*, I, 3 (1948 for 1939), 442–451.
7. Curtius, pp. 476–477, 485–486.
8. Jacob Burckhardt, in *The Civilisation of the* *Renaissance in Italy*, trans. S. G. C. Middlemore (London and New York, 1928), pp. 139–153, dealt with the idea of fame. Owing in part to Burckhardt's influence, many would say that the sense of the author was shaped largely by the rise of humanistic individualism and by the imitation of ancient writers like Horace who boasted that their works would outlast their own times; hence they might say that Chaucer's awareness of himself as a writer is a harbinger of the Renaissance. But in fact the sense of the author antedates the revival of the classics and the rise of humanism; it is quite as possible to regard it as a cause, rather than a result, of the "revival of learning."
9. See *The Works of Geoffrey Chaucer*, ed. F. N. Robinson, 2nd ed. (Cambridge, Mass., 1957), p. 837. All quotations are from this edition.

go. One might quote the sentiment of the Knight's Tale, "Thanne is it best, as for a worthy fame, / To dyen whan that he is best of name" (A.3055–56), as evidence of Chaucer's interest in a just reputation as a reward for good labors; still of course the labors are not poetical ones and Chaucer is not speaking of himself. On the whole it does not appear to me that Chaucer put more stock in lasting fame than did any late medieval author; he does not claim to confer fame on others, and his hopes of fame for himself are suggested only with the utmost modesty. In the Man of Law's Prologue, the lawyer mentions Chaucer by name and reels off an impressive bibliography of his works, but he takes a rather condescending tone toward the poet, who he says "kan but lewedly / On metres and on rymyng craftily" (B.47–48), and prefers him to Gower only because he is more moral. Again, the passage gives a hint of Chaucer's hope of fame, but it is sardonic indeed to make one's critics talk like J. Donald Adams.

Another aspect of the changing sense of the author in the late Middle Ages comes about as the result of technological progress. In the earlier Middle Ages a manuscript was read by few and copied seldom, but with the rise of professional scriptoria in the fourteenth century and the invention of printing in the fifteenth, the writer could begin to imagine an audience going unpredictably beyond his immediate milieu. People could then conceive of the writer as having the power to address and influence an ever increasing body of readers—a "public."[1] The writer could imagine himself no longer a scribe, a maker of books or a transmitter of authorities, but the originator of an irreversible process. Here again Chaucer is in the transitional stage of an important cultural change. Certainly in the *Troilus* he takes the position of a scribe or pedant transmitting from an "authority" matters of which he claims no personal experience. This was, as Professor Bethurum has shown,[2] generally his pose in his earlier poems. On the other hand, it is distinctly a pose. Chaucer might not have made extravagant claims for the originality of the *Troilus*, but it is clear that he felt he had created something. Seeing himself as the originator rather than the transmitter in a process of publication through copying, he even expresses anxiety over the accuracy of the process:

> And for ther is so gret diversite
> In Englissh and in writyng of oure tonge,
> So prey I God that non myswrite the,
> Ne the mysmetre for defaute of tonge.
> And red wherso thow be, or elles songe,
> That thow be understonde, God I biseche!
> (v.1793–98)

Again, in the *Canterbury Tales*, we get a sense of his hope that he will be received well by an unseen audience of readers. In the General Prologue he warns us,

---

1. The *OED* reports the earliest uses of the word in the fifteenth century, and in this sense only in the sixteenth century.

2. Dorothy Bethurum, "Chaucer's Point of View as Narrator in the Love Poems," *PMLA*, LXXIV (1959), 511–520.

But first I pray yow, of youre curteisye,
That ye n'arette it nat my vileynye,
Thogh that I pleynly speke in this mateere,
To telle yow hir wordes and hir cheere,
Ne thogh I speke hir wordes proprely.

(A.725–29)

There is the same kind of anxious apology just before the Miller's Tale, and here Chaucer suggests,

whoso list it nat yheere,
Turne over the leef and chese another tale.

(A.3176–77)[68–69]

To be sure he wrote with oral delivery in mind, and in many ways the expectation of oral delivery colored his style. But it is evident that he expected also to be copied by unseen hands and read by unseen readers. To some extent this was true throughout the Middle Ages; the formula "readers and hearers" is enough to suggest it.[3] Chaucer conceives of his function as we should expect a writer of the fourteenth century to do—with an increased sense of an unpredictable and irreversible process of communication going beyond his milieu and beyond his time, but with nothing like the feeling which the printing press was to encourage.

These changes in the idea of authorship—this steadily increasing expectation of being read and admired—created a corresponding change in the idea of anonymity. In the earlier Middle Ages anonymity was a mark of the scribe's or writer's humility: it showed his deference to the "authorities" he transmitted. He viewed himself as a mere agent in a process of transmission and preservation. Writers who mention their own labors often deprecate them—one thinks of Einhard, who tells us that although his powers are almost nil he is willing to risk the opinion of the world in order to preserve the deeds of Charlemagne. By the twelfth century we can find a writer like Bernard of Morval, in the prose dedication of his De contemptu mundi, asking for criticism and defending his use of rime on the ground that it commends moral precepts more readily to the mind. Bernard argues, too, that the Bible contains lyrics and quotes Horace that writing should instruct and delight. He claims to have been inspired to his work by a vision, and

3. On the tradition of oral delivery and its influence on Chaucer, see Ruth Crosby, "Oral Delivery in the Middle Ages," *Speculum*, XI (1936), 88–110; "Chaucer and the Custom of Oral Delivery," *Speculum*, XIII (1938), 413–432; and Bertrand H. Bronson, "Chaucer's Art in Relation to his Audience," *Five Studies in Literature* (Berkeley, Calif., 1940), pp. 1–53. For an excellent analysis of Chaucer's estimate of himself with relation to his audience, see Rosemary Woolf, "Chaucer as a Satirist in the General Prologue to the *Canterbury Tales*," *Critical Quarterly*, I (1959), 150–157. It is not necessary to suppose that the printing press and silent rapid reading caused modern writers to stop thinking in terms of oral delivery. Writers still read orally, if only to

their wives, and they may well imagine themselves speaking aloud as they compose. We write "I should like to say" and similar expressions without implying oral delivery. Language is by nature spoken, and a writer who writes with any degree of fluency is bound to "hear" spoken discourse as he writes. The difference between medieval and modern in this respect, as in others, is a matter of degree. Cf. Jordan, "Chaucer's Sense of Illusion," p. 21, n. 3. On the oral-aural component in western culture, see Marshall McLuhan, *The Gutenberg Galaxy: The Making of Typographic Man* (Toronto, 1962); Walter J. Ong, *Ramus, Method, and the Decay of Dialogue* (Cambridge, Mass., 1958), and *The Barbarian Within* (New York, 1962), esp. pp. 68–87, 220–229.

boasts of his ability to sustain the metrical pattern at such length. All of this sounds very modern for a twelfth-century monk writing at Cluny, and Bernard injects much of his own strong personality into his indignant denunciation of the evils of his time. Yet he does absolutely nothing to preserve his name: it is mentioned only in the salutation to his abbot. Scribes did no more, for it is not certain that he wrote "Bernardus Morvalensis" rather than "Morlanensis" or "Morlacensis." Nor has anyone discovered what Morval might have been.[4]

By Chaucer's time, of course, writers are much less reserved about mentioning their own names. A fashion has taken shape. The new interest in names of writers is reflected by the appearance, in the early fifteenth century, of the De scriptoribus ecclesiasticis by Johannis Trithemius, a biographical dictionary which contains chiefly dates, lists of works, and stereotyped praise of each man's piety and learning. Chaucer himself likes to name authors and praise them. At the same time, anyone who has worked with fifteenth-century manuscripts will know that while the names of authors may be more frequently recorded than in previous times, there are still many manuscripts which omit altogether the writers' names. It would be interesting to have some statistics about the decline of anonymity after the fourteenth century. What is important, however, is the increasing sense of the author: when curiosity about the author could be assumed as a normal attitude among readers, it permitted the author to use anonymity not merely to avoid criticism or persecution, but to whet the interest of his public. Gulliver's Travels is the classic example: the reader is purposely led to seek out in the text the true views of the anonymous author which lie behind the literal statement of the pseudonymous one. It is the sense of the author, considered as a cultural phenomenon, which makes possible a tension between the persona or narrator and the understood or felt personality of the author. And Chaucer is the first English poet to use the full artistic possibilities of this masked presentation of self.

Chaucer saw himself, then, as an originator of literary works who could hope for a continuing audience and reputation. He speaks of himself with modesty and, usually, with self-deprecating humor; but he does not seek anonymity—indeed, he provides us, in the prologue to the Legend of Good Women, in the Retraction of the Canterbury Tales, and in the Man of Law's Prologue, with lists of his writings. He did, however, mask his personality. This seems like a kind of anonymity, but it is not anything like the simple, unintentional anonymity of, say, the Gawain-poet. We should do better to call it masquerade.[5]

What is distinctive in this element of Chaucer's style begins, perhaps, with The House of Fame. Here the narrator is actually called "Geffrey"; he

4. See Bernard of Morval, De contemptu mundi: A Bitter Satirical Poem of 3000 Lines upon the Morals of the XIIth Century, ed. H. C. Hoskier (London, 1929), pp. xv, xxii, xxxv–xxxix.

5. See Ruth Nevo, "Chaucer: Motive and Mask in the 'General Prologue'," Modern Language Review, LVIII(1963), 1–9.

is a plump, bookish fellow with little experience in the high courtly practices of love. The portrait is humorously autobiographical—for our author is a bourgeois, a customs-clerk; and his audience is composed of knights and ladies, or of people like himself who are knowledgeable about court fashions. What *is* out of character, of course, is the narrator's obtuseness and insensitivity. This, I suspect, was a humorous development of the half-comprehending, naive reactions which one finds in the conventional "dreamer."[6] Such a narrator serves the artistic function of throwing attention on the subject matter: the audience perceives the *meaning* of the facts, while the narrator does not. And of course it is high comedy for the writer to adopt the mask of a fool when his artistry shows him to be anything but.

The device is essentially the same in the *Troilus*, but there are refinements. The narrator is a devotee of books, and a "servant of the servants of love." He himself is unsuccessful as a lover, on account of his "unliklynesse," yet he stands in wide-eyed and somewhat envious admiration of the affair as he transmits it from his "auctor." He is no longer the conventional dreamer of the earlier poems—he is a *reader*. What Professor Bloomfield has brilliantly described in his article on "distance and predestination" in the *Troilus*[7] is, after all, the common experience of those who read: the alternation between emotional involvement in the illusion and aesthetic distance from it. The "narrator" of the *Troilus*, this reader with his old book in hand, is therefore like ourselves: we are, as the English say, "reading Lollius with him." He is closer to the events than we are (for he has already read the book from which he draws his tale), but he is willing at times to remove himself from our attention and let us look on directly with him as the story unfolds.

Pandarus is a kind of mirror image of this narrator. He, too, is an unsuccessful lover, taking a vicarious enjoyment in place of a real one. He reacts to the story quite as the narrator does—fearful for Troilus, eager over the progress of the affair, exercised in the consummation scene, helpless and dejected by the way things turn out. And, as the narrator manipulates the events of his story, Pandarus manipulates the events themselves. But the similarities between Pandarus and the narrator all merely emphasize one enormous difference between them. Pandarus is a pagan who believes in a pagan philosophy of *carpe diem* ("cache it anon," he says at one point), whereas the narrator is a Christian. Pandarus is of their time, the narrator of ours. Hence Pandarus is of no use when things go wrong. His morality, which consists chiefly of the notion that one should take advantage of Fortune while one may, can provide no better consolation to Troilus than another affair. He "stant, astoned of thise causes tweye, / As stille as ston; a

---

6. On the early development of the device, see Bethurum, esp. pp. 511–516; Alfred L. Kellogg, "Chaucer's Self-Portrait and Dante's," *Medium Ævum*, XXIX (1960), 119–120; David M. Bevington, "The Obtuse Narrator in Chaucer's *House of Fame*," *Speculum*, XXXVI (1961), 288–298; and Charles A. Owen, Jr., "The Role of the Narrator in the 'Parle-ment of Foules'," *College English*, XIV (1953), 264–269.
7. Morton W. Bloomfield, "Distance and Predestination in *Troilus and Criseyde*," *PMLA*, LXXII (1957), 14–26. Cf. E. Talbot Donaldson, *Chaucer's Poetry* (New York, 1958), p. 966.

word ne kowde he seye" (v.1728–29). At the end, the narrator, like any reader, sees a lesson in the story shaped by his own age and culture: he is a Christian, and he learns from his story the error of "payens corsed olde rites," though he had been carried away at first by enthusiasm for them.

Now this narrator, this reader and learner, *is Chaucer*. We learn this from the epilogue, where he speaks in his own person—"Go, litel bok, go, litel myn tragedye." To say that the narrator goes off stage at the end and Chaucer steps on to speak the envoy *in propria persona* is simply to misread the text: At the end of the envoy, after expressing his worries over the diversity of English, Chaucer says "But yet to purpos of my rather speche," and then, going back to what he had been saying, "The wrath, as I bigan yow for to seye . . ." What is this if not an explicit statement that the "I" of the epilogue is identical with the "I" who has told the story? We could, of course, say with Professor Jordan that the narrator *becomes* Chaucer at the end.[8] But what would be the point? Do we not rather discover here, if we had any doubt before, that it was Chaucer speaking all along? It was Chaucer the enthusiast of courtly love, who is now convinced that Christian love is best. And why is this so different from the real live Chaucer of the fourteenth century? We know that he *was* a lover of books. And he *did* have a certain "unliklynesse" as concerns courtly love, because it was aristocratic behavior and he was not an aristocrat. At least for a time he did take the poetry of courtly love seriously. But also, quite early in his career, he began to search for other materials and other styles. And he wrote Christian poems throughout his life. One cannot really find anything in the *Troilus* (except "Lollius") which makes the narrator *factually* different from Chaucer the man. The difference is simply a matter of tone. It is the humorous exaggeration of his bookishness and "unliklynesse" that makes him seem different from the presumably "real" Chaucer of the epilogue—the Chaucer we *think* we know.

This element of humorous and exaggerated self-presentation is carried a step further in the narrator of the *Canterbury Tales*. In the *Troilus* Chaucer unmasks himself at the end, but in the *Canterbury Tales* he avoids any direct self-revelation, except in the Retraction. Rather than unmask himself, he unmasks the pilgrims. And his knowledge of them is based upon direct observation.[9] He is not a "dreamer" here, not a "reader" either; he is a returned traveller. Now returned travellers always have a certain air of omniscience. When the narrator says, as he does of the Merchant, "Ther wiste no wight that he was in dette," we do not have to think it out of character or charge it up to an omniscient author: returned travellers report gossip and surmises along with facts. It is the most natural kind of storytelling in the world, utterly realistic and utterly convincing. As a dreamer in the earlier dream-poems, Chaucer had been reporting what was an illusion

8. Robert M. Jordan, "The Narrator in Chaucer's *Troilus*," *ELH*, xxv (1958), 255.

9. On the narrator's stance in the General Prologue, see Ralph Baldwin, *The Unity of the Canterbury Tales* (Copenhagen, 1955), pp. 55–57, and Edgar

Hill Duncan, "Narrator's Points of View in the Portrait-sketches, Prologue to the *Canterbury Tales*," *Essays in Honor of Walter Clyde Curry* (Nashville, Tenn., 1954), 77–101.

to begin with; as a reader in the *Troilus*, he claimed only to be translating and adapting an old story. But in the *Canterbury Tales* he claims to be reporting real events in which he has been a participant, things he can remember. And yet, while he claims this, we enter into the most improbable illusion in the world: that each of thirty people can tell tales in rimed verse as they ride horseback in a group—through open country.

What this means is that the "fictive illusion" of the *Canterbury Tales* is less real and less convincing, despite its contemporaneity, than the intense events of the ancient, doomed city in the *Troilus*. All that was far and strange in Troy was made to seem near and real; but on the way to Canterbury, something in the author himself endues the familiar world of his audience with a strangeness. As we read the General Prologue we perceive that the author does not think what the narrator says. Our curiosity about the author is brought into play; we wonder about his real opinions. Chaucer even throws dust in our eyes by telling (as pilgrim) a dull tale like *Sir Thopas*, which we know he intends (as poet) to be a spoof, then following it with the quite serious *Melibee*. Again, he titillates our sense of the author by having the Man of Law drop his name and discourse on his works. Indeed, he conceals himself so skillfully that we continue, almost six centuries later, to argue about what he really thought. For just as soon as Chaucer the returned traveller is removed from the fictive illusion, just as soon as we are listening directly to one of the pilgrims, we think we detect Chaucer the man in the pilgrim's words. For example, when we read the Miller's Tale we are delighted by all the echoes of the Knight's Tale in it. Is the Miller poking fun at the Knight's Tale? or is Chaucer poking fun at it? Or is Chaucer poking fun at the Miller for not understanding the Knight's high seriousness? or is it all three at once? And even in the Knight's Tale, for all its high style, we are faced with lines like these on Palamon's imprisonment:

> And eek therto he is a prisoner
> Perpetuelly, noght oonly for a yer.
>   Who koude ryme in Englyssh proprely
> His martirdom? for sothe it am nat I;
> Therfore I passe as lightly as I may.
>   It fel that in the seventhe yer, of May
> The thridde nyght, (as olde bookes seyn,
> That al this storie tellen moore pleyn)
>   (A. 1457–64)[599–606]

Is the Knight merely being humble? If so, why the reference to riming? or is the Knight being ironic, making fun of his own tale? Or is it Chaucer himself speaking? and if so, is he making fun of the Knight, or of himself? We want to say to Chaucer, as the Host does, "What man artow?" But it is an essential part of the style of the *Canterbury Tales* that no real answer to the question is ever given. And it is probably time we stopped trying to decide who is speaking where.

What I am arguing is that Chaucer the man is present in the *Canterbury Tales* not "objectively" through any explicit representation, but dynamically—through an implied relationship between himself and his audience. And his role is precisely what it must have been in reality—that of a bourgeois addressing his social betters. From all the biographical facts which we know about Chaucer, exactly two major ones emerge: that Chaucer was a bourgeois who successfully established himself as a civil servant, and that he was a poet who wrote for the court. His aristocratic audience, which certainly admired him, would still have looked upon him as a social inferior. In such a milieu a man of wit is on guard not to show any bourgeois vices—literal-mindedness, uncritical gregariousness, pedantry, naiveté, inexperience, or pretentiousness. It is the perennial problem of the bourgeois: he does not want to appear bourgeois in the eyes of the upper class, but he knows that the most bourgeois thing he can do is to show discomfort about his status or, worse, attempt to deny it. I can think of only two ways to get out of the dilemma. One is good-natured clowning with an edge of modest self-deprecation; the other is to be a sober, useful fellow and let your betters like you for what you are, not what you say you are. In the *Canterbury Tales*, and to an extent in the earlier poems, Chaucer adopts both these attitudes. He presents himself in the General Prologue as an exaggerated bourgeois type—uncritical, affable, admiring the rich and powerful, even impressed with successful thievery. He presents with humor exactly those bourgeois qualities which the average bourgeois would conceal from aristocrats, makes them into an elaborate joke, and parades it before the court. In doing so he tactfully conceals his wit, his intelligence, his learning, his philosophical depth, his wisdom—traits which could hardly have escaped any member of his audience. To make it easier, he pokes gentle fun at other bourgeois—the sober Man of Law, for example, or the genial Franklyn. His own tale of Sir Thopas illustrates the method perfectly. He presents himself as a bourgeois dunderhead attempting to tell an aristocratic tale of knightly deeds. And in the tale itself the joke revolves around the notion of a Flemish bourgeois ineptly playing knight. The real and necessary implication is that Chaucer himself really sees it all not from any bourgeois point of view but from that of true knights and ladies. He leaves his audience to assume that he is indeed *au courant* with their aristocratic attitudes. In a word, he leaves the audience *to create him in their own image*. In the *Troilus*, as Professor Payne has lately shown,[1] the narrator carries on a kind of running dialogue with us the audience—implies what kind of an audience we are and draws us into the poem so that we become a part of its reality. But in the *Canterbury Tales* Chaucer does something different: he draws the audience into the work not by engaging in a dialogue with us but by expecting us to intuit what he thinks, to project ourselves into the role of the implied author, to overreach ourselves and become one with him.

1. Robert O. Payne, *The Key of Remembrance: A Study of Chaucer's Poetics* (New Haven and London, 1963), pp. 227–232.

I will venture a step further and suggest that in one fundamental respect the naive narrator is wiser, has a truer vision, than this "implied author" with whom we align ourselves—that in the narrator Chaucer has isolated and presented one important trait of his own personality, his interest in people and his tolerant humanity.[2] Everyone is accustomed to say that through the narrator Chaucer presents the surface appearance and lets the pilgrims themselves show the underlying reality. But is it not equally true that the wide-eyed narrator, blind as he may be to the vices of his companions, sees the good side of them with a strange clarity? This—if you care to be allegorical—is quite consistent with medieval theology. Chaucer had it from St. Augustine that all created things are fundamentally good—that evil is parasitic, a deprivation of goodness rather than an entity; that one should on this account "hate the vice but love the man." So, in the masquerade of the literal-minded, gregarious pilgrim, Chaucer plays a kind of Holy Fool who stumbles into Christian charity unawares. We, with the implied author, perceive his intellectual errors, but his foolish generosity infects us all the same. Through it we are made to see—in the Monk, say, or the Pardoner—the created man beneath the canker evil.

If I am right in this, then Chaucer's fragmented self-presentation leads us to grasp two things at once—that evil lurks beneath good appearances, but that good lies beneath evil. The pilgrimage begins with the narrator's doubtful notion that everything and everyone is good. It ends with a sermon whose point is that we should look to our *own* sins—and, in the Retraction, Chaucer makes his own act of penance. For Chaucer's own audience I should not be surprised if this had finally the effect of making them look within themselves and examine their own lives as Christians. To a degree Chaucer's audience might also have wondered about the elusive Master Chaucer himself—which pilgrims he liked, or thought absurd, or condemned. Since Boswell's time it is much more our tendency to wonder of the author "What man artow?" and to go in search of him. It would be *nice* to know more facts about him, but finally the most relevant information we can have comes from the style of his works. The Chaucer of biographical documents, the Chaucer of the customs-house, might for all we know have *been* literal-minded, uncritical, bookish, and fat—what might we not say, if we cared to collect anecdotes, about the Wallace Stevens of the insurance company or the T. S. Eliot of the publishing house? The Chaucer we know is a creation of our own response to his works. For that he is no less the *real* Chaucer. This is true for a reason which, as exegetes, we sometimes set aside, but which as humanists we always assume: that for every man who creates great poems there is an infinite truth, of grandeur and terror, in the adage *style is the man himself*—that there must be in him, and in those who would read him, all of the human possibilities which can be realized in his works.

---

2. The point is anticipated by Donaldson, "Chaucer the Pilgrim," p. 936. [See above, p. 491.]

H. MARSHALL LEICESTER, JR.

The Art of Impersonation: A General Prologue to the *Canterbury Tales*†

Nec illud minus attendendum esse arbitror, utrum . . . magis secundum aliorum opinionem quam secundum propriam dixerint sententiam, sicut in plerisque Ecclesiastes dissonas diversorum inducit sententias, imo ut tumultuator interpretatur, beato in quarto dialogorum attestante Gregorio.

In my judgment it is no less necessary to decide whether sayings found [in the sacred writings and the Fathers] are quotations from the opinions of others rather than the writers' own authoritative pronouncements. On many topics the author of Ecclesiastes brings in so many conflicting proverbs that we have to take him as impersonating the tumult of the mob, as Gregory points out in his fourth *Dialogue*.

Abelard

In his much praised book *The Idea of the* Canterbury Tales, Donald R. Howard has isolated a perennial strand in the Chaucer criticism of the last thirty years or more—isolated it, defined it clearly, and given it a name. Discussing the Knight's Tale, he remarks:

Chaucer . . . introduced a jocular and exaggerated element that seems to call the Knight's convictions into question. For example, while the two heroes are fighting he says "in this wise I let hem fighting dwelle" and turns his attention to Theseus:

The destinee, ministre general,
That executeth in the world over all
The purveiaunce that God hath seen biforn,
So strong it is that, though the world had sworn
The contrary of a thing by ye or nay,
Yet sometime it shall fallen on a day
That falleth nat eft within a thousand yeer.
For certainly, our appetites here,
Be it of wer, or pees, or hate, or love,
All is this ruled by the sight above.
This mene I now by mighty Theseus,
That for to hunten is so desirous,
And namely at the grete hert in May,
That in his bed there daweth him no day

† Reprinted by permission of the Modern Language Association of America from *PMLA* 95 (1980): 213–24.

That he nis clad, and redy for to ride
With hunt and horn and houndes him beside.
For in his hunting hath he swich delit
That it is all his joy and appetit
To been himself the grete hertes bane.
For after Mars he serveth now Diane.
                                    (1663–1682)[805–24]

All this machinery is intended to let us know that on a certain day
Theseus took it in mind to go hunting. It is impossible not to see a
mock-epic quality in such a passage, and hard not to conclude that its
purpose is ironic, that it is meant to put us at a distance from the
Knight's grandiose ideas of destiny and make us think about them.
This humorous element in the Knight's Tale is the most controversial
aspect of the tale: where one critic writes it off as an "antidote" to
tragedy another puts it at the center of things, but no one denies it is
there. It introduces a feature which we will experience in many a tale:
we read the tale as a dramatic monologue spoken by its teller but
understand that some of Chaucer's attitudes spill into it. This feature
gives the tale an artistry which we cannot realistically attribute to the
teller: I am going to call this *unimpersonated artistry*. In its simplest
form it is the contingency that a tale not memorized but told impromptu
is in verse. The artistry is the author's, though selected features of the
pilgrim's dialect, argot, or manner may still be impersonated. In its
more subtle uses it allows a gross or "low" character to use language,
rhetoric, or wit above his capabilities. (Sometimes it is coupled with
an impersonated *lack* of art, an artlessness or gaucherie which causes
a character to tell a bad tale, as in *Sir Thopas*, or to violate literary
conventions or proprieties, as in the Knight's Tale.) The effect is that
of irony or parody, but this effect is Chaucer's accomplishment, not
an impersonated skill for which the pilgrim who tells the tale deserves
any compliments.[1]

Having generated this principle, Howard goes on to apply it, at various
points in the book, to the tales of the Miller, the Summoner, the Merchant,
the Squire, and the Manciple. He is in good and numerous company. One
thinks of Charles Muscatine's characterization of certain central monologues in *Troilus*: "the speeches must be taken as impersonal comments on
the action, Chaucer's formulation, not his characters' "; of Robert M. Jordan, who, having presented an impressive array of evidence for a complicated Merchant in the Merchant's Tale, argues from it, like Dryden's Panther,
"that he's not there at all"; of Anne Middleton's exemption of selected passages of the Physician's Tale from the pilgrim's voicing; of Robert B. Burlin's praise of the Summoner's Tale despite its being "beyond the genius of

---

1. Howard, *The Idea of the* Canterbury Tales (Berkeley: Univ. of California Press, 1976), pp. 230–31.

the Summoner"; and of many other commentators on the Knight's Tale, some of whom I mention later.[2]

Now in my view this "unimpersonated artistry" is a problem, and a useful one. Howard's formulation—an attempt to describe an aspect of Chaucer's general practice—is valuable because it brings into the sharp relief of a critical and theoretical principle something that is more diffusely present in the practical criticism of a great many Chaucerians: the conviction, often unspoken, that at some point it becomes necessary to move beyond or away from the pilgrim narrators of the *Canterbury Tales* and to identify the poet himself as the source of meaning. If the assumption is stated this generally, I probably agree with it myself, but Howard's way of putting it does seem to me to reflect a tendency, common among Chaucer critics, to invoke the poet's authority much too quickly. Howard helps me to focus my own discontent, not with his criticism (much of which I admire), but with a more general situation in the profession at large. If we consider "unimpersonated artistry" as a theoretical proposition, it seems open to question on both general and specific grounds; that is, it seems both to imply a rather peculiar set of assumptions to bring to the reading of any text and, at least to me, to be an inaccurate reflection of the experience of reading Chaucer in particular.

"Unimpersonated artistry" implies a technique, or perhaps an experience, of reading something like this: we assume that the Canterbury tales are, as they say, "fitted to their tellers," that they are potentially dramatic monologues or, to adopt what I hope is a less loaded term, that they are instances of *impersonated* artistry, the utterances of particular pilgrims. After all, we like to read Chaucer this way, to point out the suitability of the tales to their fictional tellers, and most of us, even Robert Jordan, would agree that at least some of the tales and certainly the Canterbury frame, encourage this sort of interpretation.[3] We read along, then, with this assumption in mind, until it seems to break down, until we come across a passage that we have difficulty reconciling with the sensibility—the temperament or the training or the intelligence—of the pilgrim in question. At that point, alas,

2. Muscatine, *Chaucer and the French Tradition* (Berkeley: Univ. of California Press, 1957), pp. 264–65. In a more general statement on the *Canterbury Tales*, on pp. 171–72, Muscatine observes: "No medieval poet would have sacrificed all the rich technical means at his disposal merely to make a story sound as if such and such a character were actually telling it. The *Miller's Tale*, to name but one of many, would have been thus impossible." See also John Lawlor, *Chaucer* (New York: Harper, 1968), Ch. v. Jordan, *Chaucer and the Shape of Creation* (Cambridge: Harvard Univ. Press, 1967), Ch. vi. Jordan is, on theoretical and historical grounds, the most thoroughgoing and principled opponent of the notion of consistent impersonation in Chaucer's work. In this connection the book just cited deserves to be read in its entirety, as does Jordan's "Chaucer's Sense of Illusion: Roadside Drama

Reconsidered," *ELH: A Journal of English Literary History*, 29 (1962), 19–33. Middleton, "The *Physician's Tale* and Love's Martyrs: 'Ensamples Mo than Ten' in the *Canterbury Tales*," *Chaucer Review*, 8 (1973), 9–32. Burlin, *Chaucerian Fiction* (Princeton: Princeton Univ. Press. 1977), p. 164. Elizabeth Salter's reading of the Knight's Tale, in *Chaucer: The Knight's Tale and the Clerk's Tale* (London: Edwin Arnold, 1962), pp. 7–36, is perhaps the most consistently developed in terms of the "two voices" of the poet. See also Paul T. Thurston, *Artistic Ambivalence in Chaucer's Knight's Tale* (Gainesville: Univ. of Florida Press, 1968).
3. Howard states the position admirably (pp. 123–24). I suppose no one would question that the Wife of Bath's and Pardoner's tales virtually demand this approach.

I think we too often give up. "This passage," we say, "must be the work of Chaucer the poet, speaking over the head or from behind the mask of the Knight or the Miller or the Physician, creating ironies, setting us straight on doctrine, pointing us 'the right weye.' " Unfortunately, these occasions are seldom as unequivocal as the one case of genuine broken impersonation I know of in the *Tales*, the general narrator's "quod she" in the middle of a stanza of the Prioress' Tale (VII. 1771)[147]. Different critics find the poet in different passages of the same tale and often have great difficulty in deciphering his message once they *have* found him—a difficulty that seems odd if Chaucer thought the message worth a disruption of the fiction.

Thus, Howard, whose observations on the critical disagreement over the humorous element in the Knight's Tale are well taken, offers an interpretation of "The destinee, ministre general . . ." that is in fact uncommon. His account of the ironic tone of these lines in context is at least more attentive to the effect of the language than are the numerous readings that take the passage relatively straight. Even within this group, however, the range of proposed answers to the question "Who's talking here?" is sufficiently various to raise the issue I am interested in. To mention only those who discuss this particular passage, Frost, Ruggiers, and Kean are representative of the large body of criticism that remains relatively inattentive to the whole question of voicing in the tale.[4] They share a view of the passage as a piece of "the poem's" doctrine, to be taken seriously as part of an argument about man's place in the cosmos. Of those who, like Howard, find something odd about the passage, Burlin suggests that the speaker is Chaucer, who intends to suggest by it that Theseus is a man superior to Fortune but unaware of Providence (p. 108), while Neuse, the only critic to attribute the speech unequivocally to the Knight, maintains that it differentiates the latter's implicitly Christian view of the story from Theseus' more limited vision.[5] Who *is* talking here, and to what end? One might ask what the consequences for interpretation are if one concedes both that the passage makes gentle fun of the machinery of destiny, at least as applied to so trivial an event, and that it is the Knight himself who is interested in obtaining this effect. Howard's suggestion to the contrary, the passage is not really directed at Theseus' hunting but at the improbably fortuitous meeting in the glade of Theseus, Palamon, and Arcite, described in the lines that immediately follow (I. 1683–713) [825–55]. This encounter is one of many features in the first half of the tale that show that most of the plot, far from being the product of portentous cosmic forces (Palamon and Arcite are consistently made to look silly for taking this view), is generated by human actions and choices, not least by those of the narrating Knight in conspicuously rigging events and manipulating coincidences. The Knight, as Neuse points out (p. 300), is adapting an "olde storie" for the present occasion,

4. William Frost, "An Interpretation of Chaucer's Knight's Tale," *Review of English Studies*, 25 (1949), 290–304; Paul Ruggiers, "Some Philosophical Aspects of *The Knight's Tale*," *College English*, 14 (1958), 296–302; P. M. Kean, "The *Knight's Tale*," in her

Chaucer and the Making of English Poetry (London: Routledge and Kegan Paul, 1972), II, 1–52.
5. Richard Neuse, "The Knight: The First Mover in Chaucer's Human Comedy," *University of Toronto Quarterly*, 31 (1962), 312–13.

and the irony here reflects his opinion of the style of those "olde bookes."
To him that style embodies a dangerous evasion of human responsibility
for maintaining order in self and society by unconsciously projecting the
responsibility onto gods and destinies.

The point is that a notion like "unimpersonated artistry," by dividing
speakers into parts and denying them the full import of their speaking, puts
us in the difficult position of trying to decide which parts of a single narrative are to be assigned to the pilgrim teller and which to the "author," and
in these circumstances it is not surprising that different critics make the cut
in different places. All such formulations involve finding or creating two
speakers (or even more)[6] in a narrative situation where it would appear
simpler to deal with only one. The procedure seems to me theoretically
questionable because it is unparsimonious or inelegant logically: it creates
extra work, and it also tends to lead to distraction. Narrative entities are
multiplied to the point where they become subjects of concern in their own
right and require some sort of systematic or historical justification such as
"unimpersonated artistry" or the deficiency of medieval ideas of personality,[7] and before long we are so busy trying to save the appearances of the
epicyclic constructs we ourselves have created that we are no longer attend-
ing to the poems that the constructs were originally intended to explain.
Therefore, I would like to preface my more detailed opposition to "unimpersonated artistry" with a general caveat. I call it Leicester's razor: *narra-
tores non multiplicandi sunt praeter absolutum necessitatem.*

Naturally I do not intend to let the matter rest with this general and
essentially negative formula, though I think its application would clear up
a lot of difficulties. I want to use the space my principle gives me to argue
that the Canterbury tales are individually voiced, and radically so—that
each of the tales is primarily an expression of its teller's personality and
outlook as embodied in the unfolding "now" of the telling. I am aware that
something like this idea is all too familiar. Going back, in modern times,
at least as far as Kittredge's characterization of the *Canterbury Tales* as a
"Human Comedy," with the pilgrims as dramatis personae, it reaches its

6. See, e.g., Jordan, *Shape of Creation*, p. 181,
where what is apparently envisioned is Chaucer the
poet projecting Chaucer the pilgrim as the (intermittent?) narrator of the Knight's story. For an instance
of how far this sort of thing can go, see A. P.
Campbell, "Chaucer's 'Retraction': Who Retracted
What?" *Humanities Association Bulletin*, 16, No. 1
(1965), 75–87.
7. Jordan once again provides the clearest example
of this historicist form of argument, but D. W.
Robertson also uses it, e.g., in the Introduction to
his *Chaucer's London* (New York: Wiley, 1968), pp.
1–11, where he both specifies and generalizes such
statements in his *A Preface to Chaucer* (Princeton:
Princeton Univ. Press, 1962) as the following: "The
actions of Duke Theseus in the Knight's Tale are
thus, like the actions of the figures we see in the
visual arts of the fourteenth century, symbolic actions.
They are directed toward the establishment and

maintenance of those traditional hierarchies which
were dear to the medieval mind. They have nothing
to do with 'psychology' or with 'character' in the
modern sense, but are instead functions of attributes
which are, in this instance, inherited from the tra-
ditions of medieval humanistic culture" (pp. 265–
66; see also the discussion of the Friar's Tale that
immediately follows). This whole line of argument
probably originated with Leo Spitzer's "A Note on
the Poetic and the Empirical 'I' in Medieval Authors,"
Traditio, 4 (1946), 414–22. Spitzer's argument is
drawn from particular textual investigations and is
relatively tentative about its conclusions. Judging
from his remarks on Boccaccio, I am not at all sure
that Spitzer would see Chaucer as a representative
user of the "poetic 'I,' " but in any case I think his
successors, unlike him, are arguing from "history"
to texts, not the other way around. Spitzer's formulation has become fossilized in these Chaucerians.

high point in Lumiansky's *Of Sondry Folk*[8] (and apparently its dead end as well, since no one since has attempted to apply the concept systematically to the entire poem). Moreover, as I said before, we are all given to this sort of reading now and then. I think one reason the idea has never been pushed so hard or so far as I would like to take it is that the voicing of individual tales has almost always been interpreted on the basis of something external to them, usually either some aspect of the historical background of the poems (e.g., what we know from other sources about knights, millers, lawyers, nuns, etc.) or the descriptions of the speakers given in the Canterbury frame, especially in the General Prologue. Such materials are combined in various ways to construct an image of a given pilgrim outside his or her tale, and each tale is then read as a product of the figure who tells it, a product whose interpretation is constrained by the limitations we conceive the pilgrim to have. The specific problem of historical presuppositions, the feeling that medieval men *could not* have thought or spoken in certain ways, I would like to postpone until later, because the assumptions involved are often relatively tacit and well hidden and the problems they present are easier to handle in specific instances. It is clear, I hope, how such assumptions can lead to the kind of constraint on interpretation I have just outlined and how such a constraint puts us in danger of arguing from inference back to evidence, in Robert O. Payne's useful phrase,[9] when what is desired is an understanding of the evidence—the text—in front of us.

It is the specific problem of the Canterbury frame, however, that has been the more stubborn obstacle to reading the tales as examples of impersonated artistry. Since I do not mean by this phrase what either the critics or the defenders of similar notions appear to have meant in the past, the topic is worth pausing over. The issue is generally joined over the question of verisimilitude, the consistency with which the fiction of the *Tales* can be felt to sustain a dramatic illusion of real people taking part in real and present interaction with one another. The critic who has most consistently taken this dramatic view of the poem is Lumiansky, who locates both the "reality" of the pilgrims and the "drama" of their relations with one another outside the tales themselves, preeminently in the frame. He ordinarily begins his discussion of a given tale and its dramatic context with a character sketch of the pilgrim drawn from the General Prologue (and from any relevant links) and then treats the tale itself as an exemplification and extension of the traits and situations in the frame. He is attentive to such details as direct addresses to the pilgrim audience within a tale (such as the Knight's "lat se now who shal the soper wynne") and to a degree to the ways tales respond to one another, as in Fragment III, or the Marriage Group. This approach leads to an account of the poem as a whole that doubles the overt narrative of the frame and, in effect, allows the frame to tyrannize the individual tales: what does not fit the model of actual, preexisting pilgrims really pres-

8. G. L. Kittredge, *Chaucer and His Poetry* (Cambridge: Harvard Univ. Press, 1915), Ch. v; the famous phrases are on pp. 154–55. R. M. Lumiansky, *Of Sondry Folk: The Dramatic Principle of the Canter-* bury Tales (Austin: Univ. of Texas Press, 1955). 9. Payne, *The Key of Remembrance: A Study of Chaucer's Poetics* (New Haven: Yale Univ. Press, 1963), p. 3.

ent to one another is not relevant to the enterprise and is variously ignored or dismissed. Other critics have not been slow to point out that this procedure neglects a great deal.[1]

The objection to this "dramatic" model that I would particularly like to single out is its disregard for the poem's insistent, though perhaps intermittent, *textuality*, for the way the work repeatedly breaks the fiction of spoken discourse and the illusion of the frame to call attention to itself as a written thing. The injunction in the Miller's Prologue to "turne over the leef and chese another tale" (I.3177)[69], the more interesting moment in the Knight's Tale when the supposedly oral narrator remarks, "But of that storie list me nat to write" (I.1201)[343][2]—such interruptions not only destroy "verisimilitude" but call attention to what Howard has named the "bookness" of the poem (*Idea*, pp. 63–67), as do, less vibrantly, incipits and explicits, the patently incomplete state of the text, or "the contingency that a tale not memorized but told impromptu is in verse." Now this conspicuous textuality (by which I mean that Chaucer not only produces written texts but does so self-consciously and calls attention to his writing) certainly militates strongly against the illusion of drama as living presence. It is no doubt this realization, coupled with the counterperception that some tales do seem "fitted to the teller," that has led Howard and others to adopt formulations like "unimpersonated artistry" in order to stay responsive to the apparent range of the poem's effects. Such a notion allows the critic to hover between "bookness," which the French have taught us always implies *absence*, and what Howard calls "voiceness": the *presence* we feel when "the author addresses us directly and himself rehearses tales told aloud by others: we seem to hear his and the pilgrim's voices, we presume oral delivery" (*Idea*, p. 66). If we cannot have presence fully, we can at least have it partly. But when and where exactly and, above all, *whose?* As I have tried to suggest, a phenomenon like "unimpersonated artistry"—which is, remember, an *intermittent* phenomenon—tries to save the feeling that someone is present at the cost of rendering us permanently uncertain about who is speaking at any given moment in (or of) the text: the pilgrim, the poet, or that interesting mediate entity Chaucer the pilgrim.

It seems to me that the "roadside-drama" approach, the critiques of this approach, *and* compromise positions (whether explicitly worked out like Howard's or more intuitive) have in common a central confusion: the confusion of *voice* with *presence*.[3] All these views demand that the voice in a text be traceable to a person, a subject, *behind* the language, an individual controlling and limiting, and thereby guaranteeing, the meaning of what is expressed. The language of a given tale, or indeed of a given moment in a

---

1. Jordan is particularly good at evoking the element of "the girlhood of Shakespeare's heroines" that often finds its way into this sort of interpretation; see "Roadside Drama," esp. pp. 24–26.

2. Quotations from Chaucer are from F. N. Robinson, ed., *The Works of Geoffrey Chaucer*, 2nd ed. (Boston: Houghton, 1957).

3. In what follows I ought to acknowledge a general obligation to the work of Jacques Derrida, perhaps more to its spirit than to any specific essay or formulation. For a representative discussion of the problem of presence and a typical critique of "logocentric metaphysics" see "Writing before the Letter," Pt. I of *Of Grammatology*, trans. Gayatri Chakravorty Spivak (Baltimore: Johns Hopkins Univ. Press, 1976), pp. 1–93.

tale, is thus the end point of the speaker's activity, the point at which the speaker delivers a self that existed prior to the text. For this reason all these approaches keep circling back to the ambiguous traces of such an external subject—in the frame, in the poet, in the facts of history, or in the "medieval mind." But what I mean by "impersonated artistry" does not involve an external subject.

In maintaining that the *Canterbury Tales* is a collection of individually voiced texts, I want rather to *begin* with the fact of their textuality, to insist that there is nobody there, that there is only the text. But if a written text implies and enforces the absence of the subject, the real living person outside the text who may or may not have "expressed himself" in producing it, the same absence is emphatically *not* true of the voice *in* the text, the voice *of* the text. In writing, voice is first of all a function not of persons but of language, of the linguistic codes and conventions that make it *possible* for an "I" to appear.[4] But this possibility means that we can assign an "I" to any statement. Language is positional. It always states or implies a first person in potential dramatic relation to the other grammatical persons, and it does so structurally—qua language—and regardless of the presence or absence of any actual speaking person. Thus, by its nature as a linguistic phenomenon, any text generates what it is conventional to call its speaker. The speaker is created by the text itself as a structure of linguistic relationships, and the character of the speaker is a function of the specific deployment of those relationships in a particular case to produce the voice of the text.

This kind of "voiceness" is a property of any text, and it is therefore theoretically possible to read any text in a way that elicits its particular voice, its individual first person. Such a reading would, for example, try to attend consistently to the "I" of the text, expressed or implied, and would make the referential aspects of the discourse functions of the "I." To put it another way, a voice-oriented reading would treat the second and third persons of a discourse (respectively, the audience and the world), expressed or implied, primarily as indications of what the speaker *maintains* about audience and world and would examine the way these elements are reflexively constituted as evidence of the speaker's character. We would ask what sort of person notices these particular details rather than others, what sort of person conceives of an audience in such a way that he or she addresses it in this particular tone, and so forth.

One might conceive of a study that undertook to work out a poetics of the speaker in literature. It would be a classic structuralist enterprise, moving from linguistic structures to a systematic demonstration of how it is possible for literary speakers to have the meanings they do. But since I do not believe, for reasons I will not go into here,[5] that such an enterprise

---

4. See Emile Benveniste, *Problems in General Linguistics*, trans. Mary Elizabeth Meek, Miami Linguistics Series, No. 8 (Coral Gables, Fla.: Univ. of Miami Press, 1971). Chapters xviii and xx are espe-

cially helpful, but the whole section (Chs. xviii–xxiii, pp. 195–248) is of value.

5. One might observe in passing that many "structuralist" discussions of voice in literature seem plagued

would succeed, and since in any case it is not where my interests lie, I would like to move back to Chaucer by way of a further distinction. While any text can be read in a way that elicits its voice, some texts actively engage the phenomenon of voice, exploit it, make it the center of their discourse—make it their content. A text of this sort can be said to be *about* its speaker, and this is the sort of text I contend that the *Canterbury Tales* is and especially the sort that the individual tales are. The tales are exemplar of impersonated artistry because they concentrate not on the way preexisting people create language but on the way language creates people.[6] They detail how what someone says "im-personates" him or her, that is, turns the speaker into a person, or better, a personality (I prefer this word to "person" because "personality" suggests something that acts like, rather than "is," a person). What this implies for the concrete interpretation of the poem is that the relation that I have been questioning between the tales and the frame, or between the tales and their historical or social background, needs to be reversed. The voicing of any tale, the personality of any pilgrim, is not *given* in advance by the prologue portrait or the facts of history, nor is it dependent on them. The personality has to be worked out by analyzing and defining the voice created by each tale. It is this personality in the foreground, in his or her intensive and detailed textual life, that supplies a guide to the weighting of details and emphasis, the *interpretation*, of the background, whether portrait or history. To say, for example, that the Miller's Tale is not "fitted to its teller" because it is "too good" for him, because a miller or the Miller would not be educated enough or intelligent enough to produce it, is to move in exactly the wrong direction. In fact, it is just this sort of social typing that irritates and troubles the Miller himself, especially since both the Host and the general narrator social-typed him long before any Chaucer critic did (I. 3128–31, 3167–69, 3182)[20–23, 59–61, 74]. The characters in his tale repeatedly indulge in social typing, and the Miller types several of them in this way.[7] The Miller's handling of this practice makes it an issue in the tale, something he has opinions and feelings about. The end of the tale makes it quite clear how the maimed, uncomfortably sympathetic carpenter is sacrificed to the mirth of the townsfolk and the pilgrims; he is shouted down by the class solidarity of Nicholas' brethren: "For every clerk anonright heeld with oother" (I. 3847)[744]. One could go

---

by the same confusions as Chaucerian ones. See, e.g., Roland Barthes, "To Write: An Intransitive Verb?" in Richard Macksey and Eugenio Donato, eds., *The Structuralist Controversy: The Languages of Criticism and the Sciences of Man* (Baltimore: Johns Hopkins Univ. Press, 1970), where he remarks of the discourse of the traditional novel that it "alternates the personal and the impersonal very rapidly, often even in the course of the same sentence, so as to produce, if we can speak thus, a proprietary consciousness which retains the mastery of what it states without participating in it" (p. 140). There is not space here to deal with this extraordinary idea, but see Jonathan Culler's sympathetic and skeptical

discussion of this notion and related ideas in *Structuralist Poetics* (Ithaca: Cornell Univ. Press, 1975), pp. 189–205.

6. There are a number of tales—the Prioress' is one and the Shipman's another—that suggest how this happens whether the speaker intends it or not.

7. E.g., "A clerk hadde litherly biset his whyle. / But if he koude a carpenter bigyle"; "What! thynk on God, as we doon, men that swynke"; "She was a prymerole, a piggesnye, / For any lord to leggen in his bedde, / Or yet for any good yeman to wedde" (I. 3299–300, 3491, 3268–70) [196–97, 388, 165–67].

on to show how the Miller's sensibility in the tale retrospectively and deci-
sively inflects the portrait of him in the General Prologue, making it something quite different from what it appears to be in prospect, but the same
point can be suggested more economically with the Physician. When we
read in the Prologue that "His studie was but litel on the Bible" (I.438), the
line sounds condemnatory in an absolute, moral way. Reconsidered from
the perspective of the tale, however, the detail takes on a new and more
intensive individual life in the light of the Physician's singularly inept use
of the exemplum of Jephthah's daughter (VI.238–50). Retrospectively the
poet's comment characterizes a man of irreproachable if conventional morality
whose profession channels his reading into medical texts rather than sacred
ones and who uses such biblical knowledge as he has for pathetic effect at
the expense of narrative consistency: he forgets, or at any rate suppresses,
that Jephthah's daughter asked for time to bewail her virginity, whereas
Virginia is being killed to preserve hers. The situation in the tale is a good
deal more complex than this, but I think the general point is clear enough:
it is the tale that specifies the portrait, not the other way around.

The technique of impersonation as I am considering it here has no necessary connection whatever with the question of the integration of a given
tale in the Canterbury frame. The Knight's mention of writing in his tale is
indeed an anomalous detail in the context of the pilgrimage. It is often
regarded as a sign of the incomplete revision of the (hypothetical) "Palamon
and Arcite," supposedly written before Chaucer had the idea of the *Tales*
and afterward inserted in its present position in Fragment I. The reference
to writing is taken as evidence that the Knight was not the "original" speaker
and, in a reading like Howard's, that he is still not always the speaker.[8] As
far as it goes, the argument about the chronology of composition is doubtless valid, but it has nothing to do with the question of whether or not the
tale is impersonated, a question that can, and ought to, be separated, at
least initially, from the fiction of the pilgrimage. Details like the Knight's
"write" are not immediately relevant because they do not affect the intention to create a speaker (they may become relevant at a different level of
analysis later). Impersonation, the controlled use of voicing to direct us to
what a narrative tells us about its narrator, *precedes dramatization of the
Canterbury sort* in Chaucer, analytically and no doubt sometimes chrono-
logically. The proper method is to ascribe the entire narration in all its
details to a *single* speaker (on the authority of Leicester's razor) and to use
it as evidence in constructing that speaker's consciousness, keeping the
question of the speaker's "identity" open until the analysis is complete. It is
convenient and harmless to accept the frame's statement that the Knight's
Tale is "the tale the Knight tells" as long as we recognize that it merely
gives us something to call the speaker and tells us nothing reliable about
him in advance.

---

8. See Alfred David, *The Strumpet Muse* (Bloomington: Indiana Univ. Press, 1976), pp. 77–89.

I want to conclude an already perverse argument with a further perversity. I have argued that we ought to reverse the ordinary common-sense approach to the relations between foreground and background in the poem and see the pilgrims as the products rather than as the producers of their tales. I have suggested further that Chaucer's fiction may explain, rather than be explained by, the facts of fourteenth-century social history. I now want to maintain that the poet is the creation rather than the creator of his poem. More perversely still, I want to put a nick in my own razor and reintroduce a version of the double narrator in Chaucer. I do this in order to question a notion more widespread and apparently more durable than the various versions of "unimpersonated artistry," the notion of Chaucer the pilgrim. I must admit to being less sure of my ground here. For one thing, I am challenging an idea first put forward by E. Talbot Donaldson,[9] who has for years been producing the best line-by-line interpretations of Chaucer that I know, using what amounts to the very technique of reading I have been urging here.

Nevertheless, it seems clear on the face of it that issues of the sort I have been discussing are raised by the notion of Chaucer the pilgrim, the naïve narrator of the General Prologue and the links, who so often misses the point of the complex phenomena he describes in order that Chaucer the satirist or the poet or the man can make sure *we* see how very complex they are. The idea leads to a multiplication of speakers of the same text, not serially (though some critics have considered this possibility too),[1] but simultaneously. It requires that in any given passage we first decide what Chaucer the pilgrim means by what he says and then what Chaucer the poet means by what the pilgrim means. Here, too, there is often confusion about the distinction between the voice of the text and a presence behind and beyond it who somehow guarantees the meaning we find there.[2] Descriptions of Chaucer the poet sometimes take on a distinctly metaphysical cast, as in this passage from Donaldson's *Speaking of Chaucer:*

> Undoubtedly Chaucer the man would, like his fictional representative, have found [the Prioress] charming and looked on her with affection. To have got on so well in so changeable a world Chaucer must have got on well with the people in it, and it is doubtful that one may get on with people merely by pretending to like them: one's heart has to be in it. But the third entity, Chaucer the poet, operates in a realm

9. Donaldson, "Chaucer the Pilgrim," *PMLA*, 69 (1954), 928–36; rpt. in his *Speaking of Chaucer* (London: Athlone, 1970). Howard discusses the topic in his "Chaucer the Man," *PMLA*, 80 (1965), 337–43. [See above, pp. 484–92 and pp. 492–502.]

1. See Rosemary Woolf, "Chaucer as a Satirist in the General Prologue to the *Canterbury Tales*," *Critical Quarterly*, 1 (1959), 150–57.

2. I suspect that this confusion has to do with a natural desire on the part of critics to evade the feelings of contingency and responsibility that haunt the act of interpretation. If the voice of the text is assumed to be that of an external subject, one justifies what one reads out of the text on the authority of a poet who must have "meant" to put it in. See Donaldson's brilliant and humane critique of stemma editing on similar grounds in "The Psychology of Editors of Middle English Texts," *Speaking of Chaucer*, pp. 102–18.

which is above and subsumes those in which Chaucer the man and
Chaucer the pilgrim have their being. In this realm prioresses may be
simultaneously evaluated as marvellously amiable ladies and as
prioresses.   (p. 11) [See above, p. 491]

But the "higher realm" Donaldson is talking about is and can only be
the *poem*, the text—as he himself knows perfectly well—and Chaucer the
poet can only be what I have been calling the voice of the text. Donaldson
is, as always, attentive to what the text *says* here, in particular to the tensions among social, human, and moral elements that the General Prologue
undeniably displays. The division of the speaker into pilgrim, man, and
poet is a way of registering these tensions and their complexity, of suggesting
"a vision of the social world imposed on one of the moral world" (p. 9)
[p. 490], and I can have no objection to this aim. I do not see the need,
however, to reify these tensions into separate personalities of the same speaker,
and I think this way of talking about the narrator of the General Prologue
is misleading because it encourages us to treat him *as if we knew who he
was* apart from his utterances. The general personality traits of Chaucer the
pilgrim have themselves become reified in the Chaucer criticism of the last
twenty years, and this frozen concept of the character has fostered a care-
lessness in reading that Donaldson himself rarely commits.

If I were going to try to characterize the speaker of the General Prologue
myself, I would follow the lead of John M. Major in calling him, not naïve,
but extraordinarily sophisticated.[3] I doubt, however, that this characterization, even if accepted, would go very far toward solving the problems of the
poem, because it still does not tell us much about who the speaker is, and
that is what we want to know. The notion of Chaucer the pilgrim at least
offers us an *homme moyen sensuel* with whom we can feel we know where
we are, but I think that it is just this sense of knowing where we are, with
whom we are dealing, that the General Prologue deliberately and calculat-
edly denies us. For a brief suggestion of this intention—which is all I can
offer here—consider these lines from the Monk's portrait, a notorious locus
for the naïveté of the narrator:

> He yaf nat of that text a pulled hen,
> That seith that hunters ben nat hooly men,
> Ne that a monk, whan he is recchelees,
> Is likned til a fissh that is waterlees,—
> This is to seyn, a monk out of his cloystre.
> But thilke texte heeld he nat worth an oystre;
> And I seyde his opinion was good.
> What sholde he studie and make hymselven wood,
> Upon a book in cloystre alwey to poure.
> Or swynken with his handes, and laboure,
> As Austyn bit? How shal the world be served?

3. See Major's valuable and neglected article "The Personality of Chaucer the Pilgrim," *PMLA*, 75 (1960),
160–62.

> Lat Austyn have his swynk to hym reserved!
> Therfore he was a prikasour aright . . .
>   (I. 177–89)

The Monk's own bluff manner is present in these lines. I agree with most commentators that he is being half-quoted, that we hear his style, for example, in the turn of a phrase like "nat worth an oystre!" Present too are the standards of his calling, against which, if we will, he may be measured. The social and moral worlds do indeed display their tension here, but who brought these issues up? Who is responsible for the slightly suspended enjambment that turns "As Austyn bit?" into a small firecracker? For the wicked specificity with which, at the beginning of the portrait, the Monk's bridle is said to jingle "as dooth the *chapel* belle"? Who goes to such pains to explain the precise application of the proverb about the fish, "This is to seyn . . ."? Who if not the speaker? But these observations do not permit us to say that he is *only* making a moral judgment or only making fun of the Monk (the two are not quite the same, and both are going on). A sense of the positive claims made by the pilgrim's vitality, his "manliness," is also registered by the portrait.[4] The speaker's amused enjoyment of the Monk's forthright humanity is too patent to let us see him as just a moralist. The way his voice evokes complex possibilities of attitude is neatly caught by "And I seyde his opinion was good": that's what he said when he and the Monk had their conversation, but is he saying the same thing now in this portrait? Did he really mean it at the time? Does he now? In what sense?

The point of this exercise is not merely to show that the speaker's attitude is complex and sophisticated but also to stress how obliquely expressed it is, all in ironic juxtapositions and loaded words whose precise heft is hard to weigh. What we have, in fact, is a speaker who is not giving too much of himself away, who is not telling us, any more than he told the Monk, his whole mind in plain terms. The tensions among social, moral, and existential worlds are embodied in a single voice here, and they are embodied precisely *as tensions*, not as a resolution or a synthesis, for we cannot tell exactly what the speaker thinks either of the Monk or of conventional morality. What we *can* tell is that we are dealing with a speaker who withholds himself from us, with the traces of a presence that asserts its simultaneous absence. The speaker is present as uncomprehended, as not to be seized all at once in his totality. He *displays his difference* from his externalizations, his speaking, in the very act of externalizing himself. It is this effect, I think, that creates the feeling of "reality" in the text, the sense that there is somebody there. In literature (as in life) the reality of characters is a function of their mystery, of the extent to which we are made to feel that there is more going on in regard to them than we know or can predict. Criseyde is a well-known and well-analyzed example in Chaucer,[5] and I suggest that the general

---

4. See Jill Mann's excellent discussion in *Chaucer and Medieval Estates Satire* (Cambridge: Cambridge Univ. Press, 1973), pp. 17–37, esp. p. 20.
5. See Arthur Mizener, "Character and Action in the Case of Criseyde," *PMLA*, 54 (1939), 65–81, and Robert P. apRoberts, "The Central Episode in Chaucer's *Troilus*," *PMLA*, 77 (1962), 373–85.

narrator of the *Canterbury Tales* is another. His lack of definition may also explain why he can be taken for Chaucer the pilgrim. Because his identity is a function of what he leaves unspoken—because it is derived from implication, irony, innuendo, the potentialities of meaning and intention that occur in the gaps between observations drawn from radically different realms of discourse[6]—there is a temptation to reduce his uncomfortable indeterminacy by forcing the gaps shut, by spelling out the connections. But suppressing the indeterminacy in this way involves reducing complex meanings to simpler ones. One infers "Chaucer the pilgrim" by ignoring the things the speaker "does not say" (since, after all, he does not *say* them—only suggests) and by insisting that he "means" his statements in only the plainest, most literal sense. Such an interpretation does not fail to recognize that the complexities of meaning are there; it simply assigns them to "the poem" or to "Chaucer the poet," thus producing what I am arguing is a contradiction: the simple and naïve narrator of a complex and sophisticated narration.

In fact, however, not only the General Prologue but the whole of the *Canterbury Tales* works against a quick or easy comprehension of the speaker. It is to suggest how it does so that I am going to reintroduce a sort of double narration. First of all, though, it should be clear that there is only one speaker of the entire poem and that he is also the poem's maker. The conspicuous textuality of the work makes this fact inescapable. It may be that Chaucer would have "corrected" anomalies like the Knight's "But of that storie list me nat to write" and that he would have supplied a complete and self-consistent set of links between the present fragments to round out the Canterbury fiction. It seems much less likely that he would have revised the Man of Law's promise to tell his rime-royal tale in prose or the "quod she" in the middle of the Prioress' Tale or the "turne over the leef" passage in the Miller's Prologue or the inordinate and undramatic length of the Melibee. And I am quite certain that he would not have altered the fundamental "contingency that a tale not memorized but told impromptu is in verse." What is at issue here is not simply a neutral medium that we are entitled to ignore. If pentameter couplets are the *koiné* of the poem, stanzaic verse (especially rime royal but also the Monk's stanza and even Sir Thopas' tail rhyme) functions as a formal equivalent, a translation into writing, of a different level of diction: it identifies a speaker with pretensions to an elevated style, in life as well as in storytelling. If it is functional in the poem that one kind of verse be sensed as verse, why not other kinds, and prose as well? The poem's insistence on these distinctions has interesting

---

6. This observation suggests that a paratactic style is particularly conducive to producing the kind of effect I am describing, because the information (syntax) that would *specify* the connection between statements is left out. See Erich Auerbach, "Roland against Ganelon," in his *Mimesis: The Representation of Reality in Western Literature* (Garden City, N.Y.: Anchor-Doubleday, 1953), pp. 83–107. Parataxis is one of the main descriptive techniques of the General Prologue, particularly noticeable in the three central portraits of the Shipman, the Physician, and the Wife of Bath, but widely employed throughout. Further, the structure of the Prologue itself is paratactic (composed of juxtaposed independent portraits), and so is that of the poem as a whole (composed of juxtaposed independent tales).

implications for the problem of oral delivery. The *Canterbury Tales* is not written to be spoken as if it were a play. It is written to be read, but read *as if* it were spoken. The poem is a literary imitation of oral performance.[7]

One effect of this fundamental textuality is to keep us constantly aware that the frame, the reportage, is a patent fiction. There is no pilgrimage, there are no pilgrims. Whether or not Chaucer ever went to Canterbury, whether or not the characters in the poem are drawn from "real life," what we have in front of us is the activity of a poet, a maker, giving his own rhythm and pattern, his own shape and voice, his own complex interpretation to the materials of the poem. And that maker *is the speaker of the poem*, the voice of the text. There is no one there but that voice, that text. The narrator of the *Canterbury Tales* is the speaker we call Chaucer the poet, though it would be more accurate—I cannot resist, this once—to call him Chaucer the poem.

This being said, it is also true that one of the first discoveries we make when we try to characterize this maker and speaker on the evidence of his discourse, to begin to specify the voice of the text, is that he is an impersonator in the conventional sense: he puts fictional others between himself and us. This is the sense in which the tales are double-voiced: each of them is Chaucer impersonating a pilgrim, the narrator speaking in the voice of the Knight or the Reeve or the Second Nun. They are his creatures, voices that he assumes; he gives them his life.

But it would be as accurate, from another perspective, to say that he takes his life from them, and the amount of time and effort spent on making the pilgrims independent, the sheer labor of consistent, unbroken impersonation to which the poem testifies, suggests that this is the more compelling perspective, for Chaucer as for us. The enterprise of the poem involves the continual attempt, continually repeated, to see from another's point of view, to stretch and extend the self by learning to speak in the voices of others; and the poem itself is, among other things, the record of that attempt.

I have tried to evoke, however briefly, the incompleteness—the indeterminacy and the resistance to classification—of the voice that speaks in the General Prologue. One corollary of this quality is the cognate incompleteness of the Prologue itself, one of whose principal themes is the insufficiency of traditional social and moral classifying schemes—estates, hierarchies, and the like—to deal with the complexity of individuals and their relations. The speaker not only embodies this insufficiency, he recognizes it and feels it: "Also I prey yow to foryeve it me, / Al have I nat set folk in hir degree / Heere in this tale, as that they sholde stonde" (I.743–

---

7. I have neglected B. H. Bronson's criticisms of Chaucer the pilgrim and related matters (see esp. his *In Search of Chaucer* [Toronto: Univ. of Toronto Press, 1960], pp. 25–33), because my assumptions about the relations between literary and oral cultures in Chaucer's poetry start from a position very nearly opposite to his. I agree with him, however, that the problem of performance in Chaucer is worth further study; in fact, I think it is a central theme throughout the poet's career. In the *Canterbury Tales*, the frame exists precisely to provide a literary representation of the ordinarily extratextual and tacit dimensions of storytelling in writing. The poem presents not merely stories but stories told to an audience that is part of the fiction, and this circumstance allows Chaucer to register the effects of a range of conditions of performance.

45). From this insufficiency he turns to the pilgrims. He sets them free to speak in part to free himself from the constraints and uncertainties generated by his own attempt to classify them—an attempt that, however universal and impersonal it may look at the beginning of the Prologue, is always only his view and one too complex for him to speak by himself. The Prologue does not do justice to the pilgrims. By the same token and for the same reasons it does not do justice to the narrator and his understanding of his world. In the tales, therefore, he slows us down, keeps us from grasping him too quickly and easily, by directing our attention to the variety and complexity of the roles he plays, the voices he assumes. He is, we know, each of the pilgrims and all of them, but he seems to insist that we can only discover him by discovering for ourselves who the Knight is, who the Parson, who the Pardoner and the Wife of Bath.

We may be impatient to know the speaker of the General Prologue, but as the voice of the poem as a whole, he is the last of the pilgrims we may hope to comprehend, and then only by grasping each of the others individually and in turn and in all the complexity of their relationships to one another. The relation of the voice that speaks in the General Prologue to the personality of the poet is like that of an individual portrait to its tale and that of the Prologue itself to all the tales. It is a prologal voice, a voice that is only beginning to speak. Chaucer's Prologue, like this prologue of mine, needs the tales to fulfill itself in the gradual and measured but always contingent and uncertain activity of impersonation, in both senses. The speaker of the *Canterbury Tales*—Chaucer—is indeed as fictional as the pilgrims, in the sense that like them he is a self-constructing voice. He practices what I have called the art of impersonation, finally, to impersonate himself, to create himself as fully as he can in his work.

GEORGE LYMAN KITTREDGE

[The Dramatic Principle of the *Canterbury Tales*]†

The Canterbury Tales exists in fragments, which no one has ever succeeded in fitting together. Different manuscripts arrange them in different ways, and modern scholars have exhibited much ingenuity in trying to make out the right order of the several stories. Of late, there has been a disposition amongst the learned to believe either that Chaucer made more than one tentative arrangement, or that he never settled the matter in his mind at all. These are questions, however, that need not now detain us. The plan is clear enough for our immediate purposes. We may profitably study the tales in groups, without regard to disputed problems of order.

†Excerpted by permission of the publishers from *Chaucer and His Poetry*, by George Lyman Kittredge, Cambridge, Massachusetts: Harvard University Press, Copyright © 1915 by George Lyman Kittredge; © 1970 by the President and Fellows of Harvard College. Pp. 146–56.

We know, at least, that the series begins with the Knight, the Miller, the Reeve, and the Cook, and ends with the Manciple and the Parson. Within these extremities, we can make out several groups, each of which holds together. One of the longest of these begins with the Shipman's Prologue and ends with the Nun's Priest's Epilogue, containing the tales of the Shipman, the Prioress, Chaucer himself (namely, two, Sir Thopas and the Melibee) the Monk and the Nun's Priest. This group is admirably organized. Another, still longer, which is called the Marriage Group, begins with the Wife of Bath's Prologue and ends with the Franklin's Tale: the order is Wife, Friar, Summer, Clerk, Merchant, Squire, Franklin. The Physician's Tale and the Pardoner's also form a group; so do the Second Nun's and the Canon's Yeoman's. The Tale of the Man of Law stands, in a manner, by itself, with an elaborate introduction which makes it clear that it was to begin the day. By common consent it is placed after the Cook's fragment. It will not be possible, in the limited time at my disposal, to consider every group of tales. I shall make a selection, therefore, with a view to illustrate Chaucer's art in the two main points of character and dramatic method.

There has been a rather active discussion, for more than a hundred years, concerning the probable source of Chaucer's scheme of the Canterbury Pilgrimage. The result is a *non liquet*. Several possible models have been pointed out, and others are turning up continually. The *pros* and *cons* in every case have been argued with learning and ingenuity. So far as I can see, however, the advocates of each new source, though they have found it easy to demolish the arguments of their predecessors, have not been quite so successful in constructing acceptable theories of their own. There is, then, no single collection of tales to which we can point, with any confidence, as that which gave Chaucer the hint.

This condition of things should not surprise us. It is what we ought to expect, and the inference is easy. The plan of attaching stories together so as to make a collection is very old, very widespread, and very obvious. It was a traditional bit of technique, both in literature and in folklore, ages before Chaucer was born, and in all four quarters of the world. And furthermore, it was a bit of technique that accorded with actual practice. What could people do, in old times, but tell stories, when they were assembled and had plenty of leisure? The practice, indeed, has not died out, even in these days of novels and newspapers, and it was universal and inevitable, under all sorts of circumstances, when these time-killing but unsociable inventions did not yet exist. Chaucer's problem was not, to hunt through literature for an idea which confronted him, unsought, at every turn in life. That he knew collections of tales may be taken for granted; that he often followed convention is a matter of course. He had some knowledge of the literary device, and much knowledge of the immemorial habit of mankind.

That the particular frame which Chaucer adopted resembles this or that frame which preceded it in literary history, signifies nothing—except that some things in life are more or less like other things. Chaucer had no need to borrow or to invent: he needed only to observe. His genius appears, in the first place, in making a good choice among his several observations, in perceiving the advantages of one particular frame over all others. Pilgrims were as familiar sights to Chaucer as commercial travellers are to us. There is not one chance in a hundred that he had not gone on a Canterbury pilgrimage himself. And pilgrims did, for a fact, while away the time in story-telling. Newton did not learn that apples fall by reading treatises on pomology.

The most tantalizing of all the parallels, by the way, is Sercambi's *Novelle*, for which the frame is likewise a pilgrimage. But it is hard to get an historical point of contact. Dates are right enough, and geography does not interfere. It is even conceivable that Chaucer and Sercambi met in Italy, though there is no evidence either way. The difficulties are less tangible than dates and places; but, such as they are, they cannot be surmounted. Yet, after all, Sercambi's scheme is a precious document in the case, though not in proof of imitation. What it does show, is that it was possible for a writer of far less originality than Chaucer to hit upon the device of a pilgrimage as a convenient frame for a collection of stories.

Before the idea of a pilgrimage occurred to him, Chaucer had twice undertaken to compose a series of tales. The results lie before us in the Tragedies, afterwards assigned to the Monk, and the Legend of Cupid's Saints, otherwise known as Good Women. Both works exhibit, in the most striking fashion, the orderly habits of mediæval literature. They likewise prove, beyond cavil, the docility of Chaucer himself, the instinctive readiness with which he deferred to technical authority and bowed his neck to the rhetorical yoke. The lesson is salutary. We perceive, in this great poet, not a vast, irregular, untaught genius,—an amiable but terrible infant, impatient of regulation, acknowledging no laws of structure, guided by no canons of criticism. Quite the contrary! Chaucer was a conscientious student of literary form. He submitted with patient eagerness to the precepts of his teachers. Schematism was the governing principle of their instruction, and he had no wish to rebel. Thus he got the training which enabled him, when the time came, to give free rein to his vivacious originality without losing his self-control.

From these considerations there emerges a rule of judgment that is of some value for our guidance in interpreting Chaucer's final masterpiece, the Canterbury Tales. It may be stated in the simplest language: *Chaucer always knew what he was about.* When, therefore, he seems to be violating dramatic fitness,—as in the ironical tribute of the Clerk to the Wife of Bath, or the monstrous cynicism of the Pardoner's confessions,—we must look to our steps. Headlong inferences are dangerous. We are dealing with a great literary artist who had been through the schools. The chances are that such details are not casual flourishes. Somehow, in all likelihood, they fall into decorous subordination to his main design.

This design, as we know, is a pilgrimage to Canterbury. I have spoken of it, for convenience, as a "frame." That, indeed, is the light in which it is commonly regarded. We read each tale by itself, as if it were an isolated unit; often, indeed, as if Chaucer were telling it in his own person. At most, we inquire, in a half-hearted fashion, whether it is appropriate to the character of the Knight, or the Sumner, or the Franklin. Very seldom do we venture to regard the several stories from the dramatic point of view. Yet that is manifestly our paramount duty.

Many and great were the advantages that Chaucer discerned in his plot of a Canterbury pilgrimage. They stand out in sharp contrast against the monotonous background of his two earlier experiments, the Tragedies and the Legend, to which we may return for a moment.

Each of these is unified not by structure but by subject matter. The unity, therefore, is not organic, but mechanical. In the Tragedies,—for the idea of which Chaucer was indebted in equal measure to the Romance of the Rose and Boccaccio's *De Casibus*,—we have a number of sombre sketches, rather declamatory than narrative, of exalted personages whom Fortune brought low. In the Good Women,—a singular cross between the *Legenda Aurea* and Ovid's *Heroides*, with a charming prologue, which reverts for its machinery to the French love-visions,—we read the lives of famous ladies of ancient days who suffered death, or worse, for love of faithless men. In both works the plan is absolutely rigid. Variety in form or matter is excluded by the convention adopted (tragedy, in the one; legend in the other) and by the limitations of the theme. Movement is impossible, for there is no connection between the parts. Dramatic presentation is not attempted, or even thought of, all the stories being told by one person, the poet himself.

Turn now to the Canterbury Tales, and the change is startling. It results, in the last analysis, from Chaucer's adopting the scheme of a Canterbury pilgrimage. The stories are no longer alike in form or subject, nor are they all in one key. There is infinite variety, because they are told by a variety of persons. Every reader may discover something to his taste, both in style and substance, as Chaucer himself protests in his apology for the Miller, "who tolde his cherles tale in his manere." Those who do not fancy low comedy may find enough of polite history, as well as of morality and religion.

> And therfore, whoso list it nat yheere,
> Turne over the leef and chese another tale;
> For he shal fynde ynowe, grete and smale,
> Of storial thyng that toucheth gentillesse,
> And eek moralitee and hoolynesse.
> Blameth nat me if that ye chese amys.
>   (A.3176–81) [68–73]

But this is not all. Chaucer's adoption of a Canterbury pilgrimage was not a mere excuse for story-telling. Most readers, I am aware, treat this great masterpiece simply as a storehouse of fiction, and so do many critics. Yet everybody feels, I am sure, that Chaucer was quite as much interested in the Pilgrims themselves as in their several narratives. This, no doubt, is what Dryden had in mind when he wrote, comparing Chaucer with Ovid: "Both of them understood the manners, under which name I comprehend the passions, and, in a larger sense, the descriptions of persons, and their very habits. For an example, I see Baucis and Philemon as perfectly before me, as if some ancient painter had drawn them; and all the pilgrims in the Canterbury Tales,—their humors, their features, and the very dress, as distinctly as if I had supped with them at the Tabard in Southwark; yet even there too the figures in Chaucer are much more lively, and set in a better light."

I am much deceived if Dryden is not here treading on the verge of the proposition that the Canterbury Tales is, to all intents and purposes, a Human Comedy. Certainly he is calling our attention to something that distinguishes Chaucer's work from every collection of stories that preceded it. It was much, as we have seen, that Chaucer had the judgment, among the infinite doings of the world, to select a pilgrimage, and to parcel out his tales to the miscellaneous company that met at the Tabard on the way to Canterbury. It was more, far more, that he had the genius to create the Pilgrims, endowing each of them with an individuality that goes much beyond the typical. If we had only the Prologue, we might, perhaps, regard the Pilgrims as types. The error is common, and venial. But we must not stop with the Prologue: we must go on to the play. The Pilgrims are not static: they move and live. The Canterbury Pilgrimage is, whether Dryden meant it or not, a Human Comedy, and the Knight and the Miller and the Pardoner and the Wife of Bath and the rest are the *dramatis personae*. The Prologue itself is not merely a prologue: it is the first act, which sets the personages in motion. Thereafter, they move by virtue of their inherent vitality, not as tale-telling puppets, but as men and women. From this point of view, which surely accords with Chaucer's intention, the Pilgrims do not exist for the sake of the stories, but *vice versa*. Structurally regarded, the stories are merely long speeches expressing, directly or indirectly, the characters of the several persons. They are more or less comparable, in this regard, to the soliloquies of Hamlet or Iago or Macbeth. But they are not mere monologues, for each is addressed to all the other personages, and evokes reply and comment, being thus, in a real sense, a part of the conversation.

Further,—and this is a point of crucial significance,—the action of the plot, however simple, involves a great variety of relations among the Pilgrims. They are brought together by a common impulse, into a casual and impermanent association, which is nevertheless, for the time being, peculiarly intimate. They move slowly along the road, from village to village and inn to inn, in groups that are ever shifting, but ever forming afresh. Things happen to them. They come to know each other better and better. Their personalities act and react. Friendships combine for the nonce. Jokes are cracked, like the Host's on the Pardoner, which are taken amiss. Smouldering enmities of class or profession, like that between the Sumner and the Friar, which was proverbial, blaze into flaming quarrels. Thus the story of any pilgrim may be affected or determined,—in its contents, or in the manner of the telling, or in both,—not only by his character in general, but also by the circumstances, by the situation, by his momentary relations to the others in the company, or even by something in a tale that has come before. We lose much, therefore, when we neglect the so-called prologues and epilogues, and the bits of conversation and narrative that link the tales together. Many more of these would have been supplied if Chaucer had not left his work in so fragmentary a condition; but such as we have are invaluable, both for their own excellence, and for the light they throw upon the scope and details of the great design.

* * *

GEORGE LYMAN KITTREDGE

[The Marriage Group] †

* * *

One other act of Chaucer's Human Comedy is complete (but for the story of Cambuscan) and highly finished. It begins with the Wife of Bath's Prologue and ends with the Tale of the Franklin. The subject is Marriage, which is discussed from several points of view, as the most important problem in organized society. The solution of the problem brings the act to an end.

The dominant figure in this act of the Comedy is the Wife of Bath. It is she who starts the debate, and the participants keep her steadily in mind, and mention her and her doctrines more than once. Even the comic interlude which breaks into the discussion is occasioned by her prologue. Nowhere is the dramatic spirit of the Canterbury Pilgrimage more evident than in this Marriage group of tales. Nowhere is it more important to heed the relations of the Pilgrims to each other. Neglect of this precaution has led to a good deal of misunderstanding.

The Wife's ostensible subject is Tribulation in Marriage. On this, she avers, she can speak with the authority of an expert, for she has outlived five husbands, worthy men in their degree, and she is ready to welcome a sixth when God shall send him.

> "Yblessed be God that I have wedded fyve!
> Welcome the sixte, whan that evere he shal." [44–45]

Somebody—was it one of the clerics in the party?—has told her lately that she should have married but once. This dictum rankles: she finds no war-

† Excerpted by permission of the publishers from *Chaucer and His Poetry*, by George Lyman Kittredge, Cambridge, Massachusetts: Harvard University Press, Copyright © 1915 by George Lyman Kittredge; © 1970 by the President and Fellows of Harvard College. Pp. 185–201, 205–10. We have abridged Kittredge's argument by omitting his discussion of tales not included in this volume, some of his lengthy citations from Chaucer, and a few shorter references. His ideas were first and most fully presented in "Chaucer's Discussion of Marriage," *Modern Philology* 9 (1911–12): 435–67.

rant for it in Scripture, and certainly none in her inclinations. Accordingly, she breaks forth in a vehement defense of her own principles and practices. The celibate life, she admits, may be a high and holy thing, well fitted for the Apostle Paul and other saints. Out of deference to them, she accords it the palm, for form's sake; but, at the same time, she makes her own position perfectly clear. She despises the ideal of the Church in this regard, and looks down with contempt upon all who aspire to it. Human nature is good enough for her. This is her first heresy; but she is so jovial in proclaiming it that no one takes offence, however strongly some of the Pilgrims may reprobate her principles in their hearts.

* * *

The Wife proceeds, with infinite zest, to give the history of her married life, unfolding, as she does so, another heretical doctrine of a startling kind, which, in fact, is the real subject of her discourse. This is nothing less than the dogma that the wife is the head of the house. Obedience is not her duty, but the husband's. Men are no match for women, anyway. Let them sink back to their proper level, and cease their ridiculous efforts to maintain a position for which they are not fit. Then marriages will all be happy. Otherwise there is no hope for anything but misery in wedlock. She supports her contention with much curious learning, derived, of course, from her fifth and latest husband, who was a professional scholar; and she overbears opposition by quoting her own experience, which is better testimony than the citation of authorities. She had always had her own way. Sometimes she cowed her husbands, and sometimes she cajoled them; but none of the five could resist her government. And it was well for them to yield. This is happy marriage. Who should know so well as she? Once, indeed, she rises almost to sublimity, as she looks back on the joy of her life:

> "But, Lord Crist! whan that it remembreth me
> Upon my yowthe, and on my jolitee,
> It tikleth me aboute myn herte roote.
> Unto this day it dooth myn herte boote
> That I have had my world as in my tyme." [469–73]

This is one of the great dramatic utterances of human nature, as the Wife of Bath is one of the most amazing characters that the brain of man has ever yet conceived.

The Pilgrims, we may be sure, are not inattentive to the Wife's harangue. To the Prioress, her complete antithesis, it means little, either good or bad. She does not understand the language of the worldly widow. The Parson and the Clerk of course are scandalized: such heresies cannot pass unchallenged, even as a jest. Of the two, the Clerk has the greater cause for resentment, for the Wife has aimed her shafts at him directly, not in malice, but in mischievous defiance. Not only has she entered the lists as a disputant in theology, but she has gone out of her way to attack his order, railing at them especially for their satire on women. "No clerk," she declares, "can speak well of wives. It is an impossibility." And, worse than all, she has told how she had married a clerk of Oxford, an alumnus of our modest scholar's

The Wife of Bath vs. The Prioress

own university, and had reduced him to shameful subjection. The Wife is an heresiarch after her own boisterous fashion. She is not to be taken too seriously, but she deserves a rebuke; and who is so fit to administer it as the Clerk himself, whose orthodoxy is unflinching, and whose every word is "sownynge in moral vertu"? It is not our Clerk's way, however, to thrust himself forward. His turn will come, and meanwhile he rides quietly along, listening without comment, and biding his time.

* * *

The Wife's tale of What Women most Desire is a famous old story, which is extant in several versions. As she tells it, it becomes an illustrative exemplum, to enforce the moral of her sermon. Sovereignty over men is a woman's ambition, and the knight of the Round Table, who found himself in a strange dilemma, submitted his judgment to his wife's choice, with the happiest result. He lived with her in perfect joy till their life's end,—and so "I pray," concludes the Wife of Bath, "that those may die early who will not yield themselves entirely to petticoat government." Mediæval feminism has had its say. The sermon is finished, and the moral is driven home.

Thus far the Wife of Bath has had plain sailing. She has proved her case to her own satisfaction, by experience, by authority, and by an illustrative story; and nobody seems inclined to take her to task.

The Friar compliments her in a non-committal fashion, but turns off, with a clever transition, to assail the Sumner, at whom he had been looking "with a louring chere" ever since that worthy had reproved him for laughing at the Wife's preamble. What follows, then, is a comic interlude, like that between Miller and Reeve at an earlier stage of the pilgrimage. The Friar tells a tale of a sumner who was carried off by the devil, and the Sumner, so angry that he stood up in his stirrups, retorts with an incomparable satire on begging friars, worked up on the basis of a trivial and sordid fabliau. Nowhere in the pilgrimage is the dramatic interplay of character more remarkable. For the Wife is the moving cause of the quarrel, though quite involuntarily. Harry Bailly, we note, has been content to drop the reins. The drama guides itself, moving on by virtue of the relations of the *dramatis personae*, their characters, and the logic of the situation. To all appearances the discussion of marriage has ended with the speaker who began it. The day's journey closes with the Sumner's Tale. The Host, at all events, has no thought of reopening the debate on matrimony when he calls upon the Clerk of Oxford to begin the entertainment next morning.

The Clerk has made no sign. He is as demure, the Host remarks, as a bride at her wedding breakfast. "Cheer up!" cries Harry, "this is no time to study. Tell us some merry tale, not in the high style, of which you are doubtless a master, but in plain language, so that we may all understand it." * * * The Oxford scholar yields a courteous assent, and begins the tale of Griselda, taught him at Padua by a noble clerk of Italy, one Francis Petrarch, who is now dead and buried. God rest his soul!

The story starts quite innocently. Not until it is well underway do the Pilgrims perceive the Clerk's drift. He is telling the tale of a patient and obedient wife, whose steadfast devotion to her husband was proof against every trial. With consummate art he is answering the Wife of Bath without appearing to take any notice either of her arguments or of her boisterous assault upon his order. "Clerks," she has declared, "cannot possibly speak well of wives." Yet here is one clerk, repeating the tale told him by another, and its theme is wifely fidelity and woman's fortitude under affliction.

We should not forget that the Clerk's Tale, like the Wife's long sermon, is addressed to the Canterbury Pilgrims, not to us, though we are privileged to overhear. We must not only listen, but look. In our mind's eye, we must see the Pilgrims, and watch their demeanor. Naturally, they are interested, and, equally of course, they understand what the Clerk is doing. He is replying to the Wife of Bath,—confuting her heresies, and at the same time vindicating his own order from her abusive raillery.

One can hardly conceive a more skilful method of replying. Its indirectness and deliberation are alike masterly. The Clerk is not talking about the Wife of Bath. His tale contains no personal allusions. It is, on the face of it, simply an affecting narrative which he chanced to hear from a learned friend in Italy, and which he supposes may interest his fellow-travellers. But, as the picture of Griselda grows slowly on the canvas, no Pilgrim can fail to recognize the complete antithesis to the Wife of Bath. Besides, however you and I may feel about it, to Chaucer's contemporaries the story was infinitely pathetic. One of Petrarch's friends broke down while reading it aloud, and could not continue, so deep was his emotion, but had to hand the manuscript to one of his retinue to finish. Another read it through unmoved, but only because he did not believe that there ever lived a wife so loving, so submissive, and so patient under affliction.

This point, in truth,—the incredibility of the example,—might have weakened its force as an answer to the Wife of Bath, if she were logically in a position to take advantage of such an objection. But this she cannot well do without abandoning her main thesis, that women are vastly superior to men. She might, to be sure, retort that the story proves too much, that it shows that men are unfit to have dominion over their wives, since they abuse it so abominably. But, before she can frame any retort whatever,— if, indeed, she is not too much affected by the pathos to be mistress of her argumentative faculties,—the Clerk, who is a professional logician and a conscientious moralist, makes all debate impossible by explaining, in Petrarch's words, the true lesson. "This story is not meant as an exhortation to wives to be as patient as Griselda, for that would transcend the powers of human nature. It teaches all of us, men and women alike, how we should submit ourselves to the afflictions that God sends. The Marquis Walter was a ruthless experimenter with souls. God is not like that. The trials He sends are for our good, and we should accept them with Christian resignation."

* * *

Here is a remarkable situation. The Clerk has vindicated his order by praising women, and he has set up again the orthodox tenet of wifely obedience. But he has not said a word to the Wife of Bath, and, in the moral, he has expressly removed the story from the domain of controversy by asserting, in the plainest terms, that it is not a lesson for wives, but for

Christians in general. If he drops the subject now, he has left the Wife of Bath unanswered after all.

But he does not drop the subject. He has a surprise in store for the would-be feminist heresiarch and for the whole company. Suddenly, without a moment's warning, he turns to the Wife of Bath, and, with an air of serene and smiling urbanity, offers to recite a song that he has just composed in her honor, and in honor of the sect which she represents and of which she has proved herself so doughty a champion:—"May God establish both her way of life and her principles; for the world would suffer if they should not prevail":—

> "Whos lyf and al hire secte God mayntene
> In heigh maistrie, and elles were it scathe."

And so he declaims his Envoy in praise of feminism. It is an address to all wise and prudent married women, exhorting them to follow the precepts and the practice of the Wife of Bath.

* * *

The moment is completely dramatic. It is not Chaucer who speaks, but the Clerk of Oxenford, and every word is in perfect character. His mock encomium is not only a masterpiece of sustained and mordant irony; it is a marvellous specimen of technical skill in metre, in diction, and in vigorous and concentrated satire. None but the Clerk, a trained rhetorician, could have composed it. None but the Clerk, a master of logic and a practised disputant, could have turned upon an opponent so adroitly. The home thrust comes when the guard is down. The Clerk is a moral philosopher, and he has proved both his earnestness and his competence. It is one of the humors of literature that this Envoy is traditionally judged a violation of dramatic propriety, as being out of accord with the Clerk's character. On the contrary, as we have seen, it is adjusted, with the nicest art, not only to his character, but also to the situation and the relations among the *dramatis personae*.

Heedless criticism has thrown the Wife's Prologue into the huge heap of satires on woman piled up by successive generations of mediæval poets. This indiscriminate procedure ignores the essential element that distinguishes the Canterbury Tales from the ordinary narrative and didactic poetry of the middle ages. The Wife of Bath is an individual expressing herself in character, not a stalking horse for a satirist's poisoned arrows. Her revelations apply to herself. To extend them to wives or women in general, is as ludicrous as it would be to interpret Iago's cynical speeches as Shakspere's satire on men and husbands. We may even take the Miller to witness:—

> Ther been ful goode wyves many oon,
> And evere a thousand goode ayeyns oon badde.
> That knowestow wel thyself, but if thou madde. [46–48]

Similarly, the ironical Envoy is not to be taken as Chaucer's revolt against the false morality of Griselda's parable, but as the utterance of the Clerk, under quite particular circumstances. Nor is it, even on the Clerk's part,

an attack on wives or women. It is simply a satirical encomium on a particular person, the obstreperous widow of Bath, and on any others who may
choose to adopt her principles or join her heretical sect.

* * *

The Franklin, like the Clerk before him, has a surprise ready for Harry
Bailly and the Pilgrims. He resumes the debate on Matrimony, which had
lapsed, to all appearances, with the Host's calling upon the Squire for a tale
of love; and he not only resumes it, but carries it to a triumphant conclusion
by solving the problem. He solves it, too, by an appeal to precisely that
quality which he so much admires in the Squire, and which the Host has
scoffed at him for mentioning—the quality of "gentillesse."

This procedure on the Franklin's part is manifestly deliberate; it is not
accident, but belongs to Chaucer's plan.

The Franklin, as we have noted, feels a wistful interest in "gentillesse"—
a delightful old term which includes culture, good breeding, and generous
sentiments, or, to borrow Osric's words to Hamlet, "the continent of what
part a gentleman would see." Naturally, therefore, he selects a story that
illustrates this quality. It involves a graceful compliment to two of the Pilgrims who have held the stage in this act of Chaucer's Human Comedy,
for the plot turns on the competing generosity of a husband (who is a knight),
a lover (who is a squire), and a magician (who is a clerk), the appraisal of
merit being left to the audience.

In itself, this tale, which is an old one, throws no light on the problem
of sovereignty in marriage. At the outset, however, the Franklin makes a
definite application. Arveragus, a noble knight of Brittany, wins the love of
the lady Dorigen, who "takes him for her husband and her lord." Out of
pure gentillesse, he promises that he will never assert his authority after
they are married, but will continue to be her humble servant, as a lover
ought to be to his lady. In return for this gentillesse, Dorigen vows never to
abuse her sway, but to be his true and obedient wife. Thus the married
lovers dwell together in perfect accord, each deferring to the other, and
neither claiming the sovereignty; and it is this relation of mutual love and
forbearance, the outcome of gentillesse, that carries them safely through
the entanglements of the plot and preserves their wedded happiness unim-
paired as long as they live.

Love and marriage, according to the courtly system, were held to be
incompatible, since marriage involves mastery on the husband's part, and
mastery drives out love. * * * This theory the Franklin utterly repudiates.
In true marriage, he argues, there should be no assertion of sovereignty on
either side. Love must be the controlling principle,—perfect, gentle love,
which brings forbearance with it. Such is his solution of the whole problem, and thus he concludes the long debate begun by that jovial heresiarch,
the Wife of Bath.

[760] Thus been they bothe in quiete and in reste.
For o thyng, sires, saufly dar I seye,

That freendes everych oother moot obeye,
If they wol longe holden compaignye.
Love wol nat been constreyned by maistrye.
Whan maistrie comth, the God of Love anon
Beteth his wynges, and farewel, he is gon!
Love is a thyng as any spirit free.
Wommen, of kynde, desiren libertee,
And nat to been constreyned as a thral;
[770] And so doon men, if I sooth seyen shal.
Looke who that is moost pacient in love,
He is at his avantage al above.
Pacience is an heigh vertu, certeyn,
For it venquysseth, as thise clerkes seyn,
Thynges that rigour sholde nevere atteyne.
For every word men may nat chide or pleyne.
Lerneth to suffre, or elles, so moot I goon,
Ye shul it lerne, wher so ye wole or noon;
For in this world, certein, ther no wight is
[780] That he ne dooth or seith somtyme amys.
Ire, siknesse, or constellacioun,
Wyn, wo, or chaungynge of complexioun
Causeth ful ofte to doon amys or speken.
On every wrong a man may nat be wreken.
After the tyme moste be temperaunce
To every wight that kan on governaunce.
And therfore hath this wise, worthy knyght,
To lyve in ese, suffrance hire bihight,
And she to hym ful wisly gan to swere
[790] That nevere sholde ther be defaute in here.
    Heere may men seen an humble, wys accord;
Thus hath she take hir servant and hir lord,
Servant in love and lord in mariage.
Thanne was he bothe in lordshipe and servage.
Servage? nay, but in lordshipe above,
Sith he hath bothe his lady and his love;
His lady, certes, and his wyf also,
The which that lawe of love acordeth to.
And whan he was in this prosperitee,
[800] Hoom with his wyf he gooth to his contree,
Nat fer fro Pedmark, ther his dwellyng was,
Where as he lyveth in blisse and in solas.
    Who koude telle, but he hadde wedded be,
The joye, the ese, and the prosperitee
That is bitwixe an housbonde and his wyf? [88–133]

There is no mistaking Chaucer's purpose in this, the final scene of that
act of the Canterbury Pilgrimage which deals with the problem of husband

and wife. He does not allow the Franklin to tell a tale without a moral expressed and to leave the application to our powers of inference. On the contrary, the Franklin's discussion of the subject is both definite and compendious. It extends to nearly a hundred lines, without a particle of verbiage, and occupies a conspicuous position at the very beginning of the story, so that the tale is utilized to illustrate and enforce the principle. And in the course of this discussion the Franklin alludes, in a way that cannot have escaped his fellow-travellers, to the Wife of Bath's harangue on the thraldom of husbands, to the patience of Griselda and the theories of the Marquis Walter as described by the Clerk of Oxford, and to the grimly ironical praise of wedlock which makes lurid the frenzied satire of the disillusioned Merchant. It is clear, therefore, that Chaucer means us to regard the Franklin as "knitting up the matter," as summarizing the whole debate and bringing it to a definitive conclusion which we are to accept as a perfect rule of faith and practice.

In assigning to the Franklin this supremely important office, Chaucer acted with his usual perspicacity. Marriage, when all is said and done, is an affair of practical life. Theorists may talk about it,—divines, philosophers, men of law, harpers harping with their harps,—but we listen with a certain skepticism when they take high ground, or shut their eyes to the weakness of human nature. To the Franklin, on the contrary, we lend a credent ear. He is no cloistered rhetorician, but a ruddy, white-bearded vavasour, a great man in his neighborhood, fond of the good things of life and famous for his lavish hospitality. He has been sheriff of his county and Member of Parliament, and is perpetual presiding justice at the sessions of the peace. Such a man lies under no suspicion of transcendental theorism or vague heroics. When _he_ speaks of mutual forbearance and perfect gentle love between husband and wife, we listen with conviction. The thing is possible. The problem need puzzle us no longer.

> Who koude telle, but he hadde wedded be,
> The joye, the ese, and the prosperitee
> That is bitwixe an housbonde and his wyf?

* * *

D. W. ROBERTSON, JR.

[Christian Themes in the _Canterbury Tales_] †

* * *

Iconographic materials from the Bible * * * abound in Chaucer's poetry, where they afford a richness and depth of meaning which could not have

† From A _Preface to Chaucer_ (Princeton: Princeton UP, 1963) 373–77, 379–82. Copyright © 1962 by Princeton University Press. Excerpts reprinted by permission of Princeton University Press. Robertson's notes have been renumbered and in some cases expanded.

been achieved in any other way. Among scriptural concepts which appear in *The Canterbury Tales*, the most important is the idea of pilgrimage. Any pilgrimage during the Middle Ages, whether it was made on the knees in a labyrinth set in a cathedral floor, or, more strenuously, to the Holy Land, was ideally a figure for the pilgrimage of the Christian soul through the world's wilderness toward the celestial Jerusalem. The pilgrimage of the soul was not in itself a journey from place to place, but an inner movement between the two cities so vividly described by St. Augustine, one founded on charity, and the other on cupidity. Love moved the pilgrim's feet and determined the direction of his journey. The *Tales* are set in a framework which emphasizes this journey and its implications. The opening in April, the month of Venus, under the sign of Taurus, the house of Venus, with its showers and singing birds, suggests the love which may move the pilgrims to Canterbury toward either one spiritual city or the other. And as the journey draws to a close, with Libra's scales of justice hanging in the sky in a curious but irrelevant echo of Homer, the parson offers to show

> the wey in this viage
> Of thilke parfit glorious pilgrimage
> That highte Jerusalem celestial. [Parson's Prologue, 49–51]

The idea is reinforced from time to time in the prologue and tales. Thus the wife of Bath "koude muchel of wandrynge by the weye" both in the flesh and in the spirit; old Egeus in the Knight's Tale observes that "we been pilgrymes passynge to and fro"; Custance in the Man of Law's Tale undergoes a long pilgrimage from home; in the Pardoner's Tale the pilgrimage is seen as a quest for the death of death; and so on. The concept of the pilgrim and of the love which moves him "up a croked wey," or more directly to his home, provides a thematic background against which both Chaucer's pilgrims and the characters in their tales may be clearly seen and properly evaluated. The idea needed only to be suggested in the fourteenth century, when one of the most popular subjects for wall paintings, even in remote villages, was St. Christopher, the guide to man's spiritual voyage. As we visualize Chaucer's "folk" moving toward Canterbury, not winding through the soft intricacies of a landscape by Constable, but outlined against a background of gold leaf, we should do well to let the old words of St. Augustine echo in our ears: "Thus in this mortal life, wandering from God, if we wish to return to our native country where we can be blessed we should use this world and not enjoy it, so that the 'invisible things' of God 'being understood by the things that are made' may be seen, that is, so that by means of corporal and temporal things, we may comprehend the eternal and spiritual."

The solution to the problem of love, the force which directs the will, which is in turn the source of moral action, is, figuratively, marriage. The concept of marriage plays a large part in *The Canterbury Tales*, but to understand its significance it is necessary to know something of its wider implications. In the first place, every Christian of whatever condition should

be "married." As Thomas Brinton put it, "Every soul is either an adulteress
with the Devil or a spouse of Christ."[1] A man either preserves the marriage
contracted at baptism,[2] or abuses it. When a man is properly "married" in
this way, the "marriage" between the spirit and the flesh, or the reason and
the sensuality within him, is preserved intact, and he is also a part of the
"marriage" between Christ and the Church. In the Church, a bishop was
solemnly "married" to his diocese, and a priest was regarded as the "husband" of his flock; for both inherited in the Apostolic tradition the place of
Christ with reference to the Church. In the twelfth century, the Duke of
Aquitaine "married" the church of Aquitaine.[3] Similarly, the idea that a
prince should be a "husband" to his people gradually acquired the force of
law in France during the later middle ages. A fourteenth-century commen-
tator on Justinian wrote that "there is contracted a moral and political marriage between the prince and the *respublica*. Also, just as there is contracted
a spiritual and divine marriage between a church and its prelate, so there is
contracted a temporal and terrestrial marriage between the Prince and the
State."[4] Jehan le Bel compares the "signerie" that a husband enjoys over
his wife with that of a feudal lord over his subjects.[5] Marriage is thus a
principle of order in the individual, in the church, and in lay society; in
medieval terms, a well-ordered hierarchy of almost any kind may be thought
of as a "marriage." It follows that there are various kinds of "adultery."
When the sensuality or the lower reason rebels, the result is conventionally
termed "adultery." As Berchorius puts it, any mortal sin is a kind of "adultery." Again, a prelate who abuses his office for personal gain is an "adulterer," and so on.[6] "Adultery" implies generally what Chaucer's parson
describes as an "up-so-doun" condition in a hierarchy.

    The theme of marriage is developed first in the Knight's Tale, where
order is represented initially by the marriage of Theseus and finally by the
marriage of Palamon. Specifically, it appears here as a solution to the problems raised by the misdirected concupiscent passions, represented by Venus,
and by the misdirected irascible passions, represented by Mars. The Miller's
Tale which follows is a story of adultery in which a lecherous clerk, a vain
clerk, and an avaricious old husband are amusingly shown to suffer the
consequences of their abuses of "marriage," which include, incidentally,
Nicolas' interest in judicial astrology and Absalon's refusal to accept offerings from the ladies, as well as the actions of both with reference to Alisoun.
In the Reeve's Tale we meet an "adulterous" priest, who neglects the "lineage" of the Apostolic succession in favor of his literal lineage—

1. Ed. Sister Mary Aquinas Devlin, O.P., "Cam-
den Third Series," 75–76 (London, 1954), I, 36.
2. Cf. Odo Tusculanus, in J. B. Pitra, *Analecta
novissima Spicilegii Solesmensis* (1885–88), II, 247:
"Licet animae omnium christianorum in baptismo
desponsetur Christo, et cum eo contrahant matri-
monium spirituale." [It is lawful that the souls of all
Christians be espoused to Christ in baptism and that
they contract a spiritual marriage with Him—*Edi-*

tors.]
3. See Emile Mâle, *L'art religieux du XII^c siècle en
France*, 2nd ed. (Paris, 1924), p. 198.
4. Quoted by E. H. Kantorowicz, "Mysteries of
State," *Harvard Theological Review*, 48 (1955), 78.
5. *Li ars d'amour*, ed. J. Petit (Brussels, 1867–69),
II, 92.
6. Petrus Berchorius, *Opera* (Cologne, 1731–32),
III, 97–98.

> he wolde his hooly blood honoure,
> Though that he hooly chirche sholde devoure. [130–31]

This "hooly blood" is pretty thoroughly put in jeopardy in the tale which follows. In the Man of Law's Tale Custance escapes marriage with a pagan Sultan whose mother scorns "this newe lawe," but she achieves a more proper marriage which she succeeds in preserving in the face of adversity. The wife exerts every effort to turn marriage "up-so-doun," and we meet the results of this kind of inversion in society in the persons of the blind summoner and the hypocritical friar, who abuse their offices in "adulterous" fashion. The clerk systematically restores the order inverted by the wife, calling attention specifically to the duties of the Christian soul as it is tested by its Spouse. There are, however, as he says, few "Grisildis," and in the Merchant's Tale the fool's paradise advocated by the wife in her tale is fully exposed for what it is when an old man seeks to make of marriage a lecherous paradise on earth. Although the theme of the Franklin's Tale is "gentilesse" rather than marriage specifically, the dangers of the kind of "headless" marriage dear to the Epicurean ideals of the middle class are fully revealed. Adultery appears again in three separate guises in the Shipman's Tale. In the Second Nun's Tale there is a literally chaste marriage which is a type of spiritual virginity under Christ. Again, in the Nun's Priest's Tale, the dangers of the service of Venus in marriage are once more shown, and in this instance the idea is applied by implication to the relationship between a priest and his flock. Finally, the pastoral theology of marriage is treated by the parson. Closely related to the theme of marriage is the theme of "multiplying," which is introduced by the wife and vividly developed in the character of the pardoner, in his prologue, and in the Canon's Yeoman's Tale, where a technical term in alchemy is so used that its wider implications in other contexts become unmistakable. If we look back over these developments—and I have mentioned only the more obvious of them—it is not difficult to see that Chaucer sets the marriage theme in humanistic terms in the Knight's Tale, suggesting the proper function of marriage as an ordering principle in the individual and in society, and develops its manifold implications in the subsequent tales. Once it is seen that the elaboration of the theme of marriage in the *Tales* is thematic rather than dramatic, the false problems raised by the old theory of the "marriage group" disappear.

*   *   *

Those who undertake their "pilgrimage" in a proper spirit love reasonably, are truly "married," and are "fruitful" in various commendable ways. They are also those who "put off the old" and "put on the new." They are "new" or "young" in spirit, not "old" with the frustrating burden of vice. A man may be literally "old" in years and at the same time "young" in spirit; and a "young" man in years may be, on the other hand, "old" in spirit. But from the point of view of art, either visual or literary, "oldness" of the spirit is most easily suggested by "oldness" of the flesh, and there were in the

literary tradition, in addition to wise elders, many persons who could serve
as models for spiritual "oldness": Dipsas, Maximian, La Vieille, and so on.
It is not difficult to detect the difference between wise old persons like Egeus
in the Knight's Tale and elderly fools like old John in the Miller's Tale or
Januarie in the Merchant's Tale. The scriptural overtones of old age are
first suggested in the Prologue to the Reeve's Tale. Brother "Osewold" is
very angry with the Miller, but excuses himself on the grounds that he is
too old to "pley." The subject of age seems to fascinate him, and he gives
us an account of it. Old men like himself, he says, desire "folie" even when
they cannot perform it, a fact of which we are reminded later by the parson
with peculiarly medieval vividness. The "wyl" of the aged is green, Oswald
says, even though nothing else about them is very vigorous. When he has
finished his little essay, the Host reprimands him:

> "What! Shul we speke alday of hooly writ?" [47]

The reeve has neither mentioned nor quoted the Bible. Harry's question is
undoubtedly meant to call attention in a humorous way to his usual lack of
perceptiveness, but it also reminds the audience of the Scriptures and of
what they have to say about old age. As the reeve describes it, age, with its
desire for folly, is very much like old age in St. Paul. Those who are "old"
in spirit, it will be recalled, are associated with the old law or the law of the
members and belong to the "lineage" of the bondwoman, described by St.
Augustine as "the generation of Cain." When the reeve tells a tale about
how this lineage, masquerading as "hooly chirches blood" is "bigiled," he
is in a very real sense talking about himself and the fate of his own antiquity.

One of the most famous passages in *The Canterbury Tales* is the wife's
disquisition on her lost youth:

> But Lord Crist! whan that it remembreth me
> Upon my yowthe, and on my jolitee,
> It tikleth me aboute myn herte roote.
> Unto this day it dooth myn herte boote
> That I have had my world as in my tyme.
> But age, allas! that al wol envenyme,
> Hath me biraft my beautee and my pith.
> Lat go! farewel! the devel go therwith!
> The flour is goon, ther is namoore to telle;
> The bren, as I best kan, now moste I selle. [469–78]

The idea for this passage was undoubtedly suggested to Chaucer by a passage from a speech by one of the wife's literary ancestors, La Vieille:

> Par Deu! si me plaist il encores
> Quant je m'i sui bien pourpensee;
> Mout me delite en ma pensee
> E me rebaudissent li membre
> Quant de mon bon tens me remembre
> E de la joliete vie
> Don mes cueurs a si grant envie;

Tout me rejovenist le cors
Quant j'i pens e quant jou recors;
Touz les biens dou monde me fait
Quant me souvient de tout le fait,
Qu'au miens ai je ma joie eüe,
Combien qu'il m'aient deceüe.[7]

Chaucer has added the significant word *pith* and expressed the thought of
the last line in terms of *flour* and *bren* in order to emphasize the poetic
significance of what "age" has done to Alisoun. But both passages contain
a concept of rejuvenation or *renovatio*, explicit in the French and implied
in the second sentence of the English. And this renewed youth is brought
about by the memory of former joys. This is not, of course, in itself a
scriptural concept, but it is an inversion of a very common idea. In Psalm
27.7, we read, "The Lord is my helper and my protector: in him hath my
heart confided, and I have been helped. And my flesh hath flourished again.
. . ." The *Glossa major* takes this as a reference to Christ, who flourished
when He was born without sin and again at the Resurrection.[8] The actions
of Christ set a pattern for others to follow. Thus in Ps. 102.5 we find another
renewal: "Who satisfieth thy desire with good things: thy youth shall be
renewed like the eagle's." This renewal, the *Glossa* says, is made possible
by Christ,[9] and it naturally involves the removal of an "oldness." St. Paul
urges us (Eph. 4.22ff.) to "put off the old man" and "be renewed" so as to
"put on the new man." When the wife, therefore, having invoked "Lord
Crist," begins to talk about how good it feels to remember the "good things"
of youth and then laments that age has bereft her of pith and "flour," leaving only bran, it is clearly and amusingly apparent that she has taken the
name of Christ in vain and neglected her opportunity to "flourish again" in
a true *renovatio*. The passage is neither sentimental, nor a lament on Chaucer's part for the joys of his lost youth; it is a jocular little complex of scriptural iconography designed to fill out the implications of the inversion
represented by the wife. "Renewal" through the desires of the flesh must
necessarily prove to be illusory, and it is this illusion that the wife holds out
as a prospect of "parfit joye" in her tale, wherein a knight of strong carnal
impulses allows an old hag who offers to satisfy his "worldly appetit" to win
sovereignty over him so that she appears to him to be "fair and good." The
wife's inverted *renovatio* sheds light on other "old" characters in the *Tales*.
That old man the pardoner can, like Shakespeare's Falstaff, refer to "us
yonge men," but we know that he, too, lacks "pith" and steadfastly refuses
to be renewed. Januarie's abuse of marriage is another refusal of "youth,"
although Januarie tries very hard to regain the "youthful desires" of the "old
man." The theme reaches its climax in the Pardoner's Tale, where the Old
Man himself appears, knocking on the ground, his "mother's gate," and
vainly seeking that death and that renewal which alone can restore his youth.

* * *

7. For a translation of this passage from the *Romance of the Rose*, see p. 313 [*Editors*].
8. Ed. J.-P. Migne, *Patrologia Latina*, vol. 191, col. 281.
9. *PL*, 191, col. 920. The explanation is involved, but we need not be concerned here with its details.

GABRIEL JOSIPOVICI

Fiction and Game in the *Canterbury Tales* †

Chaucer differs from most other late medieval artists in that his rhetorical play is genial and ironic rather than hectic and desperate. Nevertheless * * * the irony does not always imply an overall control. It is, in fact, only in his last work that he manages to overcome the apparently impossible conditions with which, as a story-teller and a devotee of the truth, he is faced, and he does this by making explicit the notion of art as game which had been implicit in his work from the very beginning.

By distinguishing himself from his narrator Chaucer, as we have seen, turned the ensuing fiction into a game between himself and the reader. He is able to introduce this notion of game more easily and effectively in *The Canterbury Tales* because here the game played with the reader coincides with another game, played within the fiction, by the pilgrims themselves. Thus the kind of relationship Chaucer establishes between himself, his poem and the reader is mirrored in the relationship established within the poem between the pilgrim story-tellers, their tales and their audience.

It is the Host who first suggests that the pilgrims play a game in order to relieve the boredom of the journey to Canterbury, and it is he who lays down the rules for this game when the company assents to his suggestion. Each pilgrim is to tell two tales on the way to the shrine and two on the way back; the teller of the best tale is to be given dinner by all the other pilgrims; and anyone who fails to abide by the decisions of the Host is to pay a forfeit. The pilgrims agree to these rules, and, with the drawing of the shortest 'cut' by the Knight on the following morning, the game is on. The ensuing tales, then, are not simply stories told to pass away the time on the road to Canterbury; they are part of a game, with rules of its own, which all the pilgrims have agreed to play. As with the game the poet and the reader have agreed to play, it takes place in the context of real life, but the participants are answerable to none of the laws which govern real life, only to those rules which they have agreed upon beforehand.

The Host, who has set himself up as arbiter, has, it soon transpires, very clear ideas as to what it is he requires of a story. His words to the Clerk sum up his attitude:

> Telle us som myrie tale, by youre fey!
> For what man that is entred in a pley,
> He nedes moot unto the pley assente.
> But precheth nat, as freres doon in Lente,

† Reprinted from *The World and the Book: A Study of Modern Fiction* by Gabriel Josipovici with the permission of the publishers, Stanford University Press. © 1971 by Gabriel Josipovici. Reprinted by permission of Macmillan, London and Basingstoke. We have expanded some of the references in his notes.

To make us for oure olde synnes wepe,
Ne that thy tale make us nat to slepe. (*CT* IV 9–14)

His first requirement is that the story must not be boring. He is willing to
listen to a tale in the high or the low style, in prose or in verse, a saint's life
or a fabliau, but if he considers it boring then he has no hesitation in cutting
it short and asking for something better. The ultimate crime of the story-
teller, in his eyes, is that of sending his audience to sleep, since to do so is
to destroy the very raison d'être of the story—as he points out to the Monk,
you can't very well tell a tale if there aren't any listeners.

It is partly for this reason too that the Host warns pilgrim after pilgrim
not to preach. A sermon, for the Host, represents the height of boredom.
But there is another reason for his objection to preaching, which is related
to this but is not to be confused with it. What the Host really objects to is
that the preacher has designs on his listeners. Although Harry Bailly never
loses a chance to attack or ridicule preachers, he has nothing against them
as such. He simply feels that they have no place in his game. For, believing
as they do that what is not true must be false, they fail to understand that a
game stands outside this antithesis, and hence themselves tend to disregard
the rules under which a game is played.

The Parson seems to be the chief offender in this respect. In the general
prologue we are given a picture of him as an ideal figure who, with the
Knight, the Plowman and the Clerk, forms a contrast to all the other pilgrims by virtue of the fact that with him word and deed are one: 'first he
wrought and afterwards he taught'. In all the other ecclesiastics and in most
of the laymen the gap between word and deed is more or less large, and
one of the functions of the irony in the general prologue is to reveal the
degree of deviation. Yet this idealised picture of the Parson is contradicted
on at least two separate occcasions in the body of the text before the Parson
tells his own tale which brings the poem to a fitting conclusion.

In the epilogue to the Man of Law's Tale the Host turns to the Parson
and asks for a tale, 'By Goddes dignitee'. The Parson's only answer is to
reprove him for swearing, whereupon he turns to the other pilgrims in
mock surprise and warns them that 'they shal han a predicacioun', and that
'this Lollere here wil prechen us somewhat'. At this the Shipman leaps in
and swears that no one is going to preach in this place. The Parson subsides
into silence, but the next time he and the Host clash it is he who wins the
victory. For some unknown reason Chaucer changed his mind about the
number of tales he was going to tell and in the Parson's prologue it emerges
that all the tales have been told except his own. The Host thus turns to him:

'Sire preest,' quod he, 'artow a vicary?
Or arte a person? sey sooth, by thy fey!
Be what thou be, ne breke thou nat oure pley;
For every man, save thou, hath toold his tale . . .
Telle us a fable anon, for cokkes bones!' (*CT* X 22–9)

But once again the Parson rebukes him: he will take part in the 'pley', but
only on his own terms:

> 'Thou getest fable noon ytoold for me;
> For Paul, that writeth unto Thymothee,
> Repreveth hem that weyven soothfastnesse,
> And tellen fables and swich wrecchednesse . . .
>
> For which I seye, if that yow list to heere
> Moralitee and vertuous mateere,
> And thanne that ye wol yeve me audience,
> I wol ful fayn, at Cristes reverence,
> Do yow plesaunce leefful, as I kan.' (*CT* x 31–41)

The figure who emerges from these two scenes is hardly that of the ideal
ecclesiastic of the general prologue. He is a type as familiar as the Friar or
the Summoner, a medieval Puritan, rigidly opposed to any form of swearing and to all but overtly moral tales on the grounds that they are lies and
thus conducive to sin. He is no different, in fact, from the real-life author
of the Wycliffite sermon which condemned the playing of Corpus Christi
plays and argued that only things done 'in earnest' were relevant to the
Christian life.[1] Yet in saying this I am aware that I raise a problem, since
the Parson, at this stage in the poem, is clearly intended to be a figure of
authority, whom the reader, like the pilgrims, is asked to respect. After all,
he ends the tales, and he ends them with a sermon, designed, as he says

> To shewe yow the wey, in this viage,
> Of thilke parfit glorious pilgrymage
> That highte Jerusalem celestial. (*CT* x 49–51)

I feel though that there is a clash of interests here similar to that found in
The Book of the Duchess: here a Dantesque scheme of movement upwards
to a final goal comes into conflict with the very Chaucerian scheme of
seeing the whole work as a game, mirroring the game played by the pilgrims
themselves, and therefore without beginning or end in any strictly linear
sense. This last scene and the Parson's actual sermon do not present us with
quite such a blatant cutting off of the main themes of the rest of the work
as we find in *Troilus*, because the themes of truth and falsehood, art and
life, are still present. What does happen is that they are resolved in terms
of the very order and hierarchy on whose validity, or at least availability to
man, grave doubts had been cast by the rest of the poem.

What the Host objects to in the Parson, then, is his tendency to destroy
the game by substituting his own rules (which, he insists, are the rules of
God and hence govern the universe) for those agreed upon by the pilgrims.
But Harry Bailly is not really as disinterested himself as he would have us

---

1. See V. A. Kolve, *The Play Called Corpus Christi* (Stanford: Stanford UP, 1966), 18. The whole of his
second chapter, 'The Corpus Christi Drama as Play and Game', is relevant to this discussion.

believe. To begin with there is the question of the prize dinner. Whoever wins, at least part of the proceeds will go to the keeper of the Tabard, since he has undertaken to prepare the prize meal. But there is another, less obviously material advantage, which accrues to the organiser of the game: his role as referee allows him to indulge his love of mockery and sarcasm, his need to command and control, all under cover of the rules. Thus he can insult the Cook and Monk to their faces while avoiding censure by immediately reminding them to 'be nat wroth for game; / A man may saye ful sooth in game and pley'. The Parson refuses to play the game. He confuses fiction and falsehood and stands firm in his determination to preach a sermon rather than tell a tale. The Host plays the game, but he is even more at fault than the Parson since he plays it for his own ends. So long as it is he who makes the jokes he is only too eager to invoke the game as an excuse; but as soon as the joke turns on him he forgets all about the game and its rules in his blind anger at the joker. This is just what happens at the climax of the Pardoner's Tale: as the Pardoner finishes, Harry Bailly finds that for the first time the joke is on him, and he does not like it.

The Pardoner's Prologue and Tale stands at the centre of *The Canterbury Tales* and demonstrates the final twist of Chaucer's convoluting irony. Quite simply, the Pardoner tells the assembled company of pilgrims that he is going to fool them with his words, and then he goes ahead and does so. As the pilgrims drink in the conclusion of his moral tale of the three rioters who come to a bad end, and submit to its inevitable application to the present:

> Now, goode men, God foryeve yow youre trespas,
> And ware yow fro the synne of avarice!
> Myn hooly pardoun may yow alle warice,
> So that ye offre nobles or sterlynges,
> Or elles silver broches, spoones, rynges. . . . (*CT* vi 904–8) [590–94]

they automatically reach into their pockets, their hearts warm with the glow of goodness, to buy themselves a pardon—only to be brought up short by the sudden realisation that the Pardoner is only going through his old routine, explained to them at some length only a short while before:

> Myne handes and my tonge goon so yerne
> That it is joye to se my bisynesse.
> Of avarice and of swich cursednesse
> Is al my prechyng, for to make hem free
> To yeven hir pens, and namely unto me.
> For myn entente is nat but for to wynne,
> And nothyng for coreccioun of synne. (*CT* vi 398–404) [85–91]

The reaction of the Host when this dawns on him is violent in the extreme:

> But, by the croys which that Seint Eleyne fond,
> I wolde I hadde thy coillons in myn hond
> In stide of relikes or of seintuarie. (*CT* vi 951–3) [638–40]

At this the Pardoner grows speechless with indignation and a fight seems
about to ensue when the Knight intervenes, reminding Harry Bailly of what
he had himself so often said to cover up for his own insults, that all that
had been said had only been said 'for pley and game':

> Namoore of this, for it is right ynough!
> Sire Pardoner, be glad and myrie of cheere;
> And ye, sire Hoost, that been to me so deere,
> I prey yow that ye kisse the Pardoner.
> And Pardoner, I prey thee, drawe thee neer,
> And, as we diden, lat us laughe and pleye. (CT VI 962–7) [648–53]

It would be a mistake to imagine that the Host is angry because the Pardoner has asked him for money. What arouses his indignation is the feeling
that the Pardoner has fooled him. And in this he is surely right. The Pardoner is not out to make money out of these pilgrims or he would never
have revealed to them so candidly his methods for doing so beforehand.
What he wants to prove is the power of words, of his rhetoric, and in order
to succeed he must make the pilgrims see that he has been able to fool them
in spite of their previous knowledge of his methods. In that moment, between
the conclusion of his tale and the outraged cry of the Host, the moment
when the rhetoric wears off just enough to be recognised as such, he finds
his satisfaction. And, just as the power he is allowed to exercise over others
under cover of the game is more important to the Host than the money he
might make out of the prize dinner, so, we may be sure, the Pardoner
would not have foregone his mental triumph for all the relics in the world.

The Pardoner has not fared well at the hands of the critics. A good example
of the kind of treatment he has received is to be found in a brilliant essay
by R. P. Miller, 'Chaucer's Pardoner and the Scriptural Eunuch'.[2] Miller
begins by analysing the Pardoner's actual tale in terms of the exegetical
tradition we examined in the previous chapter. He takes as his guiding line
the notion now familiar to us that there are two ways to read any text, a
foolish natural way and a spiritual way, which is the way of the Christian
exegetical tradition. The tale itself is a simple and traditional one, but Miller
shows how, read correctly, it is rich in the themes that interested Chaucer
and the Middle Ages. Three rioters see a corpse being taken to burial and,
on asking who it is who has killed the man, are told that it is Death, who is
devastating the countryside. At once they decide to set out and slay Death.
In their search for him they meet an old man who tells them that Death is
to be found up a twisting path under a tree. They follow these directives
and find not a man but a treasure. Forgetting their search for Death they
make plans to carry away the treasure but secretly plot to kill each other in
order to have more for themselves. Inevitably all three succeed and all three
die. Their literal death, one could say, is the result of a prior spiritual death,
which made them constantly interpret literally what they should have inter-

2. In *Chaucer Criticism*, ed. Schoeck and Taylor (Indiana: University of Notre Dame Press, 1960) I. 221–
44.

preted spiritually: the injunction to slay death ('Death, thou shalt die'); the 'old man' whom they meet; the treasure under the tree up the crooked path, etc. The clues are thick on the ground, but the rioters fail to read them because they are foolish natural men, and their own death is the result of their failure to alter, to become spiritual. In the same way, Miller argues, the Pardoner himself, who should be a 'eunuch in God', is in fact only *physically* a eunuch, while very much the reverse in spirit. As a false eunuch masquerading as the true one he is even more to be condemned than the three rioters whose story he tells. And Miller concludes that

> the Pardoner's Tale fits generally into a scheme of opposition between Charity and Cupidity in *The Canterbury Tales* as a whole. The extreme maliciousness of the Pardoner as a person sets him at the far end of the scale among the pilgrims. As a type he is even more definitely evil. He is the false eunuch who stands and points the way up the wrong road. He represents the way of cupidity, malice, impenitence, spiritual ste-rility—just the opposite of the way of the Parson and his spiritual brother, the Plowman. He is that Old Man as he lives and exerts his influence in the great pilgrimage of life. And, as the *vetus homo* he is to be opposed to the Christlike figure of the *novus homo*, the true guide— the 'povre Persoun of a toun'.[3]

In the way it brings together the figure of the Pardoner as he is described in the general prologue and the themes of the Pardoner's own Prologue and Tale, Miller's article is exemplary. The only thing he forgets—and it is crucial—is that the Pardoner meets the requirements of the game so much better than the Parson. St. Augustine, who asked how a horse could be a true picture unless it was a false horse, knew better. For is not Miller's reading itself the result of an overliteral interpretation of the text? Does he not look simply at the content and forget the tone and context in which it is delivered? For in one sense the Pardoner is the only honest pilgrim in the group. Only he plays the game to its limits while still recognising it as a game. Although at one level his Prologue and Tale are aimed at making a fool of everyone, at another level it is not aimed at anyone at all except those who refuse to recognise it as a mere tale told as part of the game, a rhetorical exercise designed to demonstrate his virtuosity. To read it as Miller does is, in a way, to read it like Harry Bailly: as a personal affront which can only be met by showing up the evil of the teller. But the tale was only told in play and the right reaction is the Knight's: to accept the joke and learn from it. There is perhaps some excuse for the Host; his reaction is the kind one makes every day to the realisation that one has been fooled. But for the *reader* of Chaucer to react in this way is to reveal a misunderstanding of the whole nature of Chaucer's art. For if the reaction of the Host is similar to that which one makes in everyday life, that of the Knight is of

3. Ibid. 240–1.

the kind which games try to foster and which an art like Chaucer's or Rabelais's or Sterne's tries to produce.

Miller's error lies in his belief that because Chaucer is concerned with true and false readings and interpretations, it is up to us to read his work in the 'true' way. This is certainly the way to read Dante or Langland, but then, as we have seen, their major works describe the movement *towards* the truth. In Chaucer there is never any movement, the hero never grows into understanding or enlightenment. And this suggests that his work is not so much governed by the opposition of true and false readings, as itself an exploration of the relationship between them. In other words the right and wrong ways of reading the world is the principal *theme* of his work, as of this tale.

The tale itself, as Miller rightly saw, is about the failure to distinguish the spiritual from the literal; but since it is told by the 'literal' Pardoner, does that not mean that we must *reverse* the values in the tale? Once again we see that Chaucer has removed any vantage point superior to the poem and from which we can judge its value. For the tale itself of course we have just such a vantage point, and it is pretty easy to see just where the rioters go wrong. The short sermon set into the beginning of the tale reveals its solid base in Christian exegesis:

> The hooly writ take I to my witnesse
> That luxurie is in wyn and dronkenesse.
>   Lo, how that dronken Looth, unkyndely
> Lay be his doghtres two, unwityngly. . . .
>
>   Adam, oure fader, and his wyf also,
> Fro Paradys to labour and to wo
> Were dryven for that vice, it is no drede. . . . (CT vi 483–507)
>   [169–93]

The focus here is the same as that of a Hugh of St. Victor or a Dante. We don't have to be particularly well up in Christian theology to know where we stand. But then we ask who speaks these words and the answer is: the Pardoner, the man who boasted that his only 'intent' in preaching was not to free people from sin but to gain money for himself! The content of what he says is unimpeachable, but set in the context of his aims it takes on a new dimension. And it is not enough for us simply to step back and readjust our vantage point, for now there is no solid base from which to operate: we are tossed backwards and forwards from the words to the speaker, and our interpretation changes every time our position does. And we now see that the schema literal / spiritual with which Miller operates is not really adequate. It only works if we have some criterion for distinguishing the two; without such a criterion we are thrown back onto a world where nothing is literal, everything depends on interpretation, and where no clear criterion of interpretation seems to be present.

There had been other tales in *The Canterbury Tales* told with a different end in view from the winning of the prize dinner: the Miller had told a tale about a carpenter who married too young a wife and so rode for a fall, and the carpenter-Reeve had retaliated with a story about a miller who also got his deserts. The pilgrims were able to sit back and laugh at the knaves who fooled others only to be fooled in turn through a lack of self-knowledge, and the reader could laugh confidently with them. But the Pardoner has designs on the whole company of pilgrims and so, implicitly, upon our-selves, the readers. When we have laughed with the Miller at John the carpenter, and with Chaucer and the Reeve at the Miller, and with Chau-cer at the Reeve, we suddenly find, as the Host found, at the close of the Pardoner's Tale, that the joke is on us. At this point there is only one way of escape: to acknowledge that one was led up the garden path and learn from the game. What we learn is not a thing, a body of doctrine, but an attitude, the attitude that simultaneously accepts the need for, and denies the reality of, stories.

V. A. Kolve, writing of the Corpus Christi play cycles, has sensitively brought out the notion of play and game which pervades the genre:

> The aim of the Corpus Christi drama was to celebrate and elucidate, never, not even temporarily, to deceive. It played action in 'game'— not in 'ernest'—within a world set apart, established by convention and obeying rules of its own. A lie designed to tell the truth about reality, the drama was understood as significant play.[4]

How similar and yet how different is Chaucer's own conception of game, implicit in all his major works and explicit in *The Canterbury Tales*! He too creates 'a world set apart, established by convention and obeying rules of its own'. But his world is not one that celebrates and elucidates the struc-tures of the universe and God's plan for mankind. Rather, it is a world which mimes our natural propensities for misinterpretation (the result mainly of our belief that the meanings we find in the world are somehow inherently there), and, by miming, relieves us of them. To read the Pardoner's Pro-logue and Tale as *either* sheer characterisation and entertainment *or* as the exploration of a theological truth, is equally wrong. Both look for the mean-ing of Chaucer in the subject-matter, but where, in Dante, form and con-tent inevitably coincide, since his poem is a model of the universe, in Chaucer, on the contrary, the theme is their perpetual failure to coincide. Chaucer's aim is similar to Dante's or to that of the anonymous writers of the miracle plays: a redirection of the reader's or viewer's will. Like Dante, Chaucer places false interpretations within his work as guides to the truth. But where Dante could present this truth at the climax of the poem as the discovery of the meaning (and meaningfulness) of the universe, Chaucer's truth lies solely in our response to the work itself, the creative recreation in our minds of the author's rhetorical play. Chaucer forces the reader out of his man-locked set, but the other, truer world to which he introduces him

4. Op. cit. 32.

exists only in the moment of creative encounter with the poem, the moment when we recognise the 'set' for what it is.

In a famous letter to Vettori, Machiavelli wrote:

> On the coming of evening I return to my house and enter my study; and at the door I take off the day's clothing, covered as it is with mud and dust, and put on the garments of court and palace; then, in this graver dress, I enter the antique courts of the ancients, where, received by them with affection, I feed on that food which is only mine and which I was born for.
>
> (10 Dec 1513)

When Dante met the ancients it was simply as men who had spoken the difficult truth through mastery of their art. He had no need of special clothes or of a special setting. The world was a book, written by God, and knowledge was therefore unitary and everything was ultimately reconcilable with everything else, Roman with Jewish history, Lucan and Virgil with the Bible. For Machiavelli, on the other hand, books and the world have parted company. He gets through his daily tasks, but only because they are something that has to be done; his real life begins when he changes his clothes and enters his study, takes down his books, opens them and enters their world. In Chaucer there is neither the optimism of Dante nor the Stoic serenity of Machiavelli. In his pages books and authors, paintings and frescoes and reliefs, the wisdom of the ancients, the sayings of the Fathers, the proverbs of the people, all jostle each other, struggling for a place at the front. His reading may not be wider than Dante's, but it is far more obtrusive: he makes us constantly aware of the superabundance of things in his world, and the things include books and pictures. With all these objects mimicking each other, contradicting each other, tumbling and falling over each other in their haste to emerge into the light of day, one question detaches itself. It is never explicitly raised by Chaucer, but his very silence on this point in the midst of so much sheer talk forces it on our attention: What are all these books *for*? Are they for our instruction? Our delight? We can, like the Wife of Bath, tear the pages from one book as we back our transgressions with words out of another, but after reading Chaucer we can never again be at rest with those mysterious objects. Nor is he himself at rest. The abundance of his invention seems to reflect his awareness of the irresponsibility of words, of sayings, of stories, and his desire to exorcise each and every false voice that rises within him in order to draw attention to that which cannot be spoken, since to speak is to falsify and destroy it. This unease has of course absolutely nothing to do with a change from script to print, as some crude theorists like to argue. Chaucer never dreamt of print and the tension is as evident in his work as in that of any post-Gutenberg writer. His unease stems from the clarity of his vision and the honesty of his response, and out of it he creates his narrative art.

Geoffrey Chaucer: A Chronology |

1327	Reign of Edward III begins.
1337–1453	The Hundred Years War with France.
1340–46*	Chaucer's birth.
1348–50	The Black Death. Epidemics of plague recur throughout Chaucer's lifetime.
1357	Chaucer in service as a page in the household of Elizabeth de Burgh, countess of Ulster.
1360	Edward III contributes to Chaucer's ransom after his capture in France. Chaucer carries letters to England from Calais for Lionel, earl of Ulster.
1366*	Chaucer marries Philippa Roet.
1367	For the first time, the king addresses Parliament in English. Edward III grants to Chaucer, his "valet," an annuity of twenty marks for life.
1369	Chaucer in service as an esquire in the royal household. Takes part in John of Gaunt's campaign in northern France.
1370	Chaucer travels on the continent in the king's service.
1372–73	Chaucer commissioned to establish an English seaport for Genoese trade; to this end and for other matters of the king's business, travels to Genoa and Florence.
1374	Edward III grants Chaucer a pitcher of wine daily. Chaucer leases a house above Aldgate. Appointed Controller of Wool Custom and Subsidy for the Port of London.
1377	Chaucer goes to France and Flanders on the king's secret business. Assists at the negotiations at Montreuil-sur-Mer for peace and in Paris for the marriage of Prince Richard. Reign of Richard II begins.
1378	Chaucer sent to Lombardy on a mission concerning the war.
1381	Chaucer receives a gift of twenty-two pounds from Richard II for his diplomatic service in France. Peasants' Revolt.
1385–86	Chaucer sits as Justice of the Peace for Kent.

†The principal source for Chaucer's biography is the *Chaucer Life-Records*, ed. Martin M. Crow and Clair C. Olson (Austin: U of Texas P, 1966). See also Albert C. Baugh, "Chaucer the Man," *Companion to Chaucer Studies*, rev. ed., ed. Beryl Rowland (New York: Oxford UP, 1979) 1–20.
*These dates are conjectural.

1386   Chaucer elected to Parliament as Knight of the Shire for Kent. Retires as Controller of the Port of London. Richard II's power weakened.

1389   Richard II regains power. Chaucer appointed Clerk of the King's Works, with responsibility for construction at Westminster, the Tower of London, and several castles and manors.

1390   Chaucer is among those charged with responsibility for the walls, ditches, and other works on the Thames between Woolwich and Greenwich.

1391   Chaucer retires from the clerkship. Appointed deputy forester of the Royal Forest of North Petherton, Somerset.

1393   Richard II awards Chaucer ten pounds for "good service."

1394   Richard II grants Chaucer an annuity of twenty pounds for life.

1398   Richard II's final gift to Chaucer: a "tonel" (252 gallons) of wine a year for life.

1399   Richard II deposed. Upon his accession to the throne, Henry IV renews Richard's gifts to Chaucer and grants him an additional annuity of forty marks. Chaucer leases a residence in the garden of the Lady Chapel of Westminster Abbey.

1400   A sixteenth-century tomb in Westminster Abbey records Chaucer's death as occurring on October 25 of this year.

Selected Bibliography

The amount of published material devoted to Chaucer is enormous, and this highly selective bibliography can only be an introduction to it. We have included general works in a variety of areas and specific studies of the tales (and their tellers) that appear in this volume. Within each category, arrangement is chronological rather than alphabetical. Books excerpted in this volume and articles reprinted in this volume are not included in the bibliography.

MODERN EDITIONS

Skeat, W. W., ed. *The Works of Geoffrey Chaucer.* 7 vols. Oxford: Clarendon Press, 1894–97.
Manly, John M., and Edith Rickert, eds. *The Text of the* Canterbury Tales, *Studied on the Basis of All Known Manuscripts.* 8 vols. Chicago: U of Chicago P, 1940.
Robinson, F. N., ed. *The Works of Geoffrey Chaucer.* 2nd ed. Boston: Houghton-Mifflin, 1957.
Baugh, Albert C., ed. *Chaucer's Major Poetry.* New York: Appleton-Century-Crofts, 1963.
Pratt, Robert A., ed. *The Tales of Canterbury.* Boston: Houghton Mifflin, 1974.
Donaldson, E. Talbot, ed. *Chaucer's Poetry: An Anthology for the Modern Reader.* 2nd ed. New York: Ronald Press, 1975.
Fisher, John H., ed. *The Complete Poetry and Prose of Geoffrey Chaucer.* New York: Holt, Rinehart and Winston, 1977.
Ruggiers, Paul G., and Donald C. Baker, eds. *The Canterbury Tales: A Facsimile and Transcription of the Hengwrt Manuscript, with Variants from the Ellesmere Manuscript.* Norman: U of Oklahoma P, 1979.
Benson, Larry D., gen. ed. *The Riverside Chaucer.* 3rd ed. Boston: Houghton Mifflin, 1987.

BIBLIOGRAPHIES AND BIBLIOGRAPHIC ESSAYS

Hammond, Eleanor P. *Chaucer: A Bibliographic Manual.* 1908. New York: Peter Smith, 1933.
Griffith, Dudley D. *Bibliography of Chaucer 1908–1953.* Seattle: U of Washington P, 1955.
Crawford, William R. *Bibliography of Chaucer 1954–63.* Seattle: U of Washington P, 1967.
Baird, Lorrayne Y. *A Bibliography of Chaucer, 1964–73.* Boston: Hall, 1977. See also Fisher's edition for a 1964–74 bibliography.
Baugh, Albert C. *Chaucer.* 2nd ed. Goldentree Bibliographies. Arlington Heights: AHM Publishing Corp., 1977.
Fisher, John H., et al. "An Annotated Chaucer Bibliography 1975–76." *Studies in the Age of Chaucer* 1 (1979): 201–55. Subsequent issues of this annual contain yearly annotated bibliographies.
Rowland, Beryl, ed. *Companion to Chaucer Studies.* Rev. ed. Oxford: Oxford UP, 1979.
Leyerle, John, and Anne Quick. *Chaucer: A Selected Bibliography.* Toronto: U of Toronto P, 1984.

SOURCES AND BACKGROUND MATERIAL

Bryan, W. F., and Germaine Dempster, eds. *Sources and Analogues of Chaucer's* Canterbury Tales. Chicago: U of Chicago P, 1941.
Rickert, Edith. *Chaucer's World.* Ed. Clair C. Olson and Martin M. Crow. New York: Columbia UP, 1948.
Loomis, Roger S. *A Mirror of Chaucer's World.* Princeton: Princeton UP, 1965.
Benson, Larry D., and Theodore M. Andersson, eds. *The Literary Context of Chaucer's Fabliaux.* Indianapolis: Bobbs-Merrill, 1971.
Miller, Robert P., ed. *Chaucer: Sources and Backgrounds.* New York: Oxford UP, 1977.

LANGUAGE

Tatlock, John S. P., and Arthur G. Kennedy. *A Concordance to the Complete Works of Chaucer and to the Romaunt of the Rose.* 1927. Gloucester: Peter Smith, 1963.

Kökeritz, Helge. *A Guide to Chaucer's Pronunciation*. 1954. Toronto: U of Toronto P, 1978.
Jones, Charles. *An Introduction to Middle English*. New York: Holt, 1972.
Ross, Thomas W. *Chaucer's Bawdy*. New York: Dutton, 1972.
Elliott, Ralph W. V. *Chaucer's English*. London: Deutsch, 1974.
Davis, Norman, Douglas Gray, Patricia Ingham, and Anne Wallace-Hadrill. *A Chaucer Glossary*. Oxford: Clarendon Press, 1979.
Burnley, David. *A Guide to Chaucer's Language*. Norman: U of Oklahoma P, 1983.

COLLECTIONS OF CRITICAL ESSAYS

Wagenknecht, Edward, ed. *Chaucer: Modern Essays in Criticism*. New York: Oxford UP, 1959.
Schoeck, Richard J., and Jerome Taylor, eds. *Chaucer Criticism: The Canterbury Tales*. Notre Dame: U of Notre Dame P, 1960.
Owen, Charles A., Jr., ed. *Discussions of the Canterbury Tales*. Boston: Heath, 1961.
Brewer, D. S., ed. *Chaucer and Chaucerians: Critical Studies in Middle English Literature*. University: U of Alabama P, 1966.
Burrow, J. A., ed. *Geoffrey Chaucer: A Critical Anthology*. Baltimore: Penguin, 1969.
Economou, George D., ed. *Geoffrey Chaucer: A Collection of Original Articles*. New York: McGraw-Hill, 1975.
Hermann, John P., and John J. Burke, Jr., eds. *Signs and Symbols in Chaucer's Poetry*. University: U of Alabama P, 1981.
Boitani, Piero, ed. *Chaucer and the Italian Trecento*. Cambridge: Cambridge UP, 1983.
Jeffrey, David Lyle, ed. *Chaucer and Scriptural Tradition*. Ottawa: U of Ottawa P, 1984.

GENERAL CRITICAL STUDIES

Manly, John M. *Some New Light on Chaucer*. New York: Holt, 1926.
Lowes, John Livingston. *Geoffrey Chaucer*. 1934. Bloomington: Indiana UP, 1958.
Lawrence, W. W. *Chaucer and the Canterbury Tales*. New York: Columbia UP, 1950.
Tatlock, John S. P. *The Mind and Art of Chaucer*. Syracuse: Syracuse UP, 1950.
Baldwin, Ralph. *The Unity of the Canterbury Tales*. Anglistica 5. Copenhagen: Rosenkilde and Bagger, 1955.
Lumiansky, Robert M. *Of Sondry Folk: The Dramatic Principle in the Canterbury Tales*. Austin: U of Texas P, 1955.
Muscatine, Charles. *Chaucer and the French Tradition*. Berkeley: U of California P, 1957.
Bronson, Bertrand. *In Search of Chaucer*. Toronto: U of Toronto P, 1960.
Curry, Walter Clyde. *Chaucer and the Mediaeval Sciences*. 2nd ed. New York: Barnes and Noble, 1960.
Brewer, Derek. *Chaucer in His Time*. London: Nelson, 1963.
Payne, Robert O. *The Key of Remembrance: A Study of Chaucer's Poetics*. New Haven: Yale UP, 1963.
Ruggiers, Paul G. *The Art of the Canterbury Tales*. Madison: U of Wisconsin P, 1965.
Jordan, Robert M. *Chaucer and the Shape of Creation: The Aesthetic Possibilities of Inorganic Structure*. Cambridge: Harvard UP, 1967.
Whittock, Trevor. *A Reading of the Canterbury Tales*. Cambridge: Cambridge UP, 1968.
Burrow, J. A. *Ricardian Poetry*. New Haven: Yale UP, 1971.
Kean, P. M. *Chaucer and the Making of English Poetry*. 2 vols. London: Routledge, 1972.
Robinson, Ian. *Chaucer and the English Tradition*. Cambridge: Cambridge UP, 1972.
David, Alfred. *The Strumpet Muse: Art and Morals in Chaucer's Poetry*. Bloomington: Indiana UP, 1976.
Howard, Donald R. *The Idea of the Canterbury Tales*. Berkeley: U of California P, 1976.
Gardner, John. *The Poetry of Chaucer*. Carbondale: Southern Illinois UP, 1977.
Owen, Charles A., Jr. *Pilgrimage and Storytelling in the Canterbury Tales*. Norman: U of Oklahoma P, 1977.
Cooper, Helen. *The Structure of the Canterbury Tales*. London: Duckworth, 1983.
Shoaf, Richard Allen. *Chaucer and the Currency of the Word*. Norman: Pilgrim Books, 1983.
Kolve, V. A. *Chaucer and the Imagery of Narrative: The First Five Canterbury Tales*. Stanford: Stanford UP, 1984.
Pearsall, Derek, *The Canterbury Tales*. London: Allen & Unwin, 1985.

GENERAL PROLOGUE

Bowden, Muriel. *A Commentary on the General Prologue to the Canterbury Tales*. New York: Macmillan, 1948.

Cunningham, J. V. "The Literary Form of the Prologue to the *Canterbury Tales*." *Modern Philology* 49 (1952): 172–81.

Baldwin, Ralph. "The Prologue." *The Unity of the* Canterbury Tales. Copenhagen: Rosenkilde and Bagger, 1955. 17–64.

Woolf, Rosemary. "Chaucer as Satirist in the General Prologue to the *Canterbury Tales*." *Critical Quarterly* 1 (1959): 150–57.

Brooks, Harold F. *Chaucer's Pilgrims: The Artistic Order of the Portraits in the* Prologue. London: Methuen, 1962.

Jordan, Robert M. "Chaucer's Sense of Illusion: Roadside Drama Reconsidered." *ELH: A Journal of English Literary History* 29 (1962): 19–33.

Nevo, Ruth. "Chaucer: Motive and Mask in the *General Prologue*." *Modern Language Review* 58 (1963): 1–9.

Richardson, Cynthia C. "The Function of the Host in the *Canterbury Tales*." *Texas Studies in Language and Literature* 12 (1970): 325–44.

Lenaghan, R. T. "Chaucer's *General Prologue* as History and Literature." *Comparative Studies in Society and History* 12 (1970): 73–82.

Morgan, Gerald. "Rhetorical Perspectives in the *General Prologue* to the *Canterbury Tales*." *English Studies* 62 (1981): 411–22.

Nolan, Barbara. " 'A Poet Ther Was': Chaucer's Voices in the *General Prologue* to *The Canterbury Tales*." *PMLA* 101 (1986): 154–69.

THE KNIGHT AND HIS TALE

Lowes, John L. "The Loveres Maladye of Hereos." *Modern Philology* 11 (1913–14): 491–546.

Cook, Albert S. *The Historical Background of Chaucer's Knight*. 1916. New York: Haskell, 1966.

Pratt, Robert A. "Chaucer's Use of the *Teseida*." *PMLA* 62 (1947): 598–621.

Frost, William. "An Interpretation of Chaucer's Knight's Tale." *Review of English Studies* 25 (1949): 289–304.

Muscatine, Charles. "Form, Texture, and Meaning in Chaucer's *Knight's Tale*." *PMLA* 65 (1950): 911–29.

Owen, Charles A., Jr. "Chaucer's *Canterbury Tales*: Aesthetic Design in the Stories of the First Day." *English Studies* 35 (1954): 49–56.

Underwood, Dale. "The First of *The Canterbury Tales*." *ELH: A Journal of English Literary History* 26 (1959): 455–69.

Neuse, Richard. "The Knight: The First Mover in Chaucer's Human Comedy." *University of Toronto Quarterly* 31 (1962): 299–315.

Salter, Elizabeth. *Chaucer: The* Knight's Tale *and the* Clerk's Tale. London: Edward Arnold, 1962.

Westlund, Joseph. "The *Knight's Tale* as an Impetus for Pilgrimage." *Philological Quarterly* 43 (1964): 526–37.

Helterman, Jeffrey. "The Dehumanizing Metamorphoses of *The Knight's Tale*." *ELH: A Journal of English Literary History* 38 (1971): 493–511.

Hanning, Robert W. " 'The Struggle between Noble Design and Chaos': The Literary Tradition of Chaucer's *Knight's Tale*." *Literary Review* 23 (1980): 519–41.

Jones, Terry. *Chaucer's Knight: The Portrait of a Medieval Mercenary*. Baton Rouge: Lousiana State UP, 1980.

THE MILLER AND HIS TALE

Tillyard, E. M. W. [Plot and Character in the *Miller's Tale*.] *Poetry Direct and Oblique*. 1934. London: Chatto and Windus, 1945. 85–92.

Donaldson, E. Talbot. "Idiom of Popular Poetry in the *Miller's Tale*." *English Institute Essays 1950*. Ed. Alan S. Downer. New York: Columbia UP, 1951. 116–40.

Block, Edward A. "Chaucer's Millers and their Bagpipes." *Speculum* 29 (1954): 239–43.

Jones, George F. "Chaucer and the Medieval Miller." *Modern Language Quarterly* 16 (1955): 3–15.

Harder, Kelsie B. "Chaucer's Use of the Mystery Plays in the *Miller's Tale*." *Modern Language Quarterly* 17 (1956): 193–98.

Birney, Earle. "The Inhibited and the Uninhibited: Ironic Structure in the *Miller's Tale*." *Neophilologus* 44 (1960): 333–38.

Kaske, Robert E. "The *Canticum Canticorum* in the *Miller's Tale*." *Studies in Philology* 59 (1962): 479–500.

Olson, Paul A. "Poetic Justice in the *Miller's Tale*." *Modern Language Quarterly* 24 (1963): 227–36.

Rowland, Beryl. "The Play of the *Miller's Tale*: A Game Within a Game." *Chaucer Review* 5 (1970): 140–46.

Beidler, Peter G. "Art and Scatology in the *Miller's Tale*." *Chaucer Review* 12 (1977): 90–102.

Gallacher, Patrick J. "Perception and Reality in the *Miller's Tale*." *Chaucer Review* 18 (1983): 38–48.

Ross, Thomas W., ed. *The Miller's Tale*. The Variorum Chaucer. Norman: U of Oklahoma P, 1983.

THE REEVE AND HIS TALE

Hart, Walter M. "The *Reeve's Tale:* A Comparative Study of Chaucer's Narrative Art." PMLA 23 (1908): 1–44.
Moffett, H. Y. "Oswald the Reeve." *Philological Quarterly* 4 (1925): 208–23.
Tolkien, J. R. R. "Chaucer as a Philologist: *The Reeve's Tale.*" *Transactions of the Philological Society* (1934): 1–70.
Muscatine, Charles. "The *Reeve's Tale.*" *Chaucer and the French Tradition.* Berkeley: U of California P, 1957. 198–204.
Kaske, Robert E. "An Aube in the *Reeve's Tale.*" *ELH: A Journal of English Literary History* 26 (1959): 295–310.
Copland, Murray. "*The Reeve's Tale:* Harlotrie or Sermonyng?" *Medium Ævum* 31 (1962): 14–32.
Olson, Paul A. "*The Reeve's Tale:* Chaucer's *Measure for Measure.*" *Studies in Philology* 59 (1962): 1–17.
Delany, Sheila. "Clerks and Quiting in the *Reeve's Tale.*" *Mediaeval Studies* 29 (1967): 351–56.
Friedman, John B. "A Reading of Chaucer's *Reeve's Tale.*" *Chaucer Review* 2 (1967): 8–19.
Brewer, Derek. "The *Reeve's Tale* and the King's Hall, Cambridge." *Chaucer Review* 5 (1971): 311–17.
Olson, Glending. "The *Reeve's Tale* as a Fabliau." *Modern Language Quarterly* 35 (1974): 219–30.
Plummer, John F. " 'Hooly Chirches Blood': Simony and Patrimony in Chaucer's *Reeve's Tale.*" *Chaucer Review* 18 (1983): 49–60.

THE WIFE OF BATH AND HER TALE

Shumaker, Wayne. "Alisoun in Wander-land: A Study in Chaucer's Mind and Literary Method." *ELH: A Journal of English Literary History* 18 (1951): 77–89.
Eisner, Sigmund. *A Tale of Wonder: A Source Study of* The Wife of Bath's Tale. Wexford, Ireland: John English & Co., 1957.
Silverstein, Theodore. "The Wife of Bath and the Rhetoric of Enchantment; or, How to Make a Hero See in the Dark." *Modern Philology* 58 (1960–61): 153–73.
Pratt, Robert A. "The Development of the Wife of Bath." *Studies in Medieval Literature.* Ed. MacEdward Leach. Philadelphia: U of Pennsylvania P, 1961. 45–79.
———. "Jankyn's Book of Wikked Wyves: Medieval Antimatrimonial Propaganda in the Universities." *Annuale Mediaevale* 3 (1962): 5–27.
Miller, Robert P. "*The Wife of Bath's Tale* and Mediaeval Exempla." *ELH: A Journal of English Literary History* 32 (1965): 442–56.
Harwood, Britton J. "The Wife of Bath and the Dream of Innocence." *Modern Language Quarterly* 33 (1972): 257–73.
Kernan, Anne. "The Archwife and the Eunuch." *ELH: A Journal of English Literary History* 41 (1974): 1–25.
Matthews, William. "The Wife of Bath and All Her Sect." *Viator* 5 (1974): 413–43.
Carruthers, Mary. "The Wife of Bath and the Painting of Lions." *PMLA* 94 (1979): 209–22.
Robertson, D. W., Jr. " 'And For My Land Thus Hastow Mordred Me?': Land Tenure, the Cloth Industry, and the Wife of Bath." *Chaucer Review* 14 (1980): 403–20.
Patterson, Lee. " 'For the Wyves love of Bathe': Feminine Rhetoric and Poetic Resolution in the *Roman de la Rose* and the *Canterbury Tales.*" *Speculum* 58 (1983): 656–95.

THE CLERK AND HIS TALE

Jones, H. S. V. "The Clerk of Oxenford." *PMLA* 27 (1912): 106–15.
Severs, J. Burke. *The Literary Relationships of Chaucer's* Clerkes Tale. New Haven: Yale UP, 1942.
Sledd, James. "The *Clerk's Tale:* The Monsters and the Critics." *Modern Philology* 51 (1953–54): 73–82.
Heninger, S. K., Jr. "The Concept of Order in Chaucer's *Clerk's Tale.*" *Journal of English and Germanic Philology* 56 (1957): 382–95.
Salter, Elizabeth. *Chaucer: The* Knight's Tale *and the* Clerk's Tale. London: Edward Arnold, 1962.
McCall, John P. "The *Clerk's Tale* and the Theme of Obedience." *Modern Language Quarterly* 27 (1966): 260–69.
Cunningham, J. V. "Ideal Fiction: *The Clerk's Tale.*" *Shenandoah* 19 (1968): 38–41.
Grennen, Joseph E. "Science and Sensibility in Chaucer's Clerk." *Chaucer Review* 6 (1971): 81–93.
Kellogg, Alfred L. "The Evolution of the *Clerk's Tale:* A Study in Connotation." *Chaucer, Langland, Arthur: Essays in Middle English Literature.* New Brunswick: Rutgers UP, 1972. 276–323.
Utley, Francis Lee. "Five Genres in the *Clerk's Tale.*" *Chaucer Review* 6 (1972): 198–228.
Frese, Dolores W. "Chaucer's *Clerk's Tale:* The Monsters and the Critics Reconsidered." *Chaucer Review* 8 (1973): 133–46.

Taylor, Jerome. "*Fraunceys Petrak* and the *Logyk* of Chaucer's Clerk." *Francis Petrarch, Six Centuries Later: A Symposium.* Ed. Aldo Scaglione. Chapel Hill and Chicago: U of North Carolina and The Newberry Library, 1975. 364–83.

Middleton, Anne. "The Clerk and His Tale: Some Literary Contexts." *Studies in the Age of Chaucer* 2 (1980): 121–50.

Morse, Charlotte C. "The Exemplary Griselda." *Studies in the Age of Chaucer* 7 (1985): 51–86.

THE FRANKLIN AND HIS TALE

Gerould, G. H. "The Social Status of Chaucer's Franklin." *PMLA* 41 (1926): 262–79.

Sledd, James. "Dorigen's Complaint." *Modern Philology* 45 (1947): 36–45.

Blenner-Hassett, Roland. "Autobiographical Aspects of Chaucer's Franklin." *Speculum* 28 (1953): 791–800.

Baker, Donald C. "A Crux in Chaucer's *Franklin's Tale*: Dorigen's Complaint." *Journal of English and Germanic Philology* 60 (1961): 56–64.

Gaylord, Alan T. "The Promises in *The Franklin's Tale*." *ELH: A Journal of English Literary History* 31 (1964): 331–65.

David, Alfred. "Sentimental Comedy in *The Franklin's Tale*." *Annuale Mediaevale* 6 (1965): 19–27.

Mann, Lindsay A. " 'Gentilesse' and the Franklin's Tale." *Studies in Philology* 63 (1966): 10–29.

Berger, Harry, Jr. "The F-Fragment of the *Canterbury Tales*." *Chaucer Review* 1 (1966–67): 88–102, 135–56.

Peck, Russell. "Sovereignty and the Two Worlds of the *Franklin's Tale*." *Chaucer Review* 1 (1967): 253–71.

Kearney, A. M. "Truth and Illusion in *The Franklin's Tale*." *Essays in Criticism* 19 (1969): 245–53.

Hume, Kathryn. "Why Chaucer Calls the *Franklin's Tale* a Breton Lai." *Philological Quarterly* 51 (1972): 365–79.

Kee, Kenneth. "Illusion and Reality in Chaucer's Franklin's Tale." *English Studies in Canada* 1 (1975): 1–12.

Morgan, Gerald, ed. *Geoffrey Chaucer: The* Franklin's Tale. London: Holmes & Meier, 1981.

Specht, Henrik. *Chaucer's Franklin in* The Canterbury Tales: *The Social and Literary Background of a Chaucerian Character*. Copenhagen: Akademisk Forlag, 1981.

THE PARDONER AND HIS TALE

Curry, Walter Clyde. "The Secret of Chaucer's Pardoner." *Journal of English and Germanic Philology* 18 (1919): 593–606.

Brown, Carleton. Introduction. *The Pardoner's Tale*. Oxford: Oxford UP, 1935.

Sedgewick, G. G. "The Progress of Chaucer's Pardoner, 1880–1940." *Modern Language Quarterly* 1 (1940): 431–58.

Kellogg, Alfred L. "An Augustinian Interpretation of Chaucer's Pardoner." *Speculum* 26 (1951): 465–81.

Kellogg, Alfred L., and Louis A. Haselmayer. "Chaucer's Satire of the Pardoner." *PMLA* 66 (1951). 251–77.

Miller, Robert P. "Chaucer's Pardoner, the Scriptural Eunuch, and the Pardoner's Tale." *Speculum* 30 (1955): 180–99.

Stockton, Eric W. "The Deadliest Sin in *The Pardoner's Tale*." *Tennessee Studies in Literature* 6 (1961): 47–59.

Beichner, Paul E., C.S.C. "Chaucer's Pardoner as Entertainer." *Mediaeval Studies* 25 (1963): 160–72.

Steadman, John M. "Old Age and *Contemptus Mundi* in *The Pardoner's Tale*." *Medium Ævum* 33 (1964): 121–30.

David, Alfred. "Criticism and the Old Man in Chaucer's *Pardoner's Tale*." *College English* 27 (1965): 39–44.

Howard, Donald R. "The Pardoner and the Parson." *The Idea of the* Canterbury Tales. Berkeley: U of California P, 1976. 333–87.

Patterson, Lee W. "Penitential Literature and the Pardoner." *Medievalia et Humanistica* ns 7 (1976): 153–73.

McAlpine, Monica E. "The Pardoner's Homosexuality and How It Matters." *PMLA* 95 (1980): 8–22.

Leicester, H. Marshall, Jr., " 'Synne Horrible': The Pardoner's Exegesis of His Tale, and Chaucer's." *Acts of Interpretation: The Text in its Contexts, 700–1600*. Ed. Mary J. Carruthers and Elizabeth D. Kirk. Norman: Pilgrim Books, 1982. 25–50.

Storm, Melvin. "The Pardoner's Invitation: Quaestor's Bag or Becket's Shrine?" *PMLA* 97 (1982): 810–18.

THE PRIORESS AND HER TALE

Brown, Carleton. *A Study of the Miracle of Our Lady Told by Chaucer's Prioress.* London: Chaucer Society, 1910.

Lowes, John Livingston. "Simple and Coy: A Note on Fourteenth-Century Poetic Diction." *Anglia* 33 (1910): 440–51.

Schoeck, Richard J. "Chaucer's Prioress: Mercy and Tender Heart." *The Bridge: Yearbook of Judaeo-Christian Studies* 2 (1956): 239–55.

Steadman, John M. "The Prioress' Dogs and Benedictine Discipline." *Modern Philology* 54 (1956–57): 1–6.

Beichner, Paul E., C.S.C. "The Grain of Paradise." *Speculum* 36 (1961): 302–7.

Gaylord, Alan T. "The Unconquered Tale of the Prioress." *Papers of the Michigan Academy of Science, Arts, and Letters* 47 (1962): 613–36.

Ridley, Florence H. *The Prioress and the Critics.* University of California English Studies 30. Berkeley and Los Angeles: U of California P, 1965.

Langmuir, Gavin I. "The Knight's Tale of Young Hugh of Lincoln." *Speculum* 47 (1972): 459–82.

Friedman, Albert B. "The *Prioress's Tale* and Chaucer's Anti-Semitism." *Chaucer Review* 9 (1974): 118–29.

Frank, Hardy Long. "Chaucer's Prioress and the Blessed Virgin." *Chaucer Review* 13 (1979): 346–62.

Collette, Carolyn P. "Sense and Sensibility in the *Prioress's Tale*." *Chaucer Review* 15 (1981): 138–50.

Wood, Chauncey. "Chaucer's Use of Signs in His Portrait of the Prioress." *Signs and Symbols in Chaucer's Poetry.* Ed. John P. Hermann and John J. Burke, Jr. University: U of Alabama P, 1981. 81–101.

THE NUN'S PRIEST AND HIS TALE

Curry, Walter Clyde. "Chauntecleer and Pertelote on Dreams." *Englische Studien* 58 (1924): 24–60.

Young, Karl. "Chaucer and Geoffrey of Vinsauf." *Modern Philology* 41 (1943–44): 172–82.

Severs, J. Burke. "Chaucer's Originality in the *Nun's Priest's Tale*." *Studies in Philology* 43 (1946): 22–41.

Donovan, Mortimer J. "The *Moralite* of the Nun's Priest's Sermon." *Journal of English and Germanic Philology* 52 (1953): 498–508.

Lumiansky, Robert M. "The Nun's Priest in the *Canterbury Tales*." *PMLA* 68 (1953): 896–906.

Manning, Stephen. "The Nun's Priest's Morality and the Medieval Attitude toward Fables." *Journal of English and Germanic Philology* 59 (1960): 403–16.

Lenaghan, R. T. "The Nun's Priest's Fable." *PMLA* 78 (1963): 300–307.

Allen, Judson B. "The Ironic Fruyt: Chauntecleer as Figura." *Studies in Philology* 66 (1969): 25–35.

Scheps, Walter. "Chaucer's Anti-Fable: *Reductio ad Absurdum* in the *Nun's Priest's Tale*." *Leeds Studies in English* 4 (1970): 1–10.

Pratt, Robert A. "Three Old French Sources of the Nonnes Preestes Tale." *Speculum* 47 (1972): 422–44, 646–68.

Donaldson, E. Talbot. "The Nun's Priest's Tale." *Chaucer's Poetry: An Anthology for the Modern Reader.* 2nd ed. New York: Ronald Press, 1975. 1104–8.

Gallacher, Patrick. "Food, Laxatives, and Catharsis in Chaucer's Nun's Priest's Tale." *Speculum* 51 (1976): 49–68.

Pearsall, Derek, ed. *The Nun's Priest's Tale.* The Variorum Chaucer. Norman: U of Oklahoma P, 1984.